"Lumley ex_____ life and horrors worse than death. The exciting py_____ nale appears to bring final resolution to some long-running subplots."
—*Publishers Weekly*

NECROSCOPE: DEFILERS

"The genuinely evil Wamphyri, Lumley's original portrayal of paranormal powers, and a long, thundering climax assure that the hefty book will handsomely reward readers."   —*Booklist*

NECROSCOPE: INVADERS

"The amazingly prolific Lumley kicks off a new branch of his Necroscope series. Necroscope fans will find themselves reading as fast as Lumley can type, and new readers may apply as well with this inaugural Jake Cutter entry."
—*Kirkus Reviews*

BRIAN LUMLEY

"I'm impressed with Lumley's talent. He's obviously one of the best writers in the field . . . [and] should attract major attention [from] those looking for a series comparable to the Anne Rice "Vampire" books."   —John Farris

"Brian Lumley's skillful mix of epic fantasy and vampire mythology offers wide-angle horror of a scope too rarely seen in modern fiction. His Wamphyri are vicious, savage, ruthless, and unrepentantly evil—a feast for the horror fan."
—F. Paul Wilson

"The voice of the vampire—powerful, unscrupulous, passionate—is sometimes the most enjoyable aspect of any vampire novel. [Lumley] revels in every telling detail, in stories-within-stories and convoluted histories of the self-mutating vampires."
—*San Francisco Chronicle*

Necroscope
AVENGERS

BRIAN LUMLEY

TOR®

A TOM DOHERTY ASSOCIATES BOOK
NEW YORK

This is a work of fiction. All the characters and events portrayed in this book are either products of the author's imagination or are used fictitiously.

NECROSCOPE: AVENGERS

Copyright © 2001 by Brian Lumley

A Tor Book
Published by Tom Doherty Associates, LLC
175 Fifth Avenue
New York, NY 10010

www.tor.com

Tor® is a registered trademark of Tom Doherty Associates, LLC.

ISBN: 0-812-57019-7
Library of Congress Catalog Card Number: 2001017386

First edition: June 2001
First mass market edition: May 2002

Printed in the United States of America

0 9 8 7 6 5 4 3 2 1

*This one is for that master of dust-jacket artwork,
my good friend Mr. Bob Eggleton.
Bob, I just can't help wondering where we'd be,
without all those marvellous skulls!*

Invaders
and
Defilers

A RÉSUMÉ

What Has Gone Before:
Invaders and Defilers

THREE YEARS AGO, THREE GREAT VAMPIRES—
two Lords and a "Lady" of the Wamphyri, the alien origi-
nators of the alleged vampire "myths" or "legends" of
Earth—entered our world via a transdimensional Gate under
the Carpathian Mountains. Having split up following their
covert "invasion," the trio went their own ways. Lord Nephran Malinari ("Malinari the Mind") enthralled an Australian billionaire to set himself up in a casino aerie in the
exclusive resort of Xanadu in the Macpherson Range. Lord
Szwart, a metamorphic "fly-the-light" in the truest sense of
the term, headed for London, settling in a forgotten Roman
"temple" in the deepest, most inaccessible bowels of the city.
And Vavara—"beautiful" mistress of mass hypnotism—defiled an order of nuns by infiltrating their fortresslike monastery on the Greek island of Krassos.

Their plan to overthrow the planet, reducing it to a vampire paradise, was in essence a simple one: to plant gardens
of deadspawn fungi and bring them to deadly maturity. Nur-
tured on the life fluids (the mutated DNA) of sacrificed vampire thralls or lieutenants, these toadstools when they ripened
and spawned would release a myriad of spores into the
Earth's atmosphere, to be breathed by an unwitting human
race! Then, as men became blood-lusting monsters who hid
from the sun during daylight hours and hunted by night, and
nation fought nation as the world sank into chaos, and no
one—least of all the mazed, blood-addicted victims—was
able to understand or even consider fighting the incurable
"disease" that was converting them . . . then the Great Vampires, the Wamphyri, would emerge from the shadows and
come into their own.

3

As in the earliest days of their predawn Vampire World of Sunside/Starside, their thralls and lieutenants would go abroad in the world, carrying their monstrous plague with them as they consolidated their masters' (and mistress's) territories, where the laws of the Wamphyri would be the only laws. Malinari would take Australia, expanding into all the islands around and eventually Asia, and Vavara would take the Mediterranean and Africa, spreading east to form a border with Malinari. As for the metamorphic horror that was Lord Szwart: while it would seem he had been disadvantaged, with only the British Isles, France, Spain, and the northern and westernmost regions of Europe coming under his control, as he deployed his forces west across the Atlantic, he would quickly seed the Americas with his deadspawn, and when the time was ripe he would move his power base to New York. The metropolis's sprawling underground network would provide access to all parts of the city whether in daylight or darkness, while its greatest building would be Szwart's aerie, its every window lacquered black and draped against the sun.

These had been the ambitions of the Wamphyri, and they had seemed infallible; *their* dreams, and an unwitting mankind's as yet unrealized nightmares. But despite their legendary cunning and leechlike tenacity, the three Great Vampires had not reckoned with E-Branch.

E-Branch (E for ESP): a top-secret arm of the British intelligence services, many of whose psychically talented agents had dealt with vampires before, and not only in this world but also in Sunside/Starside. Ben Trask, the members of his London-based organization, and a small handful of people in the Corridors of Power were the only human beings who knew of the alien invasion. And because of the planetwide panic any disclosure would cause, they didn't dare speak of it to anyone outside their circle.

But having traced Malinari to Australia (and with the ever-grudging assistance of their Minister Responsible in Whitehall: his help in covertly informing an Australian counterpart of the problem and enlisting military aid), Trask and an E-Branch task force had ventured down under to confront Malinari in his aerie. There in Xanadu they had destroyed his fungi garden (though not without the timely assistance of Jake Cutter, a young man whose extraordinary powers were not yet fully developed or even understood) but The Mind himself had escaped.

As for Jake Cutter (though more especially from Ben Trask's necessarily cautious point of view):

Jake seems an entirely wrongheaded man with something of a chequered background. Having fallen foul of a gang of international drug-runners and suffering at their hands, he was bent on settling old scores when strange circumstances brought him into contact with E-Branch. (He was in fact pursuing a vendetta with this criminal organization's powerful leader and several of his close colleagues—people who had raped and murdered a girl of Jake's acquaintance, with whom he had had a brief but passionate affair—and had been responsible for a series of violent, extremely ugly deaths in their higher echelon.)

But the leader of the gang—a Sicilian vampire named Luigi Castellano—had laid a trap for Jake, causing him to fall into the hands of the Italian police. Incarcerated in a Turin prison, Jake had soon discovered that Castellano was not without influence there, and that Jake's demise had been scheduled for the very near future.

Then, during a jailbreak (also arranged by Castellano), when it seemed certain that Jake must die under fire from the guards . . . a weird reprieve, a miraculous escape: Jake's first taste of things to come, and the beginning of his transition.

Something he took to be a ricochetting bullet—a flash of golden fire—struck him in the forehead. But instead of falling dead he fell into something else entirely and was conveyed through the Möbius Continuum (a means of metaphysical teleportation) to Harry's Room at E-Branch HQ in London.

Harry's Room:

The long-dead (?) Necroscope Harry Keogh was once the

most important member of E-Branch. On those occasions when he stayed at the London HQ, he had a room of his own, as did many espers. Harry's Room, however, has always been (and still is) *different* from other rooms. Perhaps to signal their regard for their much loved, highly respected ex-member—or perhaps because the room continues to retain something of the Necroscope's personality—it has been left untouched and unoccupied, exactly as it was in the time of Harry's residence.

And so it was a singular event for Ben Trask and his espers to discover a bewildered stranger *inside* the locked room of the Necroscope, in the heart of security-conscious E-Branch HQ! And it had to be more than a mere coincidence . . .

Jake's advent had come at a propitious moment (or at least, everyone except Trask thought so), for it was only a short time later that Nephran Malinari was discovered in Xanadu, his playboy retreat and aerie in the mountains of the Macpherson Range. And teaming Jake up with Liz Merrick, a young, attractive, budding telepathic receiver whose powers, like Jake's, were still developing, Trask took them to Australia as part of his task force.

It was during the course of this largely successful operation that Jake discovered the truth of what Trask and his people had suspected all along: that indeed he had inherited something of Harry's powers. For when the original Necroscope had died on Starside, his metaphysical personality—the sidereal *intelligence* that was Harry—had fragmented into many golden splinters or darts, one of which had entered into Jake! Now in his dreams Jake could converse with the "dead" Necroscope through the medium of deadspeak. Then, too (not yet aware that his dreams were of crucial importance, that they had real meaning in the waking world and were much more than disturbing symptoms of paramnesia and a crumbling mentality), Jake had felt obliged to ask Trask just what, exactly, a Necroscope was.

But while Trask had been willing to explain something of a Necroscope's powers to Jake—his ability to teleport, and the unearthly "gift" which enabled him to converse with the dead—there were certain other things that he dared not speak of. For as the director of E-Branch for many years, Trask had developed an enquiring and skeptical mind; he knew how very deceiving outward appearances can be, and how even the most innocent seeming of men (*especially* the innocent ones: for example, the original Necroscope) may be susceptible to the greatest evils. Moreover, Trask had never had much faith in coincidence or synchronicity. He believed that things usually had good reasons for happening, and that *when* they happened might be equally relevant . . .

Jake had come on the scene at a propitious time, certainly—but for whom? And wasn't it simply too much of a coincidence that at the advent of a trio of Great Vampires out of Starside, a new Necroscope should also put in an appearance? So, had Jake arrived of his own (or Harry Keogh's) accord, by "coincidence," or had he in fact been sent to infiltrate E-Branch? What was it of the original Necroscope—how *much* of Harry, what element—had entered Jake? Something of his light side, from his earlier life, or something of his far more dangerous side from a later, darker period?

For one of the several things that Jake didn't yet know was that at the end of the Necroscope's time on Earth he had been a vampire in his own right—Wamphyri! And probably the greatest of them all! And not only Harry but two of his sons: they, too, had been vampires, changeling creatures, on Starside in a weird parallel world . . .

Thus Trask's doubts—or more properly his natural caution, coupled with his inability to read the young Necroscope despite that his own weird talent made him a human lie detector—held him back from bringing Jake more fully into his confidence. For if Jake was *not* the real thing, if he had *not* inherited Harry's mantle to become the fantastic weapon against the Wamphyri that most of Trask's agents believed him to be, but rather possessed the potential to become the exact opposite . . . then Trask might yet have to kill him!

Hence his great quandary, for if on the other hand Jake

7

was the real thing, and if he was made privy to everything, then he might easily shy from the knowledge—the *full* knowledge—of what he was becoming and what he would be capable of doing, and would be lost to E-Branch forever. For while it takes a special kind of man to accept the responsibilities of a Necroscope, the role of caretaker to the dead, it takes an *extra* special man to accept that the Great Majority will do almost anything for love of him . . . *including the agony and horror of self-resurrection, of rising from their graves in order to protect him!*

After the Australian venture, when Jake was given the comparative "freedom" of E-branch HQ—if not access to all of its many secrets—the first thing he did was desert the cause in order to pursue his own agenda: his vendetta with Castellano. But the fact was that Jake didn't see his leaving as any kind of treachery; his reasons for walking out on Ben Trask and E-Branch were more than one, and not least self-preservation.

First, the Harry Keogh influence had been replaced by something of a far more disturbing nature: Jake was finding himself under constant attack from a deceased vampire lieutenant called Korath (once Korath Mindsthrall), an ex-minion of Malinari. Dead and sloughed away in a subterranean sump in Romania, Korath had used deadspeak to tell Jake the histories of the three Wamphyri invaders from Starside—but in the process he had also tricked his way into semiresidence in Jake's head. Only let Jake relax and let his mental shields down, Korath would be there with him in his mind, dreaming his dreams, conversing with him, attempting to influence—to "guide" or "advise" him—and generally sharing his waking world experiences. Jake could send him away, back to his sump, but he could never be absolutely certain when Korath was or wasn't there.

The only good thing to come out of this was that Korath had "inherited" something of his former master's mentalism; endowed with eidetic recall, he'd memorized the mathematical Möbius formula given to Jake by Harry Keogh—which for some reason Jake was unable to grasp—and had thus become his reluctant host's one and only key to the metaphysical Möbius Continuum's mode of trans- or *tele*portation.

And so he and Jake had worked out a compromise. All Korath wanted—or so he had led Jake to believe—was revenge on his former master and the other Great Vampires for killing him as a means of accessing our world. But since Korath was incorporeal, a dead creature whose sole contact with the living was through Jake and his deadspeak, the new Necroscope was the only one who could possibly exact such a revenge. Jake couldn't go about his business without Korath, and Korath would have no existence at all without Jake.

One other problem with Korath: if Ben Trask found out about his coexistence with Jake, it might yet be a case of having to kill two birds with one stone—or more properly one man and a parasitic mind-thing with however many bullets were required to do the job.

But even that, self-preservation, wasn't Jake's only reason for quitting the Branch. In fact he was *driven* to leave by some unknown but increasingly insistent force which demanded that he pursue his own—or perhaps someone else's?—agenda. Moreover, the longer he remained with E-Branch, the greater the chance of a romantic attachment to Liz Merrick, with whom he'd developed a semitelepathic rapport. The last thing Jake needed was to be close to someone he couldn't touch for fear of a dead vampire's voyeurism!

In Jake's absence, while he used the Möbius Continuum to pursue and harass Luigi Castellano's Mediterranean-based drug-runners, E-Branch had tracked down Malinari and Vavara to the tiny Greek island of Krassos. This time, as distinct from the Australian operation, Trask's task force was a very small one, and politically and economically (even climatically, in an El Niño year), there were huge problems to be overcome. But with the help of a Greek friend of theirs from an earlier adventure—an Athenian police inspector called Manolis Papastamos—finally E-Branch located and burned Vavara's monastery aerie, while her deadspawn garden was dynamited and buried in a series of explosive attacks.

But at the same time there had been two major setbacks. In London, Ben Trask's newfound love of only a few days' duration, the telepath Millicent Cleary, had been kidnapped by Szwart and his minions down into his Roman temple dedicated to dark gods in a forgotten cavern deep under the city. And in Krassos, Liz Merrick had been taken by Vavara when that mistress of evil made her escape from the blazing monastery. It had looked like the end for both of these brave women. But:

In Sicily, where Jake had finally rid the world of Castellano and his organization—and in the process discovered why he had felt so driven by his vendetta: that this had been part of a task begun but left unfinished, even unremembered, by the original Necroscope—the *new* Necroscope "heard" Liz's desperate cry for help. Across all the many miles between them, Jake *heard* it. It was the rapport which existed between them, which had boosted Liz's developing telepathic talent.

But when Jake required Korath to show him the Möbius equations in order that he might use the Continuum to find Liz and rescue her . . . *then* Korath had sprung his trap!

Korath had already discovered that Jake couldn't be bribed or threatened when his own life was at stake, for without Jake there would be no Korath; so whatever else the vampire did, he would try to keep his host alive. But Jake would definitely be open to persuasion if another's life were at risk . . . and more especially if that other was the woman he loved. Now Jake knew Korath's real objective: access to his inner mind—to be one with him, a part of him—and perhaps permanently!

Jake couldn't refuse . . .

Without Korath's help, Liz was as good as dead . . .

In order to view the equations, create a Möbius door, teleport through the Continuum and rescue Liz, he must first accept this dead but incredibly dangerous thing's conditions. And this despite Harry Keogh's warning: that he must never let a vampire into his mind . . .

But there was no longer any other way . . .

He went along with it, gave Korath access to the very core of his mind and welcomed him in "of his own free will" . . . and only then discovered how he had been duped, that he would have been able to conjure the formula all along—if Korath had not been blocking his every attempt!

Too late now, though, to do anything about it, for Liz was in trouble on a small Greek island hundreds of miles away . . .

Jake was in the nick of time. In Krassos, he reunited Liz with her E-Branch colleagues, who then informed him of the plight of the telepath Millie Cleary in London. Using the Continuum, Jake returned Trask and company to their London HQ, where the espers combined their weird talents to locate Millie. Still alive, her psychic aura was well known to Liz who was then able to contact her and determine her precise whereabouts. Now it was up to the new Necroscope.

Taking Millie's coordinates from Liz's mind, Jake "went" to the distraught telepath in her previously unknown temple prison. There he found not only Millie, but also Lord Szwart's terrible deadspawn garden, which (after a nightmarish confrontation with the "Lord of Darkness" himself) he managed to destroy by bringing about an explosion of natural gas.

So now, and despite that the plans of the Wamphyri were in disarray, the main question had to be: how many of the invaders themselves had survived? Had Vavara died when her limo crashed, throwing her into the sea? Had Malinari been trapped below, in Vavara's garden, when it was buried? Had the metamorphic Szwart suffered the true death in a Roman temple whose destruction had even registered on the seismographs at Greenwich?

Now, too, with Ben Trask and his people in Jake's debt, it was time for a showdown. Time for Jake to give up *his* secret—the fact that he harboured a vampire intelligence in his mind—and ask for E-Branch's help, but also time for him to demand to know the full story: why had Trask been so reticent in his dealings with him, and what had been the problem with the previous Necroscope that the Head of Branch hadn't dared talk about it?

Harry Keogh's ability to raise the dead? But Jake had found that out for himself; indeed, it accounted for the grey streaks at his temples, and the hint of fearful, forbidden knowledge in his eyes. But he knew that wasn't the entire story. Perhaps one day the teeming dead—that Great Majority of human souls gone before—might believe in Jake, have enough faith in him that he could ask them, but for now he was asking Ben Trask.

Or he would have been.

But at a meeting in Trask's office, when all Jake's questions might finally have been answered:

An urgent message from the Minister Responsible: something had come up which he knew would "interest" E-Branch. His usual British understatement, for in fact the minister knew that it was something which *only* E-Branch could handle.

And now read on . . .

1
The Sun, the Sea, and the Drifting Doom

AT SOME 35,000 TONS AND JUST OVER 700 FEET from stem to stern, the *Evening Star* was a Mediterranean cruise ship without peer. Her eight public decks were all served by elevators, and with her casino, gymnasium, outdoor pools, bars, gift shops, sports deck—all the usual amenities—the *Star* was the pride of her line. Of an evening, her 1,400-plus passengers could choose to relax in the Moulin Rouge lounge or the All That Jazz show bar, dance the night away in the Sierra Ballroom, or simply sit and be serenaded, watching the sunset from the panoramic sundeck.

This being the *Star*'s last voyage of the season, however, last night had been a little different. A mid-cruise "extravaganza," the extra glitz of its shows and its grand finale—a fireworks display from the stern, lighting the Aegean sky with dazzling spirals and brilliant, thunderclap bomb-bursts—had been one of the highlights of the voyage; the locals ashore in Mytilene on the island of Lesbos had enjoyed it as much as the passengers aboard. Add to this cuisine straight out of a gourmet's dream of paradise, and it was easy to see why the onboard partying had gone on and on through the night, and why the run on the champagne locker had seemed unending . . .

But all good things *do* come to an end.

Now . . . it was early morning of a Monday in October, and in the galley breakfast was being prepared for those who still had the stomach for yet more food, while those who didn't slept off their excesses. A few younger passengers were up and about, making the most of the pools while yet they had them to themselves, and as if emulating their energy a pod of dolphins, like so many silver minisubmarines, played chicken on the bow wave, crisscrossing the prow just beneath a sparkling surface that was so flat calm it might well be a horizon-spanning plate of diamond-etched glass. While the sun had risen no more than half an hour ago, already the deck rails were warm from its rays.

Perfect!

So thought Purser Bill Galliard where he strolled the main deck for'ard, having risen early to prepare the shore excursion roster for the *Star*'s midday visit to the picturesque island of Límnos. Thus far the cruise had gone precisely to plan, without a hitch, and Galliard had wanted to do his bit to ensure things stayed that way. Now that he'd finished with the Límnos documentation, he could take it easy for an hour or so, at least until the bulk of the passengers were astir and those who desired to go ashore were readying themselves for terra firma.

Now in the very prow of the ship, forty feet above and forward of the spot where the knifelike stem sliced the water, he leaned on the deck rail and looked out across the vast curve of the ocean. No land in sight, but Galliard came from a long line of deckhands; he knew how quickly land masses could take shape on the horizon, especially in the Aegean, looming up as if from nowhere into cloud-capped mountain ranges. And with the cooling breeze of the vessel's forward motion in his face, and the hiss of parted waters in his ears, he reflected on the trip so far.

Most of the passengers were middle-aged, comfortably well-to-do, generally easygoing Brits, and the crew was composed of a British captain, officers and senior stewards, supported by a largely Greek Cypriot body of deckhands, engineers, chefs, and an "international" lineup of entertainers. The passengers had flown out from England to Cyprus, joining the cruise in Limassol. After a week of sailing they would return to Cyprus before flying home.

Sailing from Limassol on Thursday evening, the *Evening Star* had cruised all day Friday, providing an ideal opportunity for the passengers to get to know the vessel and fellow holidaymakers. Saturday it had been "all ashore who's going ashore" in Vólos on the Greek mainland, and Purser Bill had taken time out to visit friends in their villa at the foot of Mount Pelion, also to pick up some gifts in Vólos's bustling bazaar for the folks back home. Sunday they'd cruised to Lesbos and Mytilene, where the sightseers had gone ashore again, and last night had been the food and fireworks fest.

That brought Galliard up to date. The next port of call in some four hours' time would be Límnos's new deep-water harbour, and tomorrow they'd be through the Dardanelles on their way to Istanbul. But that was to look too far ahead, and cruises such as this were best taken one day at a time.

As he thought these things through, Galliard had been idly scanning the forward horizon. A moment ago—if only for a moment—he'd caught sight of something in direct line ahead. The fact hadn't made a great impact on him; shipping of one sort or another can be found any time in Mediterranean waters, and just about anywhere. Anyway, it had been a flash of white on a glittering surface . . . maybe a dolphin had leaped clear of the water and the splashdown had caught his eye. But—

Purser Galliard stepped to one of two telescopes mounted on the rail and focussed ahead. For a while there was nothing, but then . . . now what was that? A Greek caïque? Just sitting there, all these miles from the nearest island? Nothing peculiar about the boat itself; the islands were full of them—like gondolas in Venice—but they usually stuck pretty close to shore. This one looked becalmed, and it simply shouldn't be here.

The canopied boat was maybe three-quarters of a mile ahead—but dead ahead—and it definitely wasn't moving!

Galliard took out his on-board communicator and pressed 1 for the bridge three decks higher. His call sign was recognized, and a voice answered, "Bridge. What can we do for you, Purser Bill?" It was Captain Geoff Anderson, informal as ever.

"You might try swinging her a tad to port and calling full stop on all engines," Galliard told him at once. "We're about a minute and a half from running someone down!"

"Wait," came the terse answer, and ten seconds later: "Well done, Purser Bill. We would have seen and cleared her okay, but if they need help we'd have had to slow down and come about. So you've saved us some time and a little embarrassment, possibly. Now for your trouble you can arm yourself with a hailer and get down starboard onto B deck, okay?"

"Aye, aye, Cap'n," Galliard answered with a grin, heading at the double for his office amidships. After only a few paces, he was gratified to feel the gentle shudder of a sudden deceleration, the barely noticeable shifting underfoot as the *Star* began veering a few degrees to port . . .

From just below the surface of B deck (the vessel's basement) a section of the hull had been rotated outwards to form stairs. And from the bottom step, Purser Bill Galliard threw out a line to the tattered-looking man in the shade of the caïque's canopy. Accompanied by three stewards and a deckhand, Galliard watched as the figure of the man in the caïque made fast the line, then began to haul his boat in alongside.

"That's okay," Galliard called out. "I'll do that. You just sit tight."

"Water," the shaded, crumpled-seeming man answered him, his voice a dry croak. "The lady and I . . . we're burning up."

A lady? That must be the second figure, lying supine between the thwarts. Even as Galliard drew the caïque alongside, he saw her jewel-green eyes flicker open to fix his own, in the moment before a luminous glow suffused her face, making it indistinct. And:

God, she's beautiful! he thought . . . before wondering where that idea had come from, since as yet she was barely visible in the shade of the boat's canopy, which made a jet-black contrast with the blinding sunlight.

"Shade," said the gaunt, ragged figure of the man, standing hunched under the canopy. "The sun. We have . . . suffered!"

16

"We have juice," said Galliard, passing a pitcher down. "Sip a little. It will ease your throats, give you strength. But how long have you been out here?"

"Too long," said the other, sipping and passing the pitcher to the woman, then reaching out a hand to Galliard. "Help me to get her up there."

The purser took his hand, and felt its chill. Strange, on a day as hot as this to feel a hand so cold. Stranger by far that the hand seemed to smoke in the sunlight! But Galliard was much too busy, too concerned, to wonder about the apparent contradictions here. The woman was heavily muffled; wrapped head to toe, she seemed almost mummified as she struggled to her feet, tottering where she emerged into the light. Galliard leaned forward, held to the rail with one hand and caught her round her slender waist with the other. She stepped—was lifted up—from the boat to the stairs, and her man-friend close behind, apparently eager to enter into the shade of the ship.

"But what on earth happened here?" Galliard enquired, as he and the stewards assisted the pair up into the ship and towards the elevators, and the deckhand left to go about his business. "I mean, that you got into trouble, adrift way out here?"

"We ran out of fuel," said the man, throwing off the jacket he'd been using to cover his head. "We were taken by an unusual tide off Krassos. We used up our fuel trying to get back to the island. A little jaunt turned into a nightmare."

His story sounded incredible: that even in this mad El Niño summer they'd been lost in the Aegean—adrift and going unnoticed through all the regular shipping routes—long enough to have become so dehydrated and *so* badly burned. But on the other hand it must be true, for the condition of the pair admitted of no other explanation.

Galliard looked sideways at the tall, dark, would-have-been handsome man; "would-have-been" because the skin was peeling from his blackened face, and his sunken cheeks were pitted almost as if by small meteorites. The woman's condition . . . was harder to describe, similar yet different.

17

She was burned, too, blackened in places—as if by real fire as opposed to strong sunlight—and yet that strange glow obscured most of her facial ravages. She had thrown off some of her upper wrappings, revealing her face, and now breathed so much easier in the electric light of the ship's bowels. But despite that she was close enough to lean on Galliard, still he couldn't make out her features.

And riding the elevator up through four decks to the fifth, the bridge deck, Purser Bill frowned and shook his head. He continued to support the woman (also to wonder why, like her companion, she felt so cold) but was aware now of something weirder far. Despite that he somehow "knew" she was beautiful, she *felt* decidedly unlovely. Her waist where his arm circled it, and also her body where he supported it, they were hard, angular, bony!

But now, breaking into his thoughts as Galliard shrank back a little from these far from ordinary people:

"Take us to the Captain, Purser Galliard," the man growled, his voice firmer now and commanding. "And don't let the details concern you. All will become clear—shortly."

"You . . . you know my name?"

"But of course I do, just as you told it to me," the other answered (despite that Galliard was sure he'd told him no such thing.) And through all his burns, somehow the enigmatic stranger managed to smile a leering smile.

They left the elevator and headed for the bridge, at which the purser's weird sensation of suspended reality—of all of this not really happening—eased off a little. Then, releasing the woman and drawing farther apart from her, he turned to the stewards, saying, "Lads, there's something not quite right, in fact totally wrong . . . here?"

And far more so than Galliard had suspected, or so it appeared. For the stewards—all three of them—seemed dazed, in a world of their own. Having taken the woman's weight, now they were wholly intent upon her, unable to take their eyes off her. And they weren't listening to Galliard at all!

Just beyond a sign saying OFFICERS AND CREW MEMBERS

ONLY, Purser Galliard came to a stiff-legged halt and turned to face the man he had so recently rescued. "What—?" he started to say, and stopped. For the tall stranger had moved so quickly, taking his face between his cold, burned hands, that the purser hadn't been able to avoid the contact. Following which it was too late anyway. And:

Your knowledge of the vessel, the words flowed like a river of ice in Galliard's trembling mind, freezing him solid. *Of its Captain and other officers. Of anything that might be dangerous to me and my . . . companion. I need to understand your communication capability with the outside world and other ships—ahhh! your radio room,* yesss!*—and the location of any weapons that you are carrying. Do not think to deny me, Purser Galliard, for the pain I can cause you will not be denied! Give me everything I want and suffer no further, or suffer all that I can bring to bear in the knowledge that I shall* still *get what I want!*

Galliard fought—or rather, he fought to move, to cry out, to break free—but it was useless. The icy power of this creature, the alien nightmare of his sucking hands, feeding on the purser's knowledge, held him rooted to the spot. But he sensed what was happening to him, felt the flow of his thoughts—in fact his memories—going out of him, and knew that the chill they left behind them was the emptiness of a mental vacuum, as cold as the spaces between the stars.

You are correct, the Thing (surely not a man) told him. *My mind is a great storehouse of memories, only a small number of which are mine. But knowledge is power, Bill Galliard, without which I'm at the mercy of a strange environment. So don't hold back now, but let me have it all, everything. Then, as I "remember," so you shall forget— even how to hurt. For as Nephran Malinari reads a book, so he tears out its pages!*

"You men," Galliard gasped, swiveling his bulging eyes to stare at the three stewards, at the same time trying to shrink down into himself away from his tormentor, but held up—held fast—by the monster's hands. "You men . . . you

have to . . . to *do* something! You have to fight it! Fight
them!"

One of the stewards had heard him. His eyes focused as
he staggered back away from the woman and looked at the
purser in the hands of the demoniac stranger. "Purser Bill?"
he mumbled, blinking rapidly. "I mean, what the hell . . . ?"

The woman at once went after him, seemed to flow upon
him, her slender hands reaching out like long, raking claws.
And as for the first time Galliard saw her actual face . . . so
his jaw fell open. Beautiful? But she was the worst possible
nightmare hag! Her eyes were green as jewels, but they
burned crimson in their cores, as if lit by internal fires. And
her *jaws* . . . her *teeth*!

Her face closed with the steward's shoulder in the joining
with his neck, and Galliard heard her lustful snarl as she bit
him there. *Then* he knew what they were—monsters out of
myths and legends, but real for all that—and fought harder
still. A mistake, for he left the man-creature no choice. And:

You have a saying, said that one in Galliard's mind, *which
has it that the eyes are the windows of the soul. It may be
so; I who am without a soul cannot say for sure—but they
are most certainly a means of entry to the brain! And likewise the ears: routes of access to the inner mind, these organs. The ears that hear*—(his index fingers extended
themselves, projecting deep into the purser's ears, their knifelike nails slicing a way in through flesh and cartilage)—
and the eyes that see. (Now his thumbs turned purple, vibrating as they elongated and dislodged Galliard's eyeballs,
penetrating the soft tissue behind them to sink into the
purser's brain.) *I want to know what you've heard and all
that you've seen. Painful, aye—but didn't I warn you not to
resist me?*

Galliard's screams were thin, high-pitched wailing
things—more like the whining of a small child than the agonized denial of a tortured man—as his mind was drained
and he "forgot" all that he'd ever known about the *Evening
Star.* And with his face hideously altered, he crumpled to

the floor as Lord Malinari of the Wamphyri finally withdrew his brain-slimed fingers.

By then Vavara, Malinari's "partner," if only for the time being, had dealt with the second steward. But the third was recovering from her hypnotic spell. Blinking his eyes and shaking his head, he peered slack-jawed at his shipmates where they had slumped to the deck in blood that fountained from severed arteries in their necks; also at the spastically twitching, crumpled figure of the purser, his eyes flopping on his bloodied cheeks, while his cries turned to a vacant moaning as his cruelly depleted, crippled brain closed down his survival systems one by one.

But already muffled enquiries were sounding from beyond the reinforced door to the bridge. Someone in there must have heard the purser's strangled, inarticulate babbling, and Malinari saw at least two outlines in motion behind the frosted glass of the door's upper panel. With no time to waste on the third steward, he grabbed him and swung him out through a hatch and up against the deck rail. And stiffening his hand and arm to a ramrod, the vampire slammed bone fingers into his victim's chest, rupturing his heart. Then, after yanking his hand free, a push was sufficient to topple the steward backwards over the rail, sending him plummeting to the promenade deck twenty feet below.

Down there, a half-dozen or so early risers were leaning on the rail, taking in the view. As Malinari snarled his hatred of the seething sunlight and snatched himself back into the shade, he saw their startled, horrified faces glancing up at him. *Hah!* As yet they hadn't the slightest notion of what real horror was. But they'd know soon enough. Oh, yes, they *would* know! And gritting his awesome teeth against the agony of his seared forearms and face, Malinari returned to Vavara—

—In time to see her trying the handle of the door to the bridge. As Malinari had learned from the purser, however, this was a security door with a voice-activated lock; Vavara's hiss of frustration wasn't a voice or code that it would recognize. But she wasn't much known for her patience,

21

either, and before he could caution her against it she'd balled a fist and struck furiously at the pane of frosted glass.

Fortified against ordinary shocks or blows, still the pane caved in, shattering as if struck by an axe. Vavara's hand continued on unhindered, caught at the throat of a blurred figure on the far side, and drew him headlong through the razor-sharp, dagger-rimmed frame. Deeply cut about his face and arms, shouting his pain and shock, he was sent skidding along the deck in his own blood, only coming to a halt at Malinari's feet.

Malinari dragged him upright—scanned his bloodied, wide-eyed face, his tattered, spattered ship's uniform—and said, "Not Captain Geoff Anderson, no. Merely his under-ling. But you *are* going to take us to him, aren't you?" And he propelled him back towards Vavara at the door.

Vavara's guise was down now; furious, she showed her-self in all her horror. Her forked devil's tongue wriggled behind teeth like twin rows of knives; her eyes flared red; her clawed hands brooked no resistance as she sank fingers like rusty fishhooks deep into the First Mate's cheek, lifting him up onto his toes. And:

"Open this door," she hissed, "lest I'm tempted to toss you through it. For I refuse to climb in the way you came out!"

"It's voice-activated," Malinari told her. "Let him speak."

"Speak, then," said Vavara. "Speak now, or lose what's left of your face!"

"D-d-door!" the man gasped, and a buzz sounded from within, followed by a series of clicks. When the clicks stopped, Vavara turned the handle, thrust her shoulder at the door, and when it sprang open hurled the Mate ahead of her onto the bridge.

Captain Anderson was there; he was using a telephone at the traditional, mainly ceremonial wheel. Taking one look at Vavara and Malinari where they stood framed in the door-way, he dropped the phone and made a clumsy run for the radio room in a soundproofed, glass-walled wing of the bridge. Calmly following him, Malinari caught up with him just as he uttered the command that opened the door. And taking Anderson by the scruff of the neck, he thrust him ahead into the radio room.

An operator sat at the console with earphones on his head. With starting eyes he glanced around, saw the Captain hurtling towards him, was slammed back into the console. Winded, he toppled from his chair as Anderson rebounded from him, and in the next moment Malinari stood over both men.

Grabbing the radio operator by the hair, Malinari drew him to his feet and almost casually enquired of him, "Have you sent any messages? About a becalmed caïque, perhaps, and a rescue at sea?"

"N-n-no!" the radio man gasped. "I . . . I was waiting on the Captain's orders."

"Eh?" said Malinari, raising an eyebrow. "What's that? This one's orders, do you mean?" Grabbing Anderson by the throat, he exerted the massive strength of a Lord of the Wamphyri and tore out his windpipe. The Captain died in a crimson welter of blood and mangled gristle, which Malinari draped over the bald, sweating head of the radio operator. And as that one shrank back and down, the Great Vampire effortlessly took up the Captain's body by the shoulder and hip, hoisted it overhead for a moment, then slammed it down onto the radio console with such force that the entire bank of dials and switches flew apart under the impact. Then, as a sputtering shower of electrical sparks ensued, and a whiff of acrid smoke drifted from the wreckage, Malinari said:

"Thus you have a new Captain. You may call me Captain Malinari. Or better still, Lord Malinari."

"The . . . the radio!" the other sputtered hoarsely. "You've destroyed it! And not just the radio but navigation. Satellite navigation was routed through these controls!"

"Oh, I know!" Malinari nodded. "So now we're not only dumb, but we're blind, too—that is, unless we go to manual. Can you by any chance pilot this vessel?"

"I'm not q-q-qualified." The man wiped blood from his face, his hand trembling violently. "But y-y-yes, I think so."

"Excellent," said Malinari. "The purser thought so, too. So if you'd told me otherwise . . . well, that would have gone quite badly for you. So perhaps you'll now consult the charts, find a suitable rock, and dock us?"

"A rock?" The man looked this way and that. "Dock us?"

"Wreck us," Malinari nodded. "Bring us up aground."

"But first he must see us under way again," said Vavara, as she entered the room. Seeing her in close proximity, the radio operator shrank down more yet.

"So then, things to do," Malinari told him. "You have your orders. But try not to fail me, or I may put you over the side where you will be drawn into the propellers. And whatever else you do, do not think to disobey me. That would prove even more . . . unfortunate."

Hooking the man under the chin, Vavara drew him upright and let him see the gape of her jaws and smell her breath. And, "Very well, then," she glared at him. "Is all understood?"

He couldn't speak, and so simply nodded his head.

Releasing him, she turned to Malinari. "I think I hear running footsteps. Are they coming to their senses, do you think?"

He shrugged. "Very possibly. As you'll recall, the Captain was on the phone speaking to someone when we broke in. Also, I killed a steward and hurled him down a deck. That should definitely have alerted them to the fact that something is amiss."

"Then perhaps it's time we introduced ourselves," she said. "To the rest of the crew, and then to the passengers."

"Aye," Malinari agreed. "To all of them eventually. Myself, I am sorely in need of refreshment, and I've heard the cuisine aboard these pleasure cruisers is superb."

"Cuisine?" she laughed throatily. "Then you shall have your choice. What's your preference, blonde or brunette?"

"Redhead, I think," Malinari leered. "There are bound to be a few among the fourteen hundred on board. But first there's an arms locker we should see to—just a few small arms—in the purser's cabin on the main deck. We should heave that overboard, I think. Our leeches have work enough with all our burns, without that they're overtaxed healing bullet holes, too!"

"I agree," she answered. "As for the rest—the passengers and crew—it won't be long before they discover that the only safe places are on the open decks, out in the sunlight."

"Safe while it lasts," Malinari nodded thoughtfully. "And at least until tonight. By which time—if we're assiduous in our work—we shall have a good many thralls to instruct, vampires in the making."

As they left the radio room and made for the shattered door to the bridge deck, the radio operator came staggering in their wake. Malinari glanced at him, reminding him, "Now don't let us down, will you? If in five minutes' time this ship isn't making headway, I'll know where to come looking for an answer. Oh, and as for that rock I mentioned: the Aegean has plenty of them, as I'm sure you're aware. So find one on your charts—the nearest one will do—and take us to it."

He pointed at the telephone dangling over a varnished spoke of the wooden wheel where the Captain had let it fall. A second spoke supported the First Mate's limp body; it was sunk deep in the socket of his right eye, having got stuck in his skull when Vavara had slammed him facedown onto it. Now he hung there like a wet towel, with his blood pooling around his knees.

But the phone was squawking like a tiny strangled chicken, making shrill enquiries. And: "Carry on, then." Malinari pushed the radio operator forward. "Do something—speak to whoever it is—tell lies and live. But remember, if you intend to survive this, don't do or say anything too rash." And with a final monstrous smile, he followed after Vavara out through the door and into hell.

Hell for the passengers and crew of the *Evening Star,* but to the Wamphyri a way of life and of undeath which they had kept mainly suppressed for far too long . . .

2
The Survivor

THREE DAYS LATER...

Gunnery Commander John Argyle was thirty-eight years old, a good six feet two inches tall, immaculate in lightweight, warm-weather order, blue-eyed, blond, and crew-cut beneath his flat-topped naval officer's cap... and plainly annoyed. As a man who had gone to sea at eighteen and climbed up through the ranks to his current position—in which he was a stickler for regulations and discipline in general—it was these despised "civilians" or, in ratings' belowdecks parlance, "landlubbers," who were the cause of his considerable displeasure.

More to the point, however, it was the fact that the Captain had seen fit to detail *him* as escort to this polyglot party of nonnautical and apparently seriously disturbed people. Only add to this their implied VIP status... it did nothing to curb Argyle's feelings of resentment. For in his estimation—based on previous, mercifully infrequent contact with such "VIPs"—the abbreviation usually stood for Virtually Incompetent Plebs!

And as for *this* foursome...

... Well, what was one to make of them?

Three of them sun-browned and one pale as a ghost; three of them comparatively "old men" and one little more than a girl or "young woman" at best; three of them Caucasian and one as Chinese as they come—in his looks if not in his accent, which was "pure" Eastender London—and all of them wont to converse with his or her fellows in a kind of double-talk as alien as Martian to the down-to-earth gunnery officer!

Argyle realized that he'd been scowling just a moment

after the leader of his charges—a slightly overweight, broad-shouldered, somewhat lugubrious-looking man called Trask—gave him a much sharper, sideways look and said, "Can't we get in closer than this? I'd like to get down there, 'alongside' or whatever, and see if we can take a look in through the bridge's windows." His voice over the headphones was tinny, but even so there was a definite bite to it.

The group of five was standing in the midsection observation bay of a Royal Navy antisubmarine jet-copter, hooked up to a safety rail with the boarding door open. In front of them and below the oval door frame, the silvery curve of the streamlined starboard pontoon was plainly visible; to anyone suffering from vertigo, it would seem the ideal launching platform into oblivion! Trask and his colleagues had been in a great many far more dangerous places, however, and the height and frequently dizzying motion when the chopper manoeuvred were the least of their concerns.

"We can indeed get down there and 'alongside or whatever,'" Argyle eventually answered. "In normal circumstances we'd even be able to land on her—God knows she's big enough! But we've already tried that, remember? And if this really is a new variant strain of the plague . . ." He let it taper off, shrugged, and went on, "Well, it *isn't* a good idea. It could be airborne, and this chopper's fan is disturbing an awful lot of air. You don't want to be breathing plague germs, do you?"

Now Trask looked at Argyle more closely, even penetratingly, and there was something in the older man's keen green eyes, and in his frown, that warned the gunnery officer not to appear too defiant. But if Argyle couldn't say it, he could at least think it:

Get in closer, my backside! What, to a fucking plague ship? What a fucking idiot! A Virtually Incompetent Pleb, indeed!

But even as Argyle smiled (albeit inwardly) at his own wit, again Trask's eyes were flashing their singular warning. And:

"So, you're an expert in these matters, are you?" He

cocked his head a little on one side. "You know all about this plague, right?"

"I know enough to stand well back from sudden death," said Argyle, stiffening at Trask's dry tone, his deadpan expression. "I know that if it's killed off an entire shipload of passengers and crew in the few days since the ship sailed from Cyprus—taking them all out before they could even tell us what was going on—and that if a chopper only has to touch down on the deck to cost the lives of a pilot, two aircrew, and the ship's doctor—"

"You *know* nothing!" Trask snapped, cutting him off. "You're merely guessing, and you're being deliberately obstructive. You don't much care for me and my people, and you think that you're wasting your time with us. We're sightseers—sensation-seekers, that's all—and you'd much rather be back on *Invincible* in the Officer's Mess with your shipmates, than looking after a gaggle of dumb boffins. And as for us: since we can't possibly achieve anything here, we'd do best to bugger off home and let the Navy handle things their own way . . . right?"

For a moment Argyle's mouth fell open in astonishment. This sudden outburst—despite that it was mainly correct—seemed to confirm his original opinion. But since he was here to cater to these people, pander to their needs . . . he gritted his teeth and said, "Let me assure you, Mr. Trask, that I'm only—"

"Don't you go 'assuring' us of anything!" The girl standing beside Trask spoke up, narrowing her eyes where she stared into Argyle's face as intensely as Trask himself. "Mr. Trask's right: you've been thinking your nasty, pig-headed thoughts all along. You consider us high-powered, mentally impoverished bureaucrats or something: morbid thrill-seekers swanning around in the Mediterranean, who'll eventually report back to our bosses in Whitehall and make out we've actually done something. But at the end of the day it'll be you who gets stuck with the job."

Argyle frowned back at her, rubbed at his chin awhile, finally grinned wonderingly . . . *and* genuinely! Both Trask and the girl, they'd come pretty close. "Actually," he answered, "I was thinking you might be Lloyds underwriters or something. From Mr. Trask's expression, I would have guessed he was calculating his personal losses!"

Relaxing a little, Trask shook his head. "My *future* losses, possibly . . . and not just mine or Lloyds but the world's. So let me straighten you out, Commander. We're not the bureaucrats and utter assholes you might think we are. But this time around we *are* the experts. Yes, there was, and probably still is, a plague here, but it didn't originate in China and it isn't what you've been made to believe. In broad daylight like this—high noon, as it were—it can't do us any harm. The only mistake the Navy made, which in the circumstances was pretty much understandable, even if it wasn't what you'd been advised to do, was to send in that recce chopper in the twilight after sundown."

"Would you care to explain?" Argyle had begun to sense something of the other's authority now. Just looking at this man he knew he wasn't exaggerating, waffling, or just plain lying, yet at the same time he wasn't saying too much, either. So what the hell was going on here? What was it all about? "You see, if you really want me to commit this aircraft, placing the pilot, your people, and myself in danger, I really should know what—"

But again Trask cut him off. "No, you really shouldn't! You see, Commander, even if I were to tell you, it's doubtful you'd believe me—and I certainly wouldn't blame you. But if or when you've seen something of it for yourself . . ."

"Seeing is believing," said the girl. "Well, in most cases, anyway, where people aren't quite so stiff-necked, locked in to their own little worlds. But at least it's encouraging that you *are* actually beginning to think now, and not just snarling away to yourself."

The Commander gave a small start. For it was a fact that he had been "snarling away to himself"—getting all hot under the collar—and it was also a fact that he was "actually beginning to think now." Which made one too many times that Trask and the girl had seen through him. But *right* through him, to the core!

"Who on earth are you people?" Argyle stared at Trask, then at the girl—also at the tall pale man, and at the yellow one—and began to feel more than a little foolish as he tried to grin and frown at the same time, and only succeeded in blinking his confusion. The way they looked back at him (not in contempt, no, but rather, what, sympathetically?) made him feel very much cut down to size. So that again he felt prompted to enquire, "I mean, all I was told is that you're E-Branch. So what does that make you? Mind-readers? Psychics or something?"

Or something, obviously.

For the girl only smiled and looked away; likewise her colleagues, the tall man and the small yellow man both, while Trask said, "Now maybe you'll be so good as to have the pilot take us in closer? There's no danger, Commander. Not as long as we don't try to alight on this lady, and even then not until nightfall."

The "lady" Trask had referred to was a cruise ship that had beached herself on an unnamed island—or more properly a fang of sun-bleached rock—between the island of Áyios Evstrátios, itself little more than a boulder, and the popular Greek island resort of Límnos ten miles to the north. Except E-Branch's best bet was that she hadn't simply run aground in some kind of accident but that she'd been wrecked deliberately, and it was just possible that the wreckers were still aboard. As for a mutating strain of the Asiatic bubonic plague: that was the cover story, certainly, but as Trask had stated it was a very different kind of plague that he and his party expected to find here. They had even dared hope (albeit remotely) that they might also discover its source here . . . *and* put an end to it forever.

"What do you think, David?" Trask asked the smallest of his colleagues after Argyle had ordered the pilot to take them down and in a little closer. "How does it look to you?"

"Mindsmog," said the other at once, his voice taut as piano wire over the headsets. "The ship is full of it, stem to stern. This is where they escaped to, definitely. But I find it doubtful that they themselves are still here. It's too thin. There's no heavy presence or presences that I can detect, just a lot—a *hell* of a lot—of individual sources. Not that we can put a great deal of faith in that. For it was the same on Krassos for a while until we learned what we were doing wrong, or what they were doing right. Our 'old friend' is good at shielding himself, while she . . . I don't need to remind you what *she* can do! Still and all, I reckon they've moved on. They must surely have known they'd make one hell of a target sitting here. So I don't think we need worry so much about them as what they've left behind."

Trask offered a grim nod of agreement. "They're on the run, and they're all through with doing things quietly, covertly. We hit them in Australia, Krassos, London, and ruined their plans. Now they're deliberately giving us work—leaving a trail, yes, but one of destruction—in the full knowledge that while we're dealing with problems like this . . ."

". . . We can't concentrate on tracking them," the yellow man, whom Argyle knew to be called David Chung, finished it for him. "Yes, that sounds about right . . ."

"Liz?" Trask glanced at the girl; and totally bewildered by their double-talk, Argyle looked at her, too. Now that a little of his venom had been drawn, that wasn't at all hard to do. Liz Merrick, as she'd been introduced to him when first the Commander met up with these people, was maybe five seven and about as pert as a girl can get—as he'd found out the hard way. She'd be twenty-something; she was all curves, long-legged and willow-waisted, and when she smiled (she *had* actually smiled when they had been introduced, but that hadn't lasted long) it was like a ray of bright light. Her green eyes were a very different shade from Trask's—deep as a beer bottle, deep as the sea—but her stare could be equally unnerving. Her hair, black as night, and cut in a boyish bob, had the shine of natural good health to it . . . and Argyle suspected that if he had photographs of her in a swimsuit he could earn himself a month's salary selling them to HMS *Invincible*'s crew! Come to think of it, it appeared that at at least one member of the crew had already contrived to get to know her a little better; she was wearing ship's fatigues three sizes too big for her that had never looked nearly this good on any sailor of Argyle's acquaintance!

As he was thinking these things the chopper performed a jig in a small thermal, and for a moment the beached and apparently derelict pleasure cruiser sidestepped out of view. In that same moment Liz glanced at Argyle, and said, "That's better. But now if you'll try to keep your mental observations low-key, this is one 'Virtually Incompetent Pleb' who's trying to concentrate."

Argyle's jaw fell open. Dumbfounded, he could only stare at her. But the shipwreck had swung back into view maybe a hundred feet below and a hundred yards away, and as Liz focussed all of her attention on it her forehead had wrinkled into a deep frown of intense concentration. Taking one hand from the safety rail, she lightly touched her fingertips to her temple forward of her right ear—

—And in the next moment gasped and jerked back on her line as if she had been physically thrust backwards, rebounding when the nylon safety line reached full stretch!

Trask caught her arm—Chung, too—as she steadied herself and made a wild grab for the safety bar with her free hand. She couldn't have fallen anyway, but some kind of temporary disorientation had completely thrown her. And:

"Liz?" Trask said again, no longer her superior but more an anxious father- figure now, as he continued to support her. "Are you okay?"

She took a deep breath and tried a wan smile, but under her tan she was visibly paler, as if the blood had drained from her face. Argyle, believing he knew what this was, said, "It's just motion sickness, very much akin to seasickness. I see plenty of it. She's not used to the rhythm of the chopper, that's all."

Trask barely glanced at him, then spoke to Liz again. "What was it? What did you get?"

"People," she answered. "Hundreds of them—men, women and children—all of them in shock, not knowing what's happened to them but knowing enough not to come out on the decks in the sunlight. It'll be 'instinctive' by now; the filthy stuff in their blood will have done it to them. And the terrible craving: it's already there!" She offered a small, involuntary shudder. "It's horrible, Ben . . . it makes your skin crawl! In the last twenty-four hours they've all of them infected each other. Now they're hungry again. Soon they'll separate into factions, and then . . . and then . . ."

"I know," said Trask. "I know. A mini-bloodwar!"

And Argyle said, "Hungry? People on the ship? But you can't possibly know that! And anyway you must be wrong. This is a big pleasure cruiser and the galley will be full of excellent food. It's only been a few days, and if there's still anyone alive on that vessel they'll—"

"—Most of them will still be 'alive,' " Trask told him. "If not as we understand life. And yes, they'd be perfectly capable of surviving on the ship's food . . . except they'll be driven to go for something more to their liking."

Most of this had flown right over Argyle's head. "Not as we understand life?" He frowned. "I'm not sure I understand *any* of what you're saying! You can only mean they're incurable, better off dead."

"Something like that," Trask answered after a moment, sighing his resignation.

"But—" The Commander was plainly confused, very uncertain now, and feeling well out of his depth.

"—*But* I want to get in a whole lot closer," Trask told him yet again. "And I do intend to look inside." He tapped a fingernail on a pair of binoculars slung around his neck. "Those huge panoramic windows in the bridge will do nicely."

Standing in line, hooked up in their safety harnesses, from left to right the five were Argyle, Trask, Liz, Chung, and last but not least the tall, pale, almost cadaverous figure of a man called Ian Goodly. Now the latter spoke up. "We'll have to sink her, Ben. According to the charts, this rock is only the tip of a steep-sided submarine mountain. If we were to send her to the bottom here, the abyss would finish it for us. In fact, there is no 'if' or 'were' or 'would' about it. Though I hate to have to say it, that's how it's going to be: the only way we can ensure that nothing of this ever, er, resurfaces."

"You've seen it?" Trask said, sharply.

"Oh, yes," said the other. "The ship-to-ship missiles going in, the explosions, the stem going up in the air, and the rapid slide backwards off those rocks."

"Sink her!?" Now Argyle exploded. Finally he had had enough of this gobbledegook. "What? You're talking about having *Invincible sink* her? You must be out of your tiny minds, you people! This is an ultramodern pleasure cruiser and even her lifeboats are worth millions! Just looking at her I'm sure she can be refloated, then sailed or towed away—that is, of course, after we've made sure she's clean. But even if she's too badly holed, still the salvage contract alone would be worth—"

"—Nothing," said Trask. "Nothing is coming off that ship."

"You *are* fucking crazy!" Argyle exploded again. "And if you don't mind, next time I start a sentence I'd like to be able to finish it! I'm getting heartily sick of—"

"Commander?" the pilot's voice sounded in his headphones.

"Oh! . . . Bloody hell! . . . *Yes?*" Argyle snapped, still glowering his fury at the four.

"The air-sea rescue chopper has spotted something starboard of the wreck," the pilot came back.

"Something?"

"Someone," the other specified. "A living someone, still on board and active. Do you want me to patch you through?"

"Yes," said Argyle. "Of course. Patch us through. We may as well all hear what's going on. Who knows? That way *I* might actually get to learn something, too!"

"Roger," said the pilot. "And I'll take us starboard of the wreck so you can see what's happening."

The air-sea rescue helicopter had accompanied them out

from the carrier HMS *Invincible* where she lay at anchor like a small landmass in her own right on the horizon some five or six miles away. Starboard of the wreck, about the same distance away from her as Argyle, Trask and party were to port, now the big rescue chopper sat like a great hawk on the air, with the ripples from her downdraft spreading out in choppy concentric circles on the surface of the dead-calm sea.

Along with its regular crew, the rescue chopper carried two other members of E-Branch's contingent: a roguish, leathery old Gypsy by the name of Lardis Lidesci—possibly of Hungarian or Romanian descent, if Argyle was any judge of ethnic origins—and a young Englishman called Jake Cutter, who seemed to stand somewhat apart from the rest of the team, as if he wasn't quite one of them. Like the others he had a very definite "attitude," but where theirs seemed intense beyond the demands of the situation, his was . . . different. Argyle had spoken to him on first meeting, and it had seemed to him that Cutter wasn't all there; not meaning that he was in any way mentally deficient, but just that he appeared very much preoccupied despite that he tried to hide it. And while the Commander had no way of knowing it, he'd hit the nail right on the head.

Preoccupied: to engross or fill the mind of (someone) or to dominate (someone's) attention, thoughts, mind, et cetera, and so on. And therefore from a defining viewpoint, Jake Cutter could be said to be *very* preoccupied. But for the moment at least he *was* concentrating . . . on what could be seen through his binoculars: that tiny human figure on the shielding collar—almost a small deck in its own right— that protected the upper deck from the hot stench of the ship's slipstreamed "chimney" array, a delta-shaped set of six massive exhaust flues high over the stern.

Right now, however, with the engines at a standstill, there were no exhaust fumes, and the small, lonely figure was leaning or propping itself up against an open service hatch in the foremost chimney, from which he had emerged only a few seconds ago. Jake could see now that it was a man, but he looked so tattered and dirty in grimy coveralls that it had been hard to tell. And he was looking up openmouthed at the two helicopters in a kind of stunned disbelief. Or was he simply in shock?

"Mr. Cutter?" (The pilot's voice crackled in Jake's headset, causing him to start.) "Mr. Trask is asking to speak to you. I'm patching him through now."

"Roger," said Jake, as he leaned out a little from the open hatch to watch the antisubmarine jet-copter come *whupwhupping* through one hundred and eighty degrees to the starboard side of the wreck, giving it a wide berth. And in the next moment:

"Jake?" Ben Trask's harsh, gravelly, unmistakable voice was sounding in his ears. "Where is he? Where's this . . . survivor?"

"Our side of the exhaust flues," Jake answered. "In fact he just a moment ago climbed out of one! You should be able to see him by now. He looks done in."

"Yes, we see him," said Trask. "But done in by what? By his experience, or by the sunlight?"

"Doesn't look like he's shrinking from the sun to me," Jake answered. "He's just shrinking, on the point of collapse. Maybe you should let Liz take a look at him."

"Wait," said Trask. And a few seconds later: "She says he's in shock. He's almost a blank in there, his mind shot to pieces. So he probably is a survivor!"

"I can go down on their rescue gear and get him off there?" Jake suggested. "Or I could do it my way and get him off faster still."

"No!" Trask answered at once. "Keep the Continuum as a last resort. Send down the gear by all means, yes, but if he's going to make it off that ship it will have to be under his own steam. You see that chopper standing idle on the promenade deck?"

"I know, I know," said Jake. "That's what happened the last time someone landed on her. They stayed landed."

"Right," said Trask grimly, and Jake sensed his nod. "So we won't be making the same mistake. If this one *really* wants off, he gets off on his own. By the time you've reeled him in Lardis will know if he's okay or not. If he *is* okay, then it's a lucky break—not only for him but also for us. And if he isn't okay, well, Lardis will be able to handle that, too. It's one hell of a drop back down to the deck or onto those rocks. Either way it won't make too much difference."

"Ben," said Jake, "you know this is a rescue chopper, don't you? I mean, the crew heard what you said just then, and if you were the captain I suspect you'd have a mutiny on your hands!"

"Yes, I know it's a rescue chopper!" Trask answered. "And I also know what we could be dealing with here, as do you. So for now, just you get that gear down to him and then we'll see what we'll see. And meanwhile, Commander Argyle and I will be taking a shot at looking in through the panoramic windows at the sharp end . . . that's the bridge, to you."

"Roger and out," said Jake, sourly.

"That boss of yours," one of the rescue crew spoke to Jake, after the pilot had reverted to an onboard frequency. "What is he? Some kind of monster?"

"Anyone who doesn't know Trask or his work," Jake answered, "might easily make that mistake. But no, he isn't a monster. He does know an awful lot *about* monsters, though. Don't ask me to explain more than that because I can't."

"And don't ask us to lower the gear," said the other. "It's our job, sure, and God knows we'd like to get that guy off. But if he's a carrier . . ." His shrug was by no means callous; on the contrary, if anything it was helpless. "Commander Argyle is the only one who can give that kind of order."

Jake looked at him. The sailor was a young petty officer, a fresh-faced twenty-two-year-old with fair hair and freckles. He was also an expert at his job, and he knew the rules. Only this time he was torn two ways, between knowing what he'd *like* to do and knowing (or believing he knew) the dangers inherent in that course of action. It was the difference between his training—his duty and natural instinct to save life—and the knowledge that the life he wanted to save might be a plague-bearer, someone who carried the seeds of death. And that was a feeling that Jake understood only too well.

"No sweat," he said. "So we'll simply sit tight here—me, you, and your mates—and wait for the order from your Commander Argyle. I understand your position, but the order *will* come, I can promise you that. So even if we can't lower the gear now, still we should have it ready."

"It's already ready!" said the other, scathingly. "On a job like this and once we're airborne, it's always ready."

"Whoa!" said Jake, ruefully. "What would I know? I'm just a civilian, right?"

The rescue team was made up of three petty officers, and as far as they were concerned, Jake Cutter and Lardis Lidesci were precisely that: "just civilians," alleged "experts" who'd doubtless get in the way at their earliest opportunity. As for their boss—this Trask bloke and Co. on the sub hunter-killer—well, Gunnery Commander Argyle would sort *them* out, for sure!

The three glanced at each other where they sat hooked up in their safety rigs, then looked again at Cutter and his Gypsyish companion. And even though Jake wasn't a telepath—not in the fullest sense of the word—still it wasn't hard to guess what they were thinking:

If this was what experts in tropical diseases were supposed to look like . . . well, it had them beat all to hell!

Jake was wearing a shirt, a flying jacket, jeans, and cowboy boots; in fact he *looked* something of a "cowboy" to the crew of the air-sea rescue chopper. Long-legged, he had narrow hips and a small backside, but the rest of him wasn't small. He was well over six feet tall—maybe six four, if you included the heels of those boots—and had long arms to match his legs. His eyes were chestnut-brown; likewise his hair which he wore swept back and braided into a pigtail. His hair wasn't all brown, however, but had contrasting, even startling shocks of white at the temples: this was a recent thing, a change that had taken place in him almost overnight. His face was lean and hollow-cheeked, and he looked like a week of HMS *Invincible*'s meals wouldn't do him any harm . . . but on the other hand the extra weight would certainly slow him down; and Jake Cutter looked fast. His lips were thin (some might even say cruel) and when he smiled it was hard to make out if there was any real humour in it. His jaw was angular and thinly scarred on the left side, and his nose had been broken high on the bridge so that it hung like a sheer cliff—like the straight strong nose of a Native American—instead of projecting. But despite his lean and hungry look, Jake's shoulders were broad, his chest deep, and there was more than enough of strength in him both physical and psychological. Indeed, his mental powers bordered on the metaphysical, occasionally crossing those borders into realms that other men had never dreamed of visiting and certainly wouldn't care to.

As for Jake's companion:

The Old Lidesci was short, barrel-bodied, and almost simian in the great length of his arms. His lank hair, once jet-black, was greying now and in places turning white; it framed a leathery, weather-beaten face with a flattened, suspicious nose that sat uncomfortably over a mouth that was missing too many teeth. As for the ones that he'd kept: they were uneven and as stained as old ivory. But under shaggy and expressive eyebrows Lardis's dark brown watchful eyes glittered his mind's agility and defied the ever-encroaching infirmities of his body.

And if Jake had seemed a little cowboyish in boots, jeans, and his deliberately contrived casual manner, then what was the rescue helicopter's crew supposed to make of Lardis? The Lidesci's mode of dress was outlandish, like a cross between that of a frontiersman out of the Old West and a European Gypsy of that same era! It was all greens, browns, and greys; all tassels and tiny silver bells that jingled when he moved, so that the overall impression was that of a total outdoorsman, a fighting man, and a wanderer in endless woodlands. As if to verify that last: in a cutaway sheath under his left arm, Lardis carried a wicked-looking, razor-

sharp machete, its time-blackened ironwood grip etched with
several rows of notches . . .

While the crew had spent a little time wondering about
Jake and Lardis, Commander Argyle and the larger E-Branch
contingent aboard the hunter-killer had descended to within
thirty feet of the stem of the stranded vessel and were looking through binoculars into the spacious bridge. For perhaps
thirty seconds Jake watched the jet-copter hovering there,
fanning the air over the stricken ship. But then, as the aircraft
suddenly gained altitude, performing a slow spiral up and
outward, Trask's voice was again patched through to the
rescue chopper. And if anything it was harsher than ever:

"Where's that rescue tackle? I want you to get that man
off there, and I do mean right now!"

"Fine," Jake sent back, "but the crew needs Argyle's say-
so on that."

Ten seconds ticked by, and then Commander Argyle's
voice—stuttering and quite obviously shocked—said, "G-g-
get him off there. Get that man off that b-bloody ship, and
be bloody quick about it! But listen in: no matter how long
it takes, *no one is to go down there*! He has to make it on
his own."

And once again Trask, saying, "Jake, the same rules are
in force. If he isn't what he would seem to be, let Lardis
handle it his way. Is that understood?"

"Only too well," said Jake. "Over and out . . ."

3
The Trouble With Harry

DOWN BELOW, ON THE SHIELDING COLLAR OF
the exhaust array, the rescue bucket had swung to and fro
in front of the survivor's face half a dozen times without
him seeming to notice it. But as finally it collided with him,

almost sending him sprawling, he appeared to wake up. Then, looking up at the chopper sixty feet overhead, and fending off the bucket and harness as once again it made a swing at him, he reached up an imploring hand, blinked his eyes, and seemed to be trying to say something.

The winchman directed the pilot on his headset: "Take her down just a few more feet. Good! Now hold it steady—hold it right there!" And as the gear clattered down and skittered on the collar, jerking this way and that immediately in front of the survivor, a second petty officer with a loud-hailer called down:

"Don't try to grab the bucket or it may haul you off your feet. Just sit yourself in it—your whole body weight—and adjust the harness straps. Then try to sit back and hang on to the chains. That'll help you feel secure. And don't worry, we won't let you fall."

The "bucket" was more like one of those aerial chairs that children ride at fairgrounds. Suspended from four leather-clad chains, it had a back and sides but no legs. A webbing harness was fitted to the interior, with a safety belt dangling loose. And *like* an aerial chair, even a child could see how to use it . . . or should be able to. But the man below was in shock.

As the bucket danced in front of him—now bouncing on the collar, now twitching to knee height, finally swinging out and away from him—he took a dazed, stumbling step toward it and tried to grab at it. After that . . . it was only sheer good fortune that saved him; one more staggering step would have taken him to the rim of the collar some twenty feet above the bridge deck, and the rescue tackle might easily have dragged him over the edge. But as it happened the chair spun around him, struck him behind the knees, and scooped him up.

And slumped in the bucket, with his arms and legs dangling loose—and likewise the straps of the harness, which he hadn't fastened—he was winched toward safety, or to what would have been safety in any normal or routine rescue situation. But even as the gears wound him in and he flopped there, with his vacant eyes staring up at his rescuers from a pale, dirty, slack-jawed face, so Trask's harsh, apparently emotionless voice was in the crew's ears, telling them:

"From now on you do *exactly* as Jake Cutter and the Old Lidesci tell you to do. They are acting on my orders, on authority conveyed to me by your Gunnery Commander Argyle. The man you're bringing up from that ship may or may not be infected with this . . . this terrible disease. But the old man called Lardis is the world's foremost expert in such things and he will know. In any event his decision—and whatever action he takes—has my full backing. Anyone attempting to interfere will not only be liable to severe disciplinary action, he may well be placing the lives of your entire crew in jeopardy!"

The rescue crew's members glanced at each other but made no comment, and the bucket came up within reach of the hatch. Then Lardis yelled across to the man in the bucket: "You, I want you to give me your hand. Reach out and give it now!" He leaned out of the hatch on his safety strap and offered a gnarled, purple-veined left hand to the survivor. The fingers of that hand were heavy with rings of purest silver.

The man in the bucket looked at Lardis, then at his hand. A flicker of vague recognition passed over his face, and his lips formed the word "Szgany!" But still his arms continued to hang loose in the downdraft, and in another moment his eyes had gone vacant again.

Lardis glanced at the three petty officers. "Swing him in a little, but carefully." And to Jake: "In the event he makes any sudden move—tries to jump aboard—you know what to do."

Nodding his understanding, Jake took out a specially modified 9 mm Browning automatic from an inside pocket of his flying jacket and cocked it—at which the fair-haired, freckled petty officer gasped and said, "What the fuck . . . !?"

"Just do as Lardis said," Jake told him, aiming his weapon directly between the eyes of the man in the bucket. And

without further protest (for the time being at least), and beginning to understand just how serious this business was
beyond any normal course of duty, the winchman swung the
pulley arm in toward the hatch.

In that selfsame moment the survivor moved! He grabbed
hold of the Old Lidesci's hand (but so suddenly that Jake
almost shot him), gave a wild inarticulate cry, and babbled
something which to Jake sounded utterly unintelligible.

"What did he say?" said Jake anxiously. "What did he
say?"

"He called me 'father,' " Lardis grunted. "Said he'd cried
out to me and was glad that I've answered his call. Very
complimentary! He doesn't seem to be afraid of silver, either. But we're not finished yet."

Using his free hand, he took out a small aerosol dispenser
which he passed to Jake. And drawing his machete, he said,
"he has my hand, this one, but if he should squeeze it too
hard—perhaps with a fiend's strength—then I shall have
his!"

Jake leaned out a little on his line, showed the dispenser
to the man in the bucket, and said, "This shouldn't do you
any harm. Close your eyes and don't breathe for a moment."

Continuing to cling to Lardis's hand, the man looked to
him for reassurance. "Do as he says," Lardis told him. And
dangling there on thin air, the survivor closed his eyes.

Jake sprayed him in the face, a full burst of two or three
seconds . . . and nothing happened. But the rescue crew
wrinkled their noses and again looked at each other. What,
garlic? Well, something that smelled like garlic, anyway.

The man in the bucket opened his eyes, took a deep
breath, didn't seem at all affected.

And Lardis said, "Now the acid test. Except it isn't acid,
but blood!" And without pause he slid the razor-sharp blade
of his weapon lightly over the back of his own wrist. And
showing the survivor what he'd done—the slow drip of his
blood into the abyss—he said:

"No, I'm not your father. But I readily understand why
you would cry out to him. So perhaps we can be brothers,

you and I? Perhaps we already are, of a sort. 'Szgany' you called me. Aye, and you're right. So what do you say? Can we be blood brothers, my friend from this world's so-called 'old' country, and doubtless from a long line of Szgany fore-fathers?"

The other said nothing, simply watched as Jake sprayed the blade of Lardis's machete . . . before it descended to the survivor's wrist and cut a thin red line there!

And the freckled petty officer burst out, "Now what kind of fucking voodoo barbarism is this!?" Reaching past Jake, he made to grab at Lardis . . . and felt the barrel of Jake's gun digging into his ribs. And:

"Let it be!" Jake warned him through clenched teeth. "What? Didn't you hear what Trask said? Man, you're under orders."

"But . . . but this is just a very frightened man!" the crew-man protested, drawing back.

"Just a man, aye," Lardis agreed, with a curt nod. "Only a man—but a damned lucky one!" And, as he sheathed his machete, "You can bring him in now."

Meanwhile the survivor had done absolutely nothing. He continued to sit there, looking unemotionally at his wrist without really seeing anything. And if that could be called a reaction, it was his only one.

They swung the rescue tackle in, secured it and closed the hatch, then gentled the rescued man out of the tangle of chains and webbing. He immediately toppled into Lardis's arms, and the old man fell back with him onto the crew's padded bench and sat there cradling him.

"We have him," Jake told Trask on his headset. "He seems to be okay."

"Has he said anything?" Trask's voice had lost something of its sharp edge.

"Said anything?" Jake answered. "Hell, no, nothing I could understand. Just looking at him, I'd say he still doesn't believe he's alive!"

"Well, don't *let* him say anything," Trask said. "Don't

even ask him anything, not until we're back aboard *Invincible* and we can talk to him in private."

"Roger that," said Jake. And to Lardis: "*Is* he okay?"

"Oh, yes," the old man answered, wonderingly. "In fact he's already asleep!"

"Probably for the first time in three days," said Jake.

"Probably, aye," Lardis replied gruffly. "And certainly for the first time in three long nights . . ."

Aboard the aircraft carrier *Invincible,* Trask's contingent had bunks next to a large stateroom used for ship's orders groups. They also had use of the stateroom, which was where the medics saw to the survivor.

On landing, however, Trask had been called to see the Captain. Which meant that he arrived at the stateroom some fifteen minutes later. Briefly looking inside and on seeing the medics, he called his people out into the cramped privacy of the corridor, all except Lardis who stayed with the survivor.

And Trask was plainly bitter as he told his colleagues, "We have to go back to the *Evening Star.*"

"We *what*?" said Liz, very obviously concerned. "Are you saying I missed someone else? Ben, I can't see how that's possible. Okay, I know I overlooked the survivor, but in all that horror, confusion, and mindsmog . . . I mean, he was just one small human mind—that's if you can call that crawling void a mind! But I swear that while he was being rescued I scanned the entire ship stem to stern, and—"

"—This has nothing to do with survivors." Trask shook his head, cutting her off. "It's a safe bet that there aren't going to be any more of those. But the Captain's had 'a request' from our Minister Responsible, which of course was relayed to *Invincible* through the Admiralty. And the Admiralty, not being quite as 'diplomatic' as our Old Man, has made it an order."

"We've been ordered back to that ship?" Goodly spoke up in his typically high-pitched, piping voice. "But why?

The ship's doomed, Ben. I've already seen it going down. It *will* happen!"

"I know," said Trask. "And we've got to ensure we're not on board when it does! But that's not the worst of it."

"So what is the worst of it?" said David Chung, nervously.

Scowling, Trask leaned back against a bulkhead, scratched his forehead, and said, "As if we haven't enough on our hands, now there's this." And then, resignedly: "People, it seems that someone in high places—someone who should have known better, if not our Minister Responsible then maybe one of *his* superiors, possibly the Prime Minister himself—has let something of what we did on Krassos and what we're trying to do on HMS *Invincible* slip. That would be bad enough, but it seems it's slipped all the way to some high-profile boffin at Porton Down."

"Porton Down?" Liz frowned—then opened her eyes wide and gasped. She was plainly shocked.

Jake glanced from face to face and saw the same expression on all of them. "What?" he said. "Porton Down? Isn't that some kind of—I don't know—some kind of research establishment where they mess about with . . . with . . . ?" But there he paused, for he'd suddenly remembered what they messed about with.

Trask nodded his bleak corroboration. "Yes, I suppose it's accurate to say they 'mess about' down there in Wiltshire, for certainly they handle some of the messiest stuff on this small planet. We're talking about the Porton Down Centre for Applied Microbiology and Research. And that same person in high places—the bloody idiot—has agreed with them that we should get them a sample!"

"A sample?" David Chung had backed off a pace. "A sample of what? Don't tell me they—"

"But I *am* telling you," Trask answered. "And it's not only a sample they want but preferably a live one! Oh, if it was up to me Ian's cruise missiles would be on their way right now—and the *Evening Star* on *her* way, straight to the bottom! But now that the Admiralty's involved it's no longer up to me. If we don't go in—and I do have the right to refuse, as the message makes plain—then the Navy will do the job their way. But do you think I'm going to allow that to happen?"

"Not a snowball's chance in hell," said Jake, fully in the picture now. "The idea of a thing like that getting loose on a ship of war like *Invincible* . . . it doesn't bear thinking about. There's more sheer destructive firepower on this ship than was used in both world wars!"

"That's right," said Trask. "And a lot more than enough to start World War Three! So since we're the only ones who really understand what we're up against—"

"We're going in," said Liz, with a small shudder.

"But not you," said Trask. "Not this time."

"But—" she began to protest.

"No buts about it." Trask shook his head determinedly. "You put ten years on me when Vavara got hold of you on Krassos, and frankly I've no years left to spare. Anyway, this won't be like anything we've ever done before. On the Australian job, most of those vampires we tackled had Wamphyri or lieutenant overseers. They knew what they were doing. Likewise on Krassos. This time, the poor creatures we'll be dealing with are barely thralls . . . not even that, for only three days ago they were people holidaying in the Med. Now they're undead in the Med, and the ones who changed them are no longer here to offer them any kind of guidance. So if we should be attacked en masse—"

"It will be a slaughter," said Jake. "And it'll be us doing the slaughtering. We'll be armed, and they won't be. We'll know what we're about, and they'll still be coming to terms with the unknown, the utterly horrific."

But Liz shook her head. "They know what they are," she said. "Oh, they're confused for now, terrified as yet . . . but they do know. And that hideous hunger is growing in them. Down there in the dark, in the bowels of that ship—all eight decks—we'll look like so much fresh meat to them."

"Except slaughter isn't our job," said Trask, "and we won't be doing it or having it done to us. Nor will we be going belowdecks. Not too far below, anyway. Our job is to get a sample—just one—and once we've got it and we're out of there, we'll call in Ian's missiles. *That* will be the slaughter."

"I wish you wouldn't call them 'my' missiles," said Goodly. "I can't help what I saw, can't stop what will be." And:

"My God . . . all those people!" Chung shook his head, looked small and pale and sick.

And Jake said, "Am I missing something here? I thought we'd already agreed that we won't do it, that we simply can't afford to bring something like that out of there?"

"Nothing living," said Trask. "When we're in the air again, we'll tell them we have a sample and they can sink the ship. By the time they find out the sample isn't alive it'll be too late to do anything about it."

"A dead sample?" said Liz.

"An undead one, yes." Trask stared at her. "They want infected blood, flesh, brain tissue. That's why they're asking for—Jesus!—an entire 'specimen.' A person, for God's sake! But we won't let them have one. Oh, they'll get what they want, but it won't be walking on two legs, and it definitely won't be thinking, calculating, and just waiting for its first opportunity."

"Flesh, blood, brain tissue?" Jake frowned and continued to look puzzled.

But Trask only glanced at him and said, "No need to concern yourself. It'll be more work for Lardis. For where that kind of thing is concerned, the Old Lidesci really is the world's foremost expert. And not only on this world . . ."

They had been scheduled to go in that evening well before dark. It would have been sooner, but Trask's one stipulation had been that he must be allowed to speak to the survivor first. *Invincible*'s medics, however, had temporarily sedated that one in the hope that sleep would be conducive to recovery. Used to dealing with physical rather than mental trauma—and lacking the guidance of the vessel's chief medical officer, assumed dead on the *Evening Star*—they believed that sleep, a universal panacea, would be equally effective here. Perhaps it would be, but meanwhile their patient would be out for the next three or four hours.

After the E-Branch members had talked through and finalized details for the coming mission, as Goodly and Chung returned to the stateroom, Trask took Liz and Jake aside to talk to them in private.

"Things seem to be coming to the boil far more quickly than we expected," he said. "And it really does appear that Malinari and Vavara have thrown caution to the wind. As for Lord Szwart: well, we don't know about him; we can't say for sure whether he was trapped and died below when you destroyed that temple under London" (he glanced at Jake, for once appreciatively, ungrudgingly), "or whether he escaped. But we do know that these creatures are tenacious beyond any other species. The other two . . . well, obviously they're undead and well and until recently were living on that cruise ship. Or rather, on its passengers."

"Both of them?" said Jake. "Look, I may not be as quick on the uptake as you people, but how can we be sure it wasn't just one of them?"

"Because when we returned to England," Trask told him, "our good friend Manolis Papastamos remained on Krassos with his men to prepare the way for our follow-up team. On the other side of the Palataki promontory, in a bight under the cliffs, they found evidence that suggested a boat had been kept there. There was a tunnel leading back into that labyrinth under the Little Palace, too. That was where Vavara was going when we forced her car off the road and into the sea not far from Palataki. The assumption has to be that she swam the rest of the way, or maybe clambered along the base of the sheer cliffs." He shrugged and added, "No easy task, not even for a strong man. But there you go . . . Vavara is Wamphyri, after all."

"And Malinari?" said Jake.

"Ian Goodly had a close encounter with him under Palataki," said Trask, "so we know he was definitely there. That was just before the fireworks. But the point is, if Ian had time to get out of there and climb to the surface before the dynamite blew that place to hell—"

"—Then so did Malinari," Jake finished it for him.

"Correct." Trask nodded. "And since he didn't emerge on the surface—"

"—It looks like he made his way to that cave and escaped by boat."

"Along with Vavara, yes," said Trask. "Let's face it, Wamphyri or not, it would be damned difficult for just one of these creatures to take over a ship as big as the *Evening Star*. But both of them together . . . Nephran Malinari, with his powers of mentalism, and Vavara with her mass hypnotism? They could do it, all right. And they did. And when they met with resistance, with someone, or thing, or situation they couldn't control—"

"—Then they resorted to mindless violence," said Liz. "And there's nothing so violent as a Great Vampire."

"As witness the mess they made of that bridge," said Trask, grimly. "I feel sort of sorry for Commander Argyle. He was just a bit too full of himself . . . until he saw that bridge. It's as you told him, Liz: seeing is believing. Now he's on our side. I heard him advise the Captain to give us carte blanche, but that was before the Admiralty entered the picture—or should we say before Porton Down came in on it."

"This Porton Down," said Jake. "I mean, how is it an outfit like that has so much clout?"

"But that's where they found the answer to HIV," Trask told him. "It's also where they brewed up the antidote to the plague out of China, the new Asiatic bubonic. Hell, they do good work! So maybe I'm overreacting. Maybe we should have thought earlier to open this thing up, ask for outside help. Maybe our Minister Responsible—or whoever it was who let the cat out of the bag—has done the right thing after all. I just don't know."

"God, I'd certainly like to think so!" said Liz, with feeling. "You'd think we'd be hardened to it by now, but I for one never will be. Frankly, I'd far rather squirt aerosols or fire drugged darts than shoot silver bullets!"

"You and me both," Jake agreed. "Surely anyone would rather cure than kill."

"Do you really think so?" said Trask, looking morose again. "Perhaps you'd like to mention it to the Wamphyri. *Huh!* That'll be the day!" And then, changing the subject:

"But that isn't what I wanted to talk to you about. That's something else, and it really can't wait. It's waited too long already. I don't know, maybe it's this Porton Down thing that's brought it back into focus, but it is important that we keep it there."

"What's bothering you?" said Jake.

"Actually, you are!" Trask answered. But then he managed to grin, however sardonically. "No, I don't mean in the old way—and yet, yes, perhaps in the old way, too. Okay, I'll explain. You were down there under London with Szwart and Millie, and—"

"—And we haven't been checked out since," Jake cut in. "Is that it? You're worried we might have been infected?" His voice was suddenly wary, thoughtful; likewise his narrow-eyed expression. And Trask couldn't help but think how much he looked like the Necroscope Harry Keogh. In another moment it had passed and he was just Jake again, except "just" didn't do it justice. For of course Jake, too, was a Necroscope. And in this world he was *the* Necroscope, the only one.

Trask shook his head. "I'm worried that the longer we leave it the less I like it," he said. "Jake, I owe you more than any man should owe anyone, and no way I can ever repay you. But you have to understand that my concerns, my duties, go much farther than personal debts, loyalties, and friendships. I *am* concerned, yes—for you, and for Liz, your partner; for the branch, too, and all the good people in it—but mainly for humanity. Maybe I've been caught up in this game for too long, I can't say, but at least I've learned a few half-decent tricks. In my time with E-Branch . . . Lord, I've seen some bad shit! So far I've managed to step clear, and that's what I'm trying to do now. That's *all* I'm trying to do now."

"Hold on," said Jake. "It seems to me you've missed someone out of these 'concerns' of yours. I'm talking about Millie. She was down there under London with Szwart a lot longer than I was. So if you're worried that maybe I'm a little more than I should be—and *if* that's the case, personally I know nothing about it—then I'd suggest you stop worrying about me and check Millie out first!"

A cruel thing to say, perhaps. Harsh words: but as he spoke them Jake deliberately held Trask's gaze, staring directly into his deep green eyes. And Ben Trask—being what he was, a human lie detector—knew that Jake spoke only the truth and straight from the heart. If anything had got into Jake in that forgotten Roman temple deep under London, he honestly wasn't aware of it. But on the other hand only four days had passed since then, and weird things had a habit of getting into Jake Cutter.

As for Millie Cleary, the newly discovered love of Trask's life: "Millie is being checked out right now," he said. "That's why she's not with us. It was my excuse to keep her out of this . . . that she required extra decontamination and a complete physical. Not that I really needed an excuse—Millie was in a hell of a state when you brought her up out of there. You, however—as you just a moment ago demonstrated—seem in fine fettle. At least *you* think so. And anyway I needed you out here with us."

"So let's get to it," said Jake. "What is it you require of me? What's the bottom line? What do you want me to do?"

"Nothing much," Trask shrugged, perhaps a little uncomfortably. "Just that as soon as we're done here and back in London, you let us treat you the same as Millie: let us put you through a one hundred percent decontamination programme, a full medical checkup, and . . . and . . ." But there he paused.

"And?" said Jake, thinking *here it comes!*

"And that you give us your fullest assistance in trying to

help you with . . . with your *other* problem, the one you told me about on our way out here."

Oh, ha-haaaa! He's talking about meeee! A loathsome deadspeak voice chuckled in Jake's head. *This idiot believes that he can erase, remove, or otherwise dispose of me, as if I were some kind of mental disorder. Well, I'm not, and he can't! And telling him about me was a great error. These so-called psychiatrists you told me about can only do you enormous harm. Aye, for as you very well know, Jake Cutter, I'm no figment of your imagination—no alter ego, no Mr. Hyde playing to your Doctor Jekyll—but as real and as valid as you are. The only difference being that while you're alive, I'm dead!*

"But very much alive in me," said Jake. "And I really don't want or need you! And incidentally, I note you've accumulated a pretty good knowledge and understanding of this stuff: figments of imagination, alter egos, Jekylls and Hydes, and et cetera."

All from your reading materials, Korath answered. *This, er, sudden "penchant" of yours for psychology—especially schizophrenia and the like.* Hah! *And you've never once suspected that I was "reading over your shoulder," as it were. For the fact is that until I speak to you, you simply don't know I'm there; you don't know if I'm awake or sleeping. But in any case there's no way round it. I'm here in your head whether you like it or not, Jake Cutter, and neither your Mr. Trask nor all his psychiatric specialists put together can ever change that. Oh, ha-ha-ha!*

"Bastard!" Jake muttered darkly, as Korath retreated. And: "Him again?" Liz enquired, quietly.

"Him!" Jake growled. "Korath-once-Mindsthrall. "And believe me, I want rid of him just as much as you do . . . well, short of prefrontal lobotomy, that is!"

Trask shook his head. "That doesn't come into it," he said. "Don't even think of it. We wouldn't subject you to anything of that sort. But if we can find a way to shift this . . . this personal demon of yours—"

"He says you can't," said Jake. "And he makes a very

valid point. He isn't something I just dreamed up. He's no figment of my own imagination. He *was* a lieutenant of the Wamphyri, one of Malinari's creatures, and he was almost ready to ascend. That's probably why Malinari wanted rid of him and rammed him headlong into that pipe under the Romanian refuge. Christ, what a way to die! But Harry Keogh and I, we talked to him there, and learned the histories of the Wamphyri . . . well, of Vavara and Malinari, anyway."

"But that was a mistake," Trask nodded. "For even dead vampires are dangerous to such as you."

"That's right," said Jake, ruefully. "When they're alive— or undead if you prefer—you can't have physical contact with them. They radiate corruption like some kind of ultimate contaminant, like plutonium, so that even their presence is poisonous. And when they're dead, you daren't even talk to them."

"I couldn't anyway," said Trask wonderingly, as always at a loss in this kind of conversation, still unable to fully accept the concept of a Necroscope.

"And I shouldn't have," said Jake. "But that wasn't my idea. It was Harry who put me up to it."

"But did he do it deliberately?" Liz wanted to know. "If so it might bear out Ben's earlier concerns that it's Harry's dark side that may be influencing you."

Jake shook his head. "No, and perhaps 'put me up to it' was a bad choice of words. He 'suggested it,' yes, but only because he wanted to find out about our invaders. And who better to get it from than one of their own? It was for my protection, and it was my mistake. In fact it was Harry who warned me never to let a vampire into my mind. Damn good advice! But when Harry wasn't there, then Korath persuaded me otherwise. With such as him the word 'devious' takes on a whole new level of meaning!"

"You're satisfied, then," said Trask, "that what the Necroscope gave you was for the general good? For your good, and the world's both?"

"For my good?" Jake lifted an eyebrow. "Well, I can't

say I entirely agree with that! But let's face it—you, me, Liz, all of us—without it we'd have been dead for quite some time now out there in Australia."

"That's true," said Trask.

"And it's also true that for all I hate Korath and want rid of the bastard," Jake went on, "still he played his part in all of that."

Trask nodded and said, "But for his own ends, as you've now discovered. Best to get it straight in your head, son: vampires don't do anything for nothing . . . except maybe kill. They don't need a reason for that, it just happens as the mood takes them. What I'm saying is, Korath wasn't doing us any favours."

"I know," said Jake. "To save me he had to save all of us, but I'm the one he really cares about. That is: I'm the one he needs. Without me he's nothing, just a bunch of polished bones circulating in black water in a night-dark sump in some burned-out, godforsaken Romanian sinkhole!"

"Yes," Trask agreed, "but whatever else you do, don't ever go feeling sorry for him. Which takes us back where we started. You said you want rid of him, and so do we all. Are you willing to let the best specialists we can find have a look at you? I'm not talking quacks but people like Grahame McGilchrist, who you met in Australia. Back home in London, we have some of the best in the world."

"Whatever you say," Jake answered. "Just as long as they're not going to slice my brain open, I don't really care. And yes, I'll help all I can. But I know that whatever we do Korath will fight me all the way. He's fighting for his 'life,' after all."

Trask nodded, and said, "Then that's it. We're all done for now. We can join the others, see how our survivor is doing."

"Not so fast," said Jake, taking Trask by the arm before he could turn away. "We're not done yet."

For a moment Trask stood stock-still, frozen there, staring fixedly at Jake's hand on his arm. Then he sighed, relaxed, and said, "Very well. I gave you my word after you'd saved

Millie's life, and a promise is a promise. What is it you want to know?"

But with a heartfelt sigh of her own, Liz spoke before Jake and said, "Well, thank goodness for *that!* And not before time."

Jake stared at her, then at Trask, and said, "Just look at you. You *know*, don't you? I mean, both of you—all of you know—even before I've asked my question! Okay, what is it that you haven't dared to tell me about Harry? What's this down you have on him?"

"A down? On Harry?" Trask offered a wry smile and shook his head. "No such thing, Jake. I was one of the last people to see him in this world—I watched him *leave* this world, by a route you haven't discovered yet—and while it was my duty, while I had every right to stop him, I didn't even try but let him go."

"You let him go?" Jake frowned and did a double take. Shaking his head, he looked from Trask to Liz and back again. "What are you talking about, you let him go? He was E-Branch's greatest hero, or so I've been led to believe. Yet you make it sound as if he were a criminal, almost as if he were some kind of . . . of . . ." As Jake stumbled to a pause, so his frown fell away and his eyes went wide.

"Some kind of vampire?" said Trask, queryingly. "The answer is yes, and believe me I do mean *some* kind of vampire, the most powerful ever! Harry Keogh, Necroscope . . . but he was also Wamphyri, Jake, Wamphyri!"

"That's right," Liz nodded. "And now you understand why Ben didn't tell you. Because you're too valuable and he didn't want to scare you off, didn't want to lose you. Yes, Harry Keogh was a hero. And yes, he almost single-handedly won the first battle that E-Branch ever fought against vampires. Me, I wasn't around then, but I've read up on it. When we get back to London, there are some files you'll want to read up on, too, now."

Jake still couldn't take it in. "But . . . Harry? A vampire?"

"Right at the end of his time here, yes," said Trask. "He'd got too close to them and let them get too close to him. He was Wamphyri, but he made me a promise and he kept it. And he carried on the fight in Starside. Ask Lardis Lidesci about it. He's been biding his time, just waiting to tell you."

"You're telling me" (Jake felt his Adam's apple bobbing up and down) "that the man, ghost, thing, or whatever who gave me my powers—deadspeak and the Möbius Continuum—was the revenant of a vampire?"

"And now perhaps you can understand my concern," said Trask. "You see, all of Harry's life was like a tragedy, especially at the end. And the trouble is it didn't stop with him. Even while he was winning it seemed like everything around him was turning to so much shit. Nathan Kiklu—or perhaps it's easier to think of him as Nathan Keogh, one of Harry's sons in Sunside/Starside—finally redeemed him. Which is to say, Nathan put right most of the things that had turned sour for Harry; he squared it for him, with both the living and the dead alike."

"His sons, yes!" said Jake, with a snap of his fingers. "I remember now: the bits that were missing from those first files I read, the ones that you'd had doctored especially for me. The material that was missing was about Harry's sons."

"Because it's like Liz told you," Trask answered. "I didn't want to lose you. Letting you know about Nathan was okay, but I certainly couldn't tell you about the others."

"The others?" Jake was frowning again. "Harry's other sons, you mean?"

Trask nodded. "You see, Jake, even after Harry died on Starside, the curse remained. Both Harry Jr., and Nestor Kiklu, too, Nathan's twin brother, they both of them—"

"—Were vampires?" Jake knew it was so, and his hollow face turned really pale now.

"They *became* Wamphyri," Trask told him. "Maybe it was sheer bad luck, the curse, call it fate or whatever you will. But . . ." And not knowing what else to say, he shrugged and fell silent.

And in a little while, feeling obliged to pick it up where Trask had left off, Jake said, "*But,* now there's Jake Cutter— a Necroscope in his own right, Harry's heir apparent, with some weird leftover of the original lodged in him, not to mention a nightmarish thing called Korath Mindsthrall—and Jake has got himself involved in killing vampires, too. It all sounds just a little bit familiar, right? So what is it you're trying to say? What, like history is repeating itself or something?"

"Not this time, Jake," said Liz, moving closer and reaching out to him. "No way—not if we have anything to say about it. That's why you've got to accept Ben's help, and in turn give us your assistance with those tests back in London."

"That's it," said Trask. "End of story. Now you know almost everything. And anything you don't know, just ask and I'll tell you—right now if you like. Or do you need some time to think about it first?"

Jake thought about it, then took a very deep breath before answering, "Yes, I have a question. How soon are we going back to London . . . ?"

4
The Survivor's Story

AFTER CHECKING THAT THE *EVENING STAR*'S LONE survivor was sleeping comfortably and apparently well—at least physically if not yet psychologically—Trask and his team used the extra time to get their own heads down.

While the journey out from London to HMS *Invincible* hadn't taken very long, still it had been fairly intense: a whirlwind rush from one point of departure to the next.

First they'd been airlifted by helicopter from the roof of the hotel that housed E-Branch HQ and flown to Gatwick Airport. Then a private jet—courtesy of the Ministry of Defence—had flown them to Kavála, a military airport on the

Greek mainland just a few miles north of the Aegean coast. And finally a jet-copter from HMS *Invincible* had sped them to the aircraft carrier herself.

Thus the droning sound of engines was still in their ears (now reinforced by the short haul out to the cruise ship), and similarly a dizzy and debilitating kaleidoscope of scenery and tilting ocean views all fusing into one in their memories. The overall result was a feeling of exhaustion, and the dull, near-distant heartbeat of *Invisible*'s engines at standby that came throbbing through the bulkheads was a lullaby by comparison . . .

Trask was roused at 16:30 hours and handed a communication from the Minister Responsible. Relayed through Admiralty channels and encrypted by them, the message had been unscrambled in *Invincible*'s radio room, so that Trask was able to read:

FOR YOUR EYES ONLY:
(And: *Hah!* Trask thought, before continuing.)

Mr. Trask.

Lifeboat serial number MS 02/000000 has been discovered by fishermen, scuttled in shallow waters off Rodosto in the Sea of Marmara.

It would appear that after leaving Greek waters, she passed through the Dardanelles at night without lights, was stopped by a patrol boat which she somehow managed to set on fire and sink leaving no survivors, *and from then on played a cat-and-mouse game with various Turkish patrol vessels until they lost her in a* sea fret *off Gallipoli.*

Understandably, the Turkish authorities are somewhat miffed—especially in the light of the current heightened tension between Greece and Turkey—so you can't expect any help from them. Therefore any enquiries concerning the boat, or the ones who commandeered her, *will have to be of a covert nature.*

Suggestion: collect the PD sample ASAP, *return to base, then fly to Istanbul using the same routine you employed in Krassos: i.e., go in as tourists. There are no restrictions on British tourists in Turkey at this time. I'll arrange your flight for you. After that . . . I assume your next port of call will be Rodosto.*

Anything you need in advance, let me know and I'll have it waiting for you at your HO . . .

MIN. RES.

Trask read the message again, and scribbled underneath it: "Speak to my people. Have Bernie Fletcher and a pair of minders go out there NOW, tonight, as our advance party. Make sure they have lots of Turkish liras." Then he returned it for onward transmission to the CPO who had delivered it . . .

The survivor was awake but groggy, shivering, and still very frightened. The medics had cleaned him up, draped him in warm blankets, were pouring coffee into him when Trask and Co. went in to see him in the stateroom.

"Coffee?" Trask asked in an aside to one of the medics.

"Because he asked for it," the other shrugged.

"And has he asked for anything else, or said anything?"

"Nothing as yet."

"Then you can leave him with us." Trask dismissed them and closed the door after them.

Lardis had been with the survivor all along, but still he looked fresh as a daisy. "Why don't you try to get some sleep?" Trask asked him, taking him to one side.

"Don't need it," came the gruff reply. "Sunside days are long ones. I'm used to long hours. But when I do sleep, then I really *do* sleep, because Sunside nights are long ones, too! Anyway, I wanted to stay with him. I feel a kind of kinship."

"Oh?"

"Aye," Lardis nodded. "This one, unless I'm much mistaken, is from your so-called old country, Romania. Szgany, too, by his looks. Besides, he seems taken with me. If anyone is going to be able to talk to him, it'll probably be me. So seeing him frightened out of his wits, I decided to be close to hand when he woke up. I've seen people like him before on Sunside, after the Wamphyri raided. They usually needed gentling along for a while, and so might he."

"So can we talk to him at all now?"

"Let's find out," said Lardis.

The pair approached the survivor where he sat in his blankets, and the other E-Branch people made way for them. "Do you remember me?" Lardis asked him. "I was there when they got you off that floating town."

The other nodded. "I called you father," he answered. "But I didn't mean *my* father. When I was a boy we always called the clan elder father."

While he spoke, Trask looked him over. From what could be seen of him under the blankets he was lanky and even bony. His high forehead and penetrating dark eyes signalled his intelligence, but those same eyes also gave him away; along with his wolfish looks, raven-black hair, and light brown, large-pored skin, they more than hinted at his origins.

"You're from Romania, right?" said Lardis, but it was more a statement than a question. "A Gypsy, perhaps?"

"Was," said the other. "But when I was young my mother got married to a Greek, from Rhodes. So I was brought up on Rhodes in the village of Lindos. We eventually moved to Cyprus, and I got work as a deckhand on the cruise ships."

At which point Trask came in with, "May I speak to you?"

The other looked uneasy but shrugged his acquiescence. "If you like."

"You speak good English," said Trask.

"From school, the tourists, and . . . and the ships." He gave a small shudder. "I also speak Greek and Romanian. I even remember a little of the old secret tongue, Szgany."

"My name is Trask," Trask told him. "And my friend here is called Lardis. Lardis knows the myths of the old country, some of which aren't myths at all. I believe you know them, too. We think that's probably why you're still alive."

The survivor's shudders were coming faster now; his entire body was beginning to shake under the blankets. Lardis touched Trask's shoulder, indicating that he wanted to take over. With a nod of his head, Trask agreed. And:

"Forget about all that for now and tell me your name," the Old Lidesci said. "For as you can see, you're with friends now and you're safe."

"No one is safe!" the other gabbled. "You didn't see—you didn't hear—you didn't smell it! But the whole ship smelled of it! I saw, heard, smelled it. And I knew . . . right from the time we took them on board. I knew, but I didn't speak. I . . ." He paused, began to blink rapidly and uncontrollably, and gave a start when Lardis placed a gnarled hand on his shoulder. But then he calmed down and was able to continue. "As for my name: it's Nicolae Rusu. I go by my real father's name. His blood is my blessing."

"It most certainly has been!" said Lardis. "For without it you'd never have known, and you wouldn't be here talking to us now! And I understand why you told no one: they wouldn't have believed, and you weren't quite ready to believe yourself. Now listen carefully, Nicolae Rusu. These people here with me are experts in such matters. They know and understand such things. That ship, the *Evening Star*, is a ship of death! You know what happened, and we've come here to take our revenge. But we have to know the whole story, else we won't know what we're up against. You are the only witness."

"But I don't want to remember!" The survivor was shivering again. "I was . . . I was trying to forget when you rescued me."

"I know," said Lardis. "I understand. But tell me now—do you want it to happen again, to others? For you can be sure it will, Nicolae, if we don't stop it."

"Call me . . . call me Nick," said the other. And in another feverish burst, "You can't stop it! You can't stop *them!* I saw them, and no one can stop them!"

"Easy, easy!" said Lardis. And in a moment: "Can you

give them a name, perhaps? Do you know what we call them?"

The survivor's eyes went this way and that. "Do you really believe?" he said. "Or is it that you think I'm crazy?"

"You were crazy with fear," Lardis answered. "For a little while, at least. But you're safe now and sane. Yes, we believe. And more than that, we do what I said we do. We hunt such creatures to destroy them."

"Wampir!" said the other then, but so low they could barely hear him. *"Or obour!* The terror by night! The thing that drinks blood! Vampires . . . but no one ever dreamed of such vampires as these!"

And: "Wamphyri!" said Lardis. "Aye, we know. So then, will you tell us your story, Nick? How you survived your ordeal and what . . . what *happened* to the others?"

"Yes," Nicolae Rusu nodded. "Yes, if only to get it out of my system. And then I want to go away from here, and away from cruise ships. Back to Cyprus or Rhodes, or maybe farther still. Far, far away . . ."

"I was doing some cleaning-up on the cabaret deck near the prow when Purser Galliard called down to me to meet him starboard on B deck. But in fact I met him in the lift on the way down. He had got hold of three stewards and a loud-hailer and seemed very excited. By the time we got down onto B deck—that's inside the ship, you understand, not quite the basement but just above the Plimsoll line—the *Star* was just about dead in the water. And that was when they opened the for'ard gang: a large, watertight hatch for low-level loading. It forms steps when you let it down, allowing access from the docks or in this case permitting a rescue.

"The becalmed boat—just a boat, which should never have been out there in mid-ocean—was a thirteen-foot Greek caïque with a wide black canopy. There were two . . . *people* aboard her. When I saw the man—at first glance, just looking at him as he stepped from the caïque to the gang-way—I took fright. He was tall and dark; he could even have been one of my people . . . but something told me he

63

wasn't. It was like . . . as if my blood was running cold inside me, and I knew right there and then that we were in trouble. But what could I do or say? 'We can't let this man come aboard'? Ridiculous! Of course they *would* have thought I was mad! I myself believed that I must be out of sorts, ill, feverish, or something. I felt sick, and so very, very scared. And that was even before I saw how his hand shimmered, seeming to smoke when the sunlight fell on it!

"But after that, why, I could even *feel* the evil! It was as if every atom of my body knew that this was wrong, that *he* was wrong . . . and then I saw her, that she-creature!

"I can't remember exactly how it was. My mind was whirling. But her terrible companion helped her, and Purser Galliard lifted her up, and they were aboard. She was wrapped like a mummy, all covered against the sun, yet still I saw that she was beautiful . . . and *knew* that she wasn't! It must have been my Szgany blood—something out of the dark past—like a strange memory of times I've never known. But it was as if I could see through her tatters to the *Thing* beneath them. And she was ancient, and ugly, and terrifying!

"Perhaps I looked sick? I can't remember. In any case, once they were aboard Purser Galliard released me, told me to return to whatever I had been doing. But in fact I hurried in search of a place to be ill. Sick to my stomach, I threw up! And it had all been so weird, so inexplicable, that I still thought I was *actually* ill, that something I'd eaten hadn't agreed with me, when all it was—all it *really* was—was sheer terror! But of what?

"Anyway, after my head stopped spinning I knew I must speak to someone. I didn't know what I would say, but I must at least try to explain it to someone. Maybe to the Captain, to Captain Geoff Anderson, who was an understanding man. I knew I couldn't talk of it to the other deckhands, who would only laugh at me, or to the stewards, who would probably just brush it aside, but the Captain himself . . . well, he was understanding and patient. He'd know what to do, what to say to me and how to reassure me. And if there was something wrong with me, he'd know what to do about that, too.

"I went to the bridge . . . oh God, I *would* have gone to the bridge . . . I *almost* went to the bridge. But . . . it had already b-b-begun.

"No, no, just wait a minute, give me a chance, and it will pass. It will be okay . . .

"There . . .

"So then, I went up onto the bridge deck. The place seemed very quiet, but we'd had a big night and the people weren't up yet. It was still fairly early in the morning, and—and God, God—I'm avoiding it, and I can't help it!

"Okay, I'm okay, I can do this . . .

"In the crew-only area, the gangway that leads to the door to the bridge, Purser Galliard and two of the stewards were on the floor in pools of their own blood. The purser's face was a nightmare I'll see as long as I live. His eyes were hanging on his cheeks—hanging loose there on threads of gristle—and their sockets were black and streaming blood. Galliard's ears, too: with curtains of blood and brain fluid dripping down onto his shoulders. He was twitching—twitching his last, I would guess—but as for the stewards:

"Well, despite that they were obviously dead—I mean, no one who looks as bad, as pale, as drained as that can possibly be alive—still they were *moving,* jerking and moaning, their arms and legs twitching as if they were asleep and nightmaring!

"Nightmaring, yes—well, *I* certainly was! But I was awake, yet I hoped and prayed I wasn't . . . and the door to the bridge had been shattered . . . and there was blood on the glass, blood everywhere . . . and . . . and I could hear sounds, cries, screams—sounds of violence, destruction—from the bridge.

"And I knew then that I wasn't ever going to speak to Captain Anderson, or to anyone on that bridge.

"I got out of there. I ran—oh, I admit it—ran aimlessly, out through a hatch and onto the outer deck. Down below, people were running about, shouting about an accident. But

I saw blood on the rail and knew that it hadn't been an accident. Somewhere along the way I bumped into two stewards and tried to tell them what had happened . . . trouble on the bridge . . . Purser Galliard was dead . . . also two or possibly three stewards . . . and creatures were aboard and ravening. But they only heard half of what I said before they went running off to see what was going on. I called after them to get guns, arm themselves, but they weren't listening. Instead they told me to go with them!

"I pretended to follow them, but as soon as they turned out of sight I was gone in the other direction.

"Later, I found myself in my bunk, locked in. But you know, the doors are so *flimsy*! I couldn't stay there . . . and every so often I thought I could hear screaming . . .

"I had told the stewards to get guns. Now I thought maybe I should arm myself. I knew that there was a small-arms locker in the purser's cabin on the main deck. I didn't have the key—*he* would have that, poor Purser Galliard, or Purser Bill as we had used to call him—and I couldn't go back for it. Anyway, this was hardly the time to be worrying about keys. A fire axe would do just as well.

"My bunk was on B deck down in the guts of the ship. So I had to go up two decks to get to the main deck and the purser's cabin. It seemed to me that the safest, easiest, quickest route would be by lift. The *Star* is a huge ship; it was unlikely that I would . . . that I would come up against anything unpleasant on the way. I mean, out of all the passengers and crew on that big ship, there were only two of . . . of *them*.

"When I left my cabin, people were still moving around nice and normal on B deck. I got in the lift with a family of four on their way to a late breakfast in the Glory of Knossos dining room, also on the main deck. They were all excited, full of the thrills of the cruise, looking forward to all the onboard activities they'd planned for the day ahead—and all I wanted to do was scream at them that there wasn't going to be a day ahead—not for them, and probably not for anybody.

"We got out of the lift for'ard, and the purser's cabin was amidships past the hotel manager's office and gift shops. There was a lot of shouting going on that way, and these two children, a boy and a girl, wanted to see what all of the noise was about. I called them back to their mother and father but they wouldn't come. They were just . . . *just little kids*! So then I told their parents, 'Go and get them, and get out on the open decks in the sunlight. Keep them safe!' They looked at me as if I was weird, and I realized how I must look, all trembling and . . . and wild. They went after their kids, but far too slowly, and by then the shouting had stopped.

"Other people were on the move now; some were running, many seemed dazed, disbelieving. And then, from the purser's office, the screaming started. Oh, God . . . the screaming!

"I passed a steward who I knew. He was sitting on the floor with his legs stretched out and his back against a bulkhead. He didn't seem to see me. I went to offer help, but he didn't want any. He just looked right through me and brushed my hand aside. Then I noticed how pale he was, and the twin trails of blood on his neck, and those poisonous punctures like craters where he'd been bitten.

"The kids' parents had seen him, too, and now they began to call out for their little ones, running after them.

"Other people were down on the deck, many unconscious while some just sprawled there. I saw at least a dozen like that, and then the screaming stopped again. But finally these nice people chasing their kids reached the purser's cabin—more a kind of storeroom than a cabin proper, with plenty of open deck outside under a fancy rail-to-rail canopy—and there outside the cabin . . . it was a strange and very terrible thing.

"I was standing well back from it, but I could feel all the lure of it like a magnet dragging at me. It was the woman—no, I can't call that *Thing* a woman—the female creature, and she was surrounded by a ring of maybe ten or twelve men, women, and children alike. But they weren't attacking her. On the contrary, they were just standing there while she stepped among them. And again she looked beautiful . . . and again I knew that she wasn't at all beautiful, that she was in fact a monster!

"She was covered in a radiant haze, outlined in a dazzling corona like the sun in an eclipse. It was her disguise, I knew. She stroked the men, touched their faces, then bit them. I saw those terrible jaws like mantraps—they *were* mantraps!—and each time she struck the blood would spurt, spattering her face and neck with crimson. And God, how she drank it in, soaking it up like a sponge! Then, like men in a trance, her victims would stagger away, stumbling and going weak at the knees, until they gradually collapsed to the deck. They were so obviously fascinated, enthralled by her lying charms; and each time a man fell, another would step forward to take his place.

"The women, too. They couldn't resist her. They would reach out, touch her awful body, go to their knees before her as that loathsome *Thing* nipped at their necks, dribbling blood from her mouth down into theirs! One of them was a very lovely girl; her husband—I suppose he was her husband—seemed uncertain, he wasn't as hypnotised as the rest. Protesting, he tried to push the monster away. The she-thing took something from her robe: a sharp knife shaped like a sickle. And with a single stroke that was so fast I didn't even see it, just a blur of something that glinted and was gone, she struck. After that, nothing seemed to have changed. But as the young man began to protest again, even as he opened his mouth, a great gush of blood came out! And his throat opened ear to ear as he collapsed to the deck!

"But the most terrible thing was this: that his wife didn't even see what had happened! And while she fondled the monster's loose paps through her rags, so she in turn was deeply bitten.

"And the children, the children!

"They were all enraptured smiles where they gazed upon this 'beautiful' creature—even as she murdered or forever changed their parents before turning on them. Which included the family I had come up with in the lift; they went the same way, yes.

"As the female was finishing with those she'd hypnotised—for surely it could only be hypnotism—so the male came striding out of the purser's cabin. He was carrying the arms locker, a heavy metal trunk which he handled like a small suitcase. And that was when the two stewards who I had spoken to earlier came on the scene. They'd obviously seen something of what I'd tried to tell them and had followed the trail to its source. They had fire axes, and when they saw what was happening, all the bloody mayhem . . . then, with cries of outrage and horror, they came on and hurled themselves at the vampires.

"The monsters didn't see them until the last moment. But as the male creature reached the ship's rail with the arms locker, and hoisted it up to throw it overboard, so one of the stewards swung at him with his fire axe. The creature saw him, flung the locker over the rail and made to step aside. The way he moved—his motions were like quicksilver! But lightning fast as he was and so fluid in his actions, still the pick end of the axe went home through his trousers and into his left buttock just above the thigh. It went all the way home, right up to the haft.

"The sheer agony that would have caused any other man would surely have been enough to bring him down. But this one reached over his shoulder, backhanded the steward and knocked him away. And all he said, was, 'Ah! Ahh! *Ahhhh!*' as he drew the axe out. But I saw his face—the way his jaws extended, and the way his teeth sprouted into scythes! His colour turned to lead and his eyes were afire as he swung that axe in an arc, driving it into the steward's forehead! It got stuck there, lodged in his head, his skull. And the steward dangling—his arms and legs jerking and kicking like those of a frenzied puppet—as this creature lifted him, fire axe and all, over the rail and let him fall!

"As for the other steward: rushing headlong at the female, he had entered her hypnotic zone, penetrating the haze she wore all about her. His axe was raised overhead, but already she had him! Frozen there, solid as a statue, his mouth had fallen open. Then his stomach fell open, too, as she laughed at him and used her knife to cut through his shirt and the tight muscles of his belly, from right to left across his navel. He made no outcry—said nothing, did nothing—but simply dropped the fire axe to clatter on the red-slimed deck. And in the next moment, with an upward sweep of her arm, she'd cut him again from his crotch to his navel, so that his belly opened up in twin triangular flaps and uncoiled his guts onto the deck!

"And I ran away . . . ran and ran . . . down to my bunk . . . and out of there to a storage room with a steel door . . . then out of there and down through a trapdoor into the bilges, where I huddled against the iron plates of the ship . . . and there I stayed with the rats and the diesel stench, for hours and hours, until I think I fell asleep . . . or it could be that my mind was numb and totally insensible to everything around me.

"Eventually I came to my senses. Or perhaps not, not quite, for my senses like my manhood had deserted me. But as for what had brought me round: I think it was the insistent pounding of the engines, or more probably the sudden shock that had jolted me as they ground to a shuddering halt. I found myself slammed this way and that in the dark belly of the ship, until at last there was no motion at all, not even the gentle wash of Aegean waters against the hull. Still, I was certain that the engines had been working, and I knew that I'd felt the ship in motion.

"So what was this? This silence, this stillness? I thought— I dared to hope—that it was over and those creatures were dead. Perhaps the rest of the crew had got themselves together and gone at the monsters in a body to finish them, and now the *Star* had limped into some port or other. It had to be at least possible.

"But still I was quiet as a mouse as I left my hidey-hole, crept up through the trapdoor onto B deck's gangway, then up through the aft service ladders and hatches to the performers' changing rooms in the rear of the All That Jazz show bar; finally onto the stage, where I peered through the drawn curtains into the room itself, at the aisles, the bars, and the seating area.

"But there was no band, no entertainers, no bar stewards at their stations, and no audience. The lighting was as low as it would be during a show, but the place seemed completely empty. Except . . . I thought I could hear a low moaning—a faint cry for help, perhaps?—and a frightened, timid-sounding sobbing.

"And I thought: maybe it's someone like me, someone who has seen, heard, taken flight, and gone into hiding here. And in the gloom I sought him out.

"And I found him, yes. The show bar's Master of Ceremonies, a black American. He was sitting at a table all alone. Just sitting there in top hat and tails—his 'Cab Calloway' outfit—with his head down on his chest, and a bottle of champagne cooling in a bucket of ice on the table in front of him. He seemed to be wearing a necklace of rubies which patterned his starched white shirt and matched his crimson cummerbund. But as I moved closer I saw that they weren't rubies; they were clots of blood which had dribbled from the punctures in his neck!

" 'He gives and he takes,' he half sobbed, when he sensed me standing there and looked up.

" 'What?' I answered. 'What are you saying?'

" 'That's what he said to me,' he went on. 'He said, "I take to make me strong, and I give to make *you* strong. My essence is powerful and will soon work on you. So don't fight it, for from now on you are mine and belong to Malinari." So now I'm waiting for him to come back, for he's the only one who can help me and tell me what to do.' Then he began to sob again.

"But I'd seen his eyes and they had a faint, yellowish glow in the gloom . . .

"I made to move away, but he gripped my wrist and said, 'Do you know, I think this champagne is off." Here, try a glass, and be so good as to tell me what you think.'

"He slopped a glass of champagne for me, and I used my

free hand to sip at it for I didn't know what else to do. And then I told him, 'It seems fine to me. But I have to go now.'

" 'Go?' he said. 'But no, no, you mustn't! It's so very cold and lonely here. *I* am cold, and you . . . are so strangely warm.'

" 'But I must go,' I said.

" 'And I said you mustn't,' he answered, and again I saw the greenish-yellow glow of his eyes. And of course I knew . . .

"Then . . . I snatched myself away from him, and when he came to his feet I smashed the champagne bottle over his head! He at once sat down again, so heavily that the chair fell apart under his weight, sending him crashing to the floor. I didn't wait to see what he would do then but was off and away from that place, up through the secret ways that only a deckhand knows, to what I prayed would be the clean, sunlit upper decks.

"But when I got there, oh God . . . it was evening, and night coming in fast . . . !"

"Give me a moment, and I'll go on. But you know, I think maybe I'm getting used to the idea now? That these memories will stay with me forever? So sharing them with you . . . perhaps that's as good a way as any of relieving myself of some of the burden. It sounds cowardly, I know, but if that's the way it is then so be it. I may be a coward, but at least I'm a live coward! At least I'm not . . . not undead.

"It was evening, yes, so obviously I had indeed been asleep or in deep shock for quite some time, at least eight hours. But now . . . the last rays of the sun were falling slantingly on the upper decks, and apart from that—

"—It was as if nothing had happened! There was no sign of trouble, no trace of blood. But then of course there would't be, for these decks had been awash with brilliant Mediterranean sunlight from early morning until . . . until now.

"Now, all that remained were those last few slanting beams, and the air was that much cooler in a breeze from the north. As for having docked or run aground: oh yes—we had run aground—but not on any island worth mentioning. It was barely a rock, and the *Star* was stuck fast on it. There was no way I could get off the ship, not if I intended to go anywhere, and no easy way back to civilization and . . . and humanity.

"But then I heard commanding voices and the sounds of mechanical activity for'ard: the creaking of booms as they took the strain, and a rattling of chains. I'd heard these sounds before during ship's drills: someone—a group of people—was trying to launch a lifeboat, which could only mean one thing: at least a handful of crew members had survived, and were now attempting to get off the *Star* before sundown.

"At that point I might easily have made a dreadful mistake, but something warned me to remain vigilant. So instead of rushing to declare myself, I took off my shoes and disposed of them over the side, and keeping to the shadows crept silently toward the activity. I was on the bridge deck, open both port and starboard where the lifeboats lined the deck. To starboard, the sun was a golden blister sinking in the sea. Portside, all was now in shade . . .

"The two for'ard boats were small launches, fairly powerful vessels, each capable of towing a string of lesser boats behind them. The portside launch was being lowered. Its lights were on and I could see people inside as it slipped down out of view. I knew these people; they were all women. And I shivered as I remembered who they were: an exotic dance troupe called the Belles from Brazil . . . but in several of their more outrageous routines they were also known as Val's Vamps! And the thing was . . . they were all wearing exactly the same enthralled expression: dazed, staring-eyed, and zombielike!

"Down below, the rocks were like dark fangs jutting up from the calm sea, but directly below the launch was a deep, natural channel. And as the winch turned and the launch settled down to the water, again I heard that commanding voice. But this time I knew it didn't belong to any crew member. It wasn't the kind of voice you would expect to hear on a daily basis, but it *was* the kind I hope never to hear again, not on any day, ever!

" 'You have done well,' it said, and it was deep, oily, purring, yet in no way catlike. It was a low rumble, but one that I felt was volatile, which might erupt at any moment into lunatic laughter or a menacing snarl of fury.

" 'You've done well and your payment will be good,' it continued. 'Well, depending how well you can hunt, that is. For you all know what you are now, what you are rapidly becoming. Among my kind my bite is virulent above all others—er, mine and my "Lady" companion's—and we have given much of what we are into making you what you are. But for every one of you whom we've recruited, we know there are many others hidden away who have not felt our bite. For quite apart from the task being too great in so short a period of time—even for Great Vampires such as we are—still it was a *deliberate* omission. We have left them for you . . .'

"At that a sigh went up, or perhaps it was a gasp of denial or horror. I crept closer, until I could see everyone who stood there in the launch's now vacant stowage bay. The male and female creatures, of course: they had their backs to me, for which I was grateful, and the rest of the small crowd who were all—who had all *been*—crew members. Stewards and deckhands, even an officer or two, their faces formed a pool of greenish-yellow fire, feral in the failing light.

"And, 'Ah! *Ah!*' said the male creature. 'What's this? Did I hear a complaint? Do some among you think to deny the newfound fever in their veins, the ravening of their lust? Let me assure you, it is *un*deniable. You are not yet undead, for you've never been dead, but you are vampire thralls. And believe me the urge will grow, blossom, bloat! You can fight it, and fail. You will weaken and others will take . . . *advantage* of you. Better if you welcome it and enjoy. Enjoy it, aye, revel in it, *while yet you may!*'

74

"Again that groan went up, but the male creature ignored it and went on:

" 'For while you hunt aboard this vessel—the many hundreds who are shivering in their rooms or hidden away in other places—*men* will come who in their turn will hunt you! They may be on their way even now. You are doomed, each and every one, so what little time you have left, put it to good use.'

"And then the female spoke up, and hers was the ugly, croaking voice of a hag. 'To "good" use? No, never that, not at all. Put it to whatever use pleases you. There are women, and virgin girls, aboard this vessel. Plenty of them. You men are now vampires, with all the ferocious lust and every carnal desire that goes with it. All that was forbidden, it's yours for the taking. At last you are the masters of your own desires . . . if not your puny destinies!'

" 'We go now,' the male nodded. 'This ship, this place, this oh-so-short time, is yours. Do what you will with it . . .'

"With which he and the female thing turned from the throng, stepped easily up onto the rail with a sure balance that defied all human skills, and leaped outward to the hawsers holding the launch in position. And dressed in dark, jewelled finery stolen from the onboard stores, for a moment they clung there looking back at the changeling crew, and their eyes were red as warning lamps in the deepening gloom.

"Then, looking for all the world like great bats, they descended, their fine clothes wafting about them as they seemed to float effortlessly down out of sight.

"A minute or so more and the hawsers slackened off, as down below the launch's engines coughed into life.

"Then the double handful of ex–crew members, fledgling vampires now, looked at each other, saying nothing. But their eyes continued to flare with that feral light. And in a little while they began to lope away into the fast-falling darkness. Some of them came in my direction where I hid just inside a hatch.

"As for myself: I need hardly add that I didn't wait to see what they would do or if I could reason with them, but fled the other way. Aft and starboard, I went, to the last faint glimmer of daylight, and what little remained of sanity . . ."

5
Undead in the Med

NICOLAE RUSU HAD FALLEN SILENT, HIS EYES staring blankly into the near-distant past at terrible scenes he would never be able to forget. Trask supposed so, anyway, and let him stay that way for a minute or two. But time wasn't on Trask's side, and in a little while he said:

"Look, Nick, we understand how difficult this must be for you, but there are things we need to know. We're going back to that ship in an hour or so's time, and—"

"We?" The other started back into awareness, a tic jerking the flesh at the corner of his mouth as his eyes suddenly focussed on Trask. "Did you say *we* are going back? No—" he gave a wild shake of his head, "—no, *you* may be going back, but I am going to find a place to hide until we're under way and gone from here!" He gripped Trask's arm and tried to rise, but Lardis held him down.

"Just you hold still, son," the Old Lidesci told him then. "He didn't mean you. You're not going anywhere. I reckon you've seen enough of that ship to last a good many lifetimes. But the fact is *we* have to go back. It's our duty. There's something we have to do before we sink her."

"Sink her?" Rusu looked at him. "Really? The . . . the *Evening Star?*"

"All the way to the bottom," Lardis nodded. "And every poor bloodsucking bastard aboard her."

"But then . . . why go back?" Rusu was logical at least.

"Why not just do it? It would be a mercy to everyone on board."

Lardis looked at Trask.

But Trask couldn't tell Nick Rusu the real reason; Rusu had more than enough things to nightmare about already. And so, "We have to be sure there are no more survivors," he lied, and that came hard to him despite that it was a white lie. For to Trask the truth was all-important. "If it was you, you wouldn't want to have been left stranded on that ship, would you?"

"God, *no!*" the other shuddered long and uncontrollably. And then, gripping Trask's arm more tightly yet, "But listen, I *was* stranded on that ship, and I'm telling you there are *definitely* no more survivors. Take my word for it, they're all gone."

Trask nodded and said, "You know that, don't you, Nick? You know it because you saw everything."

"Not everything," the other shook his head. "But enough."

"Be as brief as you want to be, then," said Trask, "but tell us about it."

"But it's all a jumble," Rusu protested. "A whirling tangle of terrible images . . . three nights of hell . . . like an endless nightmare of blood and terror!"

"What if I ask you specific questions?" said Trask. "Do you think you could handle that? We really do need your help."

Rusu released Trask's arm, lay back again, said, "Ask away. And if I know the answers, I'll . . . I'll try to tell you."

"What about the other lifeboats?" said Trask. "Initially—I mean in the beginning, when Malinari and Vavara, creatures we call 'Great Vampires,' after they'd left, during that first night and the following day—surely there were other survivors? Perhaps even other crew members? How come you, or they, didn't try to launch another lifeboat?"

Rusu nodded. "I know what you mean. I thought about it, too. I even tried it, or would have if it had been at all possible."

Trask frowned. "It wasn't possible? But surely, on a modern ship like that, it can't be too difficult to launch a lifeboat? That would defeat the whole purpose."

Rusu gave a weak laugh and said, "*They* defeated the purpose! Those damned . . . what? Great Vampires? Don't ask me why they did it—it could only have been for some perverse reason of their own, perhaps to ensure that everyone on that ship was doomed—but they fixed the lifeboats, every damned one of them."

"Fixed them?" Trask repeated him. "You mean they sabotaged them before leaving? Would you care to tell us about it?" Maybe his attitude was too casual; maybe he was hardened to this kind of thing and too unsympathetic; whichever, Rusu's reaction was violent.

"No!" he snarled. "I wouldn't *care* to tell anyone about it! Jesus Christ—God Almighty—haven't I said I don't even want to *think* about it!" But as once more he tried to rise, so Lardis Lidesci continued to hold him down, saying:

"Best to get it out of your system, Nick. You have blood of the old people in you—my people, an older race than you could ever imagine, in a world you could scarcely believe—and that will see you through. But if you try to keep these memories all bottled up inside, keep them to yourself . . ." He shook his head. "They'll only do you harm."

And now Rusu gripped Lardis's arms, staring deeply into his eyes. "I . . . I trust you, father," he said. "And I believe you. So very well, I'll try . . ." And in a little while he continued:

"That first night wasn't so bad. I mean, it was bad, but it wasn't the worst. They were still fighting—that is, fighting what was happening to them, not fighting each other, not yet—and while a few were hunting, others hadn't quite succumbed and were still trying to protect their loved ones. Later . . . my God! Later they'd be *converting* their loved ones! But it hadn't come to that just yet. As for the lifeboats:

"You saw the *Star*, the way she'd brought up on those rocks, that little island? I believe it was done that way intentionally, so that there'd be no chance of getting off her once she'd run aground. And it was just *their* good fortune that they could get away in that one launch. But no, there's no sense in that, and it seems far more likely it wasn't so much luck as planned that way. As for the rest of the lifeboats:

"Apart from a handful at the stern end, what good would it have been to lower them onto rocks? And the situation was such that even if it could be done, there was no way we could carry a boat over *that* moonscape to the water. I'll explain the 'we' later. But the rocks . . . well, you saw them. They were jagged, with deep fissures. Over a sandy beach, yes, it would be possible, but no way a half-dozen men could manhandle a heavy boat across even twenty or thirty feet of terrain like that! When I saw those rocks . . . it was a miracle that my hidey-hole in the bilges hadn't been ripped open. And me with it!

"Anyway, I got through that first night. I spent the whole night on the heat-and-fumes baffle—that big collar under the exhaust array—from where I was able to see . . . to see what was going on. But I . . . I don't want to go into that, not just yet. Let it suffice to say that there *were* other survivors, at least for that one night. And somehow it passed, and it could be that I even managed to sleep a little until it was morning.

"Blessed morning—and oh, the wailing when the sun came up over the horizon! And the way the decks cleared of that moaning, howling, screaming crowd! They just melted away, back down into the night-dark guts of the ship. Except for a handful that came out, creeping like mice into the sunlight for'ard. And that was where I joined them.

"They were the 'we' I mentioned: the handful who had lived through it. And there were probably plenty of others down below locked in their rooms, who didn't *dare* come out—and who could blame them for that? But I didn't think they'd last through the second day, poor bastards—not with a horde of vampires prowling the lower decks, bars, lounges, and all . . .

"And it's a funny thing—or maybe not so funny—but some of them, for whom it was already too late . . . they seemed to be trying to pretend that it wasn't happening! They had the tannoy systems going, and we could hear the Cab Calloway look-alike in the jazz bar doing his stuff. All those old numbers: 'Minnie the Moocher,' 'The Scat Song,' and . . . and you know, all that jazz? But I don't like to think what his audience looked like—how they showed their appreciation—or what they were drinking!

"Okay, 'we': myself, two other deckhands, a ship's engineer, and a junior steward. That's it, all that was left of humanity aboard the vessel. Survivors other than the crew wouldn't know where to hide, so like I said they'd be shivering in their cabins. But by now the hunting must be well under way, and those doors were oh-so-flimsy. Or maybe they'd be safe, at least during daylight hours. We didn't know enough to say for sure.

"About the lifeboats:

"The engineer—I don't know his name, didn't get to know any of their names; we never got around to asking—but anyway, he said we should go aft and see if we could lower a boat. This was a hell of a hard man; he was full of grit, so determined to live through this thing that he lifted our spirits. Well, for a while at least.

"But those perverse bastard things, those—what was that you called them? Wamphyri?—they'd taken care of all that. The winches had all been sabotaged, and to be doubly sure the boats had been wrecked, too. Any of them that were hanging over clear water, they'd been holed in far too many places to fix.

"So that was that. We were stuck there in the middle of the ocean, on a ship full of vampires . . ."

As Rusu faltered to a halt and his eyes began to glaze over again, Trask prompted him: "But what about the radio? How is it there was just one brief call for help . . . and then on a mobile-phone frequency?"

Rusu jerked alert again. "Eh? Oh . . . the mobile-phone thing? That was me. As for the ship's radio: well, the first place your bloody Great Vampires headed for was the bridge. The radio room is in an annexe, and after what I had seen as I approached that place . . . I'm assuming they took care of communications first.

"And then there was my cell phone . . .

"I'm afraid my using that was completely illegal, the first time I've ever been glad to break the law!"

"Illegal?" Trask didn't understand. "To call for help?"

"To use a cell phone. On her last trip before this one, just a week or so ago, the *Star* had trouble with all the sunspot activity. Satellite navigation, ship-to-shore and onboard communications were all very badly affected, made worse by passengers using cell phones. Since the prognosis was for another—perhaps even worse—spell of sunspot activity, cell phones were banned on this trip. Passengers weren't allowed to bring them on board. But mine was already on board, in my quarters."

Trask glanced at his colleagues and nodded. "We experienced something of the sunspot problem ourselves. But in your case—in your position—surely it wasn't a case of breaking the law? You and your handful of survivors, you were the only legitimate or lawful people aboard."

Nicolae Rusu grinned however weakly. "I was making a joke," he said, "trying to be flippant. I mean, do you really think I gave a damn that the Captain had ruled cell phones out? The Captain was dead, and most everyone else undead! But my cell phone was down in my quarters, and we didn't know what would be waiting for us down below."

Trask blinked his surprise. "You went back down there?"

"Had to." Rusu shuddered. "I'd told the engineer about the cell phone and he insisted we go below and retrieve it, that it was our one last chance. He'd found two Verey pistols and some flares, and if we made torches—and if we carried fire axes—we should be able to make it. As it turned out, our going down there was a mistake; it gave us away, told those bloody things that there was a bunch of people up top who hadn't been got at. And when night fell . . . when night fell again, they would remember that.

"Anyway, we waited until midday, when the sun was sizzling hot on the decks and its glare was reflecting off the rocks and the sea, blazing in through all the windows and portholes. Only then did we dare go below . . .

"As I told you, my bunk was on B deck down in the guts of the ship. There were passenger cabins down there, too, but crew quarters weren't nearly so sumptuous. By then the elevators had quit working and we had to use the stairwells. That was okay at first and there was plenty of light from outside. But when we'd got down through the main deck onto A deck, by then the light was very poor. The emergency lighting was still working, but it was flickering, weak, and failing. And the cabin configurations were such that they had the portholes, which kept almost all of the natural light from the gangways. Most of the cabin doorways were open, however—in fact a lot of them had been ripped off their hinges—so that at least a little light from outside did shine through. But . . . but the light was red! The light shining in from outside, that came in through the open or wrecked doorways into the gangway, was red!

"And when we checked one of the cabins we saw why. A girl's body was in there. She'd been savaged, raped, murdered. But . . . but raped? No, it was worse than that. I could never have imagined anything so bad. She'd been just about torn apart. And her blood and guts had been used to smear the porthole, to keep out the light. And part of her face, her lips and her tongue . . . it looked like they'd been eaten!

"Her heart had been cut out of her with—I don't know—with a fire axe, judging by the mess it had made. But whatever, she wouldn't be coming back to life. And, God help us—when we came out of that cabin and looked down the gangway—every door that was open, wrecked or just plain massing . . . the light that was filtering in through them was that same shade of red!"

As Nicolae Rusu paused, David Chung said, "Ben, we need to get on. We're only fifteen minutes from the *Evening Star,* but the light will start fading in about an hour and a half. We have to get through with our business and airborne again before *Invincible* can finish this thing. Surely we've heard enough now from Nick here? I mean—"

"No!" Lardis interrupted. "Let him finish. It can't hurt us to know, and I think in the long run it will be good for him. I feel a certain kinship, and it's no more than I'd do for one of my own on Sunside."

Looking at Lardis, Trask nodded. "We owe him to let him get this out of his system. We have the *Star*'s schematics, so we're not going in blind. Also, it isn't as if those poor bastards on that wreck are . . . *experienced*. They're neither lieutenants nor even true thralls. They're just . . . just vampires, and we've had far worse to deal with in our time. And anyway, as night begins to fall the first of them will be on the prowl. Who can say, it might even make our task easier to have one of them come to us, instead of having to hunt one down." He nodded again and turned back to Rusu. "So I'll leave it up to you, Nick. If you want to go on, we're listening."

Rusu was no longer trembling. His eyes were fully focussed, and he looked a lot steadier now. "You must be very brave men," he said. "Which makes me feel like the world's worst coward."

"No need for you to feel that way," Trask told him gruffly. "We really do know what you've been through."

"But knowing what's waiting for you on that ship, and then to go back to it . . . ?"

"It's our job," said Lardis. "It's what we do."

"Rather you than me," said Rusu. "But if that's the way it is—if you'll risk your lives that way—then what have I got to lose? All I'm doing is telling my story."

"Out with it, then," said Lardis, "for time's wasting."

And Rusu nodded and quickly went on:

"Some of the cabins on A deck that still had doors . . . we could hear movement behind them. But not knowing what was waiting for us in there—not knowing if they were survivors or . . . or something else—we didn't wait around but crept on down to B deck. And this far, despite all the many hundreds of people and crew on that big ship, we hadn't seen a single one. Not one that was living, anyway.

"But dead people? Oh, there'd been plenty of those.

They'd littered the stairwells, men, women, and kids, and all of them so badly mangled that they were past *any* kind of recovery. I mean, they were just dead, *really* dead! Most of them were either old ones or very young ones, and all of them were weak ones. They'd paid the price first, of course. And as for the living, if you want to call them that—the ones we hadn't as yet seen, not in daylight hours, anyway—well, plainly they weren't just drinking blood but eating flesh, too. Some of those corpses . . . *God,* they'd been well chewed down! The stairwells, the gangways, and the cabins; there was blood and guts everywhere. The whole ship stank of blood and shit and death.

"But the worst, most nerve-wracking thing by far was this: we knew that for every corpse we'd seen there were at least two others who were still 'alive,' sleeping or hiding there, crouching and listening there, red-mouthed, feral-eyed, and full of a feverish, hideous strength there. And of course that was why we crept . . .

"We made it down onto B deck . . . and then everything went wrong. By then the light was very bad. Only our torches, electric and flaring both, sustained us. We had thought to go unobserved, unheard, unobstructed—*huh!* But when they're no longer human it appears their senses become far more highly tuned. And already they were accepting what had happened to them, becoming organized, and sorting themselves into groups and hunting parties. So maybe they had been aware of us all along, and B deck being in the guts of the ship, down in the darkest levels, that was the obvious place to spring their trap.

"We reached my cabin and found the door hanging open. Everything inside had been turned upside down, thrown about all over the place, so it took me a while to find the cell phone. While I searched through the jumble the others kept watch, and just as I found what I was looking for under a pile of my clothing, so I heard one of the other deckhands hiss a warning; he thought he'd seen movement in the shadows at one end of the gangway. A moment later, the big, burly engineer cursed and fired a Verey light. He was good at cursing—every other word was 'fuck' or 'shit' or 'bastard'—but I'd never in my life heard anything like the stream of abuse that came out of him then! The reason why was obvious, and when he reached into my cabin, grabbed me and dragged me out into the gangway . . . I saw it for myself.

"Back the way we'd come, down the aft stairwells, the vampires were massing—but I do mean they were *massing!* The engineer's flare had glanced off a bulkhead, gone skittering almost all the way along the gangway. And there it was sizzling away, spinning about all over the place—like a blob of raw sodium on water, or a drop of grease in a hot pan—creating a brilliant, dazzling ball of light in a wreathing cloud of pink smoke. And leaping and dancing in the smoke, skipping to avoid contact with the thing, a dozen or more people—men and women both, or things that had been people—were outlined in its glare. And behind them, crowding the stairwell, a sea of feral faces swam in a secondary darkness made luminous by their firefly eyes!

"But I had the cell phone and we were out of there, or so we thought, all of us making a stumbling run for the for'ard stairwells—where another group was waiting for us! But a group? I mean, they were a nightmare horde! They came spilling, spewing, spawning from the stairwells into the gangway; a milling crowd of gaunt, staring, feral-eyed faces like so many grinning zombies, and all of them reaching for us with outstretched arms and eager hands!

"We had the big engineer with a Verey pistol in front, and the steward with the other pistol at the rear. And only one way out now: through the middle of that . . . that awful undead horde of blood-lusting monsters.

"The engineer had reloaded; he fired his Verey pistol; the shot went right through the vampire crowd, setting some on fire as it passed before ricocheting off the stairwell bulkhead and leaping back into the press. There it flared up, sputtering and jumping like a Chinese firecracker—issuing smoke and blinding light, and setting fire to everything it touched—

causing the milling once-humans to scatter like shell-shocked rats.

"Simultaneously, the steward had fired *his* pistol into the massed ranks of the original pack at the aft end of the gangway. They had recovered from their panic and were loping after us to close us in. In fact we *were* closed in from both ends, and only the incendiary Verey lights and our fire axes—and our terror—gave us any chance at all. But I think the best weapon of all was our terror.

"The big engineer led the charge; he tucked his pistol into his belt and was into them in a moment, his axe swinging with a will. The other deckhands flanked him, which just about filled the width of the gangway, leaving the steward and I to turn our backs and bring up the rear. And while it lasted . . . Jesus, but it was a slaughter!

"Mad with blood-lust those creatures surely were, but they seemed to have little or no sense of direction; their orientation was shot, their blood and senses were out of kilter because of the poisons that coursed through their veins. Oh yes, their senses had been enhanced . . . but they hadn't yet learned how to put them to best use. Yes, they were that much stronger, but as yet they didn't seem to recognize that fact. And the strangest thing of all: I don't think they cared a damn!

"All they cared for was blood. That was the fuel that drove or powered them. They'd tasted a drug which made man-made drugs seem puny by comparison, which—combined with the alien stuff that had been transfused in them—was instantly addictive and caused their craving. They wanted *our* blood! But in their blind lusting they'd forgotten or ignored a simple fact: we wanted to keep it! And our axes did terrible work.

"But their strength . . . and their numbers . . . we piled them up and then had to climb over them! And through all the crimson hell of it, we were awash in their blood!

"How we made it to the for'ard stairwell, I don't know, but that was where we lost the first of our group. One of the deckhands up front . . . he fell . . . went shooting past me feetfirst down the stairs. Kicking and screaming, slipping and slithering in spilled blood, he crashed into the ravening horde behind us. And because we were facing that way, me and the steward, we . . . we saw the end of it.

"Still shrieking—and I shall hear his screams forever— the deckhand was grabbed up by the red-spattered crowd. It was as if a press of red and grey and feral yellow came together on him. One moment he was thrown aloft, buoyed up by all the hands that grasped him, and then he was dragged under. It was like—it was as if—he had fallen into a huge vat of dense, swirling paint: at first the surface was solid and supported him . . . but then the skin broke and the colours opened to engulf him. Whole and pale he was absorbed, only to be tossed up again . . . but no longer whole! Pieces of him, bites out of him, had gone missing in the space of only two or three seconds. Then all of him went missing, as he was dragged under again, devoured and lost to us forever.

"Two of us in front and two behind, back to back, we fought all the harder up that stairwell. And as daylight began filtering down to us so the pressure slackened off. Suddenly—almost unbelievably—we were fighting on the A deck landing, where lances of glorious yellow light slanted down from above, stinging and blinding our attackers. On the way down, those beams of light had seemed faint; now they were quite literally the light at the end of the tunnel. Then, just as it looked like we might make it without any more losses—damn, damn, *damn* it to hell!—that was when we lost the young steward.

"In the briefest of brief lulls, he'd put down his axe and was trying to reload his Verey pistol. But his hands were slimy with blood and shaking so feverishly that precious shells were spilling from his grasp and pockets both. And that was it: the terror that had been his mainstay now cost him everything, for in the moment before he could shoot he was tripped. Someone—or rather some *thing*—had kept low and crept up the steps to snatch his axe where he'd dropped it, and now used it to catch him behind the ankles.

"As his feet shot out from under him he gave a wild cry and finally managed to fire the pistol diagonally across the stairwell. The ball of fire made a hissing zigzag of heat and smoke down the stairs, ricochetting off walls and bulkheads alike before the final explosion and brilliant starburst. But as burbling cries of fear and hissing warnings went up as the vampires below me retreated in confusion, so they took the steward with them, dragging him by his ankles. It was the last I saw of him, and now there were only the three of us.

"The way below was temporarily clear, so I joined the other two facing forward where they drove just three or four vampires before them. Considering the amazing strength of these terrible creatures, you might find that hard to believe or imagine: that we could force them back. But in the main they were still thinking like men; their near invincibility had not as yet dawned on them. Moreover, there was light pouring down from above—real light, reflected sunlight—so that as well as having to avoid our bloody axes, the vampires were also hindered by stray ultraviolet rays which, however watered down by reflection, worried and blinded them.

"By then we were almost exhausted; even our terror could no longer fuel our desperate fight for survival. And on those last few steps up to the main deck, with salvation in view, that was where the big engineer's massive strength finally gave out. And at the same time—as the creatures above us realized they were being driven up into raw, seething sunlight—it was the moment they chose to launch themselves in a body down upon us.

"One of them threw himself at me, another at the other deckhand; we were able to hold our axes overhead, impaling them and using their impetus to hurl them down the stairs. The other two were relatively small men; one was fat and balding. The big engineer cursed and swung at him, caving in his chest, but his axe somehow got caught fast in his ribs. And as the gibbering thing flopped down on him along with the last of the four, their combined weight drove him backwards, sent him stumbling into darkness. And below us, the pack that trailed us took the opportunity to reach up into the light, grab him and drag him down. The last I saw of him was his snarling clenched teeth—his straining, blood-spattered face—as with his last ounce of strength he somehow managed to toss his Verey pistol up to me.

"Earlier, he had given me a box of four spare cartridges to carry in case he ran out. Knowing he was finished, I rammed one of these into the pistol, snapped it shut, and fired it directly down the centre of the stairwell. But I didn't look to see what was illuminated by the flare, for I already knew.

"Then my last human friend and I were up onto the main deck and racing—or rather staggering—along the gangway to where it came out into broad, blessed daylight at the prow. And there we fell in a sprawl on the open deck, gasping and sobbing until we could breathe again. . . ."

"I was covered in blood! It suddenly dawned on me that my flesh and clothing were drenched in the blood of vampires! And so was my friend. We climbed—but we would certainly have run if only we'd had the strength—up three flights of exterior stairs to the open upper deck on the very roof of the ship, where without pause we went amidships and threw ourselves into the large swimming pool.

"In the water, we tore our clothes off and bathed our shuddering bodies. And we floundered from one patch of water to the next as each in its turn became tinged with red. This cleansing seemed to take forever, but when we were done we got out in the sunlight to dry.

"Incredibly, I was unharmed—which is to say I had no cuts, bites, or punctures—but my friend . . . he wasn't so fortunate. During the fighting, he'd been bitten in the shoulder and upper arm, and a shallow cut in his forehead was still oozing blood.

"Seeing his wounds he became very scared, even more so than during the fighting, and asked me, 'Do you think . . . think that maybe I . . . ?' But I didn't know enough to answer him, not right then."

* * *

"My cell phone wouldn't work. The batteries had run down, and my splashing about in the swimming pool hadn't much helped things. Ridiculous that after all the trouble we'd gone to—the price we'd paid to recover the damn thing—I had forgotten it was in my coverall flap pocket! Obviously it was my state of mind, the fact that I'd been in fear of my life and completely panicked.

"I took the cell phone to bits and dried it out, and while I was putting it together again sent my friend looking for fresh batteries. Fortunately I'd carried the Verey pistol in my hand, retaining sufficient common sense to leave both it and the cartridges beside the pool. At least *they* hadn't suffered any water damage.

"As for my friend:

"At two-thirty in the afternoon he still hadn't come back. Meanwhile I had fallen asleep from sheer exhaustion, but there in the sunlight, half in the shade of an awning, I knew that I was safe. And despite that there had been slaughter last night, the decks were amazingly clean; it seemed the vampires had seen fit to clear up after themselves! Apart from a few stains, the ship looked freshly swabbed down. Or had they simply been keeping their house in order?

"Earlier there had been, oh, maybe a hundred or more bodies floating in the sea. These had sunk or drifted away now; but in a narrow bottleneck where the sea met the rocks, I saw that the water was alive with motion. When I looked closer, I saw a huge raft of crabs and small fishes in a feeding frenzy down there. Nothing goes to waste in the sea . . .

"The *Evening Star* is a monster of a ship. *Hah!* Unfortunate choice of words . . . let's just say she's big. It wouldn't make much sense for me to go looking for the other survivor; he could be anywhere, could even be—might even have gone—missing? Myself, I didn't intend to go anywhere belowdecks again, and certainly not into any dark places. But I didn't know about my friend. While he had *seemed* to understand what was going on, maybe he hadn't understood enough.

"And suddenly I found myself in a panic again. I was alone! I was stark naked! My cell phone was my only hope, and it wasn't working because I had no batteries!

"I got a grip of myself, or at least as much of a grip as I could get. There were gift shops on the main deck, but that was three flights of stairs down. Fortunately the shopping area was dead centre of the ship, almost directly below the pools. Also, the central main deck was above the porthole level and had windows that let in lots of God-given daylight. More to the point, so far I hadn't seen a single changeling creature on that level—well, with the exception of the original pair of Great Vampires when they were rampaging, and they'd now left—and with the sun high in the sky, I prayed I wouldn't see any more. And I didn't.

"When finally I got my nerves under control, and after I'd descended to the central area of the main deck, I saw why there were no vampires down there. For indeed the windows let in lots of light, and most of the shop façades and interiors were lined with chrome or mirrors that reflected it. To my eyes the effect was no more dazzling than a well-lit shopping mall, but to them . . . I supposed it must seem like hell!

"I went to a gift shop which I knew stocked every kind of photographic accessory. For some reason I thought I'd find the place wrecked, but that wasn't so. Indeed, it was almost fully intact . . . except for the shelf which had housed the batteries. That had been stripped clean . . .

"Quickly then, I tried the other shops, but to no avail.

"And so I returned to the open upper deck, but not before I'd taken socks and shoes from a shop, a shirt and fresh coveralls from the laundry, and raided a refrigerator in the *Star's* main dining room to stuff my pockets with food and a bottle of decent wine. The power had been off for some time but the food was still good and cold.

"And still I'd seen no sign of my friend. So that I found myself wondering if he was my friend after all . . . or anyone's friend, for that matter."

* * *

"I thought about using the Verey lights. Crazy! What good would it do to fire them off in the daylight? And I doubted very much that I'd be able to do it at night . . . if I did it would be the *last* thing I did! Anyway, I needed the Verey pistol as a weapon. Apart from a fire axe, it was my only weapon.

"After eating I felt heavy and tired, from nervous exhaustion or whatever. And anyway, I reckoned it would be a good idea to get as much sleep as I could right there and then, for I had no idea how much I'd get later. And dusk was only some three or four hours away. But I did spend another hour looking for batteries without finding any. I supposed that I might find some on the bridge . . . but after just a few seconds in there I couldn't take any more. And now *I* knew what hell must look like.

"I climbed up to the exhaust baffle and opened a maintenance hatch in the lead stack. I had been in there before, scaling out the flue between voyages. The burning stench of greasy diesel residue was sickening, but with the engines at a standstill it was just about bearable. I couldn't have gone in there when the ship was running; I would have suffocated and fried in a matter of seconds. But these engines wouldn't ever be running again. Not as long as the ship was parked on these rocks. There was a ledge in there where I could even lie down, but not until I had to. Not until nightfall.

"And so I slept out on the collar, in the shade of the big exhaust array, while in the west the sun slid down the sky . . ."

6
The "Entertainment,"
and Leave it to the Marines

DAVID CHUNG, EVER THE MOST NERVOUS OF THE
team, said, "Ben, we have to get on."

Glancing at his watch, Trask answered, "We can spare a
few more minutes. Let him carry on."

Lardis nodded and said, "I agree. Let him get it right out
of his system. And anyway, if it's vampires you're after
you'll need the night. It's like you said, Ben: with the sun
up, you'd have to hunt 'em down. But when the sun's down
... they'll come looking for you!" And winking encourag-
ingly at the survivor, he prompted him, "Nick?"

Rusu had gone from strength to strength. In the presence
of men such as these he felt safe for the first time in three
long days and nights. He was actually looking around now,
making eye contact, actually seeing people. One of *Invincible*'s medics had left a pack of cigarettes and a lighter on
a table. After lighting up and taking a deep, soothing drag,
Rusu looked at Lardis, gave a curt, decisive nod, and continued where he'd left off.

"So there I was asleep on the collar ... until I heard this
voice whispering, 'Hey, wake up!'

"I started awake and saw it was the other deckhand. He
was up the maintenance ladder, just his head and shoulders
visible, and he was staring at me where I lay. I was a little
chilly and started shivering, and I could see by the length
of the shadows that the sun was almost down. Both myself
and ... and my *former* friend, we were covered by the
shadow of the exhaust array. And the way he was staring at
me—all intent, and unblinking—it was unnerving.

93

" 'Where've you been?' I asked him. 'Did you have to hide up or something? Did you get trapped?'

" 'Hide up?' he said, looking surprised. 'Trapped?' And then he gave himself a shake and seemed to come more alive. 'Trapped, yes! Down below. But they didn't see me, and I fell asleep waiting them out. Later, I couldn't find you. But then I remembered where you came from this morning. And . . . and here you are.'

"As he climbed up onto the collar, I sat up and backed off until I came up against the exhaust array. 'What about the batteries?' I said. 'Did you find any?'

" 'The batteries?' Echoing my words, he sat down cross-legged facing me. 'Oh, yes—the batteries!' He'd rigged himself out with some ill-fitting clothes, and reaching into a pocket, he produced three or four brand-new blister packs of different-sized batteries. The price tags were still on them, and labels with the name of the gift shop. I looked at them, then at him, and he nodded. He knew what I was thinking. And:

" 'See,' he said, 'it's a matter of survival. After all that fighting—what with getting myself wounded and bitten and all—I couldn't say for sure if I was . . . if I was okay, you know? So I thought it through and decided to wait and see.' His voice had fallen to a slow, monotonous, husky drone; he sounded as if he were drugged. But even as he spoke he crept a little closer.

"I had been using my shoes wrapped up in my new shirt as a pillow. Now I reached out, carefully pulling the bundle toward me. He watched me and said nothing, so that in a little while I prompted him with, 'You weren't trapped below at all, were you? You were just worried about yourself, right?'

" 'Something like that,' he said. And: 'Are you going to try the batteries?'

"Then, as I took out my cell phone and opened up the blister pack containing the batteries it used, abruptly he moved closer still, and his next few sentences tumbled out of him all urgent like and garbled. 'How do I look? You've *got* to tell me! I have to know if I look ... okay? See, I don't feel too good. I don't feel very well at all ...'

"My fingers felt like rubber as I fitted the batteries, but the tiny pilot light on the phone at once lit up. It was working! 'You look just fine,' I told him. A lie, because he looked like shit, but I daren't say that. I *wanted* him to be okay, and as yet there was very little to say he wasn't—but at the same time I wasn't taking any chances.

"He cocked his head a little on one side, smiled and said, 'I look fine? Oh, really? You think I look okay?' But his smile was all wrong.

" 'Yes, I really think so,' I lied again, and began dialling my family's number in Limassol, Cyprus. The phone burped once, twice, three times ... and I could have screamed my frustration out loud, except I didn't dare. But after the fourth burp, finally it was answered, by my mother.

" 'It's Nick.' I barely croaked the words out, then cleared my throat and repeated them. 'It's Nick, aboard the *Evening Star*. Mother, listen very carefully. We're in trouble. Tell the company that the *Star* is shipwrecked on a rock, but I don't know where. Tell them we've been boarded by—'

"But that was as far as I got, for moving so fast I barely saw it, my good 'friend' reached out and slapped the phone out of my hand. As it fell to the collar he brought a clenched fist down on it so hard that the thing splintered into little shards of plastic! And:

" 'That's enough,' he said, in that terrible monotone. 'See, I still haven't made up my mind. I can see you're scared of me, and maybe you've a right to be. I still don't know for sure.'

"But I knew for sure. For by now the sun had sunk more yet, and as the gloom deepened so his eyes were beginning to shine a gleamy yellow!

"Trembling, I left my shirt in a little pile and pulled my shoes on. And he said, 'Are you going somewhere? Myself, I was thinking of just ... of just waiting here for a while.'

" 'Waiting for what?' I asked him. 'Another fifteen or twenty minutes and they'll be coming out onto the decks.

So you and I, we have to hide ourselves away.'

"He didn't seem to be listening. His feral eyes had gone to an empty carton of milk and the rind of an orange, the remnants of my last meal. 'I see you've eaten,' he said.

" 'Are you hungry?' I asked him. 'If so, I have some food.'

" 'I found food below,' he answered. 'It just made me throw up. So either it was off . . . or I am.'

"Coming to my feet with my shirt in my hands, I unfastened the top of my coveralls. 'It's getting chilly,' I said, making to put my shirt on.

"He had come to his feet, too. The way his eyes roved over my upper body before focussing on my neck . . . I knew there was nothing anyone could do for him. Or if there was, I would have to be the one who did it.

"Then, the way he leaned toward me telegraphed his intention, but knowing how very quick he was I beat him to it. As he himself had pointed out, it was a matter of survival. I'd kept the Verey pistol wrapped in my shirt, my finger on the trigger. In the act of reaching for me he saw the weapon's muzzle poised only inches from his face, and as his mouth fell open in a big round O of surprise, so I fired at him point-blank.

"The charge hit him in the left eye and lodged there, half in, half out of his skull, ejecting its hot gasses and driving him backwards to the rim of the collar. There he stood flailing his arms, until the final brilliant starburst cooked his brain and went on to incinerate his head from the inside out.

"As his arms flew wide he stiffened, then slumped down into himself, toppled backwards over the rim, and went crashing down onto the pool deck twenty feet below . . .

"After that I stood there for quite a while—oh, perhaps a minute—before I could get anything working again. But shadows were creeping and I knew I must get moving. The trouble was that I couldn't leave this man I'd killed lying where he was in full sight of who or whatever would soon be coming out into the night. If they saw him there, then they'd start looking for who *put* him there.

"I went down the steel rungs breakneck, dragged the perfect and normal-seeming body with its blistered, bubbling, and barely recognizable head to the rail and dumped it overboard. No time to spare then as I climbed back up to the exhaust array, opened the hatch a crack for easy and rapid access, then stretched myself out flat on the collar to observe the night's proceedings. This wasn't simply morbid curiosity; I needed to know just how much these creatures had got it together in order to gauge the odds against my surviving. So in a way I suppose it *was* morbid curiosity after all.

"The sun was no more than a blister on the sea now, and the shadows were everywhere, lengthening by the second.

"I knew where to look: the stairwells for'ard and amidships. As for the aft stairwells: they were behind the array and there was nothing I could do about that but listen. And I listened so intently that I thought my ears might burst from the silence.

"Then it was time—that preternatural moment when the sun disappears and the gloom deepens—not yet night but no longer daylight, the ever-deepening twilight preceeding *their* time. It stretched itself out into minutes, and the minutes into half an hour. The shadows gradually merged together and became pools of darkness. Beginning in the east, the stars were flickering into being one by one . . .

"And then . . . there was movement!

"Something crept in the dark. Many somethings. Low-burning, lambent candles that weren't candles at all but eyes!

"They came up out of the stairwells onto the decks . . . two groups that I could see and one that I could hear . . . a rustling like bat wings unfurling. The association with bats seemed very obvious. And then I saw those blots of darkness moving out from under the collar and spreading along the deck, that sea of vampires on the swarm, that host of horror!

"Between these groups there must have been . . . oh, it seemed a thousand of them, men and women alike! And God only knows how many remained below. As for those who had come up aft—I could see that they were cautious, curious, and supposed they'd heard my Verey pistol. I lay very still as they lifted their heads to sniff at the air, the lingering cordite and sulphur stink. Some of them paused at the spot directly below me where my ex-deckhand friend had fallen. There would be blood and shit there, of course. And I saw them follow a trail, go to the rail and look over. But as yet none of them had looked up. Fearing that they might, I drew back out of sight—the trouble with that being that now I didn't know what was going on down there! But I was still able to look forward toward the prow, see what the other two groups were doing.

"The silence was broken when the aft vampires found their voices and began to talk, all in the same husky monotone of my ex-friend. From what they said it was fairly obvious that they suspected someone—an entirely human someone—was up here on the open deck. Mercifully, they didn't seem too concerned. But then again, with their numbers why should they be concerned?

"Meanwhile, the two groups amidships and for'ard had more or less held their positions; none of the members of the three factions was mingling with the others. So it looked like they'd formed into three quite separate bands. And for a fact they had chosen or accepted leaders, for there were those among them who strode about giving orders. Good, for it was just such an order that saved my neck.

"My blood froze when I heard boots clanging on the rungs of the exhaust array's maintenance ladder. The sound paralysed me, freezing me solid. Some curious vampire bastard was climbing up to see what he could see, probably to act as some kind of lookout for the rest of the aft group!

"I had already loaded my Verey pistol; now I rolled onto my back, with my shoulders slightly raised and the weapon pointing down between my feet. The moment a face appeared over the collar's rim, I was going to send the bastard to hell! After that I would have only one shot left and would have to try to bluff it out. Only one way up onto the collar, and me waiting at the top with a deadly weapon. Perhaps after I'd taken out a second man, then they'd give it up. But if they should send up a *third* man . . . well, that would be the end of me.

"But it didn't come to that, for as I heard the boots climbing higher, suddenly a gruff voice called out, 'You there! Come down from there and bring on the entertainment.' God! The first thing I thought was that he knew I was there and was talking to me!

"But . . . 'the entertainment'? Sweet Jesus!

"Then I heard the boots pause as someone hesitated, and finally I started to breathe again as they went clumping back down the metal rungs.

" 'The entertainment' consisted of the last handful of human beings, captives of the vampires. They'd been saving them, keeping them back, for this. And despite that I was now mindless with terror—or perhaps because I was—I had to know what was happening. Turning over onto my stomach again, I inched forward until I could see over the edge of the collar. A handful of survivors were dragged up from below decks, mainly girls and young kids. They were all naked, sobbing, and clinging to each other, incapable of accepting what was happening to them. For even now—to *me*, let alone to them—it was beyond belief, as I watched mass rape turn to murder, and blood-lust to cannibalism!

"But there are some sights that simply weren't meant to be seen, acts that could blind a man simply by watching them, and living human flesh being carved and passed around in rough red lumps is one of them . . .

"Well, I didn't go blind, though I'm sure I wished it. And there was the same monstrous activity in the other groups amidships and for'ard; they had captives, too. And all of them went the same way. But those monsters—those monsters who had been men—they made it last. And it lasted, and it lasted.

"And all the while I lay there, half-delirious yet scarcely daring to breathe, where finally I curled myself up into a ball at the foot of the exhaust array . . .

* * *

"Their moaning woke me up. It was the twilight before the dawn, and they were moving off in dribs and drabs, disappearing back down into the darkness as the first pink flush lit the eastern sky. And I had made it through a second night.

"Well, and it seems I made it through last night, too, but not on the collar. From dusk till dawn I was breathing all that stale diesel stench inside the leading exhaust stack. I'd found a way to jam the maintenance hatch behind me. And you know, for all that the place is a rat-hole, it was the only place on the ship that I felt safe? There was just the once I stuck my head out, and that was last night in the twilight when I heard that first helicopter coming in. To the crew of that chopper, it must have looked like the *Star* was abandoned, like a modern *Marie Celeste*. But when they touched down and the rotors slowed to standby, God, I wanted to leap out of hiding, wave my arms and stamp my feet, yell and warn them off! But I didn't, and you know why I didn't. They were at the stem and I was at the stern . . . they wouldn't hear or understand me, but I knew there were those who would.

"You want to know what happened to the people in that helicopter? It was like darkness fell on them, swift as the shadows when a cloud passes over the moon. And the pilot, poor bastard? They dragged him out of there onto the deck, and fell on him in a swarm. And that crew were gone as if they'd never existed. So that when I ducked back into my hidey-hole and jammed the hatch shut again I was feeling so suicidal that it was all I could do to keep from tossing myself down the flue onto the iron guts of the big engine and finishing it. And I vowed that I wasn't coming out again, that I would rather shrivel and die there in the greasy stinking darkness than be drained off like so much juice from a ripe fruit!

"And the fumes in there got to me. I don't know if I slept or what. If I ate anything I immediately threw up. When I drank it was all I could do to keep it down. But I wasn't coming out, not ever, not even when it was daylight again. I'd quite literally resigned myself to dying in there. What with the fear and the fumes—I don't know—I suppose I was out of my head.

"When I heard your choppers circling I thought it was some kind of dream, a mental mirage, and for a while did nothing. My head was swimming and I could scarcely get to my feet. The luminous dial of my watch told me it was daylight, and the sound of the choppers was getting louder.

"Suddenly the survival instinct kicked in and I had to know. When I came out of hiding onto the collar, the fresh air nearly did for me. After all that shit I'd been breathing, it was like good wine, a champagne overdose.

"And the rest ... well, the rest you know. So if what you've told me is true and you're going back there, what can I say but God help you?"

Rusu lit another cigarette, inhaled deeply and trickled the smoke out through his nostrils, lay back and fell silent.

And Trask said, "Thanks, Nick. You have helped us, but even if you hadn't I think you've helped yourself."

Lardis nodded and said, "You'll dream this stuff for a long time, Nick, but eventually you'll find a way to switch off. The mind is clever at switching off. There's a thousand things that I no longer let myself dream."

"One last thing," said Trask. "This story you've told us—don't tell it to anyone else. They wouldn't believe you anyway, but if they did it might prevent us from doing our work. Do you understand?"

"My lips are sealed," said Rusu. "It's like Lardis said: I have to find a way to switch off and forget."

And then, as Trask and his people left him he gave one last shudder and added: "But I don't think I ever will ..."

Out in the gangway, a CPO was waiting for them. "Sir," he spoke to Trask, "the Captain wants to see you on the helipad ASAP. I'm to take you up there."

Trask nodded his understanding. "It's late and he's getting worried."

Poker-faced, and possibly bridling a little, the CPO looked at him. "I shouldn't think so. The Captain of HMS *Invincible* is a man who doesn't get worried too easily. I only know that he's been swapping messages with the Admiralty and the Fleet Air Arm for at least two hours now, and that your escort has been assembled and is waiting on the helipad."

"Our escort?" Trask raised an eyebrow but the CPO had nothing more to say . . .

They were marines, and all six of them dressed in alien-looking nuclear, chemical, and biological warfare suits, nite-lite headgear and long-snouted gas masks, carrying NATO standard 7.62 mm laser-sighted self-loading rifles . . . and Trask just didn't want to believe it when *Invincible*'s Captain McKenzie told him these men were his escort.

"What?" The Head of E-Branch could scarcely contain himself. "You've been briefed by Gunnery Commander Argyle—who I'm sure must have explained something of what we saw on the *Evening Star*'s bridge—yet you still expect me to take these men with me, and not one of them knowing a single damn thing about what's happening here?"

Captain Arthur McKenzie wasn't used to being spoken to like this, but on the other hand he did recognize Trask's authority. Unfortunately, however, with the sun already touching the horizon, there was no time left for polite explanations. And, "No," he answered, "I don't expect anything of you, Mr. Trask. But the Admiralty, the Fleet Air Arm, and even your own ministerial superior—they do. And on this occasion I'm only following orders. One of these soldiers is a qualified helicopter pilot. His duty is to bring back the stranded chopper. The other five . . . have their orders."

"What orders?" Trask was dumbfounded.

"First, to protect you," said the straight-backed, bearded, broad-shouldered, and unblinking Captain, "and second to immobilize and secure at least one living specimen—which is to say an infected person—from that vessel and return him or her to *Invincible* for onward conveyance to London and the proper authorities."

"Authorities? Meaning the boffins at Porton Down?"

The Captain nodded. "Who we would assume are the experts in such matters."

Trask shook his head. "I can't believe the Minister Responsible—I mean my, er, ministerial superior—would hamper me in this way."

"Hamper you?" Now McKenzie bridled. "By giving you the protection of these marines, these superb soldiers? Well, allow me to inform you, Mr. Trask, that the only reason you're going back to the *Evening Star* at all is that your 'Minister Responsible' pleaded your case with *my* superiors! And what's more, if you don't board this helicopter now— without wasting any more valuable time—as your host and the Captain of this warship I may take it upon my own shoulders to redefine the orders I've received. In which case I'm empowered to let these men go without you!"

"Captain," said Trask, a note of desperation creeping into his voice now, "look, you really don't understand. This *infection* we're talking about isn't anything like you've been led to believe it is."

McKenzie nodded. "I know what you're going to say, Mr. Trask. For indeed Commander Argyle did brief me. And yes, I'm aware of what you saw on that bridge. The Asiatic plague has mutated and does to men what rabies does to wild animals . . . turns them into killers. But you see, two of my marines are also carrying dart guns with a powerful sedative that will knock a man down in seconds. And so that I'll be able to follow their progress, the WO has an audiovisual transmitter in his headset: a camera linked to *Invincible*'s screens. So I'll be with you in a lot more than spirit. And believe me, I won't allow you to interfere. You may advise by all means, but leave the work to the marines. I think you can be fairly certain that they won't, er, 'hamper' you."

As he finished speaking the Captain turned away and whirled his hand over his head. And on the helipad the rotors of a Mark VI Sea King twitched into life as the marines boarded in single file.

Trask looked this way and that and licked his lips. "And

is that it? You're not going to listen to—?" He was about to say "reason." But:

"—That's *it!*" Captain McKenzie cut in. "On my next signal she takes off—with or without you. There are extra NBC suits aboard. I'd advise you to put them on, even if you don't get to set foot on the *Evening Star*."

"What?" said Trask. "What did you say? Even if we don't get to set foot on . . . ? Hell's teeth! We're the only people who know what's going on here, and you—"

Jake Cutter took his elbow. "Er, Mr. Trask? Sir? The Captain is right. We're fortunate that we have the opportunity to watch the operation from beginning to end. I'm sure that will suffice for our, er, Minister Responsible? And now we really should get aboard, right?" His grip on Trask's arm was like iron.

Trask looked at Jake, and as the downdraft from the chopper built up he turned to the telepath Liz Merrick. Half shrugging, she leaned forward and whispered, "You'd be making a mistake to think McKenzie's bluffing. For just a moment back there, he was even thinking to throw you in the brig! A passing thought, yes, but if we're going it has to be now."

Trask stamped for the big chopper's ramp, but as the others got aboard he turned and shouted, "Captain McKenzie, these men, these marines . . . they're not my responsibility."

"Of course they're not!" the Captain shouted back.

And Trask nodded. "Just you remember that," he said, before climbing aboard.

A marine with a Warrant Officer Class 2's insignia on the wrist of his NBC suit told Trask, "Sir, it will take you maybe ten to fifteen minutes to get into one of these suits. And we're only fifteen minutes to target."

"Target?" said Trask, whose thoughts were elsewhere.

"Our destination," the other shrugged. He had pulled aside his headgear and gas mask in order to talk. Most of his men had done likewise for easy breathing en route to the *Star*.

Trask was still feeling sour but the mood was quickly

falling off him. For after all, it wasn't these people's fault that they were caught up in this. They were just following orders—however stupid those orders might appear to be. Also, from what Trask had been told, he knew he couldn't blame the Minister Responsible, either. And it was easy to see what had happened here: the minister didn't have carte blanche in this thing; since HMS *Invincible* was involved, he'd had to work through the Fleet Air Arm and the Admiralty both. So, what would he have been able to tell them: that E-Branch had priority here, and they were going up against vampires? Not likely! Which meant that it all boiled down to a military (or more properly naval) operation.

To these six men, however, it wouldn't seem like a military mission at all; they were simply doing their bit to help out in an emergency situation, giving aid to the civilian authorities. And on second thought maybe Trask *should* blame the Minister Responsible after all. For he had governmental power, the power to swear both the Admiralty and the Fleet Air Arm to secrecy . . . *if* he'd had the balls to use it. Or maybe it was the case that too many people were already in the know. And then again maybe something had changed—changed drastically—since Trask and his people had been sent out here.

But what or whichever, it was a fucking mess! These six men thought they knew what they were doing, thought it was going to be easy. They'd been tasked to knock down some kind of unarmed, rabid civilian animal and take him to a vet to have him checked out . . . just like that.

But it wasn't just like that at all . . .

"You and these men," Trask suddenly blurted it out, "you're all in grave danger! You aren't in possession of all the facts. Your superiors don't *know* all the facts. Only set foot on that ship without knowing what you're doing, and—"

"—Oh, we know what we're doing, sir," the Warrant Officer cut him short. "Our orders were very simple."

Jesus! thought Trask. *Simple? So were the minds that issued them!* And out loud: "Listen to me. I'm telling you that some of you might not be coming back from that vessel!"

The WO narrowed his eyes. "And I'm telling you that that's what we call spreading alarm and despondency among the troops. If you were one of mine, you'd be on a charge. And in any case I'm obliged to report what you just said."

"But—"

"Just ten minutes to target." The WO turned away, and then turned back again. "And if you're not in a bloody suit when we get there, I'll be confining you to this chopper—sir!"

Trask barely managed to keep from exploding. "We have our own 'bloody suits,'" he said, "which aren't nearly as complicated as yours." And to his own people: "Spray yourselves down, apply nose-plugs, and weapon up. Liz—I want you on guard from touchdown. We all stay together as far as possible, and always within sight and easy reach of Jake."

All twelve passengers—marines and E-Branch people alike—were standing, belted, hooked up to safety rings in the ceiling of the aircraft; a purely precautionary and standard safety measure, for except from a little vibration the ride so far had been as smooth as silk. It would be relatively simple for Trask and his people to unhook themselves and suit-up in NBC gear.

Instead, Ian Goodly and David Chung took out small aerosol canisters and commenced spraying down their fellows. As the gas spread out the marines wrinkled their noses, backed off, began sliding away on their safety rings and pulling their gas masks into position over their mouths and noses.

"Shit!" one of them said, disgustedly.

"No," Liz told him. "It's just garlic. You don't need your gas masks . . . not yet, anyway."

And as Goodly and Chung finished their spraying: "We never use anything else," said Trask. "That's us all 'suited up.'"

"That's a shame," said a marine junior ranker. "See, I was sort of looking forward to helping the little lady on with her suit. Helping her get dressed, I mean."

"Or undressed!" Another marine sniggered.

"Watch your dirty mouths!" their WO told them. But:

"It's okay," Liz smiled at him however tightly, and turned to the one who would have liked to help her dress, or undress. "I feel perfectly safe with the soldier boys here—especially this one. You see, he has to come on all sexy because he isn't. Oh, he has the gear all right, swinging away down there, but in fact that's all it does. He's so worried that his wife is probably being banged by the big policeman who lives next door back home in Portsmouth, that he just can't get it up. But still he likes to pretend he can." And smiling sweetly at the marine in question—who stood swaying there with his bottom jaw hanging loose and his eyes bugging—she added, "So what does that do for your privates, Private?"

Now the man leaned towards her. "Private?" he said. "What? Private soldier? So what do you know? In the marines it's just 'marine,' sweetheart!" But with his colleagues staring at him, he quickly realized that while he had corrected her error he'd said nothing to address the insult! So . . . could she in fact be right? "Why, you *bitch!*" he spat then, going white and yanking on his tether to get closer to her. But Jake Cutter, hooked up opposite him, quickly got in the way.

"Later," Jake husked, showing his teeth. "We'll talk about this later, you and me, when we're back on *Invincible.*"

"My pleasure!" the other spat.

"I very much doubt that," said Jake. "But it will certainly be mine."

"Knock it off, everybody!" the WO snapped. "Five minutes to target."

And in Jake's head: *Back on* Invincible? Korath-once-Mindsthrall's deadspeak voice echoed his astonishment, his disgust. *This one insulted your woman, accepted your challenge, and yet he's still standing? Your reaction should have been immediate, instinctive, final! By now he should be writhing on the floor, choking on his own blood! Sometimes you disappoint me, Jake.*

I'm not here for your pleasure, Jake told him. *And anyway, this isn't Starside. Also, and if you'd been paying attention, it might have dawned on you that these people will be lucky to get back to* Invincible *in the first place.*

Ah! said Korath. *Now that's more like it. You have let him live knowing that he faces a far worse death on a ship full of vampires!*

Oh, for Christ's sake! Jake sighed. And not wanting to get into a full-blown argument or Wamphyri word game with his dead "familiar," he added: *Yes, sure, whatever you say.*

Then he glanced sideways at Liz.

Sorry, she'd sensed his probe, no longer deadspeak but telepathy, the rapport they had between them. *It's just nerves, I suppose. It doesn't take too much to set them jumping. I think I'll probably always be like this when we... when we're going up against Them.* Then she shrugged and added, *Despite that what I said about this poor jerk is true, still it was cruel of me.*

Forget it, Jake answered. *And anyway, my nerves are jumping just as badly. And maybe I'm just as cruel. I mean, for a while there I was actually enjoying the idea that this marine* fuck *is on his way into hell! And the fact is, he may well be.*

But not us?

Again he glanced at her. *Yes, probably us, too. But at least we know what we're doing. We know what's waiting for us...*

7
Collecting the Specimen

THEY FELT THE SUDDEN DECELERATION, SENSED their gradual descent towards the *Evening Star*. The WO was listening to the pilot on his headset; in answer to information received he said, "Roger that," slapped a magazine into the housing on his rifle, and spoke to his team. "Remember, ladies: these weapons are for show. The infected people on this ship may be loonies but still they'll know what rifles are. And what the hell, the way you're dressed will most likely scare the shit out of them before they even notice your rifles! So then, you may fire warning shots if neccessary, but *only* if it becomes neccessary."

"Oh, it will!" Trask murmured under his breath, then spoke out loud to his agents: "People, if your weapons aren't already loaded, do it now."

"*That* won't be neccessary," the WO spoke up. "You can belay that last. I told you to suit up, and you didn't. Therefore you aren't going anywhere."

Trask shook his head. "You can't confine us, can't order us around. We're not military personnel, we're civilians and don't come under your jurisdiction. You don't have the power to—"

"Williams," the WO cut him off, and the man Liz had taunted stopped glaring at Jake and came to attention.

"Yes, sir?"

"You're on rearguard," said the WO. "Stay back, and keep an eye on this lot. Make sure that they and the pilot stay safe."

"Yes, *sir!*" Williams snapped, and armed his rifle.

"Sergeant Major," Trask grabbed the WO's arm, made one last desperate effort to get through to him. "Those NBC suits aren't any use in this situation. I mean, they're *tar paper,* for God's sake! They can only slow you down. And as for the men and women on that ship—"

(The chopper touched down and the whine of its rotors began to reduce in pitch.) "—on *this* ship," Trask went on, "they're not mad. This isn't like rabies or any other disease we've ever come across. These people won't just attack you—they'll fucking *eat* you!"

The WO shook himself loose, scowled one last time at Trask, then ordered his men out onto the *Star's* deck.

As the door slid open, the pneumatic boarding ramp reached out and down, locked into position, and the marines disembarked. Williams stayed on board, guarding the door and looking at Jake, Trask, and the rest of the E-Branch personnel with a narrow-eyed expression that said, "Just you try something."

The Sea King had landed on the sun deck midway between the two swimming pools. The sun was gone, dusk coming in fast, and the shadow of the island's central fang had draped itself like a shroud over the ship.

"Mr. Beamish, sir," the WO's voice shouted over the throb of rotors on standby. "The stranded chopper's up front on the main deck. She's all yours. We'll see you back on *Invincible*."

"*Christ!*" Trask shouted, and tried to shoulder his way past Williams at the door. "Don't let him—"

But Williams planted the butt of his rifle in Trask's stomach and cut him short. "*Ugh!*" said Trask, doubling up. And when he spoke again his words were a gasp: "Don't let him . . . let him go alone!" Too late, for the marines had already dispersed; the WO and one other towards the starboard stairwells, two others to port, and Lieutenant Beamish crouching low where he skirted the main pool, running along the shadowy open deck toward the prow.

And as Jake unclipped himself, cursed and made to grab hold of Williams, the marine stuck the muzzle of his weapon into his gut, took first pressure on the trigger, and said, "Don't tempt me. Don't even think about it!" His eyes had gone very wide and a nervous tic jerked his pale face in the oval frame of his NBC headgear. "Don't give me any reason at all to pull this trigger—because I just *might,* fuck-head!"

And looking inside Williams's mind, Liz saw what she'd previously missed: that impotence wasn't his only problem. He was a coward, too, scared shitless. And his trigger-finger was trembling like a leaf in a gale!

WO2 Bently switched on the miniature camera situated centrally between the lenses of his nite-lites. As yet the thermal-imaging nite-lites were simply goggles, attachments for the gas mask that protected his mouth and nose, but he need only trip a tiny switch to see in infrared. Lacking a lighting system, the *Evening Star* would be dark below decks, getting darker as the gloom of twilight deepened. And now that Bently and his men were aboard the *Star,* they had also switched on interunit communications; not only could they speak to each other, but their conversations would be heard aboard *Invincible.* Similarly, anything the WO saw would also be seen by Captain McKenzie.

"Get below," Bently told his people now. "One flight down, and we meet up on the bridge deck. Any contact, which is to say on *first* contact, waste no time but dart the target and report, then get him or her back up topside to the Sea King. That's all we're here for. Clear?"

"Roger that," the answer came back from the marines on the larboard stairwell.

Then the sounds of boots clattering on the stairs, and:

"Switch your nite-lites on now," said Bently, as his teams joined forces again between the bridge-deck landings. Then, speaking into his headset: "Lieutenant Beamish, sitrep." Normally Beamish would be his superior, but in the current situation Bently had command while the officer was just another man, a pilot whose only task was to rescue the stranded chopper.

"Y-yes, Sergeant-Major?" came the shaky reply. But shaky?

"Is there a problem?" Bently snapped. "I want a sitrep!"

"I . . . I thought I saw some movement up ahead of me," Beamish answered. "Weird, flowing motion, where the exterior stairs go down to the forward sun deck. The light is bad and the decks are still warm—their heat is interfering with the nite-lites and blurring my vision. Probably better if I rely on my natural eyesight. I'm switching the nite-lites off now and approaching the stairs. And . . ."

Bently waited a moment and repeated him, "And?"

"And there's . . . there's no one here," came the reply, and what sounded like a broken sigh of relief.

"Can you see the chopper?" Bently also sighed, but managed to keep it to himself.

"Yes. The shadow of the upper deck is falling right across her, but . . . but I don't think there's anyone there."

"When you get down there," said Bently, "a couple of warning shots into the air should clear the way—that is, should you need to clear the way."

"Understood," said Lieutenant Beamish.

Bently looked at his men: like molten red and blue ghosts, wavering in his nite-lites. "Okay," he said. "There are no passenger accommodations on this deck, so we'll split up again and go down one flight to the next landing. You pop-gun people, make sure you're ready with your darts. Somewhere on this damn great spook of a ship there are supposed to be a couple of thousand people . . . that is unless they've all jumped overboard! So let's find just one of them and then get the fuck out of here!"

In the ghostly subdued fluorescent lighting of HMS *Invincible*'s Ops Room, Captain McKenzie and two of his officers were following Bently's progress on a wall screen and listening to sitreps and conversations as they came in. Radio procedure had gone out the window, but the Captain wasn't worried. With only a handful of marines involved, all of them well known to his fellows, the SOPs would only have slowed communications down. Captain McKenzie could also speak to Bently if he so desired, but so far he hadn't deemed it necessary.

The thermal imaging of Bently's camera displayed the wooden panelling on the walls of the stairwell as a softly fluctuating peripheral neon glow, gradually brightening as he descended and left what little natural light there'd been on the bridge deck behind.

Then, as Bently reached the promenade deck and the picture on the screen stopped jerking with his motion, the voice of one of his portside men came up loud and clear:

"Sir, there's debris in the larboard stairwell. It's almost choked. Wooden lockers or dressers torn out of the ship's bunks by the looks of it. And there are bodies. We can see . . . we see a great many dead bodies. No, wait! One of them's alive. It's a woman. She's in a bad way, trying to stand up, asking for help. No need to dart this one. She's all done in."

"Stay there!" (Bently's voice.) "We're between the landings below you. We'll cross over to your side and come up."

"Roger that," came the answer, as the picture · on the screen jerked into motion again and the narrow walls of softly glowing neon began to flow by, but more rapidly now.

And then Lieutenant Beamish's voice, or rather his stuttering, choking, terrified shriek: "God Almighty! Oh, sweet Jesus! Yahh! Yahhhh! *Yaahhhhh!*" Followed by four rapid-fire shots, and a new, hitherto unknown, triumphantly guttural voice saying:

"Oh, we've got you now, soldier boy!"

Then, briefly, Beamish's panting growing louder and louder in his throat mike . . . and what sounded like a sharp intake of breath at the beginning of a fresh bout of shrieking . . . until a tearing sound cut it off before it could get started—

—And finally silence . . .

"What?" Bently asked of no one in particular. *"What?"*

And from the portside party: "Sir, we've got the woman— I think. But these dead 'uns—I don't understand it—they've got body heat. They're showing up on our nite-lites!"

"What do you mean you *think* you've got her?" (This was from Bently. Suddenly things were on the move—moving too fast for him—and he was having difficulty staying ahead of them.)

"She . . . she's hanging *on* to us," came the reply. "And God, she's strong! And the dead 'uns under this busted furniture . . . they're not dead! *They're fucking mobile!*"

"We're coming up!" Bently yelled over the muted but frantic clatter of booted feet on polished wooden stairs. And: "Mr. Beamish?" he commenced calling. "Beamish? Lieutenant Beamish? Where are you? . . . Where the fuck are you?"

But Beamish didn't answer . . .

* * *

Aboard the Sea King, the face of the marine called Williams was a picture of fear. He had heard Lieutenant Beamish's last transmission; also the gunfire and Beamish's screams, which he would have heard anyway and without the aid of his radio.

The E-Branch team had heard them, too, and now Trask turned to the locator David Chung, and said, "What do you make of it?"

"Make of it?" Chung flinched from the suddenness, the sharpness of Trask's tone. The locator's face had turned a very pale shade of yellow. "They're everywhere, that's what I make of it! They're under us and all around us. We're in the midst of them. The only place where they aren't is above us . . . which is where *we* should be! They're on all the lower decks—maybe even this deck—hiding in the shadows. It's not dark enough for them up here yet, but it's *getting* darker all the time! And I can feel them creeping."

"Liz?" said Trask.

"They're like one big mind," she answered. "One big silent but seething mind. And there's only one thought in that awful, awesome mass mind: blood! The picture I'm getting is red, Ben. It's red with blood!"

"Ian?" said Trask, turning to the precog.

Ian Goodly was white as death itself. Swaying this way and that where he was still hooked up, he said, "I see what Liz and David saw: a sea of red. But it's not for us. We . . . we're getting out of this."

"What the fuck are you lot talking about?" Williams's eyes swivelled this way and that. He leaned out of the big chopper's door, looked toward the *Star*'s prow to see if he could discover what had happened to Beamish. But his weapon remained pointing at Jake's middle, only inches away, and Jake couldn't make his move.

And now, too late, you see that I was correct, said Korath in Jake's mind. *If you had knocked this one down, Necroscope—if you'd crippled or killed him—he wouldn't be blocking your way now.*

And I'd be a murderer, Jake answered. *Anyway, it's easy to be wise after the fact.*

But I was wise before *the fact,* said Korath.

"Williams," said Trask, "you've got to let us off this helicopter. You heard those screams, those gunshots, but you don't have any idea what they meant. They meant that Beamish is dead. And any time now the same thing will apply to your Warrant Officer and friends. They don't know what they're up against, and we're the only ones who can help them."

Taking Trask's elbow, the cadaverous Goodly shook his head and said, "No, Ben. When I said *we* would get out of this, I was talking about us, E-Branch. I didn't say anything—didn't *see* anything—of them except for the pilot. Obviously he will make it, too. But as for the rest of them, no. Not even this one." He looked at Williams . . . looked pityingly at him.

"So if you're right," said Jake, glancing first at the precog and then at Williams, "it should be okay to tell him what's going on." (He almost added, "For after all, he isn't going to be repeating it to anyone, now is he?")

"What the fuck *is* all this mumbling?" Williams was sweating now, shaking in his boots. "What? You're trying to talk me down or something? I have my . . . I have my orders."

"To hell with your orders!" Jake told him, without waiting for Trask's say-so. "You want to know what we're talking about? We're talking about vampires. That's what this so-called infection is all about. The ex-passengers and crew of this ship have become vampires—and all of your mates are meat!"

For a moment Williams's brow was lined in a frozen frown—before his lips turned down in a sneer of disbelief. "You fucking . . ." he began to say. But then, as gunshots sounded from the port stairwell, his eyes went wide again and he leaned from the door to look in that direction. With the barrel of the marine's rifle momentarily deflected, Jake saw his opportunity.

Making a grab for the weapon, he simultaneously lashed out at the man holding it. Jake hit hard, a blow to Williams's face that drove him even farther out of the helicopter. The Old Lidesci had been expecting some such; the razor-sharp blade of his machete hissed where it sliced through the marine's safety harness. Windmilling his arms, Williams uttered an outraged cry as he released his rifle, crashed down onto the boarding ramp, and bounced off onto the deck.

Crowding the doorway, Trask and his people looked down on the fallen marine. For a moment he lay there in the shadows—the shadow of the Sea King, itself in the shadow of the jagged central fang of the little island—with his face contorted in rage. Then he made to get to his feet.

But among those gradually lengthening shadows were several much darker ones that were moving a lot faster, and pale, eager hands were already reaching for Williams from under the bulk of the helicopter!

He didn't see what grabbed him, but he certainly felt those powerful hands closing on his ankles, the terrible *urgency* with which they dragged him out of sight.

Williams screamed high and shrill—just once and briefly—a scream that quickly gurgled down into silence. And all across the *Evening Star*'s decks the shadows came alive!

In that same instant the tableau of frozen faces in the Sea King's doorway shattered into motion, as Trask yelled, *"That* is what we're here for! We want one of those! Ian and David, guard the door and look after the pilot. Liz, Jake, Lardis . . . you're with me . . ."

Three minutes earlier, and one and a half flights down the port stairwell:

WO2 Bently and his number two had been forced to slow down where broken furniture littered the stairs. Now, as they clambered their way up toward a right-angled bend, a deafening burst of gunfire sounded from just around the corner.

Brought up short by the sound of the shooting, the spanging of ricochets, and the terrified cries of men-at-arms around the bend, Bently's thermal imaging showed him a tall man staggering into view, his head a crimson blob that appeared to be spraying red out the back like the tail of a comet. Both the Warrant Officer and his subordinate were so astonished that they fell back against opposite walls as this figure passed between them, somehow staying erect as it went stumbling down the stairwell.

But the junior rank had to know what this thing was that he was seeing. And in the deep gloom of the confined area he switched off his nite-lites in favour of normal vision.

"*G-God!*" he said then, despite that he still wasn't absolutely certain. But what the thing had looked like before it fell over and went tumbling down the stair like a scarecrow released from its pole . . . was a man in an evening suit with the back of his head blown off!

And that wasn't all the junior ranker saw. For creeping *up* the stairs, following close behind him and his superior, an incredible swarm of silent night-black figures filled the narrow passage wall to wall and as far back as could be seen!

Bently saw them, too—the weird ebb and flow of their low body heat in his nite-lites—and the red blaze of their feral, triangular eyes!

Then, over a renewed outburst of shooting and screams from around the bend—coming right into Bently's ear from the receiver in his headset—he heard his underling's hoarse, terrified whisper, "*Wh-what the hell? What are they, s-sir? Shall I d-dart one?*"

Bently switched his rifle to rapid-fire, and with his mouth half-open breathed, "Dart one? Throw your popgun away, son, and cut the fuckers down!"

Which was perhaps three seconds before the wave from below, and another from above, washed over them . . .

Trask and Jake went down the ramp side by side, turning off at the bottom to fire into the darkness beneath the helicopter. In the gloom under there, a whole nest of triangular eyes—maybe ten pairs—shrank back from them, their owners squealing their terror of the hot death that the two men poured into them. Jake fired full metal jacket, and Trask snub-nosed silver. And vampires or mere mortals, flesh and blood simply couldn't withstand the onslaught. The shadows shrank back, and the deck behind the Sea King turned darker as the vampire flood dispersed in every direction, taking cover in every hiding place.

At the same time Liz and Lardis had come down the ramp more slowly, spraying aerosols until the air was hot with the stench of cordite and garlic. Of Williams there was no trace; wherever the "shadows" had gone, he had gone with them.

Vavara's spawn, most definitely! Korath told Jake. *Her essence is in them . . . and copiously! See how easily they disguise themselves, melting into shadows and darkness?*

"But they're barely thralls," said Jake out loud.

Aye, but a good many are hers, *taken by Vavara or those she took first. And as I said, she wasn't sparing with her essence.*

Trask, who thought Jake had been speaking to him, answered, "Vampires, thralls, lieutenants: I don't give a damn what they are—they're undead and should *be* dead!"

A fresh burst of shooting and muted screaming sounded from the port stairwell. Looking that way, Jake said, "Shouldn't we try to do something about those poor bastards?"

No, said Korath. *It's far too late. There were only four of them, whelmed under by a horde. Even with your superior weapons you wouldn't stand a chance. And moment by moment the darkness deepens. Even here on the deck you are far from safe.*

Jake looked all around, and Korath was right: the "shadows" were creeping again, and feral gleams lit the deeper gloom.

"You heard what the precog said," Trask answered hoarsely, as the chaotic chattering of gunfire ceased and its echoes were replaced by gurgling screams, which in their turn were abruptly smothered. "We can't help anyone. They're gone, Jake."

"Look!" Liz cried.

"Help me!" a young girl's plea rang out, as she came staggering from the direction of the exhaust array in the stern of the ship. "Oh, won't somebody please help me! I've been hiding from them! Hiding from . . . from all the rape and the murder!"

She was maybe eighteen, had a beautiful figure, and in normal circumstances would be lovely. Now her makeup was streaked from her tears, and her cocktail dress was hanging by a single strap, leaving her right breast bare. Her blonde hair was everywhere, stringy and unkempt, falling over her face and shoulders as she came stumbling. Her panties, snagged on the buckle of a shoe, trailed her left ankle.

The sight of her stopped Trask and his people short. "Jesus *Christ!*" Liz heard Trask's gasp. And: "Thank God I don't have a daughter, because she could be it."

For Liz this was a new situation; she'd never seen anything like it before; automatically, she stepped off the helicopter's ramp and moved toward what looked like a second survivor. Jake, on the other hand, had been in precisely this situation before, in Australia, and he wasn't about to be taken in a second time. Side by side with Liz, he advanced on the girl as she came on, arms reaching.

Even so, it was a hard thing to do: to point the rifle at her and pull the trigger. So hard that at first he couldn't do it. What if she really was a survivor?

"You poor thing!" said Liz, moving quickly forward.

"Liz!" Jake cautioned her, but needlessly, for in fact she knew exactly what she was doing. Then, when it seemed that the girl was about to fall into her arms (and as the eerily mobile pools of shadow on the deck crept forward in the rapidly deepening gloom), Liz lifted her hand to arm's length, and instead of gathering the "poor thing" up sprayed oil of garlic directly into her face.

The effect was immediate and dramatic.

Before, the girl had been slumped, staggering, her shoulders drooping, her eyes mainly hidden in tangles of matted hair. Now: it was as if Jake really *had* pulled the trigger! She shot upright straight as a rod, her hair straightening in an effect that was almost electric, flying out from her head and framing it in spiky tufts. Her eyes, previously weepy and disguised by running mascara, opened wide in shock and fear, blazing yellow as boiling sulphur pits. And Liz said:

"Surrounded by thoughts as red and evil as hell, I had to close my. mind to them or lose it altogether. And so I couldn't be sure—until now."

And merely pointing his weapon, scarcely taking aim at all, Jake pulled the trigger. On rapid-fire his weapon stuttered an obscene war cry, ripping the girl's heart to pieces inside her. Her feet left the floor and she flew backwards two full paces. But before her heels touched down and tripped her, Lardis Lidesci was looming up alongside with his machete already raised.

"Poor lass!" he said, as his blade made a gleaming arc.

Liz and Jake—even Jake—turned their faces away. Shooting the girl had been one thing: instinctive, a necessity, even a mercy. But what Lardis must do was calculated butchery.

Then Trask was shouting, "That's it, let's go! We've got to get out of here right now!" And all four E-Branch agents on the ground could see why:

The shadows were no longer creeping but rising up! Up from the stairwells and the lower decks—up over the four-bar railings at both sides of the ship—up into view! The vampires had thrown caution to the wind now; they came on like a flood, with their yellow Halloween eyes lighting the night and illuminating their sallow, hollow-cheeked faces.

Scything among them, Jake's bullets cut a swath as he emptied his magazine. Liz and Trask, too, with Lardis between them, firing silver death as they backed up the ramp to the Sea King, whose vanes were turning faster and faster.

As they got aboard David Chung slammed and secured the door—slammed it on the horde that swarmed after them—while Ian Goodly signalled the pilot it was time to go. But the pilot had seen enough and needed no special urging. He withdrew the ramp, fed power to the engine, began to lift off. The Sea King felt a little sluggish, and Trask switched on the intercom to ask:

"Is everything okay?"

"No," the pilot answered. "Those mad things are clinging to the undercarriage! And the ones on the deck up front are trying to disable the fan!"

Jake, who had run up front, rapped on the pilot's interior window until it was slid open. Looking out through the cockpit windows, he saw what the pilot meant: among the crush of vampires crowding the decks around the swimming pools, several had chair legs and other pieces of broken furniture which they were hurling up at the gleaming blur of the blades. And:

"Drop your nose," Jake told the pilot. "They want your fan, so let's give it to them!"

"But . . . but they're people!" the pilot shouted.

"No," said Jake. "They *were* people. Now they're things and better off dead. So do it, or we're all dead."

And as finally a wooden chair leg hit the fan and flew into a thousand splinters, so the pilot got the message. Then he did as Jake had suggested: floated the big chopper forward, dropped its nose, and went ripping like a horizontal buzz saw along the deck. And Jake had a clear view of the ensuing carnage.

The cockpit's windows turned red, yellow, and black as blood and guts sprayed back from the whirling blades, and the screams of the vampires could be heard even over the thunder of the big helicopter's engine. Then she was rising, but still sluggishly, lopsidedly, as the *Evening Star* was left below and behind.

"Now what?" Trask's anxious voice on the intercom.

"God knows how," the pilot answered, "but I think we've got a bunch of those things still hanging on underneath!"

"Yes," Trask told him. "They're good at that. But there's

a cure for it. Take her up a couple of hundred feet into the sunlight."

And up they went until the sun was once more visible low on the western horizon, and its cleansing beams reached out to the dragonfly plane. Golden fire blazed in through the windows, but more importantly on the creatures that were clinging impossibly to the undercarriage and other projections.

Liz was "listening" to them. With them, she felt the seething of the sun, and heard their cries, then their sighs, as one by one—perhaps thankfully—they let go and went fluttering down the sky. Striking the sea from that height would be similar to crashing down on concrete. None would live through it.

But in any case, she didn't stay with them that long . . .

In the Sea King's belly, Lardis Lidesci wrapped the girl's head in a jacket from one of the NBC packs, while Trask spoke to the pilot and asked to be patched through to *Invincible*.

On a spare headset, Captain McKenzie sounded much subdued. "I saw something of what went on belowdecks," he said. "And it seems I owe you an apology. As for those poor lads, my marines, God only knows what I owe them." (Trask sensed the sad shake of his head.) "But Trask—I've got to know—what was so secret that I couldn't be told?"

"I tried to tell you," Trask answered. "And in fact we did tell your marines. But . . . they had their orders."

"As I had mine," said McKenzie. "So why couldn't the Admiralty tell me? I mean, a plague's a plague—but that had to be something else again."

"It was," said Trask, "and it is. But listen, you won't be blamed. Heads higher up might roll, but not yours. And while it won't be much consolation, we did get their bloody specimen."

"It cost the lives of my boys," said the Captain, quietly.

"And probably saved a million more," Trask told him.

"Really?"

"This thing could have wiped us all out," Trask said. "And I do mean everyone. Until that ship is on the bottom, it still can."

"Just tell your pilot to keep that chopper out of the way," said McKenzie, "and I'll have my Gunnery Commander take care of that right now."

"Good," said Trask. "And then you can have a party ready in NBC suits to wash the chopper down when we land, and we'll also need access to your decontamination chambers, all six of us and your pilot, too. And . . . and a large, airtight plastic bag, for the specimen."

"Roger all that," said McKenzie.

Following which Trask and his people crowded the Sea King's windows . . .

It took but a minute.

The cruise missiles came in low, like purring, short-finned flying fish over the wine-coloured sea. Swift and deadly in the gloom of twilight, of a dull, metallic grey, they carried death in their bellies but nothing so terrible as their target.

In the final seconds before they struck home, just six feet above the Plimsoll line on the *Evening Star*'s hull, Trask remembered what Ian Goodly had said about "The ship-to-ship missiles going in, the explosions, the stem going up in the air, and the rapid slide backwards off those rocks."

And as usual the precog had been right, for that's exactly how it was. The massive, thunderclap explosions that ripped the *Star*'s hull open, cracked her back, and lifted her stem into the air; twin fireballs going up amid a shower of twisted wreckage; the fires raging within the vessel and all along her decks; and finally the shuddering, slipping, and sliding, as all those tons of metal, that once proud ship, keeled over backwards and began her last short journey to the seabed.

Then there were only the fireballs, rising still, and a few scraps of burning debris drifting over the island, and fires in the sea itself, where fuel had spilled and ignited. And perhaps among those fires a degree of splashing, but that wouldn't last for too long . . .

8
First Warning

AFTER SOME WRANGLING WITH THE GREEK authorities, the Minister Responsible had sent a private jet out to the military airport in Kavála on the Greek mainland. It was sitting on the runway, its engines ticking over, when one of *Invincible*'s helicopters dropped Trask and his agents off a little after midnight. Along with the plane was a British Embassy official and two "specialists" from Porton Down. The former was there to lend substance to E-Branch's claim to diplomatic immunity if necessary, obviating any last-minute difficulties which might have arisen with the airport staff, namely the Greek military. The Porton Down people were there to take charge of the "specimen."

Mr. Teale was a small, bald, middle-aged, bespectacled microbiologist of an apparently nervous disposition, and Mr. Kline was his young pimply-faced assistant. Aboard the jet, when the Old Lidesci presented them with a girl's head in a plastic bag inside a steel pot with a clamp-down lid from HMS *Invincible*'s galley, Teale came very close to having a heart attack. He had been bursting with questions since first meeting Trask and his people on the runway, none of which had been answered. But now:

"What in God's name . . . !" he protested. "I was assured that you people would obtain a living specimen!"

"A person, you mean?" Trask answered him coldly. Obviously Porton Down hadn't been told everything, or at any rate the people they had sent hadn't been told everything. Teale and his assistent still seemed to believe they were dealing with a mutant strain of the Chinese plague.

"An infected person, yes," said Teale, "in a harmless, se-dated, or comatose condition. We have with us certain respiratory items and a full-body protective 'suit,' in essence a body bag, in which we intended to convey this . . . this *absent* specimen."

Trask wasn't in the mood for this, and answered, "Well, you see, she wouldn't come under those or any other conditions. And since she had the will and the power to infect every single one of my team, everyone on HMS *Invincible*, and eventually everyone on this planet, we decided her head would have to suffice." And before Teale could reply, "Listen," Trask went on, as patiently as possible. "Myself and all of my people, we're sort of tired. I'm sure you know how it is: the last day or so hasn't been too easy on us. Now, we were told to bring back infected blood, infected flesh, and a little brain tissue, preferably alive. Well, here we have infected blood and likewise infected flesh. As for brain tissue: we've brought you an entire head."

"But alive?" Teale scowled where he sat towards the rear of the jet with Kline, and took up the plastic bag, all bloody and smeared within, from inside the steel container. "The specimen was supposed to be alive—preferably *alive*—Mr. Trask!"

Now Trask might have lost it, but before he could explode:

"Alive?" the Old Lidesci grunted, taking the bag from Teale and dangling it in front of his face. "So, you think it's dead, do you? But if I were to take this machete of mine and cut this bag open—and if you should perhaps get a little of this blood in your eyes, mouth, nose, or any other of your body's openings—then, in three days' time, you'd probably change your opinion. Anyway, it's all yours now. But do take care of it, won't you?" And dropping the bag back into the container, he ambled back to his seat up front with the rest of the team. And:

"If I were you," said Trask, "I would make sure that lid is clamped down just as tightly as it will go. And I would keep it that way all the way back to Porton Down. For as my friend just told you, it's all yours now. And believe me we're very glad to be rid of it."

Then, without another word, he trailed the Old Lidesci back to his seat near the front of the executive jet, where the rest of the E-Branch team were already falling asleep. And from then on, there was no more conversation with the people from Porton Down . . .

At Gatwick Airport, Teale and Kline—and the specimen— were whisked away in double-quick time in a police helicopter, while Trask was met and collected by the Minister Responsible himself in another chopper courtesy of the Ministry of Defence. At 2:45 A.M. on a wet, early November morning this was a rare privilege indeed, and when they were under way Trask asked:

"To what do I owe the honour?"

The Minister Responsible looked surprised. "What, no shouting match?" he said. "No cursing, or demanding to know what the hell I think I'm doing? No questions about what's been going on over here while you've been swanning around in the Med?"

"Swanning?" said Trask, beginning to bridle.

"It's a joke!" the Minister told him. "Though how I managed it at this time in the morning and under these circumstances is a mystery even to me!" And suddenly Trask noticed how drawn the Minister seemed, how pale and hollow-eyed.

"So, I'm not the only one who's been having a rough time of it," he said. "Anyway, I'm too tired for shouting matches, cursing, and all that. And as for the latter, I don't much go along with it. Unless it's used under considerable stress it's a sure sign that a man's vocabulary is on the blink."

"Really?" said the Minister. "Well, right now I don't think I've ever heard so much silly fucking shit in my entire life!"

Which was more than enough to give Trask pause. And looking at the Minister more closely now, he said, "In your case it has to be considerable stress. So, would you care to tell me what's up?"

And as the Minister sat there turning it over in his mind— getting his thoughts in order—Trask continued to look him up and down, studying him more closely yet. For already his talent was twitching away, telling him he was about to become privy to certain truths that he could well do without.

The Minister Responsible . . . a man who usually kept himself to the shadows, who, over the course of Trask's thirty years in the mindspy business he'd only met face-to-face on half-a-dozen occasions, and always in emergency situations. Even in the Corridors of Power—where obscurity frequently rules—the Minister's duties, his "responsibilities," were obscure. He *might* be "someone in civil defence." He was *probably* "a boffin from the MOD." He "takes care of things that no one else has time for—I think." In low whispers in those selfsame Corridors of Power, that was how he'd frequently heard his presence explained away, for except for the Very Top People in successive governments he was literally a man with no name, no precise portfolio. Even to Trask—and likewise to various heads of departments *almost* as secretive as E-Branch—he was simply the Minister Responsible.

He was in his mid-sixties, small and dapper, his thinning dark hair brushed back and plastered down in a fashion at least forty years out of date. He wore—he had *always* worn—patent-leather black shoes, a dark blue suit and light blue tie, and a waistcoat with an old-fashioned fob watch. His once round, open face was thinner now and deeply lined, and his forehead creased with the worries of far too many years. His bright blue, penetrating eyes—which was how Trask would always remember them—were a little rheumy; his lips were turned down at the corners, and his shoulders were weighted, slumped and weary. His general aspect was harried.

"But you must have wondered what the hell was going on back here?" he began. "What with this Porton Down thing, conflicting or very ambiguous orders, and Old Uncle Tom Cobley and all trying to get into the act? You must have thought that I'd let you down?"

"I considered it," Trask admitted. "But then I gave you

the benefit of the doubt. Actually, I was coming around to the same conclusion myself."

"Conclusion?"

"That perhaps we should get in some help with this thing," Trask explained. "That while in the past we've somehow muddled through, perhaps those times *are* past, and what we really need is some new blood—if you'll pardon the expression—coming in on this. Someone or some outfit with new ideas, a new perspective. Instead of trying to kill the disease at source, maybe we'd do better seeking a cure. And if that were the case, then who better than the Porton Down crowd? They have always understood the secrecy thing, the security aspect, and they've had many marvellous successes. So if they could beat AIDS and come up with a jab against the new bubonic, why not this, too?"

"Very understanding of you," said the Minister Responsible. "But I think I should tell you that I've always been more than satisfied with your work, Ben. It may not have seemed that way at the time, but—"

"—But, we did get results," said Trask, taken aback by the 'Ben' thing. (It had to be something big, for the Minister Responsible to be calling him Ben.)

"Indeed you did," said the other. "And personally I would be perfectly happy to let you go on getting results, but . . . something's come up, and it's something that could take this entire thing right out of my hands and make me just another player. In fact I've got a meeting with—well, all sorts of people: heads of the National Health Service, Security, Civil Defence; chiefs of the Army, Navy, Air Force; the police, you name it—in just half an hour. So since we're only fifteen minutes from E-Branch HQ, where I'll be dropping you off, I'd better get on with it."

"I'm all ears," said Trask, and shivered. Because right out of nowhere he had gooseflesh. He (or his talent) knew that this was going to be very bad.

"You'll still be our main man, of course," the Minister continued. "The man who knows it all—who has done it all—the man with all the field experience. You and all your people. But from now on there'll be a great many more people involved. Yes, we'll keep as tight a lid on it as we can, but sooner or later, and probably sooner, the public will want answers. Oh, we'll do as we have always done: lie to them. But unless we get to grips with it, our lies will eventually catch up with us. That is, of course, if it's what we think it is."

Trask was beginning to feel frustrated now. "Fine," he said trying not to snap, "but as yet I've no idea what you'll be lying about! Okay, I can tell you're not really stalling . . . so what *are* you doing? Why don't you get to the point?"

"I was giving you the background," said the Minister, "letting you see that we haven't been sitting on our backsides doing nothing since this thing broke, since the first couple of cases were reported . . ."

"Cases": that was the catchword. And Trask repeated it:

"Cases? Something has happened while we've been gone? What, in the last twenty-four hours? Cases of what?"

"Even before you'd gone," the Minister answered. "There was a handful three days ago, another half dozen leading up to your leaving, and ten that we know of while you've been away. But at first it didn't connect . . . I mean I didn't tie it in with your work, with what you'd told me about that thing under London . . ."

At which the truth hit Trask like a hammer blow! For "that thing under London" could only refer to Szwart, the destruction of his lethal fungus garden in an unknown, abyssal Roman temple deep under the city. But before he could voice his suspicions:

"We've given it a name, of course," said the Minister. "The symptoms suggested it. We've also ascribed a cause; we borrowed it from the American experience in New York in the fall of ninety-nine, right on the turn of the millennium."

Grey-faced, Trask nodded. "I think I remember that. The hot summer and rains brought up a swarm of so-called killer mosquitoes out of the sewers and underground systems. They carried a bug that invaded the brain, and several New

Yorkers died of it. And we've had the same problem this past summer with mosquitoes here in London."

"Yes," said the Minister. "So we've blamed them. And we've called it a kind of sleeping sickness, *encephalitis lethargica*. But that's a lie, too, or we think it is, though we'd rather it was the truth. For the fact is we can't be sure *what* it is. But you and I, we can take a pretty good stab at it, right?"

Trask's thoughts were flying. He thought of Millie Cleary, and of Jake—Jake's debriefing after he'd rescued Millie from Szwart's subterranean lair—and felt his blood cooling in his veins as he recalled the final part of Jake's story:

"I was barely in time," (Jake had said.) "Szwart had opened a flue to the surface—some kind of natural conduit for a wind blowing up from hell—and that nightmarish mushroom garden was about to spawn. One by one, the black-capped domes of the mushrooms were flattening out, their gills opening, and their first red-coloured spores beginning to drift free. By the time Szwart showed up a stream of red spores was floating in his direction, carried on a draft of that foul, stinking air. But after I tore down that wall and let the methane in—and after I'd lobbed my grenade—well, obviously I couldn't hang around waiting to see what happened next . . ."

Then the Minister was looking at Trask, asking him, "What's on your mind?"

"Jake's report," said Trask faintly, almost to himself.

The Minister nodded. "And remember, I've read that report, too. So when I heard about these cases—would you believe, in the bloody newspapers, midday yesterday?—and when I'd checked their locations, how they were all clustered close to old underground railway stations, then I saw the connection.

"After that, well, I wasn't taking any chances. I couldn't afford to simply wait and see—the responsibility was just too great even for a Minister Responsible. An epidemic is one thing, Ben, and even a plague. But a plague of vampires? So you see, I had no choice but to advise and then to *seek* advice. Since when I've been on the move nonstop. Or to use an old Army expression, my feet haven't touched the ground."

"What are the symptoms?" said Trask, his head full of pictures of Millie stumbling about in a dark cavern, breathing red, vampiric spores. "How does it affect its . . . its victims?" *God, let it be something else!*

"They sleep," the Minister shrugged. "They can't be got out of bed, or barely. They're sluggish, slow-moving, tired. Sleeping sickness, Ben. That's what it's like."

"But for how long? And then what?"

"That remains to be seen. It will either stay, go away, or change into . . . something else. And meanwhile, we have them in isolation wards."

"But who takes care of them?" Trask gripped the Minister's arm. "Are they in close contact with their nurses?"

"They're in isolation wards, Ben!" the other said again. "I mean, I'm no doctor, but I've been given to understand it's all rubber gloves and face masks and . . . and *isolation,* for goodness sake!"

"Lord, I hope so!" Trask muttered, biting his top lip. "But is that it? Nothing else? No other symptoms? Maybe we're simply starting at shadows."

"Shadows?" said the Minister, himself starting, and giving himself a shuddery shake. "Ah, yes—stupid of me! *Huh!* Maybe I could do with a good night's sleep myself!" And his eyes seemed more deeply sunken yet, as he nodded and said, "Yes, there are other symptoms. For one, they don't much care for daylight."

"And?" Trask prompted him.

"And they very quickly go off their food . . ."

Trask licked his lips. His mouth felt bone dry, desiccated. "But their doctors must have examined them?" he said. "What was their prognosis, before you'd voiced your own theory, that is?"

"Flu," said the Minister. "Sleeping sickness, malaise, malingering."

"And then, after you'd spoken up? I mean, what did you tell them to look for?"

"What did I tell them to—?" Snorting, the Minister slumped back into his seat. When his wry chuckle came it was barely audible and more than a little hysterical. "Ben, now tell me: just how *big* is one of these bloody spores? Does it invade the lungs or some other organ? When it's in the host body, does it infect the blood first, then the brain, or both simultaneously? How do we detect a metamorphic organism that can fuse with human flesh and blood? How long does this metamorphosis or mutation take? We don't have any answers, Ben—and you want to know what I told them to look for?"

"So what are they working with?" Trask was licking his lips again. "*How* are they working? Trial and error? God, I hope not! This is just too fucking dangerous for common or garden laboratory experiments."

"Common or garden?" said the Minister. "Not at Porton Down, Ben. They're the best in the world."

"But this shit isn't from our *fucking* world!" Trask said.

The Minister sat up straight again and said, "I suppose I'll have to put that last down to considerable stress, right?"

Trask ignored that and said, "I'll ask you again: what have the scientists at Porton Down got to work with—I mean, apart from what we've just sent them?"

"They have a whole specimen," the Minister answered. "But a dead one, of course. An old tramp who spent his last few months wandering in and out of King's Cross with a brown paper bag and a bottle of methylated spirits."

"*Huh!*" said Trask. "They asked me for a live one."

"To make comparisons, I suppose," said the Minister.

"But a dead one?" Trask was suddenly worried; or rather, he was more worried than before. "How did he die?"

"He was found asleep on the station. They couldn't wake him up, took him into hospital. He died a few hours later."

"When was this?" Trask said, anxiously now.

"He was one of the first," said the Minister. "Knowing his lifestyle, there was no need for an autopsy. They'd begun looking for someone to claim him when I dropped my bombshell. After that, Porton Down asked for him."

"So by now he's been dead for . . . for what? Something like three days, maybe?" But Trask had placed heavy emphasis on the word "dead."

"Something like that, yes."

"Then you had better have another word with the Porton Down people," said Trask grimly. "If they haven't already started to slice him up, they should watch his body very carefully! On the other hand if they *have* cut into him . . . then maybe they should start watching each other . . ."

"Don't go over the top with this thing, Ben," said the Minister. "I know how bad it's looking, but we've called our best in on it. And as I said, it's all rubber gloves and face masks and what have you."

"Which won't help one little bit," said Trask, "if this old gentleman of the road wakes up and starts biting people!"

"Point taken," said the Minister. "And I *will* speak to Porton Down—from your place, before I go on to my meeting."

Trask's mind was racing ahead now. "Okay," he said, "so I'm in the picture. Now, what do you expect of me and mine?"

"Well," said the Minister, "I've had more time to think it over than you, and I do have a couple of ideas."

"Such as?"

"Our Gypsy friend from the vampire world," said the Minister. "I've been given to understand he can somehow smell these creatures out, right?"

"Lardis Lidesci isn't just 'our Gypsy friend,' " said Trask. "In his own world he was a chief, who in his time was very much feared by the Wamphyri. As for smelling them out: no one can be that certain, but there are tests which can be applied, yes. On the other hand, I don't suppose they go much on witchcraft down at Porton Down. Except it isn't witchcraft but alien chemistry. So if it's a surefire litmus test they're needing, tell them to try silver and garlic."

"Yes," the Minister nodded, and at once slapped his knee in anger. "Damn it all, why didn't I think of that! It's just that it all seems so way out, so over the top. I've been your Minister Responsible all these years, and still it's as if your work has been some kind of fantasy. I just haven't got the imagination for it. But yes, I'll tell them that, too. And then we have your locators."

"Mindsmog?" said Trask. "That may be more difficult, uncertain. If these people have been infected with vampirism, it may take its time showing. Maybe a group of them in close proximity would register on David Chung's mental screen, I can't say. But we must certainly give it a try. And then what? Supposing we do find a vampire plague brewing in these poor people? Well, I can tell you what the Old Lidesci's answer would be to that!"

"Yes, I know," said the Minister, quietly. "It might yet be our answer, too, if the microbiologists don't come up with something in very short order." He paused a moment, then went on:

"Anyway, as for you and yours: that's all that will be required of you at this time. But as soon as you've rested up—or even before that—I want you back out in the field doing what you and your people do best. Here at home, we'll deal with whatever's coming, but your job is the same as always: to deal with the ones who have brought it upon us. You are our avengers, and despite all the menaces, in a way I envy you."

Trask looked out of the window. They were descending toward the lights of central London. Like a vast bright spiderweb, the city's wetly gleaming electric network spread out in all directions, rotating with the helicopter's motion and seeming to rise to meet them.

Behind those swimming lights dwelled all that was known and human. While in the darkness between them lurked something utterly inhuman, a different kind of spider in the man-made web of the city and indeed the world.

"There are many millions of people down there," said Trask, quietly. "How is it such a small handful of us has become responsible for so many?"

"Not easy, is it?" said the Minister. "And now you know how I have felt, and for more than thirty years . . ."

Millie Cleary and Paul Garvey, both telepaths, were at the helipad on the roof to meet Trask and the Minister Responsible. The chopper's downdraft turned the rain aside, blowing it horizontally at Millie. It grabbed at her umbrella and turned it inside out, then flattened her blouse to her upper body and her skirt to her legs, highlighting her trim shape in the strobing beams of the landing beacons. She didn't seem to mind getting wet.

Trask and the Minister vacated the chopper, and ducking low ran for the roof shelter with its stairwell leading down to the top-floor complex which was E-Branch HQ. Trask caught up Millie along the way, and Paul Garvey took the Minister's elbow, guiding him in out of the rain. Behind them, the helicopter's pilot remained on board, slowing his machine's big fan to a tick-over *whup—whup—whup* while waiting on the Minister's orders.

On their way down the stairs Millie dug her heels in, dragging Trask to a halt in order to hug and kiss him. "Slow down," she said then. "Look, the Minister has put us in the picture as much as he was able and we're doing what we can; not that there was much we could do with you and the others away. And now that you're back there's nothing much *you* can do, either, not tonight, and not by way of work. So will you please, *please* stop forging ahead, at least until I've told you that . . . that it feels very good to have you back?"

Trask knew that last to be an understatement; the way Millie was pressed to him told him that much, without his talent so much as whispering it.

Millie. Upon a time she'd been like a kid sister to him; he had always had time for Millie. She'd been here even before Zek, but always in her kid sister role. And *because* of Zek—and the job, of course—she'd never let Trask know how she felt about him. Not until recently.

Millie was in her mid to late forties but looked five years

younger. A very attractive blonde, her hair was cut in a fringe low over her forehead, flowed onto her shoulders and framed her oval face while partly concealing her small, delicate ears. Her eyes were blue under pencil-slim, golden eyebrows, and her nose was small and straight. Millie's teeth were very white, if just a little uneven in a slightly crooked, frequently pensive mouth. Five feet six inches tall, amply curved and slim-waisted, she'd always made Trask feel big and strong, and sometimes clumsy. He had always liked her a lot—indeed, a great deal—and now knew that he loved her . . . which made him feel a little guilty.

His wife Zek had passed almost three years ago, but she had been such a huge part of his life—indeed, Trask had sometimes believed she *was* his life—that it still didn't feel like she was gone; it felt like she was still there, and maybe watching. And the last thing Trask wanted was that Millie be seen as someone who was filling a gap. It was his loyalty, that was all; it was the "truth" of his love for Zek, an undying love, which had yet made room for another . . .

He held her at bay for a moment, then said, "Come on. We've work to do, you and I. The rest of the team are on their way in by limo from Gatwick. There's not much traffic on the roads, so we've got maybe an hour before they get here. By then I want to be able to delegate tasks. From tomorrow morning at first light we're going to be working overtime as never before."

Behind them as they reached the security door—where Trask blinked rain from his eyes before positioning his face in front of the retinal scanner—they heard the Minister's very audible sigh of relief. He'd obviously been listening to what Trask and Millie had said to each other, and as he and Paul Garvey caught up with them:

"She's right, Mr. Trask," he said. "It's *always* very good to have you and your people back. And despite that things are more complicated now, it's also good to see that your— is 'enthusiasm' the right word?—that your energy is undiminished."

But here in front of "the minions," as it were, Trask noted

that the formalities were on again. Smiling to himself, however wryly, he said, "Thank you, Minister." And then to Paul Garvey, as the steel doors hissed open and they all four passed through into the HQ's main corridor: "See that the Minister gets to use one of our secure telephones, will you, Paul? And then he'll be needing an escort back up to the roof."

Then, as Garvey and the Minister turned right for the Duty Officer's room, and Millie and Trask went the other way, toward his office at the very end of the corridor, the Minister paused and called out, "Oh, and Mr. Trask, there's one other thing that seems to have slipped my mind. You'll find you've a rather important visitor. Normally we'd accommodate and, er—look after him elsewhere, but it seems he's intent on staying with you! So since your HQ is probably as 'safe' as anywhere in the city, he's all yours. I'm sorry about this—that in addition to what I've already handed you, I'm dumping this on your plate, too—but in the current situation . . ." He could only offer an awkward shrug.

Trask had half turned back. *Now who—?* he was about to ask, but Millie "knew" what was on his mind and preempted him. "He's in your office," she said. "And he seems a very nice man. Well, considering some of the tricks he's had to pull to stay so long in power."

And Trask knew the truth of it at once. His "visitor" could only be—"Premier Gustav Turchin himself!" he said, as he and Millie reached the open door to his office and the man in question stepped into view to meet them.

Upon a time Turchin had seemed an unshakable rock of a man. Blockily built, square of face, and short in the neck—with a shock of black hair, bushy black eyebrows, darkly glinting eyes over a blunt nose, and an unemotional mouth—he'd been a veritable bulldog. But that had been some years ago, since when the Russian Premier had faced up to many problems in his vast, ever-turbulent postcommunist homeland. Some of these problems, when they had coincided with E-Branch's, had served to bring the two men together in several mutually beneficial endeavours.

The understanding between them and the respect they had for each other were still very apparent, but as for Turchin himself—his physical appearance—there had been changes. He was much thinner, less bright and sharp of eye, and his hair had turned an iron-grey. The last time Trask had spoken to him in person—in Australia, only a few weeks ago—even Turchin's voice had lost something of its former authority. The intellect was still there (and still lethal, as Trask had soon discovered), but the dynamism was failing. Seven years of political power in a bankrupt country teetering on the brink of anarchy had taken their toll of him. When things went wrong, which they had, and frequently, then he had become a prime target for every disaffected, disillusioned citizen, some of whom were powerful members of the once-mighty military.

The one thing that had stood him in good stead was the fact that he had inherited control of what was left of "The Opposition," Trask's term for E-Branch's Russian equivalent: the leftovers of a once-powerful mindspy organization with headquarters in Moscow. The original Soviet outfit back in the '70s had been Leonid Brezhnev's baby and very effective at first, but successive failures, most of them down to the Necroscope Harry Keogh, had disenfranchised the organization almost to extinction. Turchin, always the visionary, had given its members his patronage when no one else wanted anything to do with them. In their turn they now gave him their support. But even The Opposition hadn't sufficed to save him from his current dilemma.

Trask was privy to what had happened:

Close to retiring, a Russian army general, Mikhail Suvorov, had learned that a parallel world called Sunside/Starside was a huge open-cast gold mine compared to which the Klondike had been a worthless bag of frozen dirt; also that beneath the Perchorsk ravine in the Ural Mountains, a man-made singularity or "Gate," the result of a failed nuclear experiment, would provide access to all of this previously undreamed wealth, and also a possible invasion route into an entirely new and "defenseless" world.

As the C-in-C of two military gulags at Beresov and Ukhta, punishment garrisons straddling the Urals east to west, General Suvorov had been perfectly placed to take charge of Perchorsk's decommissioning when Turchin had ordered the place flooded. But the soldiers he'd sent in to do the job had been other than the team of "military engineers" which he'd made them out to be. In fact they were hardened long-term criminals, and he had offered them the choice of serving their sentences or serving him. Thus after they'd stripped the massive lead shielding from the complex's power plant, and after the legitimate engineers had moved out, Suvorov's crew had stayed on as "caretakers" at Perchorsk.

Having then drained the complex to allow the general and a team of geologists and soldiers passage through the Gate, these men were still there waiting on his return and the rich rewards he'd promised them. But they would have to wait a long time; for in fact Mikhail Suvorov was dead on Starside, where Nephran Malinari of the Wamphyri had sucked him dry of all knowledge of Earth and of the Gates and of life itself.

However, when General Suvorov had entered Starside—despite the fact that Gustav Turchin had let him proceed unadvised of the dangers that might be lurking there, but *suspecting* that such might be the case—he had not been so naïve as to simply step off into a parallel universe without some kind of lifeline or at least a connection to his home-world.

And so he'd told a handful of military cronies that he was onto something big—something *so* big that it could even change the course of history and elevate Russia to her former might as a world superpower—*but,* in the event he was gone for too long, they should start asking questions of the Premier.

Recently, they had been doing just that, and now it seemed Turchin had had enough of it . . .

"Ben," he said, reaching to engage Trask in a none too

firm handshake. And then, a little nervously, "Well, and here I am!"

"And it couldn't be at a worse time," Trask answered, looking around his office. "I see they somehow managed to leave you on your own with all my little secrets?"

Turchin lifted a bushy eyebrow and followed Trask's gaze to a large wall screen, then to the filing cabinets, the computer, the intercom, and other gadgets on his desk. And, "Ah!" he said. "But no, for your Mr. Garvey switched them all off from his Duty Office. Anyway, I was not alone. And in any case, how could you even think it? Is there no honour, not even among mindspies?"

Trask allowed himself to grin. "You're an old fox, Gustav," he said, indicating that the other should take a seat.

"Too old," Turchin answered. "And now I have gone to ground, or rather I've been driven to earth. Oh, and incidentally, when Mr. Garvey turned off your toys, it seems he also turned off the central heating. I've been feeling the cold a long time, Ben—even before I got here—and now I'm tired of it. This charming lady was helping me warm up a little."

"I was doing my bit to entertain the Premier," Millie said, indicating the glass of whiskey and a half-empty bottle of Wild Turkey standing on a corner of Trask's big desk.

"Yes," said Trask. "And warming him up with some of my best booze, at that! But do help yourself." Then he noticed Turchin's overcoat and fur hat hanging from the horns of a coatstand just inside the door; they were still wet.

"And so am I," said Millie, in that new, very disconcerting way of hers. Her telepathy, with which she read his mind: something she'd previously kept under control . . . or at least Trask had always *assumed* she kept it that way. And when he remembered some of the things he had thought about her backside (the delicious way it moved when she walked) and occasionally, when he'd been thinking these things, the way she'd looked at him in that less than innocent way of hers . . .

Now, as she headed for the door, he saw that she was

blushing, but she covered her confusion by saying, "I think perhaps I had better change out of these wet things. Anyway, I suppose you two have plenty to talk over in private."

"Ah, privacy!" said Trask drily. "Yes, I remember that."

"Personally," said Millie, as she stepped from the room, "I think it should all wait till morning. You'll only manage a few hours' sleep, Ben." (That last pointedly.) "And Mr. Turchin looks very tired, too. The Minister's people delivered him to us only a few minutes before you arrived, and I gather his getting here was a bit, er, circuitous?"

After she'd gone Turchin said, "The lady in your life. And unless I miss my guess, a telepath at that. The slightly purple bloom under her eyes gives her away. I think you are very fortunate, my friend."

"Is it that obvious?" said Trask:

"The telepathy?"

"No, the other thing."

"Ah, yes—very!" said the Premier.

"Well, then," said Trask, uncomfortably. "And now let's get to what's not so obvious. What *exactly* is going on, Gustav? And what, if anything, have you brought with you? Only please don't tell me you've brought trouble, because right now I have plenty of my own . . ."

9
Turchin's Trade-Off.
the Sleeping . . . and the Undead?

STILL ON HIS FEET, TRASK SAID, "FIRST LET'S GET things back on line." Shouting down the long, echoing corridor, he called for Paul Garvey to reactivate his office. And closing the door and seating himself face-to-face with Turchin across his huge desk, he said, "There, and now we can be more comfortable."

Then, as grilles in the skirting boards began blowing warm air, and various small lights flickered into life on the office equipment, he took out another glass from a desk drawer, topped up the Russian Premier's drink (while wondering if he still was or would be the Premier), and poured a double for himself. And: "Okay," he finally said, "now I can hear you out."

"I take it I am not being recorded?" Turchin was still very nervous.

"Almost everything is in this place," Trask told him, pressing a key on a small console. "But now we're not, no."

"Good!" said Turchin. "Next—and in the event things don't work out—can you guarantee me safe haven?"

"Political asylum?" Trask raised an eyebrow. "I don't see a problem with that. On the other hand, the 'if things don't work out' bit tells me you don't intend to stay here, not if you can help it. So obviously you have plans. But before we get to that . . . who knows you're here?"

"Your Minister," said the other at once. "And you, and your people. I'm supposed to be attending another Earth Year Conference in Paris. It starts tomorrow, and my talk is scheduled for the day after that—which means that in about thirty-six hours' time people will begin to wonder where I am."

"How did you get away from your, er, minders?" In Australia Trask had experienced some small problems in getting to see the Premier in private, so his defection should have been even more difficult.

"After that little diversion you created in Australia," the other answered, "causing those ex-KGB 'security men' to lose me, I took the opportunity to accuse them of gross incompetence and sacked them. I still command—or should I say commanded—that much power at least. As for my new 'minders,' as you call them: I contrived to choose them from among my own people."

"The Opposition?"

Turchin shrugged. "Let's call them minor talents, shall we? Tomorrow night they will announce my disappearance

142

and in their turn apply for political asylum in France."

"So . . . it will take your opponents back home some time to figure out where you've gone."

"That's part of the plan, yes."

Trask shook his head. "You really are the fox, aren't you? But I won't ask you the details of how you got here; I'll just take Millie's word for it that your route was circuitous."

"And tiring—and very boring!" said Turchin. "But take it from me, if I left any trail at all it won't be an easy one to follow. Oh, they will trace me eventually, but I think it will take several days."

"And then they'll want to know why we're hiding you," said Trask. "Why we're protecting you, and what from. Or far worse, they'll want to know why we've coerced or kidnapped you. So in offering you political asylum, we could be about to initiate a major international incident."

"You are covered," Turchin said at once. "For if our plans fail, then I shall announce my own defection—on television, the BBC, if you like. But on the other hand, if we succeed—"

"—*We?*" said Trask. "And *our* plans?"

"I would not have come to you if there was any way I could do it by myself!" Turchin threw up his hands. "But it seems you have a short memory, Ben. Out in Australia, didn't you give me to understand that if I helped you, you would help me? Well, I tried to help you, and for my trouble got a man killed by that slimy drug-runnning dog Castellano in Sicily! Also, I promised to discover what I could about the current situation in Perchorsk—and I have done so. In short, I've attended to my part of our agreement in full. Indeed, when you see what I have done you'll agree I have more than fulfilled my commitment. All very well, but now I need *your* help. You should remember, Ben Trask, that I could have done as Suvorov did. And knowing the dangers, I would have stood far more chance of success. Instead I chose to go along with you and Nathan, and protect Sunside/Starside! You should remember these things."

"Calm down," Trask told him. "I haven't forgotten. I'm

just calculating the odds before I place my bet, that's all. And the odds are good. Let's face it, with all the border disputes, the anarchy, the infighting between various Moscow mob 'families,' which amounts almost to war on the streets, and the rest of the problems you have in Russia right now, merely political shenanigans can't mean all that much. Why, your enemies may not even notice you've gone missing!" And then, realizing how that must have sounded: "I simply mean that—"

"I know what you mean," Turchin cut in. "That I'm not even a figurehead anymore, merely a puppet. And there are plenty of other toy Premiers-in-waiting just looking for the opportunity to jump onto the strings. Yes, and you are right. So if I can't be important in Russia—if I can't help guide my homeland into true and lasting democracy—then let me be of assistance here. Believe me, Ben, if you want to close the Perchorsk Gate—and close it forever, so that it can't be reopened—you need me. And if we can do it my way, according to my plan, then I'll be able to go home in triumph with all the political, er, 'shenanigans' behind me."

"I do want to close the Perchorsk Gate," said Trask. "Yes, I desperately want to close it, and for good. Even though it's like closing the stable door after the horse has bolted . . ."

"The horse?" said Turchin. "Bolted? Explain."

"Okay," said Trask, "now listen. You already know what I've been doing; you know *my* problem. You know about all three problems, because I told you about them in Australia. But you don't know what's gone on since then, and how bad things have got. So what if I were to tell you that all of the troubles you've left back home don't hold a candle to the real threat? And then suppose I told you that it's no longer a mere threat but a reality, and that it's happening right here and now?"

Turchin gulped at his drink, stared hard at Trask and said, "It is? Here and now? A plague of vampires, capable of creating monsters such as those that once invaded Perchorsk?"

"Eventually they could, definitely," said Trask. "And it's more than likely they will—*once they've created sufficient of their own kind!*"

Now Turchin gasped, and said, "But what are you saying? Are you telling me they've come out in the open? Are you saying . . . they're recruiting?"

"Oh, they've been recruiting ever since they first got here," Trask answered. "But always covertly, in secret, in hiding. A gradual, stealthy, very insidious infiltration. But that was then and this is now. Now . . . it's as if they don't care who knows about them! And in a way it's my fault, or E-Branch's."

"Your fault?" Turchin frowned.

And Trask nodded. "You see, we've been too successful."

"I don't follow you." Turchin was plainly lost. "How could you be too successful?"

"By destroying everything they've been working for," Trask told him. "By taking everything away from them, until now they have nothing left to lose."

"And you have done that?"

Then, briefly, Trask explained about Malinari's, Vavara's, and Szwart's fungus gardens—how they'd been destroyed, first in Australia, then on the Greek island of Krassos, and finally in a forgotten subterranean vault under London. "Except we may have discovered the London garden just a little too late," he finished off.

And yet again: "Explain," said Turchin, attentive as never before.

And Trask told him about the strange new malady in London, perhaps in the world, and also what he feared it might be.

Then, after a moment's dumbfounded silence, "But . . . is it under control? I mean, can you contain it?" Turchin's face was very pale now.

"What are you thinking?" Trask said. "That perhaps you've jumped out of the frying pan into the fire?"

"No!" Turchin shook his head, and continued, "Give me some credit, Ben. My thoughts don't always revolve about myself. But frying pans and fires? *Huh!* Actually, I was thinking about this entire world going up in flames!"

"My thoughts precisely," Trask nodded. "Which might explain my coldness, and why I've been less than the perfect host."

"Indeed," said the other, quietly.

"As for containing it," Trask went on, "that's not going to be my problem. It's already in hand—or so I'm informed by my higher authority—and I'm to continue tracking down our three invaders. So even if your defection works out to be a temporary one, still it's come at a bad time. I could have used your help, Gustav. With your agents as colleagues or even 'comrades'—no longer The Opposition—they could have come in very useful."

"You can still count on my help," said Turchin. "My people have been working on it ever since we, er, joined forces in Australia. As I said: I've kept my word. My espers are not without their resources—which I set up for them a long time ago—and they *will* be able to pass on information. Well, as long as I am here to receive it in person, that is."

"Then what more can I say?" said Trask. "Except that you're very welcome."

"Good!" said Turchin. "And now, if you've finished bringing me up to date, I think it's time I explained my plan."

"Okay," said Trask. "Let's hear it. Best to have all of our cards on the table."

Turchin nodded and steepled his hands in front of his chin. A moment's thought, and then he began:

"I'm sure you'll remember the trouble we had with Chechnya twelve years ago, when poor old Boris Yeltsin was in power?"

"Of course I do," said Trask. "The Western world gave Russia a hard time because of its heavy-handedness."

"Yes, but as I recall Russia was no more heavy-handed than NATO in Kosovo," Turchin replied. Then, waving a hand dismissively, "Anyway, please let's not argue about it. The point is, the Chechens have never forgiven us. And less than a fortnight ago there was a Chechen raid on one of our missile sites . . . oh, yes, we've retained a few. One of my agents—I suppose you'd call him the Russian equivalent of your Mr. Chung—is nuclear-sensitive on a worldwide scale, and when he became aware of a weapon or lethal amount of weapons-grade uranium on an unscheduled move across the Russian countryside—specifically toward Moscow—that was when I had my people step in. To cut a long story short, I prevented a raggle-taggle Chechen suicide squad from trying to destroy Moscow!

"Heads might have rolled in the military, but I kept quiet about it for two reasons. One: panic among the civilian population, and two: I had my own idea how this bomb might be used. Er, need I say more on that point?"

"I don't think so," said Trask. "Even a small nuclear explosion inside the Perchorsk complex would be enough to bring down a million tons of rock. And if that won't block the Gate, then nothing will."

"Correct," said Turchin. "And so I gave back the missile's casing and engine but secreted the actual warhead away until I could devise a means of smuggling it into Perchorsk. Naturally, the Major in charge of the site—more properly a dump—was delighted to accept my suggestion that the purloined missile had never been equipped with a warhead in the first place; it was either that, or—"

"—His would be one of the heads doing the rolling," said Trask.

"Indeed. And between us we kept the whole business hushed up."

"Where is this warhead now?" Trask enquired. "And for that matter, *if* we could get it into Perchorsk, how would we arm it? Obviously it was designed for an aerial delivery system."

"As to where it is: don't ask," said the other. "Even with your talent you probably still wouldn't believe me. And I have already seen to its conversion. Even now—or especially now—there are plenty of out-of-work scientists in Russia who will do almost anything to avoid starvation. As for getting the bomb into the Perchorsk complex . . ." The Premier looked at Trask in a certain way, his eyes narrowed, his manner conspiratorial. "But nothing is impossible, eh, Ben? Where there's a will there's a way, eh? A will or a skill, whatever?"

"Meaning?" said Trask, knowing perfectly well what Turchin meant—that even a job like that wouldn't pose much of a problem for a man who could access the most inaccessible places at will, someone such as a Necroscope, for instance—but unwilling to reveal anything unnecessarily this early in the game.

"Meaning—" Turchin frowned and glanced away for a moment, then narrowed his eyes more yet and said, "meaning exactly what I said. That if one wants it badly enough, one can usually find the means to an end. To any end. But for now, let it suffice to say that I don't think it will be a problem—or rather that I *hope* it won't be a problem—and leave it at that."

"As you wish," said Trask, keeping a poker face and hiding his pleasure at the fact that Turchin looked more than a little perplexed and wrong-footed now. "And anyway, we need to get on. So is that it? Your plan? To get this bomb of yours into Perchorsk and detonate it there? I can see how that would solve one of my—one of *our*—major problems, but I still don't see how it will get you reinstated and strengthen your power base back home."

"Leave that to me," said Turchin. "As long as it's done on my mark, believe me, all of my personal problems *will* be solved. My position will be unshakable, and détente will reach heights never before realized. Which will be of benefit to both of us personally, and most certainly to our countries, our world."

Trask nodded, and said, "That's assuming our countries and our world are still ours."

"I understand," said the other. "But at least no more vampires will be coming through the Perchorsk Gate."

"Nor the Gate in Romania," said Trask, "which was blocked when Malinari and the others came through."

"And that will leave our hands free to deal with the invaders who are already here," said Turchin. "With them and with whatever they've spawned here. We'll make that our priority."

"It's already been my priority for some three years now," Trask answered. "And will continue to be until I—" (he came close to saying, "until I've had my revenge," but caught himself and said,) "—until I'm finished with them."

"Then I think we are all done here," said Turchin. "Except I have brought you a small gift." He took out and opened up an old-fashioned silver cigarette case with a spring clip holding in place twenty cardboard-tube-tipped Russian cigarettes, then held it out over the desk toward Trask.

"I don't smoke," said Trask.

"Nor do I," said Turchin. "Well, not these filthy things." With which he spilled the cigarettes into a wastebasket. "Not now that I can get some of your excellent British and American varieties." And then he pulled on the clip to remove the wafer-thin, scrolled silver plate in the tray of the box. And there, coiled in that secret place like so many pubic hairs, lay roll upon roll of microfilm. And carefully replacing the plate, he snapped the case shut and passed it across the desk to Trask.

Trask raised a querying eyebrow. And:

"The Perchorsk schematics," said Turchin. "That place is a vast underground complex, a veritable maze. I'm sure that when the time comes to go in, you wouldn't want to lose anyone down there. Especially not with an atom bomb ticking off its countdown, eh?"

Standing up, Trask put the case in his pocket. "My people will be arriving shortly," he said. "I'll need to talk to them before letting them get a few hours' sleep. Or maybe Millie was right and I should leave it till morning. They've had a fairly stressful time and need a break . . . and so do I. And after all, there's very little we can do tonight."

Pressing an intercom button on his console, he said, "Paul, I take it you've arranged accommodation for our guest?"

"I'll meet you in the corridor," Garvey's voice came back.

As they left his office, Trask took Turchin's arm and said, "Just one other thing. You said we'd have to wait to deploy the bomb 'on your mark.' Can you say why, and when that will be?"

"Shortly," said the Russian Premier, ex-Premier, or Premier-in-Waiting, whichever. "Believe me, I, too, am eager to see this thing finished. But ask yourself this: what use to spring a rat trap if the rats are not inside it?"

Again Trask raised an eyebrow, but Turchin put a finger to his lips and said, "Ask no more questions, my friend. My plans are laid, and it would do you no good to know any more. In the Kremlin we have a saying, 'Ignorance is innocence, while knowledge is culpability.'"

"We have the same saying," Trask replied, "but it comes out a lot less obliquely than yours and from a very different viewpoint. 'What you don't know can't hurt you.'"

"Precisely," said Turchin, and for a brief moment his dark, intelligent eyes glinted as brightly as ever they had in former and perhaps better times. A brightness cold as the cutting edge of a razor, that boded ill for somebody or bodies . . .

Along with Paul Garvey, Trask saw Turchin to his room— nothing less than a hotel room, because E-Branch HQ occupied the entire top floor of what had once been an hotel— and saw him settled in. "In the morning," he said, "we'll make sure you've got some of your favourite booze and whatever else you need to make your stay comfortable."

"You are very understanding," said Turchin.

"One last thing," said Trask. "Go where you like in the HQ, except where you shouldn't go. It's not that I don't trust you, but the place is full of alarms."

"I shall go nowhere that I am not invited," said the other.

As Trask and Garvey returned along the corridor towards the Duty Officer's room, Garvey asked, "Do you really trust him?"

"You're the telepath," Trask answered, "what did you sense? Me, I couldn't detect a single untruth in anything he

150

said. The man's as happy as can be to be avoiding all that deep political shit back home."

"Actually, he was thinking how much he owes you," said Garvey. "But he was also wondering how much he can trust you!"

"In his shoes," said Trask, "I'd be doing the same thing."

The elevator monitor showed an ascending cage; the rest of the team members had arrived. But suddenly Trask felt too tired for briefs, debriefs, or almost anything else. In the wee small hours of the morning, what good would it do anyway?

"I'll want an 'O' Group at eight A.M.," he quickly said, as Garvey made to enter the Duty Office. "Make sure they all know, will you?" And then, on second thought: "Better make that nine. What's an extra hour, anyway?"

"You've got it," said Garvey.

And before the elevator could stop and its doors hiss open, Trask put on a little speed and made it to his own room. Inside, he was about to switch the light on when Millie said, "We don't need it. Why don't you take a shower, freshen up, and then come to bed while I'm still awake? But better hurry, because I can't promise I'll stay awake too long!" She was already in his bed.

He showered, then called Paul Garvey and said, "If anything happens before morning . . . let it!"

"You've got it," said Garvey again.

Indeed I have, thought Trask, getting into bed and Millie's loving arms.

She *was* still very much awake. And oddly enough, Trask discovered he wasn't all that tired, either. Not yet . . .

"Don't you ever sleep?" Trask asked the Minister Responsible at 8:30.

"This morning, for about an hour," said the other, gruffly. "What are *you* complaining about? I've allowed you as much time as I could."

"Oh? In preparation for what?"

"I'll need you and your people ASAP."

"Specifically?"

"A telepath, and a locator. And, trying to think ahead—"

"The precog?" Trask was awake now, and making a poor job of getting dressed while cradling the phone between his cheek and his shoulder.

"Well, it wouldn't hurt to know what we're in for."

"Wouldn't hurt me, either!" said Trask. "So what's happening?" (He believed he already knew, while hoping he didn't.)

"Some of our sleepers are starting to wake up," the Minister answered. "They look more or less normal, a bit pale—and they still don't much like daylight—but other than that . . ."

"Garlic?" said Trask, as Millie came out of the shower and stood looking at and "listening" to him.

"And silver," said the Minister. "We've tried both, with no positive reaction as yet."

Trask breathed a sigh of relief. "So what you're asking for is—what? Confirmation that these are just people and we were barking up the wrong malady? Or do you think we should start looking for mindsmog? Yes, I can see that. It would explain why you want a locator."

"And now that our specimens are waking up, it might also be a good thing to know what they're thinking," said the Minister. "And to know if they're answering our questions truthfully."

Trask nodded. "Which involves me and my telepaths," he said. "Okay, but I have an 'O' Group in twenty minutes."

"Fine," said the Minister, "but I'd advise you to make it a quick one. There'll be a chopper on your roof in an hour's time with seats for five. I'd suggest your Mr. Goodly, Mr. Chung, yourself, and a telepath of your choice."

"Me!" Millie's sweet mouth silently framed the single word, while she continued towelling her hair.

"Where will we be going?" said Trask.

"Bleakstone, in Surrey."

"What, a prison for madmen? Psychotic murderers, arsonists, rapists, and lots of other very irresponsible citizens? Is that where you've put the sleepers?"

"Where better?" said the Minister. "I told you they were in isolation. They have a wing to themselves, where they're in the care of a very specialized staff."

"See you on the roof," said Trask, and put the phone down.

"Me!" said Millie again, out loud now and determinedly.

And Trask couldn't see any reason to deny her. It wasn't as if there'd be any real danger, not this time. Except: "There'll be some pretty sick thoughts floating around in that place," he warned her.

"Oh, really?" Millie answered, as she began to get dressed. "Well, it's very obvious you're no telepath, Ben Trask. I mean, if you really want to know sick, why don't you come with me on a walk through the city sometime."

"But I mean *sick* sick," said Trask.

"Yes," said Millie, "and so do I. It's not the ones on the inside that I've ever felt concerned about. Not until now, anyway . . ."

Bleakstone was on the South Downs not far from Arundel. A relatively new institution, the medical authorities had weathered a storm of protest during its planning and building. But that had been nine years ago, and in the interim Bleakstone had earned a reputation as a second Alcatraz. Not one inmate had ever broken out.

"We're landing half a mile away, near the road into Petersfield," said the Minister, as their helicopter passed high over the grim grey prison walls. "Closer than that, we might disturb the delicate equilibrium of the place. The last thing I want is to excite its regular inmates."

"There are some really twisted types in this place, right?" said Trask, looking down on the fortresslike complex with its towers, exercise yards, and frequently windowless cell blocks.

"The worst," said the Minister. "Down in the guts of Bleakstone, literally underground, that's where they keep the truly menacing ones. They feed them, keep them as clean as possible, sedate them when they're not behaving, and watch over them for the rest of their lives until they die naturally. That's about all they can do. But frankly—having read some of their case files—if it was up to me I'd speed that latter process up a little."

"You'd take out the 'dying naturally' clause," said Millie a little coldly, causing the Minister to glance at her. And:

"I fully understand why you would find that objectionable," he told her, "and ordinarily I would agree that it's a drastic solution. Please don't think I'm some kind of heartless brute, Miss Cleary, but consider yourself fortunate that *you* haven't read those case files . . ."

They were picked up on the road to Petersfield by a uniformed prison guard in a vehicle that looked like an ambulance on the outside and a reinforced cage on the inside, and driven a half-mile farther out into the countryside and down a private track to Bleakstone Prison. One hundred and fifty yards from its entrance they passed through tall electrified gates and a barrier operated from a security post, where on both sides of the road triple-coiled razor wire stretched off into the distance following the contours of the land. By which time the general mood was ominous in keeping with the gaunt aspect of the high walls that loomed ahead.

"How about it?" Trask asked Chung, as massive steel doors opened inwards, allowing them access.

But the locator could only shake his head. "There are too many distractions," he said. "I mean, this place was frightening enough from the outside! And there's lots of steel in here and a hell of a lot more concrete. I'm thinking about how grim it is instead of concentrating on what it might contain. Maybe when we actually get to see our suspects . . . ?"

"And you?" Trask looked at Goodly as the vehicle came to a halt.

The precog was as cadaverous, pale, and sunken-eyed as

the stylized undertaker he always seemed to epitomize. "There *is* a very definite . . . atmosphere here," he said. "But it's as David says: it conjures up pictures of its own, so that I can't even be sure my talent is involved. I see pain—a lot of it—but I'm not sure that the pain I feel isn't mine."

"Yours?" said Trask, as the driver opened up the back door of the van to let them out. "You mean you're hurting?"

"It could be just the atmosphere," said the precog. "I mean the 'now' atmosphere. Or it could be tomorrow's pain or the day after that . . . or any future time. I can't say if it's significant."

"In this place," said their driver, who could have no idea what Goodly was talking about, "everyone hurts sooner or later. And if you work here it's sooner. You need eyes in the back of your head—which wreaks havoc with your bleedin' nerves! But if you'll accompany me, gentlemen, the doctors should be waiting for you."

He led the way from the exercise yard through an arched entrance with the legend "West Wing" carved into its keystone, down a long, clinically tiled and antiseptic-smelling corridor that reminded Trask of nothing so much as a recently disinfected toilet in London's mainly defunct underground rail system, past several security doors to a junction of passageways lined with various offices, laboratories, surgeries, and storerooms. Here, at least, the place was starting to look more like a conventional hospital.

Finally they were shown into a room under a sign that said simply PSY, and Millie murmured, "Now if that was PSI, I think I might feel a lot more at home."

Two men in casual clothing, presumably psychiatric specialists, were seated in swivel chairs before a reinforced observation window or one-way viewscreen. As their visitors filed into the room one of them quickly rose, put a finger to his lips, and cautioned them, "Be reasonably quiet, if you will. Despite that these rooms are soundproof, the patients sometimes sense vibrations."

"Vibrations?" Trask glanced at Millie, thinking, *Perhaps it should be PSI after all!*

155

"Or someone can't spell very well," she answered, "and that sign should read PSYLENCE!"

"Pardon?" said the man on his feet, looking from one to the other enquiringly.

"I do apologize," said Trask. "But . . . vibrations?"

"Ah!" said the other. "I meant in the floor. When there are a number of people in this room, they sometimes feel vibrations in the floor. The patients, that is." He indicated the screen.

Then, while Trask's team moved carefully toward the screen, the Minister Responsible produced a governmental ID card, which served as his introduction, and indicating Trask said, "My good friend and his team here are experts— or the closest thing we have to experts—in the recognition of this, er, malady." And he quickly added, "Always assuming, that is, that your patients are indeed carriers."

Hearing what he had said, Trask was appreciative. He didn't want his or his agents' names bandied about in public. The anonymity of the Branch was everything, and if or when things broke (God forbid) he didn't want to be quoted as any kind of source. So now he and his espers were simply "experts."

He turned to the doctor, who had introduced himself as Doctor Burton, offered his hand, and said, "I take it that you and your staff—that is, Bleakstone's staff—in general— have been fully briefed in this matter? I don't want to sound overbearing or come off like some kind of witch-finder, but if this is what we think it might be, then I honestly can't put enough emphasis on the potential dangers you're facing here."

Doctor Burton was tall, young, and good-looking, with a wide forehead and intelligent blue eyes. Now as he took Trask's hand and shook it, his forehead wrinkled up and he said, "We've been briefed, yes. But I have to tell you, sir, that what we've been told sounds more like the mouthings of some of our inmates than the legitimate—"

"I know!" Trask cut him short. "I know just exactly what you mean. And *that* is the greatest danger of all: that you find it too incredible. Has anyone given it a name?"

"Not up front," said the other. "But we aren't simpletons. The alleged symptoms and method of transmission speak for themselves. You do understand that I'm a doctor of psychiatry? Yes, I see that you do. Well, this isn't the first time I've met up with vampires—neither myself nor my colleague here—but on those occasions they came to us *looking* for help. They weren't brought to our attention by . . . well, by 'experts.' "

"And of course they were only sick people," said Trask.

"Sick in their heads, yes." Doctor Burton nodded.

"And do I look sick in my head?" said Trask. "Do my people? Does the Minister here?"

"No, of course not, not at all!"

"Then please take my word for it," Trask nodded, "and treat these patients of yours with extreme care—at least until we've found a way to clear them. Or not."

The second psychiatrist, small, thin, and fragile-looking, was on his feet now. Introducing himself as Jeoffrey Porter and offering his chair to Millie, he stood with his colleague at the back of the group while Trask sat beside Millie, with Chung and Goodly on their flanks. The Minister Responsible hovered to one side. Keeping silent, he left the rest of it to his "experts."

Now it was Millie's turn, but Trask knew he didn't need to say so. Like a waft of sweet air she was in his mind, something he would never have noticed except he had come to recognize the feel of her, but in the next moment the sensation passed as she left him to go probing elsewhere. And:

"He's not thinking anything very much," she said. "But what thoughts there are seem a little frightened, also angry . . . and . . . concentrated? I believe it's mainly anger and frustration."

But Trask wanted to know: "Concentrated as in 'forced,' as in 'deliberate'? Frustrated as in 'trapped'? What do you reckon?"

She glanced at him out of the corner of her eye. "You

mean, is he trying to throw us off the track? But if he doesn't know we're here I don't see how he can be. Anyway, doesn't that presuppose a certain talent?" She meant telepathy.

Trask frowned. "This early in his development . . . it seems unlikely." He shook his head.

The "he" they were talking about was a youth seated in one of two easy chairs in the room on the other side of the screen. The room wasn't much larger than a cell and sparsely furnished. Between the chairs stood a small round table with an ashtray, a packet of Marlboro cigarettes and a box of matches, plus a cake stand decked with cheese biscuits and a small selection of hors d'oeuvres, mainly small sausages and cubes of cheese on miniature skewers. In one corner a door stood open, displaying a wash basin and toilet, while the actual door to the cell was closed and fitted with a small barred window. Despite that the furniture wasn't screwed down or in any way secured, the windowless walls were padded.

"The mirror must be a dead giveaway," Trask murmured to no one in particular. And Doctor Burton—who was still trying to work out what Trask and Millie's brief, very cryptic conversation had been about—answered:

"It isn't a mirror but a pastoral scene. Very tranquil. As for the furnishings: they rather depend upon whom we're observing. And since there is no real evidence of aggression in these sleepers . . ." He let it taper off, then added: "Oh, and in order to comply with our briefing, the ashtray is of silver and those hors d'oeuvres contain plenty of garlic."

"Good," said Trask. "But the lighting is artificial."

"True," said the other, "but since the day is overcast . . . there was nothing we could do about that. And anyway, we think it likely that this photophobia is a natural part of the awakening. No one is partial to a bright light shining in his eyes the moment he wakes up. It could well be a symptom of the real disease—I mean, in the event your suspicions are erroneous."

Trask said nothing but thought, *They don't believe.*

And Millie murmured, "Who can blame them?"

The youth in the room was fidgeting a little, looking this way and that. His expression was trapped, bewildered, annoyed; angry, as Millie had said. Maybe eighteen years of age, he was dressed in casual, mismatched clothing and badly scuffed shoes. He was pimply and spike-haired, with an unevenly cropped beard that gave him a goatish look.

"Where did we find him?" Trask wanted to know.

"He was one of these so-called aggressive beggars on one of London's mainline stations," Doctor Burton answered. "We've had him for three days now, but he's only recently awake. He's been in this observation room for about half an hour . . . which probably explains his fidgeting."

"Has he eaten?" said Trask. Synchronicity, because even as he spoke the youth took up a skewer, clenched his uneven teeth on a sausage and piece of cheese, and commenced chewing.

Now Trask's agents leaned forward, intent on watching what would next occur . . . which was nothing. The youth finished off the skewer and took up another.

And Doctor Burton sighed heavily, saying, "Ah, well. And so much for *that* theory!" It wasn't hard to detect a heavy note of sarcasm in his voice.

Hiding his annoyance on the one hand but sighing his relief on the other, Trask said, "How many sleepers do you have here?"

"Sixteen in all," said the doctor. "But so far only four of them have woken up." And then, as the door with the barred window began to open: "Here comes another right now. We desired to see how they would interact, so we chose two entirely different types or classes. Perhaps this will be more interesting. And we know for sure that this one is a smoker. He's also a lawyer, by the way, and he's been threatening lawsuits since the moment he woke up!"

10
Messing with the Mechanisms

THE LAWYER WAS AS TALL, PALE, AND ALMOST
as cadaverous as Ian Goodly. That was where any similarity
ended. For while in the precog's eyes there was this warmth
belying his looks, in the lawyer's eyes there was only a cold,
malicious glint. And he, too, was angry.

Shown or rather ushered into the cell by two burly, white-
clad interns who then left and locked the door behind them,
he stamped his feet, brushed himself down, then whirled and
hammered on the door, shouting: "Who the *hell* do you people think you are? D'you think you can get away with this?
Do I look as if I'm suffering from some mutant bug, some
new strain of . . . of this Asiatic plague? I had my bloody
shots the same as anyone else! Maybe they're what put me
down! So do I have to sue the bloody National Health Service, too? God *damn!*"

His pinstripe was crumpled, tie askew, shirt collar flap-
ping loose, and he hadn't yet shaved. Three days' stubble
made his chin look blue against the pallid parchment of his
hollow cheeks. Now he whirled again, this time to face the
youth who sat there looking at him. "And who are you?" he
snapped.

"Don't you go takin' an attitude with me, mate!" said that
one. "It looks like we're in the same boat. They said as how
I might 'ave contacted some-bleedin'-thing. Meself, I dunno
what they're on about."

"That's 'contracted,' " said the lawyer, as he flung himself
into the empty chair. "And what they're on about—what
they're up to—is holding us in isolation against our will.
Certainly against mine! Here," (he dug in an inside jacket
pocket to produce a card and passed it across the table) "If

you're in need of representation once we're out of this place, contact me. By God, but these bastards are going to make me rich!"

"Well, I could certainly use some o' that," said the other, pocketing the card and reaching for a third skewer.

Then the lawyer patted his side pockets, shook his head in disgust, and pointed to the cigarettes. "Yours?"

"Naw," said the youth. " 'Elp yerself."

The lawyer lit up, then reached over and drew the ashtray to his side of the table. His contact with the silver was only momentary, because it didn't require to be any longer, but his expression never wavered. He showed no sign of pain or revulsion whatsoever, except at being detained in this place. And:

"So much for *that* theory, too!" said Doctor Burton on the other side of the screen.

"Well?" Trask looked at Millie, and beyond her at the precog where he stood, then turned and looked at Chung. "Is there anything? Do we have anything at all?"

They said nothing, looked undecided, which he took to be a negative. But then Millie said, "And how about you? You're the one who can usually tell the difference between true or false. So are they on the up-and-up, or what?"

Trask shook his head and frowned worriedly. "I'm stymied," he said. "Maybe it's because I'm looking too hard. Or it could be that I'm relieved it isn't obvious. But in any case this is getting us nowhere and we've other things to do. So that's it, we're finished here."

"Do you people always talk to each other in code?" Doctor Burton inquired, as he showed them out into the corridor where their driver was waiting.

"Er, we've worked together for many years," Trask told him. "I'm sorry if we appeared to be rude."

Not so much as rude but weird as hell! thought Burton, who had seen some weird ones in his time. But then Millie turned to him with a curious expression on her face and said:

"And we're also sorry if we seemed weird. People are always accusing us of that!"

The two doctors accompanied them to the exercise yard, and as the team was getting into the back of the van Goodly paused, turned to Burton and said, "Please remember what you have been told. This visit hasn't proved anything, that's true—but it hasn't disproved anything, either. You should watch all of those sleepers very closely. And the longer you detain them, the more closely you should watch them. If things are to develop at all, it may take some time."

"Can you say how long it will be?" said the other. "I mean, before we can clear them? This facility has its priorities, you understand. We do have other work to do."

And the Minister Responsible replied, "Of course we understand, but especially in a place like this *you* must understand that public safety and the government's priorities come first. I'll let you know as soon as I'm able. Until then, nothing has changed."

"As you will," said Burton, a little sourly . . .

On the way back to the chopper, Trask turned to the precog and asked, "Were you having second thoughts back there?"

"I was having thoughts, certainly," said Goodly.

"Which is more than I can say for myself," said Millie.

"And I got a kind of—I don't know—mental fuzziness?" said Chung. "But nothing specific. Nothing I could put a finger on."

"But it didn't feel right, right?" said Trask.

All three of them could only shrug and look blank, and the Minister Responsible said, "I do hope I haven't made a terrible mistake . . . or rather, I do!"

And Trask said, "But best to err on the side of prudence."

And still unwilling to let it go, he went on: "Well, it didn't feel right to me. Not at all!" And turning again to Ian Goodly, "What do you mean, you were having thoughts?"

"I mean I was wondering about something," said the precog. "We know what effect the vampire's bite has, also what happens to a victim who is totally drained of his blood, and even what occurs with the introduction of a leech into the human system. All such things are well documented. But where spores are concerned. . . . we know so very little."

"Go on," said Trask.

"When I was a boy," Goodly went on, "my uncle had a farm in Yorkshire. In the woods nearby was a large pond where the lower branches of the trees trailed in the water. I remember watching moorhen chicks hatching out in their nest. The first thing they do, these little fellows, after they've broken free of the eggshells—"

"—They jump in the water and swim," said Trask. "I think I know what you're getting at."

"So do I," said Millie. "The devious nature of the vampire. Is it inherited? Is it instinctive in them from the very beginning? Do they 'know' to protect themselves without knowing why? And is that what happens to these sleepers while they're unconscious? Do they become aware, if only partly?"

"But that lad ate garlic!" said the Minister.

"Maybe the changeover isn't complete as yet," said Trask. "And the lawyer touched silver." ·

"But briefly," said Trask. Then, sighing, he sat back. "The simple fact is," he said, "that we don't know. But one thing is for sure: we *do* know we can't take any chances. Just as soon as you get the opportunity, I think you should call Burton and his colleague and make your point a lot more strongly. For example, I didn't like the way those two interns just thrust that lawyer chap into the observation room. That was contact . . . and it was very *close* contact. I certainly hope the boffins at Porton Down are being a bit more careful."

"So do I," the Minister nodded.

And the precog said, "One other thing. I'm simply hazarding a guess, of course, but that sensation of pain that I was feeling . . ."

"What about it?" said Trask.

"Well," said the other, "considering the sort of place that Bleakstone is, and also the volatile nature of its more regular inmates, if anything ever *did* break loose in there—"

"—The result would be a whole world of pain for someone," said Trask, very quietly. "Yes, I see what you mean . . ."

In the observation cell in Bleakstone, the lawyer was quieter now. He stood up, took three paces to the large picture on the wall, pressed hard with his fingertips against the glass that covered it, and said, "Hmm, bulletproof! And it's not simply a picture. It's very odd, but do you know I sensed them there watching us? They seem to have gone now."

"I know," said the pimply youth. "I knew they were there, too, but I don't know how I knew."

"Something is telling me we should watch ourselves," said the lawyer, returning to his chair. "We must watch what we do and say, or we could find ourselves in big trouble."

"But if we play it cool," said the other, "sooner or later they'll 'ave to let us out."

The lawyer nodded, then cocked his head on one side in an attitude of listening, and said, "Ah! Those doctors are coming back. So let's be patient until we find out what's happened to us and what's going on here . . . until we know why those others were . . . what, frightened of us?"

"Suits me," said the youth. And, as the lawyer reached for the hors d'oeuvres, "Don't! They're not . . . not right for us."

"Really?" said the lawyer, as he paused and picked up the cigarettes instead. This time he left the ashtray alone. There was a burning in his thumb and forefinger, and there was something about the ashtray that he didn't like. But now they must stop talking, for the doctors were back in the room beyond the pastoral picture.

Then, when the youth stood up, the lawyer asked him, "Just where do you think you're going?"

"That's between me and Ma Nature," said the youth, closing the toilet door behind him.

And all unseen, as quietly as possible while shuddering in every fiber, he emptied his seething, burning stomach into the toilet bowl . . .

* * *

Back at E-Branch HQ in the afternoon, Trask called Liz Merrick into his office and told her to close the door and sit down.

And without pause: "How are you getting on with Jake?" he asked her.

"As well as can be expected," she answered, just a little stiffly. "And he hasn't been looking at all sleepy, if that's what you're asking."

"No," said Trask, "and neither has Millie, thank God!"

"But if you're worried about them," Liz said, pointedly, "then surely you should be even more worried about me. I was with Vavara and her women for quite a while, and for part of that time I was unconscious."

"Yes, and I've been with you most of the time since then," said Trask, "and I do trust my own five senses—not to mention my sixth. You're okay, Liz, I'm sure of that. But surely you must understand my concerns about Jake? And I'm not just talking about Szwart's vampire spores."

"But we've been over this before," said Liz, "and Jake's ready to take whatever tests you've set up for him. He's more than ready—he's eager!"

"That's not the whole thing," said Trask. "Look, I don't want to get personal, but . . . I mean, I don't quite know how to put this."

"You don't have to put it," she answered. "You've *already* put it. You've been trying not to, but you've been thinking it ever since I walked in here. No, we haven't slept together . . . not yet. But don't think I don't want to!"

Trask relaxed a little, and said, "Liz, I'm sorry. But you know we're into this too deep now to let personal feelings get in the way. It's just too important. And believe me, there are no words to express how relieved I am that you've had the good sense to—"

"—Good sense nothing!" she said, hotly. "I want him more than I ever wanted anything." And now she was flushed and there was the silvery gleam of tears in her eyes. "Jake's the one who is holding back. *He* is the one who's got all the 'common sense,' the guts, fortitude, and bloody pride! Oh, Jake wants me—and goodness knows he could have me—but not while Korath's there. Not while that damned, godawful, leering vampire Thing is there sharing his mind with him. That, in the main, is what's holding him back: the fact that he won't share me! And it's why we have to see that he gets rid of it."

"But only one of the reasons," said Trask.

"For me, right now, it's the only reason I need," said Liz. "Yes, I love him dearly. And just as you love Millie—just as you *have* Millie—so I want Jake."

And suddenly Trask felt guilty. Here he was warning Liz off Jake, but he'd spent last night with Millie. And Liz was right: the danger was the same on both sides.

Standing up, he moved round his desk, took her in his arms, and as she sobbed a little said, "It's all a matter of priorities, isn't it, sweetheart? Maybe my priorities have been wrong and I've put my head before my heart, but I thought my reasons were good ones."

"Oh, they were, they were!" she said into his shoulder.

"And maybe I've been selfish, too," Trask went on, gruffly. "I just didn't want to admit—not even to myself— that Millie might be . . . that she could be in trouble, too."

Liz drew away to arm's length, and said, "What's next, Ben? I don't want to search your mind for it. I'm frightened what I might find in there. So just tell me: what are we going to do?"

"To hell with the tests!" he told her then. "They can wait. I don't think they would prove anything anyway. I saw that this morning. So this time let's get the priorities right. We have a job to do, and I need my agents on it in full force, which includes Millie and Jake. But an idea has been growing in me. It's a kind of . . . a kind of prayer I've been saying to myself, over and over again, ever since those damned Things came through the Gate from Starside: if only Harry Keogh were here. Oh God, how I wish the original, the real Harry were here!"

"But he isn't," said Liz.

"No, but he could be," said Trask. "Something of him *could* be, through Jake Cutter."

Liz's jaw fell open a little. "Jake's been in contact with him once or twice, but—"

"—But he couldn't handle him," said Trask, "didn't understand him, let him go."

And now her eyes opened wide. "You think we can somehow get Harry back, enlist his aid?"

"We can try," said Trask, excited now. "Indeed, we have to try. And you know, Liz, we've done some very marvellous things, here in E-Branch."

He released her, pushed her towards the door. "Now get out there and whistle me up some agents. Chung, Goodly, and Millie. And Jake, of course. See to it they're all together in the same place—" he glanced at his watch, "—in fifteen minutes' time."

"In the same place?" she repeated him. "But where?"

"In Harry's Room," Trask told her. "Where else . . . ?"

"We're only missing Zek," Trask said, when the specified agents had convened in Harry's Room. Those few words—in addition to the location, which in E-Branch was the holy of holies—served immediately to quell any speculation among those gathered there. Except for Jake Cutter, everyone present now knew more or less why he or she—why they as a group—were here.

"We're missing Zek *and* Nathan," Ian Goodly corrected Trask. "They were powers, those two, and especially without Nathan our task will be that much harder. But we can make up for them—in numbers, at least—with Liz and Millie. So whatever it is you have in mind, Ben, and since this time we're not attempting to move a world, it strikes me we have a good team."

Jake Cutter was mystified. "Er, don't I fit into this somewhere?" he said. "I mean, what's going on?"

"Jake, there are some things we need to know," Trask told him, "questions we have to ask. But the real expert—the only one who might be able to answer our questions with any kind of genuine authority—is no longer available, no longer with us. We do know, though, that Harry Keogh was irresistibly drawn to you, that he found an affinity with you and your mind. We know that for sure, because of what you've experienced, what you've become."

"A Necroscope?" said Jake, with precisely the kind of naïvety that conjured pictures of the young Harry Keogh himself.

"*The* Necroscope," Trask answered him. "The only Necroscope, on this planet, anyway. So, you want to know where you fit into this? You're the focus, the magnet, and this room is the genius loci. Or maybe you're that, too. I don't know."

Uncertainly, Jake glanced from face to face, finally found Liz's and paused there. She nodded eagerly and said, "It could clear a lot of cloudy water, Jake, and tell us a lot of things we badly need to know. That is, *if* we can help you to find the original Necroscope, or him to find you . . ."

And now he got it. "So this is—what? Some kind of experiment—part of those tests we talked about?"

"In a way," said Trask. "I suppose you could say that, yes. But that's not all it is. We want to know about vampire spores—without finding out the hard way! Since Harry was converted by spores, who better to ask? We'd like to know what's happening in Sunside/Starside, where Nathan and other friends of ours are fighting the selfsame battle against vampires. Also, we're interested in Harry himself: where is his principal focus now; and if you're his legacy to us, does he intend to carry on his work through you, and how? And last but not least, we'd really like to ask his advice about your unwanted tenant. For you see, Jake, we believe that Harry was once in the same fix—that he was possessed by the spirit of Faethor Ferenczy—and so might be able to suggest a way to get rid of this Korath creature."

(At which a night-dark something immediately surfaced from the depths of Jake's mind and gurglingly enquired, *Oh, really? Does this fool* really *think so? Hah!*) But Jake was accustomed to it; he ignored it, nodded his partial understanding of what Trask had told him, and asked, "So how will we go about it? Do you intend to play gadgets and ghosts again, where Harry's the ghost and I'm the gadget?"

"There is no other way," Trask answered. "You're our only connection with Harry—you and this room, which was once his. Can you smell the musty air in this room, Jake? Harry breathed it. So if there was ever a place where his essence lingers on, this is it. When he first discovered you he brought you here—not once but twice. It's like a nexus, binding whatever's left of him to our world. Genius loci, like I said."

"His spirit of place," said Jake.

"And yours, now," said Trask. "As to how we'll go about it: this isn't the first time we've done this sort of thing. As Ian hinted a moment ago, the last time was on Starside. Then we had Zek and Nathan's help, and without Nathan we couldn't have done it at all. We moved a world, Jake, turning it on its axis until the sun shone on Starside! The end of vampiric life, throughout all the Vampire World. So we thought—*huh!* But this time we're not looking to move anything, merely to attract something. It's like recovering a lost file in a computer. We are the disks, so to speak, and also the power source, and Harry—"

"—Is the lost knowledge," said Jake. "And I'm the monitor screen. But can it damage me? I mean, what if it blows my chip? What if my mind overloads or something?"

"In our experience," said Trask, "the mind of a Necroscope, of *the* Necroscope, is a hard thing to overload. Without wanting to put you down, I have to tell you you don't know half of what Harry knew, or Nathan . . . and *they* didn't know half of what The Dweller knew! You're young; your brain can accept a lot of knowledge yet. So I don't believe there's any danger in it for you. Indeed, it could well be your opportunity to grow, to learn the rest of it. But I can't make you do it. The decision is yours."

"Let me think about it," said Jake. "Just give me five minutes to think it over—or rather, to *talk* it over."

"With Korath?" said Liz, reading it in Jake's mind.

"Surely you know he'll try to talk you out of it?" She was anxious now.

"Yes, and I fully expect him to," Jake answered. "But often as not Korath's word games and arguments supply as much information as they conceal. They let me learn things. For example, if he wants me to do something, then it's invariably to his advantage. And if he doesn't it's usually to mine. I only need a few minutes." And:

"Go right ahead," said Trask. "We'll give you some privacy, and when you're ready you can call us back in." He indicated to the rest of the team that they should leave, was last to go and closed the door behind him.

Then Jake pulled a wheeled chair out from under an ancient-looking computer console, sat down in it, and looked around the room. He looked around *Harry's* Room, and wondered why it looked and felt so familiar. For what was it after all but a small and outdated hotel room? Oh, it had been fitted out with a computer console, but that had been a long time ago, in Harry's time.

Genius loci? Well, maybe. On those previous occasions when he'd been in here, he hadn't really had the time to think about it. But now, on his own, with nothing pressing . . .

. . . *Nothing pressing?* said Korath, apparently or ostensibly astonished. *These "friends" of yours want to call up some freak out of space and time, some ghost who has already tried to take over your mind more than once, and you don't feel any pressure? What, are you insane? You'd swap me for him? But why should you, when I'm nothing more than Trask named me—an unwanted tenant? That's all I am, Jake—a tenant to whom you've let a room, for which you're now sorry while I'm very grateful. But as for this Harry: how do you know he doesn't want the whole house? Oh, and by the way, I heard what you said about me. About my word games and arguments. But of course they're to my advantage! Naturally they are! Isn't that the very nature of arguments?*

Jake shook his head and chuckled however wryly. He

couldn't help it. And: "You know something, Korath?" he said. "If Malinari and those others hadn't rammed you into that pipe—if you had somehow managed to die a 'natural' death—do you know how you would have ended up? You're so twisted, they would have had to screw you into the ground!"

Ah, a joke! said Korath. *While considering my expulsion—*

"Your exorcism," Jake corrected him.

—you find room for crude jests! Be warned, Jake: whatever else you do, don't make an enemy of me. And remember this: that whatever Trask says about the human mind's capacity, its mechanisms are delicate things. The mansion of your mind is furnished, and I am in here with all your treasures! Suppose I should, er, stumble and bring something crashing down? Ah! Who can say what damage such an "accident" would inflict upon you?

"Treasures?" said Jake, a little warily.

Memoriesss, Korath hissed. *Habitsss, instinctsss—and what of emotionsss? For example: can human love become lust? Ah, but the dividing line is narrower than you think. Far narrower than the centuries separating you from barbarous ancestors. So then, what if I were to pick the lock on the primal "you," the avatar that lies buried in your genes, to let him loose?*

"You've been reading over my shoulder again," said Jake.

But so illuminating! said Korath. *So fascinating, and oh so revealing of your current penchant. All those great heavy books on psychology—*

"—Were required reading," said Jake. "If I were carrying a tapeworm I'd need treatment, medicine, a physical solution. But in your case—since you're a *mind*worm—the answer has to be metaphysical: some kind of exorcism, yes. But I wasn't about to let anyone else mess with my mind before first reading up on it myself. And it was useful. I learned quite a bit."

And I have been learning about you, said Korath darkly. But then, as if afraid of divulging too much, he quickly continued, *As for the books: the reason for my interest is simply stated. Since you sought an answer to me, I must seek an answer to the answer!* (And "despairingly"): *But see how low I am fallen! How are things come to this, that I am now considered a mere parasite?*

"But you always were," said Jake. "You and every other vampire who ever existed. So stop playing with words and *listen* to me. Do you know why I'm bothering to talk to you at all?"

To torment me? To gloat over me, perhaps for the last time, before these mentalist friends of yours attempt my removal? Ah, but what if they fail? What then of our relationship, our 'partnership,' Jake? Do you think I'll ever trust you again?

"About as much as I trust you," said Jake. "But in any case you're wrong. I'm not gloating, not yet. For I know well enough that you won't be a pushover. But on the other hand, if they do succeed in banishing you back to that black sump where Malinari left you . . . well, I just want you to know that I won't let you rot there. That's why I'm talking to you."

Hah! said Korath. *Another "joke," for I have already rotted there!*

"I meant," said Jake, "that I'm not about to let your bones lie there in the dark. I wouldn't sentence anyone—not even a rabid dog—to an eternity of night. And despite that you're a loathsome parasitic Thing, you have saved my neck several times over. For that . . . well, I owe you a decent grave at least. And I'll see that you get one. You can take that as a promise."

And after a moment's silence: *Your vow?* said Korath wonderingly, yet with something in his voice which hinted that Jake's offer hadn't been totally unexpected.

"My vow, yes," Jake gave a deadspeak nod—and frowned. For he was just as surprised at himself as Korath should have been.

What? said Korath, trying not to gurgle his pleasure, which by all rights should have been his astonishment. *Are you really offering to take my bones out of there? But why? And what's in it for you?*

"As to why," Jake shook his head. "I'm not at all sure. You can put it down to my ridiculous, probably ill-founded sense of fairness, I suppose. Fair play, Korath: a human folly, yes. But if I 'befriend' you—if I show you mercy—maybe the teeming dead will give you some leeway, too. Who can say, in time they might even review your case. Maybe they won't exclude you."

Ah! said Korath. *And now I think I understand! For you have known the misery of exclusion, too—though never to the extent that I knew it before you discovered me in my sump. Indeed, the Great Majority are wary of you still.*

"Thanks to you," said Jake. "But compassion goes a long way with the dead. If I can show a grain of mercy even for a creature as terrible as yourself—"

Then they will think well of you, said Korath. *Yes, I see.*

"Do you see?" said Jake with a frown. For now, suddenly it seemed to him that Korath was supplying logic for feelings and emotions that he himself didn't understand.

Oh, yes. I see . . . several things, said the other, his dead-speak voice hardening again. *But mainly I see a clever ploy to quell my fighting spirit, making it easier for your friends or this Harry Keogh to cast me out.* Hah! *For if a man believes in heaven, he will die that much easier. Alas, Jake, but the Wamphyri, their lieutenants and thralls, have no such faith. Even if there were a heaven, there'd be no room in it for them. No, you shall do your worst, I'm sure. And I shall resist you with all my strength, no matter what you promise.*

"I expected nothing less," said Jake with a shrug. "But if they do find a way to kick you out, I'll keep my word anyway."

As you will, said Korath. *But if they should fail—which they will—do not expect leniency on my part. For I am what I am, and above all else tenacious.*

"Then that's it," said Jake. "Conversation over. I'm out

of here. And with a bit of luck so will you be, and very shortly."

Let the battle commence, said Korath, *with no quarter asked and none given. I fight for my existence, with whatever weapons are to hand!*

"As you will," said Jake, equally resolute.

But ... I mean ... in the event of my failure—which isn't going to happen—but if they actually do find a way to cast me out ... ? (An uncertain quaver in the dead vampire's voice now, as even in these final moments he sought to find an advantage.)

Jake gave a sad shake of his head, and before he opened the door to call Trask and the rest of the team back into the room, sighed and said, "No need to concern yourself, Korath. Speaking for myself—if *only* for myself—a promise is a promise."

"How did it go?" said Liz.

"Much as I expected," Jake answered. "He doesn't want it to happen. But on the other hand, I don't think he's too afraid of it, either. Even if you get Harry back here—if you can manage to invoke him—Korath doesn't think he'll be any real problem. If he did I'm sure he would have argued a hell of a lot harder. But no, while he's not about to take any chances, Korath really doesn't believe Harry can expel him. Frankly, neither do I. For the fact is Harry Keogh is *less* than Korath. Oh, he was a power in his own time, yes, but now he's scattered, diffused, thinned out. While Korath, however incorporeal, is real and embedded in my mind. I should know. I invited him in, after all."

"Of your own free will," Liz nodded. "In order to save me."

"Whichever." Jake shrugged. "But he's in there."

"And you did, er, *talk* to him?" said Trask, who for all his time as the Head of Branch, and despite all the evidence of his "six" senses, still found the concept of the Necroscope fantastic, so that he had to force himself to accept it.

"Yes, I did," said Jake. "And I went easy on him, made

him a promise. I told him whichever way it went, that when I get an opportunity I'll shift his bones out of that sump and give them a decent burial."

"You were trying to bargain with him?" said Ian Goodly.

"No," said Jake, "but he has my word on it anyway. The way I see him—the way I remember him when Harry first introduced us—is as a frightened creature trapped in a night-dark place forever. Soulless but sentient, and totally lost and alone. The Great Majority won't have anything to do with him; his thoughts go unheard; madness brings no relief. I can't imagine any worse torture, and it's never-ending. So, I'm going to bury his bones where I can go and talk to him now and then."

"I don't understand," said Trask. "This creature is ruining your life; he has to be the ultimate voyeur; there's no privacy with him in there, no thought you can think that he won't eavesdrop. As long as he's around you can't ever have a life of your own!"

"I wouldn't *have* a life of my own, but for him," said Jake. "And not just me." He looked at Trask and the others pointedly.

Trask shook his head in disbelief. "Man, you're even beginning to sound like him! Can't you see what a word game this is? It's a circular argument, Jake. You feel you owe him because he saved our lives? But it was Korath who put our lives at risk in the first place, when he messed with your numbers!"

"Maybe, but I still think he can teach me things." Jake was as stubborn as ever.

And Millie came in with, "Are you saying you don't want rid of him after all?"

"Of course I want rid of him!" said Jake, while yet wondering if that were really so. But then he looked at Liz and said, "Damned right I do! But I want him where I can access him. In a place where I can still talk to him—but on my terms. You see, of all the Great Majority, he is one of only a very small handful who'll have anything to do with me. I mean, what's the good of deadspeak if I can't use it?"

At which Trask relaxed a little, sighed his relief, and said, "You know, Jake, you really had me going there? In fact I think you had all of us going!"

But as Trask spoke, suddenly Jake noticed the selfsame look on all their faces: a worried look, fading now, that said for a moment there they hadn't known what they were dealing with. And he could understand that well enough, for he'd just this moment realized that neither had *he* known what he was dealing with!

Feeling weak and cold, Jake reached for the chair to steady himself. "I . . . I'm not myself," he said, as he sat down with a bump. "Not at all myself." And he absolutely meant it.

Liz was there beside him at once, her hand on his shoulder. "What is it, Jake?" she said, trying to probe him. His shields immediately went up, turning aside her telepathy. And Millie's, too. For all five of them were focussing upon him now: the precog's weird talent, attempting to scan his future, Chung like a lodestone, and Ben Trask doing his best to read the "truth" of it, whatever it was. But none of them getting through, because his shields were that good. And the only trouble with that was that Jake hadn't raised them!

"It was something he said to me," he choked the words out, his face writhing.

"Korath?" Liz gripped his shoulder harder still. "What did that bastard say to you?"

"He hinted he could mess with my mind," Jake answered. "And that could be why he's been keeping so much to himself recently. He's been practising. And now, I think he's actually doing it!"

"Messing with your mind?" Trask snapped. "How?"

"He called my mind a furnished mansion," Jake growled, "and said he's inside with all my treasures: my memories, habits, and instincts. He wanted me to consider what would happen if he had an 'accident' that brought something crashing down, and he wondered what the result would be if he released my primal avatar, the basic, instinctive, animal *meeee!*"

Jake's lips had drawn back from his teeth in an utterly uncharacteristic snarl. Glaring his hatred at his—his what? His tormentors?—he thrust Liz away from him, came surging to his feet.

Which was when Trask hauled off and hit him, and the lights went out . . .

11
Calling Harry Keogh

ON COMING TO, JAKE FOUND HIMSELF BOUND TO the chair with computer cable. And with his jaw still aching from Trask's knockout blow, and likewise his head where it had slammed into the wall, the last thing he needed was Korath's deadspeak voice hammering away at the back of his mind:

Didn't I warn you? What, "friends" of yours, these people? The very first time you act as your own man—attempt to regain something of your independence—and what happens? This Trask, whom everyone holds in such high regard, strikes like the treacherous dog he is! After all you have done for them . . . no, after all we *have done for them, to knock you unconscious and tie you down? And now perhaps you'll stop this ridiculous charade, come to your senses and begin to fight back. And I shall be with you all the way . . .*

But fully in the picture now, Jake brushed Korath aside and looked up groggily at the people surrounding him. Three of them wore wary, watchful expressions; one other (Liz) was very obviously concerned—she was dabbing at Jake's lip where he'd bit it when he was hit—while the last, Ben Trask, looked as mean as Jake had ever seen him. And:

"For an old man," Jake mumblingly told the latter, "you hit pretty damned hard!"

"Consider yourself lucky," Trask growled. "After what I

saw just five minutes ago, it's a wonder I didn't shoot you dead!"

"But you didn't, because you recognized the 'truth' of it," said Jake.

"Barely in time," Trask nodded, "before you got completely out of control. It was what you said, about your primal avatar, the basic, animal you. Also what you said about not being yourself. I didn't see the truth of 'you' because your shields were up, but I could still read the truth of your spoken words. Damn right you weren't yourself! That was *him* pulling your strings."

"He's done it," said Jake. "Found a way to get at my 'mechanisms,' knows which buttons to press."

"Which means that from now on," Liz said, "you're going to have to keep a very tight grip on yourself. If anything doesn't feel right—doesn't feel like you—that'll be him, and you'll have to fight it all the way."

"It means a lot more than that," Trask growled. "Unless we can shift this bloody thing or find a way to block it, Jake is going to be useless to us, and to himself. In fact he won't *be* himself! There's no way we're going to work with someone who's likely to turn on us at any moment, most probably at a crucial time. Also, it strikes me that this time—this first time—Korath wasn't in complete control, that he was clumsy. I don't know, maybe he was desperate and pushed too hard on the pedals. But if he's only just learned how to drive, and if that was the result, how soon before he memorizes the owners' manual and gets it down pat?"

"The one thing he's not short of is memory," said Jake. "He got it from Malinari whose talent is eidetic. That's how Korath remembers the Möbius equations, those numbers which I guarantee would baffle any of you. If Harry Keogh hadn't passed on, well, whatever it was to me, they'd baffle me, too."

"Which in turn means that what we're attempting here has to be now or never," said Trask. "It seems to me we've caught this just in time, before it's had a chance to really take hold. But on the other hand, if we should fail . . ." He looked at Jake, and his expression was bleak.

And Jake said, "I'll spend the rest of my life in a cell?"

"Try a straitjacket," said Trask, "strapped down to a bed, anaesthetized and immobilized. Permanently!"

"What?" Jake's jaw fell open.

"Figure it out for yourself," said Trask. "A mind under the control of a vampire—a mind like yours, capable of doing the things only you can do—running completely amok? Not a hope in hell, Jake. Madness and the Möbius Continuum just don't mix. If you got loose we could never take you again. And we could never know what you'd do next, or who you'd be doing it for."

You see? You see? I was right! Korath howled, but only Jake could hear him. *Are you blind? Can't you see I was only protecting you? You must not let them dabble, Jake. You can't let them fool with your mind. I'm embedded now— melded with your inner being—a part of your very identity. If they attempt to rip me loose, who knows what else might go with me? Have you forgotten what you said about pre- frontal lobotomy? Mightn't this work out the same? And if so, will you ever again be yourself?*

"Oh . . . why don't you . . . shut the *fuck* up!" Jake groaned, then shook his head wildly, bared his teeth, and began to rock to and fro in his chair.

"It's Korath again!" Liz gasped, going to her knees beside Jake. "It's him. I don't know what he's saying or trying to do, but I can feel him there—raw and ugly, like a running sore—festering in Jake's mind!"

"Are Jake's shields down?" Trask yelled, as the precog and the locator grabbed Jake's arms, holding him still. And:

"Yes!" all four of his espers answered as one person.

"He's fighting with Korath," said Liz. "A mental struggle, as if with himself. He's fighting to *keep* his shields down, so that when we find Harry he can let him in."

"But apart from that it's a complete and utter shambles in there," Millie said, falling back and leaning against the wall.

"His thoughts are spinning—like a wall of whirling numbers—a mathematical cry for help."

"But his aura is awesome!" said Chung. "He's a giant dynamo running wild."

"And his future—his immediate future is—*ahhh!*" The precog staggered. Clutching at Trask with one hand, he held on to Jake's arm with the other. But the hand and arm that held Jake were vibrating as if from an electric shock.

"What do you see?" Trask barked.

"I see . . . I see . . . *I see Harry!*" said the precog.

And suddenly Jake was still, and everyone in the room knew instinctively what he or she must do.

Jake's chair stood central. The E-Branch team closed in on it, joined hands and made a circle around it. And as on several previous occasions they acted as a body—or rather as a mind, one mind—willing it to happen.

Chung was the locating force; his probe went out, searching for a once well-known, never-to-be-forgotten psychic signature. Trask clung to the truth of things—willing that it *come* true—and sought to dispel all lies and evil. Millie and Liz linked minds as well as hands, and followed the locator's probe where it washed out from him on its mission of discovery. And Goodly held them together, carried them all forward, second by second, into the ever-devious future.

Jake's eyes were wild, wide, bulging; his teeth were clenched in straining jaws; sweat dripped from his chin. "The bastard is . . . he's *fighting* me," he groaned. "But he isn't . . . he isn't going to win!"

And in his mind: *No!—Ah, No!—Nooooooo!* Korath howled his denial, then fell abruptly silent. For something had come. Something was here.

Jake's eyes closed; every straining muscle went slack; his head fell forward onto his chest . . .

The light in the room dimmed. The temperature fell. In the space of mere seconds the room was cold. But it was more a psychic than a physical chill. And Jake . . . was no longer Jake. Or rather his outline in the chair seemed to have taken on a different shape.

"Harry!" Chung breathed, where he almost hung between Trask and Millie. "His signature was faint but unmistakable. He came speeding from—oh, from far away—and I can't say if it was space or time or both. Or neither. I mean, he was here, and yet he wasn't, isn't. I mean . . . I don't know *what* I mean!"

"From space *and* time," said the precog, looking as gaunt as ever in the sudden gloom. "From a different space, perhaps, and a time between. But on the other hand he has always been here."

"This was his place," said Trask, in a hoarse aside to Liz on his left, she being the only one present who had never actually known the original Necroscope. "And I knew that if we were to find him it would have to be in here."

"But how can we be sure it's him?" said Liz, her voice shivery in the eerie hush of the place. "What if it's Korath making fools of us all?"

"*I* can be sure it's him," said Chung.

"And me," said Trask. "Now tell me, Liz, Millie: is Jake in there or not?" He was asking them to probe the apparition telepathically.

The "apparition." That was the only way to describe it. On the one hand it was Jake, tied to a chair. But he was scarcely solid; his outline shimmered, lit from within by the only real light in the room. And superimposed *in* Jake—seeming to drift or hover within and around his slumped figure—the neon-blue foxfire outlines of a boy were plainly visible, his young features picked out in the glow from within. He was a three-dimensional transparency, a hologram, a faint but otherwise perfect computer image in outline. Consisting of myriad luminous traceries, he was like an electric etching on glass or water, all of him drifting within and without the host body. So that now Jake really was the gadget, for the moment at least inhabited by a ghost.

Tentatively, Liz and Millie had attempted telepathic contact. But their first instinctive thought had been simply, *Who?* Even knowing who, still they had asked the first question that entered their stunned minds.

The boy's face—he would be maybe eleven or twelve years old—had been contemplative, lost in some reverie. It was as if he'd been daydreaming, as if he hadn't known he was here at all, or barely, until they'd "spoken" to him. But now his eyes blinked behind his plain prescription spectacles, focussed and gazed translucently out of his hologram at the people surrounding him. Even so, it would have been difficult to say whether he saw them or not, until he said:

"No need for that. Just use your natural medium of speech. Now that I'm here, I'll hear you anyway, even as you hear me." He said it, and they heard it—all five of them heard it—as clear as crystal. But his lips hadn't moved at all! Telepathy, but so advanced it left them all agog, awed in the presence of a boy—this "mere boy"—who spoke with a child's sweet voice, a man's authority, and a superman's skill in all five of their minds simultaneously. And:

"Harry?" said Trask, sure yet unsure.

The young boy's face turned toward him, frowned for just a moment and concentrated its near-immaterial gaze, then smiled its recognition and said, "But surely, Ben, you of all people *know* that I am, or was, or that I will be." Then he turned his face again—turned his whole body, yet without moving a luminous limb or twitching an immaterial muscle—to look at the locator.

"David Chung," he said, more certainly now. "You sent your probe to guide me home."

"Home?" said the locator, still astounded by what he'd achieved, knowing that while it was a team effort, his talent had been their mainstay, their carrier wave. "Your home?"

"Home to you, this now, this place," said Harry. "Only one of many homes." Then, sensing a query, he turned to Millie and smiled. "I remember *you* well," he said. "You were always sorry for me, and I for you. We were both looking for something that couldn't be found." (And Trask could swear that just for a moment the apparition's eyes glanced sideways at him.)

"But . . . how could you expect us to recognize you?" Millie asked him, wonderingly. "The Harry we knew was older."

Harry looked down at himself—at his scruffy, threadbare, ill-fitting, secondhand school jacket—and seemed puzzled by what she'd said. Or perhaps by what he saw. He fingered a shirt where the top button was missing and tugged gently on a frayed, tightly knotted tie bearing a faded school crest.

"The Harry you knew?" he murmured, frowned again and asked of no one: "Was I older . . . ?" But then the outlines of his empty eyes narrowed in dawning understanding, and: "Ah yes!" he said. "Of course! It's just that being as I am, or not being, it gets confusing. And different times and places, I mix them up. There are so very many times and places, Millie. The myriad Universes of Light are full of them. And I . . . well, I have to be here and there. But rarely all here, and never all there. So tell me now . . . is this better?"

His last three words were "spoken" in an entirely different and far more mature voice, but one strictly in keeping with the metamorphosis that was taking place.

The schoolboy Harry, with his ignis fatuus freckles, neon-rimmed eyes, and starry spectacles gradually faded, and another, later Harry took shape. This one—the one they knew—suited Jake's figure much better, which was probably why their picture of him seemed that much more clearly defined. They saw the neon outlines, but they also saw what they desired to see, what they remembered best. Or perhaps they saw only the image that *Harry* wanted them to see, the one that he projected.

The figure superimposed on Jake was the same "boy" for sure, but he'd be twenty or maybe twenty-one years old now. Of a wiry build, he would weigh somewhere between nine and a half and ten stone and stand seventy inches tall. His hair, springing from a high brow and roughly brushed back, was the same sandy, rebellious mop as before, and despite that his nose and jaw had firmed up and were now more angular—in keeping with cheeks that were hollower— still his boyish freckles were visible as a handful of luminous dust motes high in the contours of neon cheekbones.

More than any other feature, Harry Keogh's eyes were especially interesting. Looking at the E-Branch team, they seemed to see right through them—as if *they* were the revenants and not the reverse! But they had been oh-so-very blue, those eyes, even unnaturally so, so that one might think their owner was wearing lenses; not the electric-blue of this neon image, no, yet somehow the neon reinforced the memory. And for all that the apparition *was* in the main a hologram memory of the Harry that Trask and E-Branch had known, still there was something in those eyes that said they had seen a lot more than any twenty-year-old had any right seeing.

This then was the man himself, or what remained of him, the ex-Necroscope. But in fact they'd known him far more intimately in his second incarnation, when Harry had revitalized and inhabited the brain-dead body of Alec Kyle. In short, he was as they *seemed* to remember him, those of them who were fortunate enough to have known him.

But Liz hadn't known him, only what she'd read and heard of him. His gaze had gone from Trask to Chung and then Millie, and skipping the precog it now settled on Liz. And:

"A new one," he said. "New to the inner circle. We've never met before, or after. This is the one time, the one place. It's a real pleasure."

"And for me," she answered, tremulously. And then: "No, we never met, but I could sense you there when you were talking to Jake. He is the reason we've called you here, because he needs your help."

"Jake?" And again the apparition frowned.

"Your focus," Liz told him. "Your . . . your genius loci?"

"Ah, Jake!" Harry let his electric arms float wide, looked down into himself and said, "*This* Jake!" Then he looked at Liz again. "And so we have met after all. I remember now: his mind was full of you—and of one other. But she was only a memory. And now there's only you."

"I wish there was only me!" said Liz, and she almost

broke the circle by starting forward. "But there's Korath, too."

"Korath?" said Harry. But this time, while his lips didn't move his eyebrows came together in a grim frown. "Yes, I remember him, too. And how I warned Jake not to have anything to do with him. But are you saying that Korath is in here?"

Now Trask spoke up, saying, "Harry, Jake's problem is only one of the reasons we brought you here. An important reason—considering what's happened between you—but only one of many. And Korath isn't the only vampire we're having to deal with. In fact we could be about to suffer a plague of vampires. Which is why there are things we still need to know about them."

"About those three who came through the Gate with Korath?" (Harry was very focussed now; he seemed more conscious of when and where, and the importance of his presence here.) "But Jake was there with me when I talked to Korath. He knows about them, all of their history. Except . . . that was while he dreamed. Are you saying it didn't take, he didn't remember?"

"It took eventually," said Trask. "He did finally remember it all. But Malinari, Vavara, and Szwart, they're only the start of it. Or rather, they're the source of what could end up being the real problem."

"They have been at work? Here in your world, in this world, in what was my world?" Intent on Trask, Harry was leaning forward now, half in and half out of Jake, and his neon eyes were brilliant in their passion.

"Right now, they're running wild." Trask nodded. "We did a lot of damage, wrecked three years' worth of what they had been doing here. Now it looks like they've gone on the run, and they don't care what havoc they leave behind them. Also, we mightn't have been as successful as we thought . . ."

"What have they done?" Harry growled now. "What corruption have they spilled here?"

And Trask told him about Szwart—his cavern under London, his fungus garden, the spores that he might have sent drifting up into the city's night air.

Then Harry groaned and his neon outlines wavered, becoming even more indistinct before slowly firming up again. And Trask commanded his people, "Hold on to him, all of you!"

"Hold on, yes." Harry nodded. "Other times and places call. Other worlds and other hosts. So you had better ask your questions, Ben, while I'm still here to answer them."

"Spores," Trask said. "What do you know of them?"

"I fell victim to spores," said Harry. "Faethor Ferenczy's spores. He'd been dead a long time but it made no difference. I made the mistake of thinking I could simply talk to him because he was dead and gone, so how could he possibly harm me? Also, I slept where his fats had rendered down in a fire. But his metamorphic filth was still there, lying dormant in the ground. His vampire essence 'knew' I was there; it put up black toadstools; I breathed their spores, and the rest you know. You were one of the last to see me in your world. You, Zek, and poor Penny."

This was the closest the ex-Necroscope had come to reality, to making real sense, and Trask believed he knew why. Dispersed throughout all the Universes of Light, still his basic instinct was to do what he'd done in life. And in life he couldn't abide the thought of vampires. This was what had taken him to Jake in the first place—a task left unfinished in life—and Jake's vendetta with Luigi Castellano had provided Harry with an opportunity to put things right. The scarlet vampire lifelines which he'd seen merging with Jake's blue human threads in future time—which was now recent-past time—had been those of Castellano and his gang, and despite that Harry hadn't remembered the lost years, when he'd destroyed Castellano's vampire forebears at Le Manse Madonie, still he'd sensed something of the continuity of their evil.

But vampires are vampires, and they all leave the same crimson trails in Möbius time. The ex-Necroscope had confused Luigi Castellano's trail with Malinari's, Vavara's, and

Szwart's, for which reason he had taken Jake to visit Korath-once-Mindsthrall where Malinari had murdered him . . .

These thoughts were only semioriginal to Trask—who previously hadn't been privy to all the details—but as he thought back on what he did know, so Harry "read" his mind and was able to fill in the blank spaces. And:

"My lost years!" he said. "And so at last all is explained. In my lifetime it would have destroyed me, and the teeming dead knew it. So they protected me, for my mind's sake. However mistakenly, it seems they've gone on protecting me . . ."

As he finished speaking he wavered again, rapidly fading to a neon mist. And Trask cried, "For God's sake keep him here! We may not be able to get him back!"

And as his espers concentrated on Harry, so he once again firmed up. "Spores!" Trask gasped then. "We need to know about them."

"What more can I tell you?" Harry shrugged, but not negligently.

"After you were infected," Trask pressed him. "Did you fall asleep? Did you sleep for any length of time? For that seems to be what's happening here. We have these . . . sleepers. Also, did you know you were infected? Were you aware, and did you try to protect yourself from that time forward as a vampire?"

"It's all so very hard to recall," said Harry. "This world, this life, this existence . . . one out of many. But did I sleep? I seem to remember that I was *made* to sleep, drugged. It didn't last. Protect myself? I remember feeling threatened, certainly. I suppose I must have protected myself, but since I was preparing to go up against Janos, another Ferenczy, surely that was only natural."

"I meant," said Trask, "did you try to conceal yourself—to hide what you'd become—from men?"

"Not to any great extent." Harry shook his head. "But then, how might I conceal myself from E-Branch? From David Chung? No way! From poor Darcy Clarke's telepathy? Impossible! My vampire signature was written in my mindsmog. But Darcy . . . I did protect myself from him, yes. How could I know it would lead to his death?"

"You see—" said Trask, becoming frustrated now, "I need to know—is there any way to *detect* a spore's infection? I mean, in the early stages, are there any positive symptoms? How can I tell if a man has breathed mutative vampire spores and is commencing to change? And how long does that change take? In short, how much time do we have?"

"A lot of questions," said Harry, wispy again, "and I don't have any answers, not as gospel. I can speak only from personal experience."

"Then that must suffice," said Trask. "How was it for you? How long after breathing Faethor's spores did you know for certain that . . . that you were in trouble?"

"Just a few days," said Harry. "But without the Möbius Continuum I might not have suspected it for quite a while. In fact the actual . . . *condition* came on quite slowly. Its 'symptoms,' as you call them—my love of the night, a liking for raw meat, and the redness in my eyes—were things that came later. And as you know, Ben, I fought them."

"For us," said Trask.

"And for myself," said Harry. "For if I'd submitted, then I wouldn't be here, or there, or anywhere now. No, for you would have seen to that."

"But you won," said Trask. "We all saw it, how you escaped into the myriad Universes of Light."

"I wondered if you would," said Harry. "I tried my hardest to show you. And you—all of you, your talents—did the rest. But the Continuum was my medium, and in the end it was my saviour, too. But escaped? No, I died . . . and went on."

"The Möbius Continuum," said Trask, returning to what Harry had said earlier. "You said that it gave you your first indication of your condition. How, exactly?"

"When I disposed of Faethor along the future-time streams," Harry answered, "I stood at the threshold of a future-time door and watched my blue life-thread unwinding out of me. But it was tinged with red. There was that of the vampire in me . . . and it was growing!"

Trask grasped the concept immediately, grasped the truth of it, and said, "Jake has access to the Continuum!"

"Of course," said Harry, looking puzzled, "for I gave it to him. In your world, your now, Jake *is* the Necroscope."

"But just like you, in your time," Trask continued, "he may have pushed it too far, come too close . . ."

"I see," said Harry, slowly. "And now you would like him to test himself, by following his thread into the future and checking that its colour stays true. But if Jake is in fact infected . . . do you think that's wise? And in any case, it may be pointless."

"How so?"

"Because Korath is in him, at the moment suppressed— as is Jake himself—by my presence. Let me explain. Before I got rid of Faethor my life-thread was tinged red. We both supposed this was his fault: that being a part of me, his presence was tangible, made visible, in Möbius space-time. But I tricked him into leaving my mind, and when he left erected impenetrable shields. Still he clung to me, but I dislodged him and sent him into the loneliest future any creature has ever known. But while Faethor was gone, my thread was still tinged red. I suppose it had been his plot to usurp me entirely; which is possibly Korath's plot, too, this time with Jake as the vessel."

"So if Jake's lifeline is red," said Trask, "that's because of Korath?"

"You won't know for sure until he gets rid of Korath," said Harry. "But in any case, your advice to Jake should be to avoid trying to read the future."

At which Ian Goodly said, "As you avoided me?" He sounded a little hurt.

"The future is a devious thing," said Harry, turning now to the precog. "Oh, I know that your talent has often stood you in good stead, but you of all men must surely be aware that it can also let you down. I wasn't so much avoiding you, Ian, as finding you hard to read. In many ways your mind is much like mine: it won't stay fixed in one time."

"I can't help what I am," said Goodly.

"Nor should you apologize for it," the other answered. "But as for myself: I was wary of the future. I only rarely followed future time-streams, and then not to the end. And as it happens this was a wise precaution, because if I'd known the end of it, I might very well have ended it myself, and much sooner."

"You would have saved yourself a lot of pain," said Goodly, believing that he understood.

"And saved the pain of others," said Harry. "Having me as a friend was a dangerous business."

The apparition's neon outline was wavering again, his blue-neon filaments fading. Trask cautioned the others to leave the questioning to him, urged them to concentrate instead on keeping the ex-Necroscope's revenant focussed in the here and now, and returned anxiously to his previous theme:

"Harry, you said we can't be sure of Jake—whether or not he's contaminated—until he gets rid of Korath. Is that possible? I mean, *how* can Jake rid himself of this monster? And if he can't, could you perhaps do it for him?"

And beside him, Trask heard Liz's fervent prayer, "Oh yes! God, yes! Please let it be so."

Harry's neon glow was an intermittent pulse now. Like some failing light source he came and went. And similarly his telepathic voice in their minds, fading and strengthening moment by moment but never coming back to its full strength. The lure of this space-time was weakening, and likewise the team's hold on him. And as he retreated from them psychically, so their needs retreated from him; his answers took longer, and his responses became more vague.

"Listen everyone!" Trask snapped. "You have to concentrate as never before, else all our efforts go for nothing. *Keep him here!*" And then, to the fading image: "Harry? Can you hear me? Can you answer me?"

"Harry?" said the other queryingly, like a faint echo from far away. "You want to speak to Harry? But there are—or

190

have been, or will be—a great many Harrys. Which one is it you're looking for?"

"It's *you* we need!" Trask cried.

"But I'm in so many, and so many are in me," said the apparition. "So take your pick. Is it the one you see, or—"

And the boy was back, elbow on knee, chin in hand, strange eyes staring into some ill-defined distance. "—This one?" he said in his boy's voice, which Trask was gratified to note was a little stronger now. "Or maybe one of these?" Harry said, in a barely remembered voice, as he metamorphosed into a startled-looking Alec Kyle, a previous Head of Branch. His guises—his incarnations or host bodies in however many worlds and times—came and went in rapid procession:

A brawny black-haired Szgany youth with strangely familiar features . . . an old, white-haired mage . . . a baby in a crib in a garret room with a sloping ceiling . . . a gaunt, crimson-eyed spectre of a man in mummy wrappings . . . a Thing with tentacles and a naked, throbbing three-lobed brain . . . a furry, wolflike creature with triangular eyes, whose hands were those of a man . . . a burned, smoking figure in the shape of a crucifix, tumbling endlessly, head over heels in darkness. Until finally—

"—Or perhaps this one?" Harry grunted, in the obscene but far stronger, sardonic tones of the Wamphyri! And there he sat as Trask had last seen him in the flesh, the monstrous Vampire Lord that Harry had been before departing Earth for Starside.

For comparison Jake Cutter's central outline, the shape of a full-grown man, was like that of a child, a waif, within the thing's neon framework. Harry (the awakened, vampire Harry, as once was) was wearing an entirely ordinary suit of ill-fitting clothes which seemed at least two sizes too small for him, and his upper torso sprouted massively from the trousers. Framed by a bulging jacket which was held together at the front (barely) by one straining button, the wedge-shaped bulk of his rib cage was hugely muscular. His open-necked shirt had burst open at the front, revealing the ripple of muscle-sheathed ribs and the powerful depth of his chest; the shirt's collar stuck up from his jacket like a crumpled frill, made insubstantial against the corded pillar of his leaden neck. His flesh (for all that he was immaterial, a hologram) gleamed a sweaty grey-blue, while his face—

—Was the absolute embodiment of a waking nightmare!

Harry looked at Trask through halogen, Halloween eyes that seemed to drip sulphur, and smiled. At least in the alien world of Sunside/Starside—especially Starside—it might be called a smile. But here on Earth, in London, at E-Branch HQ, it was a writhing of thin scarlet lips, a flattening of convolute snout, a slow gape of mantrap jaws.

That face . . . that mouth . . . that crimson cavern of jagged teeth, like shards of white, broken glass! And:

"No," Trask croaked from a suddenly dry throat. "No, Harry, we don't need that one. Never that one!"

"Good God Almighty!" Liz gasped from beside Trask, physically repelled by the sight of the thing in the chair. Her hand jerked out of Trask's grasp as she backed away, and the apparition began to fade faster yet, guttering like a spent candle.

But behind Trask and Liz the door to Harry's Room had just that moment opened, and now a sixth figure joined the five. It was Lardis Lidesci, and filling the gap between Trask and Liz, he grabbed up their hands and growled, "I felt called here, by my seer's blood. It told me *he* was here, Harry Hell-lander!"

And the three-dimensional neon hologram at once firmed up; the vampire Harry morphed back into the twenty-year-old Harry; his hollow eyes fixed themselves on Lardis, and he said, "It's been a long, long time, old chieftain."

And Trask breathed a sigh of relief. The image was as firm as ever, and perhaps more so. Reinforced by Lardis's presence, it was proof indeed of a seer ancestor's blood, still coursing in the Old Lidesci's veins. And Lardis, no stranger to strange things, knew what he was doing here; the fact that this apparition had spoken to him hadn't thrown him at all.

"Still you come and go in that weird way of yours," the old man grunted, nodding his head. "But weirder far now . . . because I saw you die at the Gate on Starside! You, Karen, and The Dweller. Along with Shaithis and Shaitan and all that was theirs."

"True," said Harry. "But death isn't like that, and I have gone on."

"Gone on, *and* gone into!" said Lardis. "And is this really you here and now, gone into Jake? You did me and mine no harm, Harry Hell-lander, not even at your worst, and I can't believe that you're seeking to usurp this poor lad."

"Nothing of the sort!" said Harry. "For I was called here, even as you have been called. That of me which is now in Jake, it's for the good, or so I'm given to hope. And this image you see is just a facet, and transient." And then to Trask, "But I can't stay here indefinitely. You asked me something, Ben, and I may have the answer."

And eagerly now Trask said, "The answer to Jake's problem? How he might expel this Korath?"

The other shook his immaterial head. "There's no way he can do that, not while Korath clings like a leech to his inner mind. It was the same for me: I couldn't dislodge Faethor Ferenczy. I had to trick him out into the open and then keep him out. But I did manage to shut him down. I blanketed him, trapped him in an empty room in the manse of my mind, and so excluded him from my affairs."

"You could do this at will?" Trask licked his dry lips.

And Harry nodded. "The mind has unsuspected mechanisms for which it has no use. Like the appendix they're mainly obsolete, redundant. Or perhaps they're as yet undeveloped? Anyway, while I can't say whether they're atavistic or futuristic, in certain psychically talented people such as you and your agents they're very strong. You call them shields, and Jake Cutter's shielding mechanisms have enormous potential. Despite that I was drawn to him—that he was to be my successor, as it were—his shields were so strong that for a while they defied even me. Jake knew instinctively how to use his shields externally, to keep telepaths and other psychics at bay, but there's at least one more trick that he hasn't mastered. Perhaps I could show him how to turn his shields inwards."

"To isolate the thing within him?" Freakish as the concept was, still Trask managed to grasp it.

"Precisely," said Harry. "It's the same principle that lets us switch off unpleasant or traumatic memories, which after all have origin in our minds. It's just that the switch needs turning up a little, or tuning to a higher degree."

And Liz broke in, "Can you really do that?"

"I can try," Harry told her.

"Which might *confine* Korath," said Trask, "but it won't get rid of him."

Harry nodded. "It can only be done step by step. But assuming that Jake *does* find a way to expel Korath, there's another, even finer mechanism he might employ. Again a kind of shielding is involved—but shielding carried to the nth degree! And even though Korath has managed to gain access previously, he'd never get in again." Harry paused to look at Trask expectantly. And:

"I think I may have seen something of this mechanism—this talent—at work," said Trask, narrowing his eyes thoughtfully.

"And so you should," said Harry. "Upon a time, in E-Branch, there was just such a man. By virtue of his 'talent'—the fact that no one could get at him—he was even the Head of Branch, albeit briefly. But he was a traitor, a double agent whose actions gave him away, and you caught him before he could kill me. I think you remember him well enough, Ben."

"Norman Harold Wellesley," said Trask. "A psychic blank. He couldn't be read, couldn't be located . . . he was quite literally a zero in the psychic aether!"

"The same," said Harry. "Well, when he was dead he tried to make amends for his past misdeeds by offering me this metaphysical defence mechanism. I accepted it, and in my turn now offer it to Jake, to use at will. Except—"

"—Now please, Harry," Liz cut in, her anxious grip tightening on Trask's and Lardis's hands. "Don't make conditions, but if you can do these things, *please* do them now!"

"—Except," Harry went on, "if he is in fact infected—"

"—Then it will make him stronger still," said Trask, his face suddenly gaunt and ashen.

At which everyone looked at him. For this was his decision. And for good or bad, Ben Trask had never been afraid of making decisions . . .

12
Starside—a Wolf's-Eye View

TRASK LOOKED RIGHT BACK AT HIS AGENTS, especially at Liz, and said, "I know that in the end it's my decision, and that it's now or never. But now *as* never before I need your input, each of you in turn, and as quickly as possible. But remember this: if we let Harry do this, and if Jake is . . . *other* than he appears to be, then Baron Frankenstein will have been a veritable saint compared to us! What we'll be making might well be indestructible. Jake is the Necroscope, yes, but what if he's a vampire, too, or even Wamphyri? Immune to our talents—invisible behind Norman Wellesley's shields—we'd never be able to read or locate him. And he knows almost everything there is to know about us. You really do need to consider that . . ." He paused to let it sink in, and finished off: "That's it, enough said. Now we have to get done with this. So starting with Liz we'll work right to left. What's it to be, people?"

And almost before he'd finished Liz was speaking. "Jake is Jake," she gasped. "He isn't anything else. No one knows Jake's mind like me, and if there was something wrong with him—other than this Korath—then I'm sure I would know it. Also, this is Jake's last chance. Korath knows his mind's mechanisms and from now on, when Harry's finished and gone from here, he'll be able to control him. There's only one way to fight Korath: by taking those controls away from him, giving Jake the power to lock him away, to exclude him from his thoughts and actions. If we don't we'll have lost our greatest weapon. And if that's the case . . . if that's the case . . ."

She was almost sobbing now, and on her left the precog took over from her. "We'll be taking a chance," he said, "but it's a chance we have to take." And, enigmatic as ever, "Always remember this: whatever we say or do, the future is laid out for us. What will be has been."

Millie spoke up. "I'm with Liz, and anyway we've no choice. If we don't do it Korath will have Jake, and then . . . then we'd have to kill him. Don't misunderstand me; Jake saved my life in Szwart's hideous garden under London; he's saved all our lives, but still there's no escaping the facts. Yes, we'd *have* to kill him, for with Korath in command it would be just like Ben said: Jake would be— if not truly, then virtually—a vampire with the incredible powers of a Necroscope, and access to the Möbius Continuum. So I vote we ask Harry to do whatever needs doing."

It passed to Chung, who said, "From the moment Jake came to us I felt that the Necroscope was back. I mean *the* Necroscope—this one apparently sitting here—the one who held us together through some of our darkest years. In Jake there was nothing of darkness. Rebelliousness, yes, but then he had a mission of his own. How I see it: if we had left him out of things he wouldn't be in this mess now. And God knows we owe him. I mean, Millie's right, we'd all be dead without him! So let Harry do his thing. I'm with Liz."

And then it was Trask's turn. "So it's fairly obvious," he said, "that even if I was against it I'd be outvoted. Not only that, but as a team we'd be finished. A classic case of 'united we stand,' and all that. But in fact I'm for it. Just listening to you people—listening to your hearts speaking way over your heads—reminded me that this isn't the first time I've had to make a choice like this . . ." He looked pointedly at Harry's neon image, and Harry replied:

"The last time it was me, right, Ben? And you took a chance with me. Well, maybe your luck is holding. As for Jake . . . consider it done. All it took was a tweak here and there."

"Consider it done?" Liz repeated him. "You mean—?"

"—I cornered Korath in an empty room, and locked him in," said Harry. "And if sometime in the future Jake can find a way to expel him, then he'll be able to lock him *out*—permanently. But that's a maybe, for no one can second-guess the future."

Then his eyes went to Lardis Lidesci, and he said:

"Old warrior, these people are in your debt. Without you I might have drifted free of my focus and slipped away. Moreover, I'm personally in your debt. Following the battle at The Dweller's garden, my son and I relied greatly on your strength, you and your Travellers. Also, it was your people who took care of me when my son . . . after my powers . . . when they failed me. It seems to me I owe you, and I sense a great need in you. A need to know. I drew on your strength, now you can draw on mine."

Lardis nodded and said, "My thanks, Harry Hell-lander, but there are needs and there are needs. There's a seer ancestor's blood in me, that's true, but it can't let me see into another world. You spoke of the battle at The Dweller's garden. All of us here have seen some battles since then. I suspect that even now there's a war going on in Sunside/Starside. Your son—but this time a son you never met—is fighting it. Or maybe it's too late, over and done, and you never will get to meet him."

"A son of mine?" said Harry. "Oh, I've sensed him, sensed *them,* upon a time or times. But if I'm in him then he's in me, and not so distant after all. How long since you saw him, this son of mine?"

"Three long years," said Lardis. "Since the day he left me here. I can't think other than he's dead and the war lost."

"One of them is dead," said Harry. "The dark one. I sensed his departure. But the other? Ah, no. He lives on."

"Nathan?" Lardis gasped. "Alive? But . . . how do you know?"

"I've been in many," said Harry once again, "and there are many in me. Do you want to know how it's been these three long years, in Sunside/Starside?"

Lardis's jaw fell open. "Do I want to—?" he gasped. "Only tell me what I must do!"

"Sit down," said Harry. "All of you, on the floor. Hold me here in your minds, and concentrate. And if there's that of me in Sunside/Starside—some child of me or mine—and if it can speak, I'll find it and you shall hear it."

And as they all sat down, he looked from face to face with his hollow hologram eyes, and said, "Are you ready now? Yes, I see that you are. Good, for now we go."

Which was all the warning they had before the darkness set in. Then, after seconds or aeons of searching:

Voices . . .

At first faint and far distant, but gradually swelling out of the darkness, and the darkness itself brightening to a grey opacity.

A gruff man's voice, speaking Szgany, but the translation was instantaneous through Harry's telepathy. "Misha, lass, you need sleep. You're so thin and weary that if he ever comes out of this he won't recognize you anyway. Do you see that look in his eyes? No you don't, do you? Those strange eyes of his: you could fall into them forever. But there isn't *any* look in them any longer! They're just vacant. It was a hell of a hard knock on the head he took; it's still a wonder to me it didn't split his skull and let his brains out! Since when we've done all we can for him, until there's nothing left. Now it's up to him."

"Six months," a female voice answered (but in fact it said "Twenty-five sunups"). "Six months ago, and the war against Starside finally won . . . and then this had to happen. For all that Nathan is and all that he's done, why is the world so cruel to him? Can you answer me that, Andrei Romani?"

"Maybe that's the way of it with his kind," said the other. "His father, and his brothers—Nestor and The Dweller—they didn't have much luck, either. A necromancer the one, and Necroscopes the others, none of them came to a good end. It's such a terrible thing, to be able to talk to the dead and conjure them from their graves. Now he talks to no one and conjures nothing. Oh, he walks, however dazedly, eats, sleeps, and perhaps dreams. But it's you who clothes him each morning, who walks him, feeds him, and tends his every need. And you're the one who's paying for it."

"Let her be, Andrei," said a second female voice (which Ben Trask and his people recognized at once). "It isn't intentional, I know, but you're just a blunt man and your words are hurtful. Can't you see her pain?"

"I talk this way because I'm *tired* of seeing her pain!" the male voice answered. "There are plenty of others, including myself, who would share her duties, but Misha won't let them. She does it all herself."

"Oh, and is that so strange?" said the voice of Anna Marie English, ecopath. "And if you were in Nathan's shoes, wouldn't I do the same? He's her husband and she loves him."

"But all to no avail," the other protested. "Does he hear, see, know anything at all that's going on about him? It's been six months now. He makes so little progress, and Misha suffers. Me, I'm only a 'blunt man' if you say so, but I'd gladly share her suffering. And plenty of others like me. But . . . what can I do?"

"The best thing you can do is leave them alone," said Anna Marie. "Misha can cope, and if or when she can't I'll be here."

"*Huh!*" Andrei snorted. "See what's become of the clan Lidesci now. With Lardis away a Romani is chief, but who will give heed to a chief whose own wife turns a deaf ear, eh? And a wife of alien spheres at that!" His words might sound severe, but it was just his Szgany gruffness. "Well then, so be it. I'll leave you women to it. But the moment you see any sign of improvement in the lad—any sign at all—I want to know about it. Meanwhile I've a town to rebuild, else when Lardis gets back I'm in big trouble!"

That last was as Szgany as a man could get—like "a bit of old Irish" in Anna's world—but it was meant as encouragement. For with the Necroscope in this twilight state, an almost total amnesiac, the Old Lidesci never would be back. In speaking that way Andrei had put the cart before the shad, which was just his way of saying that all things were possible. Anna Marie English understood this well enough, and after he had gone she said:

"Pay no mind to my husband. He means no harm. Why, he loves Nathan as much as Lardis himself! He's a worrier, that's all."

"Oh, I know that," said Misha. "But between the two of us, Andrei's not alone in his worrying. I mean, this is my Nathan, and look at him. Does he hear anything, do you think? And does he see anything? I mean *really* see anything? He's not blind, I know that, because he steps aside if things are in his way. Or is it merely instinct that keeps him from harming himself like that? Deaf, dumb, and oblivious, what's to become of him, Anna Marie?"

"He's to get better, that's all," said the other. "And now that the war is over and the vampires defeated, destroyed, you needn't fear that Nathan will come to harm during his recuperation. If we had access to my world, to its physicians . . . but no, that's ridiculous, a forlorn hope. Nathan *was* our access!"

The opacity had cleared a little and was comparable now to a heavy, swirling fog. In the fog, two roughly female outlines were visible, one of which was seated while the other moved to and fro, wringing its hands. Trask and his team had determined from the conversation that they viewed the scene from Nathan's point of view and through his eyes. Likewise, they supposed he must be hearing what was said, for *they* could hear it. But did it make sense to him? Did he understand it? The voices of Anna and Misha seemed deadly monotonous, as leaden as the foggy medium that carried them; Nathan might just as easily be tuned in to some strange form of Muzak as speech. And when the shrouded figures moved, his eyes scarcely followed them at all.

And now Harry spoke, but only to Trask and his people. For this was some fantastic probe that he was using—a combination of all their talents—while the "real" Harry was here at E-Branch HQ. "I understand how they must be feeling," he said, "for his mind is a blank to me, too. It's completely run-down, out of order, its polarity reversed. If an intelligent, thinking mind might be compared to a dynamo, Nathan's has spun to a halt, been deactivated. I feel that I'm standing in a deserted house where nothing works, or at best in a rudimentary fashion. It's possible we might learn something else from the conversation between these caring women, but apart from that—"

"—Wait!" Lardis Lidesci growled.

"Oh?" said Harry.

"My seer's blood," said Lardis. "And this is my world that we're looking into. I sense . . . something coming!"

"I sense it, too," said Harry. "And I see it!"

They all saw it:

It entered the picture from a lighter patch of fluffy grey background, brushed against Misha's legs as she reached down a vague hand to fondle its ears, came to a halt central of their arc of viewing. Misted, triangular eyes gazed in what seemed a doglike concern, and a grey tongue lolled. And for a moment—if only a moment—the picture cleared up somewhat. It seemed Nathan "saw" this one in just a little more detail. Perhaps it was a form of recognition.

Lardis knew at once what—or who?—he was seeing, while Trask, Chung, and Goodly (all of whom had visited Sunside/Starside but were less familiar with the vampire world's creatures) took a moment longer. Then they remembered. But they would have known anyway, as soon as Misha said:

"So then, Blaze, you faithful one. You've come visiting us again, to follow your uncle's progress and sit with him awhile. But as for progress: alas, it's a slow, slow business. Not much to report, I'm afraid."

And Lardis breathed, "Blaze, a wolf, one of the leaders of Sunside-Starside's grey brotherhood. A wild thing come down out of the barrier mountains. Ah, but never such wolves as this one and his brothers—or his brother, as it turned out. There were three such upon a time, Blaze, Dock, and Grinner, thus named by Nathan. The Wamphyri took Dock with his stumpy tail. Those *bastards:* they had a craving for wolf-heart, livers, and tripes!"

And Trask said, "Nathan's 'nephews.' Still hard to credit—even though I was there and saw it for myself." And:

"My grandchildren," said Harry. "Wolves of the wild! Now I understand. The last time I saw my Earth-born son, he was more wolf than man. He was forgetting what he'd been and being what he'd become, and advised me to do the same. Burned by the sun, reduced massively, he saved himself by devolving to a creature such as the one which had converted him. Vampirized by a wolf, he became a wolf. That was . . . shortly before I died."

"He died, too," said Lardis, "but not before he mated with a great white she-wolf. The three brothers—Nathan's nephews, your grandchildren—came out of her. But as Nathan once told me, their minds were far in advance of wolf-minds. Mentalists, they talked to Nathan and each other over great distances. And Necroscopes, they could even commune with their human grandma, Brenda, calling her the Gentle One Under the Stones . . ." Lardis paused abruptly, then went on apologetically, "But forgive me, Harry. I was forgetting that—"

"—That you were taking me back too far," said Harry, "to times and places where I've no desire to go. No, for my death released me from all of that." And then, musingly, and changing the subject: "So then, this is a child of my child."

"Indeed," said Lardis. "For you are in many, even as many are in you."

"Lardis," said Harry, "you are a very wise old man. And of course something of me must be in Blaze, too. Moreover, if anyone knows what's been happening in Sunside/Starside, and if we accept that a wolf's viewpoint will probably be very different . . . then who better to tell the story?"

Eh? (One sharp-tipped ear went up, feral eyes opened wider, and the mist-wreathed outline of a wolf head inclined itself in what could only be an attitude of rapt attention.) And: *Is that you in there, uncle?* (The thought was as clear as crystal!) *Did something stir? Are you returned to us from the darkness?*

"He senses me," said Harry. "And he has shields of his own, which he raises just a little . . . a wolf's natural caution. But he's curious, too. Blood of my blood, he can't obstruct me. Nor would he want to, if he knew my purpose."

Who is it? Blaze whined and retreated a little, his muzzle writhing back from wetly gleaming teeth, causing Misha to ask:

"Why, what is it, old friend?" But since she wasn't telepathic, Blaze couldn't answer her. And meanwhile:

"There," said Harry. "It's done!"

Like scenes in an experimental motion picture, moving from monochrome to colour, from viewpoint to viewpoint in the space of a few frames, the scene at once changed. But since this was no motion picture but remote viewing—and because the change had been unexpected and abrupt—its effect was dizzying!

Suddenly Trask and the others found themselves looking *up* at Nathan—at Nathan himself—seated on a woven chair in a shaft of late sunlight from the open door of a log cabin. Anna Marie's shadow fell partly on his pale, vacant face, and Misha moved to kneel at his side, frowning as she reached out a hand towards . . . towards them? Towards Trask and his agents?

No, of course not. She reached out her hand towards Blaze!

For they were seeing her, seeing Misha, Nathan, the entire picture now, in sharp, colourful definition. Seeing it through the eyes of a wolf! As that fact dawned, so Blaze became simultaneously aware of a stranger, an intruder, someone other than his brother Grinner or his uncle Nathan, in his mind.

At which he was galvanized, and everything devolved into a wild panic flight!

The wolf's speed was astonishing as he raced through the Szgany township called Settlement. Even from a wolf's-eye view, low to the ground—and despite that the place showed signs of recent battle or of preparation for siege, with hurling engines everywhere on top of the massive timbered perimeter walls, and fortified rocket emplacements in strategic areas where sections of the wall could be moved aside on rollers, and imitation Wamphyri warriors over staked fire-pits—still Trask, Goodly, Chung, and especially Lardis remembered and recognized it. Upon a time they had fought what they'd thought was the final battle here.

Blaze went through Settlement and out through the west gate in a headlong rush, setting all of the township's domestic dogs barking and snarling as he passed by (though not a one ventured to pursue him). It was only after he'd reached the forest's rim, where the trees gave way to rocky ground and the foothills rose umber in the early evening light, that he eased off. For a wolf of Blaze's years the run had been a great effort, but the longevity and strength of Sunside's grey brothers was legendary.

By the time Blaze paused, however, even his heart was hammering and his four limbs trembling, while the stiffened ruff of fur along his spine had only just subsided a very little. Still very nervous, he came to a halt in a patch of gorse, turned and looked back at Settlement, then settled down on his haunches to catch his breath.

Wisely, Harry had waited till then before trying to talk to this extraordinary wolf again. And:

"Don't run, Blaze," he said, as calmly as possible. "For in any case you can't outrun me. But tell me: why do you fear your own kith and kin?"

Blaze was up on his legs again in a moment, his teeth bared and the hair along his spine all spiky. But this time he didn't run. *My own kith and kin?* he growled. *Is that what I'm supposed to think? You were in my uncle Nathan, yes, but you're not him. Some Lord of vampires, perhaps, who has usurped him? Whichever, you're neither kith nor kin to me, so begone!*

"Old wolf," said Harry, "you can't run forever, and I'm not your enemy but a friend. Indeed, I'm a great deal more than just a friend. And anyway, didn't I hear the woman called Anna Marie say that the vampires are no more?"

Aye, and I've heard that *one before!* Blaze snarled. And for all that no one was there, he showed even more of his teeth. *So now leave me be, for my mind is my own and private.* He tried to raise his shields but Harry's probe was stronger.

"Nathan is my son," said Harry then. "As was Nestor. As was The Dweller, who sired you. And as for the Gentle One Under the Stones—do you still converse with her?—she was my wife, my mate, your grandmother."

For long moments then there was confusion and mental agitation, then disbelief. Until finally Blaze barked his denial. *It is of old legend among the grey brotherhood that my father, The Dweller, died fighting the Wamphyri at the Starside Gate at the time of the Great White Light ... likewise* his *father with him! No, you're not my grandfather. What, you? The One called Harry?* (He shook his wolf head.) *Not so, for his ashes are long since vanished in the past, all blown away on Starside's winds.*

"And so they were," said Harry. "My ashes, certainly, vanished into the past. But not my mind. Can't you see we're of a kind? Can't you tell we're of one blood? Who else may speak out of the beyond—or into it—but a Necroscope? I *am* your grandfather."

And now Blaze knew it was so. Whining low in his throat, he said, *I feel it now: not the lying, thought-thief probe of some rabid vampire, but deadspeak! You* are *a spirit, it's true, gone from us into another place. Nor do you speak falsely, for while we never met before, still your thoughts are ... familiar?*

"We're of one blood," said Harry again.

But . . . what do you here? (Somewhat easier in his mind now, but still puzzled, Blaze had lain down again.)

"The Szgany have friends in what was once my world," Harry told him, "and they have been worried about things here in Sunside/Starside." He showed Blaze images of Trask and the others.

I know them! The wolf's ears sprang alert. *The Old Lidesci, aye. And some of the others, too: olden allies against the Wamphyri. I even know something of their strange world, as told to me by my brother, Grinner, who ventured there with my uncle.*

"And then there's that, too," said Harry. "Your uncle Nathan's problem. If I can, I would like to help him."

Do you think you can? (A sigh of relief, which sounded as a cough or choked-back bark.) *We were cubs together, and while he is my uncle he is also my friend.*

"His mind is all askew," said Harry. "It has taken a knock, and the pictures—all memories, knowledge—have slipped from view. Except . . . I thought that perhaps he recognized you, however vaguely. Other than that, your uncle is a blank space that needs filling in. But I'm not without certain skills. If you'll walk us back to that township, back to Nathan, maybe I can help him. And along the way you could tell us how it's been with the war and all. That way all our needs might be served."

Blaze stood up, shook himself down, and said, *Huh! The tame dogs back there saw me run. They may have thought I was running from them, and some even dared to mock me. But never fear, I'll snarl at them as we pass, to remind them who they deal with!*

"An excellent idea," said Harry. "Should curs come snapping at you, bite their tender noses. If their teeth cut your flesh, cut theirs deeper. An eye for an eye. I can see there's much of me in you!"

So it would seem, Blaze answered, inclining his head. *But I am not displeased . . . Grandfather? And now we must go. My uncle Nathan is in need of your "certain skills."*

* * *

In Harry's Room at E-Branch HQ, six psychically endowed agents sat in a ring around a seventh who was temporarily "possessed" by an eighth—the revenant of a man who had been arguably the greatest psychic talent ever—to "listen" to a tale told by a wolf in an alien world. In E-Branch (never a stranger to weird events) this was probably one of the weirdest of all.

"This, then, was the way of it," Blaze began, while ambling back towards Settlement a good half-mile away. "After a time—when the world turned back again and the Northstar shone on the boulder plains as before, when our silver mistress moon sped on high in her accustomed orbit and the waters of Starside's shining lake were all drained away—then the Wamphyri returned out of the far, forbidden north.

"As mange is to a wolf, so are the Wamphyri to Sunside/Starside, feeding on the goodness until everything dies. They waged war on the Szgany of Sunside, all settled now in towns, and war with Nathan's people, the Lidescis, who were the fiercest warriors of all. But this was when my uncle was well, and it proved to be a fatal mistake on their part.

"There were three of the olden Wamphyri, come back from the Icelands. At first they had been secretive in their recruiting, striking only at remote Traveller encampments, so that for long and long their presence went unnoticed. They took of Starside's trogs, too, for their labourers, and began rebuilding among the tumbled stacks of olden Starside.

"My uncle had been away visiting the Thyre for many sunups, and at first didn't know what transpired in Starside. He wasn't neglectful of his duty with the Szgany but had a 'sister' among the Thyre, called Atwei—not a true sister, as you are surely aware, Grandfather, but a sister of the heart and spirit—with whom he visited.

"Anyway, when he returned and found out what had happened, then Nathan moved entire tribes into the furnace deserts of the south. The greatest Traveller of all—moving in that unfathomable way of his, and travelling in a single instant to wherever he desired—he took hundreds of the Szgany to safety in Thyre territory, where the watering holes and underground colonies of the desert dwellers offered sanctuary. How may I state this for a fact? Because we were there, because my uncle made myself and my brother Grinner privy to all his works at that time, and because as once before the grey brotherhood sided with the Szgany against the Wamphyri, becoming Nathan's watchers in the heights of the barrier mountains.

"But the Szgany are proud, and this was not like the olden times when the Wamphyri were awesome conquerors and could not be defeated. No, for the Szgany had knowledge of alien things. My father, The Dweller, had brought weapons of great destruction into Sunside/Starside, and while he was long dead and gone, still his human brother, Nathan, had discovered the route back to your world, Grandfather, for more of the same.

"He went, bringing weapons he was given and others that he stole back into Sunside. And the Lidescis spread the secrets of black gunpowder, guns, and rockets among all the Szgany tribes, so that their men could stand and fight. For my uncle knew that hiding among the Thyre in their furnace desert colonies wasn't good enough. There were creatures other than men that the vampires could kill for their blood and flesh—the wild things of Sunside's forests and the barrier mountains . . . such as wolves, aye!—and Nathan couldn't possibly save all of them. Also, the Thyre were his friends and he would not place them in jeopardy, knowing that sooner or later the vampire Lords would seek them out. He would not have their blood on his paws . . .

"But let me move quickly forward, for I sense that you know most of these things that I have told you, that you've had this story from some other source. And anyway, what more is there to tell? Of how my uncle finally defeated the Wamphyri? And in his triumph, even as he celebrated, of the accident and injury that shook his mind from its orbit? Both of these things? Very well, they came about in this order:

"When first Nathan had found out about the resurgent Wamphyri, he had gone up against them on his own as one man—albeit a warrior with superior weapons. Unwilling to risk the lives of friends, he had ravaged among the vampires on lone forays along routes not of this world. But as they learned what he could do, so they began to lay traps for him, and then my uncle's hit-and-run guerilla tactics became ever more dangerous.

"By then the olden Wamphyri—the three from the Icelands—had long since fled his wrath (into the Starside Gate, according to some) leaving all they'd made behind them. And oh, they had made some cruel vampires and monsters out of men! Now these blood-lusting lieutenants and thralls vied among each other, to see who would be Lords in their turn. This had left them weaker than ever . . . though never weak in the human or wolf sense, you understand. No, for they were still terrible creatures.

"Anyway, my brother and I and other leaders of various wolf packs, we had seen these aspirant Lords fighting one another on the boulder plains; we had witnessed their skirmishes and small but vicious bloodwars in the ruins of shattered aeries. And all such had been reported to Nathan, who was then prompted to make a plan. It was time, he said, to end this thing and finish them off for good in one last surprise attack, one final battle—to be fought on their own ground!

"How bold! To confront the vampires of Starside in Starside itself! Impossible for the Szgany on their own, too terrible to consider. The distances involved, and movement in the open over a pitiless boulder wastelend, and the mindless monsters waiting there. Ah, but by use of Nathan's instantaneous mode of travel, by no means impossible . . .

"In the hour when the sun rises over the mountains to shine across the territory of the vampires, Nathan armed great bodies of men and 'moved' them to the mouth of the pass into Starside. Of course, the sun hangs low in Sunside's sky, so that when its rays sweep over the mountains they never touch Starside's floor. But even so, sunup to vampires

209

is as the darkest of dark nights in a wild unknown place to men, or a deadly sliding scree avalanche to a wolf: a very terrible thing to contemplate! Which is why they burrow in their holes when the sun is up, shutting out the light, sleeping and dreaming their horrid red dreams, leaving only their monstrous guardian creatures awake and watchful. But even they stick to the shadows of Starside's boulder mounds and crumbling ruins, shrinking from the sunlight as best possible. Of course they do, for they, too, are the stuff of vampires.

"So then, in that same hour when the sun turns the mountain peaks to gold, myself, Grinner, and other pack leaders had gone creeping out onto the barren boulder plains to locate the positions of the last of our enemies. And having found them, mind to mind with our uncle, we reported their numbers, whereabouts, and fortifications to him, fixing their coordinates in his mind. At last he could move on them. And he did!

"In his special way, transporting his teams of arsonists up close, he burned the warrior creatures when they were only half-awake, scorched the grounded flyers' membrane wings to immobilize them, brought the rest of his army forward into the battle area. And all done in a trice! Szgany mirrormen in the barrier mountains reflected sunlight down into the areas where they saw flames rising; others on the ground trapped these rays in mirrors of their own, turning them on the vampires as they rose up from sleep. Grenades and bullets cut them down; men moved among them with machetes and axes; even the most dire battle gauntlet was useless against scything metal shards and silver shot! Even Nathan was surprised at how quickly the last remaining monsters caved in.

"And for all of that long sunup the Szgany gathered up vampire debris and burned it on the boulder plains in the ruins of the old Wamphyri stacks, and the smoke and stink of their fires went up to the sky, so that when night came again even the ill-omened Northstar was partly obscured. But other than the smoke and the dying fires, nothing else moved in all Starside . . .

"It was over, and not a man of the Szgany—or wolf of the brotherhood—lost or even wounded in that final victory.

"Which makes Nathan's injury that much more poignant.

"It came during the celebrations in Settlement. The Lidescis built great bonfires in the foothills, to signal the utter destruction of the vampires, the end of their reign of terror. They danced, feasted, and sent off such rockets into the skies that they rivalled the light of our mistress moon!

"But alas, such explosive devices were crude things and by no means reliable, and one such which flew awry exploded close to Nathan. He was hurled down by the blast; his skull struck a rock; unconscious, he was taken to Misha's makeshift dwelling. And there he has stayed in the care of his mate . . .

"That was many sunups ago, even as many as the toes on two wolves, and then some, since when there has been small improvement. After a while he walked, but it seems that everything is an utter mystery to him. He remembers nothing, or so little it makes no difference. And when I've looked into his head, all I have seen is emptiness. Those baffling numbers which once were there . . . where are they now? And where the uncle I loved as a cub and love as a wolf full grown? If you can help us find him, Grandfather, all Sunside will be forever in your debt . . ."

Arriving back at Settlement, Blaze paused and composed himself, then advanced stiff-legged in through the west gate. The Szgany who saw paid him no special heed. A familiar of Nathan's, Blaze came and went as he saw fit. As for Settlement's tame dogs: the look in his yellow eyes warned them off, so that he had no need for snarling . . .

13
Skin Graft—
—Clay Pigeons and Red Herrings

MISHA WAS ON HER OWN NOW, AND AS BLAZE
paused whining at the door of her "house" she looked up,
saw him, and welcomed him in. "So you're back," she said,
smiling however wanly. "What was the big hurry? Did you
have a thorn in your paw or something? Such an undignified
exit!"

He understood her words—which rang in his mind as well
as in his ears—wagged his tail a very little, and made for
Nathan where he sat in his chair. And again the young ex-
Necroscope's deep yet vacant eyes seemed to focus, if only
for a moment, on the wolf, before they once more glazed
over.

And here he is, Grandfather, Harry's changeling descendant whined again, low in his throat. *He has no shields as
such, so you can be in without him even knowing.* Huh! *But
of course you can, for he "knows" nothing! Alas, you won't
find him at home.*

"I have been there," said Harry, "and I know you're right.
My son isn't home, his house has no furniture, and the fire
is out in the hearth. It is as if it were inhabited by some
blind ghost, which looks out now and then through the windows of his eyes, seeing nothing. Surely I can do no harm
there? The least I can do is bring a little atmosphere into the
place."

When you leave me for him, will you ever return? Blaze
had sensed that this "visit" was a singular, probably unique
event.

"I doubt it," said Harry. "This time I answered a call. But

212

there are many calls, and I have been too long . . . away?"

Too long away? said his changeling grandson, who in his way was wiser than most men. *I think I understand—and anyway, it isn't my place to ask from where. Grinner, who has seen strange far places, might know, and I must speak to him of it. But when or whenever you go, know that we shall wish you a long . . . continuance?*

"You know that I appreciate it," said Harry. "But even your brother Grinner hasn't been where I shall go. How long is time, eh? Where is any- or every-where, and how far is away?"

Farewell, then, said Blaze.

And Harry was gone from one to the other in a moment—

—Gone from that sharp wolf mind with its astonishing repertory of scents and sensations, back to the grey-misted place, the "empty house," called Nathan.

In there, in that deserted echo chamber of a place, with no one else to hear except the minds of his psychic explorer colleagues from Earth, Trask spoke once more to Harry:

"What will you try to do, and how will you go about it?"

"It's just an idea, that's all," said Harry. "But you know how a skin graft works?"

"Of course," said Trask. "A patch of skin is taken from an undamaged, healthy part of the body and planted on a burned or flensed area to facilitate new growth."

"Right," said Harry. "But perhaps it's a poor analogy after all. For where a body has suffered one hundred percent burns—"

"There's no hope," said Trask. "But in this case there must be *some* hope at least. I'm sure that on the two occasions we've witnessed, Nathan recognized Blaze if only momentarily."

"But still I can only do so much," said Harry. "I have only a short time left to me. Other places are luring me."

"Then get on with it," said Trask. "Do whatever you can for him, and it won't only be Sunside that's in your debt."

And Harry got on with it.

Not skin but memories. First of Blaze, reinforcing Nathan's picture of the wolf who was his nephew, then memories of people Nathan had known—people they'd both known—transmitted from Harry's memory banks into those blank spaces that were all that was left of his son's.

It was done at incredible speed; Harry played the part of a neurosurgeon working with a laser tool, but rather than slicing or splicing nerves he welded patches (pictures?) of memory back in place on the bare walls of Nathan's mind. Pictures of Misha, taken straight from what he'd seen of her through Blaze's eyes; pictures of Trask, Chung, Lardis, and Goodly, a group once well-known to Nathan; and again pictures of Blaze himself, faithful, lifelong friend. And finally, saved until last, Harry conjured a fantastic numbers vortex—a whirling wall of mutating symbols and cyphers, the metaphysical equations of Möbius mathematics—to spiral like background static in the otherwise aching void of Nathan's mind.

And then his time was up . . .

Something had happened to Nathan, and Misha didn't know what to make of it. She didn't know what to make of Blaze, either. Wolf he might be, but she knew of his relationship with Nathan—the fact that he *was* actually a relative—and also that he was far more than just a wolf of the wild. Right now he danced, skipped, and yipped. His tail was a frenzy of side-to-side movement; his ears were up, intent, turning this way and that but always ending up pointing at Nathan seated in his chair. Now he got up on his hind legs, forepaws on Nathan's knees, black-shining muzzle inches from Nathan's nose, and stared into Nathan's eyes.

It was Nathan's *eyes* now, yes, but a moment ago it had been his movements, actions. Actions of a sort, anyway. Galvanic and by no means definitely the product of intelligence or awareness, still he had moved; lifted an arm to point at something, opened his mouth as if to speak, but only gurgled. Not much of a miracle in itself, but in a man who had done absolutely nothing for a six-month without prompting and guidance, and made no attempt to utter a single word . . . it was astonishing!

So much so that for several seconds Misha hadn't been able to move. When it had started she had been standing in the open doorway, catching the last warm rays of the sun as it sank down oh-so-slowly beyond the forest's rim. Then, very clearly, she'd heard the stamp of a foot—but a *foot*, not a paw—and Blaze the only other creature present. Blaze . . . and Nathan. Startled, Misha had looked back into the dusky unlit room to see what was happening. And what she'd seen had frozen her rigid for several long seconds.

Nathan's twitching, his pointing, his meaningless mouthing; as if he heard something, saw something, *remembered* something!

And his wolf-nephew Blaze's frantic capering—reinforcing the fact of it—letting Misha know that she wasn't dreaming.

Then she'd cried out, rushed to his side, gone down on her knees alongside Blaze, both girl and wolf staring into Nathan's eyes. And light in there! No longer the emptiness of the spaces between the stars but the light of reason! It was there for the space of a breath, two, three, before slowly fading. But it *had* been there! And before it had vanished entirely, Nathan's mouth had jerked open again.

This time, while it had been something less than a whisper, Misha knew that he had spoken. Only one word—but a word that brought her to laughter and tears in the same moment: "Misha."

And just as she'd seemed to sense weird presences this last half-hour or so, so now she sensed Nathan's presence, *knew* that he was in there, and that this was the start of his recovery . . .

There was no sensation of movement—never had been through any of what Trask and his people had experienced—but still it was a shock to every system to find themselves back in Harry's Room at E-Branch HQ, from which they'd never in any case departed!

But all of them knew that Harry had gone now, even if, like Blaze, they didn't know where.

Jake, stirring in his chair and blinking—even as the six blinked back at him—was as a man just this moment woken from a dream: he frowned, looked alarmed or at least puzzled, seemed uncertain of his reality.

"A dream?" he said, as simply as that. "Was I dreaming?"

But as the six espers disengaged and stood up stiffly: "No, it wasn't," said Trask. "And *we* weren't! Can you remember it?" Looking at his watch, he saw that more than an hour had passed. No wonder his joints were creaking!

Jake thought about it, looked from face to face as the six crowded around him, and shook his head. "I feel . . . different," he said. "But other than that—" And he shrugged.

"And Korath?" said Liz. "Is he still there?"

"Oh, he's there," Jake answered sourly. "But contained . . ." Following which he sat bolt upright and his jaw dropped. "What in the . . . ? I mean, how in hell do I know that?"

"Instinct," said Trask. "Something you had without knowing you had it." And, using Harry's terminology: "There was a certain room in the manse of your mind which you'd never had cause to visit. Harry went there and found it dark, and switched the lights on, that's all." Then, nodding curtly to Chung and Goodly, "I think you can untie him now."

"Harry was here?" said Jake, as they set about to free him from the chair.

"He took you over." Liz nodded. "Quietened you down. If he hadn't . . . Korath would have been in charge. Maybe for good."

"Or for bad." Jake licked lips as dry as dust, then got to his feet, swayed a little and grabbed Liz for support. "*Whoah!*" he said. "I feel like I've just had three or four rides on the world's biggest, fastest, nastiest roller coaster!"

"Two worlds," Trask told him, sighing his relief. And then, hardening again: "But it's not over yet."

"Oh?" Jake looked at him.

Trask nodded. "Putting it bluntly, Harry or whatever it

was of him told us a thing or two that might help us to clear you—you and Millie both." This was the simple truth, which, despite sounding cold, came out naturally. Knowing the drawbacks of his talent, however, Trask glanced at Millie apologetically. But she understood, took his arm reassuringly, made no comment.

"So, what's next?" said Ian Goodly. And despite that it was a serious question, coming from him it lightened the moment considerably.

And with a wry chuckle Trask answered, "Now here's a thing. The precog wants to know what's next!"

At which footsteps sounded, and there came a sharp knock at the door. It was John Grieve, the Duty Officer.

"Two things," he said, when Trask opened the door. "Turchin has had a call come in on scrambled, and the Russians have just broken the news that he's gone missing from the Earth Year Conference. No accusations as yet, and the word 'defection' hasn't entered into it. He's just missing, that's all."

"Where's Turchin now?" Trask came out into the corridor.

"Waiting outside Ops," said Grieve. "The techs wouldn't let him in without your say-so." Turning to lead the way, he added, "Oh yes, and there's some kind of problem with the decoder. It seems that the codes Turchin gave us are incomplete."

Trask spoke to the rest of the team. "To work, people. And Jake—don't go experimenting or anything until we're all ready to sit in on it with you. You're on trust—but not so much on trust that you're to leave the HQ. I'm sure you understand. The thing in your head may be under control now, but I'd like to be absolutely sure it'll stay that way. Ian, you'll, er, keep Jake company. Millie, Liz will be looking after you. It seems only fair, and—and I mean—oh, what the *hell!* Personalities and other considerations aside, it's simply a matter of *bloody* security!" Not much for swearing nowadays, still on occasion Trask found it the only satisfactory solution.

Jake and Millie glanced at each other, and she said, "Don't worry about it, Ben. We both understand."

Sure that they did understand but hating the situation anyway, Trask let it go and followed Grieve to the Ops Room . . .

Turchin was waiting anxiously outside the closed door with one of the techs (a member of E-Branch's technical staff, not psychically talented but nevertheless highly valued), a prematurely bald young man called Jimmy Harvey. Apologetic but rock steady, and for all that he was only five feet five or six, Harvey was blocking the door, denying access to the bulky Russian Premier.

"It's okay, Jimmy," said Trask as he approached. "Let him take his telephone call. In fact we'll be going in with him."

"Sorry about that, boss," Harvey told Turchin, opening the door for him.

For a moment the Russian scowled at Jimmy, at his lush red sideburns and bushy eyebrows—which tried desperately hard to make up for his baldness—then brushed by him, saying, "Don't concern yourself, Mr. Harvey. We all have our duties to perform. Just as long as we haven't lost what could be a most important connection . . ." And then he was into the Ops Room.

But if Trask had expected Turchin to be taken aback by the complexity of the place—its communications equipment, computer consoles, decoding devices, variously coloured telephones, wall screens, charts, and other gadgets galore—then he was the one who was taken by surprise. The Russian Premier barely paused but headed straight for a desk where another tech held out a telephone to him. More than just a telephone, its function was to descramble messages onto a screen—*if* the correct code had been tapped into the keyboard on the phone's console.

"The code that Premier Turchin gave us is incomplete," the tech at the console explained. "The message on-screen repeats, but it's still a mishmash."

Turchin glanced at the screen—at its jumble of meaningless, repetitive characters scrolling in endless procession—nodded and shrugged his heavy shoulders. "Since I could not be absolutely certain how I would be received here," he explained, "it made sense to keep a little something back. Utterly ridiculous to give my all if I was getting nothing in return."

"Understood," said Trask, just a little peevishly. "But do you think you might like to complete the code now, before your man on the other end gets fed up and stops sending?"

"Simplicity itself," said Turchin, shooting his cuffs. "It only requires my initials for authentication."

"Russian language?" said Trask. "But this keyboard has the British alphabet."

"I'm aware of your several shortcomings," Turchin smiled a fox's smile at him, "and made allowance for them. In Moscow, my own decoder's keyboards are on-screen and carry fourteen languages . . . you simply tell the computer which one you're entering the code in. Enormously useful when, er, *assisting* foreign dignitaries? But as I said, I anticipated your—how should I put it?—embarrassment? The confirmation uses British letters."

Then he spoke into the combiphone. "Turchin here."

And a desk speaker answered in Russian, saying, "Voice recognition confirmed. Are you receiving?"

"I am now," Turchin answered, tapping keys *G* and *T*.

The jumble on the screen at once reassembled itself, and a printer purred into action and commenced delivering the message in English language hard copy. It took only a few seconds, and then, abruptly, the screen went blank and the printout ceased.

"Thank you, Yuri," said Turchin into the phone, in Russian. "And now you'd better get off before they trace you."

"I'm sure they already have," said the other. "Don't worry. By the time they get here I'll be long gone . . ." The phone made a beeping sound and the line went dead.

John Grieve, standing beside Trask, had translated for him, repeating Turchin's and his agent's conversation. He, too, fell silent as Trask put a hand on Turchin's shoulder, saying, "Just assuming someone back home was eavesdropping, you've slipped up and told them who to look for—this Yuri fellow."

"Indeed," said Turchin. " 'Assuming' that was his name—but it wasn't!" And raising his eyebrows quizzically, "You've never been a conventional field agent, have you, Ben? Meaning espionage as opposed to ESPionage? Ah, but for me, being a politician in the old USSR, that was experience enough!"

Trask grimaced and answered, "You live and you learn. And I thought the Wamphyri were devious!" Then he tore off the printout and read the message:

The clock strikes twelve. The pyramids point upwards. The bats are hanging upside down. The pigeons are in flight. The moon shines silver. The waters will find their own level. The dog bites . . .

Trask read it again, twice, looked at Turchin and said, "I hope this means something to you, because it's utter gibberish to me!"

"As it was designed to be," said the Premier. "But in fact it is very simple. Seven short statements, but only the middle one means anything. The birds it refers to are made of clay."

"Clay pigeons?" said Trask. "Targets."

"Precisely, which my people have lofted to be shot at by my enemies. But these pigeons might as easily be cured fishes."

"Red herrings?" Trask inclined his head enquiringly.

"Now we are getting somewhere," said the Premier. "Red, yes—like the colour of the old USSR, and also of today's greatest enemies, yours and mine both. Ah, but *my* enemies are human. And now I must beg of you to please forgive my cautious nature, but since we need to discuss this further, I would much prefer the privacy of your office."

"Everyone here is trustworthy," said Trask.

"I don't doubt it," Turchin answered. "But the more people who know our business, the more who could talk about it . . . er, if the right pressures were applied in the right places."

"But that's to anticipate falling into enemy hands," Trask said. "Which in turn is to assume action behind enemy lines."

"But wasn't that always the plan?" said Turchin. "So maybe it's happening a little earlier than expected, that's all. And now . . . can we talk in your office?"

And five minutes later, alone together in Trask's office:

"Talk," Trask grunted.

"Very well," said Turchin. "Before leaving the Earth Year Conference, I told one of my people back home to 'let it slip' that I had become privy to vital information concerning wealth beyond all dreams of avarice. This was done in accordance with a previous arrangement."

"But you really do have just such information," said Trask. "Sunside/Starside is one huge open-cast mother lode that makes El Dorado look like the backyard of the local poorhouse!"

"Indeed," Turchin nodded. "Which my powerful military enemies already know about thanks to Mikhail Suvorov. Or should we say they know he was on to *something,* if not its nature or its location."

"Yes," said Trask, impatiently. "I haven't forgotten these things. It was some kind of vindictive safety measure that Suvorov took before he went, er, adventuring beyond the Perchorsk Gate."

"Correct," said Turchin. "Perhaps he suspected I knew more about the parallel world than I was saying—in which case he was right—which was why he told several of his military cronies that if he didn't come back to cut them in, then they should come to *me* for the answers . . . the bastard!"

"Yes, I understand all of that," said Trask. "And now that they've started asking questions you've come to us rather than tell them about the Vampire World. All very laudable—but it doesn't explain why we're in here talking in private—

or why suddenly I have this feeling that I don't know everything."

"Everything I've told you so far is true," said Turchin.

"Right," said Trask. "But that doesn't mean you've told me everything."

"It's this damned talent of yours!" Turchin burst out, and threw his arms wide. "Since I couldn't lie to you—"

"—You didn't bother to tell the whole truth," said Trask.

"But I would have—believe me I would have," said Turchin, beginning to sweat now. "If only there had been time, I promise you I *would* have."

"Eh? Time? What do you mean?"

"I mean," said Turchin, "that ever since that greedy swine Mikhail Suvorov took charge of Perchorsk, I've had a spy there. I mean that six months ago something very terrible came through the Gate—something so *utterly* terrible that if it hadn't been half-dead it might well have raged through the complex, killing everyone it found there. But Suvorov's criminal crew were lucky and it died when they burned it. And finally, I mean that those heavily armed, very dangerous ex-convicts in the Perchorsk complex have grown tired of waiting for Suvorov to return, and it's only a matter of time now before greed overcomes fear and they pluck up sufficient courage to go through the Gate looking for him. For the General . . . *and* for whatever else they can find."

Trask frowned and shook his head. "And there you've lost me. Surely if this gang of criminals at the complex has had to deal with a crippled warrior creature left over from the war in Sunside/Starside, the last thing they would want to do is go someplace where they might bump into similar things, possibly of a fighting fit variety!"

"A warrior, yes," Turchin answered. "From its description, that's what it was. A nightmarish thing like—I don't know—like a primal dinosaur, all armoured and bristling with fiendish chitin weaponry . . . but having the face of a man, albeit a face with fangs! Built to go on four legs, to do battle on the ground, it had the trappings of a mount: a saddle, stirrups, a bit in its mouth, and reins. And that's where the trouble lies. For all of the metal parts, bit, chains, stirrups, and such—"

"—Were of massive gold!" said Trask, beginning to understand.

"Gold, yes," said Turchin. "Heavy, beautiful gold. Suvorov had promised to make those men rich, and now they know what he was talking about and where it was going to come from."

"So why haven't you told me this before?" said Trask. "And what is it you're still not telling me?"

The Premier flopped back in his chair, sighed and answered, "Well then, now that the pigeons are in flight, it seems I must tell you all."

Trask's talent helped him with that one. "Which sounds like you've started wheels turning that can't be stopped, right?"

Turchin nodded. "My plans are laid, they are in motion, and there's no going back on them."

"So what's the bottom line?" said Trask. "What is it you've done, and what is it you want?"

"First, what I want," said Turchin. "These enemies of mine: there are three of them, one ex-military and two serving high-rankers. Except, they are not only *my* enemies but yours and all the free world's, too. Hard-liners—with communism, expansionism, and world domination stamped into their every fiber—only supply them with the means, precious metal enough to fuel their ambitions and start that terrible, crushing engine up again . . ." He paused and shook his head, then quickly went on. "What do I want? That's easy. I want them dead!"

For several long seconds Trask sat and stared at his guest, his expression cold and inscrutable. But Turchin scarcely required any special talent to know what the other was thinking.

"I'm not a murderer, Ben!" he burst out. "But no less than your vampires, *these* people are! Should I tell you what they're capable of? Plans so monstrous that if the west had known about them when first they were broached it could easily have started World War Three? *Hah!* You don't know the half of it! You think the CIA have hatched some feverish plots in their time, this or that assassination that didn't quite work out? But these people I'm talking about are capable of genocide. They'd think nothing of destroying entire countries!" And as he paused for breath:

"Go on," said Trask. "I'm listening."

Now Turchin was sweating freely. He mopped his forehead and said, "And so I have arrived at the point of no return. Defection is one thing, but these are my country's best kept secrets. And I am trusting them to you. They must go no further. If ever they got out no one would ever trust Russia, *or* Gustav Turchin, again. I would remain your guest for the rest of my life, which probably wouldn't be a long one . . ."

"I'm still listening," said Trask.

"One of these three men," said Turchin, "—should we call him Admiral X? You can work it out for yourself—is responsible for dumping our fleet of decrepit nuclear submarines and other radioative waste in international waters. This same man, in the late nineteen sixties through the seventies, when he was a lowly apparatchik in the USSR's Defense Department, proposed to change the world's weather patterns by detonating enormous atomic devices deep under the Arctic ice. The melting ice—fresh water, you understand, as it flowed into the Atlantic Ocean—would permanently reverse the Atlantic Conveyor, bringing Siberian temperatures to western Europe and a Mediterranean climate to the Russian heartland. Madman that he is, I know he still harbours such schemes, and that he has the fanatical will to bring them into being. All he lacks is the finances, the means. Perchorsk and the Vampire World would furnish such a means, though first he would have to cleanse that world of men and monsters alike. Ah, but with his perverse penchant for nuclear devices, I cannot see the mere destruction of an alien world as too great a problem! Well, except for our friends the Szgany, that is . . ."

And Trask nodded. "I think I can see why you'd want rid

of *that* one. And I can also see where you're making a big mistake. But go on, tell me all."

"Air defences," said Turchin. "The original plans for our answer to Ronald Reagan's SDI, his marvellous, mythical Strategic Defence Initiative, are extant still. Moreover, a certain scientist and senior officer in the Russian Air Force believes that if he were able to generate and contain sufficient energy he could make the failed Perchorsk Experiment work. All that he needs to go ahead is the funding: gold, Ben! Just think of it: an invisible umbrella, shielding an entire country, neutralizing all incoming weapons of mass destruction. After that, what could the West refuse us, eh? In any war, an impregnable force *must* conquer. But even if there was no war, the West would go broke trying to duplicate the umbrella. Total chaos whichever way you look at it.

"Finally the Army. My third and last great enemy is an ex-General, now an industrialist. A former close ally of Suvorov, he has been, is, and always shall be a hawk to the bitter end. If you think that the American General Patton was a militarist, or your own Bomber Harris, who reduced Dresden to a fiery hell, then you haven't reckoned with this man. When President Reagan made his 'joke' about nuking Moscow, this man moved a regiment of tanks into the countryside, commandeered a missile site, and sat there waiting, with his finger on the button! He had to be taken out of there by force. How fortunate that on both counts Gorbachev had a sense of humour. He ignored the first maniac's gaffe, promoted the other and privately awarded him a medal of honour . . . !"

As Turchin fell silent, Trask said, "Is that all of it? Are you done?"

"One last word," said Turchin. "These three men are intent upon discovering Suvorov's secret mother lode, his fabulous El Dorado, and I have set them a trail to follow. Nothing can satisfy them now except they follow it to its end. And its end—or more properly its beginning—is in Perchorsk. And already in Perchorsk, there's a small army of thugs just waiting to be led into the Vampire World. So then, the stage is set, and now we have to take action."

Trask thought about it for a moment, and answered, "In Australia when we talked these things over, you led me to believe that your principal interests were the same as mine—to stop any more vampires coming through into our world, to help me to get rid of those that are already here, to block the Perchorsk Gate permanently, and in so doing to secure the parallel world for Nathan and his people."

"That was what I wanted then," Turchin answered, "and it's what I want now. But it doesn't make these enemies of mine any less real. They aren't going to go away, and if I can kill two birds with one stone—or three, as it happens—well, so much the better."

"As to your enemies," said Trask, "you're trying very hard to paint them as the world's enemies, too. All these dreadful-sounding threats—the atrocities they'd enact if they had the financial means in the form of gold from Sunside/Starside. But the fact is that even if they went there and dug up a mountain of the stuff, and if they were able to shift it, still there's no way they could ever bring it, or themselves, back. The Gate itself would stop them, for it can only be used in one direction. It's a one-way ticket to hell! And as for the other Gate, at the Romanian Refuge, that's already blocked."

"You have misunderstood me," said Turchin. "I did not mean to imply that they *could* do it, but that given the opportunity they *would!* It's the thought that they *might* that drives me to distraction. Ben, there are many great sources of wealth other than Sunside/Starside. My ex-Army thug industrialist 'friend,' for example: he is already a multimillionaire. And when he's a billionaire, what then?"

"Very well," said Trask, "let's have it understood. I know what I and my people have to do. And that's exactly what we'll do given an opportunity. But as for these political enemies of yours . . . they're your concern. If they should happen to cross our paths, however—"

"But they will!" said the other. "I guarantee it."

"—then that's different," Trask went on. "But only if we have to deal with them in order to complete our mission in Perchorsk."

In answer to which the Premier said, "You can be absolutely sure of it." And the way he nodded his head—his grim expression—told Trask the rest of it.

"Those wheels you've started turning," he said. "This false trail you've set for these people. It's not so much a red herring as a carrot for three donkeys, right? And it will lead them straight to Perchorsk."

"Not directly," said Turchin. "But they'll get there eventually."

"When, 'eventually'?"

"In maybe . . . three or four days?"

"What!?" Trask was stunned. "Is that all we've got? But why did you do it? Why couldn't you wait a while longer before laying this trail of yours? You said you would have told me everything if there was time. Would a day or two more, another week, have made much difference? I have problems here at home, and we still have to track down these three great enemies of our own."

"But you're forgetting something," said Turchin. "My spy in Perchorsk. There are some three dozen desperate men up there in the Urals. They *know* that there's gold on the other side of the Gate, and three nights ago they voted to give Mikhail Suvorov's party one more week to get back with their share. If he doesn't—and he won't, because he's dead, and couldn't anyway because as you've pointed out the Gate is a one-way ticket—then they intend to arm themselves with all the weaponry in Perchorsk and go through the Gate themselves! But we know they can't win; the same dreadful fate will befall them as befell Mikhail Suvorov's party. Then, as before, their vampire murderers might start wondering where these aliens came from. And who can say? This time instead of three of them coming through the Gate—as they did at the Romanian Refuge—why, there could be an entire army of them! *That's* what I meant when I said we've run out of time!"

Trask groaned. He leaned forward, put his face in his hands and stared down at his desk. And slowly he shook his head.

"Oh?" said Turchin anxiously. "What have I said wrong now?"

Trask looked up at him and said: "Gustav, it looks like you and I have been working at cross-purposes . . . or perhaps not. I suppose it couldn't be helped. I only found out about it myself a few minutes ago."

"Eh? What are you talking about? Found out about what?"

"Found out that there are no more vampires in Sunside/Starside," said Trask. "The war is over—all of six months ago—and Nathan won it. There won't be any more Wamphyri invaders of Earth. As for that crippled warrior that came through into Perchorsk: obviously it was a 'victim' of the war. It knew it was finished and was looking for somewhere to die."

As Trask spoke, the look on Turchin's face changed from one of utter astonishment to dismay, then anger. "But I didn't *know* this!" He jumped to his feet, slammed his clenched fist down on the desk. "All I knew was what you told me in Australia—that there was a war in Sunside/Starside, and as a result of Mikhail Suvorov's expedition three Great Vampires had come through into our world. Now you tell me the war's over and there are no more vampires in Starside. But *my* thinking was that when these enemies of mine went through the Gate, then that . . . that . . ."

". . . That they'd find themselves face-to-face with the Wamphyri," Trask finished it for him. "End of story, and definitely the end of your enemies. You couldn't have devised a more cruel trap for them if you'd tried. For them or for anyone else."

Turchin thought about that and protested, "But it's like I said: I thought to kill two birds with one stone. Some vampires were bound to die in the battle with Perchorsk's criminal element, which could only help Nathan's cause: less of the monsters for him and the Szgany to deal with. Surely you can see that?"

"I can see that we have problems," said Trask. "But personally, I've so many problems my head is spinning with them. It's getting so I don't any longer know where to start. I don't even want to *think* about them any more."

"But you have to," said Turchin. "And anyway, I cannot see that this changes anything. It only means we must act that much faster. Instead of waiting until these three most dangerous men have joined up with the Perchorsk convicts and invaded Sunside/Starside—which would mean a confrontation with Nathan and the Szgany, and more bloodshed—we have to destroy Perchorsk while they are still in situ. For while vampires are one thing, these men are something else. And remember, under the command of military tacticians, the Perchorsk convicts and their weapons will be far more effective than anything Nathan's Szgany might bring to bear. Even with his weird powers, still it will be bloody."

"Bloody?" Trask shook his head. "No, it will be a lot worse than that. For there's something else I just learned: Nathan is out of it, injured, in some kind of mental limbo. So the way I see it, those wheels you've set in motion will be rolling over people who have done us no harm. Friends of mine, and at least one of yours—Nathan himself. And I can't help but think that this is all for you, that you've done this for yourself."

"For myself?" Turchin pulled in his chin and tried to look hurt. "Well, partly, yes. But mainly for my country, and yours, and for the world at large—*and* for Sunside/Starside!"

"What?" said Trask, sneeringly. "You think you can convince me that turning a gang of gold-crazy convicts loose in Nathan's world is good for the Szgany? They've just finished one bloody war, and now you would give them another?"

"But I didn't know!" Turchin protested again, beginning to stride to and fro across the floor. "And I've already supplied you with the solution. Surely we are agreed that the

Gate must be closed, if only for the safety of Nathan's world?"

"Of course," Trask answered. "Man, I wish to God the damned thing had never been created! The point is there shouldn't have been any immediate need to close it, not with the war won."

"Again you're forgetting something," said Turchin, his fist rebounding from the desk. "No matter what I have done—*despite* what I've done—that need now exists. Those convicts in Perchorsk will go through the Gate *with or without* the leadership of any enemies of mine! Of course they will. From the moment they saw the gold trappings on that warrior creature, it was inevitable. The only wonder to me is that they haven't already gone!"

"Well," Trask stood up. "What's done is done. From here on any argument would be circular, biting at its own tail. And if I thought I had things to do before . . . well, now I really have things to do, arrangements to make. You'll please excuse me."

"But first," Turchin said, as he got between Trask and the door, "first I have to know—you have to tell me—that you *do* have a new Necroscope. I'm at least correct in that assumption, yes?"

And Trask saw no point in denying it now, for soon he'd be putting Jake to use. "Yes," he answered. "Fortunately for you, me, everyone, we do have a Necroscope. He has his limitations, a few small problems, but we do have him."

The Premier's sigh of relief was quite audible. "Then this time they have earned their keep," he said.

"They?" Trask paused at the door.

"My espers," said Turchin. "When they told me of a certain heavyweight in the psychic aether—the one signature that was present every time, in every location where Luigi Castellano's organization suffered devastation—I knew it must be so."

"And so it is," said Trask, stepping out into the corridor. "We may have slipped a little behind with our gadgets, but our ghosts are still second to none . . ."

14
Submarine Sabotage—
the Threat of the Threads

IT WAS EARLY EVENING; TRASK AND HIS PEOPLE had been back from the Mediterranean for less than a day and a lot had happened in that time, yet it seemed to the Head of Branch that time was at a near standstill and everything moving in slow motion. He knew he shouldn't be here but out there in Turkey hunting for Malinari and Vavara . . . and Szwart? What about Szwart? Was it possible he had survived Jake's subterranean blast, and if so would the three of them team up again? So many unanswered questions. And so much still to be done.

As for Turkey: Trask would get a team out there as soon as possible, and meanwhile the locator (more properly a hunchman) Bernie Fletcher was in situ somewhere, looked after by a couple of Special Branch minders, policemen he had worked with before. And thank goodness for them! Trask had been a little concerned for Bernie ever since he'd sent that message from *Invincible*.

The trouble with Bernie was that while he was good at following trails, close up he wasn't nearly as good as David Chung. His talent wasn't in question; on the contrary—one could even say it was *too* effective—which was why normally Trask liked to keep him busy in the headquarters. Bernie Fletcher, yes; as Trask strode the HQ's corridor towards the Duty Office he pictured him in his mind's eye:

A burly, middle-aged, five-foot-eight redhead, Fletcher was an intuitive hunchman whose talent made him an ideal target for spotters in that it worked both ways: he could locate and track the object or enemy in question—friend or foe for that matter— but he could also be located. The fault lay in his shielding, which was almost nonexistent. At close range telepathic members of the Branch, and indeed most of Trask's espers, had little or no trouble homing in on Bernie; to them his mental activity was like magnetic north to a lodestone. As Trask had once put it:

"Let's face it, Bernie, you stand out like a sore thumb in the metaphysical aether. Man, you glow in the dark!"

Yet now he'd sent the same man into Turkey to begin tracking down two (or maybe three?) of the most dangerous creatures who had ever set foot on Earth. On the other hand, Bernie knew his limitations, and he'd be watched over by the close-protection specialists who were out there with him. And anyway, that's what E-Branch was all about; danger was no stranger to Trask's agents, and in the current situation all of them were at risk.

But still Trask's heart was beating a little faster; likewise his footsteps, as anxiety steadily mounted. Anxiety about almost everything. He hadn't been exaggerating when he'd told Turchin that it was getting so he couldn't even think. But he knew that he must, and he thanked the Lord for the others here who occasionally did it for him. Busy from the moment he'd got back to London, he certainly hoped somebody had been doing the thinking!

And as he strode in through the ever-open Duty Office door, the questions were already spilling from his lips. "John, where are we at, and where are we going? What's happening out there? Has Bernie Fletcher called in his location yet? When are we due to fly out? Have I decided who's going yet? And if not has anyone else? And finally, are there any messages for me?"

John Grieve looked up unflustered from a mass of paperwork on his desk, and answered, "Finally? I wouldn't bet on it! But to answer your questions in that order:

"We are where we're usually at: muddling through a crisis. But we're going on. What's happening out there is all sorts of things, but most importantly there's some stuff on Premier Turchin's microfilm you should know about.

Fletcher *has* called in; we do know his location; it appears he's picked up a couple of alleged 'friends' along the way. You're due to fly first class on a British Airways flight tomorrow morning. You gave a vague or tentative forecast of who would be going with you, which is likely to change when you've seen some of the stuff that Turchin brought us. And, 'finally,' there's a gang of our people in the Ops Room waiting for you."

"Waiting for me?" Trask tried as best possible to take in all he'd been told.

"Jake Cutter, Millie, and all your main men," said Grieve. "I'm not sure what they're up to, but Jake told me to tell you there's something that he and Millie want to get done with this evening, right now, in order to put everyone's mind at rest . . . or not? Also in Ops, that stuff of Turchin's is on-screen. And so, to return to your earlier question: I would hazard a guess that that's where you're going, to the Ops Room."

"I'm on my way," said Trask. And over his shoulder, optimistically: "Book a table for two downstairs, will you? Seven-thirty?"

"That only gives you forty-five minutes," Grieve told him. "Will you make it?"

"I hope to," said Trask. But as he headed for Ops, he more than suspected it all depended upon Jake and Millie . . .

Trask was right about what he'd suspected was going on in Ops. The rest of his agents had told Jake what Harry had said about red threads in Möbius time: how they showed up among the blue, and how an infected person might display a pink stain, a telltale reddening in his personal life-thread.

He arrived in the middle of some kind of argument, with the precog Ian Goodly looking as heated as Trask had ever seen him.

"I can only advise you not to!" Goodly was saying, in that piping voice of his whose pitch climbed the scales whenever he was excited. "The future can make fools of us; it has more than once made a fool of me, and I'm supposed to be the expert! Even Nathan got it wrong when he tried to forecast his future. I was with him. We were in Starside and things were looking bleak, so we looked to the future. He took me into the Continuum where we followed our blue threads through a future-time door; followed them to a place, a time, where Nathan's thread came to an end."

"But I've just been told that Nathan's alive." (Jake Cutter was on the other end of the argument.)

"Exactly!" said Goodly. "His blue thread had *seemed* to come to an end on Sunside, but that was only because he was going to step out of that universe into ours. How were we to know that a little further down the time-stream—after he had returned to his own world—his thread would stream on as before? That was something we discovered later. But at the time, what else could we think but that his life was about to end?"

"So what you're saying," said Millie, joining the argument, "is that you saw something bad that turned out good? So where's the harm in that?"

"You're not listening!" Goodly threw up his hands. "How can I explain it to you? You can't mess with the future. Even Harry tried to tell you that. His best advice was don't mess with the future. And the reason is quite simple: if you *do* see something bad you might be tempted to try to change it—and in so doing cause something worse to happen! The future isn't really a different time but a different place!" Again he threw up his hands. "God, give me the right words!" Then, seeing their unchanging, determined expressions—seeming to sink down into himself as he turned away—"But what's the use, for I can see you'll do it anyway," he said. "So I can't any longer argue with you. In any case, maybe it's meant to be. What will be has been."

"Not necessarily," said Trask, stepping forward. "Not while I'm in charge of E-Branch." And then to Jake: "Don't I remember telling you that you weren't to go experimenting or trying anything out unless we were all a part of it, all agreed on it?"

" 'All' meaning you, right?" said Jake. "Well, we were

waiting for you, and now you're here." He was looking defiant again . . . that attitude of his.

Taking a deep breath Trask stepped forward, and Millie got between them. "Ben," she said, "I'm with Jake. I'm with him all the way. He has gone along with you—been willing to do whatever you've asked of him—so now you should go along with him. And with me. This is something we need to know. It's something *you* need to know, too, Ben."

And again they were all looking at him. Liz, Lardis, David Chung, Ian Goodly, Millie . . . and Jake, of course; Trask's espers, and even the techs sitting at their machines. Everybody.

He looked at Goodly. "You've advised them not to, right?"

"The same way Harry advised us," the precog nodded. "But I can't say that I'm right to have done so, or even if I *had* the right to do so. Call it a gut feeling. I have this thing about the future, as you know. Maybe it's because I sometimes wish I *couldn't* do it that I wish they *wouldn't* do it."

"But if we don't," Jake spoke to Trask, "then you'll never be able to trust us. Me, I've just got to know. If you were in my shoes, wouldn't you? Sure you would. And this way, we'll *all* of us know what's going down. So that's that: there's no other choice. If you stop me now—if you could—then as soon as I get the chance I'll do it anyway, on my own if necessary."

Trask looked at Millie then—tried his best to look stern—but she wasn't backing down. "I've got to go with him, Ben," she told him. "For let's face it, I was down there with Szwart in that loathsome fungus garden a lot longer than Jake. And if some of those spores have been able to reach the surface—"

"—We don't know that yet!" Trask cut her off.

"But if," she came back. "Then isn't it equally possible I might have been infected, too?"

At which Liz came in on it, saying, "In any case we really do have to know, don't we? If Millie and Jake are in the clear, which I'm sure they are, then we can move on. And—"

"—And what if they're not?" Trask's voice almost cracked up, his throat was so dry. He knew how Liz felt about Jake, but it was Millie he was thinking about.

"If they're not," the Old Lidesci repeated him in his usual growl, "then we'll be able to give them . . . well, whatever help we can." And they all knew what Lardis meant.

Trask shook his head. "Nothing like that," he said gruffly, turning on Lardis. "Man, what are you thinking? This isn't some Szgany encampment on Sunside!"

And Lardis shook his head. "No," he said, "not Sunside, but it could be the same problem."

Trask didn't much like where this was going; he didn't want to scare Millie and couldn't afford to give Jake any ideas. So:

"Very well," he told them. "If you're that set on it, let's do it . . . here and now, and have done with it." There was something else in the back of Trask's mind, something he tried hard *not* to think about, keeping it firmly screwed down.

Jake looked at Millie and together they climbed up onto the stage or dais standing central in the Ops Room. With the exception of Trask, the rest of the team sat in chairs close together, where they could look up at the rostrum. And Trask said, "Jake, Millie, we've been some strange places today, but none stranger than where you're going now. Jake, you take care of her."

Jake looked down at him; their eyes met, and for once there was no animosity between them, no discord worth mentioning. And Jake said, "You, too, Ben. I mean, you take care of . . . of whatever." So maybe Trask didn't have it all that well screwed down after all.

Then, putting his arm around Millie, Jake said, "Hold on to me. You've been there before, but briefly. This time it will be longer because we aren't just going somewhere but sometime. And we'll be seeing whatever there is to see. I think that's how it works, anyway."

As what he'd said sank in, suddenly it dawned on Trask that while Jake was certainly the Necroscope, still his talents were very new to him. Did he really know what he was doing? Starting up the rostrum steps, he might have asked that very question—except Jake and Millie wouldn't have heard him.

For they weren't any longer there . . .

"Dart guns!" Trask said, even as he felt the breath of air that rushed in to fill the space where Jake and Millie had been. "In the armoury. The same kind of tranquilizers they had on *Invincible*. I want them in here, now!"

And Liz gasped and said, "You don't think . . . ?"

"It's my job to think," Trask told her. "*You* think! This is E-Branch HQ. Right now they are on their way to find out what's what. That means we're about to find out, too. Me, I don't want to find out the hard way. No, I don't think they'd rampage, not unless we put them under pressure. The darts are a safety measure, that's all, to make sure there *is* no pressure. But if they *were* to come back in a nasty mood—and God knows Jake's quite capable of it—well, need I go on? And stop looking at me as if I'm some kind of monster. I happen to be in love with Millie no less than you are with Jake."

One of the techs brought the dart guns. Trask gave them to Chung and Goodly.

"Why us?" Chung wanted to know.

"Who better?" Trask snapped. "I was beginning to think that things were getting on top of me, but now it seems I'm the only one who's still awake here! If those two get back knowing that they're in trouble, won't you know it—won't you at least be able to sense something of it—too? You know you will. So for Christ's sake get yourself in gear! Do what you do best and be on the lookout for mindsmog."

He turned to Goodly. "As for you—"

"—I'm to try reading the future, right?" said the precog. "But do you think I haven't been doing that all along? The fact is, I think I'm losing it, Ben. And it's been getting worse for weeks now, ever since we went out to Australia. The more I pressure the future, the more it resists me."

"Yes, I know," Trask nodded. "And I've been having problems with my talent, too, and so have we all. But as long as you can apply pressure to your trigger finger I wouldn't start worrying about it right now. So just get up on that dais and be ready. I would do it myself but there's something else I want to look at while we're waiting."

As he left the dais and strode across the floor towards the big wall screen, Liz caught at his arm, bringing him to a halt. "Surely you don't intend to dart them out of hand?"

Trask looked at her, shook himself loose, then glanced back at Chung and Goodly on the rostrum. They looked just as uncertain as Liz; and for that matter, as uncertain as Trask himself. And torn two ways, he said: "The hell with it! I'll leave it up to you. See what you think the moment they step back out of the Continuum onto that stage."

Then he reached the wall screen, where a tech set the great mass of information it contained scrolling for him. In the main it was a blueprint, a detailed schematic of the Perchorsk complex in its Ural Mountains hideaway. But Trask knew there had to be far more to it than that. According to John Grieve, the Duty Officer, there was something here that would make a difference to the team he wanted to take out to Turkey with him.

"Fast-forward it," he growled. And the flow of information at once picked up speed. But as the Perchorsk schematics rolled up out of sight, something very different emerged at the bottom of the picture, rapidly taking shape as it elevated itself onto the screen. And Trask recognized it immediately.

It was a skewed, blank map of northern Russia and Europe, from Severnaya Zemlya at the far right of the screen, through the Kara, Barents, and Norwegian seas, up to and including the British Isles in the west. Or rather, it would have been blank if not for a handful of tiny, concentric-ringed "targets" centred with bull's-eye dots, all of which appeared to highlight deep and occasionally not so deep oceanic locations.

Glancing at the tech, Trask raised a hand and said, "Hold it there!" . . . at which the screen froze with the map on centre stage. And then the flesh began to creep at the nape of Trask's neck. He had seen similar charts before and knew precisely what he had here: that the bull's-eye targets were deep-water sites where a down-at-heel Russian Navy had already scuppered several of its supposedly "decommissioned" but still highly radioactive nuclear submarines, revenants of its cold-war fleet. Lacking the financial or technical clout—unwilling or incapable of detoxifying these lethal hulks, whichever—somebody in the Russian Navy's top brass, probably one of Gustav Turchin's enemies, had been dumping them on other nations' doorsteps.

David Chung, never better than when he was tracking nuclear or illicit drugs sources, had been keeping tabs on such activities for years now. And quite obviously he'd have to be on this one, too. That was what John Grieve had been talking about: the locator wouldn't be going out to Turkey with Trask and the rest of the crew because he'd be working on this. And it didn't take a genius to work out why.

One of the small targets was missing its bull's-eye centre; either the bull's-eye was missing, or the target had not as yet been hit. Which probably indicated that it was a *scheduled* dump site, a theory that seemed corroborated by a much heavier, freehand circle with which "someone" (Premier Turchin himself?) had highlighted the site in question. As for its location: that was the really worrying factor.

It lay in the northern Atlantic's Rockall Deep, one hundred and fifty miles west of Ireland, which according to some oceanographers was a major junction in the Atlantic Conveyor system, a region where the balmy surface waters of the Gulf Stream collide with cold water flowing from the Arctic, sink, about-face, and join a submarine current flowing back the other way. And in the event some lunatic in the Russian Navy dumped a clapped-out and highly toxic nuclear sub there . . . given sufficient time it could poison the entire conveyor, carrying deadly Russian waste all the way back to Florida and the Bahamas and eventually depositing its lethal radiation along every Atlantic coastline!

Well, the Atlantic Ocean is a big thing, and even a massive nuclear vessel is small by comparison. But that wouldn't be the way that Greenpeace and all of the other powerful environmental bodies and lobbies would see it, especially in Earth Year, when the ecological balance of the whole planet was under discussion east to west and pole to pole. And with Russia many billions of dollars in the red and increasingly dependant on Western funds, it would be condemned as indefensible, the worst kind of pollution at the worst possible time in the history of planet Earth. Compared to the meltdown at Chernobyl—a terrible accident, a human error, which in the main had been paid for by its Russian authors—this would be seen as something else again; seen for what it was: the deliberate act of despoilers on an unthinkably massive scale . . .

Which was why Premier Turchin had released this information here, now. This was a weapon he could bring to bear against his Russian enemies. Simply by presenting the West's environmentalists with the means to prove what they'd been saying for years, he could denounce the author or authors of this thing and have them removed from office, prosecuted, and locked away for good. It was Turchin covering himself; for in the event that his Perchorsk scheme should fail, he knew that this one would succeed.

Trask turned to the tech at the screen's console. "Is there a legend, something to describe what's going on here?"

"It's in Russian," the tech answered, bringing it into view on the screen. "We think it's a timetable, encyphered, but nothing we can't crack. It's being worked on right now. However, we do have a date."

"A date?" Trask repeated him.

"Yes." The other nodded. And in all innocence: "Whatever it is that's going down here, it's all set to happen in three days' time."

And now Trask knew for certain that the locator David

Chung wouldn't be going to Turkey with him. No, for he'd be following this up instead. Indeed the locator—and perhaps Greenpeace or some similar organization, together with a whole gang of people from the government—would be doing their best to ensure that it didn't happen. Oh, they'd let it develop, gathering proof of it along the way, but at the last minute they'd step in and put a stop to it.

That was how this kind of thing usually worked, anyway . . .

In total darkness—a darkness whose like had never been experienced anywhere on Earth, or under it, or in the spaces between the stars—Millie gripped Jake's hand as tightly as she could, and floated or drifted alongside her physical guide in the metaphysical Möbius Continuum. And in a hoarse whisper (mercifully a whisper) she began to say:

"Jake, there's nothing—"

Don't! Jake at once cut her off, as her spoken words gonged like cracked bells and caused her to give a massive start where he held her. And as their echoes gradually faded away: *You only need to think whatever it is you want to say, and I'll hear you anyway.*

Telepathy? she said. *You?*

No, he answered. *Well, between Liz and me . . . there's something between us for sure. But not with you. It's the Continuum, that's all. I thought all you people had read up on it?*

You did? she answered. *I mean, I have, yes. But the reality of it is something else. The last time we were here, we were in and out. There was no time to look around . . . or to talk . . . or anything.*

There's nothing here, Jake reminded her. *The Möbius Continuum is the Big Empty. We aren't supposed to be here, not you or me or anybody. So anything we bring here or do here or cause to happen here is alien, a foreign body or event—almost a calamity—except there's no one and nothing here but the Continuum itself to experience it. It's like when you're the first person in the pool on a dead calm morning; the water is still, perfect, like crystal . . . until you jump in and ruin everything, so that it can't ever be the same again. When you speak out loud you're simply adding to the splash, that's all. But even thoughts have weight in the Möbius Continuum, which is why we can hear them.*

That's like—I don't know—like poetry, she said, sounding surprised. *It's a side of you that we haven't seen too much of. I would have liked Ben Trask to hear that.*

Oh, really?

Yes. Sometimes I think he *thinks you're soulless—oh!* (For she'd suddenly realized what she had said.) And:

Well, said Jake, *that's what we're about to find out, isn't it?*

But I didn't mean—

I know you didn't. He reassured her. And to change the subject: *Have you seen all you want to see?*

But that's what I was trying to say before, she answered. *I mean, there* isn't *anything to see, or to feel . . . or anything!*

Oh, but there is something, Jake told her. *Except you have to remain still and quiet to experience it. Do you want to try?*

Yes, Millie answered at once. *But it isn't easy being quiet when there are so many questions I want to ask.*

Questions I probably can't answer, said Jake, ruefully. *But okay, fire away. Only while you're asking keep still and try to feel the Continuum.*

She kept very still, unafraid with her hand in Jake's, and said, *If there's nothing here, why isn't it cold? And how can I breathe? And why don't I—why don't we—explode? I mean, this has to be a vacuum, the mother of all vacuums!* Following which she shivered, before slowly continuing: *Yet now, suddenly, I do feel cold. And I don't want to explode. And my breathing . . . my breathing seems a lot more difficult!*

But it's all psychological, he answered, giving her hand a squeeze. *And psychology and parapsychology don't mix. You're a telepath, and in E-Branch it's common knowledge that the unexplained really does exist . . . it's just that no one's explained it yet, that's all.*

But—

Listen, Jake said. *You're right, there's absolutely nothing here. No time for you to suffocate in, no space you can explode into. This is like a place before God. Or if that's a blasphemy, then maybe this place is God—the Mind of God, where the only influence we can bring to bear is that of willpower. See, Nothing happens here except we will it. After all, that's all there is here: you and me and our free wills. I know it's heavy stuff, but in a place where even thoughts have weight, surely our free will—our concentrated efforts of will—must be heavier still. Anyway, it works for me.*

And you may believe me when I say I'm so very glad it does! Millie assured him "breathlessly." And a moment later, *Oh! What was that!?*

He felt her small start and asked knowingly, *Is there something?*

Yes, she "whispered," shrinking down into herself a little. *Just then, I thought . . . I could swear that I felt something!*

Me, too, he told her. *That was the Continuum. It's moving us along. It wants rid of us. Since we haven't exercised our will, we must be thoughts without a purpose. Which tells me it's time we moved on.*

And she could actually feel them moving now, as if she were in tow and Jake heading in a certain direction. But as for left and right, forward and back, up and down, breeze in her face or a wind at her back: there was none of that. The Möbius Continuum made no allowance for physical points of reference.

Yet there were coordinates, and knowing them, Jake was able to move with a reassuring certainty of purpose and "direction." In short, Millie knew that they were going somewhere.

You know a lot about it, don't you? she said.

All inherited, he told her. *And the more I use it, the more I seem to remember. I don't have Harry's genes, but what-*

ever it was that made him tick, it's ticking in me, too. And before she could answer him: *We're there.*

The time-door had no frame; it was simply a hole in nothing. But beyond that hole there was something—an incredible something—which gave it a "frame of reference" if nothing else.

And Jake and Millie, they came to a halt on the threshold.

Past time, he told her then, and even his mental voice was "quiet," humbled by the very concept. *That's the world's entire past that you're looking at. It's the entire human race, all of it. Everyone who ever was, or who is now, right up to this very moment, had his or her start back there. It's where our hominid ancestors came up out of Africa—where they became men—maybe half a million years ago. That's what you're seeing back there: our ancestors, their first half-million years.*

"Back there" was the most awesome place—and perhaps even more so than the Möbius Continuum itself—for as Jake had said it was mankind's past from a primordial cradle to modern times.

It was birth and life and death, and it was blue from beginning to end. Blue life-threads sprang like neon umbilical cords from Jake and Millie's middles, sprang away into the past where they twined and wound, gradually fading into all the years gone by, mingling with and losing themselves, becoming indistinguishable among a million, a billion, six billion other threads just like them. And every one of them a life.

And way back there, where all of those myriad life-threads converged—those time-trails of humanity, coming together in a far faint neon nebula some half a million years ago,—that was where the human race had its origin.

Mankind's Big Bang, since when it had expanded—was still expanding—like the universe itself, not only in space but in time. Back there, yes: the beginning of us all . . .

It seemed to Millie that she could hear a sound, a protracted, orchestrated sighing, an *Ahhhhhhh!* as if an angelic chorus were sending its one-note hymn, its hum, its resonance out into the Möbius Continuum. But an *Ahhhhhhh* without end. Hearing that thought, Jake told her:

No, it's just that it should *be there. I don't think anyone could look at something like this without "hearing" it. We have pictures of what should be in our minds—we think we know how things should taste, smell, sound—and what you think you're hearing is the sound that goes with this. I can hear it, too.*

Millie thought she knew exactly what he meant. *Like falling stars hissing across the sky,* she said.

That's right, said Jake. *We only imagine we hear them.*

By the light of the past, Millie could now see herself; see Jake, too, floating in a blue haze on the time-door's threshold. And reaching down her free hand, she hesitated for a moment before passing it through the pure blue thread that connected her with her past. That thread *was* Millie; it was her very being—perhaps her soul? And she felt a vast sense of relief on recognizing its purity. Pure for now, anyway. But then, wonderingly, unable to resist, she looked at Jake's metaphysical umbilical.

He was looking at it, too, staring at it. And before Millie could say anything:

When I came here with Harry, he said, *my thread was as blue as yours. Was as blue as yours.* And then he fell silent.

But didn't we explain that? Millie said, her eyes like his, fixed on his life-thread, no longer entirely blue but tinted— tainted?—in its core with a single, thin, pale but undeniably red filament. *Didn't we tell you what Harry told us? That crimson stain is Korath. It's the thing in your mind, Jake, trapped in your mind now. But it's no more the real you than . . . than a metal filling in a tooth when it shows up on an X-ray plate.*

Maybe, said Jake, *but still it's there, and it wasn't there before.* His thoughts were very grim now, half-convinced of something so monstrous it didn't bear dwelling upon, so that Millie found herself seeking hard for a way to convince him otherwise, to try to dispel the worst of his fears.

When you get rid of him, she said, *when Korath's gone, that red stain will disappear with him.* But:

No, said Jake, shaking his head. *Back there at E-Branch HQ, you and Liz, and Goodly and Chung, you said Harry told you that it should disappear with Korath. And that's if I can find a way to get rid of him. But meanwhile . . . how can I be sure that this is just Korath? You were there, Millie—down in that hellhole with me—and you saw Szwart's mushrooms opening up, the spores set free to drift in that wind from the pit.*

Yes! She turned to him, gripped his rough hard hand in both of hers. *And I was there longer than you! I'd been at the mercy of that creature, and of his dwarfish, hunchback companion, yet my thread is blue. You can't let this throw you, Jake. It's not the end but simple proof of something we already knew: that you have this monster in your head. But now you're controlling him, and not the reverse. He can't touch you while he's locked away. And you will find a way to be rid of him, I know you will.*

She couldn't be sure he'd been listening; his thoughts were somewhere else, working at something else. And finally he said: *If I'm infected—I mean, if I did come too close down there in Szwart's lair—then logically I might expect this red taint to be getting stronger, right?*

I really don't know, Millie answered.

And if it really is Korath, Jake went on, *nothing more than that damned vampire Thing—his presence, his taint— then it must have started when I took him on board.*

I suppose so, said Millie, wonderingly.

I have to know! said Jake. *And there's no time like now. Or rather there is time now; past time. Hold on to me.*

Which was all the warning Millie got before he launched himself through the door and back along the past-time stream.

Jake! She clung for dear life, terrified as the blue streamers hurtled past her, like neon rocket exhausts but faster yet. For they were heading into the future while Millie was going in the opposite direction.

It's okay, he told her. *I only need relax my will and we'll be pushed back the other way.*

But . . . you've never done this before, have you?

No, he answered, *but somehow—don't ask me—it feels like I have. Harry's legacy, I suppose.*

Jake's mind, his answers, felt rock solid, and likewise his grip on her. So that soon she was able to calm herself and look about. Then:

Oh! she said: *These neon stars, suddenly bursting into life . . . they're such a bright, beautiful blue.*

Bursting into life, he repeated her. *Yes, you're absolutely right. Only they're not stars. That's childbirth you're seeing. That separation from a more powerful neon source? It's the moment the infant becomes a person in its own right. Another life-thread moving into its future.*

She saw that now, and said, *Which means that the ones that go dim and blink out . . . ?*

Right again, Jake said. *And where they blink out en masse, in clusters, those are human disasters. Airplanes crash, bombs explode, buildings fall down, trains collide—whichever.*

Just like that, she said. And:

That's life, said Jake. And looking at her limned in humanity's blue light, *Why do you keep flinching?*

I keep thinking I'll collide with someone! she answered.

At which he had to smile, and said, *But you can't collide. This is a trail you've already walked. You're simply walking it backwards—in your own footsteps, if you like.*

But a moment (or an hour) later: *Jake,* Millie's voice was a "gasp," a mental exclamation, a warning. *Red threads!*

He saw them, too—many hundreds of them—expanding out of the past like a writhing horde of scarlet snakes and seeming to turn the entire horizon to blood. And there could be no mistaking the fact that as he "advanced" to meet them, so the scarlet vampire life-threads were closing in on him . . .

15
Problems Past, Present, and . . . ?
. . . Grave Conversations

FOR A MOMENT, TAKEN BY SURPRISE AND unable to explain the swift approach of the red threads, Jake shrank down into himself; and in the space of a heartbeat they were upon him!

Both Jake and Millie threw up their free hands to ward off the speeding horrors . . . only to see them blink (or indeed sink) out of existence even as they drew level. For it was only then, when he had the chance to think, that Jake understood what had happened.

It could only have been the Evening Star, *he gasped, Another human disaster—or maybe I should say an inhuman one. But at least it tells us what to expect. Next up, we'll be seeing Luigi Castellano and his creatures get theirs; followed by, or in real time "preceded" by, Malinari's victims. That will be Jethro Manchester and his family, which was when I gave Korath his initial route of access to my mind. Huh!* You know, I still can't believe I did something like that, "of my own free will" Anyway, that's what I'm here to check out. For if you and Harry and the others are right, that's where my life-thread picked up its additional splash of colour; but a purely mental thing, in no way physical. In which case I'll begin to feel halfway safe again . . . but still only halfway.*

Jake was right. In short order a further double-handful of red threads, some still showing traces of blue (for they'd only recently been recruited by Luigi Castellano to bolster his vampire forces) converged out of the neon haze of the past only to terminate in violent bomb-bursts as Jake drew level.

And now Jethro Manchester, Jake said, as he and Millie continued to plummet into the past. *That poor old billionaire, and those other poor bastards on his vampire island.*

Holding on tight, Millie said, *And you say that's where you agreed to let Korath into your mind? On Manchester's island?*

No, Jake shook his head. *I didn't actually let him in—but I did give him access. He could come to visit but I didn't have to answer his knock, didn't have to lay my soul bare to him, if you see what I mean. He didn't reside in me just yet. That came later, after my showdown with Castellano. But Korath was creeping up on me, yes.*

There was red up ahead, and Jake was slowing down now. And: *Yes, I've actually seen how he has crept up on you,* said Millie thoughtfully. *Look—your thread is as blue as mine again!*

She had no sooner "spoken" those words than the latest crimson arrivals, two of them, flared out of existence. And as Jake came to a halt he said, *That was Manchester and the bastard who vampirized him, Martin Trennier. I was more than a little sorry to see Manchester go. He fought his contamination to the bitter end; knew he couldn't win, but kept trying. As for the other: I didn't give a shit for him!*

Then, glancing at his blue thread, he went on: *After they'd died, that was when I knew Liz was in trouble. I heard her telepathic call from Malinari's casino, the Pleasure Dome in Xanadu. Up until then I was in the clear—in the black, you might say.*

Or maybe the blue? said Millie.

He nodded. *And that was when I did the deal with Korath. If I hadn't, Liz was a goner. So if we move forward a ways—just a few seconds—from here . . . there!* The first red tinge sprang into being, sullying his life-thread.

Then, turning around and looking to the future again, Jake said, *So now you can see my problem. This is where I got myself contaminated, yes, but it's obvious that the taint isn't nearly so bad back here as it is forward of this point. Here the stain is barely visible. But as we move towards our own time—*

—That's when you'll go from being in the blue to being in the red! Millie answered without a trace of humour. *But Jake, I don't think you could have been watching your thread as closely as I have. It's possible I know why your taint gets stronger as we move forward into the future.*

Oh?

Yes. I noticed it when you crossed swords with Castellano.

Now he frowned. *When I crossed swords with . . . ? What do you mean? What are you talking about? What did you notice?*

Move forward, she said, excited now. *Move forward in time, back toward the present—I mean our present—but this time keep your eyes on your thread.*

He did as Millie suggested (which was in any case the only way to go), and soon found himself paralleled by converging red threads.

Castellano and his people—again, he said sourly.

Which was when I noticed something, Millie told him. *Coming backwards in time, I saw some of the red go out of your thread! Which means that as we venture forward, this is where it should take on more colour!*

Jake saw what she meant. Suddenly, the moment after Castellano's gang exploded into scarlet bomb-bursts, the taint in his life-thread was a deeper, far more noticeable red. And he came to an abrupt halt as it dawned on him exactly what was happening here.

This was the second time Liz called for me, he said. *But by now Korath knew my affections, that I'd risk almost anything to keep her from harm.*

That was when she was under threat from Vavara, on Krassos, said Millie. *And—*

—And that was when I let Korath in all the way, Jake finished it for her. *I had to. He had the equations to the Möbius Continuum. Well, so did I, but I didn't know it. For every time I tried to use them without recourse to him—*

—He interfered (Millie's turn to cut in), *causing you to think you couldn't do it.*

Jake nodded. *So I let him in. It was this "deal" we had. He was only interested in "helping" me—helping us, E-Branch—to destroy Malinari, Vavara, and Szwart. And he said that after we had done that, then he'd go back down again, down into the true death in that sump under the Romanian Refuge. But . . . somehow I don't think he will. He won't go anywhere—not without I find a way to kick the bastard out!*

And so you will, said Millie. *But that's not the point. The point is that the more Korath takes hold the more red gets into your life-thread. A metaphysical condition, yes, but that's all it is. Physically, you aren't affected—you aren't infected!*

Slowly nodding, Jake moved them forward again, back towards the NOW. And snorting derisively, he said, *Now there's a pleasant thought. The more this bastard encroaches on me, the redder I get!*

But not any more, said Millie. *And not in the blood or the flesh. Only in the mind. It's his contamination, not yours. The reason we see it is just as I explained: it's like a metal filling in a hollow tooth. We might even forget it's there until it shows up on an X-ray. And when the tooth is pulled . . . ?*

And again Jake's nod, as he answered, *That's a much happier thought. But it doesn't change the fact that red is red. What I mean is, is my red all Korath, or is some of it something else? You see, I remember something left over from Harry; things that he knew keep coming back to me. For instance, I know how he got rid of Faethor.*

You do?

Jake nodded. *Yes. Harry had him cornered—just like I have Korath—trapped in his mind. But he tricked him into the open, where Faethor couldn't hang on. Then he told him to leave, actually gave him a chance to go back down into his grave. Faethor refused, so Harry took him down a future time-stream. The Necroscope knew that he could come back;*

because he had a thread, he could "reel himself in". But Faethor had no thread and was sent hurtling into the future down a Möbius time-stream. And for all I know he's still going.

And Millie answered, *Couldn't you do the same with Korath?*

Not a chance, said Jake. *For Korath knows that story, too. He isn't about to let himself get lured out of my mind! Anyway, that's not the point. The point is that even after Harry dumped Faethor, still his thread was red . . . it must have been because by then he was a vampire, too. And I just can't shake a certain picture I have in my mind: of Szwart's lair and all those free-drifting spores . . .*

Then, as a Möbius door loomed up out of future time, Millie said, *Jake, what can I tell you? What more can I say other than I've already said?* She shook her head. *I can only state the one simple fact: that I was down there in the darkness, in Szwart's dreadful fungus garden, a lot longer than you were. And I'm in the clear . . .*

It was meant to reassure him but didn't, not quite. But it was appreciated. And crossing the threshold to the NOW, floating in the Möbius Continuum, Jake said, *Ben Trask is one lucky man to have someone like you by his side.*

Why, thank you, said Millie. *But I think we're all far luckier to have you.*

After a moment he answered, *Let's hope you are, anyway.* And changing the subject: *But now there's something else I want you to see before I take you back.*

Millie knew what it was—the only thing it could be— and might have protested. But they were already there.

A future-time door, she said, gazing out on the vastness of all the world's tomorrows, the awesome expansion of humanity in the Möbius time-dimension: billions of blue streamers intertwining, thinning with distance, becoming a haze, like a faint blue wash on a cosmic canvas.

And that's us, Jake said, as they stood on a very different threshold—indeed, the opposite of the first—but once again a door whose unseen frame could only be determined by the panoply sprawling beyond it. *There go our life-threads into the future, our snail-trails in time. Out along there is the answer to everything.*

Out along? said Millie.

It's just a quirk of mine, he said. *We have left and right, up and down, front and back, to and fro. But time travel . . . is something else. And "out along" is how I see it, that's all.*

Why not just forward? said Millie. *It seems you've accepted backwards in time, so why not forward?*

Backwards because it's already happened, he replied. *I mean because it's history and immutable.*

But isn't the future also immutable? said Millie. *According to Ian Goodly it is.*

Maybe. Jake nodded. *But where humankind has experienced the past, we're not given to see the future. It's a hill we haven't climbed yet, untrodden ground.*

Millie shivered then and said, *We shouldn't be doing this.*

I know, said Jake. *But I look at my polluted thread and I'm tempted to see if it's going to stay red forever. You see, even now the future isn't showing us everything. We're only allowed to see so far ahead. We certainly can't see forever.*

Jake? She looked at him, and he saw her puzzled expression, her features picked out in neon blue. And:

Is that an hour we're looking at? he asked her then. *A day, a month, a year? Out along that thread of mine, the answers are waiting for me to catch up to them. But where other men have to wait it out, I can do it faster. I can travel faster than life!*

Millie felt him preparing: his mind intent upon the future, his muscles bunching, and his figure leaning forward across the threshold. Another moment and Jake would be over that threshold heading "out along" the future time-stream. But: *Don't!* she said. *Or if you must go, then first return me to E-Branch HQ. I don't want to know the future, Jake. The present has problems enough.*

For what seemed like a long time he stood poised on the rim of the unknown, leaning forward at an ever-increasing

253

angle, as if he'd heard nothing at all of what she'd said. Then he leaned back, regained his balance, and gave his head a wild shake as if to clear it. And as the tension gradually eased off—as Millie sensed his hesitation—so she was prompted to argue the point further. *Ian Goodly thinks it's a bad idea, Jake. And until now he's rarely set a foot wrong. Hasn't Harry Keogh himself warned us off the future? You know he has.*

Now Jake was himself again—almost—as he answered, *Yes, and I know what happened the last time I ignored his advice. So you win and I won't go, won't look. Not now, anyway.*

I'm so very glad! He heard her "sigh" her relief. *And Jake,* she quickly continued, *at least you know your thread is no more tainted now than it was after you first gave Korath full access to your mind. It doesn't seem to be getting any worse.*

But that was only a few days ago, said Jake. *What, a week?*

Is that all? Millie sounded surprised. *It feels like a very long time since we were down there in the dark with Szwart. But maybe that's because I'm trying hard to forget it.*

And maybe that comes easier for you, said Jake with a touch of bitterness in his voice. *Because in your case you don't have anything to remind you.*

Then he took her to a cafe he knew, overlooking a deserted, rain-swept beach in Cannes, where they drank coffees in silence before returning to London.

Or rather, before Jake returned Millie to London . . .

As Millie stepped from the Möbius Continuum, back onto the dais at E-Branch HQ, she staggered a very little. Ian Goodly at once lowered his dart gun and took her elbow, steadying her. But she had seen the gun anyway and looked at him—and at David Chung—with an expression that was something more than accusing.

Then Ben Trask came up on to the platform with them, taking her in his arms . . . or trying to. Backing away from him, Millie transferred her silent accusation to him. And even if he hadn't been what he was, Trask would have known the truth of that look in her eyes.

"They're just dart guns," he said. "Tranquilizers. I wasn't going to hurt anyone, but I wasn't about to let anyone *get* hurt, either."

"Well, as you can see, I'm hurt anyway," she answered. "Just what is it you think Jake would have done?" And before he could answer: "I'll tell you what he would have done—*if* he had been contaminated; he would have given himself over into your loving care. He would have asked E-Branch, asked you, for your help."

"Then why hasn't he come back with you?" Trask's logic, his overwhelming concern for the Branch—for people in general—overcame the guilt that he felt. "Is he . . . is he . . . ?"

"He's okay," said Millie. "At least I think so." And then, relenting as she saw the hangdog look on his face, she told him and the others gathered there everything that had happened.

As she finished, Ian Goodly said, "So, Jake didn't go scanning the future after all." The precog was visibly relieved.

"No, but he was tempted," Millie answered. "Perhaps he was afraid of what he might find—but I don't think so. I think he was simply heeding all the warnings he's had."

"So where's Jake now?" said Liz Merrick, whose anxiety for the Necroscope was such that she was almost in tears.

And Trask came in again with: "You say his life-thread was stable? That it hadn't got any worse since he let Korath Mindsthrall into his head? So what's he afraid of? Why couldn't Jake come back with you?"

"He said he wanted to go some place or places and think it over, work it out," Millie answered. Then she looked at Liz and smiled. "But he also said you'd know how to find him."

"I don't understand." Trask shook his head. "And I hate it when I don't understand! Surely he knows we need him— and especially now."

And Millie looked at him—looked at him hard and steadily—and said, "Jake thinks he's in the clear, but still he can't be absolutely sure. Have you ever stopped to consider that maybe he thinks a whole lot more of us than we've given him credit for? This could be his way of protecting us . . . by keeping well away from us. And come to think of it, Jake reminded me of something that applies to me as much as it does to him."

"Such as?" said Trask, frowning.

"That it's been only a few short days since he and I were down there, deep under London, with Lord Szwart," Millie answered. "How long does it take for the spores to take hold, fuse with us, and begin to mutate our systems? If I were as brave as Jake—if I thought I could face the future on my own—maybe I wouldn't have wanted to come back, either."

"You're brave enough," Trask told her then, as finally she allowed him to put an arm round her waist. "And as for Szwart's spores: *if* those sleepers are infected—which is something we just don't know yet—then why aren't you the same? Why didn't you sleep? . . . I mean, *if* you were infected."

She could only shrug and answer, "That's a whole lot of ifs and whys, Ben. Far too many, and I don't have any answers. Only a handful of prayers."

"You're not short on faith, I know," he said, his voice low and husky now. "And faith like that is bravery in itself. No, I think you would have come back, even if your life-thread was as red as hell's fires. That's how brave you are, Millie Cleary."

You, too, she thought to herself, as suddenly she felt the urge to cling to him, to this unswerving, rock-solid, dedicated man. *You must be brave, Ben Trask. For the fact is you can't be sure, either. Not of Jake, and certainly not of me. Yet you know where you'll be sleeping tonight, and with whom. But let's face it; you don't know what you'll be sleeping with. And to be honest, neither do I . . .*

*   *   *

Zekintha Föener—later Zek Simmons, and later still Zek Trask—was one of only a very small handful of the teeming dead who had ever spoken to Jake; on his behalf she played devil's advocate with the Great Majority, attempting to woo them to his side. Also, Zek had told Jake that all the world's knowledge was down there in the ground or blowing in the wind, and that there were plenty of dead people who went on in death to perfect what they had left unfinished in life, who *might* be able to help him with all kinds of problems and situations if only they could be persuaded to converse with him. It was chiefly Korath's fault that they couldn't.

Life they understood, for it had once been their condition. Death, too, for obvious reasons. But *un*death—a place between the two, and a fearful threat to the living who were their descendants—that was something they avoided with a will of iron. Only those few members of the Great Majority who had been close to the original Necroscope, Harry Keogh, would have anything to do with Jake, and even they were cautious, fearing excommunication from their worldwide, cemeteries-wide "church" of souls.

But on the other hand there were those among the Great Majority who would never be alone, who within their own small body—their own exclusive group—feared nothing except fear itself. Zek Föener was one of them, and the man whom she'd loved in two worlds, Jazz Simmons, was another.

On the Mediterranean island of Zante—more properly Zákinthos, from which Zek's name derived—she and Jazz Simmons had built a house and a life together following their adventures in Sunside/Starside. But no one lives forever, and Jazz had succumbed to an incurable illness. Zek's love of the island, and also of Jazz, had drawn her spirit back there on numerous occasions, and she was no longer a prisoner of the Romanian Refuge's dark, gurgling sump. Unlike Malinari's ex-lieutenant, Korath, who had been a stranger to the outer world of men before inveigling his way into Jake's mind, Zek had developed a certain mobility. And since she had been a telepath all of her life, she'd discovered

257

no great difficulty in contacting Jazz where he now lay at rest in a little cemetery overlooking the sea in Zante.

Familiar with the coordinates of the house near Porto Zoro, and having returned Millie to E-Branch HQ, Jake took the Möbius route to Zante, emerging from the Continuum on the pebbled path that led to the door of Zek's once-dwelling. Others lived there now, but he knew that Zek was as likely to be here as anywhere. He could of course simply call out to her—using deadspeak to discover her whereabouts—but that wasn't his way. Or rather, it hadn't been Harry Keogh's way, whose esteem for the dead was such that it wouldn't let him "shout" after them but caused him wherever possible to present himself close to their final resting places. As a Necroscope—*the* Necroscope—that had never posed a problem. And what had been good enough for the original was good enough for Jake.

Now he stood beneath Mediterranean pines under a night sky flecked with wispy clouds, and looked northwest at the lights of Zákinthos town where their glitter showed through the tangle of hanging branches. The sweet night air, laden with the scents of late flowers, herbs, and resin, was still misty from a recent shower; but the air wasn't Jake's medium as he softly enquired, *Zek, are you here?*

Jake? The answer came at once, from not very far away. *Yes, but not at the house. I'm with Jazz.*

Am I intruding? He felt awkward, unusual for him. It had to be more of Harry Keogh's alleged humility rubbing off on him.

Not at all, Zek answered. *In fact we were talking about you. Can you come to us?*

Her deadspeak voice was a beacon that Jake could home in on as easily as Liz's telepathy, and a moment later he stepped out of the Continuum at a location on the ocean's rim between Porto Zoro and Argassi. The clouds were clearing, and on a rocky promontory a small white church gleamed like alabaster in the light of the stars, its image reflected in the waters of the bight.

Between the beach and the dark silhouettes of gnarled

pines where they stepped down from the contours-hugging coastal road, a small graveyard was laid out in neat, regularly tended plots. Well hidden from the tourist beat in as tranquil a spot as anyone could wish for, only the gentle *hush! . . . hush!* of wavelets on sand and pebbles disturbed the place, and then like a heartbeat compensating for all the silenced hearts that were buried here.

Jazz Simmons's plot would probably seem unremarkable to any other visitor, but Jake was drawn to it as an iron filing to a magnet. And as he stepped closer:

Jake, said Zek, *this is Jazz's place. And this is Jazz.*

She could have shown Jazz as he'd been but didn't, and Jake understood that they were beyond such vanities now; it was sufficient that they were here. *It's my—pleasure?* he said, wondering if he'd chosen the right words. But apparently he had.

Mine, too, said Jazz, his deadspeak full of sincerity. *It's also my pride! You're the fourth, Jake, and there's not many of us who get to meet all four of you.*

All four of . . . ? For a moment Jake didn't quite understand, but then he did and said: *You met all of the others, too.*

Yes, I did, Jazz answered. *Zek and me both . . . but she knew them better than I did. I met Harry and The Dweller on Starside, where we all joined up against the Wamphyri in the great battle for The Dweller's garden. And I was with Harry and E-Branch out here in the Med when we went up against Janos Ferenczy. I might have missed Harry's boy, Nathan, but Zek brought him here so he could help us sort some things out that we'd never got round to while I was alive. And now there's you. So if there's any way I can, I'd like a chance to settle any outstanding debts.*

Debts? said Jake.

See, said Jazz, *I figure I owe all of your—what, predecessors?—all the other Necroscopes. I owe Harry for Zek, The Dweller for bringing us back to Earth from Starside, and Nathan for . . . oh, a good many things. But I never got around to squaring it with them. So if there's anything I can do for you, just mention it. You can collect on their behalf.*

And Zek said, *I feel the same way about it, but you already know that. So why are you here, Jake? I can feel that something is troubling you. And I really can't see why since it's obvious you've managed to get rid of Korath.*

Tongue-tied until now, on hearing that name Jake snapped out of it. *Oh, really?* he said. *You can't any longer sense Korath's presence? Previously you've said he was like a dark shadow that I was carrying with me. Something like that, anyway.*

That's right, said Zek. *I could sense him, dark and secretive against your warmth and openness. But no more. What did you do to get rid of him?*

And Jake sighed and admitted, *I didn't. Harry Keogh did. He locked him in an empty room in my mind. Put him someplace where he can't do any harm.* And then he told the pair all about it.

When he was finished Zek said, *Well, that's a start. But it isn't what's bothering you. Or if it is it's only part of it.*

And Jazz said, *Get it off your chest, Necroscope.*

Maybe that's it, Jake said then. *This Necroscope tag. Okay, so I use the Möbius Continuum, and yes, I do have deadspeak. But with me it really is a dead language! I mean, what good does it do me if the majority of the Great Majority won't listen to me? If they can't help me? Necroscope: an instrument for conversing with the dead? But there's only a small handful of you who want anything to do with me! It makes me feel—I don't know—like I'm guilty, or an imposter or something; like I'm not worthy of you. Makes me feel I can't possibly get up there with them, the real guys. Like I'm some kind of fake miming to the music.*

And Jazz said, *Well, if you're a fake, you're the best damn imitation I ever spoke to!* And then to his companion, in a somewhat puzzled tone: *Zek, didn't you tell me you thought Jake was a little, er, brash? In your own words, "a rough diamond"?*

Yes, and I told Jake so, too, Zek answered, unrepentant but wonderingly. *And so he is—or was.*

As for the cold side you mentioned, Jazz went on, *I have to admit I can feel that. But there was that about all the others, too: cold as steel sometimes, yet warm as the fires that forged them. To tell the truth, if you hadn't told me this was Jake, I would have been willing to swear it was Harry himself!* And:

There, said Zek to Jake. *That's a rare compliment. It seems you've made another convert.*

But Jake shook his head and said, *Not really. It's plain to me that you'd already been working on Jazz. Which reminds me, I remember what you said: that you two had been talking about me. So dare I ask about your topic of conversation—other than my, er, brashness, roughness, and coldness, et cetera?*

Have I offended you? Zek was at once anxious, even contrite.

No, Jake shook his head. And then he smiled. *In fact I even liked the "rough diamond" bit! But knowing that you're on my side—I mean, knowing the trouble you've been having with the Great Majority—I thought that maybe you had some news for me, something I might find useful?*

Zek "sighed" and said, *I'm sorry to have to say this, Jake, but despite everything you've achieved, still you haven't moved the teeming dead. I don't know why, but they're unimpressed.*

Everything I've achieved? (All that Jake could remember was a hell of a lot of violence and destruction!) But as always his thoughts were deadspeak, and Jazz answered them:

That, too, he said. *But surely the end justifies the means? As a result of all that violence, you and E-Branch have rid the world of a monstrous plague.*

Or at least you've started to, Zek quickly corrected him. And Jake said, *You know about all that?*

Of course, said Zek. *For that's what we were talking about when we felt your presence: all those undead, who are now truly dead, no longer a threat. We felt them come over onto our side, a great many of them. Most were im-*

*mediately excluded. The Great Majority will have no truck
with vampires.*

Which, in a nutshell, said Jake wryly, *describes my problem precisely.*

And he sensed Zek's nod. *Until you're completely rid of
the thing inside you, until our council leaders, our spokespersons, can be absolutely sure of you, nothing much is going to change.*

But Jake was frowning now. *You say* most *of the creatures we killed were excluded? So what about the rest?
Which ones didn't you exclude?*

There are always exceptions that prove the rules, Zek
answered. And because deadspeak often conveys more than
is actually said, Jake knew what she meant.

That was in Krassos. He nodded. *Those poor nuns that
Vavara defiled. You saved some of them.*

And most of the children off that ship, too, said Zek. *They
were simply, well, dead. But not all of them. As for those
nuns . . . a lot of them were too far gone into vampirism.*

Still, it seems unfair, said Jake musingly.

What does? said Jazz.

That while there's room even for vampires in the afterlife,
Jake answered, *or "redeemed" vampires, if you like, I've
got to remain a pariah. I mean, this is so frustrating! What
do I have to do to prove myself?*

Get rid of Korath, Zek replied. *He's the last hurdle, Jake.
And once he's gone, I'm sure the dead will accept you. In
fact, I really can't understand why they haven't already. But
then, I haven't been around as long as some. As a comparative newcomer, what weight can I add to the wisdom of
centuries?*

Which suggests, said Jake gloomily, *that maybe your
spokespersons know more than they're putting out for general consumption.* This was speculative and there could be
no real answer to it, but Zek tried to provide one anyway:

The Great Majority fear contamination, she said. *That
much has to be obvious. So perhaps when you and E-Branch
have dealt with the invaders from Starside . . . ?*

And Jazz said, *You're still with E-Branch, aren't you?*

I don't know. Jake was frank about it. *Being "with" an outfit like E-Branch is about as frustrating as trying to talk to the dead—er, present company excepted. I honestly don't know what goes on in their minds—or rather, I do. The trouble is, they have their suspicions, too. They're suspicious of me.*

Huh! said Jazz. *I know what you mean. It's a long time ago, but I still remember when the Branch recruited me. At that time they might as easily have called it DT-Branch— because that's what it was all about: Dirty Tricks! And when things went wrong it was usually their own agents who got shafted. I should know, because that's how I ended up in Starside. Since then, well, Zek has been trying to convince me that it's all different now, but it sounds to me like things haven't changed too much. E-Branch? You'll need to watch your step with those people, Jake. Get the job done and then get out. That's my advice.*

And Jake said, *You're saying that the job comes first?*

You shouldn't have to ask, said Jazz. *I mean, we're talking about the Wamphyri, right? If it was anything else I'd tell you to get out now. But like it or not, you are the Necro-scope, and even if the dead don't appreciate you your pow-ers were given to you for a reason. Harry gave you them to fight the Wamphyri. So what else do you need to know? Believe me, you wouldn't want to live in a world of vam-pires. If you'd seen Starside, you'd know what I mean.*

Jake nodded. *I already know what you mean. I've seen enough in this world, let alone Starside.*

So when you're done here, said Zek, *you will be going back?*

Is it that important to you? Jake asked her.

He sensed Zek's "nod." *You see,* she said, *despite that Jazz had some problems with E-Branch a long time ago, I know Ben and his people are the best sort. I'm sure of it because there once was a time when I worked with the wrong sort. Also, I know that what happened to me wasn't their fault. So if I could help them I would, and so should you. For goodness sake, Jake, that's why I'm trying to help you!*

But I haven't really left them, Jake answered. *I might possibly keep out of their way—and also out of harm's way—for a while, stand off and see how they get on, but I'm not walking out on them, no. There's someone with them who . . . who knows how to keep in touch.*

Good! said Zek. *And now? What are your plans right now?*

Right now, said Jake, frowning with his mind as well as his face, *there's someone else I want to talk to. But not here.*

From Jake's suddenly grim tone of voice Zek guessed at once who he was talking about. *Korath?* she said, her own tone apprehensive. *Do you think it wise? He's one sleeping dog you should let lie until there's a way to dispose of him for good! I mean, he's sure to play his word games with you—and you don't need reminding what happened the last time you tangled with him.*

No, I don't, Jake answered. *But where word games—more properly mind games—are concerned, it seems I've become something of a player in my own right. I'll feel far more confident in my dealings with Korath now. Anyway, I know that if he gets out of hand I can always lock him up again.*

You're sure about that? said Jazz.

I reckon. Jake nodded. *See, I can feel him in there banging on a certain door—but faintly, so that it doesn't bother me. And there's a window in that door that I can open and close. He can't escape unless I open the door for him, and until then the window lets me talk to him.*

But why would you want to? said Zek.

Because if there's anyone who knows what our three Wamphyri invaders will do next, said Jake, *it has to be Korath. The last trick up his sleeve, and it's high time he played it.*

But remember, Jake—no more deals, no false partnerships! (This from both of Jake's dead friends, spoken forcefully as by one very concerned person.)

You have my word on it, Jake reassured them. *No more*

deals, no more partnerships, no more bargaining. Not if I can help it, anyway.

So where will you talk to him? said Zek.

And as Jake conjured a Möbius door, he smiled a gaunt, grim smile and answered, *In the place that's most suited to him. The place where we first met him, you and I. A place as night-black and soulless as Korath himself, and the only place I know where he's the frightened one and I have the advantage.*

The sump under the Romanian Refuge, said Zek, "shivering."

Got it in one, Jake replied, before saying a brief farewell and making his exit . . .

The Romanian Refuge, or rather its subterranean ruins: Jake had been there once before, in something that had been a great deal more than a simple dream. The revenant of Harry Keogh had taken him there to speak to Malinari's ex-lieutenant Korath, but Jake had failed to heed Harry's warning and now Korath was locked in his mind, almost but not quite a part of him, yet sufficient of a presence that he was gradually ruining Jake's life.

In the dream, Jake had scarcely understood the principle of Möbius coordinates; he hadn't known that from then on he would automatically store such coordinates in his increasingly metaphysical mind. But now it had become as simple as moving from one familiar room into another; it would have taken just a fraction of a second to step into the Continuum at Jazz's graveside, and out again into the gloom of the sump whose hydraulic energy had once powered the Refuge. And yet Jake exited the Continuum warily, slowly, feeling the way before him and ready at a moment's notice to return to the nothingness of the Möbius dimension.

The reason for his caution was knowledge of the sump's system, the fact that it was fed by water flowing off the *Carpatii Meridionali,* the Transylvanian Alps to the north. For the seemingly endless European summer and its drought was finished, and the rains had returned with a vengeance.

While the Gate in Perchorsk (and therefore the Gate on Starside) stood open and dry, still water from the mountains might have flooded the sump. But Jake's concerns were illfounded; the water was no deeper than before; the explosion that had destroyed the Refuge had opened fresh outlets for the resurgent waters, through which they now flowed into the nearby Danube.

Jake's eyes took a little while to adjust from the velvet, dusky, starry night of a Greek island to the gloom of the sump, but gradually he was able to make out his surroundings. And he saw that nothing had changed; it was just like the first time, even though that first time had been in a dream:

The caved-in ceiling, sagging in places and in others bulging upwards from the furious force of powerful explosives; the collapsed stanchions, great tangles of shattered metal and concrete, cratered from the blast and blackened by fire. And back there along what was once the course of the subterranean river, the way completely blocked where the original cavern's ceiling had succumbed to man-made convulsions and its own great weight of fractured rock.

Up to his calves in darkly gurgling water, carefully Jake made his way to the solid, twelve-foot-thick, reinforced concrete wall of the dam which contained the dynamos and sensitive equipment that once supplied and monitored the Refuge's power. The once-smooth face of the dam was gouged, cracked, and fire-blackened in places, but it was intact. Built to withstand the pressure of waters in flood, it had also survived the pressure of the blast.

Down against the wall of the dam where the water seemed to gurgle more blackly, viscously yet, the dully gleaming, curved upper rim of a steel pipe projected some seven or eight inches above the swirl: one of the conduits that had used to feed the dynamos. From its curvature Jake could see that the pipe would be maybe fifteen inches in diameter. A child, or an incredibly thin man, or perhaps a circus contortionist, might just be able to crawl or slither through it.

As for Korath-once-Mindsthrall—he had been none of

these things but a grotesque, hulking lieutenant of the Wamphyri. Yet in order to attract attention to the sump and thus effect their escape, Nephran Malinari and his vampire colleagues had exerted their combined strength to cram Korath alive and screaming headfirst into this pipe like so much sealant into a leaky cistern; and in order to do so they'd broken the bones in his shoulders, hips, and lower legs, and folded his feet in after him!

Korath's flesh had long since sloughed away, but his naked bones were still in there, endlessly swirled and rounded by the action of the water, polished as if they'd been boiled . . .

Jake backed away from the conduit, got up onto a dry ledge of concrete that had fallen from the ceiling, used the flats of his hands to squeegee water out of his trouser bottoms, and sat hugging his knees while he considered his approach. In the end, however, there was nothing to consider; nothing left to do but open that window in his mind, speak to the monster, and try to convince him to return to his watery grave.

While Jake told himself that this was his principal reason for being here, he knew it wasn't the only one. There was also the matter of Malinari, Szwart, and Vavara: what they would do next, now that their initial plans were in ruins.

For even without their fungi gardens, still they were monstrous invaders from alien spheres, with powers enough between them to turn the Earth into a wasteland that would rival Starside. And whether Jake liked it or not, he accepted that Harry Keogh's legacy had become his burden.

Like an invisible force from within it powered him, and it would not be denied . . .

16

Romania, and Korath—London,
and Liz—
Turkey, and Bernie Fletcher . . .
and Friends?

JAKE "LISTENED" TO A PLACE INSIDE HIS HEAD, concentrated on one of the many "rooms" in the mansion of his mind. The vampire was in there—his mental stench was unmistakable—but he was no longer banging on the door. He could be asleep, but Jake didn't think so. And:

Korath, he said, as he accessed that secret inner region, *I think it's high time we talked, you and I. But since this could be the last chance you get to talk, you'd better watch what you say. And you should most* definitely *watch what you do or try to do—for you can bet your life I shall be watching.*

I bet my life a long time ago, Korath answered sulkily. *And I lost the bet. So what do you want of me now, Jake Cutter? And where . . . where have you brought me?* With that last question, a certain disquiet had found its way into his deadspeak voice.

Slowly turning his head, knowing that Korath would see what he saw, Jake scanned the collapsed cavern. Then, quite deliberately, he directed his gaze toward the sullenly gleaming rim of the conduit, like the open mouth of a great metal fish breaking the surface of the swirling water.

That place! Korath "gasped" then, and the vibrations in the psychic aether were the equivalent of a shudder. *You've brought me back to* that *place!*

Jake nodded and answered, *Knowing that you're uncomfortable here makes me feel that much more at ease, gives me the psychological advantage. And on the subject of psychology, a warning: don't go messing with my emotions. Back at E-Branch HQ you very nearly had me—you almost took control of me—but that won't happen again. Only let me feel a tweak, the smallest tweak, and I'll close this window, lock the door, and weld it shut on you. After that, I can guarantee there'll be no more visiting days.*

Huh! Korath snorted his bravado, but it came off sounding a lot less than derisive. *Do you really think it'll be that easy? Well, it won't be! You may have power over me now, but it can't last for ever. You have to sleep sometime, and when you do—*

—When I do, Jake cut him short, *nothing—but nothing— is going to happen.* And settling himself a little more comfortably on the rough concrete slab, he explained, *You see, Korath, it's an automatic thing. This new trick of mine is as instinctive as breathing. I don't even have to think about it. From the moment I break off talking to you and close this window, you're locked in, shut down, deaf, dumb, and blind. And me, I can carry on living my life as if you'd never existed in the first place. Why, I might even forget you're there!*

He let that sink in, waved a hand negligently in the direction of the morbid conduit, and went on: *You want to know something? You've no idea just how fortunate you were in that pipe. You could always eavesdrop on the thoughts of the teeming dead; you were never completely isolated; you were at least conscious of your own loathsome self. But locked in my mind, out of touch with everything . . . how long do you think you'd last before you lost even that degree of consciousness, self-awareness? How was it for you, how did it feel these last few hours? You're locked in the smallest isolation tank in the whole wide world, Korath, and it isn't about to get any bigger.*

Not a pleasant prospect, said Korath, gloomily. But then he brightened. *However, we know it isn't going to happen. It's not what you're about, for if it was you would have done it without recourse to me. No, you're not the type to bring me here simply to threaten and torture me, Jake. Oh yes, I can see the "psychological edge" that this hideous place gives you. But answer me this: why would you even require such an edge if you're as powerful as you pretend? So then, enough of all this and let's cut to the chase. Simply tell me what you want of me—and what I'm to get in return.*

Seeing his advantage slipping away, Jake gritted his teeth and said, *When I'm finally rid of you, I think I'll really miss these little sessions of ours. You're a truly remarkable creature, and in certain ways I can't help admiring you. You haven't a snowball's chance in hell but still you won't give in. Wamphyri? You came pretty damn close, and I reckon Malinari knew it. You would have ascended soon enough.*

It's true, the other readily agreed. *I had outlived my usefulness and Malinari feared I might usurp him. At least, he was aware of the possibility. Or so I pride myself. In any case, he chose his moment of treachery perfectly and found a last-minute use for me to boot. But there's more than mere flattery in what you just said. Indeed, by introducing Malinari into the conversation you've revealed your real reason for speaking to me.*

Part of it, Jake answered. *My entire reason for speaking to you is to make you an offer, give you a choice. Isolation in my mind or freedom—well, of sorts—in this sump. In return for which you'll tell me what Malinari and his invader friends will do next.*

Hah! said Korath. *And this is a choice? I remember Malinari gave just such a "choice" to a slothful, noisy thrall: he could either leap from a high window—or be thrown!*

For being idle and noisy?

Aye! Korath snapped. *Thralls are for working, not for chattering, and definitely not for thinking. Malinari loathes noise—even the whispers of secretive, perhaps renegade thoughts—as much as he loves soft or plaintive music. In his great aerie in Starside he was wont to use the one to drown the other, thus achieving a tolerable balance. But as for his own balance: that was a very delicate thing.*

You mean he's a madman, said Jake.

Of course he is, said Korath. *As were most of the Wamphyri. I thought that was understood?*

Jake nodded. *I remember your stories of Starside now, which you told to me and Harry Keogh in this very spot. At that time, however, all of this was new to me and I wasn't paying too much attention.*

Your loss, said Korath, *and too late now. You won't wheedle any more Starside stories out of me! What? My very existence—what little is left of it—under threat, and here's me giving away valuable information? You must have been practising, Jake; your word games are much improved! But be that as it may, nothing has changed. Still I ask you, what is this for a choice: to be locked in your mind or returned to this dreadful sump? Bah!*

You won't tell me what these invaders—the selfsame creatures who murdered you—will do next?

Not even if I knew, said Korath. *For my days of doing deals with such as you are over. Our so-called partnership—which you have betrayed—is as dead as I am.*

Jake couldn't leave it at that, and said, *Are you trying to tell me you don't know what they'll do next? But can't you even guess?*

Perhaps I could, said the other. *But I won't. I've done you my last favour, Jake Cutter.*

And now Jake got angry. *Favours? You've done me no favours, Korath. The only reason you got into my mind in the first place was to usurp me as you would have usurped Malinari. You planned to take over my mind, gradually squeezing me out until you were all that was left: your filthy mind in my body! Well, it didn't work, and now you're in an even tighter squeeze. So we'll leave it at that for now. I'll let you think it over and maybe—just maybe—give you another chance later.*

Later? said Korath, with a coarse chuckle. *Is there to be a later, then? You'll return to make me a better offer, perhaps—now that this one has failed?*

Oh, I'll return, said Jake, trying not to snarl. *In an hour or so, or maybe a week, or a month, I'll return. And if by*

*then there's anything left of you—if you aren't completely
out of your mind—perhaps you'll see sense and get out of
mine, while you're still able!*

Sensing that Jake was leaving, Korath rose up defiantly
and cried, *Go then! And don't bother to come back until you
have an offer I can "live" with. Oh, ha-ha-haaaargh!*

But his mad laughter bounced back on him, for Jake had
shut him in, conjured a Möbius door, and taken his departure. He had gone, yes, but nothing achieved, for even now
he'd been obliged to take Korath with him . . .

Jake had left some money, items of clothing, and other personal odds and ends, in his room at E-Branch HQ. Now he
would go there—go *directly* there, along his own special
route—pack a suitcase, leave a brief, explanatory note, and
remove to somewhere, to just about anywhere else. Since he
no longer headed Europe's most-wanted list, the world was
his oyster, with all of his old haunts available to him.

And yet he held back from returning to London, telling
himself that the night was far too young. Ben Trask and his
agents would be working late; there'd be people coming and
going; Jake might well find himself tempted to tell Liz Merrick what he was doing—which would be a neat trick, because he didn't himself *know* what he was doing!—and so
forth.

Liz, yes. It was mainly Liz. He'd probably bump into
her—no, he would definitely, deliberately bump into her—
and that was something he didn't want.

Oh, really?

Oh, he *wanted* it, all right—he would be crazy *not* to want
Liz—but he knew that it would tie him to the Branch, and
that Trask would probably try to tie him down! The man
would be intrusive, to say the least. What's more, it could
prove dangerous to Liz.

What could prove dangerous? Sex with Jake, *if* he should
get lucky . . . because then Liz might get *un*lucky.

Damn it all to hell!

And with his frustrations mounting, Jake went over it

again. His red thread: was it just Korath or something else, something much worse?

Trask's main men at E-branch seemed convinced that Jake was in the clear, but Trask himself was unsure—and he was the one who should know the truth of it, wasn't he? But then again, how could he know what Jake himself didn't know, what he was scared to find out?

And yet for all Trask's caution, tonight *he* would be in bed with Millie Cleary! But why not, since he'd already jeopardized himself? It was common knowledge in the Branch that he and Millie were lovers, and that they'd been lovers before—*and since*—the episode in Szwart's toadstool garden. So that even before Millie's trip through Möbius-time with Jake, Trask had accepted that she wasn't infected . . . or at least he'd accepted the risk that he was taking.

But as for Liz: as yet she was definitely in the clear, and Jake wasn't about to do anything to alter the status quo. Or so he kept telling himself . . .

But on the other hand, and according to Millie, so was Jake in the clear: the red in his thread was Korath. It reminded him of something out of an ancient Danny Kaye movie: "the tint with the taint is in the vassal from the castle" (or more properly, in a lieutenant from a Starside aerie), "while the blood that's good has a hue that's blue."

Such was Jake's odd, not exactly humourous train of thought as he wandered a lonely beach in the Algarve where the sand was still warm, the boulevards of Paris in the dusk of evening, the dreary, rain-damp promenade in Marseilles.

Until eventually it was night not only in Greece, Portugal, and France, but right across Europe and far out into the Atlantic . . .

By 10:30 Jake had consumed three or four brandies too many in a smoky, oak-beamed pub in the heart of London, just a ten-minute walk from the hotel that housed E-Branch. Because of the proximity he'd kept his psychic shields firmly in place, a precaution he intended to maintain when he rescued his belongings from his room.

Or at least, that was what he'd told himself.

But after he'd made his Möbius jump to his locked room, and as he packed his suitcase:

Jake? A voice out of nowhere, but not deadspeak. And: "Shit!" he said.

And literally reading his mind: *You weren't going to let me know you were back?* It was Liz, of course, not too far away and hurt and indignant.

It seems your talent is improving all the time, he said, in her own mode. *Either that or our rapport is getting stronger.*

Which is a whole lot more than can be said for our personal relationship, she came back at him.

He sat on his bed, sighed and told her, *I want you like mad—and I feel I'm going mad—because I reckon you want me, too. You know how I feel about you. Of course you do, because of the way you've always been able to read me. But you've got to admit it, Liz, there's a pretty good reason why . . . why we shouldn't.*

Not according to Millie, she answered. *I've been talking to her and she says that from what she saw in the Continuum you're safe. That in itself would be enough for me, but there's more.*

More? Jake could tell from the tone of her telepathic voice that over and above her resentment, still she was excited about something.

You're safe, Jake! she told him. *You really are! And if you hadn't been in such a hurry to clear out . . . but where are you? Close, I know. But can you come to me?*

That was what he had wanted to hear, Jake realized that now. It was why he'd relaxed his shields, so that he'd be able to sense Liz close by, smell her scent on the psychic aether.

But could he go to her? Lord, yes! If only to find out what she was talking about. (Oh, really? Only that? Who was he kidding?)

It was one of the shortest jumps he'd ever made, and it was only now that Jake discovered just how close she'd always been, that in fact her room was at the back of his, and only a flimsy partition wall separating them.

But now, as he homed in on her and stepped from the Continuum into normal space, nothing separated them.

Liz's bedside light was turned down low and she was sitting up in her tousled bed. She wore a shirt of some gauzy material, open in a long V in front, and the light shining through from the side silhouetted her left breast almost as if it were naked. The hollows under her eyes wore the telltale, purplish bloom of a telepath who has been hard at work, and there were also signs that she'd been crying. No need to ask what Liz had been doing. Obviously she'd been "scanning" for him, but he'd been too far away and too well shielded.

He sat down on the foot of the bed, shrugged helplessly, and said, "What can I tell you? Of course I wanted to see you, want to hold you, want us to be together, and want to ... to ... but I don't trust myself. I mean, I trust *myself* but not the thing inside me. Or the thing that might be inside me."

"Korath?" she said. "But he's locked away now—isn't he?" And after staring at him for a moment in that searching way of hers, "No, I see now that you don't mean Korath."

"Korath is locked away good and tight," Jake answered. "Oh, he would have enjoyed playing the voyeur, but that's beyond him now. I'm not so much concerned about him as this other thing of mine, this crimson stain. And I thought that was what you meant when you said something about my being safe."

"But that's *exactly* what I meant!" she said, leaning toward him so that her shirt fell open. She followed his gaze, saw her nakedness, and her first instinct was to cover herself—which she ignored. And: "Jake," she said, her voice so thickened that she could barely speak his name. "Jake, even if we didn't think you were okay, still I would want you. Our minds are already as one, or they would be if we worked together in full cooperation. And there's no longer any reason why our bodies shouldn't be as one, too."

He leaned towards her—felt love in his heart and lust in

his loins—then snatched himself away, shook his head, and got to his feet. "You don't know what you're saying!"

"Yes I do!" Liz said. "I'm saying I'd take a chance—just like Ben and Millie are taking a chance—but that it's such a remote chance now that it no longer merits our concern."

"You'd better tell me what you're talking about," he said. "And *please*, do it quickly. What's been happening here?"

"Come here," she said, holding out her arms to him.

He couldn't any longer resist her. Stepping quickly to her side, he sat down on the bed and took her in his arms. But the way he held her, so tightly that she couldn't move, was simply to stop this thing from going any further until she'd told him everything. And now she did.

"Just an hour ago we got a message from the Minister Responsible, relayed from Porton Down. It was about that specimen you got for them. The plasma in it was . . . it was still alive; it wasn't quite dead as we understand death, if you see what I mean. And they had found similar activity in other specimens. Cells were regenerating, the blood wasn't coagulating, and the flesh—God!—was still fresh. It was all too deep for me and went right over my head. Anyway, after carrying out all kinds of tests and trying various agents on it they discovered that plague bacteria kills it dead!"

"Plague bac—?" Jake released her just a little. "You mean that new strain of the bubonic out of China?"

"The same." Liz nodded.

"What?" Jake's jaw fell open. He let go of her, sat back, let it all sink in—but in another moment he shook his head despairingly, lifted his eyes to the ceiling and gave a harsh, barking laugh. And taking her by the shoulders he said, "Well, isn't that just bloody wonderful?" And surprised by her frown, her puzzled expression: "Liz, what is it with you? Haven't you forgotten something? Some small, perhaps insignificant detail? Like out in Australia how we all had *shots* against the plague! Every bloody one of us—and by now just about everyone in the world! How can you be so happy sitting there telling me we've discovered another way to kill vampires just a couple of weeks after we've immunised ourselves *against* that agent?"

But now she was laughing, too, bringing his outburst to an abrupt halt. And: "You didn't let me finish," she said. "Those jabs we took were made of dead plague bacteria. Dead to us but *undead* to the undead! From now on if they suck on us—on anyone who has had their shots—they just won't be able to take it. The agent will reactivate in them. Nothing of their filth can get into us, and anything of us that gets into them—"

"—Will kill them?" It was too much for Jake, too sudden. And now they were both laughing, but really laughing—almost hysterically laughing—as they collapsed in each other's arms.

Then Jake grew thoughtful, sat up and said, "Then the tint with the taint really *is* in the vassal from the castle. It has to be. In him and him alone."

"What?" she said, stroking his neck with one warm hand and unbuttoning his shirt with the other.

"No, wait," he said, drawing back again. "Something's out of whack here. It isn't right. In fact it's very wrong!"

"What is?" She fell back against the bed's headboard.

"I'm talking about those people on the *Evening Star*," Jake answered. "What about them? They must have had shots. Yet they became victims, and it doesn't seem to have affected Malinari or Vavara one little bit!"

"Oh, that!" Liz said. "Well, Ben asked the Minister Responsible the same question. It seems that Porton Down didn't have the capacity to manufacture sufficient of the antidote for the entire population, so they tendered it out to other manufacturers. And of course it was all done in a big hurry. Also, a decision was taken to only inoculate people who were entering or leaving the country. If you remember, that's what the Australians did, too, at ports and airports, et cetera."

"I remember." Jake nodded. "So?"

"The *Evening Star* cruise was a package holiday," Liz went on. "All the passengers had flown out from Heathrow, where they were given their shots, to Limassol where they boarded the ship. *But* . . . certain batches of the plague antidote were defective! They were harmless enough to the people who got them, but they just didn't work. And the Heathrow batch was one of them."

She had begun to unbutton his shirt again, but Jake wasn't happy with this as yet. "Okay," he said, "but the crew of that ship weren't all Brits."

"No," Liz answered, "but Trask speculates that just as you would be turned off by the smell of rotten food, so might vampires be able to detect inedible people. He also said something about pheromones: that Malinari and Vavara would probably feel repulsed by people who weren't 'right' for them." She had finished unbuttoning his shirt and was shrugging out of her own.

"Pheromones," said Jake, looking at her ample breasts, her delicious, stiffened brown nipples only inches from his hands, his chest, his mouth. "Well, I don't know about vampire pheromones, but right now mine are working overtime!"

"Mine, too," Liz answered. And:

"The blood that's good still has its blue hue," Jake said, ready now to believe it. "Moreover, the vassal is locked in my castle."

"What?" Liz said, turning back the covers.

"Nothing," he said huskily, ridding himself of his clothes and trying to reach for her all at the same time. And a moment later when they were both naked and she opened her arms to him between the sheets, everything else was forgotten as they came together like human magnets, but warm flesh as opposed to cold steel.

Then, riding that wildest ride, they lusted and loved, and lusted again, deep into the night. There was little or no foreplay and there were very few words, only sounds of endearment. For when bodies *and* minds join like that, the sensation itself is joyous beyond any such requirements . . .

Several rooms and many walls away from Liz and Jake, Ben Trask was preparing for bed. As he left the bathroom and entered the bedroom, Millie sat up straight in bed and said, "Ben, there's something I'd like to tell you—a situation— but first you must promise not to do anything about it."

He looked at her a little suspiciously, cocked his head on one side and growled, "It's been a hell of a long day, Millie. Can't it wait?"

"Yes, but if it waits until tomorrow you'll be mad at me."

"No I won't," he answered. "Not unless it's earth-shattering, in which case you'd have told me already. But okay, since you insist, I won't do anything about it. What is it?"

"Jake's back," she said, then bit her lip as Trask came to an abrupt halt beside the bed.

He took a long moment to think about what she'd said, then asked her, "Where, back?"

"He's here at the HQ, with Liz," Millie answered. "I mean, you know, he's *with* Liz."

Again Trask thought about it, and slowly got into bed. But in a little while: "Good!" he rasped, making it sound anything but good.

"Really?" Millie seemed delighted, perhaps cautiously skeptical, certainly surprised: a mixture of all these things.

"Yes, really." Trask put the light out, then folded her in his arms. "Because she needs him in order to . . . in order to be whole, I suppose. The way I need you. And I need him— *we* need him—because he's the Necroscope. So if Liz has got him, I've got him. But on the other hand, I still think Harry could have made a better choice. And the same goes for Liz."

He felt Millie stiffen in his arms. "What?" she said. "But we know Harry's reason now: unfinished business, Luigi Castellano and his organization, those vampires we knew nothing about who were survivors of Harry's lost years. Jake and Harry, they shared the same agenda, which made Jake the *obvious* choice! As for Liz: you can't blame her for being attracted to Jake. He's a very attractive man."

"He's a bloody obstinate man!" said Trask. "He thinks only of himself, and right from the start he's been a loose cannon. But now . . . well, now he's *our* cannon."

Millie snorted and pushed apart from him. "And is that it? Is that how you see it? Just another ace card up your sleeve?" Before he could answer she broke their unspoken rule, searched his mind and saw the truth, which was integral to Trask as his blood and bones. And:

"So *that's* it!" she said. "Now that we're together Liz has taken over my kid sister role. And nobody—not even the Necroscope—is good enough for your kid sister!"

"*Huh!*" Trask grunted. Then shrugged and said, "Well, maybe you're right. Maybe I'm being overprotective. But one thing's for sure: if Liz were really my kid sister, you wouldn't catch *me* playing at peeping Tom when she was entertaining a guest in her room!"

Millie crept back into his arms and said, "Me neither, but their shields were down, and they were so very—well, *very*—that it was almost unavoidable, like psychic fireworks! I mean, it's an odds-on bet that by now the entire HQ knows Jake's back and they're together."

"Voyeurs, the lot of you!" But still Trask had to chuckle.

"Not really," she said. "And actually it's sort of nice."

"What is?"

"To know we're not the only ones? Not the only lovers?" She gave a small shrug. "Something like that, anyway. And you know, even though I was only there for a moment— just long enough to detect their togetherness," (her cool hand automatically sought and found Trask's quickening pulse, the urgency of his desire), "I know it's still flowing out of them like . . . like a river of sweet wine on the psychic aether."

Trask lay still for a moment, then turned more fully towards her and said, "Me, I can't feel a thing. Not from them, anyway. But it's pretty obvious that you can."

"Yes," Millie breathed into his neck. "And it's *very* infectious."

Which was something that Trask made no attempt to deny . . .

* * *

Bernie Fletcher's psychic shielding had always been something of a joke to the rest of his colleagues in E-Branch; Ben Trask wasn't the only one who occasionally took the mickey, accusing Bernie of "glowing in the dark." But while it wasn't as bad as all that, still at close range Fletcher's aura—the waves he gave off into the psychic aether—would be clearly "visible" to most espers. Just as Fletcher was able to locate other talented individuals, so he could be located.

Which was why Trask had tended to use him as a tracker, in situations where he could keep his distance while pinpointing the target. That was how he'd worked out in Greece and Bulgaria, when he and Lardis Lidesci had been tracking the old Gypsy, Vladi Ferengi: Fletcher had guided Lardis and his minders unerringly to the Gypsy encampment, and then Lardis had gone alone into the camp to talk to the travelling folk. In short, Bernie had always played the part of "radar" or "Asdic" to E-Branch's far more potent "flak" and "depth-charge" units, the ones who followed up with fire and fury.

On this occasion, however, Fletcher was himself "the man," a lone field agent whose mission was to get as close as possible to his target, and remain in situ until his backup squad arrived to do whatever was necessary. Not that he was entirely alone; his minders had worked with him before and were specialists in close protection; they knew something of what E-branch was about and had been sworn to secrecy.

Right now one of them, Joe Sparrow (who was anything *but* a sparrow, a burly six-footer, hard as rocks and with fists like hams), was sitting just inside their hotel room's door reading a book. And his colleague, Cliff Angel (another misnomer), was out in the town trying to find a place to buy some cigarettes. At this time of night Fletcher suspected he'd be out of luck.

"The town." Was that what this was, a town? Looking out of the bleary window, Fletcher could think of a couple of hundred places where he would rather be. For Sirpsindigi (how the *hell* did you pronounce it?), on or close to the borders with Greece and Bulgaria, was just about as drab as it gets. A town? Well, it had roads, buildings, and a main motorway running close by, but as for anything else—forget it! And Turkey itself, from what little Fletcher had actually seen of it—which he had to admit wasn't too much in the flurry of travel arrangements and bumping along third-class roads in a hired boneshaker and what all—well, at least they'd got *that* one right. By no means a misnomer!

Oh, Fletcher knew that the country was rich in antiquities, archeological treasures, and the like; he was aware of the fact that Istanbul was a Mecca for tourists, and that plenty of Turkey's Mediterranean beaches were a match for anything that the Greek islands had to offer. *But*—

But Sirpsindigi was where his tracker's nose had led Fletcher and his minder colleagues, and here the trail had fizzled out. No beaches here, no treasures, and no more mindsmog.

That puzzled him, because the scent had been so strong. He had "known" where to go; it had been as if this place, and not Bernie himself, "glowed in the dark," or rather in that corner of his mind that housed his esoteric talent. And so he'd homed in on the glow and come here, only to discover that the beacon had been doused while he was still en route.

It could be, of course, that his aura had been detected by someone or -thing. Perhaps like a bloodhound he'd been "baying" too loudly, alerting the fugitives and causing them to lie low. Bernie didn't know for sure. So all he could do now was remain here, try to pick up the trail again, and wait until Trask and Co. arrived, when with any luck they'd improve on his findings before moving on to the next location.

And meanwhile he was stuck in this godforsaken dump— this two-taxis town on the edge of nowhere—that looked like nothing so much as a barely post–industrial revolution way station just a handful of stops up the road towards civilization. Take away the cobbles and streetlights, ignore the mopeds, rickety bicycles, and foul-smelling, three-wheeler vans; throw in some mud, a batswing door or two, and a couple of tumbleweeds . . . it could easily be something out of one of those old western movies. Except they had atmosphere and this hadn't.

"You're looking down in the mouth, Bernie," said Joe Sparrow, who had stopped reading and was now cleaning, oiling, and fitting together a carbon-fibre reinforced cermet 9 mm automatic, invisible on airport X-ray machines. Finishing up and slapping in a clip, he waved the gun at Fletcher and said, "I can't understand why your people don't use these things. Those Brownings of yours are hard to smuggle and make far more noise than these cermets."

"Right now I don't even have a Browning," Fletcher answered dolefully. "Too risky trying to get it in, what with the continuing border disputes and tensions with Greece." Then he managed a grin. "That's one of the few reasons I'm glad to have you and Cliff along. True, you fart a lot and clutter the place up, but you do have the firepower."

He looked into the night again, down onto the street, where a trio of figures with their coat collars turned up against the drizzle were just approaching the hotel's entrance. One of them looked like Cliff Angel, but what with the darkness, the bleary windows, and the rain it was hard to say for sure. And: "Jesus!" Fletcher commented, shaking his head. "It's like a night at the ends of the Earth out there! Shit, if Cliff's addiction doesn't give him lung cancer he'll die of pneumonia anyway!"

Then he looked at Sparrow again, and told him, "The reason we don't use those Keramiques is simply that our ammo has a low melting point and would wreck those barrels in no time. But our modified Brownings are custom-built and suit us to perfection." He didn't mention that the ammunition E-Branch used was made of silver; while his minders knew something about the Branch, they didn't by any means know it all. If they had . . . well, it might be a lot harder to find men who'd accept this kind of work.

There came a triple knock at the door . . .

For a moment neither Sparrow nor Fletcher moved; then they jerked to their feet and looked at each other through widening, anxious eyes. A triple knock? Only three taps when there should have been four? And they both knew that Cliff Angel wasn't the kind of man who'd be playing stupid practical jokes on them.

Fletcher crossed the floor to Sparrow in five long strides and whispered, "I saw three men come into the hotel."

Sparrow nodded his understanding, and called out loudly to whoever was outside, "That you, Cliff? Hang on just a mo!" And under his breath to Fletcher: "Answer the door—but nice and casual. I'll be back here."

As Sparrow took up his position behind the door, Fletcher shrugged down into himself, roughed up his red hair as if he'd just woken up, tried to make himself smaller. Then he took the chain off the door, opened it . . . and at once took a step backwards, his green eyes going wide in shock that was only partly faked.

The first face he'd seen out in the corridor was Cliff Angel's, but it was pale and drawn. Flanking him and close behind, two slightly taller, thinner men, who by their looks might well be twins or even clones, each held one of Angel's arms. And one of them was pointing a gun into the room.

As Fletcher backed off, he noticed that the strangers were looking as nervous as he was feeling. And as they began to bustle Angel into the room, so the minder shrugged himself free of them, held up his hands before him placatingly, and said, "It's okay, cool it!" His escort immediately came to a halt, at which Angel breathed a sigh of relief and said, "Come out from behind the door, Joe. It's okay—I think!"

But even as Angel spoke so his voice had hardened, and his stiffened left hand sliced down, striking the wrist of the man with the gun with sufficient force to send the weapon flying. A moment more and Fletcher had stepped forward, grabbed the man's collar and numbed, dangling wrist in a judo hold, turned on his heel and used his shoulder as a lever to hurl him far into the room. Fletcher was no slouch when it came to unarmed combat.

Meanwhile, Joe Sparrow had loomed into view from behind the door, stuck his Keramique into the side of the other stranger's neck, and told him, "Move slow—really slow—

and I won't kill you. Not yet, anyway." And dragging him into the room, he slammed the door, then gave the frightened-looking man a shove that sent him reeling, causing him to trip over his colleague where he lay sprawled on the floor.

Cliff Angel had snatched up the fallen weapon. Aiming it at the dishevelled strangers, he said, "Okay, and now you can tell me your story again. And this time we'll see if my friends here believe it . . ."

17
Sirpsindigi and London—
Double Detente

THE TWO MEN—WHO, IF LOOKS WERE ANYTHING to go by, were white Europeans—sat gawping at Fletcher and his minders, apparently stunned by the sudden reversal of fortunes. Yet Fletcher wasn't certain about that, and Joe Sparrow had found the encounter way too easy.

With his eyes narrowed, Sparrow said, "Cliff, what the *fuck* is going on here?" Glancing at Angel, he kept the muzzle of his Keramique trained squarely on their captives. "Did these people jump you or what?"

"They did and they didn't," said Angel. "They came from an alley as I walked past. But if they really meant to take me, it was the work of amateurs. I think I could probably have made my break, turned the tables, before we got back here. I considered doing it, but then they mentioned a few things that left me undecided. If what they said was true, then I didn't want to fuck things up. Apart from which—and to be honest—I didn't much fancy the odds. Not with a gun in the small of my back."

"They mentioned a few things?" Sparrow repeated him,

frowning. "About what? What kind of things?"

"Hold your horses, Joe," Angel answered. "Let's observe the priorities. Like first I want my gun back. And the one with the mole has it."

The mark that he'd mentioned—a small dark mole on the jaw of one of the strangers—was for the moment about the only way the pair could be told apart. For it was now apparent that they were in fact almost identical twins.

Angel approached the man in question, went to one knee and reached inside his overcoat, came out with his Keramique. Next, he brought out a wallet and flipped it open. Then, standing up, he said, "Well, what do you know? At least part of their story is true. Russian ID, and this one's called, er—"

"—Vladimir Androsov," said the man with the mole, holding his arm awkwardly and grimacing. Then, looking at Fletcher, he flinched and slowly added, "Is very possible you are dislocating my shoulder."

"Don't worry about it," Fletcher answered. "I was a physio in my time and can probably pop it back again. In fact I might even enjoy it." Switching his gaze to the other twin, Fletcher jerked his head enquiringly and raised an angry red eyebrow.

"Ah, yes." Androsov carefully, painfully streched his neck, inclining his head to look at his colleague. "This is Venyamin, my brother. He is not speaking the English very much. You will please excusing his quiet."

"Listen, you," said Angel, checking his weapon and cocking it, his voice a low growl. "Please excusing *my* impatience—my quickly getting pissed off—and tell my friends here what you told me."

Androsov nodded, grimaced again, and said, "Very well. You are the British E-Branch. We are from Russian E-Branch, Gustav Turchin's men. Our listening stations are picking up the story about the *Evening Star*. We are on the same case. Turchin has said that if we are meeting up with you, we are the allies and no longer the opposition. So, Venyamin and me, we are locators. Twins, we magnify, we multiply each other's skills. That is good, but when we apart we don't working so well. We following the trail to this place, Sirpsindigi. Is not so difficult; we have the safe house in Bulgaria just across the border. But when we are getting here the trail—"

"—Disappears!" said Fletcher, starting forward. And then, to Sparrow and Angel: "These people are on the level."

He moved to help Vladimir Androsov to his feet, but before he reached him Angel said:

"Wait! So why the rough stuff? Why didn't they simply approach us, even try giving us a call?"

"This is Turkey," Androsov shrugged, and winced again. "The telephones are bugged because of the trouble with Greece. Also, the separatists and fifth columnists are on the rise. Today the Turkish man trusts no one. You are lucky you got in. But Turkey needs the tourist money. Ah, but if you are questioned, why are you in this filthy Sirpsindigi? Why are you having the weapons? What troubles are you making? We could not taking the chance to come to you in daylight, in the open."

"But at night?" said Angel. "To jump me out of an alley?"

Androsov tried to look apologetic. "We are not field agents but locators. We are finding nuclear submarines or tracking the USA's mobile ICBMs. But now this thing is starting, Gustav Turchin's agenda has changed. He is saying that the whole world—not just Russia—has the big troubles." He looked at Fletcher. "You are a locator, we know that. Your shields are, well . . ." He let it tail off, and Bernie reddened.

"I glow in the dark, right? And that's how you found me."

"No, because we *looking* for you," said Androsov diplomatically. "But your friends are . . . what, the special policemen?" He shrank down into himself. "We not KGB, not trained in their techniques. We do not know how they will be receiving. So, how to approaching? We do it like you see. A big mistakes."

"Amateurs!" said Angel. "So I was right." And now *he* helped Androsov to his feet.

Bernie Fletcher had been looking the Russians over—by no means a difficult task, for in checking out one Androsov he got an image of both. Six-footers, they were thin as rakes and angular in their features. Dark-haired, grey-eyed, and light-skinned to the point of being pale, they would be in their mid-thirties. They certainly didn't look dangerous.

Office types, Fletcher concluded, desk-bound greenhorns who much like himself had suddenly found themselves thrust out into the wider, far more sinister world of the field agent. He found himself feeling sorry for them. At least he'd had a little previous experience.

"Okay," said Joe Sparrow. "So what happens now? I mean, are we all on the same side or what?"

"Yes," Fletcher answered. "And this could be the break I've been hoping for. Working with these fellows, I might be able to pick up the trail again. A bonus for Trask when he gets here."

Meanwhile Angel was frisking the Androsov twins. Apart from the one gun he'd picked up from the floor—a Tokarev TT-33—they were clean. Examining the Tokarev, now he commented, "Will you look at this out-of-date piece of crap? World War Two shit. A stopper at close range, but that's about all."

And Vladimir Androsov said, "Why spending money on sidearms when ICBMs are making them obsolete?"

"Your philosophy, comrade?" said Angel.

"Cold-war philosophy," Androsov answered. "They—the hawks and militarists—considered the space race more important. But the American SDI was a myth, and myths are elusive. Pursuing it weakened us. Anyway, that was then and things are swiftly changing. For the better, I thinking. In current situation, you and I are no longer at war."

"These people are what they say they are," said Bernie Fletcher. "It's like back at the HQ in London: I can feel a certain kinship with them. I'm in the presence of espers, locators. You can give him back his gun."

"Sure," said Angel, and handed it over—*after* removing the clip. Androsov had seen him do it and nodded.

"Trust is coming slowly," he said.

"Fuck it!" said Angel, pacing the floor. "I'm out of cigarattes. Nicotine deficiency. I'm on edge, that's all."

And standing up, Venyamin Androsov took out a pack of Marlboros, offered it to Angel, and shrugged. "Why you no saying? I smoking plenty. American blend. Black market. Very expensive."

Angel looked at him, and a slow grin spread over his craggy face. "You mightn't speak English too well," he said, "but you certainly pick the right things to say!"

Following which, relations rapidly improved . . .

In a little while, Fletcher and the Androsovs got down to it.

In front of the Special Branch men, Fletcher didn't use the term "vampire"; and fortunately, the Russian espers didn't know what they were tracking, only what little Turchin had told them—that these mutual enemies were exceptionally dangerous. Like Fletcher himself, they'd been advised only to *locate* the source of the alien aura, then to stand off and contact or wait for E-Branch to arrive, which Turchin had known must happen sooner or later. Sooner, as it had turned out.

Now, at 2:30 in the morning local time, the three parapsychologists sat at a small table and concentrated on a map of Sirpsindigi and the outlying district. The map's legend was in Turkish, but Venyamin compensated for any deficiency in his English with an excellent grasp of the Turkish language.

"At first," Vladimir Androsov explained, "from Bulgaria, we are locating these strange—how do you say it? Like your London when the vapour is coming off the river and all the peoples are doing the coughing—these mental 'fumes,' yes?"

"Mindsmog," said Fletcher at once. "I know exactly what you mean."

Vladimir nodded. "The smog in the mind, yes. But then, when we are coming here, the—mindsmog?—it quickly goes away. We feel it fading until it has gone." He stabbed at the map with a finger. "It was there."

Fletcher looked at the map, at a district already ringed in Biro, but couldn't make head or tail of it. "It's about—what? Half a mile south of here?"

"One kilometre," Vladimir nodded. "South and a little west. Then, because the mindsmog is gone, we are thinking is not dangerous to going there. It is the better part of the town. More better than here."

"We passed through when we drove in," said Fletcher. "But I wanted to stay at a place that was less prominent."

"Understanding," Vladimir answered. "We are the same."

And Joe Sparrow, standing close to the table, came in with, "So, what did you find there?"

Vladimir looked up at him. "Nothings," he said. And then he frowned. "But there was . . . I don't know . . . somethings. Like a bad taste in the mouth, but in the mind. It soon went away."

Cliff Angel pulled a face and said, "You psychoids are very weird people! You get results, I know, but I've never been able to figure you out."

"Believe me," said Fletcher, looking up at him, "you really wouldn't want to figure this out." And then, to Vladimir. "What about physically? I mean, was there anything about that part of town that especially impressed you—or *de*pressed you? Did you take note of where you got this bad taste, its exact location?"

And now Venyamin Androsov nodded, turned to his brother and said something to him in Russian. Fletcher caught just one word, *Kino,* which he knew meant "cinema" in German. So maybe it was the same in Russian. And:

"Kino?" Fletcher repeated him. "The cinema? What about it?"

"No," Vladimir shook his head. "This place is not quite the cinema. Films are showing there, but is also the cabaret—like the opera but not the opera—ah, the burlesque? The political satire? Also, the belly-dancing, yes! Especially the girls when they are dancing."

Joe Sparrow said, "I thought the Turks were just as fond of little boys?" Fletcher's minders were far less than politically correct.

And Cliff Angel added, "Like they'll fuck anything, right?"

Vladimir nodded his head this way and that—an impatient, be-that-as-it-may motion—and said, "Possibly, but better the naked ladies, I thinking. My brother speaks true: this place is the belly-dancing, er—*Schauplatz?*" He paused to seek confirmation from Fletcher.

And recognizing the German word again: "Theatre." Fletcher nodded.

"Good!" said Vladimir. "This 'theatre' was source of mindstink, yes."

"Mindsmog," Fletcher reminded him, and the Russian shrugged his acquiescence.

"So, what's on?" said Angel.

"Eh?" Vladimir looked questioningly at the two minders.

"What's showing at the theatre?" said Sparrow.

"Ah!" said Vladimir. "The ladies, I thinking. I seeing the posters. Very crude posters, but girls, certainly. The English girls, I thinking."

"A revue?" said Fletcher. "Like a troupe? Out of England?" The twins glanced at each other, but neither one of them could say for sure.

Fletcher thought about it for a moment, then said, "If you feel like it, we could try locating something now."

"Like what?" said Angel, stealing another smoke from Venyamin's pack on the table. "At this time of the morning? Do you really think anyone will be up and about?"

And Fletcher answered, "The kind of people that we're looking for . . . they do their best work at night." Then he held out his hands to the twins. Understanding the principle, they grasped his hands and formed an unbroken chain around the table.

At that, Fletcher's minders stepped back a pace. While they weren't entirely clear what was happening—some sort of séance was as close as they could guess—still they'd

worked with E-Branch before and knew when to keep out
of the way.

And under his breath, Fletcher warned, "Vladimir, Venyamin: don't do anything rash or stupid. And remember: we
can't linger over this. We're only taking a look-see—just a
glance—and the moment we find anything we break it off.
We can't afford to alert anyone to our presence here. Is that
understood?"

"*Da.*" The brothers nodded curtly, and all three espers
fell silent.

But in another moment:

"*Whoah!*" Fletcher exclaimed, as he snatched back his
hands and jerked upright, sending his chair skidding and
almost overturning the table. And: "What the *hell* was
that?!" he said, his voice and limbs trembling. But his question was meaningless for he knew well enough what it had
been.

The Russians, too: suddenly their thin faces were even
more drawn than usual, their eyes wide and unnaturally
bright.

"A very powerful . . . somethings!" Vladimir whispered.
"Mindsmog, but deep and dark."

"And . . . evil?" said his brother, his English finally coming together. "When we are finding nuclear devices, is not
evil. Is made by men but is not evil in itself, just devices.
This thing is different. It is the people—and it *is* the evil!"

Vladimir looked at him, shrugged and said, "Venyamin
speaks now . . . he is no more shy."

"Shy?" said Fletcher. "Is that all it was with him? Well,
I am shy—*very* shy—of whatever it was we just bumped
into! Now tell me, do you think it sensed us? Did it know
we were here?"

"It?" said Vladimir, with a puzzled frown. "You are
meaning other espers, our enemies, of course?"

Fletcher calmed down, got a grip on himself. He had noticed that just like the twins, his Special Branch minders
were frowning and glancing at each other, too. And: "Yes,"
he said. "Yes, of course. I meant our enemies, who may

well be espers in their own right. Do you think they sensed our presence?"

"Not knowing," Vladimir answered. "We were in and out, just like you saying."

And Fletcher sighed his relief. Then, still a little shaken, he sat down again and looked at the map. "It wasn't the theatre or *Schauplatz* or whatever . . . er, the mindsmog, that is. Myself, I thought I detected three or four separate sources, all spread out around the town. But none near us, thank goodness!"

"Likewise," said Vladimir. "But we—Venyamin and me—we *did* feeling the faint mindsmogs in or near the Kino. And we are having the idea."

"Go on," said Fletcher.

"Is night," said Vladimir. "The Kino is closed now. Perhaps this thing we feeling is—how you are saying—left over?"

"Residual?" said Fletcher.

"Residual, yes," Vladimir nodded. "From the evening, maybe. Is possible our enemies using the place, going there during the day or in the evening times."

At which Fletcher came bolt upright in his chair. Suddenly he'd remembered something in Ben Trask's initial report on that *Evening Star* affair: that Vavara and Malinari weren't the only ones who had got off the vampirized ship. There were also those they'd taken with them. And:

"Girls!" He gasped the word out. "Dancing girls! That shipboard revue: an entire bloody troupe of dancers!"

"Eh? What's that?" said Joe Sparrow. "Girls?"

"Tell us more," said Cliff Angel leeringly.

Fletcher put his brain in gear and thought fast. Trask had told him that if he ever got a definite fix—if he was certain of his target—to keep well away or face the consequences. *He*, Bernie Fletcher, should keep well away, because he "glowed in the dark." But his minders didn't. Moreover, they looked the part. They hadn't shaved since leaving England; and with a day to go before the next performance . . . by tomorrow night they'd be perfect! They could go see the show, and fit into the audience just like a couple of Turks.

Passing through the town on the way in, Fletcher had looked the people over. The locals were shop owners in the main, small-businessmen, and farmers. The women he'd seen had been few and far between. Odds were there wouldn't be *any* women in the audience at the Kino. Also, and as far as he was aware, where Turks were concerned, belly dancers—or *any* kind of female dancers, for that matter—would be irresistible. The place would probably be packed to the rafters, and his minders just another two faces in the crowd. But if there was anything "different" about these dancers, the Special Branch men might be able to spot it.

Or one of them would. For Fletcher had remembered something else that Trask had told him: never to be on his own without at least one of his bodyguards looking out for him. As for the security of whichever minder he sent: he'd be just one more man in a motley crowd, with little or nothing to distinguish him from the rest. And of course there was always safety in numbers.

Making up his mind, he told Sparrow and Angel, "The boss is supposed to get in tomorrow. But if by tomorrow night he hasn't arrived with backup, one of you is going to get lucky. Because I need someone to go and see that show."

Angel looked at Sparrow and said, "I'll fight you for it."

But Sparrow shook his head and grinned. "Naw! Hell, you're ugly enough already! We'll cut the cards." And then, turning to the Russians, "You boys play poker? Three-card brag? Blackjack? Get out your liras, ladies, the night is young!"

"Count me in," said Fletcher, "but first I need to speak to HQ, let them know what's happening."

"Not a good idea," said Vladimir. "Like I say, Turkish telephones not secure. You will speaking in code, of course?"

Fletcher smiled and answered, "Of course—well, in a *kind* of code." Because he knew that in London, John Grieve wouldn't be too far from the Duty Officer's telephone. And working with Grieve would be a lot better, faster, and far more secure than using codes devised by even the finest cryptographers . . .

The next morning, back at E-Branch HQ, Ben Trask was taking an early Orders Group.

As he was about to begin Jake showed up, and Trask stopped him in the doorway to Ops and asked what he was doing there—was he in or out?—he should make up his mind. Trask was his usual brusque self.

Jake said, "I'm in, but I'll play it my way."

It wasn't what Trask wanted to hear, and any other time he would be angry about it. He *was* angry, but right now he had to concentrate on his briefing, and since he really couldn't afford to lose Jake he nodded and said, "Okay." And then, as they were out of earshot of the rest of the agents who were already seated, he asked how Jake would play it.

"By ear," Jake answered.

"The rest of the gang do what the conductor wants," Trask told him. "And that's me." He inclined his head into the room, indicating the people seated in front of the podium. "You see, Jake, this is something that doesn't work too well. We haven't got started and already you're holding things up."

"So go and speak," said Jake, "and I'll sit in."

"But it can't be this way always," Trask growled, gritting his teeth as he began to lose it.

"It was always this way with Harry," Jake answered cooly. "He did his own thing."

"You're not Harry," said Trask, turning away and making to head for the podium.

Jake put a hand on his arm and stopped him. "You're right," he said, "I'm not. But every day I know a little bit more about him, and I haven't been learning it from you or from E-Branch."

Trask looked at him, shook his head in a mixture of disappointment and frustration, freed himself and made for the stage again with Jake close behind. Trask was fuming, but he couldn't deny that he knew what Jake meant. The fact was that each time he looked at him, the man seemed that much more like the original Necroscope. He didn't *look* like Harry so much as *feel* like him. But—

—But he did feel an awful *lot* like him . . .

Jake had taken a seat next to Liz at the back of the gathering Trask ignored his presence, and the briefing went well. When it was over, however, and the room began to clear, Jake approached Trask again, this time with Liz in tow.

"What is it now?" Trask asked them. "And keep it brief, for as you can see we're pretty busy right now."

"Liz asked what we were talking about," Jake answered. "She wondered if I was coming out to Turkey with you. Well, I'm not, but she can get me any time. It seems that we've got it down to a fine art: if she calls I'll hear her. I think I'll be able to home in on her just about anywhere. But it would be even better if you left her out of it altogether."

"Better for who?" said Trask. "Look, she's learning all the time. She handled herself just fine out in Krassos and on board the *Evening Star*. She'll be okay. She's in. Think about it: without Liz how could we get hold of you—*if* we needed you, that is?"

"And Millie?" Jake's deep brown eyes were staring, unblinking, hard as pebbles in a pool. "Is Millie in, too?" His question was below the belt and he knew it, but Trask had a surprise for him.

"She's in, too," he said, "because I'll need all the help I can get. The team's short a very important member: our locator, David Chung. That can't be helped because Chung's the expert on this other thing that's come up. He's been on it for years, and even if I tried to pull him off I know the Minister Responsible wouldn't wear it. Yes, I have Bernie Fletcher—who appears to be doing a great job out there so far; as you heard me say just a few minutes ago, he thinks he's found the girls who went missing with Vavara and Malinari—but there are occasions when he can be a liability, too, a danger to himself and the team both. That's one more reason why we have to get moving, get out there as soon as we're able: to give Bernie support . . . and yet *again* you're slowing things up. Can't you see? It's a case of 'if you aren't actually with us, then you're in our way.' "

At which Liz came in with, "Ben, Jake *is* with us. It's just that he has other things to do that we think may be at least as important—and maybe more important—than anything else you could have him do."

And Jake said, "I'm not fighting you, Ben. It's you who has something going with me, not the other way around. I don't know . . . maybe you think I'm undermining your position or something? But if that's so then it isn't intentional. It's just that I've got some things to do, and—"

"Oh, sure, of course you have!" Trask cut in bitingly. "And a man has to do what a man has to do, and all that crap, right? So tell me, what are these very important things—things which are obviously far more important than the security of our world—that you have to do? Wash your hair and get it braided again? Contemplate your *fucking* navel? Or maybe you came too close the last time and you've realized that life's too precious, right?"

Trask rarely swore, and more rarely yet placed emphasis on his swearing. But now he was angry beyond caring, and his rage was infectious.

Jake's eyes narrowed; his jaw jutted and his fists knotted. He stepped forward, and just for a moment looked like he intended to knock Trask down . . . but he didn't. A split second more, and the anger that filled the space between the two men burned itself out. But as Jake turned to walk away, probably for good, suddenly Liz burst out, "God, how I wish you'd stop it, both of you!"

Taken aback—caught off balance by Liz's righteous rage—their jaws fell and they looked at her in surprise. Flushed and furious, her eyes almost seeming to flash sparks, she turned to Trask and snapped, "To start with, I am *not* your little sister! In my private life I can do without your protection." Following which she almost immediately softened. "But you and the Branch, you *are* like family to me." And then, turning to Jake: "They're like *family,* Jake, and while I can be part of that I'll always want to be. In fact, I believe that's why we're here. It's our purpose in life. Yours and mine both."

"Hey, I'm not arguing with you!" Jake said, shrugging but by no means casually. "I think it's why I'm here, too—at least until this thing with the Wamphyri is cleared up. But if we're to have any kind of future together, I need to be truthful with you. I still can't say if it's me who wants to see it through or if it's . . . well, something—some*one*—else who's in control. Once this Wamphyri nightmare is over and done with, I don't know if the drive will still be there. If it isn't . . . that's when we'll have to make some pretty big decisions, when our paths might head in different directions."

Trask looked at them, sensed the uncertainty in them— all the confusion of a devious future—and felt something wrenching at his heart. "Do you two love each other?"

"Yes," they answered as one. And of course he knew that it was true.

He nodded, took a deep breath, let it out slowly and said, "Then you won't let anything stand in your way. You'll work it out. And don't think I'm just an old man who doesn't know what he's talking about, because I do. I knew the risk I was taking—with Millie, I mean—after she'd been down in Lord Szwart's bloody dreadful garden. And Millie herself, she even warned me off. But you know something? I didn't give a damn. How could I give a damn? What kind of love would it be if . . . if I couldn't comfort the one I loved? And anyway, without Millie I wouldn't want to go on either. So that's how it was, and how it will be for you two if you really love each other. Believe me, there's nothing in your way that you can't move aside."

He turned to Liz. "As for E-Branch: the Branch is just the Branch, Liz. It's not the be-all and end-all that I used to think it was. And it's cost me way too much. It was here before you, and it'll be around long after you move on. I mean, hell—I'm not the first Head of Branch and I won't be the last! It'll be around long after *I've* moved on, too!"

Then, turning to Jake (and discovering that he "felt" even more like Harry Keogh), Trask said, "Now you tell me, what use are your powers if you let them set you apart from the one you love?"

"Not much damn use," said Jake, completely taken aback.

"Then don't let it happen," said Trask. And to Liz: "Let me talk to Jake alone for a moment, will you? And don't worry, I'm all done with shouting and tearing my hair."

And after she'd gone he said, "I don't care what Liz says, Jake, she's still my kid sister. But okay, so the responsibility is yours now, and you're the one who'll carry that weight. Fine, but whatever you do don't drop it."

"I'll always be watching and listening," Jake answered. "I can't do any more than that. But in your world—the world of E-Branch—it won't be an easy job." Then he grinned and said, "You know something? I always reckoned you for a hard man. But what you just said, about you and Millie, and me and Liz . . ."

"Don't go reminding me," Trask held up a hand in mock protest. "And please don't mention it again. What, do you want to ruin my reputation?"

They both laughed. Then, growing serious again, Trask said, "I really do have to be getting a move on. But before I go I'd like you to tell me: what is it you've got to do on your own?"

"It mightn't seem very much to you," Jake answered, "but I want to catch up on all those Keogh files that I still haven't had time to read. John Grieve tells me there's maybe eight hundred crammed pages of files on the original Necroscope. I want to sit down with them in Harry's Room, shut everything out and soak them up. The reason is simple: the more I learn about him, the more *yet* I seem to know. It's like—I don't know—like I'm *remembering* him, like I'm gradually understanding him that much better."

Trask nodded. "And the better you understand him—?"

"—The better I'll be able to do his job," said Jake. "And I've reached the stage where I want to do it as well as I possibly can."

"Then you'd better get to it," said Trask, "because I'm all done trying to tell you what to do. From now on you're your own man. Come to think of it, maybe your *not* coming to Turkey with us makes a lot of sense."

"Oh?"

Trask nodded. "You're a hell of a power in what we think of as the psychic aether, Jake. With your talents, you have to be. And Malinari's one *hell* of a mentalist. The rest of us might be able to creep up on him—we got away with it on Krassos for a while—but I don't think you could. He'd know you were there. So perhaps it's for the best that you keep your head down, then come on like the cavalry when you're most needed. That's the way it's worked best up to now."

"I think you're probably right," said Jake.

"Well, then," said Trask. "Those files are waiting for you, and I've got to go."

Without any hesitation, Jake held out his hand. "Good hunting, Ben," he said as they shook on it.

"Likewise," said Trask. "Break a leg, Necroscope . . ."

18
Getting to Know Harry—
and Ill Met in Turkey

THE TEAM CONSISTED OF TRASK, GOODLY, PAUL Garvey, Millie, Liz, and Lardis Lidesci. There were no techs this time around, simply because they would have nothing to do. Unlike the Australian job, there'd be nowhere to hook up their equipment, and no cooperation—not with the Turkish authorities.

Also, and especially since Gustav Turchin had come on the scene, Trask was becoming increasingly aware that the "gadget" side of E-Branch was letting him down—not the techs but the technology itself. Technology had been moving so fast in these last fifteen years that it had become too difficult, too expensive, even for governments to keep up. And so Trask's "ghosts" had come into their own and were now the mainstay of any operation.

His ghosts, yes: the talented men and women he controlled, the espers who *were* E-Branch.

The team's makeup was dictated by the situation. With the addition of Millie and Paul Garvey (and despite the unavoidable exclusion of David Chung), it could even be considered stronger than the team Trask had used on Krassos. It might seem a little top-heavy in telepaths, but with good reason.

Trask had learned from experience in Australia and Krassos; he knew that up against a mind like Malinari *the* Mind, it would take exceptional mental shielding to maintain security. Liz and Millie worked well together, and Garvey's shields might even be powerful enough to hide all three espers when they were working in tandem. Indeed, in the not-so-distant past there'd been several occasions when Trask would have liked to have Garvey working as a field agent, but Paul's personal situation had always deterred him.

Tall, well-built, and athletically trim despite his fifty-six years, Garvey had been good-looking . . . he *had* been, before he'd gone up against one of Harry Keogh's most dangerous adversaries, a psychotic necromancer and serial killer called Johnny Found, and lost the left side of his face. That had been twenty years ago; between times some of the world's best plastic surgeons had worked on Paul until he looked half-decent, but a real face is more than just so much flesh scavenged from other parts of the body. His reconstructed features had been built from his own tissues, true, but the muscles on the left (what scraps had been left by Johnny Found) didn't pull the same as those on the right, and after all these years, still the nerves weren't connecting up too well. Paul could manage a "smile" with the right side of his face, but not the left; for which reason, and even though his colleagues were accustomed to it, he normally didn't smile at all . . . and avoided all other facial expressions, too.

Since this was a purely physical condition, however, Paul's disability hadn't in any way affected his work with the Branch, and it wasn't the reason why Trask had usually kept him back at the HQ in a rear-party role. The real reason was this:

That two years earlier Garvey had taken the plunge and married a blind girl, which had made them the ideal couple. Receptive of his telepathic skills, his wife had found a new lease of life in Paul; she could "see" through his eyes! And with her he needn't any longer feel concerned about his looks; he had found an outlet for years of trapped emotions.

This was why "hard man" Trask had been protective of him . . .

But a week ago Paul's younger wife had presented him with a baby daughter, and now both mother and child were doing well in the care of her parents who lived close to a blind school specializing in postnatal studies and practice. Since this would be the way of things for some months to come, it was time for Paul Garvey to get back in harness. And just in time, too, for Trask needed him.

There was of course one other member of the team whose name hadn't come up on Trask's list: the locator—or more properly human bloodhound—Bernie Fletcher himself, who was already in situ. Complemented by Garvey's and the girls' talents, Bernie's lodestone probes would be enhanced to match the requirement . . . or so Trask hoped.

As for Goodly: the gaunt, stringbean precog had been having plenty of trouble with the future lately. This was nothing new, however, and Trask had frequently noted that when the going got tough, Ian Goodly usually got going. In his capacity as previewer of things to come, he'd rarely let Trask down.

That left Lardis Lidesci, and he was there . . . he was there *because* he was Lardis! That nose of his; his sensitivity to all things Wamphyri; his seer-ancestor's blood, and his "invisibility"—the fact that he was able to "hide" within himself, like all of Sunside's Travellers—when rampaging vampires came too close for comfort.

And finally the Brothers Androsov, Gustav Turchin's men, of whom Trask had no previous knowledge, no way as yet of checking their credentials or psychic potential. They would seem to have had little difficulty in "locating" Fletcher . . . but was that a good thing or a bad thing? All well and good, as long as no one *else* located him. Trask could only hope that their shields were better than Bernie's. He certainly couldn't fault the fact that one of them, Venyamin, bore the Russian version of his own forename! And if the Androsovs worked out as well in Turkey as Manolis Papastamos and his men had done on Krassos—

—but that was for the future, and the future was the precog's business . . .

Which took Trask looping back on himself, where he stood on the steps of a minibus in the street outside E-Branch HQ, checking his people on board prior to heading for the airport.

Liz was the last to board. She was standing with Jake just inside the anonymous-looking private entrance that was reserved for E-Branch personnel only, where they said their goodbyes and all of the things that lovers say when life intervenes to force them apart—*and,* Trask sincerely hoped, where she was reminding the Necroscope to "keep an open mind" and be alert for any Mayday call she might make.

Seated at the front of the bus, Millie sensed Trask's gathering impatience, put a hand on his arm and told him, "Let them be, Ben. We have a few minutes to spare. And now that you're on Jake's right side—well, it seems a good idea to stay on it."

Glancing at her, Trask sighed, but in the next moment grinned, adopted a mock scowl, and in his old "accustomed" fashion growled, "God, that *bloody* man!"

While in the rear entrance to the hotel, Liz had just told Jake, "I'm pregnant!"

"You're what?" He didn't quite believe he'd heard her correctly.

Liz hadn't meant to come out with it like that, but in the middle of both of them telling each other to take care, it had just popped out. "I think I have to be," she said. "After last night, I mean."

"But how can you possibly—?" he began. And:

"—I just do," she cut him short. "I know."

He looked at her for a long moment and finally said, "Well, you're a healthy woman, and I have to admit that if you're *not* pregnant—er, 'after last night, 'I mean—then I don't know what it would take!"

They both laughed and clung to each other, but then he held her at arm's length and was suddenly serious. "It's all the more reason why you shouldn't be going."

She shook her head. "All the more reason why I should. It's our world, Jake, and it'll be his—or hers—too. That's why we have to keep it that way, why we can't give it over to invaders, defilers from a different, an alien world. It's why we'll avenge the pain they've caused, the damage they've already done and get rid of them for good."

Jake knew she'd won the point—that there was no answer to her argument—and so said, "Then you'd better go. Just remember I love you, both of you, and bring yourselves back to me."

"I'll do better than that," she said. "If it all works out, I'll give you a call and *you* can bring us back!"

"And if it doesn't work out?"

"Then you'll be hearing from me anyway."

"I *will* be hearing from you," he said. "Let's face it, you and the team will need weapons eventually. So, who else do you know who can smuggle them in like I can?"

"I hadn't thought of that," she said. "But I'm pretty sure Ben has. He said to be sure and remind you to listen for me."

"As if I wouldn't," said Jake. "I'm already missing you—and you're not even gone yet."

"But time I was," said Liz.

They kissed, Liz joined the team aboard the transport, and Jake waved to her until the minibus had rounded the corner and passed out of sight into the chilly London morning.

And he hadn't been lying. The city was only just waking up, beginning to bustle, but already it felt empty . . .

Back inside the headquarters, Jake visited the archives—just a roomful of stacked shelves and filing cabinets—where, with John Grieve's help, he chose an armful of the restricted "Keogh Files." Grieve was the Duty Officer; he kept the electronic key to the locked filing cabinets, and better than anyone else knew his way around the system.

Invaluable to the Branch by reason of his *tele*-telepathy—and with the better part of his life spent in employment within HQ's four walls as a desk-jockey, where his talent had been put to its best use—Grieve's many years of prowling the corridors of E-Branch, day and night through thousands of hours of duty shifts, made him the best of all possible authorities. And in his capacity as Duty Officer he also kept the key to Harry's Room; but a real key this time, not a corneal scannner or microcoded ID tag but a piece of shaped metal that fitted the almost antique lock on the door of that very special room.

And letting Jake in, he said, "If you intend to sleep here, you'll need sheets and blankets for the bed."

"I don't intend to go that far," Jake answered, dumping the files on the dusty console of an ancient computer. "I'll use my own room for sleeping. It's just that this place has—I don't know—"

"A certain atmosphere?" Grieve nodded. "A weird ambiance? I know what you mean. We all know what you mean. Frankly, I think it would put me off. I don't think I could concentrate too well in here. But it's each to his own, and . . ." And there he paused, looking slightly uncomfortable.

"And this *is* my own?" said Jake. "Is that what you're saying? Hey, don't worry about it. Not too long ago, I might well have argued the point. But now . . . well, this place feels sort of familiar to me. And in fact it's exactly the atmosphere that I need. Where better to get to know Harry Keogh than in a room that he once occupied?"

"You're right, of course," said Grieve. "It's just that of all E-Branch's 'ghosts,' this one was—and, as we've recently seen, probably still is—the most potent."

Jake gave a little shiver and said, "It's certainly cold in here."

"Yes," said the DO. "That's as normal, or rather as usual. I could have an electric fire sent in, but I don't think you'll find it improves things very much."

"No, everything's fine," said Jake. "And if I find that the place does bother me, I can always take the files to my room."

"Suit yourself," said Grieve. "As for the files: you've got stuff there that goes right back to the beginning . . . of Harry's association with E-Branch, I mean. You even have the Dragosani file, including Alec Kyle's first—er, shall we say, 'interview'?—but in any case our first 'meeting' with Harry."

"The first time he came here in the flesh?" Jake had just opened the file in question and glanced at its handwritten—or rather hand-scrawled—A-4 pages laminated in durable plastic sleeves.

"No," said the DO, from where he now stood at the door. "I mean the first time he *appeared* here, *without* flesh! Harry was . . . incorporeal. He was dead. His first death, that is."

Frowning, Jake turned to stare at Grieve, opened his mouth to say something—and closed it again. How does one reply to something like that? And before he could ask any further questions:

"If you need anything else," said Grieve, "give me a call. There's no intercom in here but the telephone is working. Oh, and incidentally, if you should bump into Premier Turchin anywhere in the HQ, please remember that those files are for your eyes only. While Turchin knows full well what the Necroscope—er, the *first* Necroscope—did to the Château Bronnitsy and to Gregor Borowitz's Opposition, there's really no need to supply him with documentary evidence. There are wounds enough, mainly healed now, so we don't need to start rubbing salt in them."

As Jake nodded his understanding, Grieve went out into the corridor and closed the door behind him . . .

The Keogh Files:

It was all here, everything that Harry had been, and maybe something of what he still was or what he had left behind. And the more Jake turned the yellowing pages and read, the more he became involved, the more he seemed to remember. Not real memories—of course not—but pseudomemories.

He would read a paragraph and know what was coming. It was as if he'd picked up a book from his childhood, recognized the stories and knew at the end of each chapter what was coming in the next. It gave new meaning to the terms "déjà vu" and "paramnesia" . . . which in turn gave Jake pause as he read of Harry Keogh's reincarnations first in the mind of an infant son, and then in the brain-dead body of Alec Kyle.

And now . . . ?

But no, Jake was past that stage; he no longer worried that Harry might be seeking permanent residence. For if that were so he'd had ample opportunity. No, there was only one man or creature intent on possessing his mind, and the way things stood at present it was the other way around: Jake's mind possessed that creature!

And so he read on.

Of Harry's psychic ancestry, his youth, his championing of dead causes (or rather, the causes of the dead.) Of his incredible battle with the Russian necromancer, Boris Dragosani, and of his all but total destruction of the Soviet E-Branch: first when he killed Dragosani, and again when the shrivelled maniac Ivan Gerenko was in command.

Jake read of the taint that Thibor Ferenczy had transfused

into the foetal Yulian Bodescu, of the vampirism that developed in Yulian as a youth, and of his death at the hands of the teeming dead, risen from a local graveyard. He read of Janos Ferenczy, vampire bloodson of Faethor, returned to life from an urn of ashes only to be reduced to dust in a battle with the original Necroscope and a handful of centuried Thracian "friends."

He read of all of these—people?—and things, oh, and a host of others—and discovered to his amazement that he merely *reacquainted* himself, as with that old book read as a child.

As he turned the pages the hours flew, and as he became accustomed to (or less physically aware of) the room, so its ambiance seemed to adjust to him. And for the first time in a great many years it was no longer cold in Harry's Room.

Lunchtime came . . . and went, but while Jake recognized the need for sustenance he no longer had the time for it, not right now. While he was absorbed in his reading—whether learning or "remembering"—his stomach must bide its time. The late autumn day grew brighter outside, then dimmed, and the files gradually transferred from one area of the old computer console's surface to another. So that when the telephone buzzed and John Grieve's voice asked if everything was all right, "suddenly" it was 5 P.M.

Jake told the DO, "I'm going out to eat. I'll be maybe an hour. I don't suppose we've heard anything from the team?"

"No," Grieve answered. "We know their flight suffered something of a delay—actually a long one—but they did get off around one-thirty P.M. But now they'll be in at the other end. We can't expect to hear anything for a while yet; maybe when they arrive at Bernie Fletcher's location. But that could be hours yet, and even then Trask might decide that the situation doesn't warrant his contacting the HQ. By my reckoning, it will be late tonight or maybe even tomorrow morning before we hear anything . . . well, unless *you* hear something first."

"So then, we'll just have to wait and see," said Jake.

"I'm afraid so," Grieve answered. "Here at HQ, the name

of the game is patience. But there was one piece of information that came in from the Minister Responsible. I was able to pass it on to Trask at the airport just before they left."

"Oh?" said Jake.

"Yes. It's a police report. It appears a body turned up in a disused conduit under a platform at Waterloo Railway Station. As you'll know, that's the starting gate for the Eurostar, the Channel Tunnel, and Paris. Anyway, the body was so badly shrivelled it was almost a mummy; it *seemed* to have been down there a long time. Which is very odd because dental records identify it—or rather him—as a businessman who went missing only a little while ago. Actually, the night after you brought Millicent Cleary up out of the underworld."

"Szwart!" said Jake.

"Our conclusion, too," said Grieve. "Police investigations have shown that this gentleman was on his way to Paris, but he never made it. Oh, and another thing: he was naked, and everything he'd had with him had been taken . . . including his Eurostar ticket for the night train, of course."

"That bloody thing could be anywhere by now," said Jake.

"Indeed," said the DO. "He could even be in Turkey . . ."

Jake turned it over in his mind—thought about it, didn't like it—but couldn't see anything that he could do about it. So changing the subject, he said, "Right now I'm feeling starved. I haven't eaten all day. How about you?"

"I've eaten," said Grieve. "And by the way—have we given you a Branch card for the hotel diner?"

"Yes," Jake answered. "But I think I prefer a little place in the Latin Quarter."

And after a moment's silence: "In Paris?" (Grieve stuck to E-Branch protocols and didn't read minds over the phone unless there was a good reason for it.)

"Where else?" said Jake.

And after another almost imperceptible pause: "I shall be off duty when you return," said the DO, in a tone typical of his upper-class English restraint (as if what Jake had told him wasn't at all out of the ordinary). "I'll still be here in the HQ, probably asleep in my room, I should think. But one of the techs, Jimmy Harvey, will be standing in for me. I come on again at one A.M. If you need anything at that time, give me a call."

"They really know how to get good value out of a man, don't they?" said Jake.

He sensed the other's shrug, as Grieve replied, "I suppose they do. But on the other hand, they're the ones who are doing the real work, while as rear-party I'm comparatively safe here in the HQ." And then, snatching a breath and hastily following up on what he obviously considered a gaffe: "Please understand, Jake—that *wasn't* intended as a reflection on your own stance or status."

"Sure," said Jake. But in fact and however it was intended, John Grieve's comment had struck home and he'd felt it. Before he could put the phone down, however:

"Jake?" said the DO. "I really would enjoy to take you up on your offer some other time."

"My offer?"

"To eat at that little place in the Latin Quarter?"

"Damn right!" said Jake. "French onion soup, steak tartare on black unleavened bread with a little garnish, and all washed down with a glass of good beer."

"I had fish and chips!" said Grieve, sounding almost human at last. And:

"Each to his own," said Jake, smiling as he closed the conversation . . .

In fact there had been more than a "mere" delay at the airport. The VTOL aircraft that Trask and party had supposed to take had developed a fault and been taken out of service; they had been transferred to an older, much slower plane; there'd been additional holdups with baggage, arguments between airport staff and passengers, and the usual hustling and bustling that was becoming ever more the standard in the packaged holidays trade. But eventually, posing as a party of historians and amateur archaeologists, the party was airborne and heading for Istanbul.

Normally, in a British Airways VTOL aircraft, such a flight would have a duration of less than two hours; in the older airplane, flying at a lower altitude—avoiding Greece by diverting over Hungary, Romania, and Bulgaria—it took almost three. The Turkish military authorities had put a ban on all aircraft crossing their borders from Greek airspace.

Then, due to complications with altered schedules, and the simultaneous arrival of a host of other incoming flights, there had been delays getting through an overworked (and exhaustively inquisitive) customs, and a further holdup when Trask had found that the car that was waiting for them—courtesy of the Minister Responsible—was a small four-seater. Hiring a minibus and waiting on its arrival consumed a further half hour in a humid, smelly airport lounge where the facilities were something less than acceptable.

"We should have packed sandwiches and drinks," Millie said, when at last they were under way, out of the airport and heading for the northwest-bound motorway to Edirne and the border with Bulgaria.

"Sandwiches?" Trask growled scathingly. "They'd have gone a bit curly by now, I think! In another half hour it'll be dark."

"I didn't realize you thought I was that mundane," she answered archly, knowing that in fact he thought no such thing. "I was *joking,* Ben!"

"Well, I'm glad someone still can!" he answered. "We'll pull over at the first service station where we can snatch a bite to eat, and I'll try to get through to Bernie Fletcher. He's bound to be wondering where we've got to."

"Jake could have brought us first class," said Liz from the back of the minibus—and wanted to bite her tongue when Trask turned to give her one of his looks. But before he could speak: "I know, I know," she quickly went on. "If we were caught without passports, or with passports that weren't properly franked, we'd have a hard time explaining it."

"But more importantly—" Trask began.

"—More importantly," Liz breathlessly cut him short, "you don't want Jake making too many waves in the psychic aether . . . not yet, anyway. Not in Malinari's vicinity."

"Or Vavara's, or Lord Szwart's," Trask nodded. "Because for all we know, they could all three be together again by now . . ."

Ten minutes later, about 7:45 P.M. local time, the precog Ian Goodly pulled off the motorway into a service station where the team could buy some dubious-looking sandwiches from a dispenser in an alleged "cafeteria." Then, too, Trask tried to call Bernie Fletcher at his hotel in Sirpsindigi. He got the hotel, but the desk could only tell him that "Meester Fledger and other mens are outside for thee eatings, sorry."

"My name is Trask," Trask told the unbelievably slow-sounding person on the other end of the line, even spelling his name out for him. "Please tell Mr. Fletcher I called. Tell him we've had some small delays, but we're on our . . ." Which was as far as he got before the line went dead. And:

"Shit and damnation!" Trask muttered, slamming the door of the booth behind him.

Back at their table, Paul Garvey was studying a map. "It's maybe a hundred and thirty miles to Edirne, and then we take a back road to Sirp-what's-its-name. If we don't linger over this disgusting 'cuisine,' and Ian keeps us moving at sixty-five or seventy miles per hour, we can be at Bernie's hotel—er, the what?"

"The Tundźa," said Millie—

"—By a little after ten-thirty."

"Good," said Trask. "So let's not hang about, people. Eat, drink, and be merry, for tomorrow—"

"—The food might be even worse," said Millie.

"And actually," said Trask, "I think your sandwiches would probably go down a treat right now, curly or other-wise!"

At 10 P.M. in Sirpsindigi: Bernie Fletcher lay fully dressed, taking a nap on his bed. His minders had an adjacent room with access through a connecting door, but of course Cliff Angel was in Bernie's room, as was Vladimir Androsov. Angel was seated on a chair just inside the closed door; his chin kept lolling down onto his massive chest, causing him to jerk upright whenever he caught himself nodding off.

Androsov, however, was fully awake and anxiously pacing to and fro in the small room. Every few minutes would see him pause at the grimy window to look out into the night street. It had long since stopped raining, but moisture clung to the windows, making it hard to see out. The street was poorly lit and mainly deserted, and a dense ground mist was beginning to obscure the rain-slick cobbles. Very occasionally a vehicle would prowl silently by, its lights and tyres cutting tracks through the mist.

Androsov's concern was for Venyamin, his twin brother, who had accompanied the minder Joe Sparrow across town to "inspect" the girlie revue. Venyamin had a basic grasp of several tongues including Turkish, which would simplify the purchase of tickets, et cetera. But the show must surely be over by now, and the two men on their way back. The trouble was that Vladimir wasn't sure of that; he didn't know it for a certainty.

Twins (not only physically but mentally), the pair had been "aware" of each other since birth, even before they'd been able to recognize or acknowledge the fact. Separated by a great many miles—and even when sleeping—still each man had felt comfortable in the sure knowledge of the other's existence. It wasn't telepathy but a facet of their joint talent: they automatically "located" each other. Yet now . . .

. . . For the last half hour, Vladimir's mind—his awareness—had been void of all knowledge of his sibling esper's whereabouts, or even of Venyamin's existence. And that was something which had scarcely ever happened before. Deeply troubled, Vladimir decided to wait a few more minutes, then wake Fletcher—a fellow locator—and voice his concerns. And meanwhile, pacing yet again to the window, he cast a probe out into that wretched night, at the same time pressing his face to the glass and looking this way and that, scanning the street for some sign of Venyamin and Joe Sparrow.

Over there, in a dark shop doorway, something moved! But it was only a woman—perhaps a streetwalker?—waiting to make a contact. But down there, on this side of the road, keeping well in to the wall and darker shadows . . . two men? Coming this way? Yes! Their motion seemed odd, unsteady; was it possible they'd had something to drink?

Perhaps it was the minder and Venyamin. But if so . . . then Vladimir's twin was employing his shields as never before, putting so much effort into it that he even excluded his brother.

Which could only mean that he had good reason! And Vladimir at once withdrew his own probe so as not to be detected by who- or whatever it was that Venyamin was striving to keep out.

His breath had clouded the window; he rubbed at the fogged patch with his sleeve, and put his face to the glass again. No one was there, not even the woman. Only the mist, like a river of milk lying luminous in the street . . .

. . . And suddenly the short hairs were rising at the back of Vladimir's neck, and he knew that everything was wrong! It was an electric sensation, a weird feeling that for many long moments froze the Russian rigid, but then he broke free, tottered to the bed, and gave Fletcher a shake. "Wake up, English! Wake up!"

"Eh? What?" Fletcher jerked on the bed, sat up, rubbed his eyes and stared at the white-faced Vladimir. "What is it?"

But now the sensation of foreboding had gone away, mysteriously vanished, been replaced by a feeling that everything was okay. "I . . . not know!" Vladimir's face cracked open in a sick, uncertain grin. "I thinks I see some men in street. My brother and Joe, I thinks. But is too misty. Maybe I mistaken."

"Eh? Misty?" said Fletcher, hiding a yawn behind the back of his hand as he got to his feet. Then his eyes narrowed, and again he said, "Misty?" But now the word rang in his mind like a cracked, ominous bell of ill omen, and pacing quickly to the window, he said, "Why in hell . . . why would it be misty?"

"It is come from the river," Vladimir shrugged, absolutely sure now that everything was fine. "Is running close by. Hotel has the same name: the Tundźa."

"River?" said Fletcher, staring down on the street. "Just a river?" But in fact, now that he was awake, he felt nothing out of the ordinary. Indeed, and much like Vladimir, he felt quite sure that everything was perfectly in order.

"Wazzat? Eh? Eh?" Cliff Angel started awake. "Did somebody say something?"

"It was just Vlad," said Fletcher, smiling almost stupidly at Angel where he got to his feet near the door. "He thought he saw someone down there in the mist. Maybe it was Joe and Venyamin, eh?"

"What?" Angel scowled. "Are you okay, pal?"

Before Fletcher could answer, footsteps sounded and floorboards creaked on the landing beyond the door, and there came a knock—four distinctive raps on the panelling—that identified a friend.

"It's Joe," said Angel, suddenly sure of that "fact," as he unlocked and opened the door. At which there came another knock—or rather a thump—*but this time from the window!*

Three minutes earlier, downstairs in the dingy lobby, the desk clerk had been alarmed to see what at first he'd thought was a thick carpet of white smoke pouring in under the door from the street. Was there a fire in the neighbourhood, perhaps dangerously close by? It seemed the only likely explanation: a house must be burning!

If so he must alert the English party and their guests. It would be a damned shame if his only paying customers in a six-month got burned up in their beds!

The semi-invalid old man had come out from behind the desk, gone hobbling across the dusty lobby to the door, and opened it to the night. But even as he'd limped through the mist, so he'd realized that it wasn't composed of choking

315

smoke but a clammy, oddly clinging vapour. Then, looking out into the street . . .

. . . His eyes had bugged in amazement, for in all his years as owner-manager-caretaker and general dogsbody at the crumbling old Tundźa, he had *never* before seen the likes of this: in both directions, a lapping, inches-deep carpet of greasy, luminous mist! For even though the night was damp and dark, it was as if the mist glowed from within: a rotten glow like foxfire, that surged with the lazy ebb and flow of this filthily mobile stuff.

What? Had the river overflowed its banks? But surely there hadn't been that much rain? Or was this some kind of industrial pollution, or some noxious chemical that the bloody farmers had spilled? *Ugh!*

The old man had gone to close the door and shut it out, but a tall, cloaked figure had stepped or flowed into view from one side. "Eh? Eh?" The old man had limped back a pace.

And the stranger had entered—and then two more, appearing silently out of the shadows behind the cloaked, heavily muffled one. And stepping close together, moving awkwardly and robotically, these two had ignored the old man and entered the lobby, leaving the cloaked one to close the door behind them.

"Eh? What?" the old proprietor had gurgled, as the two zombielike figures made for the stairs. One of them—the one in front—was known to the old man: surely he was one of the English guests? But his mouth was yawning open, drooling from its corners, and his eyes were starting from his head!

"Wait!" the old man had cried. "What happen here?"

The pair climbing the stairs had paused, and the one in the rear had turned his head to stare at the trembling old man, his eyes burning like fire in the lobby's faltering electric light. The sight of those monstrous eyes had caused the old proprietor to stumble back a further pace. Indeed, he had stumbled directly into the arms of the cloaked one!

Then, speaking to *that* one, the one with the burning eyes

had said, "Be a good fellow, will you, and take care of things down here?" Having spoken, he had then continued up the stairs, seeming to guide or propel the drooling one before him.

And in a voice that *whooshed* like a blacksmith's bellows, the cloaked one had said, "Old man, *nothing* is happening here. Nothing that need concern you."

"But . . . something wrong!" the old proprietor had insisted, standing straighter, and turning to face the cloaked one. "The Tundźa, she mine hotel, and something . . . very . . . wrong!"

Then he'd looked up, up, at the face of the one who steadied him. But inside the high collar of the cloak, where a head should be, there'd been only a blob of inky blackness—as if a piece of the darkest night were lodged there—and the eyes that looked out of that blackness were a poisonous yellow that seemed to drip sulphur from their rims!

"Wrong?" that monstrous voice had come again, accompanied by a soul-wrenching stench. "Only the light, old fool. There's nothing wrong here but the light."

And then an arm had gone up—reaching, impossibly reaching—all the way up to the high, pine-boarded ceiling, where a hand like a claw had grabbed at electrical wiring and yanked with irresistible force.

The lobby lights had sputtered out, leaving a velvet gloom whose only illumination was that of Szwart's festering eyes and the vile phosphorescence of his breath in the yawn of cavernous jaws.

In there, too, surging up from the depths of his throat, a host of suctorial, anemonelike tendrils had greedily uncoiled themselves, fastening on the old man's head like some terrible man-eating plant or a loathsome, lethal octopus . . .

19
Terror at the Tundža—
the Future: Writ in Flames!

UNDER VAVARA'S SPELL, THE BENEFICENT AURA
in which she shrouded herself, and which extended invisibly
outward from her, the men in the Tundža's upstairs room
were taken completely by surprise. Slow-moving and slow
to react, they could only gape at what was happening as
Malinari propelled Joe Sparrow into the room ahead of him,
and Vavara came in through the shattering window.

As to the latter:

When Fletcher heard that first dull thump on the window,
he couldn't believe what he saw there: that doughy, leaflike
hand the size of a dinner plate, all covered with suckers that
stuck to the glass. And the *face* behind the hand, rising up
into view as Vavara crawled like a chameleon up the wall.
By no means the mistress of metamorphic processes, still
the climb had required only a very small effort on her part.
And she had had plenty of practice on Krassos, when she'd
been obliged to scramble across precipitous cliff faces to
escape the wrath of E-Branch.

But that had been on Krassos, while here and now—

Here and now, all had gone according to Lord Nephran
Malinari's plan. In order that no escape route or bolt-holes
would be left open to the locators and their armed watchdog,
he and Lord Szwart had agreed to enter the Tundža by the
door, while Vavara would break in through the window with
her hypnotic, lying aura preceding her, befuddling the senses
of those within . . . most of all the locators, Fletcher and Androsov. And while Szwart dealt with matters downstairs,
doubling as a rearguard to ensure that no one fled the scene,

Malinari and Vavara would attend to the coalition of enemy forces overhead.

Vavara's motive for murder—which is what they were about—was simple: revenge! Revenge for what E-Branch and its esper membership had done to her monastery aerie, her sisterhood, and her "beautiful" garden under Palataki on the island of Krassos. And similarly the Lord of Darkness, the endlessly mutating Lord Szwart: he would do anything to strike back at the ones who had destroyed his works under London. Malinari had assured his Wamphyri peers that this was the best way: to take out these people one by one, using the ones they took as bait to trap the rest.

But as for Malinari himself: other than revenge, his motive was knowledge. Knowledge of the one called Jake Cutter, no ordinary man (not even among his extraordinary E-Branch colleagues) but a Power in the psychic aether whose signature was an incredible whirligig of ever-evolving symbols, numbers, and algebraic equations. The secrets in Cutter's metaphysical mind would provide Malinari with everything he required to combat just such a Power in Sunside: the awesome talents of the one called Nathan.

For having failed on Earth, that was where Malinari and his Wamphyri colleagues were now headed: back to the Vampire World, to Sunside/Starside in a parallel universe beyond the Perchorsk Gate. But not before Malinari had got what he wanted here.

Such were his thoughts as he thrust the now almost mindless minder Joe Sparrow ahead of him into the upstairs room. Sparrow, his mind drained of what little knowledge of E-Branch it had ever contained—along with almost everything else—who moved only by virtue of Malinari's terrible hand inside his back, its hairy, wormlike fingers extending sensors into the spinal canal while others channeled themselves to the brain and loaned support to its dying motor areas. Sparrow—a mere puppet now, and Malinari the puppet-master.

Sparrow had been brought along like this—not as a hostage but as a key—in case there should be problems.

Since no such problems had surfaced, he was no longer required. And as Malinari withdrew his hand from the gaping, bloody hole in Sparrow's overcoat, he caused the hairy filament extensions that were his probes to nip at the Special Branch man's motor areas and slice through the flexible tendon that was his spinal cord, the main neural axis . . . either one of which actions would have finished the job. And utterly incapable of protest, Sparrow simply died, flopped free of Malinari's red hand and crumpled to the floor.

Meanwhile:

Finally Fletcher had reacted to the *thing* that had used a sucker hand to wrench a pane of glass from the window and send it shattering down into the street. He'd reacted—drawn back a pace and gurgled a barely articulate warning—before the hand, now *recognizable* as a hand, reached in through the empty frame and groped for the catch. But the window was jammed, literally glued shut, locked in position by multiple layers of paint and preservative, and Vavara's patience was all used up.

A warty *something*—a body as hideous as the head and face it supported—drew back from the window to swing like a pendulum against the latticework of brittle mullions and transoms, showering glass and splintered wood into the room. And shaping herself in an alien contortion, Vavara followed the debris and flowed erect before Fletcher where he staggered back away from her.

By then, in the doorway, Malinari had lashed out at Cliff Angel, a backhander with a difference. For where just a moment ago Malinari's hand had been a mass of writhing tubules, crimson with Joe Sparrow's blood, now it was a hamlike fist whose knuckles had formed into inch-long chitinous thorns. And with the right side of his face gouged to the cheek- and jawbones, its flesh hanging loose in a crimson flap, Angel had issued a bubbling, agonized shriek and gone hurtling across the room.

All of this had happened more or less simultaneously, and Vladimir Androsov, having moved to a spot that was central in the room, had seen, accepted, and finally reacted to it.

Cursing and snatching out his Tokarev TT-33, he aimed it at Vavara and jerked off a shot . . . a bad mistake. For as Cliff Angel had pointed out less than twenty-four hours ago, the Tokarev was an outdated weapon and as such it was liable at times to malfunction. Times such as now.

The gun might have been in perfect working order, but the ammunition definitely wasn't. *Perhaps* (Androsov thought, when his weapon made a damp-squib *phut!* sound, and the bullet stuck in Vavara's forehead between her eyebrows, making her jerk her head back in shock, but without penetrating to any significant depth), *perhaps the ammo was made at the same time as the gun!* And after he'd squeezed the trigger a second time it seemed he must be right, for this time there wasn't even a *phut!*—just a click as the hammer fell on a dud.

But there *was* a snarl of fury from the outraged Vavara, as she hurled Fletcher aside, reached up and plucked the offending bullet from her thinly sheathed, bone-plated skull, and headed for Vladimir with blood streaking her leathery, wizened face.

"This one," she gurgled, batting Vladimir's gun aside and grasping his throat, "this one is a dead man! I sincerely hope he is *not* the one you desired to interrogate, Malinari? For if so you're too late. He has caused me an inconvenience, and now must pay for it."

"Be my guest," Malinari answered her. "He's merely a mentalist, a locator from an outside organization. But the E-Branch locator is *that* one!" And he made for Fletcher.

So far unscathed, Fletcher saw the leer, the nameless lust, on Malinari's face and in his flaring eyes. And uttering a cry of sheer terror, he took two staggering steps toward the shattered window. The locator's intention was obvious: since a hand-to-hand fight with Malinari—or with any of the Wamphyri—was out of the question, he would vault out into the night, risking a broken neck rather than give himself up to whatever this monstrous being held in store for him.

But even as he put a hand on the naked windowsill, Malinari gripped the back of his neck, bringing him to an immediate, abrupt halt. And:

"What?" said Malinari the Mind. "Would you desert me, then, and disappoint me? But no, little man, for there are questions only you can answer. Well, for the time being at least."

Fletcher felt the iciness of Malinari's hands, their alien cold, and it was as if his brain had frozen. Turning around in what felt like slow motion, he stared petrified into that leering face, its furnace eyes, and though his life depended on it he couldn't do a thing to avoid what came next. Vaguely he was aware of a nauseating crunching, and, on the very periphery of his vision, saw the hag Vavara biting pieces out of Vladimir's broken skull. But by then Lord Malinari's hands had shifted to Fletcher's head and an involuntary, agonizing transference had already commenced.

Malinari *sucked* at him—not blood but thoughts, memories, secrets—and the contents of Fletcher's brain weren't simply duplicated but downloaded, removed, and wiped clean. Gone from Fletcher forever, they left a void as bitter cold as the hands that stole them. And absorbed by Malinari, they compressed the contents of *his* mind into ever tighter corners. The brain is a marvellous vessel that no entirely human being has ever filled to overflowing. But Malinari *the* Mind was no mere man, and his was a terrible power. Yet even he had limits.

He had the memories of many dozens of men; he "remembered" what they had known, and also recognized them as the source of his fits of madness—those spells that rushed upon him out of nowhere—those shrieking rages that ever more frequently lay outside his control. In Starside that hadn't mattered too much, but here on Earth it was a problem.

Only give himself over to his furies, his enemies would at once take advantage. Aye, and not only his human enemies. Vavara hated him with all her black heart, and as for Lord Szwart . . . but who could fathom him? Then again, who could blame them? They were after all Wamphyri; like all their kind, they sought power over others and would destroy "friends" and foes alike—murder them out of hand—if the opportunity presented itself, the time was right, and the means to hand.

But here in this man Fletcher . . . *such* secrets were his as to frustrate the efforts of any and every enemy—the secrets of E-Branch and its members: of Trask, Goodly, Chung, and especially of Jake Cutter—and Malinari *must* have them. It may well cause him almost as much pain as it caused his writhing victim; it *was* causing him pain, a pounding in his temples that threatened to explode them outwards—but he *must* go on!

And yes, yes, there it was! Jake Cutter—Necroscope? But what was this? A man who could converse with the dead and call them up out of their graves? A man who knew the runes of space and time, who had the power to move instantaneously from place to place without physically covering the distance between? Not a magician, no, for there was no such thing, but a man who . . . a man who . . . *what?*

Until now engrossed in his own hideous absorbing of Fletcher's knowledge—with his vibrating pseudopod fingers groping deep into his moaning victim's ears—suddenly Malinari became aware that something had gone dangerously awry. Halfway across the room the witch Vavara was half woman, half thing where she hunched like a great black bat over the broken corpse of Vladimir Androsov. But beyond her against the wall, another figure was getting to its knees, rising up from the floor.

It was the minder Cliff Angel, his ravaged face a mass of wet redness where Malinari's blow had flensed it to the bone. But in his hands a deadly weapon, the Keramique with which he was a marksman.

"I don't know who or what you are, you fucking thing," he choked the words out, along with blood from the torn corner of his mouth, "but the man who hits Cliff Angel like that has *got* to expect a reply! Nothing gets me back on my feet faster than being knocked down. So I hope you're ready for this, fuckface, 'cos here it comes." And he squeezed the trigger.

Vavara had become aware of Angel even as he spoke; seeing his gun, she gasped aloud, flattened herself down, then hurled herself headlong in his direction with her taloned hands reaching for him. It was self-preservation on Vavara's part—pure instinct—but hurtling below Angel's line of fire, her action had left Malinari completely exposed. And in the frozen moment of Angel's shot he had made a perfect target.

But in that same moment he'd reacted to the threat, and in a lightning-fast movement—with all the savagery and cunning of the Wamphyri—he'd turned Bernie Fletcher's head directly into the path of the bullet.

And once again Cliff Angel had been right: the Tokarev was no match for the Keramique.

The bullet passed through Fletcher's right eye, destroying his brain in its passing, and taking out the back of his skull in a fist-sized chunk. Blood and brain matter spattered Malinari's face, and his probing fingers felt the projectile's heat as it turned the subject of his investigation to so much jelly, cutting short the stream of information.

The locator Fletcher was now a "dead weight" in Malinari's hands. Thrusting his flopping body away, he gave a wild cry of rage and frustration and clapped his slimed hands to his head. Then:

"No, no, *no!*" he cried, his voice shaking with his passion. "Such knowledge—such *secrets,* Vavara—all gone now! These stupid . . . stubborn . . . *people!*"

And then, calming himself and pointing a trembling hand at the minder Cliff Angel, lolling in Vavara's taloned hands, "Is that one finished? For if not, I shall do it myself—but oh-so-very slowly!"

Vavara turned Angel's body towards Malinari and showed him the pipes torn out of his throat. "Does he *look* finished?" She grinned with jagged needle teeth and black, leathery lips, and her hag's features flowed like liquid as they morphed into the face of a beautiful young woman. "And what of us?" she went on. "What did you achieve, Nephran? Did *you* finish? I take it you did not."

Malinari took a deep breath and stood up straighter. "Take up that one's weapon," he said. "We now have two such and they may prove useful. As for being finished: we are finished here, aye. But even though I failed to get what I wanted—and despite that these people are dead and useless now—still we *can* use one of them at least, if only as a lure for the others. For these were little fishes, and the big ones are still out there. You and Szwart, you shall yet have your revenge, Vavara, and I shall have what I want."

"And for now?" She was fully transformed now, all aglow in her false loveliness.

"For now, let's get downstairs," he answered. "Lord Szwart will be waiting for us, and these E-Branch people are not very far away. I can sense them." He sniffed the air. "Their signatures are heavy in the aether. They are using their shields but I can sense that, too. For I know them now, these people. Over the reek of these cadavers, still I can sense them. Very well, go quickly and fetch our vehicle, while I wait with Szwart and attend to things here. And when we go we shall leave *our* signatures behind, so that E-Branch will know who did this."

"And so that they'll follow us?" She curled her lip. "What logic is there in that?"

"Trust me, Vavara," said Malinari, taking up Bernie Fletcher's body, tossing it carelessly over his shoulder, and heading for the door. "I *want* them to follow us. Indeed, I want them to follow us all the way to hell!"

Some twenty minutes later, Ben Trask and his agents drove into the street where the Tundźa hotel stood central, set apart from neighbouring buildings by narrow cobbled alleys that wound away into dismal back-street regions.

But just as they entered the street, Ian Goodly was obliged to pull over to the right, climb the shallow kerb and come to a halt, when an antique fire engine went clanging by, followed by a police vehicle with its strobes flashing and siren blaring.

Down the street a handful of people had gathered; they were gesticulating and pointing excitedly across the road at a burning building. A sign hanging over the entrance to the dilapidated place said TUNDŹA in two languages, Turkish and English.

Coming the other way, and narrowly avoiding the fire engine and police car, a third vehicle—a black estate car—skidded past in a blur of rapid acceleration, careened around a corner, and disappeared into the night. But as it went by—

"What?" said Liz Merrick, frowning. "Can that be the Tundźa there, burning?"

"That's how it looks," said Trask, turning to smile at her.

And Lardis Lidesci, seated beside Liz and suddenly puzzled, his wiry black eyebrows coming together in a look of amazement, said, "Eh? Eh? Have you gone stark, staring mad, both of you?"

Liz and Trask—feeling oddly buoyed up—stared at him in surprise bordering on astonishment; likewise the precog, Millie Cleary, and Paul Garvey. And the selfsame thought was in everyone's mind: what on earth was bothering the Old Lidesci?

Lardis saw it in their faces and snapped, "That *must* be the Tundźa, yes, and it's where Bernie Fletcher and those bully-boy minders of his are supposed to be staying!"

"But it will be all right, Lardis," Paul Garvey assured him straight-facedly. (For Paul's face was always straight.) "Can't you see? Everything's just . . . just fine . . . here?" But then he stopped speaking, his eyes went wide and his jaw fell open.

And suddenly the atmosphere in the minibus was electric, as the six espers felt the gradual abatement of Vavara's aura, and Trask gasped, "No, it damned well isn't! Nothing's bloody fine!" And he was first out of the minibus, hurrying past the deserted shops and dwellings toward the blazing Tundźa.

The rest of the team caught up with him when he was

stopped by a uniformed policeman, by which time the firemen were breaking in the hotel's ground-floor shutters, and the fire engine's hoses were playing feeble streams of water in through the Tundźa's door. But already it was obvious that the hotel was beyond hope. Flames were gouting from the windows on both main floors, and smoke pouring from gables in what was presumably the attic.

Trask was babbling to the policeman, "We have friends staying here. They could be inside!" And while he explained, Millie was tugging on his arm, trying to get his attention.

"Wait," said the policeman, holding up his hand. "Please to wait." Mercifully he spoke reasonable English. Then he shouted something to the closest fireman, who shouted back at him over the roaring of the flames. And:

"This fire she was set," he said, turning to Trask. "Smell the kero? Plenty kero. These old places use the kerosene—er, for the generators? Bad electricity. Often the breakdown." And he shrugged. "Your friends: if they there, I think they coming out the windows. No come, maybe not there. I *hoping* not there! You stay at Tundźa?" He looked at Trask enquiringly.

"No," Trask shook his head. "We just got here, to meet our friends. We go to look at your . . . er, your ancient things?"

"Ah! The anti-tikkies!" said the other.

"The what?" Trask didn't at first understand. But then he did, and said, "Oh! The *antiquities!* Yes—yes, of course."

"Please excusing," said the policeman. "Please be waiting here." And he went to use the police car's radio.

Finally Millie had Trask's attention. "That black car, the one that skidded by us just after Ian stopped: Liz says it was them. She says it was Vavara performing one of her illusions."

Trask knew immediately what she meant and said, "Of course it was, and who would know it better than Liz? She's been there and done that on Krassos. As for Lardis: he's Szgany. They have built-in protections against Wamphyri mentalism, and that's why it didn't work on him. But where's Liz now?"

Looking back toward the minibus, he saw Liz leaning against the wall of a shop, apparently propping herself up. But when he saw how she held her hands to her temples, he knew at once what she was doing.

"Damnation!" he gasped, striding towards her.

But Paul Garvey and the precog got to her first, and Garvey said, "It's all right, Ben—we'll cover her, shield her. She's trying to track those alien bastards."

"I know damn well what Liz is doing!" Trask burst out. "And I also know that if she carries on like that she'll get herself in a whole mess of trouble!"

Millie was hot on Trask's heels. Applying her telepathy and adding her shields to Garvey's, she said, "It's okay, it's okay . . . he's not probing back. I can't feel a thing out there, only back here." She was talking about Malinari, of course. Wherever he was now, he wasn't using his mentalism; there was no hint of telepathic intrusion.

But Trask picked up on something else that she'd said: that there was something "back here." And now he snapped, "Mindsmog? Is that what you mean? Where?"

"Only back there," Millie glanced back at the Tundźa, which was now an inferno. "Apart from this fire, they made no attempt to hide their hand in this. That place stinks of them. And Ben, *he* was here!" And she shuddered.

"Szwart?"

Millie nodded. "I couldn't be mistaken. I've been too close to that dreadful *thing* once before. His signature is a stench!"

As she spoke, Ian Goodly staggered and uttered a small warbling cry. It was a momentary thing, and he quickly straightened up. But again Trask knew what it signified.

"What is it?" he barked, taking the precog's arm and steadying him. "What did you see?"

"Fire!" Goodly gasped. "I saw Bernie's face—a *dead* face, Ben—surrounded by flames. He was melting, burning!"

"The Tundźa!" Trask gasped, turning and making to run back towards the blazing hotel. But Goodly clung to him and said:

"No, not there. He's not *there,* Ben. Not any longer."

"Then where?" Trask's face was ruddy, glaring in the light from the fire.

"I . . . I don't know," Goodly said. "It was like a scene out of a nightmare. And there were . . . there were *girls* behind him, back beyond the flames. Girls, Ben, and they were laughing and dancing a weird, frozen dance!"

"What?" Trask shook his head in dismay. "What in hell does *that* mean?"

But the precog had no answers; he could only offer a shrug of apology and blink those sad undertaker's eyes of his, those eyes that shone with tomorrow's light.

Then the policeman came hurrying toward them. "I Inspector Burdur," he said. "Ali Bey Burdur. I needing descriptions your friends, their names and so on and so forth. You are coming to police station with me. But not worrying, is not the big problem. You will following my car? On the way we make one stop."

Trask introduced himself to the heavily built, swarthy law officer, and said, "Yes, of course, we'll help you all we can. But there's something we should tell you right now. It's possible we've seen the people who did this. We believe they were in that car that was leaving just as we arrived."

Burdur nodded. "The black station wagon? I seeing it, too. Perhaps the driver eager to make room for us, and perhaps not. But . . . she was driving very fast." Again he nodded, but very thoughtfully.

"She?" said Trask. "A woman? You saw her?"

"A pretty woman, yes, Mr. Trask. But now, maybe *she* has the troubles, eh? You are knowing this person?

"No," said Trask as convincingly as possible—even though he hated lying. "We don't know her. But . . . did you say she has troubles? What troubles?"

Burdur shook his head and said, "No more questions. Now we go, and quickly. Across the town is another fire."

He looked at Trask. "A black station wagon is burning in the square near the town theatre. *Ah!* I seeing your face—you understanding!"

"*My God!*" said Goodly, under his breath, his hand shaking like a leaf on Trask's arm.

"We'll follow right behind you," said Trask grimly, as Ali Bey Burdur turned and made for his vehicle.

And then, speaking quietly to the pale, shuddering precog, Trask said, "This time, old friend, you can take it easy. I'll be doing the driving . . ."

By the time they got to the open square where the black estate car was on fire nose to tail, a second ancient fire engine had arrived and was just beginning to pour water on the flames. In the car, sitting stiffly in a rear seat, his head lolling back on the headrest, a human figure blazed like a candle, his blue and yellow flames curling out through the heat-shattered window. It could only be Fletcher, for the precog had foreseen it. And in situations like this Ian Goodly was rarely wrong.

A small, mainly muted crowd had gathered despite the lateness of the hour, and Ali Bey Burdur quickly found himself an excited witness, an elderly man who worked at the shabby-looking theatre just across the road.

There followed a rapid-fire exchange in Turkish, to which the E-Branch people were not privy, and then Burdur turned to Trask and said, "This a very horrible thing. The old man working in the theatre. He working slow, cleaning up, makes locked the doors, comes out. He standing over there in the shadows in the doorway. The car comes. Three peoples get out. No one here but the old man. The peoples pour kero in the car and outside. The old man is afraid. He sees a man in the car. He wants cry out, but the three are very strange. One is woman—he thinking. Then they set fire and go away. Is nothing else . . ."

Trask shook his head, said nothing, let his haggard looks speak for him. But the precog was moaning, "Poor Bernie. Poor Bernie . . ."

"These peoples who making the fires," said Burdur, staring hard at Trask. "Your enemies?"

"I've already told you," said Trask, obliged to lie again. "We only just got here. We have no enemies here. Perhaps these people were thieves and this is how they cover their tracks."

"And the one in the car, this poor dead man?"

"He's our friend, we think. One of them. We can't be sure. But he looked like a man called Bernie Fletcher."

And Goodly sat down on the damp kerb of the little traffic island in the middle of the square, and said, "It is Fletcher, Ben. It *is* definitely Bernie Fletcher." Distraught, the precog hadn't realized that Trask was doing his best to extricate his people from all of this.

"The tall one he seem very sure," said Burdur, frowning.

Trask took the Inspector's arm, led him away from Goodly, leaving Millie and the others to "comfort" him, and said, "You don't understand, Ali Bey. They were very good friends, Bernie and the tall one. This is a big shock to him. To all of us."

"And this Bernie came here with—how many others?—to study the anti-tikkies?"

"With two other English," said Trask. "Both men. They came to find a cheap place to stay, to use as a base."

"Well, they finding it," said Burdur. "But in wrong part of town. Now I must try to finding them, the others. You are helping, at the police station?"

"Of course," said Trask.

"Good. And then we find you a place to stay—in right part of town, I thinking."

"Lead on," said Trask. "The sooner we get done the better. We've come a long way and we're all very tired."

"Ben!" came Millie's cry of concern. Trask and Burdur came to a halt, looked back.

The car was a smoking, blackened wreck now, where very few flames continued to flicker, all on the inside. On the traffic island close by, Trask's people were assisting Goodly who appeared to have collapsed.

Trask went to them, got down on one knee, helped raise the precog up. But before he got to his feet—as he glanced once again at the gutted car, the shrivelled silhouette within, and the last few flames that persisted in springing into life from the smouldering backseat—finally Trask saw what Goodly had seen, saw what the precog had seen *twice:*

Through the buckled, empty frames of the car's windows, the advertisement over the theatre's entrance—a poster seven feet high by fifteen wide—showing the current attraction: a troupe of scantily clad dancing girls made up as vampires, all of them laughing or smiling their sly vampire smiles, and "frozen," of course, in the crude poses that the artist had given them!

But Trask knew differently, knew that in fact they weren't "made up" at all. And they certainly weren't posing . . .

Ben Trask dreamed.

In the last few moments before waking—which is often the case—he dreamed a kaleidoscopic flashback of all the events of the last twenty-four hours: of the journey to Turkey and Sirpsindigi by airplane and minibus, of the discovery of the blazing Hotel Tundźa, of Bernie Fletcher's horrific cremation, and finally of sitting in the dreary police station with Inspector Ali Bey Burdur, preparing a laborious statement.

Mercifully his statement—just the one—had sufficed; in Burdur's opinion the rest of the team had nothing of any great importance to add to what Trask had told him. Then the Inspector had spent a few minutes on the phone, found an hotel where the English party could stay for the night, given them directions and turned them loose. But he might want to question them again in the morning, and certainly he would want to tell them the results of the night's investigations. So in any case they must not leave the hotel without first speaking to him.

In all, he'd been very helpful and considerate.

But throughout the dream that picture of the burning station wagon had kept surfacing, with Bernie Fletcher's cindered silhouette picked out against crackling flames and a backdrop of dancing, laughing vampires. And Trask, knowing it must have meaning—that it was more than just a replay of a nightmarish event—had found himself striving to understand.

And in that final moment before springing awake, suddenly he *did* recognize and understand its inescapable "truth." Then, jerking upright in his bed in a cold sweat, and thinking about it as all of those jumbled images except the one faded to background static in the face of waking reality, he was annoyed at himself that it hadn't struck him sooner. For now that he had fathomed the thing . . . why, it was obvious!

The telephone had brought him awake. Of the old-fashioned, black Bakelite variety, its persistent ringing on the bedside table made a nerve-jarring clamour in the silence of the room. Yet Trask let it ring a little while longer, until finally he managed to get his thoughts in order. By then Millie had come out of the bathroom, and she picked it up first.

"It's for you," she said, passing Trask the handset as he propped himself up. "It's that policeman."

"Inspector?" he spoke into the phone. "This is Trask."

"Ah, Mr. Trask," came Burdur's thick, guttural voice. "Bad news, I afraid. We finding human remains in the Tundźa hotel. Five bodies . . . well, five *remains*, you understanding. One is downstairs, probably the owner, and four upstairs. As for the man in the car, he has the wallet. Outside burned, inside not so bad. There is a card in heat-resistant plastic. A restaurant card, for the eating place? It has his name: B. Fletcher. So, your Mr. Goodly he was right."

"And the others?" Trask was pretty sure he knew who two of them would be, but there was still hope.

"Very badly burned," said Burdur. "Also very dangerous. No sooner we, er, extracting the bodies, the floor collapse. Only way to check is with dental records. Those names you giving me—also that telephone number in London—they working on it. I expecting the fax. Is good you having connections with British police. They being incredibly helpful.

Also they asking me please to be assisting you in any way."

"I thought they might," said Trask. "There are, er, quite a few policemen in our archaeological society."

"Your society? Ah! The digging people. The ancient relics, and so on and so forth."

"And historians, too," said Trask.

"Is funny," said Burdur, with just a hint of sarcasm in his voice. "In my country the policeman is interested in the crime. He has little time for the hobbies."

"Exactly," said Trask, thinking quickly. "And we *are* interested in crime: the crimes of, er, ancient invaders." Which was pretty much the truth.

For a moment there was silence at the other end, until Ali Bey Burdur said, "Well, is all outside my, er—"

"—Your sphere of interest?"

"Exactly." And then: "So, Mr. Trask, I keeping you informed. You may going in the town if you wishing, but please to telling the desk where you going."

"And how long will you expect us to remain in Sirpsindigi?"

"Oh, only a day or so."

"Thanks for your help," said Trask.

"Thinking nothings of it," said the other. And then, before he broke the connection, "Mr. Trask, are you also the policeman? Some kind of policeman? The investigator, eh?"

"Only in connection with . . . well, with strange old things," Trask answered. "Things out of distant places and times." And:

"Of course," said the other, and Trask thought he sensed a nod of feigned understanding, and also the narrowing of suspicious brown eyes. "You are meaning the anti-tikkies, yes?"

"Yes," said Trask, "the antiquities." And when there was no answer he put the phone down . . .

20
Tracking the Wamphyri—
the Horror at the Crossing

BY 8:45 A.M. ALL THE MEMBERS OF THE E-BRANCH team were down in the three-star hotel's dining room for breakfast. The food was mainly acceptable; the alleged "continental" breakfast consisted of croissants, cheese, preserves, and coffee or tea. But the tea wasn't to Millie's liking and the coffee was a cross between the murky Turkish variety and an inferior instant brand.

"The granules," Paul Garvey commented, with his normal lack of facial expression, which made it difficult to tell if he was joking or not, "don't melt. They just turn to mud in the bottom of the cup." But he probably wasn't joking because it was true, and also because no one was in the mood for humour anyway.

"But at least it's hot," said Liz. "And with a little sugar it's even sweet."

"I'm sorry about last night," said Ian Goodly. "This talent of mine . . . sometimes I hate it! And what with Bernie and all, I just wasn't myself."

"Try to forget it," Trask told him. "And I'm not being callous, but going on about it won't help. Also, if you're feeling bad about Fletcher, well, think how I feel. I sent him and those Special Branch fellows out here. And while it's no consolation, at least we know he was dead before they torched the car."

"Yes," the precog answered. "I am positive about that. When I first saw him—I mean, when we were at the Tundźa—I knew he was dead. But I don't understand why there were two separate attacks. What was Bernie doing out on his own?"

"I don't think he was out on his own," said Trask. "I think they killed him at the Tundźa along with his minders and Gustav Turchin's men, then took him to that Kino place deliberately."

"The dancing girls?" said Millie, reading his mind without even trying.

"The troupe off the *Evening Star*, yes," Trask nodded. "Vavara's creatures now. Property of the Wamphyri."

"Malinari knew we would find that estate car and Fletcher," said Paul Garvey, "and then that we'd see the billboard. Is that what you mean?"

And again Trask nodded. "He's so sure of himself—so sure he's going to win this one—that he's leading us on. I'll give you odds that when we check it out we'll discover that the show has moved on. Malinari wants us to follow him, to go where he's going. Him and those other two freaks, and those poor girls. As to why: I can only think that he intends to trap us. But Bernie was only one man and we're many, and forewarned is forearmed."

"Which raises the question," said Lardis Lidesci, "forearmed with what—a little garlic, a little knowledge? Which in turn raises the question: *should* we be doing what he wants? *Should* we be pursuing them?"

"You know we must," said Trask. "You know that this is one trail we've got to follow, because we're the only ones who can. Okay, by now in the UK the Minister Responsible will be on it. Him and the civilian authorities, all of the security services . . . hell, and for all I know the Army, too! They'll be finding and confining sleepers—that's if there are any more, and we must hope there aren't—but if there are they'll be watching them and checking them out. At Porton Down the microbiologists and, oh, a whole gaggle of boffins, will be doing their thing, looking for answers. You see, it simply isn't enough that this new bubonic plague out of China will kill the Wamphyri. Out of the six and a quarter billion people on this planet, some four billion haven't even come in contact with the plague, and it's already waning, dying out. And at least half the population of the poorer

336

countries haven't even had shots. So there's—God!—food enough for these beasts. What's more, and as I believe I've said before, it's possible that they'll *know* who they can or can't eat."

"Pheromones," said Liz.

"Something like that," Trask nodded. "Or perhaps common or *un*common sense. Wamphyri senses are vastly superior to those of ordinary people. I'm sorry if it offends at table and what have you, but would *you* kiss a man with breath like a sewer, a sunken nose, and scabby lips? Or put it another way: don't *you* know when a piece of raw meat has overstayed its welcome in your refrigerator? It's not at all unlikely they can smell the plague, these bloody creatures!"

"In which case," said Garvey, "well, at least we know they won't be biting us. We've had our jabs. We're tainted meat."

"That may be true," said Lardis. "They won't be biting us, but it won't stop them from tearing our arms and legs off!"

"What I'm trying to say," said Trask, "is that what's happening back home doesn't apply elsewhere. Of course, the Minister Responsible will have passed all of this on to our friends in Australia, and with good old Manolis Papastamos on the case in Greece . . . who knows? Maybe the Greek authorities will listen and take some kind of covert action to isolate Krassos. We must hope so, anyway, for after what's happened back home—if it's as serious as we suppose, and I for one think it is—we just don't know what else is loose out there anymore."

"But we do know the source," said Millie.

"Right," said Trask. "And we also know that it was out and about its filthy work right here in Sirpsindigi last night. So since right now we can't tell the majority of the world's population what's happening—"

"—The job's ours," said Ian Goodly, his strange deep eyes afire now, blazing as never before. "Because we have the knowledge that almost everyone else lacks, we're it." He looked at the Old Lidesci. "We're the avengers, Lardis. Does that answer your question 'should we be going?' If not us, who else? Malinari, Vavara, and Szwart, they've thrown down the gauntlet. I say we pick it up and ram it right down their bloody throats!"

Which, coming from the thin, grimacing lips of the precog, sounded that much more impressive. And:

"Well, then," Lardis growled. "That appears to be that! For if what you just said wasn't a vow, then I've never heard one. So you, Ian Goodly, may now consider yourself an honorary member of the Szgany Lidesci, and I'm glad to have you. As for my question: but that's all it was. I was just very interested to know how everyone else felt about it, that's all. Also, and with regard to my own feelings: I don't know why we're sitting around doing sweet bugger all when we've come so very close to tracking these bastards down!"

"Sweet bugger all?" said Trask, frowning at Lardis.

"Jake Cutter," Lardis growled. "I heard him say it several times, when he was out of sorts in the HQ. Is it offensive?"

Trask shook his head. "Explicit, that's all. And as to why we're doing sweet bugger all, it's because we're stuck in this place until Inspector Ali Bey Burdur says we can go. But we're allowed out into the town, which means there is work we can be getting on with. For one thing, we can find out if my theory's right and those girls from the *Evening Star* have moved on to their next venue."

"God!" said Liz. "But what a trio of roadies they have!"

"And then there's Lardis's other point," said Millie. "We don't as yet have any weapons. When we do finally catch up to these monsters, I don't want to find myself in the same situation as last time. What, face-to-face with a thing like Lord Szwart, and completely vulnerable? That doesn't bear thinking about." She hugged herself and shivered.

"I had intended to weapon up as soon as we got settled in out here," said Trask. "There's more than enough of everything we need back in the armoury at the HQ. It's all been set aside by now, bagged up and ready to go as soon as I give the word."

"But with Ali Bey Burdur on our backs—" said Garvey.

"—Exactly," said Trask. "So we'll have to wait till we're on the move again—settled in our next port of call, wherever that may be—before we bring our secret weapon into play." He looked at Liz.

"Jake," she said. "I came close to calling him last night, at the Tundža. And again in the Kino Square."

Trying his best not to scowl at her, Trask said drily, "Oh, joy!" His sarcasm dripped. "Why, yes! What a marvellous notion! I mean, can't you just picture it? Jake Cutter, appearing right out of nowhere, and probably with no IDs? Now that really *would* give our suspicious policeman friend something to think about!"

"I know." Liz bit her lip. "But I was jittery, and we were so very close to those monsters. I'm just like Millie, Ben . . . I've been close once before. Anyway, I didn't do it."

"No," said Trask, "you tried to track them instead—which was almost as dumb *because* they were that close to us! And you have to promise me you won't do it again. Not on your own, anyway. Now listen, Liz, when I'm ready to turn you loose—when it gets close up and personal and I really need your talents—believe me, you'll be the first to know, all of you. But it will probably be a concerted effort, each and every one of us doing his or her bit. And I want us all in one piece when that time comes."

They were finished eating, not that anyone had eaten very much. Paul Garvey poured a little hot water onto the dregs in his cup, added a lump of sugar, and asked, "So what's next? I feel about the same as Lardis: now that we're out here—now that the game's afoot—I'm sure that too much inactivity is bound to get to me."

"To all of us," said Trask. "Okay, this is what we'll do. It's daylight and we're comparatively safe. So we'll form two teams. Myself, Lardis, and Ian: we'll pay a visit to this Kino place and see if my theory's correct; and if so, we'll try to find out where those girls—if we can still call them that—where they're playing next. Which leaves Paul and the ladies, bold telepaths all. You three will go up to one of the rooms, use a small-scale map of this region, and see if you can pick up the trail." Then he frowned at Liz and added, "But no deep probing. That's out. I'm talking about their *trail,* the route they took out of here, if in fact they've gone. I know you're not locators, but working in tandem, as it were ... let's see what you can do anyway. And I just want to stress it one more time: the moment you sense mindsmog you're out of there, back off and leave it at that. Oh, and there's one other thing: in case Ali Bey Burdur decides to drop in on you, you might want to make sure you're up to scratch on the local 'anti-tikkies,' okay?"

He stood up. "That's all for now, people. Ian and Lardis, if you're ready?"

And they were ...

In the Kino Square the burned-out car had been security-taped off and covered with a tentlike tarpaulin, beneath and around which the members of a scenes-of-crime team in masks and white smocks performed their gruesome tasks. Above the Kino's double doors, the billboard had been stripped and two men were busy on fragile-looking scaffolding where they were pasting up a new poster. It looked like Trask's theory was proven.

As best possible, Trask and his two avoided looking at the tented enclosure—avoided thinking about Bernie and the method of his disposal—and tried to make themselves inconspicuous as they mingled with a thin queue of Turkish men waiting in the Kino's foyer at a ticket window. The small crowd was in an ugly mood and Trask soon found out why: the revue had been cancelled and last night's show had been the last of its kind. The girls, who had been booked for another three days, had apparently quit and moved on, and these men were here to get their money back.

At the window, Trask asked if it was known where the girls had gone. What was their next venue? The harassed agent in the booth didn't understand him, became impatient, waved him aside. But a Turk who stood next in line behind the E-Branch group had heard Trask's enquiry and said,

"They gone. No one knows where. They just go. Is too bad. Was very good the show. The sexy English girls. The vampire ladies, yes?"

"Yes, indeed," Trask answered the toothy, grinning Turk. "A great pity we missed them."

Outside again, the three could scarcely avoid observing the tented enclosure which stood directly opposite the Kino. But as they paused at the kerb a police car drew up and Ali Bey Burdur got out. "Ah! Finding you," he said.

And Trask asked him, "Were you at our hotel?"

"Was going there, but seeing you here."

Goodly nodded, and said, "We were paying our last respects. Since we won't be here for the . . ." But there he paused.

"The cremation?" said Burdur. "I understanding. One cremation is enough, yes?"

"And that will be soon, I hope," said Trask.

Burdur nodded. "We having the identity. Is Fletcher. And is . . . something strange." He looked at Trask quizzically.

"Oh?" Trask tried not to sound too worried.

"This Fletcher, he have no family?"

"Distant relatives, I believe," said Trask.

"That explaining things . . . perhaps," said the Inspector.

"What things?"

"That they asking we cremate him here . . . which you knowing about? And that we do it soon, which is you suggest also."

And again Trask found himself obliged to think quickly. "In many lands," he said, "people are burning the dead—and doing it with despatch—because of the bubonic. It's becoming almost standard practice."

"Ah! The plague," said Burdur. "But surely the poor Bernie Fletcher he had not the plague?"

"No, of course not," said Trask. "But why take chances? He has no family, he's dead, it's as well he's cremated here."

"Hmmm!" said Burdur. "Same conversation I having with your people in London."

But Trask wasn't to be caught out so easily. "My people?"

"Er, I meaning the English authorities."

"Oh," said Trask. "Then I can only assume that the authorities in England will make good the expenses, too."

"So I understanding." Burdur nodded thoughtfully. And then, quickly changing the subject, "One other things. Chief of Turkish Security in Ankara—the Big Boss peoples—is speaking to me this morning. He is saying me to giving all assistance possible to Mr. Trask and his party. You having important friends!"

"Really?" said Trask, without having to act too surprised. And: *Thank God for the Minister Responsible!* he thought, for he had certainly outdone himself this time around. Quite obviously he'd broken new ground and developed some kind of alliance with Turkish Intelligence, isolated for many years now by reason of Turkey's human rights record. And Trask couldn't help but wonder how much information the Minister Responsible had passed on in order to achieve this level of cooperation.

"Yes, really," said the Inspector. "But I asking to myself, security? Big Boss security? Now what having we here, eh?"

Trask shrugged, then said, "Oh, I don't think there's any great mystery. It's not unusual when an Englishman dies abroad that our Foreign Office do their best to assist in every possible way."

"Ah, yes," said Burdur. "But assisting the dead man's *family,* usually. Is not so?"

But wanting to have done with this now—and answering the Inspector perhaps a little too sharply—Trask said, "The point is, will you help us or not?"

Ali Bey Burdur drew back a pace. "I having no choice," he said. "But was hoping you could helping me, too."

"Me help? But how?"

"The proprietor of Tundźa he dead, too," said Burdur. "And he is Turkish. The charity is beginning at home, eh? Also, the other Englishmens, and two more we not know at Tundźa. Finally, the owner of this burned car. The car he was stolen last night. We finding the owner. He dead, murdered we thinking, but . . . is a very bad, very strange thing."

"How, strange?" said Trask.

"He a young man," said the Inspector. "Young, strong, with no sicknesses. But we finding him all old and twisted. How you say it . . . ?" He sucked in his cheeks and squeezed down into himself, illustrating the word he was looking for. And:

"Shrivelled," said Trask.

"Exactly!" And when Trask said nothing: "Please, Mr. Trask," Burdur went on. "Listen, I coming clean. I having you followed when you leaving hotel. You come here, go in Kino asking about girls. For why? I not believing your anti-tikkies story—but I not thinking you the criminals. No, I thinking you the special policemans, is correct? And I also thinking I needing your help. If is bad something here in Sirpsindigi, I need knowing. So, will you telling Ali Bey Burdur what going on?"

"Ali Bey," said Trask, "I'm not a policeman. But I am concerned with security. Security of my country, and occasionally of the world. Right now the security of the world. I can't say more than that. But me and my people, we need to leave Sirpsindigi, if not tonight by tomorrow morning. If you can clear the way for us, perhaps I'll have something more to tell you."

"Is good," said the other. "Tomorrow, you going. Anythings you needing, asking me."

"Good," said Trask. "And now we're going back to the hotel. You can contact me there early tomorrow morning."

Burdur nodded. "I doing that for sure. And if I not seeing you tomorrow—" He stuck out his huge hand.

Trask took and shook it—and found Ali Bey's card in his hand. He pocketed it as the Turkish policeman turned away, and then he and the others returned to their minibus . . .

Back at the hotel, Trask and his group found Paul Garvey, Liz, and Millie seated in the foyer. Trask asked what was happening and was informed by Garvey that they'd come down to escape the confines of Liz's room, get a breath of fresh air, and stretch their legs; this following their combined effort at picking up the trail of the Wamphyri, and Garvey hinted that they'd found something.

Here in the foyer, however, with people sitting about reading newspapers and drinking coffee, and hotel staff coming and going, Garvey didn't want to say too much.

In the cranky elevator, on their way back up to Liz's room, Trask asked why everone seemed so quiet and nervous. And Garvey told him:

"Earlier, the telephone in Liz's room went on the blink, so I went down to see if they could fix it—also to fetch coffee and sandwiches. Their room service is lousy. There was this man in the foyer who couldn't seem to take his eyes off me. Well, I knew he was watching me; I could actually feel his eyes following me. You know how it is."

"Yes," said Trask, "but not as well as you do. Your talent will give you the edge every time."

"Anyway, I went to check him out," said Garvey. "I managed to get up close to him and tried to look into his eyes— just a glimpse should be enough—but he avoided me. And he was so intent on pretending *not* to be watching me, why, it was almost as if he was shielded! So I thought maybe he was a thrall, and that was scary. But I took a chance, 'accidentally' bumped into him, finally got to look him in the eyes. In one way that was a relief, but in another—"

"—It worried you," said Trask. "But far better a policeman than a vampire thrall, right?"

As they got out of the elevator Garvey said, "Well, you're obviously way ahead of me. So now it's your turn: what's happening? What did you find out at the Kino? And why are the Turkish police watching us and probably listening to our telephone conversations? I mean, I know *why* they're watching us—of course I do—but how much do they know?"

"Whoah!" said Trask, as Liz let them into her room. "You're not done yet. What did *you* find out? You gave me the impression that you'd got something for me."

At which point Millie took it up. "We think perhaps we

do," she said. "But if we're right it presents more difficulties."

"Explain," said Trask, as they all found places to sit.

And now it was Liz's turn. "When I was Vavara's prisoner on Krassos," she began, "I experienced this weird ability of hers, I suppose we should call it her 'talent,' up close. Also, I saw what lurks beneath that talent, the wrinkled hag that she is in reality. I learned something then, something we all should have realized sooner, but even then I failed to recognize its importance. This morning, however, when we began our search, suddenly it dawned on me. When Malinari goes abroad in the world he goes as a man; which is no great effort to him, because he *is* a man. He scarcely needs to disguise himself at all. As for that thing called Szwart: he lives with his condition of constant metamorphosis, and it's entirely 'natural' to him. He only wills changes in himself when it's absolutely necessary. But when the hag Vavara goes abroad she goes as a beautiful girl or woman. It's that important to her, a matter of vanity."

"Aye," said Lardis. "That's very true—but she can't stand beauty in others, which is why she mutilates her women. Especially the lovely ones." And:

"I think I see what you're getting at," said Trask. "Vavara has to keep up appearances. She's obliged to use her talent all the time. She never lets up!"

"Unless she's angry, infuriated," said Liz. "I've seen her like that, too, and close up, as I said. It isn't a pretty picture."

"You know her aura," said Trask. "You're able to recognize her psychic signature."

"I think so, yes," Liz nodded. "Well, something like that."

And now Paul Garvey took it up. "We sat at that small round coffee table there, and bonded. Then we concentrated on various areas of the map where it lay in the middle of the table, areas lying outside the town limits. We were looking for mindsmog, of course—even the faintest trace—which might perhaps indicate that the Wamphyri had passed that way. Since they probably left by road—I mean, how else could they have gone?—that's what we concentrated on: roads and crossing points."

"Crossing points?" Trask repeated him.

And Garvey nodded. "If you look at the map you'll see we're pretty close to the borders of both Greece and Bulgaria. If the Wamphyri have left Sirpsindigi—which we're fairly certain now that they have—they had a choice of going back into the Turkish heartland, or crossing into Greece or Bulgaria."

"Greece wouldn't be their best choice," said Trask, looking at the map. "The borders with Turkey are closed . . . territorial disputes and what have you. And anyway, Vavara's been there and done that, and both she and Malinari know now that we have good friends in Greece."

"That was our opinion, too," said Garvey, "so we spent only a little time sweeping west. But as for north, south, and east: we covered them extensively. And that brings us back to Liz and Millie."

The latter took it up. "There was something to the north— into Bulgaria—that I didn't much care for," said Millie. "I'm much like Liz, and my time with Szwart has left a kind of stain on my psyche. I felt, or thought I felt, something of his passing by or through. In my mind it was as if the northern area of the map lay under a shadow that was gradually clearing. Well, as you can see for yourself, the way north is a narrow route along a second-class road—and a Turkish second-class road at that—that parallels the Tundźa into Bulgaria. There's a customs post marked on the map at the border. If in fact they went that way, they would have had to pass through that border crossing."

"And you think they did?" said Trask.

"That's where I come back in," said Liz. "But before I say any more, what *did* you find out at the Kino? It seems only fair that you tell us now, Ben. Have they in fact left—or haven't they? I mean, have we three been sitting here, wasting our time and imagining things, or what?"

"You mean you don't already know?" he answered, and saw all three telepaths glance at each other with lowered eyes. Then he grinned, albeit wryly, humourlessly, and said, "Okay, under the circumstances I accept that you couldn't wait. So just to clarify matters, yes, they've left." And he quickly went on to tell them the story of the dance troupe's departure, and also of his conversation with Ali Bey Burdur, finishing up with, "So now go on, Liz. What was it you thought you sensed about that northern route into Bulgaria?"

"But that's precisely the point," she answered. "It's what I *didn't* feel! In every other direction there was motion, struggle, the massed turmoil of people, intelligences, thoughts. And Paul and Millie detected much the same thing . . . the telepathic background, the mental static of all those people. Our combined talents let us sense the backwash of humanity, all their triumphs, frustrations, and disappointments. But to the north . . . that was different. Everything was peaceful, Ben, and I knew that it was false!"

"Vavara," Trask nodded. "The route she's taken out of here, like some kind of slimy snail trail."

"That's how I thought of it, too," said Liz. "But you know, there are times when the sun lights on a snail's track that it can look quite beautiful? In this case a hideous beauty. And I can't be mistaken. That's where they've gone, and that's where she is now: in Bulgaria."

And Millie added, "I think Liz is right. It's very strange, but in combining our talents like that, we seemed to achieve a great deal more than we could possibly have done on our own. I know it's an old trick among E-Branch espers, but this time it seemed to work so much better. And I for one felt far more . . . powerful? My talent, I mean."

"Me, too," said Liz, nodding her concurrence. "There was a clarity to everything that I've never known before, but it was the negative aspect that drew my attention north."

Trask turned to Paul Garvey for the last word, but expressionless as always, Garvey could only shrug. "It's all down to the ladies," he said. "I like to think I boosted their probes, but the credit is theirs. It must be as they've said: previous close contact has given them the edge and given us a brand-new weapon. From now on David Chung must look to his laurels."

Trask stood up, said, "If those three monsters have stolen another vehicle, the guards on that border crossing post might have logged its registration number. Why, they might even know its destination. If so, I know someone who can probably supply us with both."

"Which brings us back to those difficulties I spoke about," said Millie. "Our documents only allow us to travel in Turkey. I know there aren't many restrictions on Turks travelling into Bulgaria, but we're not Turks, just guests in their country."

Trask took out Ali Bey's card from his pocket, went to the antique telephone on Liz's bedside table and began to dial the Inspector's number. "Yes," he said. "That's a very good point, and Burdur might have the answer to that one, too."

Trask got through to a grunting, unintelligible receptionist, gave his name and asked for Burdur. Following which:

"You are fortunate to be catching me, Mr. Trask," said the harassed-sounding Inspector a moment later, when he was called to the phone. "I getting back here two, three minutes ago, and now on way out again! I busy, very. Please being quickly. What is it you wanting?"

Trask told Burdur what he suspected: that last night's killers had probably departed Turkey via a little-used, backwoods border crossing into Bulgaria, and began to request documentation in order that he might pursue them. But from the moment he mentioned the border post the Inspector quit muttering to some unseen other in the police station and fell silent. Indeed, he even seemed to stop breathing. And before Trask could finish:

"You knowing the way to the crossing?" There was an undeniable urgency in the Turkish policeman's voice.

"I have a map," said Trask.

"I meeting you there," Burdur growled.

"When?" Trask was taken aback.

"Now! Packing your things, Mr. Trask. You want leaving

Sirpsindigi, leaving Turkey maybe? You leaving."

"But—"

"—I seeing you at crossing point," Burdur cut in. "Driving quickly, Mr. Trask. Is very bad business."

Trask immediately suspected the worst, and said, "I'm on my way." But the line was already dead . . .

"The scenery is Mediterranean," said Millie, staring out of the minibus's window. "And the countryside sparsely peopled, mainly farming communities. The rain last night was probably the first of the season. Just see how it's made everything look fresh."

"Nice climate," said Trask. "If the Tundźa was a sea rather than a river, I might well believe I was on some Aegean island. It's a pity the Greeks and Turks can't get along. There are incredibly nice people on both sides."

"Mundane conversation," said Paul Garvey. "It's supposed to ease the tension."

"But it isn't doing its job," said Liz. "Instead, the tension increases every time we take a wrong turning. But all these farm tracks look the same to me, and the map is too small-scale to be anything like accurate."

Liz was in the front, map-reading for Ian Goodly; Trask and the others were in the back; all six were being jostled, thrown about by a combination of their vehicle's poor suspension and a badly neglected, potholed road surface.

"At this rate," said Goodly, doing battle with the steering wheel, "it won't be too long before this old rattletrap shakes herself to bits!"

"Suggestion," said Lardis Lidesci, hanging on for dear life. "Liz, why don't you just put that chart down and simply take us there? You have the skill, after all. And Ian: surely you know, or you can guess, which tracks to take? The future can't be all *that* devious?"

Trask looked at the Old Lidesci, opened his mouth to speak, then shut it again and frowned. And finally he said, "You know, he could be right. Liz, put the map aside. And Ian, just drive. Your choice."

"Hang a right at the next crossroads," said Liz and Millie, almost in unison. But the precog was already doing it. And:

"Damn!" he said. "But you know, I think Lardis *is* right!"

They sped along a slightly better road, past the small man-made lakes of a trout farm, and crested a rise. And there, just two hundred yards ahead, they spotted a wooden structure at the side of the road, and a red- and white-striped pivoting barrier with a universal HALT! disc centrally situated. Two police vehicles were parked beside the border post, and Inspector Burdur was standing there, waving the minibus down.

As the team got out of their vehicle, Burdur came striding and gripped Trask's arm. "How you knowing?" he said.

"That they came this way?"

"Yes. How you knowing that?"

"We believe they may be heading for Romania," Trask lied—and then wondered if it really *was* a lie. For after all, they'd come *out* of Romania. But why would they want to go back there?

"You knowing plenty about these criminal peoples," said the Inspector angrily, bringing him back to earth, "yet you telling me nothings!"

"First you tell me," said Trask. "What's happened here?"

"What happening?" said Burdur. "You wanting know? You going inside, then you seeing." Wiping sweat from his brow, he nodded toward the open, fly-screened door of the border-post shack.

Guarding the door, one on each side, two nervous, trembling border patrolmen kept glancing inwards, their eyes trying—but not trying too hard—to penetrate the shaded interior. Looking at them, at these burly, sidearmed, yet badly shaken men, Trask paced to the door, then paused to look back at his people. They were watching him, uncertain what to do. Then Millie made to go to him, but Ali Bey Burdur held up a warning hand. "Not for the ladies, no," he said, gruffly.

And Trask told Garvey, "Paul, stay with Liz and Millie."

At which Lardis Lidesci stepped forward.

"You?" said the Inspector.

"I've probably seen worse," Lardis grunted.

Burdur looked deep into his eyes, and nodded. "You thinking so? I thinking so, too. You, Mr. Trask . . . I thinking *all* of you seeing worse. I think is part of your work. But me: I policeman thirty-seven years, and *not* seeing worse, never! You still want going in?"

For answer Lardis started for the door, and Burdur followed on behind.

Trask had meanwhile stepped inside. Disturbed by his entry, a swarm of blowflies whirred past on their way out, and several of them flew into his face and hair. Grimacing, he brushed them away, then passed deeper into the gloom of the place.

There was one small window looking out on the road and barrier; dirty and fly-specked, it didn't let too much light in. A cubicle at the rear contained a toilet and wash basin. The door to the toilet stood open . . . and someone was sitting there with his trousers round his ankles. Half of the shack was hidden behind a slightly elevated counter, where a second man was seated in a chair, with his head laid back as if he were asleep. Trask knew he wasn't asleep, however, and also that the man using the toilet . . . wasn't using it.

For while Trask's eyes were still adjusting properly to the gloom of the place, his talent had leaped ahead to register the grisly truth of what he was seeing. And:

"My God!" he said, when finally it sank in. His exclamation—an explosion of sound in the silent, stinking confines of the border-post shack—brought more flies swarming from the faces of the two corpses, or from what had been their faces.

For the one on the toilet had no face—just a raw, screaming mask—where the flesh had been flensed right down to the bone. And his shirt all down the front inside his open uniform jacket was a sticky crimson mess where blowflies, reluctant to give up their meal and their egg-laying pursuits, continued to swarm.

As for his colleague, lolling in his chair behind the desk: twin ballpoint pens were sticking up from his eye sockets, his face was crusted with dried blood, and his throat and windpipe had been torn free and were hanging on his chest . . .

From close behind Trask, Lardis grunted, "They were here." A completely unnecessary comment, but what more could he say?

"Yes," said Inspector Burdur from the doorway. "They were. And now you are please telling me *who* was here. I thinking you owing me that much, Mr. Trask . . ."

21
The Vampire Hunters, Memories out of Time

FEELING SICK AND MORE THAN A LITTLE DIZZY, Trask followed Lardis and Burdur out of the shack. The dizziness (he told himself) was probably due to the fact that he'd been holding his breath from the moment he'd caught his first whiff of the place. Blood and death are like that—each has its own distinctive smell—and violent death is even more distinctive, and much more pungent. And you couldn't get much more violent than this. Added to which both men had soiled themselves in the moments before they died, but only one had been in the right place to do so.

"Well?" said Ali Bey Burdur, when they were out in the open again.

Trask took the handkerchief from his mouth and put it away, and coughed for a moment or two to clear his throat before trying to speak. But the Old Lidesci—who in his lifetime on Sunside really had seen a lot worse than this, and all too often—strode across to the other members of the team and, in lowered tones, began to tell them something of what he'd seen.

"Mr. Trask?" said Burdur. "Please, I need to understanding."

"I can't tell you everything," said Trask then. "It's possible that my people back in London have already passed information to Turkish intelligence in Ankara, but I still don't know what or how much."

"If not telling everythings, then telling somethings, eh? I must knowing, Mr. Trask. Those men in there, they are having the families."

"I understand," Trask nodded. "And I'll tell you all I can, which may not be much but better than nothing. Not about what's gone but what might be coming."

"Something coming?" said Burdur anxiously. "I listening."

"But first our documents," said Trask. "We need them stamped in order to cross the border. If we're checked in Bulgaria without the proper authentication—"

"I can dealing with that," said Burdur. "These two men here are border officials. They came here to relieving the dead men. They will stamping your documents, giving you the visas. But I needing to know what is all about. I needing it now!"

"Then listen carefully," said Trask, "and when I'm finished ask me no more. Because what I'm going to tell you is *all* I can tell you. The people who did these things . . . no, the *creatures* who did these things—who killed Fletcher and the others, and who murdered the man who owned that car and these border guards—they carry a disease. But it's a disease like none we've ever seen before, and it's extremely virulent."

"A disease?" said Burdur. "A sickness? Then must be causing the madness, this disease. No sane peoples ever did things like this."

"That's right," said Trask. "They *are* insane, and in their madness they'll cause others to go mad, too. And so it spreads. That's why we have to track them down and destroy them."

"What of the dancing girls?" said Burdur. "They are having a part in this, right?"

"They were victims," said Trask. "Helpless victims. But by now the disease is in them, too. And there's no helping them."

"This is something to do with the plague out of Asia," said Burdur. "A new development—a new strain—am I right?"

"No," Trask shook his head. "It's far worse than the plague out of Asia."

"But . . . how am I *knowing* this thing when I seeing it?" Ali Bey threw up his arms in frustration. "And is it in Turkey now, this horrible plague thing?"

And Trask could only answer truthfully, for he felt certain now that it was in England. "It could be," he said. And then he had an idea. "You have rabies here, don't you?"

"The rabies? Yes. Not so much now, but still here. What are you saying? That this thing is like the rabies?"

"It's . . . *like* rabies," said Trask, "yes. But it isn't carried or passed on by dogs."

"So, how is passed on?" Burdur was insistent, and Trask had gone too far now to turn back.

"How is rabies passed on?" he said.

"Eh?" Burdur frowned—and then he gasped. "You are saying that—they are biting? They are biting like the vampire? Like the old superstitions? The old legends? *Ahhh!*" His eyes bugged. "The anti-tikkies!"

And Trask said nothing.

"Is real?" Burdur's dark skin was a shade paler. "Can I believing this thing?"

Still Trask said nothing. But Burdur knew by simply looking at him that indeed it was the truth. And:

"This happening in the night," he said. "These many things, they all happening by night. The vampires, they were here! Like your man Lardis say—*they were here!*"

"Will you see to our documents?" said Trask. "And give

us a note to cover our lease on this vehicle's use in Bulgaria?"

"Yes, yes," said the other, his eyes wide and almost vacant in the contemplation of unthinkable things. "Giving me the documents. The stamping, er, equipments—the rubber stamps—are in there." He looked at the shack and shuddered uncontrollably. It lasted only a moment, and snapping out of it he gripped Trask's arms and said, "You and your friends—what you are doing—you are the brave peoples, Mr. Trask. And I having somethings for you." He went unsteadily to his car, and Trask followed him.

"Is here," said Burdur, bringing out a thin manila envelope from the glove compartment. "This arriving by fax in the night. Big Boss Security in Ankara is say me to expecting it. I am to putting in envelope and sealing, giving to you. But . . . I keeping till now to make bargain." Averting his eyes, he offered an apologetic shrug. "Now . . . bargaining no longer required."

Trask took the envelope and said, "From?"

"Your people in London, I thinks. Is coded."

"You did look at it, then?"

Burdur blinked and answered, "Was the fax, Mr. Trask. How I not looking? But understanding, decoding, making into Turkish, I not doing. I hope is helping, or making easier your work."

"So do I," said Trask. But somehow he didn't think so.

Ten minutes later, as the E-Branch party shook hands with Burdur, boarded the minibus and drove under the raised barrier into Bulgaria, distantly, from the south, the first mournful wail of sirens could be heard. An ambulance—in excess of requirement but at least a means of conveying the dead to the morgue—was on its way, plus a scenes-of-crime team called in by Burdur.

As for the Inspector himself: he stood on the road to wave them farewell until they passed out of sight . . .

*   *   *

In the minibus, sitting up front with Ian Goodly, Trask opened the envelope, glanced at the single sheet of encyphered paper, passed it back to Paul Garvey. "There's a decoder in my briefcase," he said. "When we hit a decent patch of road, type this up and see what comes out, will you?"

And while Garvey worked laboriously and very uncomfortably at that, Trask turned to Goodly and said, "What now?"

"What's in store for us, do you mean?" The precog glanced at him out of the corner of his eye. "I can take a stab at it, make a couple of guesses, attempt to extrapolate, if that will suffice. But as for reading the future: the more I think about it, the more my mind shrinks from it. And to be honest I think I'm losing it. It could be deliberate. Maybe I've been in this game too long. 'I think, therefore I am?' Maybe it's a case of I think horrible things—wherefore I don't want to think anymore."

"Huh!" Trask grunted. "And is this the same man who almost gave Lardis a telling-off for questioning why we've got to get on with this?"

"No," Goodly gave a curt shake of his head. "This is a man who's sick to his stomach from seeing terrifying things, knowing that they're coming, and not being able to do a damn thing about it. A man who sees things but is often unable to explain them, and who knows that one day he will see his own death and the deaths of his friends, and having seen them will know that they're inevitable and utterly unavoidable."

Trask thought on that awhile, then said, "I wasn't trying to be flippant. And I'm sorry if that's how it sounded. I just don't want us to stagnate on the job, as it were. I don't want horror to become commonplace. I want us to keep working at it, eventually to defeat it."

"It's okay," Goodly answered. "And you know I'm dedicated, too. It's just that sometimes it feels like a no-win situation. We've lost too many friends down the years, Ben. Too many loved ones. And this battle we're fighting, it seems endless. I mean, after all we've done we're no further forward. Normally we take two steps forward and one back, except this time it's beginning to feel like two forward and *three* back! We're not winning this one."

And from the rear of the vehicle, "Which means we've got to try that much harder," Lardis Lidesci growled, no longer questioning but firm in his resolve.

"England might be contaminated," Goodly reminded him, without looking back. "And what of Australia, Turkey, Krassos? Contaminated, yes, with a growing infestation. Not by the Wamphyri—not yet—but victims of the Wamphyri, common vampires such as all those poor people on the *Evening Star*. Not by creatures who recognize the importance of remaining anonymous, but by people who don't know what they're becoming, who can't possibly understand these strange new forces and emotions that they feel driving them ever more strongly, hideously on. And eventually, when they succumb, when they discover their unbelievable strength and monstrous hunger . . . what then?"

"Every man for himself," said Paul Garvey, still trying to type the encrypted message into Trask's decoder. And:

"*I Am Legend,*" said Millie, quietly.

"What's that?" Trask looked back at her.

"The title of a book I read a long time ago," she answered. "It was science fiction, or fantasy, horror: a nightmarish romance about the last man in a world converted to vampirism. The once-hero was now the menace; *he* was the legendary monster!"

"I think I can see that," said Liz. "On an island of mutant three-legged people, the biped who gets shipwrecked will be the freak. It's a weird, morbid thought: that the longer we survive the more likely it is we'll become freaks, monsters. From their point of view, I mean."

"Too morbid," said Trask. "Not to mention unworkable. Where the Wamphyri are concerned there'll never be a *last* human, just as there can never be a last cow or chicken for us. And anyway, I was asking for ideas, advice . . . not for a bloody death-knell on the human race!"

"Advice I can't give you," said Millie. "An opinion, well, perhaps."

"Go ahead," said Trask.

"You were right. Malinari and the others, they're deliberately leaving a trail for us to follow. Maybe that's the idea, to pick us off one by one while they still have the chance and before the whole world finds out about them. For after all, we are the greatest threat they've had to face, the only ones who know all about them, the ones who know how to deal with them."

"No one knows all about them," said Lardis. "Not even me." He wasn't boasting or putting Millie down, just stating a fact. "I've fought them all my days and I still don't know *all* about them. But I do understand what you're saying. If they get rid of E-Branch, that's half their battle won."

"Personally," said Liz, "I think it's high time our Minister Responsible *became* responsible and told the Powers-That-Be—*his* superiors—exactly what we're up against. And that then his superiors should tell the entire world, shout it loud from every radio and television screen. Because if Ian is right and it is a no-win situation, then the sooner everyone knows about it the better. Myself, I'd rather have gangs of wandering vigilante peasants armed with flaring torches, bunches of garlic, sharpened stakes, and silver bullets—even with all the mistakes they would make, all the Dark Ages witch hunts—than see these monsters gradually, secretly, insidiously gaining ground in our world."

"I hear what you're saying," said Trask, "and I won't deny you your opinion. But you've hit the nail right on the head. A new Dark Ages, yes: that's where we could end up—and quickly—if we did start shouting it to the rooftops. But okay, we'll accept that we're being lured and that they're beckoning us on into some kind of trap. Next question: what are we going to do about it?"

"Call Jake in on it," said Liz at once. "It's too much for us alone, but with the Necroscope on the case—"

"—With Jake on the case," Trask broke in on her, "they'd have the advantage of knowing where we were, certainly of knowing where *he* was, almost all the time. Jake's psychic signature has to be the most powerful source of metaphysical radiation in the whole world. Surely you've heard how David Chung describes Jake? Like standing beside a psychic dynamo?"

"But Jake also has those incredible shields," Liz answered.

"That's not good enough," said Trask, "for we know how that works, too: if we can't find mindsmog, we look for its absence. In Vavara's case, we target the place that seems to be the most serene. When Jake puts the brakes on his aura, I'm betting Nephran Malinari can smell his tyres burning on the far side of the moon! *But*—" he went on, before Liz could continue arguing her point, "—that's not to say I disagree. Simply that I've tried to keep him out of it until the very last moment."

"But not until *our* very last moment, surely?" said Ian Goodly. "I'm concerned that the few warnings I've had in the recent past—the few forecasts I've been able to make, including last night's—have been too short-term. In Australia, when we were on that monorail, I got the warning with seconds to spare. Last night, it was the same story: I saw Bernie Fletcher's funeral pyre even as they were setting it. It's like I'm catching up on the future! And the next time . . . what if I'm too late? What if it *is* already happening, and happening to us?"

Trask nodded and said, "Very well, I'll accept the majority vote. As of now—at the first sign of trouble—Liz will call Jake in on it." He looked back at her. "In fact, it's probably a good idea if you can contact him the next time we take a break. We still have to weapon up, and I have this feeling that things will start happening sooner rather than later. So while I won't ask him to join us just yet, we can let him deliver our weapons, alert him to the situation, and request that he maintain regular contact with you—say, on an hourly basis?"

The relief Liz felt was clearly audible in her voice as she

answered, "Okay, as soon as we take a break I'll try to contact him."

Then, when the team fell silent for a while, there was only the throaty throb of the minibus's engine, and the muted, electronic *beep, beep, beep* of Paul Garvey's fingers on the keys of the decoder. And finally, when they reached a decent stretch of road where the minibus stopped swaying and bumping, both sounds settled into a more regular pattern, and the miles and the code commenced a rapid unwinding.

And the local time in Bulgaria was 11:45 A.M.—

—But the local time in England was two hours earlier when Jake Cutter came starting awake from horrific nightmares!

Now what the hell . . . ? he wondered, his heart hammering, and sweat sticking the bedsheets to his body. *Where am I? Who am I? What the* fuck *am I?*

Then, gradually, reality took over and he settled back down onto his pillows, his dreams receding, his breathing regulating itself. But those dreams!

Jake jerked back up into a sitting position, and aware that there were things he should remember, he tried desperately hard to focus on what he'd seen, felt, experienced while sleeping.

But no use, for most of it was gone, erased from memory in that part of his mind where dreams are born and die, and where they're ground down again and become grist for future dreaming. And the only things he remembered were the fearful whispers of the Great Majority, and a conversation with a faint, ever more distant and indistinct Harry Keogh . . . out of which the single fragment that stuck in his mind was this:

I never stopped fighting it. It was my stubborn attitude, I suppose. But in my time the threat was scarcely of these proportions . . . I thought that I had done all there was to do, only to discover that the fight would continue in another world. As for my world, your Earth—it seemed to me a clean and decent place when I left it, unlike now. So your fight will be twofold. Remember this, Jake: it takes a thief to catch

*a thief. And if you can't fight them on your terms, then . . .
fight . . . them . . . on . . .*

But that was all.

As for the source of the horror in the dream, its night-marish aspect: that had lain in the morbid whispers of the teeming dead, in what they'd been more than hinting. But while Jake had known what inspired his horror as he was dreaming it (*if* it was a dream), that knowledge, too, had now passed into limbo.

Mere seconds had passed since Jake sprang awake. Now, once again, the tentative knock came at his door (no, at the door of Harry's Room) reminding him of what had awakened him. Obviously, he should answer it, but instead he wished whoever it was would go away; he or they were interfering with his train of thought, and his vague and fleeting memories of the dream were fleeting that much faster . . . and were gone.

A nightmare, that's all it had been.

"Come in," Jake called out, only to discover that his mouth and throat were as dry as dust, which caused him to croak inaudibly. Clearing his throat he tried again, at the same time casting his mind back to last night:

Returning via the Möbius Continuum from Paris, he had found the bed in Harry's Room made up for sleeping, probably by Jimmy Harvey, the tech standing in for John Grieve. And propping himself up on the pillows, Jake had carried on reading through the remaining handful of Keogh files. That, at least, had been his intention. But his meal had made him drowsy; indeed, in combination with his reading, it seemed to have made him inordinately weary, and the last thing he remembered was checking his wristwatch and noting that the time was just after eight.

So what was the time now?

And as Gustav Turchin and John Grieve entered the room, he checked his watch again . . . then gave it a shake!

"It's nine-thirty A.M.," Grieve corroborated the time shown on Jake's watch. "When I looked in earlier you were dead to the world, but since there was nothing that couldn't wait I let you sleep. Now, however, it's time you were up and mobile. A bit of bumf has come in during the night which you should see, and the Premier here has asked to speak to you."

"Bumf?" Jake mumbled, trying to get it together. "Premier?"

"Gustav Turchin," said that one, holding out a hand as Jake threw the bedclothes aside and stood up a little unsteadily. "I much prefer informal meetings, but if you're not yet awake—"

"Coffee," Jake groaned, taking Turchin's hand and giving it a feeble shake. "I'm low on caffeine, that's all. I never could get it together until the coffee's done its work."

"They may still be serving late breakfast downstairs," said Grieve. "I can tell them you're on your way down, give you time to tidy up and throw some water in your face."

"Please do," said Jake, excusing himself and going into the bathroom.

When he came out Grieve was on his own. "Turchin went down to the hotel restaurant," he said. "He's waiting for you."

"Okay," said Jake. "I'll see him there. And thanks for getting me up. I must have really knocked myself out! All of that reading, I suppose."

Frowning, Grieve looked at him more closely. "Are you sure you're okay?"

"Caffeine deficiency," Jake tried to grin. "I'll be fine."

"Very well," said Grieve. "But just be careful what you say to Turchin. He's been nosing around quite a bit—I've already caught him in one or two places where he shouldn't have been—and he hasn't held on to his job in Moscow all these years without knowing one or two tricks."

"So why should I talk to him at all?" said Jake.

"Simple courtesy," Grieve answered. "Ben Trask's the only one around here who really knows him, so while Ben's away Turchin is more or less on his own. Also, I know that Turchin and Ben are working on something together, so I suppose we have to trust him that far at least."

"And the bumf you mentioned?"

"It can wait till you've had breakfast. Nothing you can do about it anyway."

"It's nothing important, then?"

"I didn't say that," said Grieve. "But at least it doesn't change anything. Not right now, anyway."

And Jake said, "Okay, I'll come see you after breakfast."

"I ordered for you," Turchin told Jake a few minutes later, as he sat down opposite the Russian in an alcove exclusive to the Branch.

"What did you order?"

"Ham, eggs, and hash browns. Oh, and a pot of coffee, naturally."

"Nothing natural about it," said Jake, smiling despite his sudden headache. "It's an addiction!"

"We all have them," Turchin shrugged. "With me it's politics. Ever since I was a boy."

"Here in the West," said Jake, "we sort of look on Russian politics as something of a bloodbath."

"Communism's aftermath," said Turchin. "A defunct ideology, thank God! And a pointless one, because it's obvious there will always be those who want to be *more* equal. But . . . it still has its adherents. And that's one of the reasons why I'm here."

"Here at this table?" Jake didn't think so.

"Here in England. Here with E-Branch."

"You have a problem with some less than democratic politicians back home, right?"

"You're quick to catch on," the Premier nodded. "Except it isn't just me but the world."

"Which sounds pretty similar to our problem," said Jake.

"I know about your problem," said Turchin, leaning forward a little. "And yours and mine—disparate though they may seem—pretty soon they're going to come together . . ." Then, as their food arrived, he fell silent. But between mouthfuls:

"Why are you telling me . . . whatever it is that you're telling me?" said Jake.

"Because you're the Necroscope," said Turchin at once. "And because you'll be helping me—us, E-Branch, the world, if you insist, which you should and rightly so—to put things back in order."

Jake swallowed what was in his mouth, pulled a face, gulped some coffee down, and sat back. "Necroscope?"

"Oh, come, come!" said Turchin. "What am I, a child? I have met and talked with Nathan Kiklu, who Trask calls Keogh, son of the original Necroscope. And every time that I've passed you in the corridor, or seen you in the distance, I've felt that I was seeing him again. No, you're not him— not anything like him—but the feeling persists. With Liz Merrick, Millicent Cleary, or John Grieve, I know I'm in the company of telepaths. The bloom under their eyes gives them away. And you—"

"—What gives me away?" said Jake.

"You do," Turchin told him. "You have that quality. Not the bloom under *your* eyes, no, for that's lack of sleep, or perhaps too much? But it's *in* your eyes, certainly. You've seen strange things, Jake Cutter. And the things you can do . . . are stranger still."

Jake shook his head. "I'm not buying that. I look at myself and I see a man, just a man. Surely I can't look all that different to you?"

"But you haven't denied it," said Turchin. And: "Very well, let me tell you. Last night I went to your room to talk to you. You were out but the door was open."

Jake nodded. "I forgot to lock it."

"I understand," said Turchin. "Doors are something you must forget about quite often—considering you don't need them. But let me go on. I knocked, entered, saw the files. Don't worry, I didn't read them. But I did see what they were, and I also know that E-Branch has a fledgling Necroscope. So, I left your room, occupied my time with this and that, and waited on your return. When you didn't come back I thought to reenter your room—er, *perhaps* to glance, but just a glance, you understand—at those files. Ah! But there you were on the bed, fully clothed just as I see you now, and fast asleep. Well, I did not want to disturb you. But I am not without powers of reason, Jake, and since you had left Harry's Room and returned to it without using the door . . . two and two made four. You had to be Ben Trask's new Necroscope."

Jake nodded and said, "He calls you an old fox."

Turchin shrugged and offered a half-smile. "But any fox who has even *managed* to grow old would have to be a very wise creature, wouldn't you agree?"

"I suppose so," Jake answered. "He would have had to kill a whole lot of chickens along the way, too."

Again Turchin's shrug, as he finished his food. "Well, such is politics. But . . . are you done eating?"

Jake pushed his plate away. "It's tasteless," he said, with a grimace. "Maybe I ate too well last night—in Paris."

"In Paris?" For a moment Turchin didn't get it, but then he did and his jaw fell open. "In *Paris!* Ah! Then I am right!"

"Steak tartare," said Jake. "Damn, it was good!"

"Jake, please listen," said Turchin urgently, as the Necroscope refilled his coffee cup. "We must talk, and seriously."

"I'm listening," said Jake. And Turchin repeated his story, the one he'd told Trask only two days ago. "So the problem is," he finished off, "that while I now have the means to close down the Perchorsk Gate forever under millions of tons of rock, I do not have a means of delivering the weapon. Trask knows all of this—he knows the time restriction, too—and I am sure that by now he would have requested your help in this matter if his mind was not concentrated on the evil that already exists. But he's reluctant to tie my problems in with his own and fails to see the benefit of killing two birds with one stone, er, as it were. He would prefer to seal Perchorsk in his own time, which is all very well but it still leaves me on the hook."

"Two birds with one stone?" said Jake. "But I thought

there were three of these enemies of yours—three political, or ex-military types—who are standing in your way?"

Turchin shook his head in anxious frustration. "But they're only in my way in the sense that they'll put Russia back thirty years, and likewise détente. And in *your* way in that the Perchorsk Gate will remain open, and others will find out about it."

"I still don't see it," said Jake. "If they go through that Gate that's them gone—there's no way back. They'll no longer be of any concern, no longer a threat to you."

"That's only if they all go through together," Turchin answered. "And what if they take that entire criminal element that is now controlling Perchorsk through with them? And all of them armed to the teeth? What then for Nathan Kiklu's people and his vampire world? Yes, these people would have to stay there—and they'd probably rule there, too!"

"I need to think it over," said Jake. "And in any case I'll need Trask's go-ahead."

"Which could take forever!" The Premier threw up his hands. "And time is short, and we need to prepare—I mean, *you* need to prepare—and I have to prepare you!"

"Prepare me?" Jake's eyes had narrowed.

Turchin nodded. "You need to know where the weapon is. And you need to know how to prime it. Do you know the layout of the Perchorsk complex? No? Then you need to know that, too, so that you can position the weapon to best effect. Myself, I see these things clearly, but Ben Trask . . . he sees only the need to revenge himself for what these invader creatures did to his wife!"

Jake scowled and said, "Sophistry."

"Eh?" said Turchin, who didn't know the word.

Jake, on the other hand, knew it only too well, in connection with Korath-once-Mindsthrall. A word game. Fallacious reasoning. A plausible but deceptive fallacy. And a perfect example of: "The pot calling the kettle grimy-arse," he said.

"I don't follow." Turchin looked baffled.

"You talk about Trask and revenge," said Jake, who accepted the principle of revenge well enough, "but at least Trask has a real reason for doing what he's doing. He's saving the lives of people—perhaps all of us—while you're planning to kill men for political reasons."

Again Turchin threw up his hands. "If that's how you see it then I can't any longer argue with you. I'll stay in England as a defector, my enemies—if not the three who know about Perchorsk, then others—will take control in Russia, and the world will go to hell when more vampires come through from Starside!"

Jake shook his head. "That isn't going to happen. It seems that Nathan has won the war on Starside."

"So Ben Trask has informed me." Turchin gave the impression of shrugging it off. "Ah, but as we've discovered, history has a nasty habit of repeating! This wouldn't be the first time Trask misjudged or underestimated the dangers of the Vampire World."

Jake had to agree. "You have a point," he said.

"Yes, I have," the Premier snapped. "And the point is, will you let the Gate stand open or will you close it for good? It's out of my hands now. The problem is all yours. I have the package and you can make the delivery. But without that we work together the status quo—and a very unsatisfactory status quo at that—will prevail. At least until we're toppled into a worldwide disaster."

"You sound just like Korath," said Jake.

"Who?"

"Oh, an old friend of mine. He was even more dangerous, and much more convincing, than you. But he's been neutralized, made safe—well, more or less."

Turchin stood up. "We're getting nowhere, and I'm expecting a message from my people back home. Twenty-four hours after the message comes, it could be too late to put my plan into action. If you're able to contact Trask, I would like to suggest you do so now and see what he says about all this."

"I'm waiting for Trask to contact me," said Jake. "But like I said, I'll think over what you've told me."

"Well then, for goodness sake think quickly!" said Turchin.

"First I'll be finishing my coffee," said Jake. "Then I'll talk to John Grieve, and *then* I'll think about it."

"Huh!" Turchin snorted, then turned and walked away . . .

Jake took the elevator back up to E-Branch HQ and called in at the Duty Office. After telling John Grieve what had transpired, he asked for his advice. "What do you reckon?"

"I knew Trask and Turchin had something going," Grieve told him, "but I wasn't too sure what it was—not until now. I did do interpreter on an iffy telephone call from Turchin to Trask, but even with my talent it wasn't entirely clear what was going down. I can well understand, however, why Trask hasn't reached a decision yet. It seems a very risky business."

"What does?" said Jake, whose mind was already wandering in other directions.

"Eh?" said Grieve, frowning. "What does? Are you kidding?" And again he enquired, "Are you sure you're feeling okay, Jake? I mean, doesn't it speak for itself? Exploding a nuclear device on someone else's territory—now *that's* what I'd call a risky business!"

"Oh, that!" said Jake, feeling foolish. "I thought you were talking about the other stuff: him wanting to show me the bomb, telling me how to prime it, checking out the schematics for the Perchorsk complex . . . that sort of stuff."

The frown lifted from Grieve's face, but slowly. "Well, as for the latter: you can do that any time you feel inclined. We have schematics going right back to Perchorsk's early days. We got some of it from Zek Foener, a lot more from Ian Goodly and Trask himself—after they spent a little time there courtesy of Turkur Tzonov—and a great deal more from Harry and Nathan. Unless there's been any big changes, we have the complete layout."

"Yes," said Jake, looking at Grieve—no, looking *through* him, as the Duty Officer now realized. For Jake's eyes were on something else; his eyes and mind both, they weren't here. And feeling fully justified, Grieve broke one of E-Branch's oldest rules and directed a telepathic probe straight into the Necroscope's mind.

Jake's shields were down; *strange memories stirring—not his but some other's—and scenes unravelling in his mind. The Perchorsk complex, yes. But schematics . . . no, not a bit of it. No draughtsman's blueprint this, but the real thing. Better far than any chart or plan drawn to scale, this actually was, or it had been, Perchchorsk itself. Had been—in Harry Keogh's time—but as Jake now "remembered" it!*

Grieve saw it for himself:

That huge area above the Perchorsk dam, with its incredibly massive lead shielding. The dam itself, which powered the complex's turbines; great spouts of water jetting out from the dam wall and curving down into the old riverbed. The road through the Perchorsk Pass, with a slip road winding down the mountainous contours to the complex's entrance, where great metal doors stood open on their rollers, and a fluorescent glow from within bathed the walls of the ravine in a blue light.

Grieve followed Jake's thoughts—tracked his thoughts and Harry Keogh's memories—into the Perchorsk complex. But a mere complex? More a labyrinth, surely? Roughly circular in plan and six levels deep, why, it might easily house a thousand workers, which it had in its heyday, before the experiment backfired and fried so many of them.

Evidence of that backfire was everywhere:

In a gently curving, tubelike corridor floored with rubber tiles, the ceiling and arching walls were scorched black. Great blisters were evident in the paintwork, and in places where the external bedrock had melted, the ceiling had buckled and fractured, letting molten rock squeeze through to solidify in great ugly lava blobs on the cooler surfaces of inner walls. The rubber floor tiles had burned right through to naked metal plates, many of which were buckled out of alignment. In the first moments of the accident, blow-back, meltdown, whatever, this area of the outer perimeter must have felt like a pressure cooker.

"Proceeding" rapidly along the corridor, Grieve saw that a number of lesser conduits leading inwards like spokes from the principal corridor were hung with triangular radiation-warning signs or white-on-black skull-and-crossbones discs. These were no-go areas, "hot spots" where radioactivity was so intense as to be lethal. So the heat here had been more than merely thermal. Indeed, it had been an entirely different kind of heat.

As that thought occurred—not to Grieve but to Jake, and *through* Jake to Grieve—so it conjured an instantaneous, wrenching shift in locations: to Perchorsk's magmass levels.

And Grieve found himself drifting down a wide, heavy-beamed wooden staircase into a region of sheer fantasy, where on every hand he peered into the dim recesses of a maddening confusion, a weird chaos. The lighting was only poor here, perhaps deliberately so, for what little could be seen was very disquieting and even frightening. Down through a tangle of warped plastic, fused stone, and blistered metal Grieve passed, where amazingly consistent smooth-bored tunnels some two to three feet in diameter wound and twisted like giant wormholes through old timber, except they cut through solid rock and crumpled steel girders. And Grieve knew—even as Jake knew—that something, some vast force, had attempted to bring about an alien homogeneity here, had tried to bring everything together in one similar form, or else to deform it utterly.

It wasn't so much that the various materials had been fused by great heat and fire; rather they seemed to have been *folded in,* like the banded ingredients of marbled cake, or multitextured plasticines in some monstrous child's hands . . . and Grieve saw that it was getting worse.

Beneath the timbers of a level walkway the floor was chaotically humped and anomalous, where many different materials had so flowed into each other as to become unrecognizable in their original forms. And through all the

solid mass of this earthly yet unfamiliar material, those irregular wormhole energy channels ran like the indiscrimi-
nate burrows of rock-boring crustaceans in the sea, but on
a gigantic scale.

Now Grieve found himself moving toward a dark region
which he knew (because Jake knew it) that he wouldn't much
like. But because Jake had to look, so must the telepath.
Either that or break off contact at once. But this "guided
tour," as it were, was so morbidly fascinating that Grieve
stayed with it . . . and a moment later wished he hadn't.

For in a warped, nightmarish cavern like a lunatic's dream
of hell, suddenly he saw that metal, plastic, and rock were
not the only materials which had fused together inseparably
in the uncontrolled blast of alien energy that had wrecked
the Perchorsk Project. No, for there had been men, scientists
down here, too. Pompeii must look somewhat similar to
this—if only from a limited and perhaps paleontological
viewpoint, that of someone examining fossils—but at least
the tortured figures at Pompeii had remained recognizably
human. Not twisted, compressed, elongated . . . or even *reversed,* with all of their organs visible on the outside!

But such were the moulds in the magmass. At which the
Duty Officer had had enough . . .

Seated upright behind his desk, Grieve snapped back in
his chair, cut himself free from Jake's mind like a piece of
suddenly released elastic. And:

"Jesus!" he said. *"Jesus!"* And no sign of the ex–army
officer, the oh-so-phlegmatic English gentleman now. "You
. . . you . . . you *know* that place!" he said.

And returned to the present of his own accord, Jake nodded. "Yes," he answered wonderingly, his eyes wide and
staring. "Yes, I do. And I know the coordinates, too."

"Was it in the files?" Grieve pulled himself together. "It
must have been in those files."

"Something of it," Jake answered. "But not like that. That
was the real thing. Little by little, I seem to be remembering,
that's all."

"Remembering what Harry knew?"

"It has to be," said Jake. And then he, too, pulled himself together. "Don't waste your time trying to figure it out, John. Myself, I gave up on that a long time ago. Anyway, you said you wanted me to see something that came in overnight?"

At which the Duty Officer opened a drawer and handed Jake a decoded copy of the Minister Responsible's memo to Ben Trask . . .

22
News from Porton Down—
the End of Things—
Jake: Remembering . . .

AT A BULGARIAN GAS STATION-CUM-RESTAU-rant and rest rooms midway between Topolovgrad and Jambol, still following the Tundźa in a direction due north, Ben Trask and his task force had paused to take refreshment and dust themselves off. The sun was high in a blue sky and the day had turned quite warm. It was Trask's best opportunity to read the Minister Responsible's deciphered message without the constant interruptions of the minibus's jarring motion—or so he had reckoned. But as for interruptions:

As his party sat down at a wooden table with a sun umbrella in the restaurant's beer garden overlooking the river, a waiter bustled into view and enquired, "Do we having a Mr. Trask?"

Trask answered, "I'm Trask. Is there something?"

"Telephone," said the other, smiling. "I having the number. You should please be calling, er, a Mr. Burdur?"

Trask looked at the others and said, "Ali Bey. It could be important. Order something for me, will you?" And then he followed the waiter indoors to the telephone.

Burdur was waiting for the call. The phone at the other end was snatched from its cradle at the first ring, and: "Mr. Trask? Ben, is it you?" Burdur's voice; Trask sensed his excitement.

"Yes, what is it?" he said.

"Ben, last night another vehicle stolen. Being seen heading toward border post. I thinking this your, er, quarry?"

"Good!" said Trask. "Do we have the make and number?"

"The number, yes," said Burdur, and Trask quickly scribbled it down. "As for the make . . . it is unmistakable. Forgetting the make, my friend, because you are certainly knowing this vehicle when you seeing it. Knowing it at once, immediately. It is the big black hearse!"

"A hearse?" Trask repeated the Inspector, and pictured the vehicle in his mind's eye. A long, broad black car—indeed a limo—with benchlike seats in the back for the pallbearers, and windows curtained in black velvet. Such a conveyance would be ideally suited, certainly to the needs of Malinari, Vavara, and Szwart. And it would be just spacious enough—if a little cramped—for their recent recruits, the girls from the vampirized cruise ship. Then again, if that troupe had been in any way *diminished* . . . there would be more than sufficient room.

"Ben?" Burdur's voice came again. "Ben Trask, did you hearing me? It is the funeral vehicle, this stolen car."

"I heard you," Trask nodded, if only to himself. "A hearse, and very much in keeping, too."

"I wishing you luck, my friend," said Burdur then. "And I hoping my problems are going with—" and here his voice sank low, almost to a whisper, "—going with the vampires!"

"I hope so, too," said Trask. "Goodbye."

"Goodbye," Burdur answered, and Trask heard his telephone go down . . .

Back at the table in the beer garden, after Trask had told the others about his conversation with Burdur, finally he was able to read the Minister Responsible's message.

And at E-Branch HQ in London, Jake Cutter, Necroscope, was reading it at almost the same time:

Trask—
Just in from Porton Down, where they have had every available microbiologist working on it since square one, the following information:
(1) Their initial assessment was only partly correct. Large doses of plague bacteria will destroy these creatures, but only after an extended period. The first tests were carried out on incomplete samples—such as the one you obtained from the Evening Star*—and that was where the error occurred. Tissue separated from a carrier (ergo, without will) succumbs much more readily and totally.*
(2) The sleepers we saw at Bleakstone: one of them was a lawyer, and rather than suffer his threatened lawsuit the idiot psychiatrists let him go! He is still at large. The other sleeper, when he began to react to our recommended agents, was sent to Porton Down, making him the perfect test medium. Sorry if I sound less than sympathetic toward him. He is in any case alive, but highly dangerous now and caged.
(3) Unfortunately, however, he is not the only one at Porton Down. As you are aware, the Civil Authorities are on this now, and in the last twenty-four hours have discovered a great many more sleepers—and worse! Here once again, however, we were mistaken in our understanding of the problem. Some of the "sick" people we've discovered have not "slept" at all, while others slept only after considerable amounts of time had passed since they were in the city's underground tube system where we must presume they contracted their conditions.
*(4) Worst of all, we now have our first cases of— forgive me if I still refuse to use what must eventually become the official term—*transmission, human to human. *They are* biting, *Ben, and passing this thing on.*

And not only in the UK. I've been in contact with our Australian friends and they are reporting cases, too. Also, Mr. Papastamos has voiced his further suspicions about Krassos. I can only assume that eventually we shall hear from Turkey and wherever else you are obliged to pursue the instigators. But pursue them and destroy them you must, for they are the source of this scourge.

(5) Finally, with reference to Note (1) above. Until now we had thought we were safe with our anti-Pasteurella pestis shots. This is no longer the case. The presence of the antidote in your bodies may well deter the enemy, but it won't stop him and it certainly won't incapacitate him. Moreover, with regard to those shots, they weren't always reliable. Quite apart from the defective batches, perhaps twenty percent of people treated don't have a reaction—they simply don't take. The easy way to check is to think back and ask yourself, "Did my shot raise an itchy blister and leave a tiny scar?" If it didn't, then it didn't take and your blood is pure . . . and delicious.

That's all for now. I have nothing else for you. If you have anything for me be careful how you deliver it. Not all of the world is as stable as we like to believe we are . . .

Good hunting—
M. Res.

Trask read it again, this time out loud albeit in muted tones, so that he wouldn't be overheard. And slowly the implications began to dawn on him, and on the others . . . those of them who were still seated at the table.

"Where's Liz?" he asked then, noting her absence.

And inclining her head toward the riverbank, Millie said, "She's behind those trees there. She wanted a little privacy, in order to contact Jake . . . and here they come right now."

"What?" said Trask, frowning as he glanced in the direction Millie had indicated. "I don't see anyone."

"Neither do I," Millie answered, matching frown for frown. "I don't *see* them, but I do hear them. She's no longer alone."

And as Liz and Jake came into view, Paul Garvey looked at Millie and said, "Damn, you're good!"

But still frowning, she didn't answer him.

They all greeted Jake in as reserved a manner as possible, and he took a seat with them. Liz had obviously explained something of the situation to him, because the first thing he said was, "So, you're hot on the trail again." He sounded something less than enthusiatic about it.

"Very hot," said Trask, "and it's time we weaponed up. Not here but in some quiet lay-by a little farther up the road. If you ride with us you'll have the coordinates without having to rely on Liz."

"Right," said Jake dully.

"Is something wrong?" Liz said. She wanted to read him but knew better; he had asked that she respect his privacy before, and anyway his shields were up in force. But *why* were they up, in the presence of so many friends?

In the next moment Liz knew why—guessed something of it, at least—when suddenly Jake said, "Did you get the Minister Responsible's memo?"

Trask nodded. "Oh, we got it," he said, grimly. "The world is going up in flames, and all we've got is a bucket of water. Well, at least we're no longer alone. Slowly but surely everyone is going to have to be put in the picture. And who can say—maybe they should have been told right from the start."

Jake's tone and expression hadn't changed, as now he said, "So, you've read about the shots." Then, *wanting* them to know, he dropped his shields and looked at Liz, Millie, and Paul Garvey. Since it was an invitation, they looked and saw what was on his mind.

Millie turned pale in a moment, but in the next she said, "It still doesn't prove a thing, Jake."

And Liz took his hand and told him, "Don't even think it!"

"Don't think what?" Trask growled, knowing that something was very wrong here.

Jake opened his mouth to speak, but Millie at once cut him off and said, "Jake, let me tell him."

Shaking his head, he answered, "I'm the one who could have a problem. So it's my place to talk about it."

"But you're not the *only* one who might have it," she said. And as simply as that a great weight was taken from his shoulders—the weight of loneliness, of being on his own—for he knew what she meant, which until now he'd scarcely considered.

"What the *hell* is everybody talking about?" the Old Lidesci snapped. And Trask said:

"For pity's sake, spit it out!"

Millie looked him straight in the eye and said, "Those jabs or shots or whatever, and the itching blisters they're supposed to raise? Well, mine didn't." And:

"Nor mine," said the Necroscope.

Finally Trask saw the "truth" of it and supposed he'd understood what they were saying all along but hadn't dared admit it, not even to himself. And even now—now that it was out in the open—he didn't intend to let it interfere with what they were doing here.

"So what's that supposed to mean?" he blustered. "What does it change, eh? Nothing. So you believed you had a small measure of protection and now it's gone. So what? *Nothing* can guarantee complete protection against these ugly bastards!"

"That's not it, Ben," said Millie. "Not all of it, but only a small part of it. And you know it."

And that was true, too. After she and Jake had taken their first trip together in the Möbius Continuum, they'd been informed of their immunity as a result of the shots they'd had, Jake in Australia and Millie in London. That had given them peace of mind. But now . . . now it appeared their shots had been invalid. Likewise their peace of mind. And probably everyone else's.

Trask sank down in his chair a little—also in his soul—

and said, "Jake, what's the damage? Have you checked it out?"

Jake nodded. "On my way here," he said. "It didn't take any time at all, not in the Möbius Continuum. I stopped at a future-time door, looked through it, saw my blue thread winding out of me into tomorrow."

"And?" said Trask.

"And . . . I don't know," Jake's hands made an ambiguous gesture. "My thread's still blue. But the taint, the red stain . . . I couldn't be sure. It might have gained a little ground. There isn't any sure way I can measure it."

"Well, you were sure enough that you felt safe to come here to us!" Liz burst out, clutching at his arm.

And Ian Goodly said, "You didn't actually go *in* through the door, did you? You didn't venture into the future?"

"No," Jake shook his head. "I accept now that you know what you're talking about, you and Harry Keogh both. What's the good of looking for trouble if you can't avoid it?"

"Exactly," said the precog. "No good at all."

"But of course there is a way to put your mind at rest once and for all," said Millie. "Or if not yours, mine."

At which Trask, knowing what she meant, immediately came in with, "We've tried that once and it proved absolutely nothing." And now, for all that his voice was rough, there was fear in it and even desperation.

"But that was then," said Millie, "and enough time has gone by that it might be worth checking again. I was trapped down in that underworld a lot longer than Jake, so it's far more likely I would get infected than him. Another short trip in the Möbius Continuum with Jake could put everyone's mind at rest. We could go take a look through that future-time door again—this time paying particular attention to *my* thread—and if I'm still in the clear then surely Jake must be."

At which Goodly uttered a small inarticulate cry and rocked back in his chair, which promptly gave way beneath him. He went sprawling, and Garvey, closest to him, was quickly at his side, helping him to sit up.

"What is it?" Trask was next to kneel beside the dazed precog. "What did you see?"

Goodly shook his head as if to clear it, blinked at Garvey and Trask, managed to get to his feet. Millie helped steady him into her chair, and Trask sat down beside him, with his hand on the precog's arm. "You saw something, I know you did," he said. "What was it, Ian? What's the future got in store for us now?"

Slowly the dazed, disoriented look left Goodly's face, and he gripped Trask's hand tightly. But before he could speak the waiter came running with a tray of sandwiches and drinks.

"Ah, the accident!" he said, putting the tray on the table. "I am seeing it! The faulty chair! I am so sorry!"

"It's okay," Trask told him. "He'll be okay." And when the waiter had left: "Ian, you did see something, right?"

"Yes," Goodly nodded, still visibly shaken. "I saw the end of things, Ben. I saw what was . . . what was probably the end of me!" Naturally pale, now the precog was as sallow and sallower than Trask and his people had ever seen him, his face as gaunt as a funerary mask stripped of its gold.

"The end of things?" Trask repeated him. "Of you? What are you trying to say, Ian? Describe what you saw."

There were other tables out on the lawn; a number of travellers had seen Goodly's fall and were beginning to look interested in Trask's team, in these strange, serious-looking people at the crowded table.

"We should take the food and leave," said Liz. "Too many of these people are starting to wonder about us. I can hear them."

"Me, too," said Millie. "Over there—that group of four— it's a Bulgarian policeman and his family. The man doesn't much care for foreigners. He's off duty right now, but he's thinking about coming over and checking us out anyway. Things could get complicated."

"Damn it to hell!" Trask muttered. "Okay, leave some money and we'll go."

"Money?" said Garvey, looking at Liz and Millie curiously, but without putting a strain on his ill-matched features. "You mean Bulgarian money? We haven't changed from our Turkish liras yet! And paying in plastic will only slow us down."

But now the waiter was back, and he saw Trask staring at a bundle of Turkish banknotes in his hand. "Is good," he said at once, taking the notes, counting off some small denominations, and handing the wad back. "Is no problem the exchanging."

"Thanks," said Trask, giving him a little extra.

And in a few breathless moments—which seemed to take as many hours—they managed to bundle the precog out of the beer garden and across the parking lot to the minibus . . .

Paul Garvey drove, with Jake and Liz sitting alongside and the others in the back. And again Trask asked Goodly, "Now can you tell us what that was all about, Ian? What knocked you off your chair like that? The end of things? That sounds pretty ominous to me. What *exactly* did you see?"

"Exactly?" said the precog, more in control of himself now. "It doesn't work like that, Ben, not always. Anyway, we were in a dark place—or maybe not so much dark as confined. To me it came over as dark. As to what I saw: oh, I *saw* things, alright! But there were sounds, too. And despite that it was jumbled, it was all so real that I could almost . . . almost smell *them!*"

"Them?" Trask grasped his arm. "The Wamphyri?"

Goodly nodded. "But especially him, Malinari!"

"Go on," Trask urged him. "I promise not to interrupt."

And the precog began telling what he remembered of it:

"It was dark and enclosed, or that was my perception of it. But don't rely on that; it could be figurative, or symbolic. I sensed that we were all there together—wherever—in close proximity. But so were the Wamphyri, all three of them."

380

"What about those sounds?" said Trask, his promise already forgotten. "What did you hear?"

"Screams," said the other, "from not too far away, but distorted by . . . by angles? Shapes? Anyway, they were death cries, Ben! The sounds of people dying in agony. It was like . . . like the gloom was alive, but alive with death? It sounds insane, I know that, but that's how it felt: as if we were trapped in an unlit madhouse, and all the maniacs running loose."

"Go on," said Trask, as Goodly paused to moisten his lips.

"Then things quickly changed," said the precog, glancing at Liz and Jake in the front seats. "There was gunfire . . . but not ordinary gunfire. It was loud, deafening, devastating. Malinari had Liz; she was struggling with him, desperate to get away."

"And where was I?" said the Necroscope, turning to stare at Goodly wide-eyed and apprehensive. "Was I there at all?"

"You were there . . . and you weren't," said Goodly.

"What?" Jake snapped. Fearful for Liz, his anger was mounting. "What the fuck is that supposed to mean? Either I was or I wasn't. And if I wasn't, then where the hell else would I be?"

"Don't take it out on me, Jake!" Goodly threw up his hands. "I didn't see it all. And what I did see happened in—I don't know—in a weird, fast-moving, kaleidoscopic fashion. It's so easy to confuse the order of things. I mean, you can't read the future like a book. The chapters can get all tangled, and occasionally the first few pages come last!"

Jake calmed down and said, "Go on anyway. Tell us more."

"I . . . I think Szwart had got you trapped," said the precog. "That was before you . . . before you weren't there."

"You mean he'd taken me somewhere?" Jake was frowning, trying hard to understand.

"Maybe," Goodly answered. "Maybe that's it. I think so, but I don't *know!* It was all gunfire, madness, and mayhem—like a very bad dream." Mentally exhausted, he sighed and slumped down in his seat. But they weren't finished with him yet.

"Hey, Ian," said Paul Garvey, keeping his eyes on the road. "How did I figure in all this?"

"I know you were there," said Goodly, "and I think you were in some kind of trouble, but that's all. I'm sorry."

"Oh, great!" said the telepath, with a shiver in his voice.

"And is that it?" said Trask.

"That's about it," Goodly answered. "The only other thing I remember is Malinari again. He called me a 'scryer,' laughed at me and said that for all my alleged talent I hadn't seen any of *this* coming! I think he may have been bleeding, but nothing too serious. And he slopped some of his blood on me. I *think* he hit me with something. But hit, or maybe *bit* . . . I just don't know. And after that darkness, and then nothing . . . nothing at all. I must have passed out, and that's when I toppled my chair."

"Christ!" said Trask, under his breath.

But Jake wanted to know, "When you say Szwart 'took' me, is that 'figurative or symbolic,' too? Or are you really saying I'm not going to survive this?"

"You can't ask me things like that, Jake." Goodly shook his head. "I'm sorry, but I won't second-guess the future . . ."

"When?" said Trask. "Tonight? Tomorrow? Any idea at all?"

"I can't be precise," said the other, "but it would have to be soon. Yes, it would have to be very soon."

And Lardis, silent until now, said, "Was I there, precog?"

Goodly looked at him and said, "Yes, all of us were there."

And now the Old Lidesci spoke to Jake. "Son, I've liked you from the beginning. You remind me of the other Necroscopes. Oh, you're different, yet you're the same, too. The dead asked favours of them, but apparently the dead don't know you as well as they knew Harry, Nathan, and The Dweller. So it's me the living asking a favour of you now. Since you're the one who stands the most chance of surviving what's coming, promise me this: if you do get out alive you'll tell my Lissa how I've always loved her and always will. For that's the way it is, isn't it? What we've done in life, we'll continue to do in death?"

"But no one needs die!" Ian Goodly suddenly piped, his normally high-pitched voice even higher, shriller. "We can bring it all to a halt right now, turn around, go back the way we came!"

"Oh?" said Trask grimly. "And is that the way it works? Did I really hear you say that, Ian? You, of all people? The precog himself? The one who has always insisted that what will be has been, and what has been *seen* will be? Or is this sheer desperation?"

And in the front of the vehicle Paul Garvey said, "We can't turn back now in any case. We've already managed to arouse this fellow's suspicions more than enough."

"What?" said Trask. "What do you mean? Whose suspicions?"

Looking out of the rear window, Millie answered for Garvey and said: "It's the policeman from the guesthouse. Him and his family. They're behind us in that beat-up Volkswagen. And he's still wondering about us."

"I don't have my passport," said Jake. "And even if I did, it wouldn't be franked."

"Time you were gone from here," Trask told him. "If we get stopped we'll plead ignorance about you. Let's face it, if this nosy bastard counted seven of us and it turns out there's only six—well, obviously he miscounted."

"Okay," said Jake, ducking down a little in his front seat. "But the next time you have Liz call me, make sure it's a secure location and I'll bring the weapons with me."

"That's agreed," said Trask. "And however things go it will be before nightfall. And now you'd better get out of here. That car's starting to overtake."

"Understood," said Jake, crouching down a little more, into a Möbius door that he'd conjured under the minibus's dashboard. Turning around as his body disappeared, he looked up at Liz who bent to kiss his face.

Then she drew back as he passed beyond sight. And much like the Cheshire cat in *Alice,* the last thing to go was Jake's half-grin, half-grimace.

The ancient Volkswagen drew up alongside and began to overtake, its driver looking across, frowning at Paul Garvey in the minibus's driver's seat. Garvey looked back at him, pulled over a little, waved him on. And the car passed by, accelerated, and began to pull away.

"Ease off, but gently," Trask told Garvey. "Let him go."

And Millie said, "It's okay. He's satisfied that we're not quite as weird- and suspicious-looking as he first suspected."

"So Jake needn't have left us," said Liz regretfully.

But Trask, relieved that he'd gone, told her, "It's just as well. We must be a big enough presence in the psychosphere without having Jake along. Anyway—and as Ian has pictured it for us oh-so-graphically—Jake will be with us for the Big One. At least part of the time, anyway."

"The Big One?" growled Lardis then. "I can remember another time when you knew a Big One was coming."

Trask nodded. "That was on Sunside/Starside," he said gloomily. But then he brightened and added, "We didn't stand a snowball's chance in hell then, either, but we came through it."

And the precog said, "I'd be obliged if everyone would forget what I said about turning back. You're quite right, Ben: it was fear, desperation. I panicked and felt like a cornered rat; I was instinctively looking for a way out, despite that I know it doesn't work that way. What I saw is how it will be."

"Maybe sooner than you think," said Liz from the front.

"Come again?" said Trask.

"Up ahead," said Liz, "on a heading just a little bit east of north, perhaps—I don't know—twenty-five or thirty miles in front of us? That's where they are."

"You're right," said Millie, her eyes shuttered, eyelashes fluttering, and her brow furrowed in concentration. "It's them, alright. And they've stopped moving."

"What?" said Trask, utterly perplexed. "What the hell is

384

it with you two? Are you suddenly locators or what?"

"Maybe it's because we've done so much work in tandem," Liz answered, looking back. And:

"That could be it," said Millie. "But whatever it is, we're definitely getting good at it!"

And Paul Garvey at the wheel said, "I can see I'll soon be out of business. Just a second-rater compared to you ladies."

At which Trask felt a sudden chill—a sure sign or symptom of his talent in action—but he didn't know where it had come from or what it meant. All he knew was that there was a "truth" here somewhere, and that he shouldn't have missed it.

But he had, perhaps because he really didn't want to recognize it . . .

In Jambol there was a major Y junction, with roads heading off in both northwest and northeasterly directions. This wasn't a problem; Liz and Millie were as one in their decision, and when Garvey linked with them telepathically, he readily agreed their choice of route. "The northeast fork it is," he said.

Trask looked at his map and said, "Karnobat."

"Eh?" Lardis Lidesci grunted. "What's that you say?"

"The name of a town," Trask told him. "And it fits right in with the distance Liz specified."

"Karnobat?" said Garvey, still driving. "Not only that, but it's pretty descriptive, too. A carnivorous bat. In fact, three of them!"

"Well, that's where they are," said Liz and Millie together. "And as for their mindsmog, they're not even trying to hide it. They have to be laying a trail for us, it's as simple as that."

"Ian." Trask turned to the precog. "You said it was dark— in your forecast, I mean."

"I said it *felt* dark," said the other. "But that might have been my interpretation, the colour of my mood, the sheer terror that the vision inspired in me."

"Well, to me dark is dark," said Trask. "So whatever it was will probably happen at night. That's how *I* have to reckon with it."

"You'll excuse me," Goodly answered with an audible shudder in his voice, "if *I* don't want to 'reckon with it' at all. Personally I'd like to forget it!"

"And you also said it would be soon," Trask reminded him.

"But I can't say how soon," said the precog.

"It could easily be tonight," said Garvey, without looking back. "Suggestion. Even if we can't let Jake stay with us right now, it would be a good idea to weapon up ASAP."

"That's already agreed," said Trask. "Also—assuming that Millie and Liz are right about the Wamphyri calling a halt somewhere in front—I think we should slow down and approach them with a bit more caution. They could be resting up for the night ahead. It's possible that what Ian saw was their plan coming to fruition. So while I know the future's immutable, that isn't to say we should ignore it completely. Forewarned is forearmed."

"So then," said Liz, "if we're also assuming they're asleep right now—er, hitting the hay while the sun shines?—there's no reason why we shouldn't call on Jake to deliver our weapons at our very next opportunity—"

"—Like, in that copse that's coming up on our side of the road," Millie finished it for her.

And Trask leaned forward, tapped Garvey on the shoulder, and said, "Pull over, Paul. We'll make camp here, finish those sandwiches we never got to start, and take a decent break. Frankly, I'm bone weary. I didn't sleep much last night—I don't think any of us did—and we've all been shaken about in this rattletrap until we're numb from head to toe. An hour or two's sleep will do us all the world of good."

By which time Garvey had pulled off the road and driven on deep into the copse, finally drawing to a halt where a bank of dense brambles hid the minibus from view.

Climbing stiffly out of the vehicle, Trask said, "Boys and

girls, take a break. As for me: Nature calls and I must answer. But before that—" He took Liz aside and told her, "Liz, I've had second thoughts about Jake delivering those weapons. Now I know how much you love him, but the time isn't right. You know as well as I do that in daylight we have nothing to fear. That means we don't need those guns just yet."

"But—" she began to protest, only to have Trask wave her protests aside unspoken.

"No buts," he told her. "Look at it this way: we've already aroused one policeman's suspicions. What if we were stopped for some reason, or had a breakdown or something? What, and the minibus loaded down with guns? There'd be no explaining it. And if those three monsters are asleep, we don't want to go disturbing their dreams with Jake's psychic aura. It's a bit of a paradox, I know, but on the one hand we're too close to them to call him in, and on the other we're too far away. We'll need Jake in our darkest hour, and not before then. So love has to wait."

Then, before going off into the trees, he called out to the others, "I'll be back shortly. Meanwhile, I suggest you take it easy, make yourselves as comfortable as possible."

And Liz walked off on her own a short distance, sat on the knotted stump of a felled Mediterranean pine, and despite knowing that Trask was right tried not to sulk . . .

An hour earlier at E-Branch HQ in London, Jake had taken charge of the canvas sackful of arms that John Grieve had put together for him. Then, while waiting for Liz to contact him again, he'd returned to Harry's Room where he was reading through the final batch of Keogh files—including Ben Trask's report on Harry's departure from this world—when Gustav Turchin knocked on his door.

"What is it now?" he asked the Russian Premier after inviting him in.

Turchin was in a highly agitated state. "That message I was waiting for has arrived," he said. "Time is running out. I need your decision now."

"I can't give you a decision," said Jake, without admitting that he'd completely forgotten about Turchin's problems in favour of his own. "It's not my decision to give. But it's likely I'll be seeing Ben Trask in just a little while, and I promise you I'll mention it to him then. The one thing I can tell you: there's no need to worry about Perchorsk's schematics. I . . . I believe I've sort of memorized them."

"What?" Turchin frowned. "You've memorized them? Since you and I last spoke, and from those files? Is E-Branch's intelligence really so good, then?"

Jake smiled a crooked smile and answered, "Yes, it really is. And I . . . well, I suppose I'm a quick study."

Turchin had to accept it as the truth; there wasn't a lot he could do about it if it wasn't. And so he said, "Very well, then all that remains for me to do is show you where the bomb is and instruct you in arming the thing."

"I take it the bomb is in Russia?" said Jake. "Just how do you plan to take me there?"

"What?" Now Turchin looked confused. "But surely you would be taking me! *You* are the Necroscope. You have the use of this . . . this Möbius Continuum thing."

"You don't know much about it, do you?" said Jake.

"I know nothing at all about it!" Turchin snapped. "I only know what I've seen: that when Nathan Kiklu came to see me, he emerged out of nowhere. And that when he left he simply disappeared. Him and a lean, slavering wolf out of Starside that he called his nephew! What *should* I know about Möbius Continuums, Gateways, and Necroscopes with wolves of the wild for kin? I'm a politician, not a bloody magician!"

"Coordinates," said Jake, calmly. "I can't go where I have never been, because I don't know the coordinates. I'm not talking about map coordinates or grid references; they mean nothing to me. I'm talking about coordinates that I keep up here, in my head," he reached up to tap his temple. "Which means that since I've never been to Russia, I'm afraid I can't take you there. I suppose we could do it by trial and error—taking small Möbius jumps one at a time—but that could be dangerous and it would take time. *And* I'm expecting Ben Trask's call, which could come in the next ten minutes. So . . . you'd better think again."

"This is infuriating!" Turchin threw up his hands. "At this very moment my enemies could be on their way to Perchorsk—my one chance to settle with them for good, and the perfect opportunity to close the Gate at the same time—and Trask is unavailable to me. He promised his help; I kept my part of the deal and he has let me down. Is there no honour?"

"Maybe among thieves," said Jake, "but apparently not among murderers."

"Haven't I told you it wouldn't be murder?" Turchin snapped. "These are mad dogs I want rid of, not true and honest citizens. They are *dogs,* Jake, and they're shitting all over our world. I gave Ben Trask the information that has sent your locator David Chung out on his mission to save the ocean deeps from pollution—to save *your* British fishing grounds, the American coastline, and all the waters in between. I have made myself an outcast, a defector, to come here and bring you people warnings and important information. I sent a man of mine out of Russia into Sicily to get himself killed seeking out Luigi Castellano so that you, personally, could take revenge. Have you forgotten these things? These are the sacrifices that I have made. So don't you talk to me of personal revenge. For what of yourself and Ben Trask? Ah, but that is different, eh? Well, I think not. And why should I be excluded?"

Which gave Jake pause. Not only what Turchin had said about revenge, but more especially what he'd said about sending a man out of Russia into Sicily, and sending him to his death. Georgi Grusev had been his name, and he'd come out of his tomb to save Jake's life in the cellars of Castellano's stronghold. And Jake really had forgotten about all that in the light of more recent problems. Forgotten about it until now.

"Georgi Grusev," he said.

"Yes." Turchin nodded. "He was dead before you got to

Castellano. You never met him, but that doesn't alter the fact that he did try to help you."

"Oh, but I did get to meet him," said Jake quietly. "He was dead—you're quite right—but still he got to help me. And I owe him. Which I suppose means that I owe you."

Turchin's dark eyes lit up at once, and he said, "You'll do it, then?"

"That's something I can't promise," Jake answered. "I don't know which way Trask will move on this. But we should certainly try to prepare for it. One thing's for sure: a nuclear explosion in Perchorsk's guts would very definitely close the Gate."

Turchin threw his head back and drew a deep breath. "Common sense at last!" he sighed. "Good, so how do we go about it? How do we use this Möbius Continuum thing?"

Jake shook his head and said, "The Continuum isn't a 'thing' as such but a place. In fact it's not even a place. It's every-place. Every-where and any-when."

"Eh? What?"

"I can use the Möbius Continuum to go anywhere," Jake tried to simplify it. "But I have to know where I'm going. So where's the bomb? Until I know that I can't do anything."

Turchin licked his lips and said, "And so we get to it. The location of the bomb is of course a secret. If it gets out—if the wrong people should get to know what I've done, or even the right people—then I'm finished. But very well: the bomb is at my dacha in Zhukovka, not far out of Moscow."

"Zhukovka?" Jake knew of the place; he'd been reading of it in the Keogh files. "There are several dachas on a pine-covered hillock overlooking the Moscow River. You're not the first head of Russia's E-Branch to have a dacha there. Gregor Borowitz had one, too. He died there, when Boris Dragosani murdered him . . ."

But there the Necroscope paused and frowned, because Turchin's mouth had gradually fallen open while he was speaking. Now, snapping his mouth shut, the Russian Premier said, "But this is astonishing! And indeed Trask's intelligence is amazing! Gregor Borowitz's place stood deserted until I took it over and refurbished it. Yes, yes—I have the very same dacha!"

At which Jake's head began to whirl, and as if suffering an attack of vertigo he swayed dizzily where he sat on his bed, as suddenly out of nowhere he remembered, remembered—

—Remembered . . .

23
Transitions

GREGOR BOROWITZ'S DACHA. OH, JAKE "REMEM-bered" it alright. But now that he had this thing in proper perspective—now that he knew definitely that these weren't his memories at all but the original Necroscope's—and despite that these paramnesialike attacks still brought about spells of temporary disassociation and giddiness in him—he *was* finally able to accept them for what they really were.

Which meant that he was no longer apprehensive about them, and so was able to learn from them.

Borowitz's dacha (now Gustav Turchin's) was fashioned in a style that gave it the looks of nothing so much as an Austrian or Swiss chalet. Approaching the timbered, single-storey structure along a winding pebble pathway, Jake occasionally glimpsed the sluggish swirl of the Moscow River down below, where Borowitz had delighted in fishing illegally for state-owned speckled trout. Leading off from the track, the path to the rustic, oak-panelled door was paved in stone. Pausing uncertainly under the projecting eaves— hesitating, because something had warned him that what waited inside wasn't very pleasant—Jake sniffed at the fragrant blue wood smoke from nearby dachas. It hung in the bitter-cold air as if frozen there, and he could almost feel the hairs crackling in his nostrils. But of course, for it had been winter when Harry came here.

The door stood slightly ajar. Bracing himself, Jake entered, passed along a short, dark corridor, through bead curtains into a small, pine-panelled room. At one side of the room, under curtained windows that let in a little light, Natasha Borowitz lay silent in her shroud in a polished pine coffin on a low, padded bench. Gregor's wife for many years, she had died naturally.

But at the other side of the room, seated upon a couch, the old General himself . . . had not died naturally.

Jake stared at him, and Gregor Borowitz stared back through unseeing, glassy, pus-dripping eyes. He sat there upright, dead as a doornail, showing all the signs of a massive heart attack. And indeed he had suffered one. But it hadn't been natural. The Wallachian necromancer, Boris Dragosani, had done this to him—smote him with his evil eye—in order to learn all the secrets of the then Soviet Union's E-Branch.

But Jake had seen more than enough; he hadn't needed to see any of this, except to confirm what he had already known—that indeed he possessed the coordinates of the dacha at Zhukovka!

He came out of it—returned to the here and now—with a small cry, not of fear but amazement. For suddenly it was plain to him that whatever Harry had known he could know. All it required was that someone press the right button, stir the memories, and set the mechanism ticking. Harry's legacy would do the rest, and Jake . . . Jake would know!

"What is it?" said Gustav Turchin, plainly concerned. "What happened just then? Your eyes, your face . . . you were somewhere else. Just for a moment, why, I thought you *were* someone else!" He was standing beside the Necroscope, staring down at him, his hand on Jake's shoulder. And:

"Borowitz's dacha," said Jake, looking up at him. "You did say that it's yours now?"

"Yes," said Turchin. "That run-down old ruin, I had to have it refurbished. My niece is staying there now. What about it?"

"I know the coordinates," said Jake.

"What?" The Premier gave his head a puzzled shake. "How can that be? You said you'd never been there."

"But I know—I've known—someone who has," Jake answered. "And I've only just remembered."

"Ah, no!" said the Premier, wagging a finger. "No, Jake. I saw what you did just then. It could only have been telepathy. You were talking to someone else . . . someone who knows."

"Well, something like that," said Jake. "But in fact I was seeing through someone else's eyes. Anyway, I know the coordinates."

"So then," Turchin was elated. "We can go there! But . . . can we do it now, this very minute?"

Jake shook his head. "No," he said. "But when I go back to Trask and the team in Bulgaria, I'll take you with me. Then you can plead your own case."

"And you think that will be soon?"

"Before nightfall, I'm sure."

"Nightfall in Bulgaria is two hours ahead of us," said Turchin.

"Correct."

"So then, in maybe four hours' time?"

"Or whenever Trask calls," said Jake, shrugging.

"And you can hear Trask when he calls?" Turchin was finding himself swamped in E-Branch talents. "I mean, is *he* a telepath, too? My God, no wonder you have left us behind!"

Jake saw no reason to deceive him, however, and said, "It's Liz Merrick who calls to me. She and I, we have this thing."

But Turchin held up his hands and said, "Say no more. I can only take so much! Very well, I'll go back to my room and wait, but very impatiently. Don't forget me when Liz Merrick . . . when she calls for you."

"My word on it," said Jake . . .

* * *

A little less than an hour later Jake finished reading the last of the Keogh files. Titled but unnumbered, he had read them out of order—or in whichever order they came to hand—and this final file was Ben Trask's report on the Janos Ferenczy affair. That was when Harry had fallen foul of Faethor Ferenczy's deadspawn; it was when he had been vampirized. But now, knowing the whole story, Jake also knew that Harry had never surrendered to it, hadn't succumbed to its inevitability. He had been tempted, oh yes, but he hadn't given in. And that was a fact that buoyed Jake up, gave him heart, strengthened his resolve.

If—just *if*—the same thing should happen to him (or if, God forbid, it had already happened to him), Jake vowed that he would take his cue from Harry. No way Jake Cutter was going out without a fight to the finish. As in life, so in death, he accepted that now. But what of undeath?

And what of Liz?

But these were morbid thoughts, and Jake wasn't about to go venturing down these roads, either. Liz and Millie . . . they were his mainstays; *they* were sure enough of him—so why wasn't he? But then, they didn't feel the way he felt. The weird, alarming strength burgeoning in him. And the thirst . . . or was that just his imagination?

He put that thought aside, too, called for coffee, and five minutes later David Chung brought it on a tray.

"David?" Jake said, frowning as he stepped aside to let the locator in, then watching him put the tray down on the computer console and pour black coffee into two mugs. "But I thought you were out chasing Russian wreckers?"

"I was," Chung answered. "Will be again, in about an hour's time when they pick me up. Our chopper developed a fault on the way out to Tórshavn in the Faeroes, so we hobbled home to Stornoway. We were hoping to pick up our quarry coming down from the Norwegian Sea, sort of harass him from the air, let him know we were on to him, give him the chance to turn around and go home, and so avoid an international incident. But that's out now. So, I got a lift down to Edinburgh airport and flew in from there. Tonight we'll be back on the trail again, this time in a coast-guard chopper out of Glasgow. We'll be looking for our boy out near Rockall, if he's got that far by then. But it's a bit of a needle-in-a-haystack scenario . . . he has a load of anti-detection devices on board. I'll be picked up from the roof by an MOD chopper courtesy of the Minister Responsible."

Jake was still frowning. "Slow down a minute, will you?" he said. "Let's get this straight. Who are the 'we' you keep talking about, what kind of vessel is it that you're tracking, and what's this Rockall?"

Chung grinned. " 'We' are the people who can bring the truth of the situation out into the open. We can photograph this ship or ships, providing incontrovertible evidence of what this lunatic in the Russian Navy is trying to do. We can put down divers into the sea, measure the radioactivity of this clapped-out sub, and ask what the hell it's doing here when we were told it had been decommissioned and made safe ten years ago in the shipyards at Severomorsk in the Barents Sea."

Jake didn't quite follow. "And all of that *without* creating an international incident?"

"But it won't be for public consumption," said Chung. "The evidence will be delivered to heads of state—including those in Russia's military hierarchy who haven't been quite as forthcoming as Gustav Turchin—and the ball will be firm-ly in their court. The Russians will then be given a time limit in which to clean up their act, and if they don't the evidence against them will get a much wider release with very stiff sanctions brought to bear. And what with their ever-crumbling economy, that's the one thing they can do without right now."

"All nice and political," said Jake.

"Yes," Chung agreed. "And very effective. As for the actual 'we'—the people involved in the operation—well, I'm the man they turn to when binoculars, radio, radar, spotter planes, and spy satellites don't work. That's because I have this long-time hate affaire with radioactive materials. My talent is that much better when I'm dealing with lethal radiations."

"I thought it was drugs?" said Jake.

"That, too," Chung shrugged. "Poppies and plutonium. Pretty much the same to me."

"And the others in your team?" Jake enquired.

"Naval Intelligence," said Chung, "Greenpeace, a couple of high-profile ecological types, a marine biologist, and an American nuclear physicist."

"So it's that important," said Jake.

"Very important, yes." Chung nodded.

"You said ship 'or ships.' How many of these rogue vessels are there?"

"Just the one," the locator answered. "Or rather, just one on the surface—but it's the one *below* the surface that we're really interested in."

"You've lost me again," said Jake.

"They have a special ship done out like an oceanic survey vessel," said Chung. "In the rear, twin booms angle down into the sea with a cradle slung between them. The sub sits in the cradle all unsuspected. When they reach the spot where they're going to dump it, they scuttle the sub and release the cradle, 'and down goes the baby, cradle and all.'" He made an attempt to sing the last few words.

"And they told me Elvis was dead!" said Jake, grimacing.

And Chung said, "Yes, I know: I should apologize, right? I never could sing worth a shit. As for Elvis: his music is just as popular as ever. You should talk to him some time, tell him we haven't forgotten."

Jake put that aside, and serious again said, "Then there's this Rockall."

"It's a rock in the sea, a hundred and fifty miles west of Saint Kilda," the locator answered. "But according to Turchin, it's close to the route our wreckers will take. Rockall: maybe they named it that way deliberately, though personally I don't know why they bothered. God knows there's 'rock all' there."

Humour again, at a time when there was very little to

laugh about. And now for the first time Jake got the feeling that the locator's jokey attitude was hiding something else. Something a lot more serious. Behind that big grin he was nervous as a cat. And:

"What's going on, David?" said Jake, quietly. "I mean, you didn't take time out from this important stuff you're doing to come spend a couple of minutes cracking me up. So, why did you come? What's wrong?"

Chung looked at Jake, and gradually the nervous smile slid from his classically Chinese face. "I don't know what's wrong," he said. "I hoped that by coming here I might find out."

"What's on your mind, then?" said Jake.

"You are," said the locator. "And to the exclusion of just about everything else."

"Explain," said Jake.

"What's to explain?" said Chung. "I mean—*how* to explain? It's my talent, Jake—it keeps pointing me at you!"

"At me?" Jake didn't much like this at all. "Like I'm some kind of radioactive source, or maybe a heap of heroin? What do you mean, it's pointing you at me?"

"Just exactly like that," said Chung. "And yet not. I mean you're *there,* in the back of my mind, always. Like piece of me is an iron filing and you're the biggest magnet in the world."

And now Jake's eyes narrowed. "Mindsmog?" he said.

Chung opened his mouth, closed it, looked away. Jake grabbed his arms, turned the other back again. And: "Mindsmog?" he growled. "Is that what you're saying?"

"No . . . yes . . . maybe," said the other. "But that's always been there, right from square one—the moment you let Korath into your mind."

"Except it's worse now, right?" said Jake.

"Perhaps it is," the locator gasped, straining to free himself. "I can't be sure. But it isn't just the mindsmog, Jake."

"Then what?" Jake released him, flopped backwards onto his bed. "If it's not 'just' the mindsmog, what else?"

"Listen," said Chung. "When I first met you—the day you

appeared here, right here in Harry's Room, for the first time—I knew what you were, knew that something of Harry was here. It was the same with Nathan. There's a certain something about all three of you, as if you have your own psychic signatures, different again from anything else I ever detected. I mean, Trask's aura is scarcely noticeable, only to those who know what he can do. Telepathic signatures are pretty much alike; Millie is like Liz is like Paul is very much the same as John Grieve. And it's the same for locators. Any disturbance *I* cause in the so-called psychic aether will be very similar to what . . . well, to what Bernie Fletcher used to cause. The only difference being that I was better at shielding myself. But you—"

"Yes?" said Jake. "What about me?"

And Chung shook his head in a puzzled fashion. "Yours isn't just a signature, Jake. Not any longer. I mean, it's been growing. You know, I had an old hairbrush of Harry's. It was just a wooden oval full of hog bristles." He reached into a pocket and produced a four-inch sliver of wood with a few bristles attached, and said, "This is all that's left of it. During the course of the last day or two, it's vibrated itself to pieces."

"Vibrated . . . ?" said Jake. But sure enough, the broken fragment of hairbrush was thrumming in Chung's hand, shaking like a rattler's tail.

"It's my talent," the locator explained. "In the Dark Ages they would have called it sympathetic magic. It's something of yours that connects me to you, lets me know where and how you are. When I take it in hand, this is what it does. It's like a water-diviner's hazel fork." He put the thing away.

"But it isn't mine," said Jake. "It never has been."

"That's right," Chung nodded. "But it was Harry Keogh's."

"His influence over me is growing? Is that what you're saying? *Huh!*" Jake snorted. "I could have told you that much without all of this."

But the locator shook his head. "I don't think it's so much his influence over you as your strength as a Necroscope.

You've become so much more than you were, Jake. And the reason why the hairbrush shook itself to bits? Because every time I thought of you I couldn't stop from touching it—that's how much you were on my mind. And that's why I came back . . . to see if everything was alright with you."

Jake stood up, sipped coffee that was starting to go cold, and said, "Everything . . . is not all right with me. I'm worried—I'm very *worried* about me—and I think all of you should be, too."

Chung looked at him standing there, tall as (and perhaps even taller than?) he remembered. And his hair, white at the temples now and swept wolfishly back. His hawkish nose, and his lips so thin and cold. But Jake's eyes, as penetrating as they were . . . thank God they were still a deep brown!

"Jake," said Chung then. "If anything has happened to you, it wasn't your fault but ours. When you first . . . *arrived* here, we could have let you go, but it seemed you'd be such an asset that—"

"—That Trask recruited me," Jake growled. "Now that I've been involved and seen what we're all up against, I don't blame him. Nothing that has happened was his, your, or my fault but Harry Keogh's. He got me into this, and he'll get me out."

"Listen," said Chung, backing toward the door. "When Harry knew it was all over, he did the right thing." And before Jake could answer he dipped into his pocket, brought out the broken fragment of hairbrush, lobbed it across the room.

Jake snatched it from the air and said, "I'm not quitting, David."

"I know you're not," the locator shook his head. "Not without you're made to. But you're like a dynamo, Jake, and you're humming faster and faster, louder and louder. I won't need the hairbrush to find you from now on. But—"

"—But?"

"You may need it to find me. I've had that old brush since Harry left. It bears *my* signature now. If you just think of me I'm sure I'll know it." Opening the door behind him, he sidled out into the corridor.

"Why would I need you?" Jake watched him go.

"I know a thousand locations," Chung told him. "That's because I'm a locator. They're as fixed in my mind as your coordinates are in yours. Who can say, the time might come when you want to go . . . somewhere else?"

"Why would you do this?" Jake looked out into the corridor after him.

And Chung called back, "We all loved Harry, Jake. But only Ben Trask had the opportunity to help him. So now, in the event things don't work out, I'd like the chance to do my bit."

"For me or for Harry?" said Jake, as the locator headed for the Duty Officer's room.

"What's the difference?" said Chung, without looking back. And finally, "Best of luck, Necroscope . . ."

A few miles west of Karnobat in the Močurica Hills, Lord Malinari of the Wamphyri stood in the dusty gloom of a circular room and looked out eastwards through a broken window. The shadow of his tall, crumbling refuge—his, Vavara's, and Lord Szwart's—fell like a finger on the land outside. A finger pointing east.

"What are you looking at?" Vavara was curious where she sat huddled in a dark corner, away from the lances of sunlight that came slanting through knotholes in the west-facing wall.

"I'm thinking," he answered. "I'm considering our route out of all this."

"What? But as far as I can see, there is only one way out," she said. "And that's the same way we came in. So then, are you worried that we're trapped here?"

He shook his head. "This place is *our* trap, Vavara. And I'm not thinking of our immediate exit but the one we shall be taking from Burgas."

"Ah, yes," she said, her eyes flaring in the semidarkness. "Your great plan." Her sarcasm dripped like acid.

"At least it won't get us seared half to death!" he snarled. "Unlike yours, which saw us adrift in an open boat, unprotected when the sun came up!"

"The caïque had a canopy," she said. "We were mainly in the shade."

"Oh, really?" Malinari answered, sneeringly. "Mainly in the shade, you say? Well, as I recall we suffered grievously. And in another hour or so—if that vessel hadn't rescued us—there would have been precious little *left* to shade. Indeed, we would have *been* shades, lost in the land of shades, burned to cinders in a mutual true death . . . and a very painful death at that!"

"Well, we survived," she said. "Our work has gone for nothing—thanks mainly to you—but we ourselves survived. And I for one have learned a lesson from all of this. Several lessons. One: never to trust Nephran Malinari. Two: never to let another Great Vampire into my manse, not even of his own free will. And three: never to form alliances but stay on my own, even if it's the death of me. *Hah!* I would have been better off in Starside, but I let you talk me into coming here. Well, I find this world loathsome—all this sunlight, and the nights so short. If this plan of yours works I shall be very glad to see Starside again, and *overjoyed* to see the back of you!"

"The feeling *is* mutual, I assure you," said Malinari, scowling as he turned from the window and set the badly gapped floorboards groaning under his feet.

At which, up in the rafters, something stirred.

"Now see," said Vavara quietly, putting up a hand to shield her crimson eyes from a trickle of dust. "You've disturbed Lord Szwart."

And as if to prove it:

"Why waste your time in argument?" came that wheezing, ruptured-bellows voice from roughly, recently fashioned lungs and vocal chords as malleable as mud. "The sun is up, and we should be down. But Vavara, I have to agree with you: this world is an abomination. It is the light, the terrible light. There's altogether too much of it." And:

401

"There, then," said Vavara under her breath. "Are you listening, Malinari? You should be. For when one abomination condemns another, you've simply got to take his word for it."

"Huh!" Malinari grunted.

"Go to sleep, both of you," Szwart wheezed. "Wake me again, when the sun is down." And up there on a platform where rafters came together under the turret roof, an oddly shaped, flattened *thing* adjusted its outline to suit the space, letting a flap of doughy, protoplasmic matter hang like a sack over one edge. For a moment, a crimson eye formed and blinked open in the bulge of the sack, stared down into the loft's dusty interior, then shuttered itself and dissolved away.

"He's right," said Vavara in lowered tones. "We should take respite."

"Then why don't you?" said Malinari.

"Because when *you* are awake, *I* like to be awake," she answered.

"Then you must learn to trust me," he said. "Indeed, for I need you—yes, and Szwart, too—as much as both of you need me. We're all in this together, Vavara. But when it's over, by all means let's be enemies again."

"In it together, aye," she answered, sullenly. "And all of us working to the same plan ... *your* plan. That's what I don't like about it, Nephran Malinari: that we're all following this scheme of yours, but only you know the details. So then, let's be sure I have it right. Explain it once again, if you will."

"Ah, Vavara," Malinari sighed. "You may not be tired, but I am. I'm tired of our cold war, of running away from my enemies, even of this Earth which but for E-Branch could have been—oh, a most wonderful place. As for your distrust: well, I'm especially tired of that. And when we are done here—for yes, I *will* explain it to you yet again—then I at least shall take this opportunity to catch up on some sleep. But I'm also hungry, and so I'll curl me up with those women down below—perhaps sip a little here, thrust a little there, take a little and give some back, you know?—and so slip off into pleasant dreams."

"As you will," said Vavara. "What is that to me? What were they but sluts in the first place, kicking their legs and showing their breasts and buttocks? And you a horny old vampire. So go ahead, be my guest . . . 'suck what you must and fuck out your lust,' as that old Starside saying goes. But first—"

"Yes, I know," Malinari nodded, and sighed again. "First my plan. Very well, now listen:

"The psychic aether is still now. That means they are doing what we should be doing, sleeping. Very wise of them: they conserve their energies. And a while ago I sent out a probe—but a very gentle, tentative probe—to see if I might spy on their dreams without alerting them to my presence. What dreams I discovered, while yet they were vague, were fraught with all kinds of terrors, all manner of doubts and suspicions . . . the much of which concerned ourselves, of course. Other than that they were unclear, muddied . . . well, all except for the girl's, Liz. She who was so very nearly yours on Krassos.

"Her dreams were fresh as a breeze off Sunside, come drifting over the Barrier Mountains. *Ahhhh!* How very sweet and even intoxicating! For she dreamed of her lover, this Jake Cutter.

"Now, Vavara, I know how it must pain you that she escaped your clutches on that island, but in the end it's for the best. She shall be the lure. For this Jake, he is a *Power!* He's like that one in Sunside, that Szgany bastard who wrecked our every effort among the ruins of the old aeries. For all we know he's still there, doing battle with all that unpleasantness we left behind us, our lieutenants, our thralls, and various monsters. And so I ask you, what good to return to a fight we can't win? A fight we fled while the going was good? No use at all—not unless we return with superior weapons. And what greater weapons than the ones this Nathan brought to bear against us, eh?

"So then, this man—yes, a mere man, however unthinkable that may be—this man who destroyed my garden under the Pleasure Dome in Xanadu, saved his companions from the funeral pyre I had prepared for them there, and turned up yet again to ruin Szwart's plans under London—he *is* vulnerable! He has a weak spot called Liz, Vavara. When she called for him in Xanadu, he came. Ben Trask is E-Branch's leader, yes, but Jake Cutter is his mainstay.

"Do you need proof of what I say? Do you think I have some ulterior motive? Do you doubt that this Jake is the Power that I have named him? If so, then ask yourself how this 'mere man' invaded Lord Szwart's underworld, which Szwart himself thought impregnable? And not only did he invade that secret place, but he survived the explosion that destroyed it, the sabotage that he brought about. Ah, but he comes and goes in the blink of an eye, this one. He is there and he is gone, just like Nathan of the Szgany. And who can say what other skills he possesses?

"*We* can say, once we have him. And when we return to Starside, his secrets will go with us, stolen from his mind by me, Nephran Malinari. And each of us, Vavara—you, me, and Szwart alike—all three of us with the zest and strength and tenacity of the Wamphyri, plus powers to match and outmatch Nathan of the Szgany. Just picture it. We were losing the last bloodwar, our battle with Sunside, but this time . . . ?" He paused abruptly, letting the question hang there.

And in a little while Vavara said, "You paint pretty pictures, Nephran. Let's hope that's not all they are. But in any case, it will be worth it just to take possession of that girl again. I had such plans for that pretty face of hers, *ahhh!*"

"But remember," said Malinari, hurriedly, "that she is to be the bait in the trap, the lure to bring Jake Cutter out of hiding. You may not harm her. Only damage her—vampirize her—and the game is over. This Jake *kills* vampires; that is his purpose, his reason for being. Yes, and I am sure that he and E-Branch would kill Liz, too, if she were one of ours, one of us."

"And so he's in hiding, then, this Jake Cutter?" said Vavara. "And does he hide from us? Not much of a threat there, I think!"

"Oh?" said Malinari. "And did you see him on Krassos? No, but he was there. At the end, I sensed him. His signature ... it's quite unmistakable. And that girl, Liz: you thought that she must be dead—locked in the boot of your vehicle, which you saw plunge into the sea after you'd been thrown free. Now tell me this: how do suppose she survived? *Who* do you suppose saved her?"

"I understand your reasoning," Vavara answered, her voice purring now, not from pleasure but from anticipation and vicious, unnatural lust, "and you needn't fear on my account. No, for we shall make one last bargain, you and I. You shall have this Jake Cutter—all according to your plan, yes—but the girl shall be mine. In return I shall promise not to harm her ... at least until we're back on Starside. As for these powers which you say you'll share with Szwart and myself: well, make sure that you do. Only renege on your promise and you'll have both of us on your neck. You may have *my* measure, Nephran Malinari, but Szwart's? And the two of us together? I doubt it."

"So be it," said Malinari. And with a slight bow from the waist, he swept towards the timbered stairwell.

Vavara watched him step down into the gloom below, step by step lowering himself from view. But just before he disappeared their scarlet gazes met, and she read nothing in his thoughts to belie the things he'd said and promised.

But then again, he was Malinari—called Malinari the Mind—and his mind was quite unique.

Uniquely devious, too. And:

Aye, so be it, Vavara echoed him, while doing her best to keep that thought and the next one to herself. *But let me down one more time and you may be sure it will be the last. That is my vow, Nephran Malinari. Mine ... and the vow of every creature yet to be invested with my many eggs. I shall see to it ...*

* * *

But a little while later, when she slept:

Aye, sleep, Malinari thought, knowing that *his* thoughts at least were impregnable. *Sleep, Vavara, Szwart, and leave me to scheme in peace. What, you Vavara, with your hidden horde, all waiting on your flesh to give them birth—and you, amorphous* Thing, *Lord Szwart, you with your love of darkness and dread—I should gift to such as you what is rightly mine? No, I think not. I who have discovered the truth of this Jake will keep it for my own, and I'll use it to put all such as you from my sight. In the past, since time immemorial, Sunside/Starside has suffered a surfeit of feuding Lords, and Ladies, too, in excess of requirement. Just the one master, Nephran Malinari, would have been sufficient. And will be.*

And then he sent out his mentalist probes once again, this time to try and fathom something that was singular and strange beyond measure: the fact that the E-Branch signature was mutating, growing stronger, changing by the hour.

It could be, of course, simply that they girded themselves up, preparing the way mentally for the effort to come, the inevitable showdown. Or again, perhaps it was that together in a group their talents were multiplied, their metaphysical skills magnified.

Whichever, their shields were stronger . . . certain of them, anyway. The girl Liz, and the other woman: they were telepaths, and their minds should be more easily accessible, yet this was no longer the case. In Xanadu's casino Pleasure Dome, Malinari had probed Liz's mind, sending her disinformation which caused her to fall into his trap. Alas, but this was no longer possible; even sleeping her shields were up, and if her love dreams had not been so powerfully centered on Jake Cutter, then Malinari doubted his chances of reading anything of significance in them. And likewise Ben Trask's woman, this Millicent. She, too, had thrown up this—this what? This mental mist, this fog?—against outside interference. Malinari could read the identities of these women and separate out their signatures, both the women and the entire group, but their minds were near-closed.

As for Trask himself: he should be the easiest of all. His mind knew the "truth" of things. Because truth was instinctive in him, he was inclined to lay *himself* bare. Whether he willed it or not, it went against his grain to cover anything up. For incapable of accepting lies, he found it irksome, even odious, to have to protect himself in that respect. Yet now he, too, was shielded.

And then there was that Other—that old, unfathomable one—whose signature was like wood smoke that drifted this way and that, disguising his identity and even his very being. The last time Malinari had come in contact with anyone like him had been on Sunside during the hunt. Aye, for the Vampire World's Szgany were possessed of these selfsame skills. Well then, perhaps he was a Gypsy, descendant of thralls out of Sunside.

Which left just two others: the locator—whose signature was new; doubtless he was a replacement for that fool now dead in Sirpsindigi—and the one who scried on future times.

As for the latter: oddly, his signature had not changed at all! Neither his signature nor Malinari's inability to comprehend its message. There was nothing of the past there, to hint of Goodly's beginnings, nothing of the present, which might at least be indicative of current trends, but only a swirl of inchoate, half-formed images that failed to coalesce except when they occurred. And they only occurred when they caught up with the future.

But even for Goodly, how could it be otherwise? The future has ever been a devious thing.

Three of these pursuers, these avengers, then, had somehow been changed. Even four of them, when one included Jake Cutter himself. For while presently he remained distant in the purely physical sense, still his aura—his psychic signature—was alive and more vibrant than ever in the psychosphere.

It was a puzzle with several possible solutions, and Malinari would be blind if he could not at least visualize one such. But rather a fool than stretch his imagination to that extent—surely? For if *that* were so . . . it would make a total nonsense of this chase, and the leaders of E-Branch would have far more important matters to attend to . . .

One of the girls stirred, moaning in her sleep.

Malinari reached out a hand to stroke her naked thigh and whisper calming words. His leonine head lay in another thrall's lap, and he could smell her sex like a rare sweetmeat roasting in a Starside oven. For a moment he thought to have her—even to have all of them—but then thought again.

He might after all need his strength for what was still to come. The trap he had laid for E-Branch . . . problems that might arise at Perchorsk . . . others that would very definitely arise later, with Vavara and Szwart.

No, it were better that he slept now, while the cursed sun sank ever deeper in the west. Time to sleep, recoup, and dream of Starside and all the time and the power still to come.

A time of conquest—perhaps of two worlds—and then of a vampire empire spanning both. And *Powers* beyond belief which would be his and his alone . . .

Three hours later:

Malinari woke up with a start, sniffed at the air and sent a brief but powerful telepathic message stabbing in the direction of Vavara and Szwart: *Darkness falls, and they are coming!*

Then, sensing his so-called colleagues stirring, their mental awareness focussing, Malinari roused up the sleeping girls. Only six of them remained; the others had been left for undead along the way. Known as "Val's Vamps" upon a time—albeit in a very different world on a beautiful ship called the *Evening Star*—now they were common vampires fending for themselves in Turkey. As for these others, he doubted they'd be so fortunate.

And when the six were awake: "Listen," said Malinari. "That time I warned of has come. You know what you are— what we have made you—and also that the ones who pursue us will kill you if they can."

His words were greeted with sighs, groans, hisses of alarm. Naked flesh moved in the gloom; they pulled on rags of clothing and stood up among the debris of rotten sacks and mouldy grain; stood there like six strange dolls waiting for their puppeteer. And their triangular eyes glowed a feral greeny-yellow, confirming their vampire-thrall status.

"They *will* kill you," Malinari said it again. "But only if you allow it. Ah, but you are stronger now! As dancers you were fit and strong, and now even more so. For our strength is yours, given to protect you. Remember, the blood is the life and likewise the strength. If you would live and stay strong, it is the only answer. And these pursuers . . . they are filled to brimming with good strong blood!"

"Ahhhh!" came their reply, their teeth gleaming white where once-sweet lips drew back, turning their faces to sallow, snarling masks.

"Now I go up to the others," said Malinari. "If our enemies get past you to us, then we will know that you are dead. But do well and you shall earn your freedom. Freedom, aye—to go out into the world and make it your own! Is all understood?"

"Yesss, Lord," came their answer, in a concerted hissing as from one deadly throat.

"Very well," said Malinari. "Good! And now you must hide as best you might. Drape yourselves in those sacks there, or merge with the shadows and cobwebs in dark corners, wherever you may. You should find it very easy, for you are now and forever—or for as long as you may live— creatures of the night. And so I leave you, but you should know this: that you have my blessing. Long may the night and the darkness be with you."

Then, as they melted from view and their feral eyes blinked out, he went to the rickety stairwell and ascended to the uppermost level. But in his black heart of hearts Malinari knew that his blessing was a worthless blasphemy, and also that the night and the darkness would not be with them for long . . .

24
Tilting at a Windmill

ALMOST UNNOTICEABLY, THE SHADOWS HAD been creeping, lengthening for an hour or more, until finally they had merged into a smoky twilight. In the minibus all conversation—slight and muted as it had been—had fallen off completely as evening drew in.

Karnobat was just a mile or two ahead. To the north a range of purple hills paralleled the road, seeming to float on a fine mist. Traffic was very light, and what few cars there were came up from behind, flashed their lights, pulled out and ghosted by in a weird silence. Even the clatter of the noisy engine seemed muffled, and at the wheel Ben Trask was driving ever more slowly, instinct telling him that they were very close now.

"Take the next left," said Millie, suddenly alert where she sat beside Trask. "They're somewhere up in those hills."

"Then take the next left and stop!" grunted the Old Lidesci from the back of the vehicle. "Just another half-mile and we'll be into that mist. But there are mists and there are mists, and I want to check this one out."

"And now we should call for Jake," said Liz, her voice conveying the shivers that she felt, despite that it wasn't at all cold. "We should *definitely* call for Jake."

Glancing back at her, Trask raised an eyebrow but said nothing. Indicating his intentions, he turned left across the empty oncoming lane onto a rutted farm track, bringing the minibus to a halt under a row of gnarled and ancient olive trees. The mist coming down off the hills was thin here, forming swirls of vapour about their ankles as they got out of the vehicle and stood in the gathering dusk with the light of day fading in the west.

Millie was flushed, Liz, too, and Trask enquired, "Is everything okay with you two? Maybe the sun got to you. You're looking a bit pink . . . or perhaps simply rudely healthy?"

That was a new one on Lardis. "Rudely healthy?" he queried. "Is that when you fart a lot? If so, I have been rudely healthy for years now."

"I think maybe the sun did get to me a little," said Millie. "Back there where we stopped, in that pine glade, I did my best to keep out of it. Actually, this cooler air is very welcome."

Liz said nothing, but Trask couldn't help noticing that the two women had glanced at each other . . . what, speculatively?

Paul Garvey helped Lardis get down on one knee, and the Old Lidesci sniffed at the ground mist like a suspicious bloodhound before inhaling a great lungful. But then, standing up again in a creaking of bones, he shook his shaggy head and said, "Just a mist. But when I see mist rolling down off the hills like that, well, it brings back memories. Best to be cautious where these bastard things are concerned."

Ian Goodly was looking at the low hills about a mile ahead. "Windmills," he said. "And fairly large ones at that. Derelict, most of them. At least by their looks."

Trask followed the precog's line of sight and nodded. "They look typical of windmills in Greece," he said. "Not surprising, really. We're still very close to the Med."

"And closer still to the Black Sea," said Goodly. "They are ideally placed to catch the easterlies off the sea—which they would if their sails weren't in tatters. It looks like only one of them is actually working. The closest one of the four."

"Yes," said Millie, quietly, "but the one that interests me is the farthest away." And:

"Likewise," said Liz. And both women were frowning, staring narrow-eyed at the windmill in question: its broken vanes hanging like some disjointed scarecrow's arms, the uppermost rim of its turret showing a last, rapidly fading gleam of watered-down sunlight, two high windows like a pair of blindly staring eyes, and a third like a socket nose in the tapering facet that faced them. But even as they watched the windmill became a silhouette in the fading light . . .

Like Trask, Garvey had also followed Liz and Millie's seemingly rapt gaze. And now he agreed with them. "Yes, it's them," he said. "But best get out of there, girls. I sense their mindsmog thinning. They're coming awake and automatically shielding themselves."

"Get out *now!*" Trask rasped, taking the women by their arms and turning them away.

"It's okay, Ben," said Millie, gently freeing herself. "You don't have to worry. We knew what we were doing."

"And in any case," Liz added, "if this is Ian's Big One, what's coming is coming and there's no way round it. But as you yourself said, we must definitely prepare for it. So then—do I call Jake in on this now?"

"No," said Trask. "If Malinari and the rest of them—and I suppose we have to include those girls now—if they are awake up there, they'll know it the moment Jake gets here. Jake's the one ace up our sleeve, and I want to play him last. When we get to that windmill, *if* the mindsmog is still present, that's when we'll call for Jake. But right now we're just wasting time."

They got back into the minibus, and keeping it in low gear, Trask took it jarring and bumping along the deeply rutted track to the foot of the hills, then branched off along another, rising, contours-hugging track to the flattened dome of the hill.

The windmill stood behind gapped fencing in some four acres of dilapidated outbuildings and windblown, weed-grown tracks. And Trask thought, *There's no sign of life—*

"But plenty signs of undeath!" said Liz, as he put the minibus in neutral, bringing it to a halt in the long shadow of the derelict windmill.

"I know," he answered, staring through his window, looking out and up at the grim face of the ruined building. "I feel it, too, except this time it's not working, it isn't fooling me. Or rather, *she* isn't fooling me."

"Benevolence," said Paul Garvey then. "It's radiating from that place in waves. You'd swear it was a holy place."

"On the island of Krassos it *was* a holy place," the precog reminded him quietly. "Or it had been. It was supposed to be a monastery, which is how it felt to us. But in fact it was Vavara—her lying aura—a mental mask protecting the grotesque horror underneath. And that's how this place strikes me now: a rustic country scene worthy of a pastoral canvas: *Windmill at dusk,* by the Lady Vavara. *Huh!*"

"She would kill you for saying it," said Lardis. "Even for thinking it! Lady? No, for this one knows better and spurns all such titles. *Vavaaara* was her name, like the growl of some wild thing. But no Lady—never!"

"Your pastoral scene is a damned lie!" Trask spat then. And throwing the minibus in gear he circled the windmill in a cloud of dust, only to skid to a halt again on completing the circle. "Only one way in," he rasped then, "through those leaning doors there. And judging by those broken windows, several storeys to climb to the top. But this is one big place with lots of space inside. So okay, Liz, Millie—where are these bastards hiding, and what's on their bloody minds?"

"They're up there in the loft," said Millie at once. "It's humming like a wasp's nest up there. Behind the mindsmog I can smell . . . fear? Panic? Confusion? They're like—I don't know—like so many rats in a trap."

"I agree with Millie," Liz nodded. "It looks like we've got them exactly where we want them."

But Trask shook his head. "No," he said, "it's too easy. I smell a different kind of rat here. Something is trying to tell me that all's well, which in itself tells me that everything is far from well. Liz, you've been wanting to call Jake in on this for hours now, through two countries. I reckon it's about time. We need him and our weapons both. Everybody out."

They got out of the vehicle, and Liz called for Jake . . .

* * *

At E-Branch HQ, Jake heard Liz's call as clear and clearer than ever before, almost as if she was in Harry's Room with him. But the only ones with him were Gustav Turchin and John Grieve.

Jake was in his black gear, lying on his bed with his hands behind his head when the call came. *Jake? We need you now. Also our weapons.*

"Liz?" he said, getting to his feet. He had sensed her urgency, knew there was very little time to spare.

Turchin and the Duty Officer had been seated at the foot of the bed talking in lowered tones; now, as they fell silent, the Russian Premier stood up and stepped forward. "Is this it?" His eyes were suddenly wide, apprehensive.

"Yes," said Jake, grunting as he hoisted ninety-five pounds of deadly weaponry up onto one broad shoulder. "This is it. But it could be a dangerous situation."

And John Grieve said, "Sir? You'll find this easy to use, I think. Let's just hope you don't need to."

Turchin looked at him, saw the modified 9 mm Browning automatic that Grieve was holding out to him. He accepted and pocketed it, also three magazines loaded with silver bullets.

And Jake said, "Are you ready? Do you still want to come?"

"Yes—I mean no—I mean, what choice is there?" Turchin shrugged helplessly.

"Then let's go," said Jake. "Take my arm and hold on. Close your eyes and take one step forward, and don't—"

"Ahhhh!" Turchin gasped, a mere susurration that yet gonged in the Möbius Continuum.

—don't cry out, Jake finished what he'd started to say, a fraction too late. *Speech is unnecessary in the Continuum. Just thinking it is sufficient—it conveys all you want to say.*

Telepathy? Turchin was quick on the uptake. But as the head of Russia's E-Branch, so he should be.

Something of the sort, Jake answered. *The way I understand it, in a place like this where there's absolutely nothing without that it's brought here, even thoughts have weight.*

Yet I *don't have weight!* said Turchin. *My God, I'm in free fall!*

Not any longer, said Jake, guiding him out through a Möbius door.

Turchin stumbled but Jake held him upright, and the Premier opened his eyes. The gloom of twilight, following on the bright light of Harry's Room, found him stumbling again. This time Ben Trask was there to steady him, barking, "Jake, what the *hell* is going on here? Gustav Turchin? What's *he* doing here?"

"It seems I owe him," Jake answered, putting down the weapons and giving Liz a hug. "And so do you."

"We . . . we had a deal," Turchin gasped. "I'm here to ensure you take care of your end of things." And then he frowned; some weird trick of the light seemed to be affecting his eyes. Or if not his, theirs certainly. Trask, Millie, and Liz—and especially Jake—their eyes were faintly luminous, almost feral in the dusk. Or it could be an effect of the full moon drifting up from beyond the hills.

"We've no time for this," Trask rasped, turning from Turchin to the Necroscope. "Jake, the Wamphyri—all three of them, we believe—are up in that windmill, probably at the top. Liz and Millie say they're feeling trapped there, by us. I'm not so sure. I believe it's a replay of Malinari's game in Xanadu. But however it turns out we're here to destroy them, or at least to do our damnedest. Ian Goodly has foreseen something of how it's going to end, however, and while we can't say if it's to be now or later, we do know we'll all be in on it. So for now, you and me, and Ian and Paul, we're going in. That way we may manage to avoid being together, and so avoid what the precog has foreseen . . . I hope! As for what we can expect inside—"

"Those girls are in there, too," said Millie, staring up at the windmill's darkly shadowed face. "They're very scared, very excited, and *extremely* dangerous! They're Malinari's first line of defence. To get to him and those other two creatures, you'll have to get past the girls first. But we can't any longer think of them as human, and you'll be doing them a favour."

"So, then," Trask nodded, "that's it. Lardis, and Gustav—" He paused to glare at the latter, and said, "*Damn* you—you and your political objectives, your bloody interference!—you can stay down here with Liz and Millie. You'll watch that door, all four of you. And if anything comes out that isn't one of us—"

"We'll know what to do," Lardis assured him, holding a 9 mm automatic in one hand and hefting his wicked-looking machete in the other. And:

"Right, then," said Trask, picking up grenades and a specially adapted machine-pistol, "let's go."

The others had all chosen weapons, but as the four "assault troops" made for the leaning, ominous-looking doors in the base of the windmill, Premier Turchin called after them, "What about torches? It will be dark in there. Are the laser sights on your guns going to be sufficient?"

Trask hadn't considered that—hadn't really needed to—for it didn't feel dark at all. But speaking almost as one man, Paul Garvey and the precog said, "He's right," and Goodly produced a pocket torch. Then the precog said, "Oh, and by the way, it doesn't work like that."

"What's that?" said Trask, leading the way toward the windmill. "What doesn't work like that?"

"Trying to avoid the future," said the precog. But he followed on anyway.

And Jake said, "As for it being dark in there, forget it. I have enough light for everyone right here." Elevating his flamethrower's nozzle, he applied gentle pressure to the trigger and a brief, hissing lance of fire stabbed upwards into the night.

"Avoid using it," Trask warned him. "This place looks like so much kindling to me!"

A moment later, and with their weapons' crimson laser beams crisscrossing, probing the dusty, dusky gloom ahead, they were in through the doors . . .

*   *   *

Up above, Malinari turned to the hag Vavara—minus her masking guise now—and to Lord Szwart, in a less than human configuration, and said, "It worked—worked even better than I anticipated—and they're coming up. When the fighting commences just one floor down from here, that's when *we* go down . . . but on the outside! Down below, that's where they've left their weakest."

"Oh?" Szwart used his broken-bellows voice. "And meanwhile, what of their strongest? I saw that one in what I thought was a cavern stronghold, forgotten by men. He had that devil Nathan's weapons, and used them to great effect! And this is the man you would take, one of the four who are climbing towards us even as we speak?"

"Take him I will," said Malinari, "but not here, not now. I have explained how we'll go about it. Is your memory so short?"

That last was an error. Unwise to speak to one such as Lord Szwart like that, in such abrupt, demeaning terms. And:

"I remember your *other* plans!" Szwart came flowing from the darkest corner, looming large. "I remember centuries in the Icelands, the devastation waiting in Starside when finally we went back there, the ruination of all our works by Nathan Kiklu, and our flight into this place. What of *those* plans, Nephran Malinari? If anything, my memory is *too* keen, I think!"

"We've no time for arguing now," Malinari backed away. "The time of your revenge is at hand, Lord Szwart . . . but not on me! The one who was largely instrumental in my downfall—who assisted in Vavara's, and who was wholly responsible for yours, in your cavern stronghold under London—will soon be in our grasp. And I assure you he'll sacrifice his safety, aye, and even himself, for the woman Liz. *She* is our target. Only the woman Liz. As for the others . . . well, we've set our trap for them. And it only remains to spring it. The smell of kerosene rises in the air down there, yet we have blocked it from their minds and left them feeling almost invincible . . . well, with the possible exception

417

of Trask. Myself, I believe they will survive it even as they survived Xanadu, but it should at least work as a smokescreen, allowing us to slip away. Then, when we're prepared, we shall reveal ourselves one last time, at which this Jake— this Necroscope—will come after us to save his darling Liz. *Ahhh!*"

At which point Vavara came in with, "And am I really trusting my safety to you two? We are at a fearful height, and I was never the adept where metamorphosis is a requirement. Only drop me . . . I could be sorely broken."

"Oh, we'll not drop you, sister," said Malinari, "for we'll not be carrying you!"

"What!?" She was at once alarmed. "But I understood we'd be flying down from here?"

"Which indeed *we* shall be," said Malinari. "Lord Szwart and myself."

"But—"

"—*But* speed is of the essence!" Malinari cut her off. "We can't burden ourselves with you; you must climb down. After all, Vavara, your skills in *that* department lack nothing whatsoever! You managed those cliffs on Krassos easily enough when you were hurled down in the sea. And as for that hotel in Turkey . . . why, you were like a lizard creeping up that wall!"

"*Bah!*" Vavara swept to the window. "The only lizard here is you, Nephran Malinari—and I won't forget this! But what must be must be. I'll begin the descent now."

"No," said Szwart, blocking the way. "The ones who are waiting below might see you. They have weapons. They could swat you like a fly on a wall."

"Szwart is right," said Malinari. "When the fighting starts below, then you can go . . . Lady!"

"Mentalist bastard!" she hissed, her eyes flaring where she pressed to the gapped boarding of the wall close to the window.

"Oh, be quiet!" Malinari grinned, albeit nervously. "If you must do something, then use those lying powers of yours to lure them on; let them know we're 'afraid'; send the acrid stench of our fear into their minds to buoy them up. But whatever you do, don't *whine*, Vavara—for it only makes you that much more the great hag." And:

"Mentalist *bastard!*" she hissed again, all leather and bone and needle teeth where she crouched at the window, trembling in her rage. But she did as he requested, for that way lay salvation . . .

Down below, Trask and his forces had swept the ground floor and found nothing but several heaps of mouldy grain, a stack of old and rotting sacks, and some rusted ironwork and frayed belting, relics of the forsaken mill's machinery. The rickety staircase, however, showed plenty of recent footprints in a thick layer of dust; they pointed upwards, none of them coming down again. And there were at least three higher levels, and sixty or more feet of staircase to go to the windmill's top floor.

"Smell anything funny?" Trask queried in a low voice, as he began to climb the stairs.

"Just fear," said the telepath, Paul Garvey. "Maybe Liz and Millie are right and those soulless monsters are panic-stricken up there. Why do you ask? What do *you* smell?"

"Machinery, engines, oil," Trask answered. "I'm not sure. I can feel the fear, too . . . but it seems to be masking something else. Maybe I smell lies. Vavara is good at masking things, and Malinari knows no peer in the art of mentalism."

"But we do have their measure," said the Necroscope, midway between Trask and Garvey, with Goodly bringing up the rear. "If they're. up there they have plenty to fear. Szwart knows what to expect from me, and you certainly taught Vavara a lesson or two on Krassos. And anyway, we're into this now."

"But it isn't the Big One," said Ian Goodly. "This place is dark, yes, but it isn't the kind of darkness I experienced. No, for that was as deep and as dark as . . . as a pharaoh's tomb."

"Jake," said Trask quietly, "come up alongside me. We're

up to the next level and I'm not sticking my head up there without someone's here to back me up."

Feeling his way very carefully on the creaking treads, Jake stepped up beside the older man and squeezed his flame-thrower's trigger to send a brief jet of fire spurting ahead of them.

"Watch what you're doing with that!" Trask warned him again as he sniffed the hot reek of Jake's weapon. "All this dust and spoiled grain could be a problem. Under certain conditions it's like methane—goes off like a bomb!" And moving on up into the room, he sniffed again, frowned and said, "Maybe that's what I keep smelling, exhaust fumes from your flamethrower."

Jake stepped up beside him and made room for Garvey and the precog. Again their laser beams cut through the gloom, sweeping the wooden walls and floor. There was more spilled grain; a few mice leaping from their nests in rotten sacks and scurrying for the safety of mouseholes; thick curtains of cobwebs everywhere. But that was all.

"Ian," said Trask. "Is there anything?"

"The future's a blank," the precog shook his head. "But if I try too hard that's usually the way of it."

"Then you'd better quit trying and concentrate on the here and now," said Trask. "By my reckoning there are two floors to go."

The interior space had narrowed down due to the wind-mill's slightly conical construction. Central shafts in the floor and ceiling—dark square holes, which in the past had housed the belt drive—now stood empty. But as the team continued climbing the stairs, so Goodly swept the room one last time . . . and saw a thin trickle of dust and yellow grain husks smoking down from the timbered ceiling. Lit up in the light from his torch, the stream sparkled like gold dust as it fell from the central aperture.

"Look!" he whispered. And the others saw what he'd seen.

"Something stirring up there," said Garvey. And from

somewhere up above, the creaking of a floorboard voiced its corroboration.

"Those dancing girls," said Trask, his voice like a rustle of dead leaves. "Millie said we'd be meeting them first. Well, as the saying goes, it's dirty work but . . . let's do it!"

And without further pause he went headlong up the groaning stairs.

Jake was a split second behind him, both men falling into a crouch where they left the stairs. Garvey and Goodly were right on their heels, standing over them, their laser beams slashing at the gloom, seeking targets but not finding any. Or at least not yet.

The precog swept the place with his torch. He saw festoons of cobwebs . . . dusty sacking hanging from crossbeams . . . a pile of junk in a corner . . . a heap of mouldy grain . . . the eyes of mice reflecting the light of his torch—

—And then *other* eyes, feral, flaring eyes, that were too far from the floor, too big, and set too far apart to be mouse eyes! And:

"Ahhhh!" came a gasp, a sigh, a snarl—from above!

Up there, launching themselves from a crossbeam, two half-naked girls came swinging on rusty chains, their mouths gaping open and their long teeth gleaming white and razor sharp!

Paul Garvey caught a thought. It was a red thought, and it steamed:

A human heart, still beating—raw red meat!—strength!—Life!—Blooooood!—The blood is *the life!*

And Garvey's reaction was instantaneous and deadly. Swinging his machine-pistol up at arm's length, he triggered a burst that stopped one of the girls in mid-flight. With a shriek that brought down streamers of dust, she was swatted from her chain, hurled backwards by sleeting, silver-plated steel. But her companion dropped down to the floor and came on at a lope, hissing her hatred and reaching with hands like claws.

Trask and Goodly fired together, twin bursts whose strobing flashes saved them from the worst of it: the sight of the vampire girl's head exploding like an overripe melon. And away she went, swept back out of sight and toppling into oblivion.

But no respite for the team, for now it was as if the shadows themselves were coming alive, and coming at them from every direction . . .

Vavara was halfway down the windmill's flank.

Moving crabwise and so descending diagonally, she turned a corner of the five-sided structure and thus passed from line of sight of the E-Branch group below, who in any case were preoccupied with guarding the door. And in shadows cast by an overly bright moon, she clung to warped, often crumbling fascia boards, cursed the arrogance of the mentalist maggot, Nephran Malinari, and vowed terrible vengeance on him in return for all the many insults and injuries she'd suffered at his hands.

As for her "colleagues": Szwart and Malinari waited beside the empty windows from which, when the stuttering gunfire from below ceased, they would launch themselves out into the night. Experts in metamorphosis (and Szwart a past master, whose constant flux required little or no tasking from him), they would assume airfoils, glide out and down, and so descend on the unsuspecting group below. Black against the dark of night—especially Szwart—they would go all unseen until far too late.

So it came to pass. As the mechanical thunder fell silent, and the smell of cordite came drifting up from below:

"Now!" said Szwart, and the two launched outwards.

Their loose clothing ballooned—their skin and very flesh stretched—they formed webs between elongating arms and sides, between their legs, and even between the twelve-inch fingers of lily-pad hands. Like pterodactyl kites, they flew, their shapes streamlined, their webbing belling in a breeze off the distant ocean.

Malinari, the most manlike, was grotesque. But Lord Szwart was a thing born of nightmare. A scalloped blanket, a bat-shape without a bat body, a leaflike life-form with a

422

whipping rudder tail and mantalike paddles in front ... *he* was a thing of dread and darkness!

They swept out upon the air, turned, swept back and down.

And the four on the ground didn't even see them coming ...

It was Lardis who felt the first rush of air, who turned to look up, and was felled as Malinari reversed himself and rammed the Old Lidesci feetfirst. Lardis's weapons went flying; likewise Gustav Turchin's as Lardis collided with him. And both men went down, the one winded and feeling the pain of cracked ribs, the other yelping his shock, his terror, as he saw what had attacked them out of the night.

Millie backed off—backed into Liz, who was trying to fix Malinari in the sights of her Baby Browning—but before Millie could bring up her own weapon, Szwart fell on her like a living blanket.

She knew his smell—the greasy, suffocating *feel* of him—and screamed. But nothing came out, because he had wrapped her entirely, cocooning her in his webbing and cutting off her air. Unable to breathe, Millie struggled frantically, kicked, tried to throw herself down. But Szwart held her there and tightened his grip.

And Liz—cursing under her breath while hopping from one foot to the other—was unable to shoot at Szwart for fear of hitting Millie. There was no knowing which one was which; they were almost as one!

Then three muffled shots sounded and Szwart's blanket body flew open, expelling Millie who at once fell to the ground, her smoking gun spinning from her grasp. Szwart's mantle was smoking too, where her last-effort shots had singed him.

All three of Liz's friends were down, and she herself left standing. But both Szwart and Malinari were in her sights, and her hands firm on the weapon she held at arm's length. It only required a twitch of her trigger finger—or two, or three, or as many as it took to empty the clip—but the opportunity was too fleeting and she didn't get the chance.

For Vavara was there, rising up dark in the darkness, a hag out of hell with eyes like lanterns and a claw hand that almost broke Liz's wrist as it struck the gun from her grasp. And:

"There, my pretty!" that monstrous female croaked, striking again—this time at the side of Liz's head—and toppling her into a black well of unconsciousness. "And so we meet again."

"Enough!" said Malinari, quickly glancing all around.

Lardis lay still where he had fallen . . . Gustav Turchin was scrambling backwards, silently mouthing his terror and holding one hand up before him, and Millie and Liz were down and out.

"We should finish them," Vavara snarled.

"Which would be a waste of time and effort," said Malinari. "For these are the weakest and pose no great threat. But those others up there," he inclined his head, let his eyes sweep the windmill's wall to its high windows, "they have the real power. And *that* one—that Jake, that Necroscope—in particular. If he escapes this time . . . then I'll know for certain I am right and he can make us invincible. Wherefore there's time only for this—"

And loping to the leaning door, he reached inside, took up a jerrican of petrol from where it was hidden under a stack of sacking, and lobbed it inside onto a pile of grain. And taking out a Keramique from his tattered clothing, he backed away and took aim, firing once, and once again to get the range, then a third shot directly at the target.

The force of the explosion surprised Malinari. By no means expert in the dynamics of combustible liquids, he had splashed the interior walls with a little kero and now used gasoline to ignite the whole. The resultant blast wrenched the windmill to its foundations, bowed two of of its five facets outwards, and hurled shattered boards in every direction. The great door was blown off its rusted hinges by a huge lick of fire that erupted from the doorway, and Malinari and the others had to duck down and shield themselves from heat and flying debris.

Inside the damaged structure, fire raged everywhere, billowing upwards, climbing the wooden stairs, glowing yellow, red, and orange through gaps in the boarding. And:

"There," said Malinari, with a curt nod as he straightened up, acting as if all had gone exactly to plan ... which in the main it had. "And now we can go. Bring the girl."

"Good!" said Lord Szwart. "The light of that great fire is painful to these eyes of mine, and this flimsy structure could come tumbling at any moment. So by all means let's be gone from here." And he coiled up the unconscious Liz in two ropy appendages.

But pausing near the minibus, Malinari grinned monstrously, aimed his Keramique, and blew a gaping hole in the front right tyre. "A simple precaution," he said. And then, moving swiftly round the vehicle, he aimed at the rear left and fired again—only to hear his gun make a clunking sound as the breechblock sped by an empty magazine.

"Huh!" Vavara grunted. "By no means as reliable as a gauntlet, eh, Nephran?"

"You have a point," he said, drawing back his arm and hurling the weapon away. "But no matter. It served its purpose."

As they left, flowing swiftly, silently into the flickering shadows and then into the night, Lardis Lidesci and Millie were still lying motionless, dangerously close to the burning building. And the Russian Premier, having hidden himself away in one of the derelict outbuildings, was nowhere to be seen ...

Just three minutes earlier, Trask and his party had engaged the four surviving vampire girls. But they hadn't survived for long. Under a hail of devastating firepower, riddled by silver-plated steel, they had gone down one by one until the last of them had been found in her hiding place, crouched in a cobwebbed corner.

Despite that her "terrified" screams had been pitiful, terrible to hear, Paul Garvey had known better. Yes, he pitied her ... but no, he wouldn't spare her, for her thoughts were bloody beyond redemption. A single silver bullet from his gun had been *utterly* pitiless—yet paradoxically merciful—where it shattered her forehead and blew her brains out through her ears.

By which time the uppermost level of the windmill had been empty of life—or undeath—but the men from E-Branch hadn't known that. And this time it had been Jake who headed the climb up that final flight of stairs; but very calmly, coldly, with a fragmentation grenade dangling from its ring in his teeth, and his flamethrower hissing its readiness in his hands.

Up there the night breeze had blown in through windows open to the stars; Goodly's torch had swept the room, a much smaller room than the others; red rays had crisscrossed, seeking flesh-and-blood and inhuman targets, and the Necroscope had even sent a tongue of fire into the darkest corners, for by virtue of the ventilation the air was less musty, the atmosphere less incendiary here.

But there was nothing, no one.

And it was then . . . *then,* that they had known.

Trask, hearing muffled gunshots, had rushed to a window. In the darkness down below, figures moved, collided, sprang apart. But more than four of them.

"Damn it all to hell!" Trask turned to the others, his face a parchment mask. "To me, all of you! Jake, quickly. I want you to—"

Which was as far as he got before the floor lurched and the walls shook, and dust and cobwebs came streaming down in answer to the blast from below. Scorching thermals rising from the inferno came rushing, roaring, whooshing up through the stairwell and central shafts; shimmering jets of pressured, furnace heat, they bore a certain reek. And clear-minded at last, Trask knew what his mysterious smell had been: kero, or gasoline—or maybe a mixture of both—but masked by the aura of Vavara and the mentalist mind of Malinari.

Jake was crossing the floor toward Trask, but he was moving quickly, carelessly, and stepped too heavily on a rotten board. His right leg went through, toppling him sideways, and he cried out as splinters of brittle wood shot deep into the back of his thigh, just above the knee joint. A moment more to recover from the senses-numbing agony, and letting go his weapon, taking his weight on both hands, he tried to push himself up and free.

Seeing Jake's situation, Goodly and Garvey went to his assistance; but timbers groaned, and once again the floor lurched, throwing them off balance.

Ben Trask got to Jake first. And furious with himself, the fact that he'd let himself and his people be lured, fooled, and trapped yet again—but at the same time panic-stricken, galvanized by thoughts of what might be happening below, to the women and the others—the older man let his passions fuel him, took Jake under the arms and hauled him up out of the grinding, warping tangle of screeching boards. His strength was phenomenal as he dragged the Necroscope free and hoisted him to his feet, so much so that he could scarcely believe it himself.

Flames were now shooting up the stairwell, and a pillar of fire leaping from the central shaft in a fat stem that hit the domed ceiling and splayed out and down, opening like the blooming of some alien, fiery orchid. Cringing from the searing heat of its red and yellow petals, the four men came together. And:

"Do it!" Trask cried. "Jake, take us the hell out of here, down to the others, before this whole bloody place collapses!"

All four, they huddled together, arms locked around shoulders and necks, and Jake conjured a Möbius door. "Now back away from me," he yelled over the roaring of the fire, as he pushed them out of the known universe.

Instant darkness and weightlessness ... the sudden shock of drifting free in the one absolute void, the great and infinite nothingness of the Möbius Continuum—

—But a moment more found them stumbling, their legs like rubber as gravity returned. And Jake actually fell; for as his knees bent a little under his weight, so a cluster of six-inch splinters, like so many wooden daggers, drove even deeper into the back of his thigh.

They were down on the ground between their vehicle and the burning windmill. Millie lay where she had fallen, and the Old Lidesci was shielding his face from the blaze with one arm and hand, and trying to drag her away from the fire with the other. Fortunately the night breeze, grown to a wind now, was driving the flames away from them, but still the heat was unbearable.

Paul Garvey rushed to help Lardis, and as they drew Millie from danger she showed signs of recovery.

Trask was at her side at once, asking, "Millie, what about Liz? Where's Liz?"

But Millie could only lick her lips and stare dazedly into the night.

Goodly was in the minibus's driving seat. Starting her up, he called from his window, "Get in, all of you—quickly! The windmill's going to topple!"

And because he was the precog, and rarely wrong, they knew better than to argue with him . . .

25
Revelations, Reservations, Resolutions

LAST TO REACH THE MINIBUS, PAUL GARVEY came staggering, carrying Jake in a fireman's lift. Normally the Necroscope would use the Möbius Continuum, but such was his pain as jagged splinters raked naked nerve-endings and threatened to sever his hamstring tendon that his mind wouldn't focus.

Garvey reached the rear door of the vehicle in time to hear the precog's warning yell, "There she goes!" He meant the windmill.

And as eager hands reached from within and grabbed at Jake, there she went.

Trask's earlier warning to Jake, that he be careful how he used his flamethrower, was now seen to have been almost as potent a premonition as anything foreseen by Goodly. On the first floor of the windmill, the heat had dried out the old piles of grain to set them swirling, and as the perfect conditions were met so a second explosion blew out the walls of that floor and hurled blazing debris in all directions.

A heavy board came whirling, *whup-whupping* through the air. One end hit the ground; the board flexed and bounced, vibrating as it sprang aloft again, before clipping the Necroscope on the back of the head in passing. So that when Trask and the Old Lidesci snatched Jake from Garvey's athletic shoulders and dragged him inside the minibus, he was already out cold.

Then, with Garvey performing a headlong dive in through the rear doors, the precog hit the accelerator, setting the vehicle fishtailing as he turned away from the burning building. Behind them the upper floors collapsed into the ground-floor cauldron, and the structure fell on its side precisely where they'd been, spilling blazing rubble over a wide area.

But the minibus was limping, and Ian Goodly said, "As if we weren't in enough trouble, I believe we also have a puncture."

Away from the blaze he drew the vehicle to a halt, even as Premier Turchin came staggering, waving his arms, ghostly pale in the headlight beams.

"Lardis," said Trask, stepping down from the rear. "Do what you can for Jake and Millie. Paul and Ian . . . we have to change this flat. The fire will be seen for miles around. I don't want to be here when people come to investigate." Then he whirled on Turchin. "You—where the hell were you? How come *you* got away when the others were in trouble and . . . and what about Liz!" He gazed wildly all around. "Did you see what happened to Liz?"

"Liz was taken," Turchin babbled. "And yes," he nodded, "I got away. If I hadn't I'd have got dead! I didn't know what you were up against, Trask. I had no idea—couldn't possibly have guessed—what those creatures were like. It's one thing to be told about them but quite another to be confronted by them! And I panicked, I admit it."

"What about Liz?" Trask grabbed and shook him, and stockily built as Turchin was, he *was* actually shaken. Also—staring at Trask's face, feeling the anger transmitted through his hands—the Russian Premier visibly blanched.

"They . . . they had a big car," he said. "A limo, I think it was, hidden in an outbuilding. I heard the car start up, saw it drive into the open, saw them bundle Liz inside. By God, Trask, that car was like a hearse!"

"It *is* a hearse." Trask let go of him. "And Jake's hurt—Millie, too—and those black-hearted bastards have escaped me again and taken Liz with them."

Meanwhile, Garvey and the precog had removed the spare from its housing at the front of the vehicle and were working to get the minibus jacked up. And as Trask turned away in disgust from Turchin, so Millie climbed unsteadily down from the back of the vehicle and almost fell into his arms.

"Thank God you're all right!" He hugged her—but carefully—like the oh-so-very precious thing that she was. And, "Lord," he sighed, "it's bad enough Liz has been taken, a bloody disaster, but if it had been you . . . I just don't know what I'd have done, not a second time."

"Liz?" came a dazed-sounding, anxious mumble from the open rear doors. "I didn't see Liz. I thought maybe she'd got away." And then, angrily: "Ben Trask, is it you out there? What *about* Liz, Ben?"

Trask stepped to the back of the vehicle and looked inside, at Jake and Lardis. The Old Lidesci was sitting well away from Jake—sitting very quietly, in a corner up front—almost as if he didn't want to be noticed there, didn't want to *be* there. And the Necroscope had ripped open the back of his black track suit's right leg, and was sitting there with his leg up on the benchlike seat opposite, pulling long, bloody daggers of wood out of the torn flesh above and behind his knee.

But the look on his face—the very *different* look of him as he worked—was something else. Jake's hair at the temples was almost white now, giving him a sleek, wolfish look where it was swept back into a short, brown-and-white, four-ply braid at the back. His face seemed leaner, more angular, and more angry. Beads of silvery sweat stood out on his brow, and his lips were drawn back from teeth that were clenched in the right-hand corner of his mouth. But one by one, as those long, brittle splinters were tugged free and let fall to the floor, he only sighed his relief and showed no other sign of the pain that he must be feeling.

Or maybe he wasn't feeling it but staving it off. And Trask found himself thinking, *They can do that . . . can't they?*

And then there were Jake's eyes, his luminous eyes . . . !

Millie was beside Trask; she saw what he had seen, thought what he'd thought. And looking at them suddenly, sharply, Jake saw their expressions and nodded his understanding. Then, grinning wryly, mirthlessly, he drew the last splinter from his raw red flesh and said, "Oh, really? So you're thinking I'm looking a bit odd, eh? Well, let me tell you something—you should see yourselves!"

And Trask and Millie, they both knew it would do no good to deny it. It was the strife, the fighting, the passion, that had brought it on . . .

Gustav Turchin had been standing nearby. Now, very quietly, he went to where Goodly and Garvey were tightening the last few bolts on the front right wheel. And he couldn't help but notice that they, too, were looking apprehensive—no, they were looking hag-ridden—where they worked with frantic speed yet much too quietly. Working together like this, on their own, had provided them with their first real opportunity to talk in private.

Then, as they finished up and wiped their hands on a dirty rag, Trask, Millie, and Jake appeared from the rear of the minibus; and behind them the Old Lidesci, holding his damaged ribs with one hand . . . and his machete in the other!

"People—" Trask began to speak, only to pause abruptly

as Garvey leaned into the front of the minibus and brought out two machine-pistols, one of which he handed to the precog. And:

"Right," said the telepath, his voice trembling, uncertain, and very frightened. "You said 'people,' Ben, by which you mean me, Ian, Lardis, and Premier Turchin. *We* are people, all right, that's sort of plain to see—but it's equally obvious that you three aren't! Not any more. And we're pretty damn sure that Liz wasn't, either." As Garvey talked, the Old Lidesci gave the one group a wide berth, sidling carefully around them to stand with Garvey and the others.

And for several endless moments there was silence . . . until Millie said, "Well, go on then—get it over with." And she was so calm, so quiet, that her words sounded like thunder over the pop and crackle of burning timbers.

Then Lardis spoke up, and said, "If you'll just let me walk away, I think I would rather do that. And gladly."

Trask looked at him and said, "You? I would have taken bets that after all you've seen and done, you'd be the first to act. And while I wouldn't like it, I'd certainly understand it."

Sheathing his weapon, Lardis answered, "Aye, I've known bad times, but there were good times, too. And I remember Harry. He was different."

"I remember Harry, too," Trask replied. "And I know he wasn't all *that* different, not at the end. But I let him live."

And then the precog spoke up. "All my life," he said, "I've considered this talent of mine a curse—until now." And turning to Garvey he went on, "Put your weapon down, Paul. You seem to have forgotten—even as I had momentarily forgotten—that we're all going to be in this to the end. All of us together."

"But I want to stay the way I am," said the telepath, shivering for all that he could feel the warmth of the fire.

"Then read our minds," said Trask. "And if you discover any positive threat in what we're thinking, pull the trigger." Then he turned to Millie, hugged her again and asked her: "How is it you are so damned eager to die?"

"I'm not," she answered. "But how will we live? And if this is the end of us as we were—and if we have to go—then I'd like to go cleanly."

Jake had limped forward a pace—and disappeared! Stepping out of the Möbius Continuum slightly to Garvey's rear, he snatched the machine-pistol from him in a move that was one continuous blur, the incredible speed of the Wamphyri! And taking out the magazine he looked at it, frowned, and growled, "Empty?"

"That's right," said the telepath, as he backed off a pace. "Because I was afraid I might use it without giving any of you a chance to . . . well, to explain."

"What's to explain?" said Jake. "But what I would like *you* to explain: how come you'd fireman's-lift me out of trouble if you were only going to kill me later? And incidentally, that's why I haven't killed you!" And then, looking at the gun again, "Do you have a full clip?"

"Yes," said the telepath, reaching into his pocket to show Jake a full magazine.

"There, then," said Jake, giving him the gun back. "No good having the ammunition if you don't have a fucking gun!" Then he groaned, went to his knees, put a hand to the back of his head, looked at his sticky crimson fingers and said, "People—and I really do mean *people,* all of you—I think you'll have to get by without me for a while."

With which he fell flat on his face . . .

Concussed, the Necroscope lay in the back of the minibus, cared for by Goodly, with Garvey looking on, while Lardis sat hunched in a corner looking dour. Apparently drained of energy, Premier Turchin slept where he sat, his head lolling on his chest.

Ben Trask, ever the indefatigable leader, drove through the night, locked-on like a missile to the hearse and its alien occupants—how many miles ahead?—and guided by Millie who sat beside him.

After a while, the five who were still conscious conversed, tersely at first, but gradually falling into old routines, patterns of long-accustomed speech that sprang automatically from years of knowing each other, friendship, and . . . mutual trust?

That was how it had used to be, anyway.

And while they weren't forgetting—couldn't possibly have forgotten—the desperate nature of their situation, they certainly tried their best.

As if from far, far away, Jake could hear them . . . but then, he could hear diverse things, discernible to no one else. Deadspeak whispers came rolling in off a sea of fog, and there was a constant pounding in his head and faint cries of frustration, despair—even of mental degradation, madness—from somewhere deep inside . . . but not Jake's pain and not his despair.

His madness, then?

No, not that, either, though certainly his psyche felt like it was being torn in half, with both halves pulling in opposite directions.

Seeming to recognize various ethereal voices, Jake listened to the dead awhile. The ones he knew were muted, shouted down—or whispered down—by the Great Majority, who were actually *in* the majority now; for all of those who had been undecided about the Necroscope were now convinced, satisfied as to his failure, witnesses for the prosecution. And Jake the one on trial, about to be convicted. For all of their worst fears had been realized and the one light in their everlasting night, the single thread connecting them with what had gone before—the world they had known—had lost its blue glow and now burned red.

Yet still Zek—Zek Föener—Zek Simmons—Zek Trask—stood up for Jake. And Keenan Gormley, and George Hannant, and the gravel-voiced ex-soldier called Graham "Sergeant" Lane, who at different times had also stood up for Harry, and for his son Nathan; they all stood up for Jake. "All" of them, yes . . . pitiful handful that they were, compared to the Great Majority.

And among them a small but determined voice—a tiny, tearful whisper—from far away, a graveyard in Hartlepool, in the northeast of England where Harry Keogh had grown up:

The Necroscope was my friend, she said ... Cynthia, who had died a child, and remained a child despite that five cold years had slipped by. Jake didn't know her—

—But Nathan knew me, Cynthia told him, and all the others had fallen silent now, listening to her. *He was the Necroscope,* she went on, *and I was a nobody. I would have cried forever but for him. My mom and dad, too; they couldn't know there was this place, couldn't know I'd go on, and would wait for them always. But Nathan knew, and he told them. And they stopped crying, and so did I.*

He played at God! The multitude erupted then.

It was the only thing he could do! (Zek's voice.)

And anyway (Graham Lane's rough voice), *where is this God? And more to the point, where's His heaven?*

Heaven is waiting for those who believe! The Great Majority cried out against what sounded like blasphemy— though many of them had long since stopped believing.

I believe! Keenan Gormley shouted back at them. *And I would like to believe that the Necroscopes are His angels! Don't deny Jake as you denied Harry. Don't you go making that same mistake again. For if you deny Jake ... He may deny you! And your children. And their children!*

Keenan is right! (Zek again.) *And Cynthia, too. What? And has it taken the eyes of a child to see light in this eternal night? You wonder, all of you—you have your doubts, just like Graham Lane—but unlike him you keep them hidden away in your secret hearts. That's where you ask about the hell that we inhabit, instead of the heaven we were promised. But maybe it's a test, the final test, and only the worthy will succeed and go on while the rest stay here.*

But again the Great Majority cried out against her. *No! No! It isn't so! We* cannot *side with vampires. They are a plague on the living and a curse on the dead. We accept of life and death ... but never undeath! We can't place our trust in vampires!*

But I can, said little Cynthia, still only seven years old, and never to grow a day older. *I'll place my faith in this one, anyway.* And reaching out of the dark—reaching for Jake—she asked, *Necroscope? Are you there?*

He couldn't resist her. Maybe when it came to it she'd turn her back on him and run—perhaps, face-to-face, it would prove too much for her; she'd sense the darkness stirring there, back off and deny him like all the others— but in a way she was his last hope. And for a *fact* she was their last hope. And:

Yes, Jake answered, *I'm here. But you really don't know me, and perhaps they're right and you should be afraid of me.*

You're the Necroscope, she said, drawing closer. *And so was Nathan when he was here. I can't be afraid of you. You feel the same as Nathan felt. I don't care about the cold that's in you. It isn't your fault, and what's warm in you will smother it.*

Cynthia, listen to me, said Jake, warningly . . . then paused, lost for words. Because suddenly he knew her, remembered little Cynthia without ever having met her!

And the Necroscope's head whirled, painlessly this time, as a kaleidoscope of characters—Harry, The Dweller, and Nathan—merged within, briefly embodying every Necroscope avatar in the selfsame moments, and also their memories, yet at the same time strobing in fragmenting, overlapping patterns of day and night, dark and light, so that almost everything was forgotten even as it flew apart again. Almost everything.

But one of those memories remained, and Jake clung to it.

This one is for Nathan, said Cynthia, and Jake felt it like a butterfly brushing his hollow cheek. *And this one is for you.* She kissed him again, and was gone. But Jake knew that he would always remember—even as he "remembered" it now—the soft sad scent of soap and tears and innocence.

And he also knew how things were going to be, felt his injured psyche mending, bringing him back on course, saw clearly now how easy and wrong it would have been to surrender, and how hard and right to follow a child's suggestion:

To use whatever remained of that vital spark of warmth, the spark that made him human, to suppress and defeat what was cold and alien in him.

It was only a matter of will—free will—and no one more free-willed than Jake Cutter.

It was like a vow, the Necroscope's deadspeak vow, and he'd vowed it with such determination that the Great Majority backed off, fell silent, drifted out again into that great mental fogbank, and retired to wait and see. Their verdict wasn't in, not yet awhile.

But the teeming dead weren't the only ones who were waiting to see . . .

Jake moaned, turning on his side where he lay on the vehicle's benchlike seat, held against falling by Ian Goodly. But he was still hearing things, vague voices that found their way through to him—mainly the muted conversation of his "fellow" travelers, like echoes in a tunnel—but also the pounding and wailing of something or someone else.

The latter was the work of Korath-once-Mindsthrall, and the Necroscope had had more than enough of it.

Opening the window in that special door in his metaphysical mind, Jake said, *Korath? What the hell is it with you? I'm suffering enough already without all this racket.*

If he'd expected an answer it wasn't forthcoming, not immediately. Instead there was a snuffling, a weeping, an incoherent gibbering that even deadspeak couldn't decipher. But since this was Korath, Jake felt little or nothing of pity. In fact he wondered if he was still capable of it. And:

Korath? he said again. *If you're trying to get my attention you've succeeded. But I've got to tell you, the way I'm feeling right now I could do without it. And if I were in your position I'd think twice before pissing me off any more than you piss me off already. Do you hear me?*

The gibbering faded away—the snuffling and sniffing, with which it was interspersed, too—and for several seconds there was silence. Then Korath spoke, but his was no longer the voice of arrogance and incredible duplicity by which Jake had come to know him. Before, Korath had been a distraction, then a menace, a would-be voyeur . . . finally a creature bent on returning to a stolen life in Jake's body, having first removed Jake from it.

Now he was something else. A something broken beyond repair not only in life but in death, too. A creature of darkness immobilized and lost in the impenetrable darkness of a secret room in the Necroscope's secret mind. Worse than any padded cell, it had no visitors. Darker than dark, it had no light, no colours, no odours, no tastes, no touches, no sounds. It was *total* isolation—it might as well be the Möbius Continuum itself—and when Korath "pounded" with his screaming, his screaming was all he heard. In other words his own thoughts. And when all one has is one's own thoughts, it won't take very long for them to turn inwards on themselves, and on the one who thinks them.

Korath was going mad, and he knew it.

Do you know, he said quietly, when at last he'd got himself under a semblance of control, *did I ever tell you, that my once-master Malinari the Mind was wont to complain how he often felt that the tumultuous thoughts of others— their constant babble—would one day drive him insane? Well, he did, he did. And he had to control them, shut them out, else for a fact he would be a raving madman. With me . . . he got on very well with me, or so I prided myself, however naïvely. For being blessed with a modicum of shielding, a natural and most useful asset, passed down to me by my father, I had a measure of control over my thoughts. And it's no mere coincidence that I lasted longer in Malinari's employ than any other thrall or lieutenant; well, with the sole exception of Demetrakis, who was by any standard a dullard. But you saw him under the Pleasure Dome in Xanadu, and I'm sure you would agree that being crushed and drowned—which was my lot—was a far more acceptable fate than his.*

Having listened to all of this with increasing impatience,

Jake now said, *Let's get something straight, Korath, I haven't come visiting to listen to some interminable retelling of your life story. I came to tell you to be quiet—to stop rattling your cage. I have problems of my own, and you . . . you've never been other than a gigantic bloody nuisance!*

But it was as if he'd said nothing at all, or Korath hadn't been listening. For as soon as Jake had finished:

Yet now, the dead and miserable vampire continued, *if only by virtue of my imprisonment in this place, at last I'm able to understand something of Malinari's problem— though strangely, and even paradoxically, his is the very opposite of mine. We're at opposite ends of the spectrum, do you see? For where my master suffered from the myriad thoughts surrounding him, I suffer from the lack of them! And where he was plagued by all of those mental voices, I hear only my own. I used to enjoy to eavesdrop on the Great Majority, but no longer. The walls of this room of yours are impregnable, thoughtproof. I used to argue with you, and found our word games most stimulating. But what stimulus is there now? None whatsoever, and so I argue with myself. Alas, I am my own equal and the arguments go undecided. In short, given just a little more time alone in this place, and I am sure that I . . . shall . . . go . . . insane! If I'm not there already.*

And the Necroscope said, *Is it possible I feel some kind of proposition coming on?*

You have won, Korath answered. *I almost had you; on several occasions I thought that you were mine, but I cannot any longer deny the fact that you have won. And all I want now is out. You feared that I would usurp you—and so I would have—but now my only desire is to be as far away from you as possible, preferably in that detestable sump in Romania. For there at least I shall have something, if only the cold murmur of water, and the miserly thoughts of the teeming dead . . .*

And now Jake actually felt something of pity. *Didn't I promise you something better than that?* he said. *To take your bones out of there and bury them in a field somewhere, before they're washed away entirely?*

You did so promise, upon a time, said Korath. *And I gave it some thought. But in a field? In this world? Where I would feel the sun beating down on me eight or nine hours in every day? It would be worse than my sump!*

Then you must decide upon another place, said Jake. *Instead of torturing yourself and annoying me, let that be your stimulus while you wait.*

Eh? said Korath. *While I wait? Are you telling me you don't intend to release me now, this very moment?*

Not just yet, Jake answered. *And for a very good reason. We go up against the Wamphyri, Korath. Myself, Trask, E-Branch . . . a battle to the death, and you might yet be of some assistance to me.*

And if I refuse, if I have gone mad when all of this comes to pass—what then?

But the Necroscope's voice contained a deadspeak shrug, as he answered, *Then what befalls me befalls you. But meanwhile I want you to be quiet. If you distract me, you'll only be placing yourself in even greater jeopardy. So keep your wits about you, Korath, and wait.*

For how long?

Not long, I think.

Then I have no option, and I can but try, said Korath.

So be it, Jake nodded.

But as he closed the window in the door in his secret mind, already he could hear that oh-so-mournful gibbering starting up again . . .

"Damn it to hell!" said Trask for the fourth or fifth time. "We know how it happened—knew that it *could* happen—yet still we ignored it."

"And we let it happen," said Millie. "*I* let it happen. When I should have denied you, I wanted you all the more. I think it must have been fear. I *swear* I didn't know, but I was so frightened . . . I just didn't want to be alone."

"Ditto," said Trask, gruffly. "And it was my way of denying that anything might have happened to you. Yes, and it was probably the same for Jake and Liz."

"Jake and Liz?" she answered. "They were young lovers; what they did was no one's business but their own. I'm not responsible for them, but I'm certainly to blame for you."

"No." He shook his head. "If blame is to be apportioned, it was both of us."

"It was neither one of you," said the precog, from the rear of the vehicle. "It was Szwart. His spores. Yet you didn't seem to sleep, Millie. It's all very strange."

"I *wanted* to sleep," she said. "In fact I did sleep, but we thought it was simple exhaustion following that nightmare under London. And anyway I was fighting it, determined *not* to sleep."

"And Liz?" said Paul Garvey.

"Same story," Millie answered. "She had been through a lot, too, so maybe sleep was perfectly natural. And Jake and Liz . . . they'd be hard to keep apart. I wouldn't have tried to come between them."

"But *I* should have," said Trask.

"It's in the past now," said Goodly, "but it *was* the future—then. So maybe it's all one after all. Whichever, it can't be undone."

"And now the future is all-important," said Lardis. "And as for me, I can't believe I move among vampires, lacking the will to strike them down. But I've loved you people! You are like—you have become—my own."

"When this is over," said Trask, "assuming we win, that is, you and Lissa must return to Sunside/Starside through the Perchorsk Gate, before we close it forever."

"And speaking of Perchorsk," said Garvey, "has anyone given thought to where these bastards are heading?"

"I have," Trask answered. "And it fits with everything that we know about them. Their plans for Earth are in ruins; they're no longer worried about their anonymity, which is why they seem bent on leaving a trail of death and destruction in their wake; and since they came through into our world via Romania—"

"The only way back to their own is through the Gate at Perchorsk," Millie finished it for him.

"But many a mile to go yet," said Trask, "and soon they'll be into Turchin's territory. If he's still in contact with members of what used to be The Opposition, maybe we can arrange an ambush or two along the way and slow them down."

And Goodly said, "Assuming that you're right, it's odd that they've chosen this route."

"What route?" said Trask.

"We're heading for Burgas on the Black Sea coast," the precog answered. "And that's east, not north. So where land routes are concerned, this is probably the worst possible choice they could have made."

"Perhaps they intend to take another ship," said Millie.

"And if so they could be heading for Odessa in the Ukraine," said Garvey. "That might make sense. Do you really think we'll be able to follow them?"

"To hell and back, if necessary," Trask growled.

"Huh!" The Old Lidesci grunted. "And that's very possible, too. The hell bit, anyway . . ."

"And so we're decided," said Goodly. "That come what may we really are in this together, right to the end?"

"Put it this way," Trask answered. "I may need blood or raw red meat to live—yes, and Millie, too—but it doesn't *have* to be human. In another world, another time, there was this man called Turgo Zolte. Turgo refused to descend to that level. And so did Harry Keogh. They both went out fighting it, and so will we. You have nothing to fear from us. I intend to use what's in me to destroy the creatures who brought it into our world. Them and no one else. Does that answer your question?"

"I didn't ask that question," said the precog.

But Trask only grinned, however humourlessly, and answered, "Oh, yes you did, my friend. Now tell me—have I ever doubted your talent? No? So why do you deny me mine?"

"Very well," said Goodly, "but that's only you two.

There's still Liz, *if* she's managed to survive. And there's also Jake."

"He's been okay up to now," said Garvey. "But how can we be sure he'll stay that way?"

"That's a chance we'll have to take," Trask answered, glancing into his driving mirror to pierce the gloom at the rear of the minibus, where to him everything was as visible as in broad daylight. "But I've taken the same chance before, and as you're aware there's a hell of a lot of Harry Keogh in Jake Cutter."

"And talking about Jake," said Millie, "how's he doing?"

"His wounds . . . are healing," said Garvey. "The back of his thigh has formed a scab, and the split at the back of his scalp is sealing itself. And I have his blood all over my hands . . ."

"Likewise," said the precog.

At which Lardis spoke up, however gloomily. "As long as it doesn't get into your eyes, nose, or mouth, you should be pretty safe. Jake's not that long a vampire. His sexual juices are one thing—they're the essence of life, after all—but his blood shouldn't be infec—er, *infectious*—not yet a while. Not on the outside of your flesh, anyway. On the other hand, if you've been wounded, picked up a cut here and there . . ." He paused and shrugged.

"I haven't," said Garvey.

"Nor I," said the precog. "And in any case, I think that's the least of our worries. But Jake . . . he always was an obstinate, occasionally perverse sort of fellow to deal with."

"Which could be a good thing," said Trask. "And as long as his obstinate side wins out over his perverse side, I'm all for it. As for healing powers—obviously, being a vampire isn't *all* bad news."

"You're joking, of course," said Millie.

But he didn't answer at once, merely looked at her sideways through feral-gleaming eyes. Until finally—when she wouldn't stop staring at him—he sighed and reminded her, "We've got a big fight coming, Millie. I don't like being a vampire, no, but it doesn't hurt knowing we won't go down all that easily."

"Actually," said the precog, "when you're more fully—er, developed?—you should be very powerful vampires indeed. That might take some time, but with your enhanced talents . . ."

"They're already enhanced to a degree," said Garvey. "What? The way Liz and Millie were able to track these creatures down? They were as good or better than David Chung! Long-range telepathy. My own skills are puny by comparison. And as for Jake: he is going to be . . . well, something else."

And Lardis, feeling a little less withdrawn and morbid now, said, "Do you really think you can fight it and win? I mean, is it possible you'll remain avengers, and go on to rid your world of others who aren't as strong, who follow the darkness instead of the light? But if so, then what is it that's different about you?"

Trask shrugged. "What was it about Turgo, and Harry?"

Lardis thought about it, and nodded. "They had always hated vampires," he said eventually. "And what they did in life, they continued to do in undeath."

"Something like that," said Trask. "And we're the same. All of our lives—or at least, it sometimes seems that way—we've been fighting evil, so why stop now? Lardis, you spoke of avengers. Well, and don't we have enough to avenge? Look at all the poor people who have paid, and who are yet to pay, the price of what Malinari, Vavara, and especially Szwart have done. For all we know the world may still descend into chaos."

And Millie gave a little shiver and said, "For all we know, we're not even going to win the next one! For us, it could well be the last one."

"But we are going to try," said Trask grimly. "Myself, I've lost too many loved ones to vampires. Malinari and those others . . . they're *not* going back to Starside if I can help it."

"Damn right!" said the Old Lidesci. "Especially now that

we know Nathan has won his war and my people are free. I won't see them enslaved again."

And Paul Garvey asked, "But what about the others? The ones in London—and all the other sites—who've been infected? I mean, can't they be special, too? Can't they all fight it?"

But Lardis shook his head. "No," he said, "you'll find that it doesn't work that way. In Sunside, for everyone who tried to fight it there were three who surrendered at once. And remember—you *knew* what you were fighting!"

"Lardis is right," said Trask. "The vast majority of people who get infected won't have a clue what's happening to them. We know, and that's our strength. And then again there will always be a certain lunatic element—not to mention a criminal element—who might actually *want* to be vampires! I'm not a precog, but still I see a very dark future looming. I mean, think about it. Our Minister Responsible's latest communiqué wasn't exactly his usual phlegmatic response to a problem, now was it? No, the world is in dire straits, and once again we'll be the ones at the forward edge of the battle area. So you see, what's coming can best be likened to a skirmish—the first round of a fight to the finish—an opportunity to test our battle skills."

And Garvey said, "Then let's hope we're all still standing when the bell sounds . . ."

But suddenly, as they approached a junction: "Take the next left!" said Millie. "They're heading north now."

Just moments before she'd spoken, the vehicle's headlights had illuminated the legend on a motorway signpost. Straight on for Burgas on the coast, left for Ajtos, Varna, and . . . and an international symbol that couldn't be misinterpreted. It was a white airplane on a blue disk, its nose pointed to the sky.

And as Trask cut across the oncoming lane, he knew exactly what was happening here. Reading his mind, so did Millie.

"So, they're not going after a boat," she said then.

And Trask's voice rasped as he answered, "No, they're

definitely not! Twenty kilometres up this road there's an airport. That's where they're headed, and I don't think I need draw you any pictures. So fasten your safety belts, people, because I'm about to ask this beast for all she's got!"

With which he floored the accelerator and the motor howled, and the minibus leaped forward in response . . .

But Trask was asking too much of the battered old vehicle, and as the airport signs got thicker on the ground, and the lights of an air-control tower appeared just three or four kilometres up the road, so the minibus began to steam and shake, the engine clunked, and the power was gone. And they covered the last few kilometres at a limp—little better than walking pace—so that long before they reached the airport slip road, police cars from Burgas and Pomorie on the coast were already passing them, converging on the place with wailing sirens and strobing blue lights.

"It seems there's been some excitement," said Garvey nervously, from the back of the vehicle.

"I'll say there has," Trask answered him. "And I'm betting it was *bloody* exciting at that!" And:

"Eh? What?" Gustav Turchin came snorting awake. "My God, I was having this terrible dream . . ." But when Trask glanced back at him, he stiffened and fell silent.

And Garvey continued, "What do you reckon, Ben?"

"You're the telepath," said Trask, as he steered the minibus onto the slip road where she limped the last hundred yards or so to a dilapidated car park. "I'll give you one guess. No, don't guess, get over there where the action is and see if you can pick a mind or two."

Millie made to get out of the vehicle, saying, "I'd better go with him."

But putting a hand on her arm, Trask stopped her and said, "Not without a pair of dark glasses you won't."

And: "Oh!" said Millie.

In just a few minutes Garvey was back, breathless from running across the car park. "There's all hell going on in there," he said, when he'd got his breath back. "Three airport policemen are dead—torn to bits—and the pilot and copilot of a five-seater, privately owned VTOL Scimitar have been kidnapped and the plane stolen. It took off ten minutes ago and immediately vanished off the radar screens. It has to be flying way too low."

"In order to avoid detection," said Gustav Turchin, feeling a little more sure of himself now.

Trask turned to him. "I don't know if you were aleep in the back all this time or just faking it," he said, "but we believe the Wamphyri are heading for Perchorsk in the Urals in order to escape back into Starside. Is it at all possible we can contact your E-Branch, alert your air force, and have them intercept and bring these monsters down?"

"It's not *my* air force," Turchin answered. "And in any case, it's out of the question. I'll let you into a secret: in Moscow the flight controllers haven't been paid for months . . . the only reason they are still at their posts is that they'll be shot if they leave them! And that's Moscow. As for the rest of the airports—civilian and military alike—they've been getting paid in cans of pork-and-beans plundered from American relief aid to the breakaway so-called Dagestan Province! Electricity supplies are so bad that nine out of ten listening-station computers and radar posts are inoperative, and just six weeks ago a Hungarian youth landed his micro-jet in the middle of Red Square! So let's face it, if these monsters are heading for Perchorsk—"

"—We can't stop them," said Trask.

"Maybe not," said Jake, sitting up in the back of the vehicle, "but we *can* get there before them . . ."

26
Final preparations

EVERYONE GOT OUT OF THE MINIBUS, STRETCHED their legs, breathed the cool night air. The airport was a small one of its kind, and the weed-grown car park correspondingly tiny. Sooner or later—especially in the light of what had happened here—Trask's party was bound to be noticed. And the last thing they needed was a squad of suspicious Bulgarian policemen crawling all over them.

"How long will it take that plane to reach Perchorsk?" said Trask to no one in particular.

"It's maybe two thousand miles," said Turchin with a shrug. "Two and a half to three hours? I think that's about right. But where will they land?"

"It's a VTOL," Trask reminded him. "They can land any-damn-where they want to!"

"So then," said the Necroscope thoughtfully, as he massaged his stiff right leg, "we don't need to be there for at least an hour and a half, maybe two hours. Get there too soon, we could end up with Perchorsk's caretakers, that gang of ex-cons, up in arms. And by arms I do mean the kind you fire bullets with! And anyway, it's cold this time of year up there in the Urals."

"It's cold up there period," said Trask, who had been there. "And that's *any* time of year! So what's on your mind?"

"Liz is on my mind," said Jake. "Or she should be but isn't. Which tells me one of two things. She's either . . . either dead," he almost choked on the word, "or she's unconscious. If she was awake I'm sure she'd be talking to me by now and I'd be able to get a fix on her location."

"And of course you'd use the Continuum and go to her,

which might be the end of both of you," said Trask grimly. "But there is an alternative to death and even unconsciousness. She's with Vavara, Szwart, and Malinari; they could be masking her talent, interfering with her probes—which is something else you might want to consider: that they can use her as bait, and choose the best possible time to haul you into their net."

"I know that," said Jake, "and I'm pretty sure it's exactly what they want. Why else have they taken her with them? But I'd risk it anyway. And yes, I know the Möbius Continuum can get me in trouble. But it can just as quickly get me out again."

"Okay," said Trask, "and I know I won't be able to stop you if it happens. Only try to understand: Liz is on *my* mind, too—she's on all of our minds—but it won't help to keep brooding on it. So what's next?"

"You're asking me?" said Jake. "What, are my ears deceiving me? Ben Trask is asking *me* what next?"

"You're the Necroscope," Trask answered. "I can't possibly do the things you do, no one can. So I'm delegating my responsibilities, that's all."

"Fine," said Jake. "So let's think about it. First, I reckon we should listen to what Premier Turchin has to say. If only as a means of last resort, it has a lot going for it."

"Well, thank goodness someone thinks so!" said Turchin. And he quickly reiterated his plan to destroy the Perchorsk complex in a nuclear explosion.

"Including your enemies?" said Trask sourly.

"The whole world's enemies," said Turchin. "No less so than your . . . your vampires?" With which he backed off a pace, averting his eyes from Trask's, Millie's, and Jake's.

Jake nodded wryly, understandingly, and said, "Dark glasses, that's our first requirement. I know a place in Marseilles that sells them—and designer labels, at that."

"At this time of night?" said Garvey, without thinking.

"What's the time got to do with anything?" said Jake, as he took a pace forward and disappeared.

In a count of ten he was back, dumping a tray of sunglasses onto the front seat of the minibus. And, "Be my guest," he told Trask and Millie. "Take your pick. May as well look our best on what could be our last night. As for myself—since I appear to be just a little more luminous than you two—I think I'll have to go with these Ray Charles shades." He chose a pair with side panels.

Trask and Millie quickly chose suitable glasses, regardless of style, and surprisingly, so did Turchin. Then, when the rest of them looked at him wonderingly, enquiringly, he glanced from face to face and said, "Eh? What is it? I mean, don't you agree that I'm rather high-profile?"

At which point the Old Lidesci, who had been keeping watch, said, "So are we. And it looks like we've got company."

Three uniformed policemen were heading across the car park toward them, flashing their torches.

"All of you," Jake snapped. "Get round to the other side of the vehicle, and quickly."

When they were there he gathered Trask, Millie, and Turchin together and conjured a Möbius door. They clung to him—until he dumped them in the corridor of E-Branch HQ. Then he returned for the others and repeated the procedure.

And back in Bulgaria the three policemen looked at the minibus, then at the open field of scrub behind it, the slip road, and beyond that the motorway, and scratched their heads. No one was there, just the moon and the silver-gleaming emptiness, and a vehicle full of weapons and ammunition. But at least the minibus was a regular vehicle, not like that hearse they'd found on the other side of the airport, with its engine ticking over and its doors wide open like an invitation from the Grim Reaper!

It seemed a certainty that both vehicles had been the property of whichever terrorist group had hijacked the VTOL. But as for the terrorists themselves . . .

Within minutes of the team's return, the HQ was buzzing like a hornet's nest. Trask told the Duty Officer to keep everyone the hell away from his group, and took them to the Ops Room.

"Even here we're not safe," he told them, when the door had closed behind them. "Especially here. These people have various talents. It won't take them long to figure out what's wrong. Or what they consider to be wrong. So we need to move fast."

"We've lost most of our weapons," said Goodly.

And Trask nodded. "Use the intercom. Get on to John Grieve. Tell him what we need. But leave out the garlic bombs, okay? As for silver bullets . . . well, we can't do without them, so we'll just have to risk burning our fingers." Then he looked again—more closely—at the precog, Garvey, Turchin, and Lardis. And because of his dark glasses and the fact that Garvey was sticking to Branch protocols, they didn't know what he was thinking. And:

"Listen, you four," he said, taking a deep breath. "I want you to understand. You . . . you aren't necessary. I mean, you're excess to requirement. This time when we move out, I'm not asking for volunteers. And Lardis, my old friend, as for you, it's right out of the question. You'll stay here with Lissa. And all of the good people in E-Branch will look after you." And throwing up his hands, he finished off by barking, "Well, that's it! I've said what I wanted to say!"

And Paul Garvey, looking uncomfortable, answered, "But you will let us think about it, right?"

Trask's enigmatic dark glasses fixed themselves on the telepath, and for a moment there was silence. Then he said, "I'll tell you what to think about. Think about getting the Perchorsk schematics up on that big screen. I for one feel the need for a refresher. And Millie, you've never been there."

"You're letting me go, then?" Behind her glasses she raised her eyebrows.

"Do you want to?"

"Try and stop me!" she said.

"That's what I thought," said Trask. "And God knows we need you."

"You need all of us," said Ian Goodly. He had done speaking to John Grieve and the weapons were on their way. "And if I can get a word in edgewise here, aren't you forgetting something?"

"What, this 'we'll all be in it together at the end' shit?" said Trask.

"You can't argue with the future, Ben," said the precog.

And again for long moments Trask looked at his team, especially at Garvey. Until finally he said, "Okay, in the few hours we have left you can think about it. But for God's sake . . . for *God's* sake think straight! They're your lives, people—they're your lives . . ."

The Perchorsk schematics were now up on the screen. Looking at them, Trask shook a fist. "We'll be coming for you soon now, Nephran Malinari," he growled. "You're not there just yet, but when you do get there we'll be waiting."

Millie said nothing, but shielded herself and thought: *That old scar of yours, Ben? Still itching, is it? I understand. And anyway I refuse to be jealous of a dead woman. Zek Föener was a wonderful person. You're right to want revenge.*

But Trask hadn't stopped with Malinari, and continued, "And you, Vavara, you hag! I want you for Liz's sake. But especially *you*, Szwart! If everything else fails me, I've just *got* to have a crack at you!" Then, turning from the screen— and apparently unconscious of what he was doing—he glanced at Millie. Hiding her embarrassment and a smile she would not otherwise have been able to conceal, Millie's sunglasses saved her. And if only for the moment everything was all right.

Everything that mattered, anyway . . .

"Cold-weather gear!" Trask snapped his fingers. "Winter-warfare kit." And to Goodly, "Get on to the Minister Responsible. We'll be needing three sets of white parkas and trousers, our sizes."

"That will be seven sets, then," said the precog. "And yes, Ben, I really *do* have a great deal of faith in my talent. While it can be miserly in its details, rarely showing me everything, still I can rely on what it does tell me."

"Have it your own way," Trask answered, gruffly. "Just make sure that stuff's delivered within the hour." And then, nodding to himself, he muttered, "Which leaves one other item I want to take with me."

He used the intercom to speak to John Grieve. "John, are we in contact with David Chung?"

"Yes," came the answer. "I have his telephone number. He's in Glasgow, scheduled to be airborne again about an hour and a half from now. Chung and his ecological chums, they think they know where their quarry is."

"And we know where ours is going," Trask answered. "Try to get David on the blower for me, will you? Patch him through to me in Ops?"

"My pleasure," said Grieve. "And Ben . . . is there anything I can do for you? I mean, I really don't give a damn about the situation. I don't think any of us do. It looks like the world is going to hell anyway, quite apart from any other, er, local complications."

For a moment Trask was silent, then said, "Thanks, John. I want you—I want E-Branch—to know that we're on it. Everyone in here is on it. We can't say what problems we'll experience further down the line, but right now we're all on track."

"Hell, we know that!" said Grieve, his voice breaking up a little. And then, on afterthought: "Oh, and there is one other thing. Tell Turchin we had a message come through for him. The thing's a bit esoteric and goes like this: 'Nest ransacked, as expected. Egg in second nest hatched at five P.M. Moscow time, and by eight P.M. the birds had flown.' "

"And that's it?"

"That's it," said Grieve.

Trask passed the message on to Turchin, and by the time he was finished Grieve was patching David Chung through.

Trask took the call.

"It's a funny thing," said Chung, "but a little while ago I was checking out tonight's flight, looking at a map. I had

453

this feeling—a kind of premonition—and checked up on E-Branch, too. I stuck my finger on the map, London, the City. And like I said, it's a really funny thing . . . or maybe not?"

"Not," said Trask. "Not from where I'm standing, anyway. So what did you locate, David? Mindsmog?"

He sensed Chung's nod, and the locator said, "I don't suppose it's much good my asking if everything's okay down there? I mean, you know, with Jake and all?"

"Everything is . . . just fine," Trask answered, knowing full well that his tone was speaking volumes for him, telling a very different story. "With Jake, and with Millie, and with me, too. We're all just fine. For the time being, anyway . . ."

And after a long pause: "Anything I can do?" said Chung.

"Just do your job," said Trask, "and pretend it's the most important thing you ever did, even though it mightn't feel like it right now. I mean, when there's a storm blowing up, even the little hatches are important—perhaps even the most important. Every-damn-thing gets battened down, right? And anyway, we have all the help we can use at our end."

"I'll be thinking of you," said Chung huskily.

"I know you will," said Trask, "but while I appreciate your concern, it's not why I contacted you." And he told the locator what he wanted.

"Sure," said the other. "It's in my room right there in the HQ. You're welcome to it. And there's really no need to explain why you want it. Good luck, Ben."

Then Trask called John Grieve again, and had a certain item taken from Chung's room and delivered to Ops . . .

While these things were in progress, Premier Turchin spent time explaining something to Jake.

"I had fake documents 'leaked' to all three of the militarist animals who would like to unseat me," he said. "The letters hinted of a secret location—a source of untold wealth in gold—that General Mikhail Suvorov had discovered; also that Suvorov was there right now, busily amassing incredible riches while these former 'close colleagues' of his were barely surviving on cabbage soup and cheap vodka in Moscow.

"I knew, of course, that as soon as my defection, or rather my disappearance from the Earth Year summit, became public knowledge, then that my three enemies would begin hunting down this alleged El Dorado; and also that since this false information—this 'red herring,' you might say—had been leaked simultaneously to each of them, they'd be obliged to join forces on this wild-goose chase. Not one of them would dare let the others out of his sight, you see, so they'd all have to be in it together. *Hah!* The terms we use, eh? Red herrings, and wild geese? Still, I'm sure you understand.

"And where wild geese are concerned, it appears these three birds are now in flight. That message I received just now? Yes, you are correct. My apartments in Moscow have been subjected to a very thorough search. Nothing was found—because nothing was there! I didn't want to make it too easy for them, too obvious. Ah, but a man of mine in Zhukovka has been keeping an eye on my dacha there, and earlier today, about five P.M., that, too, was searched. This time they found what they were looking for."

"Your dacha at Zhukovka?" Jake frowned. "But didn't you say you'd hidden the bomb there?"

"Indeed." Turchin nodded. "And the bomb is *still* there, for if they had found it my man would certainly have reported that, too. But that's not what they were looking for! My leaked documents had mentioned all kinds of improbable things—El Dorado, yes, but also a modern scientific marvel, a means of converting base metals into gold, the philosopher's stone—hidden away in a secret laboratory somewhere in the Urals. The only thing that was missing was the location."

"Perchorsk," said Jake.

"Correct! And in a wall safe, hidden behind a picture in my dacha, was a set of schematics very similar to the ones you see up there on that wall screen. But why did I keep them secret in a safe in a dacha in Zhukovka, eh? Finally all the links in the chain that I had forged had come together, and these enemies of mine had suddenly remembered Suvorov's connection with the Perchorsk complex: the fact that he'd been responsible—or rather that he had *assumed* responsibility—for the cleanup operation when that place was finally shut down."

"And the birds have flown," said Jake. "At eight P.M. Moscow time, they left in an aircraft—"

"A military aircraft," said Turchin, "probably an air force jet-copter."

"—heading for Perchorsk," the Necroscope finished it off.

Turchin nodded. "Which means that by now they are there."

"Where they'll have come face-to-face with the hoodlums who run the place," said Jake.

"They will have *met* them, certainly," Turchin agreed. "They could hardly avoid it. But a confrontation? I think not. For my enemies are clever schemers no less than General Suvorov before them. Instead, they will join forces with Perchorsk's convicts, at least for the time being. But while they are greedy, dangerous men, these hawkish militarists, they're by no means stupid. When they see the Gate, they will doubtless recall that Mikhail Suvorov vanished a long time ago, and still has not reappeared. Gone to the alleged El Dorado? Well, perhaps. Gone to his grave? Ah! An equal possibility. So then, what to do?"

"You tell me," said Jake.

"But isn't that obvious?" Turchin replied. "They will send men who *are* stupid through that Gate, to discover what lies on the other side."

"They'll send the convicts themselves," said Jake. "All of them very heavily armed."

"Exactly," said Turchin. "And Nathan and his people in Sunside will have another battle on their hands, more Szgany blood spilled. But while the Wamphyri were monsters, as I've now seen for myself, they were *not* armed to the teeth, and they were *not* driven by the entirely human lust for gold. So then, surely you can see that my plan is the only way?

This way we can close the Gate forever, and at the same time rid the world of three ruthless militarists who—especially in the current circumstances—are an additional threat to peaceful coexistence, and therefore to the entire planet's security."

"*And,*" said Jake, "We'll also be blocking Malinari's, Vavara's, and Szwart's bolt-hole."

"That, too," Turchin answered. "And perhaps we'll even trap them, under a million tons of settling mountain . . . but only if we get there in time."

"But not too early," said the Necroscope. "Surely it would serve our purpose far better to let your 'ruthless militarists' and Perchorsk's ex-cons join forces and have a go at the Wamphyri together before we get there? Maybe we could arrive in the middle of the fighting, stand off and watch the fireworks, and step in at the last minute when there's less to be done."

"Excellent!" Turchin clapped his hands. "But how very logical! You have a sharp mind, Jake Cutter."

"I have a very *clear* mind, for once," said Jake, narrowing his eyes behind his sunglasses. "The cold, devious, and calculating mind of a vampire, eh?"

"Ah yes," said Turchin, but far more quietly now.

"And that's something I must watch very closely," said the Necroscope. *I can't afford to let the cold overcome what's left of the warmth in me. So I suppose I'll have decisions to make—choices, of which this is the first—about lesser and greater evils.*

He turned to Ben Trask who was studying the schematics, and said, "I think you'd better let me go and get Premier Turchin's bomb, if only to have it in reserve as a last resort."

Trask looked at him. "I've come to the same conclusion," he said. "But I was listening to your conversation, and I can only hope it's me thinking and speaking." And:

"I know what you mean," said Jake . . .

In Zhukovka the night was chilly and overcast.

Jake and Turchin had emerged from the Möbius Continuum some hundred yards from the latter's dacha on a wooded track. It was the same place—the selfsame coordinates—that the original Necroscope, Harry Keogh, had used all those many years ago when he'd come here to visit the murdered Gregor Borowitz, then head of the Soviet Union's E-Branch.

And now . . . Jake "remembered" it well.

"You are very cautious," Turchin whispered as he recognized the location from his own frequent visits.

"So was Harry Keogh," Jake answered, "when he came here."

"That's all very well," said Turchin, "but we'll risk being seen, out walking in this wood in the dead of night. You should have brought us a little closer than this."

"No," said Jake, shaking his head. "We're close enough for now." And then, putting a finger to his lips: "Keep very still, and very quiet."

Removing his dark glasses he lifted his head and sniffed at the air, and his eyes were feral, wolfish in the night. Then he looked all about, at the leaden sky, the silhouetted trees, the gravel path winding away, lapped at by the ground mist. And finally—as once again Jake drew on the night air, and held it in his nostrils—so his head turned in the direction of Turchin's dacha.

"Well?" said the Russian Premier, very quietly.

"A cigarette," Jake whispered. "He rolls his own, this one. He uses inferior tobacco, and he smokes them down to the tip."

"He?"

"Whoever he is, on guard outside your dacha."

"Damn!" said Turchin. "I hadn't anticipated this."

"That the authorities would be on the lookout for you?"

"*Bah!* This has nothing to do with any authorities!" Turchin replied. "Something I perhaps didn't mention: that I made provision for my cabinet to be informed that I'm not a defector but merely spending time in England where I'm avoiding the possible consequences of a death threat. Meanwhile, special forces under my control are tracking down the would-be assassins here in Russia. Therefore, since this information was restricted to senior cabinet members, whoever is waiting for me cannot possibly know it else he would not be waiting! Ergo: he is not of the authorities but obviously an underling or hireling of the three."

"This is something new," said Jake. "Does Trask know you're covering your backside like this, playing both ends against the middle?"

"It's . . . *possible* I forgot to mention it." Turchin shrugged. "But Trask is Trask; he would have known I wasn't telling all of the truth. Anyway, what has any of that to do with what we're doing here?"

"And of course the entire assassin story is so much bull?"

"Yes. *Yes,* it's bull!" said Turchin. "I'm not under threat except by these three who are on their way to Perchorsk— and we are wasting time!"

Jake nodded and said, "Okay, but you *are* the Russian Premier, after all. And this fellow at the dacha . . . can't you talk him down?"

"He isn't here to be talked down," Turchin answered. "He's here to ensure that if I send someone to retrieve those schematics—that if *anyone* goes near that dacha—he won't survive to talk about it!"

"Russian politics?" said Jake.

"Yes—no—perhaps," the other replied. "And sarcasm is the lowest form of wit!"

"And Ben Trask knows what he's talking about when he calls you a fox," said the Necroscope. "But you're right, we're wasting time. So wait here, and only come when I whistle."

Leaving the path, he moved silently into the shadows under the trees, gradually disappearing into the darkness there. And before Turchin could even begin to work up an anxious sweat . . . Jake's whistle sounded!

The Premier hurried along the familiar track, slowing down a little when he saw saw the dacha looming in the trees. There in the shadows under projecting eaves, the Necroscope was waiting for him. And at Jake's feet, crumpled to the boards of the porch, a figure in an overcoat lay partly obscured by swirling tendrils of mist. His cigarette, a mere stub, was glowing fitfully where it had rolled away from him.

Turchin looked at Jake—his gleaming eyes, his thin lips smiling in a certain way—and drew back a pace.

But Jake only shook his head. "No," he said. "No puncture, Gustav, just a punch. But I reckon he'd passed out even before I hit him, maybe half a second after I appeared out of nowhere right beside him! Now then, where's the bomb?"

"Behind the dacha," Turchin answered, "in a ramshackle old woodshed built into the hillside, a bolt-hole that Borowitz had dug for himself a long time ago. I discovered it in the winter a few years back, after letting the pile of wood get very low. I went to lift a log and it wouldn't come. Then, when I tugged harder . . . but you'll see for yourself."

They went round the dacha to the back, where Jake saw that indeed the woodshed was a ramshackle affair. There was no lock on the door, and it creaked on rusted hinges when Turchin dragged it open. Inside, at the back, an untidy pile of handy-sized logs was covered with moss and toadstools.

"You left a nuclear device in here?" said Jake.

And Turchin nodded. "Even if anyone knew I possessed such a thing, this is the last place he'd think to look," he answered. "There is nothing here to attract the attention of thieves, and even the lowliest tramp wouldn't sleep here."

"So where's the bomb?" said Jake.

"Help me," Turchin answered, "and you'll see . . . oh, and by the way, there are two bodies back here."

"Bodies?"

"The Chechens who helped me carry the thing," said Turchin, unconcernedly. "In the end they, er, attempted to overpower me. Yes. Which left me no choice but to shoot them."

Taking a deep breath, the Necroscope said, "Now tell me, is there anything else you've forgotten to mention?"

"No." Turchin shook his head. "I don't think so. I covered

them with lime, and the last time I looked in here there wasn't much of a smell."

Jake helped him shift the upper layers of logs to one side, to about halfway down the stack. The three bottom layers, however, were all bolted together.

"And now pivot," said Turchin, dragging the false wood-pile away from the sloping earthen wall at the rear. The entire façade pivoted on the left, revealing roughly concreted steps that descended into the ground.

Below, the walls were of stone under a low ceiling propped up with timbers. The floor was a crazy-paved mixture of broken garden slabs and gravel. Central, on a trolley, stood the bomb—a cylinder of shining metal some two and a half feet long by twelve inches in diameter—connected to a timing device with windows showing hours, minutes, and seconds.

And in one corner of the dugout . . . Jake saw a white-limed area of floor, where two humped human figures lay still, stiff, and obviously very dead.

While Turchin went to the bomb and wiped moisture from its casing with his handkerchief, Jake stepped into the corner and shifted lime about with the toe of his shoe. For all his enhanced sense of smell, the resultant odour wasn't too potent. But it was, of course, the stench of death . . .

"When you're quite finished over there," said Turchin, "all that remains for us to do is to wheel this thing into your Möbius Continuum, and transport it back to E-Branch HQ."

And Jake, speaking almost to himself, as if he hadn't heard what Turchin had said, muttered, "And here's a man who talks so eloquently of ruthless opponents."

"Eh? What?"

The Necroscope looked at him, his eyes burning. "I was just wondering how men who were attacking you got shot in the back," he said.

"Does it matter?" Turchin looked surprised. "I mean, aren't you forgetting something? These men were from that same suicide squad whose leaders planned to reduce Moscow to so much rubble! If they had succeeded they would have died in the blast. And if they had failed they would have been shot anyway. So what's the difference?"

"When all of this is over," said Jake, "we can no longer be friends."

"Really?" said Turchin. "Well, the way I see it—when and *if ever* this is all over—we'll each and every one of us need all the friends we can get!"

Jake thought about that and said, "I'll take the bomb while you go back out, close the door and pile the logs. You wouldn't want anyone else to come in here, now would you?"

Turchin narrowed his eyes, for several long moments remaining silent before answering, "Very well. But don't make me wait too long."

Jake said, "No, of course not."

But back at E-Branch HQ, he took his time drinking a mug of hot black coffee, leaving Turchin on his own at the woodshed in Zhukovka for a full twenty minutes before going back for him . . .

The winter-warfare kit was delivered, with black leggings to go under the white trousers. This last had been Trask's idea based on what the precog had told him: that their last stand would be made in a dark place. For Trask knew that while outside the Perchorsk complex—in the deep Urals ravine that housed it—it would be white with snow from the sky, or frozen spray from the dam, inside was a place of shadows, of gloom, and frequently of Stygian darkness. White clothing would make good camouflage for the ravine, but it wouldn't work inside the complex itself.

As the team examined and prepared their weapons, dressed in their assault gear, said various farewells over the telephones, intercom, and Internet, so the Duty Officer John Grieve came to the Ops Room door and asked to speak to Trask.

"What is it, John?" Trask asked him at the door.

Grieve barely glanced at Trask's sunglasses, before answering, "David Chung was on the blower again. He asked if we could fax him some recognition diagrams, photographs, schematics of a Russian MIKE-class sub. He believes that's what they're chasing and needs to take this stuff with him. They'll be taking off in just over half an hour's time. I have a disk with the information he requires, but I'll have to use the big screen to be sure I get a printout of the right stuff. Or, if you'd prefer not to have me in there, you can perhaps do it for me?"

"No, I can't," Trask answered. "We're pretty busy. So you'd better come in and do it yourself."

"You're sure the others won't mind?" Grieve was very diplomatic about it, or perhaps he was simply being cautious.

"We're a bit of a mix in here, John," Trask told him. "Nothing seems to have changed . . . not yet, anyway. No one will mind as long as you don't."

With which Grieve entered and went to the big wall screen's console. The screen was no longer in use; the Perchorsk schematics had been studied as best possible in the time allowed, and in a few moments more the screen was displaying a concise history of late twentieth-century Soviet submarine technology.

Grieve began printing out the photographs and other details that Chung needed, and as the various frames were displayed, so they attracted Ian Goodly's attention. Frowning, and very obviously perplexed, he moved closer, stared hard at the screen for a long moment . . . then staggered!

Having seen what had happened, Trask went to Goodly, steadied him, and asked, "What is it now, Ian? What did you see this time?"

The precog took a moment or so to compose himself and think about it before answering. Then he said, "Cast your mind back a few weeks, to a day or so before we went after Vavara on Krassos. We were in your office, you, me, and David Chung. The usual ritual: you asked me if I'd foreseen anything."

"Refresh my memory," said Trask.

"I had been having a string of glimpses, flashes, daydreams—call them what you will," said Goodly. "At the time they were more or less meaningless. They didn't relate to anything."

"Because they were scenes from the future," Trask answered. "Yes, now I remember. You mentioned black-robed figures, drifting or floating: Vavara's nuns, as it turned out, their flowing gait. And you spoke of a warren of burrows like giant wormholes in the earth, all filled with loathsomeness, like 'morbid mucus in a cosmic sinus.' I remember *that* well enough! And I know now what it meant: that place under Palataki."

"Yes," said the precog. "That's right. But as I recall it I saw something else, something that *really* didn't seem to relate to anything at all. And just a moment ago, looking at this wall screen—these schematics, pictures, diagrams of a Russian submarine—suddenly I saw it again."

And again Trask remembered, and was able to repeat Goodly's precise words from that earlier time: "You saw 'something sinking, deeper and deeper into groaning abysses of water.'"

Jake had come to stand with them, joining Grieve, Trask, and Goodly where they stared up at the schematics. And now he said, "You were seeing this boat that Chung is looking for going down into the sea. But you're a precog. Isn't it to be expected that you'll envisage things like that, in connection with what we're doing?"

"But that's just it," said Goodly. "I mean, this isn't what 'we' are going to be doing. None of us will be involved with it in any way. It's Chung's thing, not ours. Which makes it rather unusual. My visions usually relate to me and the people immediately surrounding me. It's our future, after all. Mine and whoever happens to be there to share it with me. On this occasion, however, Chung won't be there. And we can't be at Perchorsk and with him at the same time."

At which the Necroscope remembered something, went to where his discarded clothes were piled on a chair, and took the fragment of hairbrush that Chung had given him—Harry Keogh's hairbrush—from his inside jacket pocket. The thing was quiescent now, just a shard of broken wood and a few pig bristles, but he would keep it with him anyway if only as a good-luck piece. And then he returned to the others where they were still looking at the big screen.

Millie Cleary had joined them, and so had Gustav Turchin.

"All long out of date," the latter wasn't overly impressed with what was on the screen.

"It is now," Millie told him, "but it was pretty new stuff some fifteen years ago. This is a MIKE-class vessel, twin nuclear reactors using liquid lead coolant."

"Oh?" The Premier looked at her curiously, and said, "Tell me, my dear, in addition to being a powerful telepath, are you also an expert on submarines?"

"Millie is expert in a good many subjects," Trask told him. "She's a walking current affairs manual. And like she says, all of this stuff *was* current affairs, certainly to the British and US secret services some fifteen to twenty years ago."

Now Turchin was impressed. "A secondary talent?"

"No," Trask answered. "Millie is a very quick study, that's all, and she has a head for details."

"Er, such as?" Now Turchin spoke directly to Millie. It was like a challenge.

"The liquid-metal coolant system was first used in the ALFA-class attack subs," she answered. "But it was very dangerous. I mean—without wanting to be impolite—those nuclear submariners of yours paid for that coolant in a lack of lead shielding. In fact most of those Soviet subs were noisy, dirty, and lethal to the poor men who went to sea in them. The first of the MIKEs is a case in point. She's almost a mile deep southwest of Bear Island, where she's lain for the last twenty-odd years."

"Do you recall her name?" said Turchin.

"The *Komsomolets*," Millie told him. "She went down due to a fire in her aft compartments . . . the propulsion system." And:

"Best not to try testing her, Gustav," Trask grinned at his

astonished guest (grinned wolfishly, Turchin thought), "or just like that sub you'll find yourself well out of your depth . . ."

John Grieve had got what he wanted, and knowing it was very nearly time for the team to be leaving, he shook hands all round and left.

Minutes later, looking at his watch, Turchin said, "By now my enemies are well established in Perchorsk, while yours— or rather, the world's—will soon be landing there. Isn't it time we were on our way?"

Trask agreed, saying, "Anyone who wants out, now's the time to speak up."

But no one did, and Ian Goodly said, "See what I mean?"

And yes, they all knew what he meant: that the future would not be denied . . .

27
Perchorsk

IN PLAN, VIEWED OR PHOTOGRAPHED FROM space— which it had been, often, in a perilous earlier time—the Perchorsk ravine was a darkly enigmatic gash in the tortured landscape. Lying parallel with the mountains north to south, in a huge fold in the Northern Urals, the ravine was flanked by close-packed, white-capped peaks reminiscent of the shattered, fossilized spinal plates of some primal stegosaurus.

The bottom of the ravine had been a watercourse subject to severe seasonal flooding, but some thirty years ago it had been dammed to provide hydroelectric power for the disastrous Perchorsk Projekt. Upriver, the man-made lake was full, its surface leaden in starlight. But the moon was up and climbing, and soon the lake would gleam silver. Three-quarters of the waters stood open to the night, the rest lay hidden under a vast platform of reinforced concrete. During the Projekt's early days this domed canopy had supported a roof of massive lead, protection against radiation reflecting back from the sky; but since the Projekt's failure, and in the interests of the faltering Russian economy, the valuable lead had since been stripped and transported away for use elsewhere.

While the lake appeared calm on its surface, underneath it was a raging torrent. Channelled under the roof through sluice gates, the water reappeared in four shining spouts that issued from conduits in the dam wall. Flung spume, rising up from the deluge, froze, fell, or drifted back, coating the ravine's bed in feathery snow and decking its walls in curtains of glittering ice. With the bulk of its contents restrained, only a much reduced stream now followed the ancient course downriver.

On top of the dam wall, four blockhouses stood guard, each housing the controls of its respective turbine. Three of these squat sentinels stood silent and unmanned, their turbines long since fallen into disrepair. Only the fourth—the one closest to the complex—was still working, and then only very inefficiently, feeding a sporadic stream of electrical power to the complex.

Some sixty or seventy feet back from the dam wall, a dully glinting army jet-copter stood waiting on the faded yellow X of a helipad landing zone, its black-, grey- and green-mottled camouflaged shape like that of some alien dragonfly perched on the concrete canopy. The cold unblinking eyes of cabin windows stared out over the dam wall towards the yellow glow from huge steel doors in the wall of the ravine: the entrance to the complex. Behind the plane's black windows, the pilot and copilot had their orders. They had been sitting there for close on two hours now, and would continue to do so for two more if necessary, before issuing their first threats over the plane's loud-hailer.

The armour-piercing 15 mm cannons in the jet-copter's nose were also trained on Perchorsk's doors, but independent of the air mobility of the chopper, they could very quickly switch to the blockhouse. At what amounted to point-blank range, weapons like this could reduce the structure to so much smoking rubble in seconds. In which event the energy that powered the complex would be gone along with the blockhouse.

Armed night patrolmen, keeping watch from a road dynamited out of the solid rock of the mountain—the ramp that serviced the complex—shivered uncomfortably in their parkas and kept moving, making sure they weren't in the line of fire and staying well back from the light that came flooding from the half-open doors.

Inside those doors in a cavernous service bay, Perchorsk's "bosses" and their VIP visitors from Moscow sat around a blazing brazier locked in conversation, or rather in negotiations.

The three VIPs, though dissimilar in appearance, were very much of a sort in their ambitions. The only difference lay in how they would use their wealth-based power, if or when such power became available. Communist hard-liners in their time, and still hard in their hearts, they had seen their political ideologies and aspirations whittled away, Russia's status as a world leader diminished, and her armed might depleted to the point of decimation. They wanted these things back and power returned to them. And if that wasn't possible then the next best thing must suffice: personal wealth beyond all dreams of avarice. In which case let Mother Russia go to hell, for they would be out of it.

The speaker for the three was ex-General Nikolai Korolev, a big-boned, square-headed bear of a man in polished boots, a fur hat (which he persisted in wearing embellished with four stars, the insignia of his ex-rank), and a fur-lined leather overcoat. Holding his hands out to the brazier, and rubbing them briskly, he said, "So then, comrades Galich, Borisov, and Kreisky—good fellows all—allow me to thank you on behalf of my colleagues for the grand tour you have afforded us. What's more, I commend your patience in waiting out these three long years in so desolate, so isolated a place as Perchorsk. I'm sure that your, er, benefactor, my old friend General Suvorov, will be most appreciative ... that is, of course, if ever he returns."

"Oh, really?" a man called Karl Galich, seated on the other side of the blaze, replied in a voice like the purring of a big cat. "You doubt that he'll return? But why wouldn't he? He made us several promises and kept at least one—the most important of all, to set us free—else we wouldn't be here in Perchorsk now. So why should he renege on the others? It seems to me that explanations are in order: for instance, why the delay? Why has it taken *you* so long to begin looking for him, especially since the General was such a 'very good friend' of yours?"

Galich was a tall, slender, handsome man, very effeminate in his looks and sensuous movements ... but he was also a psychopath, a serial-killer axeman, who but for Suvorov's intervention would still be serving out his triple life sentence in the Ukhta penal colony.

"Patience, Karl, patience!" Korolev held up a hand. "Unwise to go rushing at things, and jumping to wrong conclusions. Yes, Mikhail is—or perhaps was—our mutual friend, and he left a trail of clues for us to follow in the event of any unfortunate accident, or even more unfortunate demise. Finally, we have put it all together and tracked him down; we now know where Mikhail went, if not why he's still there. Now you must allow us a moment or two to think things through. For after all, you've given the General three whole years! As to why he hasn't yet returned—and probably never will—we'll reach a mutually satisfactory conclusion, certainly. In view of your loyalty, your dedication to this dear old comrade, you may not *like* that conclusion, but we'll get there in the end nevertheless. And then we'll come to a decision on what to do for the best. Only rest assured, Karl, we shall honour the General's promises down to the last rouble or very last ounce of alien gold, whichever."

But as he quit rubbing his hands, sat back and appeared to engage in quiet contemplation, in fact Korolev's thoughts were elsewhere; he was reflecting on everything that he and his colleagues had seen during the course of their guided tour of the Perchorsk complex. Especially he considered the heavy rings of crudely hammered gold plainly visible, gleaming on the fingers of this cutthroat trio—Galich, Borisov, and Kreisky—self-appointed leaders of the ex-convict factions now in control of the three-dimensional labyrinth that was the Perchorsk complex. And "complex" was the right word for it, indeed the only word . . .

Korolev's coconspirators were Igor Gurevich—a physicist-cum-senior officer in the almost destitute Russian air force; a man who believed that the ill-fated Perchorsk Projekt should be resurrected as a shield against American air superiority—and Admiral Maxim Aliyev, a sailor from the cold-war school of Soviet heroes, who for his pains had been given responsibility for the "safe" decontamination and disposal of an era's once-mighty nuclear fleet. But Aliyev's mad answer to *that* specific problem was the reason why David Chung was currently out over the North Atlantic Ocean, his mind focussed on probing for massive radiation leaks.

Both of these men—who, along with Korolev, made up Premier Gustav Turchin's trio of military opponents—were in their early sixties. Gurevich was small, sharp-featured, ratlike, and swift in his movements; Aliyev was fat, bowlegged, bearded, and slow-moving, and when he walked had a sailor's swaying gait.

And right now both men, in parallel with their burly, often bullying industrialist colleague Nikolai Korolev, were thinking back on what they'd seen here . . .

The complex: roughly spherical, like a giant bubble scooped out of the bedrock, with its many levels, zones, and sectors—areas both safe and unsafe—some physically dangerous, by reason of residual radioactivity, others made fearful and *mentally* destabilizing, by virtue of sights best left unseen. Korolev and his party had "inspected" once-immaculate barrack rooms . . . pigsties now for the convict scum who inhabited them; they had visited a laboratory, once equipped with the apparatus of modern science, where nothing of value remained except some abandoned junk that Perchorsk's current crew had cobbled together into a still producing lethal potato vodka. They had seen various demarcations, signs and sigils like so much graffiti painted on the perimeter corridor walls and bulkhead hatches, offering stark warnings of passage from one "boss"-controlled zone to the next. The inhabitants of Perchorsk had separated themselves into factions, not always as mutually cooperative as now.

And of course Korolev and his colleagues had been shown the grotesque, the nightmarish magmass levels and, far more importantly, the core, the shining sphere Gate itself.

Down there in the core—where thirty years ago the world's worst yet most secret accident had occurred when an atomic pile imploded, ate itself, and created the Gate—they had also seen the stinking remains of a burned and bullet-ridden creature not of this world. Its leather and wooden saddle, reduced to little more than charcoal now, had clearly defined this thing's function as a mount . . . but for what strange species of rider? For if he was half as fierce as his beast . . .

Twice the size of a horse, but unlike any horse or beast of burden ever seen before, there was something about that cadaver where it lay on the steel, fish-scale disk surrounding the Gate—something other than its obviously alien origins—that Korolev's party found deeply disturbing. For paradoxically, *despite* its otherness, there was that about the thing's limbs, its eye sockets and entire skull, that hinted of freakish mutations and even of some unthinkable human lineage . . . which only served to make even more anomalous the creature's incredible jaws, teeth, and acromegalic paws equipped with claws like chisels.

And yet this thing from the Gate—a mere fighting brute, a mindless warrior—had worn a golden bit in its mouth, a golden plate with a spike to protect its skull, golden chains and attachments on its saddle, and a ring of gold weighing half a kilo in its armoured nose . . .

*   *   *

Sitting around the brazier, it was the ratlike physicist Igor Gurevich who, unable to suppress a shudder, blinked first. Yuri Borisov, a squat bulldog of a man seated on Aliyev's left, noticing Gurevich's discomfort, pointed at him and said, "*Hah!* But you have been two shades lighter ever since you saw that thing, eh, comrade? Think nothing of it, for you're not alone. Myself, I no longer venture anywhere near the core, for I've seen more than enough of that thing. What? It gave me nightmares! It was three-quarters dead when it burst through, but the sight of it set men screaming like women before they managed to kill it. I was one of them, and I'm not afraid to admit it. Most of those holes in its mangy skull were put there by me!"

"What, do you read minds?" Gurevich grimaced.

"No," Borisov grinned, "just expressions. I could see that thing reflected in your eyes. A creature like that, it makes a nonsense of your physics, your science, eh?"

And Korolev said, "Is that the reason why you haven't gone through? For fear of monsters like that waiting for you on the other side?" He spoke directly across the brazier to Galich.

"It could be one of the reasons." Galich's purr was more a growl now. Stung by what he considered an accusal of cowardice, a slur, he narrowed his eyes. "On the other hand, we are loyal in our way to the General. He told us to stay here and wait on his return. Myself, Borisov, and Kreisky, we've since agreed to do just that. And anyway, why should we spoil a good thing? We have a limitless supply of vouchers that we exchange for whatever we want at the penal garrison in Beresov, and compared to life in a gulag Perchorsk is a holiday camp."

"No offence," (now Aliyev spoke up) "but it's clear to me your waiting is in vain. And loyalty be damned—at this rate you could spend your whole lives here! But that alien gold you wear: can you imagine what you could do with a ton of it?"

"Oh, we have imagined," Sol Kreisky, a pockmarked, bearded giant of man—and a mass murderer of women—

answered. "And we've long since decided on the split. All that remains for us to do is figure out a way to bring it out!"

"Ah!" said Gurevich. "There is after all a problem, then?" He nodded knowingly, and went on, "I thought that might be the case. This portal is in my line of work, you see; its properties are fascinating to a scientist such as myself. When we were down there in the core, I noticed how you men stayed well back from the Gate and asked myself why. I'm still waiting for an answer. But I remember the Perchorsk accident; it was all hush-hush, and I could get no sensible answers to my questions then, either. There were various fantastic rumours, however, about a Gate with properties like those of a black hole, which once it has drawn you in permits of no return."

"There you have it," said Galich. "Yet another good reason why we haven't followed Mikhail Suvorov through the Gate."

"But not good enough," said Korolev, taking command of the conversation again. And Igor Gurevich felt the industrialist's elbow in his ribs, warning him to shut up for the time being.

"Not good enough?" said Galich. "Again you hint of cowardice. Perhaps *you* would undertake to lead us through this Gate, eh, 'comrade'?"

"And again you have misinterpreted my comments," Korolev tut-tutted. "I make no accusation of cowardice; indeed, everything you've told us so far makes perfect sense. But insomuch as you lack a scientist's understanding of the problem, your approach is wrong. You see only the action and never the *re*action—or vice versa, whichever." He shrugged dismissively.

"Oh?" said Galich. "And are you a scientist, too? Both you and this . . . this 'physicist' here? One glance at the Gate and you've figured it all out? Is that it?"

Korolev sighed, shook his head, said, "No, my knowledge of science isn't the equal of Igor Gurevich's. But then again, we don't share the same field of expertise. You see, where Igor's science is theoretical, mine is practical. I am an industrialist, and as such far better at mechanics than physics."

"Mechanics?"

"It's the science of the action of forces on bodies," Korolev explained. "Kinetics, statics, and mechanical interactions. Er, are you any the wiser?"

"Please go on," Galich purred, beginning to frown a little. "By all means enlighten me."

"First tell me," said Korolev, "is it a fact that once you enter that sphere you have to go on?"

Galich nodded. "First the General and his expedition, they experienced this problem. They thought it might be a temporary effect and proceeded anyway. But then, they had no choice. And eventually three of ours followed them—well, in fact we made them go through. There *is* honour, you see, even among thieves, and we had caught them stealing. So, they had a choice: go and see what Suvorov was doing—see if they could help him in any way—or refuse and die. We were testing the General's theory that this was a temporary thing. But . . . it wasn't."

And now Gurevich came in again, with: "And yet that creature had no trouble at all when it came through from the other side." (And again Korolev dug him in the ribs.)

"I know," said Galich, still frowning. "I have no explanation."

"But I have!" said Korolev. "The portal acts like a seesaw, or better still, a piston! Once up there is only one way to go, and that's down again."

"I still don't understand," Galich shook his head.

"Do you know how a slingshot works?" said Korolev.

"Of course!"

"Well, this is the same thing. Just as you can fire a stone from *both* sides of the catapult, so you can use the Gate. It's simply a matter of which way you stretch the elastic. And like a piston, you can't return until you've first gone all the way forward."

Galich was on his feet now. Excited, he was finally beginning to "understand" . . . and simultaneously falling for Nikolai Korolev's clever "explanation," his lie. "In order to return," he said, "first we must go right through to the other side? Is that what you're saying?"

"Exactly!" said Korolev.

And Gurevich, seeing the lie of the land, said, "Of course! You are precisely right, Nikolai! The Gate is a two-way shunt!"

But Galich had sat down again. And staring hard at the visitors through the brazier's flames, he said, "Then tell me, why hasn't Suvorov returned? And likewise the thieves we sent after him?"

"Which brings us back to that unfortunate conclusion," said Korolev, "but one which we must surely draw. Listen, and please try not to be offended. I understand your loyalty to the man—your loyalty to *any* man—who would set you free. But can't you see how he needed you? He *needed* you, yes, to guard this place, while he established his rights and amassed his fortune on the other side."

And as once again Galich—and also Borisov, and Kreisky—began to come to their feet:

"Now *listen!*" Korolev quickly went on. "Gold is gold, yes, but it's only one kind of wealth. I have known Mikhail Suvorov for a long, long time and I know him well. I cannot imagine he would stay long in an inhospitable world without meat and good strong booze—and certainly not without lusty, willing women! Is it any wonder that he and his party are still there? Not at all. They are taking that place for all it's worth! And do you really think there'll be room there for you?"

"But—" said Galich, his voice a growl now.

"—*But,* isn't it perfectly obvious what happened when Suvorov went through?" said Korolev, also risen to his feet. "Him and his men, his soldiers—his own heavily armed, elite special forces—they wiped out the local inhabitants on the other side, *that* is what happened! And as for that dead monster down there in the core: fatally wounded in the fighting, it escaped into the Gate and found its way here. And by now . . . by now my good friend General Mikhail Suvorov rules in a rich, beautiful parallel world that he will make his own . . . before he returns to take this one!"

"*If* he can return," Galich snarled. "You see, I've not yet accepted your theory. You're pushing it too hard."

Now, tired of this circular argument, Korolev felt obliged to play his ace card. "Then accept this," he snapped. "There's something else you haven't thought through—another possible reason why it's taking Suvorov so long to come home."

"Oh?"

This time when Korolev jabbed Gurevich, the physicist knew just exactly what to say. It had been on the tip of his tongue ever since they got here. "Mikhail Suvorov's expedition wasn't an *entirely* military operation, you know," he said. "He didn't only take soldiers with him, but some very capable scientists, too. For all we know they could be working to create a Gate of their own! And if they do . . . what price then for your loyalty and your allegiances, eh?"

Galich sat down yet again, but very heavily. "I don't want to believe it," he said after a while. "And yet—"

"And yet you *must!*" Korolev told him. "And you most surely will, when you and your men—under command of officers loyal to us—go through and take it all back again. Only this time there shall be fair shares for all. Of gold, yes, and whatever else this alien world has to offer. Now, what do you say about that?"

"I say," Galich snarled, springing up, and reaching inside his leather jacket—and Borisov and Kreisky flanking him, duplicating his actions—"I say I've had enough of military and ex-military bastards trying to make fools and dupes of us! And if this alien world is all you say it is, then what do we need you for?"

The three had guns in their hands, and likewise their men, who came surging forward out of the vast service bay's shadowy areas. But if they were armed, so were their VIP visitors. And cold metal glinted in the red firelight.

At which point there came a disturbance, shouting from outside the great doors . . .

*   *   *

Transported by Jake in two parties, Ben Trask and the E-Branch team had arrived just a minute or so earlier. On a broad ledge under an overhang on the far side of the ravine, they crouched behind drifted snow and observed the entrance to the complex.

Now Trask spoke quietly to Jake. "How come you're familiar with this ledge? I mean, these coordinates?"

"I remember them," Jake answered matter-of-factly. "Harry Keogh was here once. In fact he was all over the place. Inside that complex, it's like a maze with many levels."

"I know," said Trask. "Me and Goodly, we've been in there, too. We probably won't 'remember' it as well as you, though."

Turchin touched Trask's parka-clad arm. "You see that jet-copter? My enemies are here. Our timing couldn't be better."

"You can say that again," said Trask, "because I think *our* enemies are here, too. Or they're about to be. Listen . . ."

A moment later and they all heard it: the faint throb of a small VTOL aircraft's engines; a throbbing at first, but as it grew louder a sudden change—an obviously irregular sound—the sporadic sputtering and juddering of failing engines. And:

"Look!" Millie gasped, craning her neck and staring at the wide strip of moonlit sky, where a delta-shaped silhouette was descending on spasmodic bursts of fire.

"She isn't going to make it," said Trask. "That plane's out of fuel. Malinari and his bloody friends have pushed it all the way, pushed it to the limit—and beyond!"

"And Liz is on board!" Jake breathed. "I can make a jump."

"Can you?" Trask grabbed his arm. "Can you? Look at the way she's falling, steadying up, then falling again. There's no way you can judge it. What if your coordinates are wrong? You could end up underneath her, frying in her jets!"

"Frying or flying—*fuck* it!—I have to try," said Jake, conjuring a Möbius door.

But at the last moment Goodly stopped him. "It's all right, Jake," the precog said. "It's all right! We'll all be there at the end, remember? And that includes Liz."

"She's steadied up," Millie gasped, her hand to her mouth. "Look, she's going to land close to the jet-copter."

The VTOL Scimitar was down to their level now, maybe fifty feet above the gently domed, reinforced-concrete canopy behind the dam wall. But her vertical thrusters were sputtering again, and just when it seemed she was actually going to make it, two of them cut out entirely.

The plane yawed wildly, port wing and tail tilting, striking the concrete canopy and tearing free. If there had been any fuel left in the tanks, that would have been the end of it. But the fuel was gone, used up, and with its passenger cabin incredibly intact, the Scimitar crashed the last twelve or so feet to the deck. As she hit, torn metal screamed and bits of tailplane and crumpled wing went flying. Then she shivered and lay still, the lights in her cabin went out, and a mess of white foam came flooding from her ruptured belly, a standard protection against fire.

On the other side of the ravine, men in parkas were hauling on the service bay's huge doors, dragging them open. While from the cavern itself shouted orders came echoing, as running, gesturing figures spilled out, casting eerie shadows in the slowly widening arc of yellow light.

In a matter of seconds more than a dozen armed men were out onto the ramp, while in the bay an engine coughed into life and a tracked snowplough came rumbling into view.

With binoculars to his eyes, Turchin said, "Those three men standing together, the ones who aren't doing anything. They are the ones I want dead! If you think the Earth is threatened now, you can't imagine how much worse it will be if they should survive this."

Trask said nothing but took the glasses from him and looked where he had indicated . . .

*   *   *

The three "bosses" had finished ordering their men into action. Now Karl Galich came running, stuck a machine-pistol in Nikolai Korolev's ribs and said, "Is this your doing, 'comrade'? A task force to back up your jet-copter? Those officers you mentioned, who'll place us under their command? No way! You may have been a General in your time, but I'm very glad I didn't serve under you. As a tactician you're a total failure. Your men certainly won't fire on us while we are holding their leaders."

"Are you mad?" Korolev rounded on him. "We've no idea what this is all about! Can't you see that's a private airplane? It has nothing to do with us. As for troops: how many soldiers do you think you could cram into that thing? In any case, what on earth are you worrying about? If the people in that plane survived the crash, they're almost sure to be severely injured."

"But if they're not yours, what are they doing here?" said Galich.

"How should I know?" Korolev put away his pistol, threw up his hands, and turned to his companions. "Excuse me for enquiring," he snarled, "but can one of you perhaps explain this? Is there something I don't know? Some precaution that someone may have taken without mentioning it to me?"

Gurevich and Aliyev looked at each other disbelievingly— then at Korolev—and as a man said, "Fuck you, 'comrade'! You are the one with all the mouth, so you explain it!"

Korolev puffed himself up and looked about to explode, but before he could do or say anything else, there came a burst of static from a side pocket in his overcoat and a tinny, excited voice that said, "Chopper One to General Korolev: what's going on? What do you want us to do?"

Korolev looked at Galich and said, "There. Does that sound like this is something we planned? Of course not! Let me speak to my pilot." Taking a miniature walkie-talkie from his pocket, he extended the aerial.

Shoving harder with his weapon, Galich said, "Be *very* careful what you say."

Korolev grimaced, paused a moment to nod his understanding, then answered Chopper One, saying, "Do nothing. We have no idea what's happening. How about you?"

"No," the answer came back. "There was no call for help, no radio communication . . . that plane seemed to come out of nowhere, and it almost landed on top of us! It must be that they were in trouble and this was the only place they could land. There have to be injuries. Do you want us to help?"

But snatching the walkie-talkie from Korolev's hand, Galich answered that one himself. "No," he growled. "Do not interfere. We have it in hand. Oh, and incidentally, we also have your VIP bosses in hand. So keep your fingers off those triggers."

Meanwhile the snowplough, with a driver and three armed men aboard, had left the ramp, rumbled up onto the canopy, and come to a halt near the wrecked Scimitar. Just a moment ago the four had climbed down from their vehicle and entered the plane via a sprung hatch.

Now everyone on the ramp in front of Perchorsk's doors fell silent, waiting to see what would happen . . .

Trask and his team were waiting, too. And Paul Garvey said, "I can't see the Wamphyri being much hurt by that crash. The crew, probably, but not the Wamphyri."

"Not a hope in hell," said Trask.

"But what about Liz?" Jake muttered.

"Just try to stay calm," Trask advised him. "If your nerve-endings feel as raw as mine—which means they're almost bleeding—then I know exactly how you feel. But don't try anything rash. Those four men who just entered that plane . . . *that's* what I call rash!"

"Look," said Goodly. "What's all this? A survivor?"

The four figures, seeming inordinately bulky in their heavy parkas, had reemerged from the sprung hatch. The one in front, the smallest of the four, seemed to stagger; he could have been shocked by what he'd seen inside the wreck. But the figure immediately behind him was holding him up, apparently guiding him. The last man, the biggest of the four, moved effortlessly despite that he was carrying someone. Goodly's survivor? Liz? Jake had to hope so.

But while Goodly was the precog, he wasn't a telepath. That was Millie's department. And now she gasped:

"That's them! Those four men . . . *they aren't!* I mean, only one of them is a man. And the others are—"

"Wamphyyyri!" said Lardis Lidesci.

"Is that Liz that one's carrying?" Jake was shifting his weight from one foot to the other and back again. A feral yellow glow, escaping from behind his dark glasses, suffused his upper cheekbones.

"Take it easy, Jake," Ian Goodly warned him. "And like Ben said, don't do anything rash. This isn't the time. And it certainly isn't the place."

"If it is Liz," said Millie, "she's right out of it. But I can't scan too close or they'll sense me. The only reason they haven't so far is because they've got other things—more important things—on their minds."

"But who's the one in front?" said Trask.

"A victim," Millie shuddered. "I can't feel any mind there at all, only pain."

"Then the one behind him must be Malinari!" The words came grinding out of Trask's mouth. "Nephran Malinari, stealing all he can straight out of that poor bastard's head!"

"And the one with Liz must be Szwart!" the Necroscope growled, a rumble low in his throat. "I could be down there before they even knew it . . ."

But again the precog said, "No!"

And Trask said, "For Christ's sake let it be, Jake! Everyone down there is armed. You are . . . what you are, we know. But a bullet in the brain would pay no mind to that. It would stop you dead, the true death! And what chance for Liz then?"

The five figures had got aboard the snowplough; with Malinari at the controls, it now headed for the defended blockhouse. At first jerking, stalling, slewing this way and that, finally the vehicle answered to his touch and ran true. And since Malinari's victim—one of the ex-convicts from

the complex—was of no further use, he simply bundled him
from the driving platform. As he fell, the brain-drained
man's flopping left arm got caught in a clanking track. Immediately dragged under, he burst like a grape from the
crushing weight, and his shattered corpse was chewed by
churning metal. Flayed and flattened as the vehicle surged
on, he left a hugely spreading stain on the concrete and a
thin black trail that followed the plough to its target.

Its target, yes: the blockhouse that controlled Perchorsk's
power supply!

But aroused by the blood and the action, hothead Vavara
had given the game away. Hurling aside her parka she stood
erect in the cab of the plough, aimed a machine-pistol at the
men on the ramp and let rip with a hail of lead! Her insane
laughter could be heard even above the chatter of her
weapon and the vehicle's howling engine. But unused to the
weapons of Earth, her aim was off; her bullets struck sparks
from the face of the cliff above Perchorsk's huge doors and
sent men diving for cover, but other than that they did no
harm.

Still not knowing what was happening, but knowing what
they must do to stop it, the men on the ramp answered fire
with fire. And they were more accurate. Metal on metal, the
automatic gunfire from Perchorsk's defenders left dents in
the blade of the snowplough, scarred its sides, and had Malinari and the others cowering from the buzz and spang of
ricochetting bullets.

It lasted for a moment only, before the snowplough
crashed headlong into the blockhouse.

A wall crumbled and collapsed; figures came scurrying
from within, some from the gaping hole in the wall, others
from the door. They, too, were firing guns. But unnerved by
the suddenness of the attack and blinded by flying debris,
their efforts made no impression. Vavara, on the other hand,
had the hang of it now; she used her weapon like a scythe,
slicing among them, cutting them down. In another moment
all three of the Wamphyri had abandonded the snowplough
and were inside the blockhouse—and Liz Merrick went with

them, like a loose-limbed doll, flopping on Szwart's shoulder.

From inside, more gunshots as the lights in the blockhouse were extinguished . . . then a row of spotlights in the walls of the ravine . . . finally the lights in the service bay, blinking out one by one as the last whining dynamo died.

Then, instantly, the shadows of the ravine walls seemed to come alive, crawling blackly over the concourse, the shattered blockhouse, the face of the dam, and the entrance to Perchorsk. Which left only the streaming moonlight to save the scene from total darkness . . .

28
Opening skirmish

THE MOON WAS UP BUT STILL CLIMBING. AS YET it silvered only one side of the gorge, which left the complex side in multilayered shadows that changed from moment to moment, shrinking or lengthening, growing lighter or darker, every time a wisp of drifting cloud cleared or veiled the lunar orb.

And in the streaming, changing moonlight, smoke was issuing from the wrecked blockhouse, flowing over the dam's superstructure and eddying towards the complex.

Meanwhile, a second snowplough had set out from the service bay. Loaded with heavily armed men who clung to every available space, its headlights cut a swath through the smoke as it churned for the crippled VTOL. Once the vehicle's crew had deployed there, the men in the blockhouse would be caught in a crossfire from both the Scimitar and the service bay.

But now the smoke from the blockhouse was spreading in that direction, too—towards the Scimitar and the jet-copter—its eddies uncoiling in an almost sentient manner, like the arms of some immaterial octopus.

Almost sentient?

On the ledge in the hollow cliff under the overhang, Lardis Lidesci started and said, "Eh, what's this? Smoke without fire? Ah, but I've seen just such 'smoke' before, and far too often." The old man's Adam's apple bobbed convulsively, but after swallowing to moisten his throat he went on, "Ah no, my bully boys and likely lass, you can't fool me. That isn't smoke, not a bit of it. It's your mist, your *vampire* mist—and just look at it go! Aye, and in a moment you'll go, too, hidden in the heart of it."

The mist had reached the jet-copter; it swirled, thickened, put out other tendrils that reached for the wrecked VTOL. And:

"Now!" said Lardis. "Now!"

He was right. Barely visible shapes, fleeting figures, went loping through the mist, making away from the blockhouse towards the jet-copter. And again there came bright bursts of fire from the men now sheltering behind Perchorsk's half-open doors. They tried, but it was like shooting at shadows and had just as much effect.

The second snowplough had reached the Scimitar. Its passengers leaped free; scattering, some took up positions behind the fuselage, while others went inside. And in just a moment one of the latter used a walkie-talkie to speak to Galich:

"Three of our men are dead. The other one is missing. Probably that mess on the canopy. But God, Karl, you should see the *shit* in here! Our boys, and the flight crew—they've been cut to fucking pieces!"

Galich cursed and answered, "Those bastards who wrecked the blockhouse, they did this. Now they're headed your way. Get out of that plane and take command of the men. Hold your fire until you see those mothers coming, and then fire into that smoke, or mist, or whatever it is. Whoever they are, I want these fuckers dead!"

And Korolev, too, was back on his walkie-talkie, talking

to the crew of his jet-copter. "The stuff from the blockhouse is a smokescreen," he was shouting. "It's giving cover to a force of men who are heading your way. They have to be special forces of some sort, enemy forces. So anything you see moving between you and that blockhouse, take it out! Use those cannons and blow it straight to hell. You should have them on your thermal imaging, in which case you can open up on them right now."

In the red light from the blazing brazier, Karl Galich spat his disgust onto the floor of the service bay, stared his loathing right into Korolev's face, and said, "You'd murder your own men just to uphold a lie and save your own miserable life? Well, I reckon you're right and they are special forces. They're *your* special forces!"

"And you are a crazy fucking crab-louse!" Korolev told him, then turned his back on him in order to follow the action as it developed beyond the doors.

It was the final insult, and a fatal error. For unlike Mikhail Suvorov, Korolev knew nothing of Galich's past: his record of blind rages and serial killings, against men who had done no more than scorn or laugh at him. And twice now Korolev had cast doubts on Galich's sanity. Effeminate and feline the ex-convict might be, but cats have claws, and big cats have big claws. And almost *all* cats are wont to strike without warning.

Casually handing his machine-pistol to one of his men, Galich unhooked a small steel handaxe from his belt, weighed it in his hand, and without further pause sank it to its haft through Korolev's leather coat and deep into his back.

Amazingly, Korolev didn't die immediately but simply stood there shuddering, trying to reach behind himself with a spastic hand that couldn't quite grasp the axe's handle. Finally, falling to his knees in a flailing, agonized pirouette, he gazed up into Galich's eyes and blinked twice, his jaw hanging open.

And Galich took back his machine-pistol, stuck its stubby barrel in Korolev's yawning mouth and pulled the trigger.

Blood and brains sprayed the door in the instant before Korolev slammed into it and sat there, his head falling forward, with blood flowing over his shoulders, turning his brown leather coat red.

Only a few paces away, Igor Gurevich and Maxim Aliyev dropped their sidearms, backed away and huddled together, as Galich and his men turned their attention on them. "I know nothing—I mean, absolutely *nothing*—about any of this!" the rodentlike Gurevich squealed. "Whatever is going on here, I had nothing to do with it!"

"Nor I," Maxim Aliyev could scarcely croak his denial. "It must have been Korolev. We never could trust him. We only ever wanted to do whatever was best for everyone concerned."

"Is that so?" Galich came forward, grabbed Gurevich by the scruff of the neck and spun him toward the open doors. And the pockmarked giant Sol Kreisky did the same to Aliyev.

"Wait! Wait!" Gurevich cried. But:

"Here's your chance," said Galich. "A wonderful opportunity to prove your good intentions. Get out there and fight for us!" And he kicked Gurevich out through the doors. Sol Kreisky followed suit, and with another kick sent the pair's sidearms skittering out onto the ramp after them.

Meanwhile, the men at the wrecked Scimitar hadn't been able to fire a shot. The sinister-looking jet-copter, standing halfway between them and the blockhouse, obstructed their vision no less than the tendrils of mist that seemed intent on blanketing and blinding them.

And as for the jet-copter's crew:

In Chopper One, the pilot had penetrated the now dense mist with his thermal imaging, but too late to do anything. Fleeting figures had vanished from the viewscreen before he could adjust the range and coordinate his fire. Whoever these special forces were, they were already too close to the jet-copter to be visible on the plane's scanning devices.

Now, receiving no answer from Korolev to his frantic questions, the pilot cursed and brought his engine into whining life prior to takeoff. But again he was too late.

Someone—or some monstrous *thing*—had clambered up onto the chopper's nose in front of the black windows but behind the armaments. And now that something was pressing its face or what passed for a face to the one-way window as it tried to look inside. But Jesus Christ, the pilot felt as though it *was* looking inside, as if it could see him!

"Oh, shit! Shit!" said the copilot, having also seen that terrible face. And once more: "Shit—*oh, shit!*" as he saw the muzzle of a machine-pistol turning toward the allegedly bulletproof windows at point-blank range.

The first burst of fire sounded like a dozen hammers striking so close together they were almost one; the glass vibrated, buckled, and as if by magic a starbust of fine cracks—like a pattern in thin ice struck by a stone—appeared on the window. Then a brief pause, before the second burst shattered the glass inwards in a spray of myriad tiny cubes.

In the silence that followed when the firing ceased and the chopper's rotors *whup . . . whup . . . whupped* to a halt, the pilot could barely believe he was still in one piece. Almost deafened by the sound of ricochetting bullets—ricochets that had shut off the copilot's gibbering and reduced the flight controls to so much smoking electrical ruin—all he could hear was his own pounding heart.

But then, when finally he summoned up the nerve to take his trembling hands from his face, hands that were warm and sticky with his copilot's blood, the first thing he saw was Szwart's hideous "grin"—his entire face, melting and re-forming—as the Lord of Darkness came flowing in through the shattered window to take him by the throat . . .

By then, having left Vavara outside where she continued to make mist and watched over the unconscious Liz, Malinari was up into the near-claustrophobic fuselage. Tearing the cockpit door from its hinges, he came upon Szwart about to bite the pilot's neck.

"No!" he said. "Here, take this one while his heart's still

pumping. But we need that one." He grabbed the copilot's loose body and dragged it through into the passenger area.

Very reluctantly, Szwart released the pilot and flowed past Malinari, who in turn climbed into the cockpit.

The pilot was trembling like a jelly, massaging his bruised throat, trying hard to shrink down out of sight. "Oh mother! Oh my God!" he managed to gasp. "Who . . . who are you? I mean, what the fuck *are* you!?"

"I'm the man who will kill you," Malinari answered, "if you don't do exactly as I say. You see that wrecked airplane?"

"Yes, yes, I see it. What of it?"

"Turn your weapons on it," said Malinari. "Do it now."

"But . . . there are men from the snowplough there!"

"I know there are men there, you fool!" said Malinari. "And I know they want to kill me. But . . . very well—" His patience used up, he grabbed the pilot's head between his sucking hands. And as knowledge flowed from the pilot to the vampire Malinari, he absorbed what he needed and discarded the rest.

The targetting device was shot but the cannons remained in working order. Malinari used the manual controls to swivel the blast-shielded muzzles toward the VTOL. Notch by notch, making rapid, dull-sounding adjustments—ker-*chunk,* ker-*chunk,* ker-*chunk*—he lined the cannons up on their target something less than fifty feet away. Not quite point-blank but close enough.

Then he called back into the cabin to his grotesque colleague, "Lord Szwart, make finished in there. When I'm done with the Scimitar, we'll make a run for that second snowplough. Its heavy blade will be our shield when we drive in through what's left of those great doors."

Szwart's bloody snout rose up and he grunted, "Those doors look solid enough to me."

"But not for long," said Malinari. "This jet-copter points in the right direction, and she has more than mere cannons!"

And then he fired on the Scimitar.

A private aircraft with no armour, made even weaker by

its fall, the VTOL's shell offered no protection to the men taking cover behind it. Explosive cannon fire blew the wreckage apart, punching holes through its fuselage as if it were papier-mâché. And as the survivors ran, so Vavara was there to cut them down. For she could see through her own mist as if it were broad daylight.

And with technical skills stolen from the pilot—who now slumped drooling in his seat—Malinari armed and fired one of the chopper's air-to-air missiles.

In the service bay, a squad of desperate men was trying to close the doors when the missile hit. Half of them were killed outright as one of the doors was blown off its rollers in three massive chunks and hurled back into the bay. Sprung bolts ricochetted like bullets, and shards of sharp metal went buzz-sawing in every direction.

It was more than enough for the remaining defenders. Coughing and choking in the smoke and cordite stench, they retreated to the rear of the cavern where they took cover guarding Perchorsk's access routes . . .

On the opposite side of the ravine, the Necroscope was now more than ever concerned for Liz's safety. "If I could only see her, catch a glimpse of her through that bloody mist," he said, "I'd go to her. If she would only wake up and call me, I know I'd be able to find her in a moment."

Trask grabbed his arm. "Jake, I know this may sound stupid, but right now she's safer with them. She won't come to any harm from that rabble in Perchorsk, that's for sure. They don't know what they're up against. But we do, and it's our one advantage. So don't blow it now."

"And anyway," said Turchin, "you have other things to do."

Jake and Trask looked at him, and Trask said, "The bomb?"

"Indeed, the bomb." Turchin nodded. "The way I see it, just about every ex-convict in the complex will be dropping whatever he was doing and hurrying to defend the place— to defend himself! So if you want to destroy the core, the entire Perchorsk complex, now is the time to put the bomb down there. We should at least plant the thing before the Wamphyri get inside. After that . . . then it will be a matter of timing."

"Timing?" said Jake.

"Of course," said Turchin. "You will want to allow yourself time to get Liz out of there before the explosion."

"*And* before Malinari and the others reach the Gate." Trask nodded.

But Jake said, "You've got it backwards. No one's going to even *touch* that timer until Liz and my baby are out of it!"

"Liz and your—?" Trask's jaw fell open.

"Don't ask me," Jake told him.

"Whatever you say," Trask answered. "Anyway, what you said about getting Liz out of there first: that's understood."

"Well, okay," the Necroscope growled. And then, after pausing to calm himself: "I remember the layout in the core, every coordinate. The Gate is surrounded by a Saturn's-ring concourse of overlapping steel plates like fish-scale armour. But beneath the plates, in the bowl of the core directly below the Gate . . . well, I don't think there'll be anyone down there. It isn't the sort of place where anyone in his right mind would ever want to go. Unless they've got around to filling in the magmass, there are moulds down there— twisted human figures in the magmass—that don't bear looking at."

"That would be the perfect location," said Turchin. "But I haven't yet shown you how to set the timer. I should come back with you to E-Branch HQ."

But Jake shook his head. "No," he said, "that won't be necessary. You see, Gustav, I'm not going to be setting the timer. You are."

"Me?" Turchin was taken completely by surprise. "Why me?"

"Because you're more interested in destroying your enemies than closing the Gate, that's why. And if it's murder pure and simple that we're talking about, I'm not your hired assassin."

And after a moment: "Is that really what you think of me?" said Turchin. "Do I come over as badly as all that?"

"What difference does it make?" said Jake. "If we're talking dirty work here you'll be doing your own, and if we aren't you'll be doing everyone a favour. So what it boils down to is this: are you a member of this team or aren't you?"

"I'm here, am I not?" Turchin stood as tall as he could.

The Necroscope nodded. "And you'll be there in the complex, in harm's way with the rest of us. So is it yes or no, because if it's no I'll take you out of here right now, back to Moscow, and from now on we'll know who we're dealing with. Or not dealing with. Think it over, Gustav. For it's like you told me not so long ago: if we're lucky and there is a tomorrow, we're all going to need all the friends we can get."

But Turchin didn't need to think it over. "If you position that bomb," he said grimly, "then when the time comes, I shall prime it. As for my qualifications as a member of this team—you haven't seen what I've seen." Tapping a finger on the plastic casing of his nite-lite binoculars, he handed them to Jake and continued: "Those figures climbing the road up the side of the ravine, unless I am very much mistaken they are Igor Gurevich and Maxim Aliyev. In which case I must assume that Nikolai Korolev died in the blast when that door was destroyed, and these two are running for their lives while they still can. So tell me, Jake, since I no longer have any enemies *left* in Perchorsk, how can I be planning to murder them there?"

The Necroscope nodded again, smiled slowly, and handed the nite-lites back unused. "Okay," he said, "but don't go looking for an apology. Let's just say I'm very glad I was wrong about you on this one. That's *this* one. As for how you got this far: well, I can't say I've been much impressed by your methods."

"It's the difference between East and West," Turchin

shrugged, and grinned in that foxy way of his. "It's 'Politics,' my young friend. But I think you'll find the end will justify the means."

Jake didn't answer, but without more ado conjured a Möbius door and disappeared into it. A few loose flakes of snow where he'd been standing were picked up and swirled in the vacuum of his departure.

And Trask said, "Gustav, we're hundreds of miles from anywhere, and I'm already feeling the cold. Your old chums Aliyev and Gurevich can't possibly make it. So it looks like it's all worked out for you."

"I know," Turchin answered grimly. "They are doomed to die anyway, but not by my hand. I laid them a trail to follow, yes, but they didn't have to take it. I didn't bring those men here, Ben. Greed and their lust for power did that."

"Aye," the Old Lidesci grunted. "And that's something that holds true for both worlds, probably for all worlds. For those are exactly the same things that brought the Wamphyri here."

Paul Garvey nodded and said, "And now they're desperate to get *out* of here, no less than Gurevich and Aliyev."

"Desperation, yes," said the precog. "That's about all you can expect from them from now on. There's only one way back to Starside and they know it, and it's a defended route at that."

"That's true," said Millie, "but look—they're going for it anyway. And God help anyone who gets in their way . . . !"

From the back of the service bay, fifteen guns were trained on the open space at the entrance where one door had been torn to bits and the other stood half open. The blazing brazier, amazingly untouched by all that had happened, burned red as before, its fiery heart a marker at the far end of a seeming tunnel of darkness.

There came the rumbling growl of a snowplough's engine . . . at which six of the fifteen slipped away unnoticed deeper into the complex in search of places to hide. Or perhaps

Karl Galich—lone survivor of the three bosses, dazed and bloodied from a gash in his forehead though he was—was nevertheless aware of their cowardice. For now he raised his voice in a harsh warning: "Any man who runs without a fight answers to me. But his answer won't matter, because I'll kill him anyway! So stand and fight, you worthless bastards! And remember this: these bloody special forces—whoever they are, and no matter how good they seem to be—they're only human. They're just men, like you and me." He had no way of knowing how very wrong he was.

The rumbling grew louder, began echoing through the cavern, and preceded by a two-foot-deep, rolling bank of mist, the snowplough appeared as a silhouette against the silvery-grey oblong of the entrance. Jolting and shuddering—clattering where its caterpillar tracks lifted it up over various mounds of metallic debris, and flattening several less solid obstructions, including some that squirted—it advanced through the mist and bore down on the brazier in a cloud of stinking blue exhaust smoke.

"Use the brazier to gauge the distance and get your range." Galich's voice was hoarse with rage now, and perhaps something of fear. "When those coals are spilled, let that be your signal to open fire."

"Useless!" someone shouted back. "A waste of good lead. The plough's blade is up!"

Galich cursed and yelled back, "Then use the stanchions and cavern walls if you have to, and go for ricochets. But whatever you do, don't even think of surrendering. We've seen what they can do, these mothers. They play really rough, and they aren't the kind who take prisoners."

The brazier toppled and was crumpled under, scattering red-hot coals like a flood of rubies across the cavern's floor. And Perchorsk's defenders opened fire.

A hail of bullets struck sparks off the snowplough's raised blade; others whined viciously where they took chips out of the cavern walls or scarred the stanchions that supported the roof. But the snowplough came clattering on, neither slowing down nor deviating a single inch from its course—its unstoppable collision course with flesh and blood. And:

"We're out of here!" Galich gasped, when there was nothing left to say or do except retreat or die. But only seven out of the nine made it into the complex, while the other two left it just a little too late and went down screaming under the snowplough's bloodied tracks.

But the way had narrowed down, and Malinari was too slow in finding neutral and the brakes, so that the plough slewed sideways when it hit a wall and jerked to a halt. But no harm done, for by then all that remained of the defenders was the sound of their running footsteps, beating a hasty retreat through Perchorsk's many mazy corridors . . .

Jake dragged the trolley with its lethal load out of the Möbius Continuum onto the glass-smooth rock at the bottom of the core. The core was a perfect sphere eaten out of the bedrock when the Perchorsk Experiment went disastrously wrong and an atomic pile devoured itself. A bubble with a diameter of forty-two or -three metres, it had been all that remained of the pile, of the equipment surrounding it, and of the physicists who operated it. The core, and at *its* core the Perchorsk Gate: a second, far smaller sphere of blinding white light—a gravity-defying singularity, its outer surface an event horizon—suspended in midair dead centre of the bubble.

And slicing into the core's curved, smoothly polished floor and walls at every imaginable angle—drilled through the solid bedrock in the instant of implosion—scores of precisely circular shafts or energy channels, like wormhole escape routes for the alien forces that had been trapped here.

Now, being at the bottom of the bubble, in the bowl of the core, the Necroscope felt the blinding light almost like a physical weight on the back of his neck and looked up at its enigmatic source: the lower hemisphere of the Gate. It glared like a cosmic lightbulb—like the sun itself—but light without heat.

Even wearing sunglasses, still Jake shuttered his eyes and looked away. Blinding, yes, but the Gate's dazzle was the least of his problems. For with Harry Keogh's memories of this place, Jake also knew that if he tried to use the Möbius Continuum too close to the singularity it would create a completely ungovernable conflict of alien energies. When Harry had first come here he had done just that . . . and the resultant backlash had hurled him immeasurable light-years out into space! Then, only the long-dead August Ferdinand Möbius himself had been able to guide him home again.

Jake wasn't about to duplicate Harry's mistake, but already he knew how close he had come. For even in the act of conjuring his door prior to exiting the Continuum, he had sensed it fighting him, seen its instability, how it warped and fluctuated in the Gate's invisible force-fields.

This close, then, and no closer . . .

And now another problem. The trolley was heavy and the bomb it carried even more so, and despite the Necroscope's newfound expertise and Harry Keogh's memories, still he'd failed to arrive dead centre of the bowl. And finding their level, the trolley's wheels turned on the curved floor, and one of them tilted into a wormhole. At that the trolley jammed into immobility . . . but its clatter had been heard up above.

In the ominous silence of the core, the sound rang out with crystal clarity, its metallic echoes bouncing from the wormhole-riddled walls . . . likewise the harsh voices that reached down to Jake from above the fish-scale plates:

"What was that? Did you hear that?" The Necroscope couldn't be sure what was said for it was in Russian, but he could certainly guess. And he froze where he crouched beside the trolley. At which there came another voice, a deadspeak voice that startled him, because now of all times the teeming dead weren't much given to speaking to him:

Necroscope? Is that you, Harry? It seems like an age, and I really thought that you must be dead, too. A girl's voice—and Jake "recognized" it at once: Penny, an innocent, some poor kid who got too close to the original Necroscope at the wrong time, and ended up down here. Jake "remembered" her, and felt a lump in his throat. But Harry's emotions, not his.

No, he told her. *Necroscope, yes. Harry, no. Harry was—I don't know—my mentor? Me, I'm just Jake, Jake Cutter. But at least you were right about one thing: Harry's been gone from us a long time. Most of him, anyway.*

And from up above, where for a while there'd been a breathless silence: "Rats," someone said. "It could only be rats. The fucking place is crawling with them!" Only this time, recognizing Jake's confusion, Penny "heard" the words through the Necroscope's ears and translated them for him.

You know Russian? he said.

I have lots of friends here, she answered. *It's how we pass the time. I've learned lots of things, Harry . . . er, Jake.*

But Russian?

Physics, too, Penny told him. *It's really amazing how death focuses your concentration.*

I'll take your word for that, said Jake. And then, unintentionally thoughtless: *You were pretty stuck on Harry, right?*

Oh, yes! she answered. *Harry was taking me to a world where we'd have a great high house under a tumbling moon. He would be the Lord and I'd be his Lady. But . . . I wasn't paying attention to the things he said. This is where he lost me—or I lost him—but it wasn't Harry's fault. I've often wondered if he cried for me, wondered if he was able to.*

And knowing that Penny would feel it in his deadspeak, Jake nodded and said, *He was able to. For a little while, anyway . . .*

While overhead:

"Bloody big rats," said the first voice dubiously, "to make a racket like that! Anyway, what the hell's going on? We should have been relieved by now. What happened to the power? The fans have stopped, and now the lights in the tunnel are out. I don't like any of this."

"Like I've been trying to tell you," said the second voice, "it has to be the rats. Maybe they've chewed through a cable or something."

"And that noise down there in the bowl? Rats?"

"Could be," said the other. "Down in those wormholes there are cysts with meat in them still, all turned to leather where they're completely enclosed. And every time a cyst cracks open or gets gnawed through, it's like: hey, you furry, four-legged comrades! A free lunch!" Then, tired of the subject: "Look, if you're so fucking worried about it why don't you go down there and check it out for yourself?"

"What, are you crazy?" the answer came back. "I don't even like being *here,* never mind down *there!* But perhaps I'd better go take a look through the hatch. Just a quick look."

Jake unfroze, prepared himself to drag the trolley free of the wormhole and through a Möbius door. But at the last minute there came the tinny, bicycle-bell ringing of an antique field telephone. And: "Now what?" said the one who had been going to come and have a look.

"Better answer it," said the other. "Maybe someone's going to tell us what's happening up there."

Jake heard footsteps on the perimeter walkway, a low, muttered conversation . . . then a shout as the telephone was slammed down in its cradle. "Hey! We're out of here. It sounds like all hell has broken loose, and every available man is defending the complex."

"What? Defending Perchorsk? Against what?"

"What, am I fucking psychic? Move your arse, comrade!" Then the sound of booted feet hammering on the walkway, their echoes fading into the distance . . .

Penny, said Jake, as he carefully disengaged from the trolley and saw that it was safe and wouldn't tilt any further. *I'm going now. But before I do I just think I'd better tell you and your Russian friends that if things work out there'll be a hell of a big bang down here. I mean—*

—We know what you mean, she cut in. *It's been in your mind all along. As for these physicists: they're not at all unhappy. It seems they're finally going to find out what it's like to be at the centre of a nuclear explosion! And who can say, if there are places beyond—better places—maybe this*

*will help speed us on our way. And maybe I'll find Harry
there. Goodbye, Jake, and good luck.*

Jake climbed rungs to a hatch, got up onto the walkway
and took a look at the core. It was much as he "recalled" it
except there'd been three Katushev cannons upon a time.
Now there were only two and a stripped-down frame whose
parts had been cannibalized to service the ones that were
still working. Their squat ugly muzzles were pointing at
the Gate, of course. Jake assumed that after that warrior-
creature had come through from Starside the guns had
quickly been put back in working order, and Perchorsk's ex-
convicts had kept them manned twenty-four hours a day
from that time on.

But aware of the seconds and minutes ticking by, the Nec-
roscope had no more time for any further observations.
Trask and the others were waiting for him, and Liz (*oh, Liz!
Please, God keep her safe!*) was still in the clutches of the
Wamphyri . . .

Back on the ledge under the overhang, Trask breathed a sigh
of relief when Jake stepped out of the Möbius Continuum
and said, "Okay, I've positioned the bomb. What's next?"

"Right," Trask answered. "The way I see it, we have to
lay our ambush down in the lower levels, on the approach
routes to the core. Gustav, you'll be located with the bomb.
You'll have to be there anyway in order to prime the thing—
which you'll do as soon as we've got Liz out of the way."

In a hurry now, he turned back to the Necroscope. "When
we last saw Liz, Szwart had her. So he's all yours. It could
even be that he has a little respect for you. He knows what
you can do and was there when you wrecked his garden.
But I need someone—a volunteer—to go along with you,
because I can't help feeling that Szwart will be our most
difficult target."

"Me," said Millie at once. "I volunteer. Szwart owes me."

Since they were running out of time Trask couldn't waste
it arguing with Millie. But still his heart skipped a beat when

he answered, "Okay. And in any case we'll be fairly close together down there, all of us."

He turned to the precog, but Goodly beat him to it, saying: "Vavara is mine, Ben. I nearly bought it in her labyrinth under Palataki, so now it's my turn. Me and Paul, if he's willing. We should make a pretty good team. While I try to glean what she's *going* to do, Paul can perhaps get into her mind and corroborate what she's doing." He looked at Garvey, who said:

"Sure. Why not? What can I lose . . . except my life!?"

Finally Trask turned to the Old Lidesci. "Which leaves just you and me, old friend. You, me—"

"—And Malinari," Lardis grunted. "For Zekintha, aye."

"For all of us," said Trask. "Everyone, everywhere." And he looked at Jake. "That's it. We're ready."

"Two things before we go," said the Necroscope. "There's no power now in the complex, no lights. But we do have those three halogen lamps that we brought with us. They've got to go to the people who need them most. Millie, for one. If we get separated, the brilliant light from one of those lamps might be sufficient to back Szwart off. He can't take strong light. That leaves one lamp for Paul and Ian, and one for Lardis. As for Gustav: he'll have all the light he needs from the Gate itself."

"Good," said Trask. "So what's the other thing?"

"Not so good," said Jake. "Right now in Perchorsk, Malinari will be looking for someone who knows his way around the place. Which probably means just about any one of those ex-cons. He'll drain his victim of his knowledge, and after that he'll know as much about the complex as . . . as someone who has lived here for three years!"

"You're right, of course," said Trask. "With Malinari leading them, those monsters won't be blundering around down there. They'll know exactly where they're going. Our only advantage—that is, if we have one—lies in the fact that they don't know we're here. Not yet, anyway."

"Which leaves us with no room for error," said the Necroscope. "And no time to spare." He turned to Turchin. "You first, comrade."

And Turchin said, "What greater sacrifice, eh? The Russian Premier gives his all for his people, his country, his world!"

"Right," said Jake, moving close to him. "It'll make great headlines in *Izvestia*—if we ever get out of this."

A moment later, Jake and Turchin vanished. Following which, it took only a few seconds to transport Trask and his team into Perchorsk's leering lower levels . . .

29
The Final Battle . . . ?

BEYOND THE COMPLEX'S CAVERNOUS SERVICE bay, a tunnel lined with storage rooms led to a hatch which in turn opened on a junction of rock-hewn corridors. And from the junction onwards—right, left, and straight on—all routes except down were available. As for the latter: a boarded-over shaft in the solid rock floor was all that remained of a once-stairwell to the nether levels. Wrecked in the first terrifying moments of the Perchorsk Experiment, when shock-wave vibrations had caused bolts to shear and reduced the relatively flimsy structure to a heap of concertinaed scrap one hundred and ten feet down the shaft, it had never been rebuilt. Since there were several other routes to the core—and since in the aftermath of the disaster Perchorsk had been more or less written off, its funding cut to the bone—repairs hadn't been deemed a priority.

In the three horizontal corridors, Karl Galich had deployed six men including himself. Their instructions were simple: anything, but *anything,* that came through the hatch—an oval door five feet high set in a steel bulkhead—was to be cut to ribbons with concentrated gunfire. In Galich's own words, "I've had more than enough of foreplay, now we fuck! And if these mothers so much as stick their noses in here I'll have them in a crossfire. I want their blood and guts all over the walls and floor, in payment for what they spilled outside."

And now, from twenty-five feet away—with their electric torches and weapons lined up on the hatch—the six waited in ambush, never suspecting that just beyond the bulkhead, Malinari the Mind was listening to their very thoughts.

The complex was silent now. No humming from the motionless fans, no booted feet tramping the endless corridors, no voices echoing in the still, heavy air. But it was an ominous silence, like the dead calm that warns of a coming storm . . .

The hatch's locking wheel squealed as it was given a tentative turn. Then the wheel spun, the hatch cracked open, and was hurled back on its hinges. Torch beams stabbed at the darkness, and Galich's men took up first pressures on their triggers. But nothing was moving in the frame of the hatch. Then—

—It was mist, a corpse-white living mist that came crawling over the lower lip of the hatch, swirling into the complex. A vampire mist, coiling across the floor, and thickening as it came; until the hatch itself was obscured, its outline fading, swallowed up in the total opacity of the stuff.

It took only a matter of seconds for Galich to realize what was happening here—exactly the same thing that had happened outside—and then he drew breath and yelled, "Open fire! Into the mist. Fire right into this . . . this whatever it is!"

And his men needed no further urging. Sensing something of the alien otherness, as their skin began crawling, they were only too glad to oblige. And the clamour was deafening as they blasted away at the place where they believed the hatch to be; or rather, they hosed fire on an area which Vavara's beguiling talent had *told* them was the hatch. But it wasn't. And suddenly the four men in the corridors that angled to left and right of the hatch had adjusted their aim to target each other!

The firing commenced . . . and as quickly ceased. And in its wake there was only the hot stench of cordite and fresh blood, slumping shadows and choked screams gurgling into silence.

But in the straight-on corridor, Galich and his Second-in-Command were unhurt. And:

"What the *fuck* is going on?" Galich whispered as he loaded a fresh magazine into his machine-pistol, his hands shaking so badly he could scarcely draw back the cocking lever.

And his Second-in-Command said, "This mist is like . . . it's like living slime. Karl, I can feel it crawling on me!"

And in that same moment—from directly above them—Lord Szwart said, *"Ahhhh!"* as he came seeping down from the ceiling.

Semisolid one moment, in the next Szwart was muscle, bone, chitin claws, and mantrap jaws; and wrenching their weapons from nerveless fingers, he hurled them aside and slammed the pair up against opposite walls. Half-stunned, they would have fallen . . . but Vavara and Lord Nephran Malinari were there, flowing out of the vampire mist, their eyes burning and their overly long arms reaching with irresistible strength. And:

"This one," said Malinari, sniffing at Galich with a wrinkled snout, his fingers writhing like snakes as they grasped the ex-convict's head, "is mine! One of their leaders, he knows all the mazy ways of this place. He has learned them by heart. Now, in just a little while, I shall learn them, too."

Then, glancing at Vavara and Lord Szwart in an unaccustomed fashion—with his jaws gaping and his eyes madly ablaze—he said, "Allow me . . . allow me a moment or two before I take what we need. For I have worked my mind hard tonight, and I begin to feel . . . to feel the strain. So many voices shrieking their fear . . . my head aches with their *thunder!* How much may a single mind contain with impunity, I wonder, as often before I've wondered? How many thoughts—how much knowledge, what quantity of pain—before the brain succumbs?" And clutching Karl Galich's head in one huge lily-pad hand, he used the other to mop his livid face and brow, shaking his head as if to clear it of all the babble.

But then, seeing the way his companions were looking at him—sensing their curiosity at his apparent weakness—Malinari controlled himself and continued, "Meanwhile, before we go back for the girl, the pair of you can do as you will with that one. Aye, for the sooner *he* stops thinking the better!"

A death warrant on Galich's Second-in-Command, which Szwart and Vavara wasted no time in serving . . .

The approach route to the core. That was where Trask had determined to ambush the Wamphyri, and that was where Jake had taken the remaining members of the team after positioning Gustav Turchin in the bowl under the Gate with his deadly nuclear device. But while Trask and the precog had been here before—and Jake, too, insofar as he "remembered" it—the rest of the team were newcomers here, and as such they hadn't known what to expect.

Just as well. For in the nightmare scenario of their coming battle, the Gate's close environs made for a "perfect" setting. Perfectly nightmarish.

First to be deployed, Goodly and Garvey found themselves on opposite sides of a wide, heavily timbered, badly scorched catwalk that descended through a region of sheer fantasy. Now they formed a part of that fantasy—or more properly that horror—for they looked up at the catwalk from a grotesquely humped bed of magmass that stretched away into the dim recesses of a weird chaos, a great disorder, an utterly alien landscape.

No light here but what little came filtering up from below, from the Gate itself. For even when electricity had been freely available, it had never been routed through here. This had been the unanimous decision of various overseers over the years: that this was a region best kept unlit, which no sane eye would ever want to look at.

Yet now the telepath and the precog were very nearly a part of it, kept separate only by their clothes and the thickness of their skins. And despite that Goodly had been here once before, still he wished his skin was thicker. As for what the telepath, Paul Garvey, thought of this place . . . in fact he tried not to.

Sprawling in deep, man-shaped moulds or depressions in the magmass—finding cover in these human templates, these matrices of men who had been trapped in the backfire from the failed Perchorsk Experiment, men who had died here—Goodly and Garvey tried to avert their eyes from their surreal surroundings, only to find it impossible. For wherever they looked the magmass was there.

The precog's eyes were fixed on the catwalk, following its descent through an awesome maze of fused stone, crumpled metal, and warped plastic extrusions, where on all sides those smooth-bored energy channels wound and twisted like wormholes in soft earth, except these holes were cut through bedrock, solidified lava, and buckled steel girders. The hideous magmass, yes.

Paul Garvey was rather more successful in his mental avoidance of the magmass:

In the alien—*terrain?*—on the other side of the catwalk, the telepath was attempting to concentrate his attention in the other direction, *up* the sloping vista, where the wooden catwalk emerged from a shaft in a solid rock wall. His powerful halogen lamp was located within easy reach in the burst bubble of a magmass cyst. It was switched off for the time being, but its beam had been tested and was focussed on the night-dark shaft. If or when anyone or -*thing* appeared in that opening, Garvey's brilliant beam would reach out to define, startle, and blind it . . . or so he hoped.

So the pair were situated, and so they waited, the telepath probing for mindsmog—however warily—and the precog praying for a glimpse of the future. And both of them fearing what they might discover. They were armed, of course, with sidearms, and grenades. But neither esper felt in any way superior or even equal to what they must surely face here. Both of them were well aware of the tenacity, the audacity, of their enemy. The best they could hope for was that Paul's lamp, their protective garlic sprays, and their firepower would drive Malinari and his monstrous companions straight along the catwalk to their next confrontation. And on the way, the men from E-Branch would focus their fire on Vavara, trying to remove her from the final equation.

But why Vavara? Why the female and presumably the "weakest" of this awesome species first?

For one, because it was unlikely that she would be carrying Liz. And two, because Vavara could turn the minds of men. Trask and the others, they had to be sure that if they fired at something it was what they actually saw and not what they were made to see.

These were reasons enough. The witch must go first.

And there in the place of the magmass, the precog looked to the future and saw nothing, and the telepath searched for mindsmog—

—And found it rushing headlong, down through the tortured bowels of Perchorsk toward the core! And only himself, Goodly, and their E-Branch colleagues to halt its charge . . .

Ben Trask and the Old Lidesci were next in line. A little less than one hundred feet deeper in the heart of the complex, where the magmass was relatively free of those twisted and frequently inverted human templates—those hideous reminders of the agonies once suffered here—they'd taken up positions at the foot of a "cliff" of black, fused rock close to the perfectly circular mouth of the downward slanting tunnel that led to the core.

But for all its lack of gargoyle figures and mutant moulds, still the magmass was magmass and unearthly; so that once again the thought occurred to Trask, just as it had when first he saw this place, that the Perchorsk accident—if "accident" it had been and not a form of higher retribution—had resulted in the release of alien forces utterly outside Man's knowledge, forces that defied Earthly science.

He lay on his front behind what looked like a frozen black wave in a potholed or whirlpooled lake of magmass, and couldn't help wondering what it had looked like in flow at the moment of meltdown . . . *and* how he would have felt to be trapped in it. But since that simply didn't bear thinking about, he quickly redirected his thoughts to the Old Lidesci and wondered what he was making of all this.

Lardis had taken cover behind a once-stanchion that was now bent over in the form of a stylized magnet, and he was so quiet that if Trask had not seen him locate himself there he would be certain that he was alone. This was a Szgany survival mechanism, Trask knew, which Sunside's tribes had evolved through immemorial centuries of Wamphyri predation. In the old days—and some not so old—when the vampires were wont to come raiding out of Starside on their manta flyers, the Szgany had fled into hiding and willed themselves out of existence. They hadn't moved, they hadn't spoken, they hadn't thought—and they certainly hadn't used garlic to protect themselves! That would have been a "dead giveaway," for only cut or crushed garlic has the strong scent, and garlic can't crush itself.

Lardis was employing the same mechanisms now. He was here, and he wasn't here. When the Wamphyri came down the stairs from the catwalk and followed the base of the cliffs to the illumination from the core, they wouldn't—or shouldn't—detect him. Similarly, Trask was also protected; his talent was by no means common, and unlike telepathy and the skills of the locators, it did not disturb the psychic aether or cause him to "glow in the dark." If he could manage to keep himself to himself—"shield himself," as his espers would have it—he might remain undetected in a clump of magmass stalagmites until the last possible moment. And that would be the moment when he and Lardis Lidesci opened up on Lord Nephran Malinari.

Malinari! The name burned in Trask's mind like acid; it was a pain on his nerve-endings, a torment in his heart.

Zek's loss was something that wouldn't, couldn't, ever be eradicated—but it could be avenged. At least the pain could be salved, the torment eased, and the burning part-quenched. But not until Malinari, or Trask himself—one or the other—was dead. And only the true death would suffice.

That was why he was here and that was what he would do. For if Trask had considered himself tenacious and determined in the pursuit of this Great Vampire before, there was now that in his blood—in his no longer entirely human system—which made him far more so. And if he should be the one to die . . . well, so be it. His future along with the world's was in any case uncertain now, and his only regret would be in losing Millie, too.

But then again, perhaps she was already lost—Millie, Liz, the Necroscope, and Trask, too: all of them lost—to what continued to consume them, and consumed them ever faster, even as they waited to confront it at its source . . .

The third and last party consisted of Millie and Jake.

There in the core, Jake helped his partner settle down into the bucket seat of a twin-mounted Katushev cannon. For they had realized shortly after Trask deployed them—as soon as Millie had seen the Gate, that ball of brilliant white light suspended in the centre of the core—that she would scarcely be needing her halogen lamp! Even wearing her sunglasses she couldn't look at the singularity for more than a few seconds. But that worked to everyone's advantage: the lamp could now go to Trask or the precog, who were more in need of it. And in any case, the Katushev was a far more devastating weapon, and its lethal effects more permanent.

The only problem now was that Jake didn't know how to operate the thing . . . but he believed he knew how to find out. That would involve deadspeak, but since his every unshielded thought *was* deadspeak it required no great effort on his part.

There has to be someone down here, he said, *who understands the workings of these weapons. You Russians—you soldiers who died here doing your duty, way back in Per-*

chorsk's early days—I could use a little help.

Long seconds ticked by, and no answer. But then—

Let me speak to them, said Penny. *You see, Necroscope, even down here the Great Majority have had something of a voice, and the comrades here were warned off long ago. But if there really are other places beyond death, and if that bomb of yours really is a different kind of Gate—*

Eh? A coarse, cold voice cut her off, that of an ex–Russian soldier, which Jake understood because it was dead-speak: mental communication which, like telepathy, knows no language barrier. *Do you think that's possible, Necroscope?*

I don't know, Jake could only shrug. *If I said yes, absolutely, I'd be lying. But then again, I lived a full life without knowing there was this place—never guessing that the dead go on—so what do I know? The only thing I do know for sure, the original Necroscope died in the atomic blast of a weapon on the far side of the Gate, a weapon fired* through *the Gate from this very spot. And yes, I can definitely guarantee that he* went on, *for I'm the living proof.*

And another voice said, *I'm Gunner Golovin, or I was. Those Katushev cannons were my babies . . . I maintained them. You want to know how to fire 'em, I'm your man.*

Excellent! said Jake with feeling. *But it's only right that I should warn you: we could experience a little interference—a little deadspeak static, maybe—from the Great Majority.*

Fuck 'em! said the other. *Way down here—out of sight and almost out of our minds—we take care of our own. And what the hell, the teeming dead never much bothered with us anyway. They warned us off? So what? If there's a way out of this, we should take it. And if there isn't, what have we got to lose?*

And finally another voice, but one which Jake recognized at once. It was Zek Föener, who knew this place only too well. And she said, *Jake, the Great Majority are aware of what you're trying to do—the only thing you can do—and this time you have their blessing.*

But deadspeak often conveys more than is actually said, and Jake was adept at reading between the lines. *There are vampires in the world,* he said, *and the teeming dead want them gone. But they do mean* all *of them—all of* us*—right?*

He sensed Zek's nod. And sadly, *It's the way things have to be, Necroscope,* she said. And then, as she began to drift away, *There's just one thing, just one more little thing that you can do for me, Jake, if you will. And I'd be obliged if you'd do it before . . . before anything else happens.*

You've been my friend, said Jake. *So name it.*

And she did, and was gone.

And then Jake and Gunner Golovin showed Millie how to operate the Katushev cannon.

But just as they were finishing:

"Ahhh!" said Millie, her eyes opening wide.

"What is it?" said Jake, who believed he already knew.

She looked at him and her face was pale and drawn. But pale from what she was or from what she knew, he couldn't say. Until suddenly she projected a thought directly into his mind. Telepathy, for the first time with a person other than Liz; Millie's vampire-enhanced talent coming into play. And: *Malinari and the others,* she said. *They're coming!*

"What do you see?" Jake asked out loud. "Is there any opposition? Have any of those ex-cons survived?"

Human minds? said Millie. *Minds free of mindsmog? Only two. And strangely, they know all about these Katushev! Synchronicity, I suppose. They're creeping like a pair of terrified mice. They know that something's very wrong. The silence . . . the stagnating air . . . the lights that don't work . . . the fact that no one bothers to answer their calls. So that now they've stopped calling. Just the two of them, Jake. They're all that's left.*

"I know who they are," said Jake. "They were up here when I was installing Turchin's bomb. When the place came under attack they got called away."

"Called to their deaths," Millie now whispered, concentrating her talent on listening. "The mindsmog . . . is closing in on them. The Wamphyri know they're there. They can *smell* them!"

"Maybe you'd better get out of there," said the Necroscope, thoroughly alarmed now. "Once those men are finished, we'll be the only ones left . . . our minds. If Malinari catches you probing like that—"

"—He'll know we're here?" She looked at him and cocked her head on one side. "Do you really think he doesn't already know? I wish I could believe that, Jake. But he has Liz, and he knows that sooner or later you'll try to get her back."

Before he could answer: *"Ahhhh!"* Millie said again. And yet again, *"Ahhhh!* Two minds, snuffed out." She breathed deeply and lay back in the Katushev's seat. "Those poor men . . . they never knew what hit them. But you're right and I'm out of there now."

"How far away were they?" said Jake.

"Close," said Millie. "And by now they're closer still, for there's no longer anything to delay them. And there's one other thing you should know—I think Liz could be waking up. Just as I got out of there I sensed another mind. It was very familiar, female, afraid, and it was groping for consciousness."

"Liz? Unharmed?" He could scarcely believe it.

"She's a survivor," said Millie.

"The moment she wakes up—the moment she calls for me—I have to go to her!" said Jake.

"But only if you're sick of living," said Millie. "And only if you want Liz to die, too. Best to play it according to plan, Necroscope. She's their lure, for you. And the moment they take you, she dies—or worse."

"Damn it all to hell!" said Jake under his breath. "If only I didn't feel so bloody useless!"

"You want something to do?" said Millie. "Then why not take that lamp to the precog and Paul Garvey? They'll need it a lot more than we do. And if they don't already know about the Wamphyri, tell them. Say that they're coming and fast. And on your way back you can warn Ben and Lardis, too."

Jake had to admire her. Necroscope though he was, she sometimes made him feel like a schoolboy. "Millie Cleary," he said, "you're one cool lady."

"But not yet a *Lady*," she answered, with a wry smile. "And as long as I'm just cool and not cold, well, I'll be alright."

Taking up the lamp he did as she had suggested, but before leaving Trask in the magmass wasteland he remembered a message he'd promised to pass on. And, "Ben," he said, "Zek was here."

"Zek?" Trask started a little, then scowled and said, "What do you mean, Zek was . . . ?" But there he paused, for it had dawned on him what the Necroscope meant . . . or at least he thought so. And finally, "That was a very long time ago," he said.

"No, I mean now, a few seconds ago," said Jake. "She wanted you to know something. She said if things work out, don't waste any more of your life in remorse. And she said what you had was great but it's gone now. The living are for the living, and the dead are for the dead. She has Jazz now, her first love. She'll go to him now in Zákinthos, where she was born. And you have to go wherever your heart takes you."

Trask nodded, smiled a less than grim smile, and said, "Now she tells me, at a time and in a place such as this! But that's Zek: always the optimist." And with another nod, but gratefully now, he said, "Thanks, Necroscope."

With no time at all to spare—even at this eleventh hour— still Jake decided to make a little time. But that was *make* it, not waste it, for time stands still in the Möbius Continuum. He had an itch that couldn't wait any longer; it needed scratching, and since his course was set absolutely, what difference could it make now? It was something that the others had deterred him from doing (for his own benefit, true), but none of that mattered too much anymore, not when his future as foretold by Ian Goodly was almost upon him.

And so on his way back to the core he took the time—yet wasted none of it—to do what must be done. Then, having done it, he returned to Millie. And just one or two heartbeats after he'd stepped from the Möbius Continuum . . . then everything moved up a gear . . .

The future wouldn't be probed so Goodly had stopped trying. All he could do now was point his 9 mm Browning Special at the hole in the sheer rock wall where the catwalk emerged from the darkness and began bridging the magmass, and pray.

His bullets were silver-plated, and if he could land one of them in the right place—in Vavara's heart or one of her eyes—it should certainly stop her. Stop *Vavara*, if not the driving force within her. For she had been Wamphyri for unknown centuries, and her leech and vampire flesh would be unwilling to give in so easily. There would be a merry display before she succumbed. But if he could bring her down, pull the pin of a grenade, and ram it in the great gape of her jaws . . . that should do the trick, for sure!

The precog had calculated that he might be able to get off just two or three shots, switch on the lamp that the Necroscope had given him, use his garlic aerosol spray (mainly on himself, as protection) before the Wamphyri got it together and reacted to his presence. But by then they'd be in a cross fire, for Paul Garvey would be shooting, too.

Hopefully, with Vavara down, the other two would run for it along the catwalk. And the precog and Garvey would target their legs, try to soften them up for Trask and Lardis waiting at the shaft to the core. But if Liz was still with them—still their captive—that would be *all* that the E-Branch agents could do. And even then they'd be risking hurting Liz.

That had been the plan, anyway.

But that wasn't the way it happened.

"Jesus!" the telepath suddenly hissed from forty feet away, causing Goodly's flesh to prickle and the short hairs to spring erect at the nape of his neck. "Mindsmog! They're so close that they can't any longer shield it. It's here—*and so are they!*"

Leprous white mist—a vampire mist as dense as smoke from damp leaves in a garden fire in autumn—uncoiled itself like a living thing from the shaft in the shiny-black rock face. Expanding and putting out sentient-seeming tendrils, it rolled along the catwalk, lapped over the sides, came groping among the magmass mouldings.

Garvey's halogen lamp blazed into life, and as dense as the wall of mist was, still that powerful beam cut through it. Seen in outline, two male figures stood upright, side by side in the narrow shaft, and in the next moment moved stiffly forward. But that was as much target as Garvey and the precog needed, and as close as they wanted to get.

Their weapons came clamouring alive; their gunfire and its echoes were senses-stunning in the confines of the magmass cavern; and the two figures where they had barely emerged from the mouth of the shaft jerked and danced like puppets . . . but oddly, they didn't fall, and stranger far, their feet weren't touching the walkway's planking.

And now the precog thought, *My God! They* are *puppets!*

He had used a full clip, and so had Garvey. As they went to reload, Lords Malinari and Szwart emerged from the shaft. Following close behind, the hag Vavara came wafting, with Liz lying limp in her arms. Moving with eye-blurring speed, the first two hoisted high their human shields—the shattered corpses of the men who had manned the Katushevs—and threw them effortlessly out and down into the magmass.

Their aim was excellent. Garvey's lamp went clattering into the darkness, and the precog saw a wet, flailing, faceless mass bounce once directly in front of him, before it came slithering and flopping into his arms.

The dead man was heavy; Goodly's hands slipped in blood as he tried to throw him off; he was aware of Garvey's shuddering, gasping, inarticulate mouthings from the other side of the catwalk, where the telepath faced unthinkable problems of his own. And finally, as Goodly managed to free himself from a tangle of loose, flopping limbs . . . Malinari was there!

Malinari, no longer handsome or even remotely human, rising from a magmass matrix immediately adjacent to Goodly's own. The precog's fingers were numb, wet with a dead man's blood as they fumbled to fit a fresh clip into the grip of his gun; and Malinari crouched there, watching with scarlet eyes, perhaps amused at his antics. But then, when at last the full magazine slipped up into its housing:

"Ah, no, little seer," said the Great Vampire, taking Goodly's weapon from him and throwing it away, "I'm afraid we can't allow that. For look, look here—one of your bullets actually found its target, coming right through my poor dead friend here to strike at me! Ah, but it merely grazed me in passing. I felt its sting, its silver burn, but nothing more. And I shall heal, while this faceless thing— and you—won't. Oh, ha-ha-*haaaaa!*"

A hugely taloned hand wiped at the lobe of his fleshy right ear, and came away dripping blood. "*My* blood," Malinari nodded, "which is oh-so-scarce, so very precious. What a terrible shame to waste it, eh?" And squeezing Goodly's cheeks until his mouth popped open, Malinari slopped blood into his forced gape, gently closed it, and wiped his hand clean on the precog's lips and the rims of his flaring nostrils. Then, clamping Goodly's mouth shut, he forced him to breathe through his nose. Blood from the precog's upper lip was sucked in, and Goodly realized the worst of it: that even if he lived he was dead . . . or undead.

He tried to close his eyes, to shut everything out, but the monster's burning gaze held him mesmerized. And Malinari's jaws cracked open in a drooling lunatic grin as he said, "But there, fair's fair, little scryer, and Lord Nephran Malinari—Malinari the Mind—has been hospitable. I have given of my wine of life, and you have supped. Now I shall sup of yours. But what a great pity, and such bitter irony, eh? That for all your alleged talent, you didn't see *this* coming!"

His jaws opened wide, wider, and came down towards

Goodly's face. But then, thinking better of it, holding back on his bite for a moment, he clamped the precog's head in his icy hands and stared at him. Perhaps there was room in his mind yet, and what a bonus that would be: to be able to see into the future! Then, as his index fingers writhed like worms, lengthened, and sought his victim's ears—

—Vavara called from the walkway, "Have done, Nephran! And you, too, Szwart! Come, take this stupid girl off my hands, and let's go while the going's good. We've come a very long way but we're not done yet. Those other E-Branch people will have heard the shooting. Let's not give them time to work out what's happened to the first of their ambush parties and regroup. I'm sure there'll be hazards enough to negotiate."

Malinari looked up, flowed to his feet, growled deep in his throat. But he saw that Vavara was right. And meanwhile the precog's flopping hand had struck something hard and metallic: the handle of the halogen lamp! Malinari bent to strike a murderous backhand blow, but Goodly struck first.

Blinding white light—painful light—went streaming into the vampire's eyes in a shaft that felt solid as a bar of iron. Malinari's blow found the side of Goodly's head, but instead of crushing his skull it glanced off; enough to hurl him aside and render him unconscious, but nothing worse.

And momentarily blinded, staggering, tripping, and flailing his arms, Nephran Malinari went mewling back across the magmass to the walkway . . .

Meanwhile, Paul Garvey's problem was indeed unthinkable; it was the unthinkable Lord Szwart! Szwart, too, heard Vavara calling, but he didn't answer. Instead, through eyes that seemed to drip sulphur, he stared in alien astonishment at the telepath.

It was Garvey's face that fascinated him, that reconstructed face which looked normal enough when it was emotionless, but which now was anything but emotionless. Even a smile looked bad on Garvey, a frown frightening, and a scowl monstrous. But when the telepath showed fear . . .

Szwart had been about to kill him. (Garvey deserved to die, if only for the halogen lamp, whose fragments lay in a magmass mould nearby.) But now, looking at him—his hideously twisted features, muscles pulling in all the wrong directions, tendons jerking under unresponsive flesh— Szwart wasn't so sure that death was the worst possible punishment. Indeed, it might even be preferable. For it was almost as if Garvey formed some kind of living link with the magmass!

Szwart fashioned his vocal chords for speech, and said, "My son, my son . . . and indeed you could *be* my son! For this world has played you foul, that you should look like this. And ah, I know your torment, for I was ever ugly . . . ugliness itself, as you see! However, I have learned to live with it, and so shall you. But without my mist your beam would have revealed me, and it *hurts* me that I am as I am. You would have caused me pain—pain in these night-seeing eyes of mine, unused as they are to loathsome dazzle, but much more pain in my mind, which cringes from bright lights—wherefore I shall cause you pain, but *not* in your mind. Physical pain, aye. A little now, and a lot more later when your own kind come to kill you. Now watch."

With his head held tight in the grip of a great pincerlike hand, Garvey could scarcely refuse. And then Szwart showed him his *other* hand: a crab claw crusted with chitin, that reshaped itself even as Garvey watched. The claws flattened, fused, and elongated; they formed a pneumatic needle that slid to and fro in a bony sheath, while a pearl of greyish moisture gleamed at its tip.

"My essence," said Szwart. "Not my blood but that which is *in* my blood. When this takes hold you'll know the *real* meaning of the word 'ugliness'! And when they come to kill you, then, too, you'll remember how you tried to kill me."

And he slid the needle into the pounding carotid artery on the right side of Garvey's neck, injecting him there.

It wasn't the transfusion of a vampire egg—which of its own right causes unbearable agonies—but it was the next best, or worst, thing. And the stuff ran through the telepath's blood like quicksilver, like electricity down wires in his arteries.

As Szwart released him, Garvey tried to scream. But already he was jerking like a flatfish left stranded by the tide, paralysed by pain. And a moment later he was unconscious.

The first ambush team's gunfire—its echoes bouncing from wall to wall, floor to ceiling; its sound changing with every deflection, itself moulded by the magmass matrices—had been almost as deafening in Trask's and Lardis's ears as it had in Goodly's and Garvey's.

But when the shooting had stopped abruptly . . .

And after its echoes had subsided . . .

Then the second team had also heard the precog's involuntary cry of horror as a faceless cadaver had come flopping from the magmass, and something of the telepath's terrified gibbering when he had come face-to-face with Lord Szwart.

And now they heard only the silence . . .

Trask was armed. As well as grenades, and a machine-pistol that was loaded, cocked, and set on automatic fire, he also had a third weapon in a sausage bag at his side. As for the latter: his hopes were fading as to its use . . . but that was a personal thing, and in any case he knew that even a vampire's flesh must eventually give way to a fusillade of silver bullets.

Oh, really? But with only one exception, Goodly and Garvey had been similary armed. So what the hell had happened to them? And what *was* happening even now?

It's called fear, Mr. Trask, said Malinari in Trask's mind. *What you're experiencing is fear. For you've now seen for yourself how we deal with opposition. And as for your talents, your E-Branch skills . . . surely you've realized by now that they are worthless against the Wamphyri?*

At the first icy word or thought—almost before the message had time to sink in—Trask gave a massive start, squirming as he jerked his head to look frantically in all directions. It was as if Malinari was actually there, crouched over him, talking to him in person and not just in his mind.

And despite that no one else was present, no nightmare face staring back at him, still Trask knew that it *was* Malinari, for he'd felt those same icy thoughts before.

But how . . . !? was his first involuntary thought or exclamation. Not a reply, merely an astonished reaction.

How? The other's mental voice mocked him. *How? But am I not Nephran Malinari? Malinari the Mind? We've met once before, you and I, out in Australia. A brief meeting, it's true, but I have remembered your psychic signature, which at this range is quite unmistakable. That's how, Mr. Trask. But there's also a why . . . because you're in our way, and we haven't time to waste arguing with you or your weapons. Wherefore—mind to mind, as it were, though your mind is scarcely a match for mine—I give you one last opportunity to remove and save yourselves, you and your E-Branch people, before we move against you. Or simply stay where you are, guarding the final shaft to the core, and meet up with your fate right there. The choice is yours.*

Unused to telepathy, except with Zek and Millie—and even then never having tried to converse in his own right—Trask's mind betrayed him when, "without thinking," he thought, *Christ! This bastard knows it all!* And:

Oh, ha-ha-haaaa! Malinari's laughter slammed home, but only for a moment. And then, *So how's it going to be?* said the Great Vampire. But there was something in that cold, telepathic voice that he couldn't quite hide: a sly eagerness, and the fact that he already *knew* how it was going to be. Now Trask's talent came into its own, casting the vampire's lie aside and revealing the truth. This was no "last opportunity," just a delaying tactic.

Trask shielded himself, and was surprised that he knew how; unless it was something that came natural to all vampires. He'd left it too late, of course, for now he recognized another grim truth: that just like the locator, poor Bernie Fletcher in Turkey, he himself had betrayed his location! It had been there in his mind, in his own treacherous thoughts—his hiding place in the magmass—"near the shaft to the core!" That was how Malinari had found him.

And cold from head to toe—cold as this unmarked grave in this foreign land that he'd chosen for himself—Trask suddenly thought, *My God—I'm a dead man!*

And despite that his psychic shields were in place, at this range—this *point-blank* range—he might as well have spoken the words out loud. For he was merely an amateur while Malinari was a master. And:

Indeed you are a dead man, said that one. *But not just yet. First you'll be a hostage!*

A blanket of mist was gathering over the magmass and beginning to flow towards him, but Trask guessed there was something closer than that; "point-blank" indeed. And sure enough, he saw a lumpish black-cloaked figure—like a grounded, man-sized bat—making its weird, flopping approach over the twisted terrain.

Trask gulped the stagnant, metallic-tasting air, swallowed hard and tried to moisten his bone-dry throat. His palsied fingers groped for a fragmentation grenade . . . and a deeper shadow fell on him in his magmass mould!

He gasped, rolled over and looked up, and had barely enough time to see something furry and freakish clinging to the uneven magmass ceiling directly overhead. It took no more than a split second to realize what he was seeing, but in that same fraction of time a tentacle of mutant vampire protoplasm as thick as his forearm and hard as a rubber cosh whipped down and almost broke his wrist. The grenade was sent flying with its pin intact, and Trask's numbed right arm and hand wouldn't answer his commmands as he went to reach for his machine-pistol. But in any case the effort was wasted, for something black and viscous was descending, snatching the gun away.

And as Szwart quickly *extended* himself down from the ceiling, touched bottom, thickened and grew up from the floor like the stem of an instantaneous stalagmite, so Malinari straightened from his crouch, threw back his cloak, and reached for his greatest human enemy with a hand as broad as a plate.

Catching Trask by the back of the neck, and drawing him

to his feet, he hissed, "As for the rest of my plan, Mr. Trask—why, with the girl *and* yourself as my hostages, that should be the very simplest of things. Simplicity itself."

But Szwart had noticed something, and now in a voice that rattled and wheezed like a pair of ruptured bellows, he enquired, "Nephran, do you see what I see?" Then, leaning closer to Trask and staring at his face, he formed a member that closely resembled a hand and drew Trask's dark glasses from the breast pocket of his parka.

"Indeed I do," Malinari answered. "The feral yellow of his eyes? Yes, and I suspect the same of the girl. And what of the rest? If their powers are enhanced it answers several puzzling questions: such as how they've followed us so closely, seeming almost to anticipate our every move, and why they've proved so hard to detect and their shields so difficult to penetrate . . . even for me. It's true, I needed them to follow us, but not *so* hot on our heels! So then, it appears your garden under London met with a measure of success after all, Lord Szwart."

"Then all is not lost," Szwart wheezed. "If or when I have need to come back here, I might find this world darker and far more to my liking!" He laughed, a sound almost as awful as his looks, and stood there shaking in all his near-formless horror.

Then he pressed Trask's sunglasses to his own lumpish face, and even Malinari grimaced at what next took place, which would be self-mutilation in any other: the soft *squelching* sound, and the slow drip of morbid fluids, as Szwart forced the sunglasses back until the six-inch shafts sank right into his black protoflesh. Behind the dark lenses, the fire of his eyes was at once reduced to the glow of hot embers.

And Szwart said, "Well then, what do you think?"

"More than merely cosmetic, eh, my friend?" said Malinari.

"Indeed!" the other wheezed. "I suffered the Gate's brightness when first we came here, but the pain should be less going back!" And he laughed again.

While Malinari's only thought—kept shielded, of course—was this: *Don't laugh too loud, misshapen fool. For I sense the Necroscope close by, and talents such as his were threat enough without any help from you and your fungus garden . . .*

30
Or Merely the First of Many?

IN PERCHORSK'S CORE, THE THIRD TEAM, JAKE and Millie, had also heard Goodly's and Garvey's gunfire. That had been but a moment ago, and as its echoes died away Jake said, "It's started. This is the best possible place for you, Millie, with your thumbs on the firing studs of this Katushev! The only thing is, you can't use it until I've got Liz back. And so—"

"—And so you'll position yourself just inside the mouth of the shaft," said Millie, reading it straight out of his mind.

"Correct," Jake answered. "The Gate's dazzle should give me a small advantage at least, and with a bit of luck I'll be able to snatch Liz and get her out of here. *Then* you can use . . . you can use the Katushev . . . ?" Seeing a certain look on her face, he frowned, stumbled to a halt, and asked. "Did I say something?"

"Yes," she answered. "You seem to be assuming they're going to get this far, that's all."

And it was true, Jake had been assuming exactly that; which translated into an assumption that maybe Ben Trask and the rest of the team—

"—Aren't going to make it?" Her eyes looked right through him.

"I'm just trying to cover every angle." Jake tried to reassure her, failed, and went on: "Right now, though, I think it's a good idea you should get that armoured canopy up.

Then if you do have to shoot, and if anything shoots back, you're covered."

He went to turn away, and something squirmed in his pocket, stabbing his thigh right through his trousers.

"What the—?" Jake fumbled with his parka to thrust a hand deep in his pocket, came out with the fragment of Harry Keogh's hairbrush that David Chung had given him. There was a little of his blood on the splintered end, and the thing was vibrating in his hand.

"Chung!" said Millie immediately.

"A problem?" Jake wondered out loud.

"Should I try to reach him?" said Millie.

"No need," the Necroscope answered her, lifting his head as if he were listening to something. "I've got him. This piece of old hairbrush is both compass and range finder. I can go to him right now . . . but hell, he could have chosen a better time!"

"Still, you have to go," said Millie. "Who knows, it may be something that's important to us."

"That's true," said Jake, "but I would go anyway, because I know Chung would help me if it was the other way round. Now get that canopy up. And don't worry—I'll be back."

And a moment later he was gone . . .

Guided by instinct and the wooden shard in his hand, Jake used the Möbius Continuum and went to David Chung's coordinates. But when he got there—which took no time at all—he found something new and very odd. His Möbius door formed readily enough, but it wouldn't hold still!

This wasn't the warping effect he'd experienced upon arriving in the core; the door was firm enough and stable in itself, but it moved up and down, shifted from side to side, constantly changed its Möbius space-time location. And then the Necroscope realized why: it must be that the *locator*'s location was changing, and Jake was locked on to Chung. It was Chung's transport, the helicopter that was moving, but very erratically!

In a moment when the door held relatively still, Jake

stepped out of the Continuum into normal space, and at once lurched as the floor shifted under his feet. He staggered, saw a safety strap swaying there, grabbed at it and held on. And in the next moment three or four voices began shouting a chorus of exclamations:

"What the *hell*—!?"

"Who—!?"

"*Christ!* What's going on here?"

And then Chung's voice, saying, "It's okay. He's a ... he's a friend!"

They were seated, belted in, in the helicopter's passenger cabin, three on one side and two on the other. The seat next to Chung was empty, and as the aircraft lurched again, Jake let go of the strap and aimed himself in that direction. Chung grabbed at him, helped to locate him as he toppled into the seat, said: "Jake, we've got a problem."

"You, me, Trask, and all the rest of us," Jake answered him, breathlessly. "And we don't have a lot of time. So what's up?"

"Who *is* this person?" someone yelled above the shrilling of the chopper's engine and a bansheee howling from outside.

And another insisted, "Will someone *please* tell me what the hell is—?"

"Shut the *fuck* up!" Chung shouted at them. "All of you! You want to live? This is the man who'll save you. But if you don't want to live, just keep mouthing off ... !"

And when their mouths snapped shut he turned again to Jake. "We were okay until about half an hour ago. Then the storm came in. The weather forecast said it was going to be unsettled, but this is ridiculous! The wind is from the east, coming down from Norway, and it's getting worse by the minute. We're heading for the Outer Hebrides, but now anywhere will do—Northern Ireland, dry land—anywhere! But we're burning fuel fighting the wind, and the pilot says we may not make it."

Jake got up, grabbed a strap, leaned to look out through a window. The chopper's searchlight scanned a heaving sea, where massive waves smashed this way and that, foaming white against the black of bottomless ocean. Moonlight struggled to find its way through clouds that roared across the sky, and to the east there was nothing but inky blackness.

"How long have you got?" said Jake, stumbling back into his seat.

"Maybe twenty, twenty-five minutes," Chung told him.

Jake nodded. "If it gets tight, give me another call. Incidentally, you *did* call me, right?"

"I tried to locate you," said Chung.

"You got Harry's hairbrush," said Jake.

Chung shrugged, managed a smile and said, "Same difference, Necroscope."

"And one other thing," said Jake. "Did you find that Russki ship?"

"Not yet," Chung answered, "but I know where she is. As you know, I have this thing for radioactive materials. Well, all of our worst suspicions are proven. I keep picking up this signal, Jake, and it's a bad one. We're moving toward it right now. But a shipload? Hell, it's a whole *shitload!* And not a thing we can do about it, not in this storm."

"I have to go," said Jake, conjuring a door.

"So how are things at your end?" Chung asked anxiously, as the Necroscope lurched to his feet.

"If you call me and I don't answer," Jake replied, "that'll tell you how things are at my end."

And as the chopper lurched again he was gone . . .

Moving cautiously, Malinari led the way into the shaft's unnatural dazzle, the light from the Gate. Along the glaring catwalk he went, with Vavara and Szwart following on behind. Vavara was carrying a barely conscious Liz, while Szwart propelled a helpless Trask. But Malinari himself was for the moment unburdened, which was how he preferred it.

Back there in the magmass, he could have sworn that someone else, other than Trask, was hiding nearby. His mentalist probes had discovered no one, however, not in the magmass . . . but Jake Cutter's presence elsewhere had been more than apparent.

Then for a while the Necroscope had disappeared from Malinari's mental register, but now he was back. Indeed his return, just a few moments ago, had felt like some kind of energy surge in the psychosphere. And now, despite that he had shielded himself, his shields were so strong they betrayed him in their own right. He was in the core, guarding the Gate itself while waiting to take back his woman. And that was exactly where Malinari wanted him.

Vavara had demanded to know why she should be burdened with Liz, and Malinari's excuse for letting her do the work was very simple . . . and simply a lie: he needed to have his hands free in order to handle the Necroscope. The real reason, however, while it certainly had to do with Jake Cutter, was in fact very different: Lord Malinari knew that whoever was in charge of Liz was liable to deadly attack from the moment he—or she—stepped from the shaft into the core. Then, indeed, Malinari would need a free hand.

For the girl meant nothing, neither the girl nor Trask, but the Necroscope was everything. With powers such as his Malinari knew he could take back Starside, Sunside—even this parallel Earth in its entirety—eventually. But when next he came he'd be leading a vast vampire army of his own, and no need then for this pair of grotesque mental midgets who had been nothing but a hindrance. No, for between times he would have seen to them. As for Vavara—would-be Mother of a vampire horde—he would see to her right now, if an easy means were to present itself!

And so, having first ensured that his "colleagues" followed close behind, Malinari stepped out onto the railed walkway that hugged the wall of the core around its perimeter. But even wearing a pair of disposable cardboard sunshields that he'd picked up from a container at the entrance to the shaft, still he must put a hand up against the glare until his eyes had adjusted.

For there it was, the portal itself—shining no less dazzlingly than the natural Gate on Starside—and once across its threshold Malinari knew that he would soon be home in his Vampire World. Ah, but with what wild talents at his command? That remained to be seen.

Now he held back a little, scanned left and right, not only with eyes narrowed to slits but also with his mind, and at once detected Millie and the Necroscope. At this range their psychic signatures were unmistakable. The latter was crouched in a sort of sentry box or observation post maybe ten paces to the right, while to the left, at three times that distance, the female was hiding under the tinted-glass turret of a heavy-duty weapon. Or could it be that she was actually manning the thing? Whichever, it was time that Malinari took charge of Liz.

"Vavara," he said, letting the witch come up alongside him, and starting off across the fish-scale steel plates towards the Gate, "let me assist you with the girl."

"I need no such assistance," she grunted. "For I have seen through you, oh Lord of Lies! What? Did you think that you were the only one with powers? I feel them here, too—and more especially *him!*—but then, who could fail to detect him, eh? This is the third and last stage of their ambush. And this girl will provide a shield against whatever force of weapons they intend to use against us. So fuck you, Nephran Malinari!"

"Eh? What?" Szwart wheezed, stumbling where he followed. He now used one "hand" to hold Trask, and the other to protect his eyes from the glare. For even with Trask's sunglasses, still he could feel the light on him, revealing every hideous contour.

"The bitch Vavara would ruin our plans for her own safety!" cried Malinari. "And that is something we can't allow!"

Turning on Vavara he crouched down a little, and rising up drove the heel of a hammer hand up under her chin. Every single ounce of Malinari's prodigious vampire strength—not to mention his pent hatred of the hag—was behind that blow. And as she cried out, flailed her arms, and toppled backwards, Malinari caught up Liz.

Vavara spat blood and shattered scythelike teeth where she sprawled, and Lord Szwart stumbled this way and that, wheezing, "Eh? What? Nephran, what are you doing?"

Malinari made no answer but instead began to drag Liz—who was suddenly wide awake and struggling, however weakly—across the fish-scale steel plates towards the Gate. If the Necroscope was after all a great coward and failed to attempt a rescue, at least Malinari would not be leaving this world empty-handed.

But meanwhile Trask had recognized Szwart's difficulty. And risking his life—which probably wasn't worth anything anyway—he half-turned and reached up a hand to wrench the sunglasses from the monster's face.

Twin jets of goo spurted from the holes in that nightmarish countenance, and Szwart let out a whistling cry like steam from a kettle. He shrank down into himself and slapped both hands to his face, covering his streaming eyes, which left Trask free to make a flying tackle on Malinari. And sliding on his belly over the plates, he grabbed at that one's ankles.

Hampered by Liz's struggling, and tripping where Trask held him, Malinari cursed and managed a fumbling back-heel kick. His heel glanced off the side of Trask's head, sending him tumbling sideways. Which was fortunate for him; for Vavara was up on her feet again, hissing like a snake where she advanced on Malinari with spiderlike hands and fish-hook fingers extended.

By now Millie had seen her opportunity. The Katushev's battery-driven motor hummed into life, its turret turning smoothly as she sought to target Szwart where he stood isolated from the rest by some two or three paces. And Millie wasn't the only one in action.

The Necroscope had commenced his run, hurling himself diagonally across the steel-plated disk toward the Gate. Level with Malinari and Liz, he went to intercept them at the Gate's event horizon. But out of the corner of his eye Malinari had seen him and deliberately slowed down. For with the exception of the hag Vavara's interference, it was all working out almost exactly as planned.

Three of E-Branch's avengers—Millie, Trask, and the Necroscope—were now involved in the action, but there was still a fourth to come. For Malinari's telepathic probes had not been in error back there in the magmass cavern when momentarily they had seemed to detect a presence other than Trask's. They had in fact detected just such a presence, only to be tricked, deflected from their quarry by a Traveller survival technique. And of course, Lardis Lidesci was one of the greatest survivors of all time.

Out from the shaft he stepped, with his razor-edged machete in his clenched fist, the strap of Trask's sausage bag over his shoulder, and disposable sunglasses protecting his eyes. And no more than twenty feet ahead of him, there stood Szwart with his ropy hands held up in front of his grotesque face, his gasping, whistling voice cursing the light from the Gate.

Lardis didn't think twice—and to hell with his rheumatic joints!—as he drew back his throwing arm and let fly with all the deadly accuracy of a Szgany marksman. Coated with silver at its tip, the machete made a *whup-whup-whupping* sound as it spun end over end once, twice, three times and slammed into Szwart's back point first. But already in the process of alien, automatic metamorphosis, Szwart's being was something less than solid, and the Old Lidesci's weapon passed three-quarters *through* him, so that the first six inches stuck out in front.

Szwart drew it out point first, gazed at it through eyes in flood, then turned and glared his astonishment—then his fury—at Lardis, and took one menacing step towards him. Which was when Millie thumbed the Katushev's firing studs.

The Lord of Darkness was swatted, holed, mangled like a rag doll, snatched from his feet and thrown down, with blobs of his blood and chunks of his protoflesh flying. And under the Katushev's canopy Millie laughed and cried, bouncing in her seat like a lunatic as she eased her thumbs off the studs and the obscene cacophony of cannon fire ceased. And there on the steel plates, beginning at the spot where Szwart had been standing, lay a trail like a scarlet skid mark, leading to a steaming, immobile mound of weird flesh twenty or more feet away. And:

"Take me down under London, would you, you *bastard* thing?" Millie cried. "Vampirize *me* with your bloody spores, would you? You're done for, Szwart, but you're not going to hell alone!"

The Katushev's motor hummed again, but Millie was too late. The action had moved on, and friends and enemies alike were now too close together . . .

Malinari was almost at the Gate. Its glaring white surface, the event horizon, seemed to beckon him. But the hag Vavara was hot on his heels, her face a mask of loathing, and her chomping bottom jaw dripping blood. And not only Vavara but Jake Cutter, too.

The Necroscope was coming fast; he would arrive at the same time; and he wore a harness slung loosely over his shoulders, a bottle of incendiary chemicals on his back, and such a scowl of determination on his face that Malinari felt a sudden twinge of self-doubt. But it wasn't only Jake's look that did it—it was the squat-bodied flamethrower in his white-knuckled hands!

He had found the weapon hanging from its hook in the sentry box, and it had seemed to make a lot more sense than a machine-pistol. For no matter how lethal the latter might be against an ordinary man, it wasn't likely to unnerve Nephran Malinari, not while he was holding Liz. But the sight—the very notion—of a flamethrower just might. And in fact it had.

"Let her go, Malinari," Jake yelled. "I'm the one you want, not the girl." And pointing the flamethrowers's nozzle, he took up first pressure on the trigger and ignited the pilot light.

"I haven't harmed your lover," Malinari snarled. "Not yet. So don't worry about me, worry about that one!" And he pointed at Vavara.

For she had seen the danger, too, and came bearing down on Jake with her long arms reaching and her face a mask of blood.

"Jake, look out!" Liz cried, writhing in Malinari's arms.

She needn't have worried; the Necroscope was already swinging the flamethrower in Vavara's direction, and now he squeezed the trigger all the way home. A roaring, white-hot jet of flame—a demon's tongue of fire—licked out, striking Vavara full in the face and stopping her just as surely as if she'd slammed head-on into a brick wall.

Vavara shrieked to match the hissing shriek of Jake's lance—danced a mad dance while he hosed her down—finally slumped to the fish-scale plates in a spreading pool of her own fluids. Her smoke, steam, and stench rose up . . .

But Malinari had turned Liz to face Jake, and held her like a shield between himself and Jake's weapon. And:

"You're right," he said. "It's you I want and not the girl. But listen, do you see this face of mine? Do you see these jaws and teeth?" And he showed Jake what he meant. "One bite and the girl is gone. I can ruin her face, suck out her tongue, push my fingers in through her eyes to addle her brain. Or perhaps I'll simply drive my hand right through her and crush her heart. But on the other hand—"

"—You want me," said Jake. "And the moment you do anything to Liz you're a dead man. You know it, and I know it." He moved a step closer—and Malinari backed off until he was only a few feet from the Gate's event horizon.

"But I could do it and still leap into the Gate," the monster said.

"And if you did I'd follow you," said Jake. "All the way to hell if I had to. So tell me, can you leap faster than my fire? Even if you got to Starside I would find you there. And believe me, Malinari, no one moves faster than me. One morning as you lay down to sleep, I'd be there. With fire in my hands."

"Oh, I know, I know," Malinari gurgled. "So quite obviously this has to end here. A duel, Necroscope? Fair and aboveboard, your powers against mine? Now hear my proposal. You'll put down your weapon and kick it away beyond reach, and I'll release the girl into the hands of your good friend, Mr. Trask."

Meanwhile, Lardis Lidesci had come closer, and now he said, "Don't do it, Jake. Never make a deal with a vampire, and certainly not a Lord of the Wamphyri!" It seemed the old Gypsy king had forgotten—perhaps conveniently—that the Necroscope had become a vampire in his own right.

Jake had heard just such a warning before, but this time he had no choice. And anyway, he actually wanted it. For his vampire blood was up! "Release the girl," he growled.

"Drop the flamethrower," said Malinari.

And together, slowly, carefully, each followed the other's instructions. Jake shrugged out of his harness, let the bottle fall clanging to the floor. Malinari held Liz at arm's length, but kept hold of one wrist. The Necroscope stooped a little to let the flamethrower fall, and went to kick it away. And finally Malinari let go of Liz . . . for she was no longer of any use to him!

And in that split second—that single moment of time, as Jake sent the flamethrower and its tank skidding towards Trask—Malinari moved. He moved like quicksilver, grabbing at Jake before he could even think to avoid him. And his hands clasped Jake's head in their icy, brain-draining grip.

Lardis had a gun but couldn't use it; Liz and Trask were in the line of fire, and the Old Lidesci was by no means expert in the weapons of Earth. And in the Katushev's bucket seat, Millie was similarly hampered: if she fired at Malinari, Jake would go with him. And where Liz had been the monster's shield, now Jake took her place.

"Ahhh! *Yesss!*" Malinari hissed, as his senses-numbing hands formed themselves into great webs, and his fingers quivered and lengthened. "All of your secrets, Necroscope—everything that you know, the keys to all of your powers—soon to be mine! But what was that you said? Nothing moves faster than you? Perhaps nothing *travels* faster, place to place, but where the reflexes of muscles and mind are concerned, I think you are mistaken."

Jake slumped. The chill of Malinari's hands wasn't physical but mental: the bitter cold of ignorance leeching on knowledge; the negative pole of a powerful magnet, applied to the positive pole of the Necroscope's intelligence, his psyche. For Malinari the Mind was a creature apart, who lived not alone on blood but on the memories and deep-seated secrets of his victims, leaving nothing behind.

And already his index fingers were vibrating as they probed Jake's ears.

"All here," Malinari gurgled. "It's all right here. But ah! What's this I feel? A secret place? A *special* place, perhaps? A locked room here in the manse of your mind. Your treasure vault of powers, eh, Necroscope? But see, the key is in the lock, and now I turn it. Your secrets are mine . . ."

His fingers sought knowledge . . . and found something else. They sought magic, and found madness. Nothing—nothing at all of intelligence—transferred to Malinari, but something, some*one,* who he had long forgotten and thought never to know again. And such was his eagerness that he got it all . . . all of Korath-once-Mindsthrall, bereft in his loneliness, sucked from Jake's mind in an instant, like a speck of blood through a mosquito's siphon! But unlike Jake, Malinari had no special room in which to contain him. His rooms were full to brimming, and this latest acquisition was one too many.

"Ahhhh-*argh!*" he choked, snatching back his hands from the Necroscope's head—releasing him as if he were ablaze—to go staggering this way and that. And his crimson eyes flying open and bugging, and his great jaw dropping, gaping, as he slapped palsied hands to his head. And again. And yet again . . .

For *inside* his head—in Malinari the Mind's mind—Korath ran like the lunatic he was down every corridor, crushing every sentient thing, destroying all memories, erasing all knowledge, and leaving nothing but chaos in his wake. He was an instantaneous disease, an all-consuming virus; and

Malinari the perfect host, whose brain had been teetering on the rim of lunacy long before this fatal infection.

Liz ran to Jake where he had gone to his knees, but already he was recovering, shaking his head, "awakening," as from a bad dream. "What did you do to him?" she asked then. "What happened to him?"

"I . . . I don't know," he answered, hugging her close. "But I feel—somehow I feel—free . . . ?"

"It's something we can consider later," Trask grated as he advanced on the drooling, gibbering Malinari where he sat slapping his head, cross-legged on the fish-scale floor. "But right now there's something I need to do—something that I've wanted to do for a very long time—before we go looking for the precog and Paul Garvey and get the hell out of here."

And handing Trask his sausage bag, Lardis went with him.

A moment later, Trask thrust his hand into the idiot Malinari's battle gauntlet and flexed it, and as the cutting edges sprang erect, he raised the gauntlet high and brought it slicing down on the mad thing's neck. Again and again Trask struck home with all his strength, until the ex-monster's head leaped free and his body toppled. Then Trask shook the gauntlet loose and let it fall.

And picking up the flamethrower, Liz said, "So you finally got your revenge, Ben, and Millie got hers—but mine is still to come."

Then, as they backed off, turning away from the one grisly scene—

—Millie shouted a warning as she clambered down from the Katushev. "Behind you! Look behind you!" And for all that they had been through, still they were shocked anew at what was taking place where Millie pointed.

First: the steaming mass that had been Vavara was no longer quiet—indeed it was *unquiet*. The slumped hag's fire-blackened mouth hung open, and out onto the slimy floor poured the myriad eggs of a mother of vampires! Translucent pearly spheres like a small boy's spilled marbles, and propelled by flickering cilia, they skittered and shimmered all across the steel-plated floor, seeking blindly for brand-new hosts. Liz didn't think twice but torched them all, then turned her fire on the steaming remains of Vavara.

Yet even now it wasn't finished.

"*What the hell . . . ?*" said the Old Lidesci, his mouth falling open as he watched something black, lumpish, and ragged dragging itself to the perimeter and into a wormhole that angled acutely into the wall.

"It's Szwart!" said Jake disbelievingly. "What does it take to kill these bloody things?" Taking the flamethrower from Liz, who was done with it now, he ran towards the wormhole.

That was a mistake, for there in the darkness beyond a bend in the energy channel, Lord Szwart had quickly refashioned himself. And as Jake approached the hole—

—It might easily have been some giant octopus that sensed his presence and reached out with a nest of lashing tentacles! Jake squeezed the flamethrower's trigger, and nothing happened. The pilot light died with a noise like a damp squib. And Szwart dragged Jake headfirst into the hole.

A moment later and the Necroscope found himself inside Lord Szwart, enveloped by him! And Szwart formed eyes—several eyes—on the inside, to look at him.

"Darkness!" the vampire thing gasped and wheezed, his vestigial lungs pulsating, breathing their poison into Jake's face. "The darkness was ever my friend. It was my beginning and shall be my continuance. Where darkness lives, there goes Szwart. And you—ah, I know *you*—destroyer of my fortress under London! You come and go at will. But this time I go with you."

"*Jesus!*" Jake gasped.

"No," said the other. "Only Szwart, but be sure I have godlike power over you! The power of life and death, aye. And now, Jake Cutter—the one Malinari called Necroscope—you'll take me out of here to a place of darkness."

In that same moment Jake felt a stab through his trousers;

not anything of Szwart's doing, but a splinter of old hardwood in his pocket. Then, shielding his mind to conceal an involuntary thrill of anticipation, suddenly he knew how to kill this mutant thing!

"I can't move," he said. "Not while you surround me."

"Then I shall extrude you," said Szwart. "But heed my warning, Necroscope: don't take me where there's sunlight. It would kill me, certainly, but you would die, too—and just as painfully." With which he squirted a few drops of specially altered internal fluids onto Jake's neck. Hissing where it ate into his flesh, the stuff burned like hell, causing him to gasp in pain.

And Szwart said, "There. If you fail me, that shall be your lot: to be sucked dry of all your juices, shrivelled and burned to nothing. Do we have an understanding?"

"Yes," Jake gasped. "Yes, we have an understanding."

Szwart reshaped himself, extruded Jake inside the wormhole, but continued to hold him in a nest of whipcord pseudopods. And while Jake gulped gratefully at reasonably clean air again, the Lord of Darkness said, "So then, where shall we go?"

"I know a place of ultimate darkness," said Jake, beginning to breathe a little more easily as the agony of his seared neck gradually subsided.

"Where I may live?"

"For as long as you live," the Necroscope answered.

"Take me there now," said Szwart, driving Jake before him, out of the wormhole onto the perimeter walkway, and in through a Möbius door . . .

The storm over the Atlantic had blown itself out as rapidly as it had blown up, but the helicopter was running on fumes. David Chung had found the rogue Russian ship; now his scientist colleagues were taking infrared snapshots of the vessel, reporting its location by radio, and likewise the fact that their instruments were recording lethal radiation. It was all they could do in what little time remained to them.

Down below, stricken by the storm and hampered by its

submarine burden, the towship was wallowing in the heaving swell, listing badly to starboard, and in danger of capsizing. But the locator was intent upon only one thing: contact with the Necroscope.

And Jake came . . . but not alone.

And *not* into the chopper.

On his way through the Möbius Continuum, while Szwart assumed a man-shape, but continued to hold him as tightly as ever, the Necroscope had chosen an indirect route—moving first in one direction, then another—in order to think things through before arriving at his destination. And he'd kept his thoughts shielded in case Szwart was less of a dullard than he seemed.

As for Jake's plan: it had been somewhat complicated.

He had understood from Chung's contact—the vibrations of the hairbrush shard—that the locator was in trouble; if not Chung himself, then certainly the helicopter in which he was a passenger. If they were ditching, then it was possible that in the confusion Jake could free himself from Szwart, grab a hold of Chung, and make an exit. By now the locator and his colleagues would be wearing life belts at least, and inflatables were standard on such aircraft. Maybe they were already down in the water, while the helicopter filled up and started to sink.

In that case Jake would immediately transfer Szwart to the chopper and desert him there . . . *if* he could get away from him. Then, with the coordinates fresh in mind, he would go back for Chung and Co. and rescue them from the sea. Complicated, yes—the plan had a great many ifs, buts, and maybes—but for the moment it was the best he could do.

And one thing for sure: if it worked there would be no more trouble from Szwart. For there's no darker or deadlier place to be than under the crushing weight of a mile of water . . .

That had been the Necroscope's plan, but as he conjured his Möbius door he saw that once again it was slipping and sliding, bucking and heaving—*and* slowly but surely descending—and so guessed that the helicopter must be settling toward the sea.

He made a quick decision, dissolved the door and moved away from it, and at coordinates of his own conjured another. Except this time, without pause, he proceeded through it into the dark Atlantic night and the blustery aftermath of the storm.

His calculations were a little off. Emerging in midair, he tasted salt and felt the slap of spume from driven wave crests, saw the helicopter's fan glinting overhead some little distance away . . . and then fell; Jake and Szwart, plunging into a trough between waves, sinking under the water and slowly surfacing.

Then: "What? Eh?" Szwart gasped and spluttered, tightening his grip as their heads broke the surface. "Are you mad, Necroscope? Do you *want* to die?"

"A mistake," Jake lied, as choppy water slapped him in the face. "But I can get us out of this."

"Then do it now, at once!" said Szwart. "For that was your *last* mistake, Jake Cutter. I won't allow another."

At which moment Jake spied the Russian ship.

As the heaving ocean lifted them up, Necroscope and monster together, Jake saw the stricken vessel; saw members of her crew in goggles and safety harnesses, risking their lives where they hung from a framework of buckled steel booms at her stern. They were working at frantic speed with acetylene torches, trying to cut through the trailing towlines. And behind the ship, lolling in the swell with the tip of a rusty conning tower breaking the surface, there was the doomed old sub herself—where Jake had hoped she would be.

Then, breaking in on his concentration, Szwart told him, "I can't swim. Nor can you, not with me clinging to you. So get me out of this now, Necroscope, or we both go down together."

"As you will," said Jake.

He judged the distance, saw the last hawser sliced through and go splashing down into the sea, attempted to recall everything that he'd seen of Chung's target on the big screen in E-Branch HQ's Ops Room. That great nuclear submarine—but more especially its reactor compartments: those lead-lined rooms that no sane engineer would ever enter except in the most desperate of circumstances.

And then—as the conning tower slipped under for the last time and a wave lifted them high—the Necroscope conjured his door, prayed that he'd got it right, and again entered the Möbius Continuum.

He needn't have worried. Chung's hardwood shard was vibrating itself into a hundred even smaller fragments in his pocket, and as before it was his compass and his range finder.

"EH?" said Szwart. "WHAT . . . ?" Like a thunderous grunting in the Continuum's nothingness.

Darkness, Jake answered, as he fashioned his most dangerous door and guided Szwart through it. *That is what you asked for—isn't it?*

And dark it was—pitch-dark, oily, metallic—and burning with a heat that couldn't be felt by men, except in the passing of time. But Szwart felt it, and he couldn't understand it.

Astonished, he relaxed his grip, and the Necroscope at once leaned away from him and through a Möbius door. The one pseudopod that managed to come snaking after him was lopped off as he slammed the door behind him.

And Jake was free in the Möbius Continuum.

While in the corporeal world, below the waves:

There was heat in the reactor compartment, the same energy that fuels the sun—but *without* the sun's light. Little wonder Szwart couldn't understand it, but he *could* feel it. And as the groaning sub nosed ever deeper, he felt it eating into him.

Mercifully, perhaps too mercifully, he wouldn't feel it for long. Already his mutant flesh was sloughing from him, steaming away into nothing, while his bubbling screams went all unheard, drowned in fathoms of ocean . . .

* * *

Down in Perchorsk's core, Lardis had found another flame-thrower and was busy filling the air with foulness, removing every last trace of Malinari and Vavara. Trask had told him (perhaps optimistically, because optimism was all he had left) that this was futile; as soon as the Necroscope got back the entire Perchorsk complex would be consumed utterly in an awesome nuclear explosion. But that had made no great impact on Lardis.

"A job isn't done until it's finished," the Old Lidesci had answered. "And I've been finishing such as these bastards for a very long time. It needs doing, so leave me be."

And who could say he was wrong? For even as Lardis worked Malinari's neck grew fat as a leech wriggled free of the stump, and his body burst open in a nest of pulsing grey and purple pseudopods that lashed frenziedly at the air before they melted. And likewise with the hag; her crisped outer shell cracking open—steam jetting from the rupture—while her pale blue and yellow guts heaved and tossed, full of a mindless "life" of their own.

But Lardis had carried on, and finally had his way.

Meanwhile, Turchin had come up from the bowl under the Gate and gone with Trask, Millie, and Liz in search of Garvey and the precog. And they had carried them back to the core. Both of the men had been "sleeping," but a special kind of sleep. And Trask said to Millie, "At least we didn't go through that."

"No," she answered, "but it all works out the same anyway."

"I know." He nodded grimly, and sighed. "We're all vampires now. And out there in the world a lot more are being made—and making others—as we speak. But that fight is still to come."

"A good many fights," she agreed. "Us against the rest, and I'm frightened. How do you think it will go, Ben, that's assuming we can get out of here?"

"The fighting . . . or the rest of it?"

"The rest of it," she answered quietly. "The blood."

"Harry abstained," Trask reminded her. "As did The

Dweller. Likewise Turgo Zolte, until Shaitan forced him. It doesn't have to be human blood, Millie. If we don't slip too far back towards the Dark Ages—and if science doesn't take too much of a battering—maybe we'll be able to synthesize something. And if not . . . well, people have been meat-eaters ever since the Good Lord gave us incisors!"

"Okay," she said, "I'll accept that. But where do we start? And what do we do? The human race is facing extinction, Ben."

"We start at E-Branch," he answered. "That is, if our people will accept us! That's our power base. And while the world goes to hell we'll look for a solution—we'll find a way to survive *and* keep our humanity. As for the more distant future: you'd do better asking him." He nodded toward the sleeping precog. "When he wakes up, his powers should have been enhanced quite a bit."

"Talking about survival and the future," said Liz, breaking in excitedly on their conversation, "he's okay—Jake, I mean! And he's on his way back here right . . . now!" Liz's powers, too, had been enhanced.

Jake stepped out of the Möbius Continuum a different man from the one they had known. His hollow, handsome face was grey now; and his hair—where it swept back like wings from his temples—was white. It formed into a brown-and white-banded braid at the back. And as for his eyes . . . they were no longer feral but uniformly red. Red as blood.

"I lost my dark glasses," he said, as Liz went to him. "But I can replace them. Right now, though, I think it's time we all got out of this hellish place."

Everyone agreed, and Gustav Turchin went back down through the trapdoor under the Gate to set the timer on his device; ten minutes should be enough. In his absence, Trask took Jake aside and said, "You know, twice you've had my heart in my mouth. Are you insane or something? First to take on Malinari's challenge, then to go chasing after Szwart like that?"

But Jake only smiled, and Trask knew the truth of it. "You did it!" he said. "You checked out the future!"

"That's right," said Jake. "I didn't go far, but far enough to see that my thread goes on way past tomorrow and a day. It's a red thread, sure enough, but it does go on. And as it goes it gathers other threads to it; doesn't *make* them, you understand, just gathers them up. Yours and E-Branch's, I suppose. And they all go on together."

Then Turchin came scrambling back up through the trapdoor, and in the next few seconds and three trips Jake conveyed the entire party back to the surface. Up there, the locator David Chung was waiting—Chung and his scientist colleagues—*and* a British search-and-rescue helicopter, sitting there on the dam wall.

Inside the chopper the wide-eyed pilot told Jake, "I've got just enough fuel left to take off. But I'll really have to give her the gun with all these extra passengers aboard. I mean, I'm still not sure we can make it. So, what do you want me to do?"

"We have to be mobile," the Necroscope shrugged. "I suppose the easiest way would be to take off, and then fly her out over the dam wall."

"Over the gorge, you mean?"

"That's right," Jake nodded.

"And you can do that, er—that whatever you did—again?" The pilot's face was chalk-white. He wasn't even sure where he was, or *if* he was, or what this blood-eyed creature was. But:

"Trust me," said Jake.

And because he'd already been privy to one miracle tonight, the pilot did trust him. And when the engine shut down over the gorge he simply closed his eyes . . . and kept them closed even as the chopper yawed a little and fell—

—All of six inches to the roof of E-Branch HQ.

And not quite by coincidence, just a few minutes later and thousands of miles away in the Urals, the mountain over Perchorsk gave a massive shudder and subsided by almost exactly the same amount . . .

By Way of an Epilogue:
Not so Very Devious After All

FOR A FULL SEVENTY-TWO HOURS, THE PRECOG Ian Goodly lay asleep, and Paul Garvey woke up just an hour or so before him. For both men it had been the sleep of change following a direct infusion of blood or essential essence from a Great Vampire; a three-day fight between the men and their raging fevers, which inevitably they must lose while yet surviving. They wouldn't die—not the true death—but they would wake up undead.

Paul Garvey wasn't alone in his anguish. A telepath, as he tossed and turned and fought his fight, other minds accompanied him. Liz, Millie, and John Grieve, they stayed with him through his torment, spelling each other, willing him on and constantly reminding him of his humanity. They didn't try to converse, but simply topped up his troubled mind with positive and fortifying thoughts, so that when he woke up he would remember what he was and not what the alien thing in his blood wanted him to be. And when they weren't succouring Garvey, the three were counselling each other.

As for the precog: he was a different case entirely. Search as they might, the greatest minds in E-Branch couldn't find *his* mind; it wasn't there but traversing future times, searching in its own right. And in the last hour or so, before he opened his eyes, Goodly dreamed the strangest of dreams.

This is how it went:

He was reading a newspaper report on the plague . . . but not the Asiatic plague. In the Mediterranean—in the air, on land, and across the Aegean—the Greeks and Turks were at war, each blaming the other for the vampires come among them. In Australia, the authorities had blockaded the east coast from Gladstone to Coffs Harbour, and were shooting anyone or -thing attempting to leave. China had launched its first nuclear missiles against the new vampire-infested "red" Russia, and there was continuous night-fighting all along their borders. The Bulgarian authorities operated a dusk-till-dawn curfew, and anyone caught walking the streets after dark was shot on sight and burned.

In the British Isles—with the exception of Northern Ireland, where as yet the two main parties had failed to agree on any mutually satisfactory countermeasures—the various governments had long since declared a state of emergency, giving the police and military previously unthinkable, draconian powers of arrest, confinement, and execution. Sales of home security systems were rising exponentially, while those of sunglasses, contact lenses, and sun-screening creams had been banned. Ounce for ounce, the price of silver was double that of gold, garlic was selling on the black market for seven pounds the clove, and for the first time in decades the churches were filled to overflowing, while holy water was disappearing from their fonts in equal measure.

Despite that he had rarely been allowed to see so much, the precog looked at the date on the paper: 13 March 2014—just a little over two years!

He was reading the newspaper while riding into the city on an evening bus. Outside, the streets were almost deserted; a handful of people—but a very small handful—were hurrying to their homes or other destinations and no one looked at or spoke to anyone else. There were posters pasted on the walls of every street corner; except for their headers, in blood red, six-inch letters, Goodly couldn't read what they said.

He didn't need to, for the headers alone said it all:

PUBLIC WARNING NOTICE.
ARE YOU AWARE OF THE TIME?
BETTER CHECK YOUR WATCH NOW!

Then he felt a bump and gave a start. The man seated beside him had fallen asleep, his head striking Goodly's shoulder. And a nervous woman behind him tapped him on the other shoulder and said, "I think . . . I think someone should tell the driver." And for all that her voice was a mere whisper in his ear—or perhaps because it was—still it contained a whole world of fear.

Goodly did as she suggested; as he moved from his seat, the sleeping man lolled sideways, falling across both seats without waking up. The driver took his bus off route to a gloomy building (once a police station, the precog felt sure) with bricked-up windows, and tall, new chimneys that were pouring out smoke, stopped and got out. And in a while three men came and carried the sleeper off the bus.

"There are so many of them," the woman whispered again, and Goodly turned to look at her. But seeing his face her eyes went wide. Then she stood up and stumbled into the aisle calling for the driver.

A dream or a vision, whichever, it was time to move on. And Goodly left his newspaper, the woman, and the bus behind him as his mind carried him further still into the future . . .

Previously, the precog had recognized some of the streets. Now, too, he recognized them, yet at the same time didn't, or didn't want to. Not in their current disorder. But disorder? "Destruction" was the better word for it! It was still London—a sign on a heap of rubble where a chimney of bricks stood central told him that much: the junction of Oxford and Regent streets!

Goodly was still in a vehicle, but it wasn't by any stretch of the imagination a bus. Its windows were dark-tinted slits in the thick metal walls of an armoured personnel carrier, a half-track rumbling through the shattered remains of the city's once bustling streets. He seemed to be the commander of the vehicle, and there were half a dozen combat-clad men with him, excluding the driver. Outside, it was a dirty, dingy daylight.

One of the men, his Second-in-Command, was David Chung, and his eyes were as brown as always. The rest of the crew was made up fifty-fifty of vampires and human beings, most of whom Goodly recognized as E-Branch agents of old. Which meant that they were quite capable of working together, if only because they'd always worked together in a common cause.

Looking at Chung, however, he thought, *Good for you, David! Keep it as long as you can, my friend. You may grow older faster than I do, but you'll always be you and no one and nothing else making decisions for you without you realizing it.* Then:

"Stop here!" said Chung, and the vehicle kicked up dust and debris as it slewed to a halt. Then a motor hummed and the roof slid open, and four high-powered weapons elevated into position with their gunners crouched under smoked, sun-screening plastic canopies, scanning all the quadrants. Since the sun hadn't been visible for a six-month, the canopies were a purely precautionary measure, and overhead the leaden, lowering clouds remained black- and yellow-streaked with poisonous smoke.

"Over there," said Chung, pointing, his eyes narrowed, brow wrinkled, and radiation-sensitive mind focussed. "It's there in that street, dumped there by the last heavy rains. It's bad, so you can't afford to hang about. Get those signs up quick as you can and then get out of there. We can't have any of our patrols going down there."

Two men in radiation suits left the vehicle carrying warning triangles and metal staves. They worked quickly, hammering the staves into the ground at the entrance to Chung's "street"—an avenue of piled rubble stretching away out of sight, with two or three gutted buildings in various stages of collapse—hung the signs on the staves and ran back to the half-track.

"Decon as soon as we get back home," the locator told them as they climbed aboard. And when the vehicle rumbled into life again, he turned to the precog. "Maybe it's my imagination but you seem awfully quiet. What's up?"

"Er, daydreaming," Goodly heard himself saying. "I wasn't here for a minute . . . or a couple of years."

Chung nodded. "I know. Just a handful of years since those bastards brought this hell down on us."

"A handful?"

"Well, six actually. Sometimes it seems like yesterday, and other times it's forever, like it's always been this way." Then it was back to business again. "Is there anywhere else you want to check before we go back under the dome?"

Goodly wanted to say, "The dome?" but figured he'd find out soon enough.

And he did, and then was glad he'd kept silent.

For soon they were into a part of the city that he definitely recognized. Ahead of the vehicle, suddenly the air was full of a shimmering distortion; and the buildings beyond it—while they were gradually falling into disrepair—were still more or less intact.

As they drew to a halt before the shimmer, Chung spoke into a walkie-talkie. "Hello the barrier. Let us in."

There was no barrier as such that the precog could see, but the uniformed man beyond the shimmer gave a nod, spoke into his own walkie-talkie, and a moment later the distortion went away.

"Ah!" said Goodly then, beginning to understand. And frowning, Chung turned to him and asked:

"Are you sure you're okay?"

But the precog never got to answer. Not in his "dream," for his mind had moved on again. He had moved it on . . .

This time Goodly—the current, time-travelling Goodly—wasn't himself present. At least not as a viable, corporeal presence.

On the first occasion, on the bus, he'd experienced a true vision. For in that world as he had foreseen it, he definitely wouldn't have been riding a bus . . . not with red Wamphyri eyes! The next time, in the half-track, that had been him; he'd actually played himself, inhabited that future Goodly and seen out through his eyes. This meant that he was learning; his vampire-enhanced talent was growing, exploring its own potential.

Now, this third time out, his talent reverted to its previous parameters, so that he "saw" the future without the future seeing him. Also, the time and location weren't randomly thrust upon him but determined by the precog himself. And *knowing* that he did it, he went to E-Branch HQ, into the Ops Room, during an introductory briefing by Trask.

Ben Trask, on the podium, leaning on the lectern exactly as the precog had seen him so often before, now talking to a handful of new recruits. David Chung and Paul Garvey, Gustav Turchin and the Minister Responsible, Jake, Liz and Millie—even Goodly *him*self!—they were all there, standing at the back watching the proceedings, along with many other members of old E-Branch. And a few of them were still entirely human.

As for the six seated people, four men and two women: they were fatigued, dirty, and their eyes were feral. They were vampires, yes, but only recently.

"The reason you're here," Trask told them, "is because you managed to hold out, because you lasted all this time out there on your own, fighting back and refusing to give in despite that the country is overrun. In short you've done what we've done—or what we haven't done—you haven't succumbed. You've refused to kill other men in order to prolong your own existence. That, and only that, is what sustained you. You're vampires, yes, but you're human, too. And we need you because there are so few of us. It's your choice: to stay and work with us, or to go out in the streets, where you'll live till you die the true death. For while *you* haven't taken the blood of your fellow men and women, there are millions in the world who have. They're killing themselves off and we can't stop it, because once they've tasted it . . . well, that's the end of it.

"But in this place, under this dome of energy, that doesn't happen. It isn't allowed to happen, and if you ever forget that . . . then *we* will kill you. Survival of the fittest, yes. And we are, and we intend to remain, the fittest.

"We have food. We have healthy animals—a farm of sorts, a Noah's Ark—and we're learning how to synthesize blood. We've got scientists here, geneticists and microbiologists, and we're getting better at what we do all the time. There's got to be an answer, a better way, and because we *know* it's there we'll find it . . . that's a fact. You can be a part of our future, too. And believe me, we do have a future." Trask paused to glance at the other Goodly standing at the back of his audience, smiled knowingly and continued. "We know that quite definitely, that there *will* be a future. And meanwhile, as for what we've got here:

"This place is our protection, a dome of energy half a mile wide that covers all of central London. It was a foreign invention originally, but it didn't work for them; in fact it caused a disaster. But with the help of a Russian friend— the man who brought us the specifications—we've *made* it work for us." Now he glanced at Gustav Turchin, an older, much less robust Turchin of course, but still human. For now as then, the old fox was tenacious in his own right.

Trask gave him a grateful nod, and carried on:

"The power source is a nuclear generator buried deep underground beneath what used to be our seat of government. A secret national emergency measure from cold-war times, it remained inactive until . . . well, until the emergency. Let's face it, there couldn't have been a greater emergency.

"We learned of this power source from one of our oldest and most learned members," now Trask turned his gaze on the crimson-eyed Minister Responsible, "a man who is still with us to this day—as we hope you'll be with us from now on.

"And that's it. For the time being that's all I have to say. But as I've already said, you have a choice: stay here and work with us, or return to the streets, the terror, the end of humanity. Except here humanity—albeit a different humanity—will go on."

That was enough for Goodly. Having heard what he had wanted to hear, so did the precog go on: into the future, but further, much further than ever before . . .

* * *

This time the precog's mind found its own way. For Goodly could home in now on his target times and subjects as surely as David Chung homed in on radiation or people of his acquaint. And when he knew he'd reached a point of revelation, there he paused.

Once again he was the ghost, not participating in the scene but simply viewing it. It seemed to him that he was in a classroom—or perhaps a church, or a cross between the two—but it was only dimly lit, with tall windows set high in the walls, so that the light came slanting in overhead, crisscrossing, without reaching down to the children. And for the time being, that worried him: that the light wasn't reaching them.

The teacher, or preacher, was a woman. She wore dark-tinted spectacles and held a chalk in a white-dusted hand. She was the only one who stood in a pool of reflected light that loaned her something more than a dusky outline. And behind her on a blackboard, there were names and words that Goodly couldn't help but recognize: Perchorsk . . . Necroscope . . . Liz . . . Porton Down . . . Trask . . . New Eden . . . E-Branch . . . the Minister Responsible . . . and last but not least, Goodly!

It was the end of the lesson, and now the teacher was testing her charges. She took up a rod, pointed it at a word on the blackboard, and said, "Gordon Clarke?"

A small boy stood up. Like all the children he was a featureless blob in the gloom. "Perchorsk," he said, in his little boy's voice. "The bad blood came from Perchorsk, and those who brought it died there. The true death, aye."

As he sat down the pointer moved on, and the teacher said, "Jimmy Chungskin."

Another small figure stood up, reciting, "The Minister Responsible. He Ministered the Power and gave glory to The Dome."

"Annie Goldfarb," said the teacher, moving her pointer. And a small girl answered:

"Liz. She was wife to Jake, mother to Harry Jakeson. He was a Necroscope, the fifth of his line."

The pointer moved on; the teacher called a name. And, "Porton Down," a tall, eager boy jumped up, his voice like a chant. "Jake the First brought Wise Men out of Porton Down; they were the Keepers of the Blood; and he brought others who understood the power of the sun, to harness it and make The Dome."

"Alice Techschild," said the teacher. And:

"E-Branch," came the answer. "Ben Trask was its father, and E-Branch mothered and fathered us all."

"John Garviskin," said the teacher, her pointer on the move across the blackboard. "Er, but *without* reading my thoughts, if you don't mind!"

"Eden," a well-built boy tried not to snigger. "They called The Dome 'New Eden,' which means 'Innocence' and a 'New Beginning.' And when The Dome failed they went out into the land, and found the clean places and built again."

"Too smart by far, John," said the teacher, after he'd sat down. "Don't think I didn't feel your probe, clever-clogs . . . !"

Then once again, for the last time this session, she moved her pointer and said, "Jake Jakeson?"

"Goodly," said that one, in a strong, sure voice. "He foresaw it all, all of this, and was able to guide them, Trask and the Wise Men and all. And without his future, we wouldn't have had one. Goodly and Trask and the host of E-Branch, they could have had eternity, but in choosing the blood that is true, they relinquished their years to retain their humanity, as we shall give of ours, for our children's sake."

And the teacher nodded and said, "So ends the lesson. Time to go home."

Then it was a race for the door, and Goodly went with them out into . . . into the sunlight!

Out into the broad green fields under blue skies, where for the first time he saw their eyes—those *different* eyes of the children of E-Branch—which so perfectly reflected the nature of their genetically altered blood.

Some of them were yelling, "Jake, this time we'll beat you home!"

And Jake Jakeson—the spitting image of another Jake from another time, except for those amazing eyes—answered, "Not a hope! Why, I'm already there!"

But the teacher grabbed his arm, shook a finger, and said, "Jake Jakeson the Twelfth, or is it the Thirteenth? Why, you're just like your father—and his, and his before him, like all of them have been—for two hundred and fifty years, according to the books. Now listen to me. By all means beat your friends home, but do it on your own two feet and running! Beat them by *running,* Jake, like all the rest of us, and not by just . . . by simply going there! You're to stay fit and strong, do you hear? But you'll only do that by using your God-given muscles as well as your talents." (This despite that the boy was the strongest, fittest-looking child that Goodly had ever seen!)

"Yes, ma'am," Jake said, looking up at her with his oh-so-innocent eyes . . . those uniformly *azure-blue* eyes!

She let go of his arm and turned toward the precog—then gave a small start, so that just for a moment he thought she'd actually seen him there. For like all of them, the teacher was talented, too. But then, frowning, she blinked, shook her head, and turned to call one last time after Jake—

—Two seconds too late. For while the other children were streaming out over the fields toward their homes, Jake Jakeson was no longer there.

And neither was the precog Ian Goodly. For there was nothing left to see, and only one place left to go . . .

E-Branch's entire higher echelon, its most senior members, were standing at Goodly's bedside. His scarlet eyes moved from smiling face to face, knowing they would find no one missing—only to find someone missing! And the first thing the precog said as he came fully awake, was:

"Lardis?" For in those future times there'd been no mention, no hint, of Lardis Lidesci.

Ben Trask laid a hand on the precog's arm, and said,

552

"Don't concern yourself about Lardis. He's back in Sunside, Lardis and Lissa both, taken there by Nathan."

"Nathan recovered, then?" said Goodly, struggling to sit up. And as Trask helped him: "But of course, he *must* have! For with the exception of The Dweller, he is the only one who ever moved between worlds without using one of the Gates." Then he frowned and asked, "So what about it, Ben? What about the Gate?"

"Gone," said Trask. "It all worked out fine, and we did our job, stopped those alien bastards at Perchorsk and stopped them dead." Then the smile slipped from his face. "As for the world: there's nothing good to report, I'm afraid. It's going to hell, and fast."

"I know," said Goodly, taking Trask's hand and standing up. "And we've an awful lot to do."

"The trouble is finding a place to start," said Jake Cutter as he stepped forward, hand in hand with Liz.

But the precog only smiled, albeit wryly, and said, "No big deal, Jake. But there'll be work for you—work for all of us—and the sooner we get to it the better."

"Ian?" said Trask anxiously. "What's going on? Are you sure you're—?"

"I'm fine," Goodly cut him short. "And now if you're ready, I want you to get the Minister Responsible in on this, and call in every available agent, and then . . . and then—"

"Yes?" said Trask.

"Then I'll tell you all just exactly how it's going to be," said the precog.

And that's just exactly how it was . . .